Grace Livingston Hill

THE STRANGE PROPOSAL
A VOICE IN THE WILDERNESS
MARY ARDEN

THE STRANGE PROPOSAL

Living Books®
Tyndale House Publishers, Inc.
Wheaton, Illinois

This Tyndale House book
by Grace Livingston Hill
contains the complete text
of the original hardcover edition.
NOT ONE WORD
HAS BEEN OMITTED.

3-in-1 ISBN: 1-56865-181-3

Living Books is a registered trademark of Tyndale House
Publishers, Inc.

Printing History
J.B. Lippincott edition published in 1935
Tyndale House edition/1994

Library of Congress Catalog Card Number 94-60395
ISBN 0-8423-5944-3

Printed in the United States of America

JOHN Saxon saw Mary Elizabeth for the first time as she walked up the church aisle with stately tread at Jeffrey Wainwright's wedding. John was best man and stood at the head of the aisle with the bridegroom where he could see everything.

First came the ushers stealing on the picture with earnest intent to get the business over, then the four bridesmaids in pale green crisp organdies,—and then Mary Elizabeth! She was wearing something soft and delicately rosy like the first flush of dawn in the sky, and bearing her armful of maidenhair fern and delicate blossoms like a sheaf of some lovely spring harvest. She preceded the bride, Camilla (on the arm of her father's old friend Judge Barron) as if she delighted to introduce her to a waiting world.

But John Saxon had no eyes for the lovely bride, for they had halted at Mary Elizabeth and held there all the way up the aisle.

Mary Elizabeth had eyes that were wide and starry, fringed with long dark lashes under fine level brows. There was a hint of a smile on her lovely unpainted mouth, a little high-born lifting of her chin, a keen interest and delight apparent in her whole attitude that distinguished her from the rest of the bridal party. To her it was all a beautiful game they were playing and she was enjoying every minute of it. There was none of that intent determination to get each step measured just right, each move made with the practised precision that characterized the procession of the bridesmaids. Mary Elizabeth moved along in absolute rhythm, as naturally as clouds move, or butterflies hover.

The wide brim of the transparent hat she wore seemed to John Saxon almost like the dim shadow of a halo, as she lifted her head and gave him a friendly impersonal glance before she moved to her place at the left of the aisle head.

The bridesmaids wore thin white hats also, but they were not halos, they were only hats.

John Saxon suddenly remembered the bride whom he had not sighted as yet except as background, and lest he seem to stare at Mary Elizabeth, he turned and looked back down the aisle to Camilla. Camilla in her mother's lovely old embroidered organdy wedding dress of long ago; Camilla, wearing the ancestral Wainwright wedding veil of costly hand-wrought lace, and John Saxon's orange blossoms from his own Florida grove; Camilla, carrying Jeff's white orchids and looking heavenly happy as she smiled up to answer her bridegroom's welcoming smile.

Yes, she was a very lovely bride, with her gold hair shining beneath the frostwork of lace and waxen blossoms! How splendid they were going to look together, Jeff and Camilla! How glad he was for Jeff that he had found a girl like that!

Then he stepped one pace to the right and front and took his place in the semi-circle as had been planned, with the old minister standing before them against the background of palms and flowers that the old home town people had arranged for Camilla's wedding.

He raised his eyes again to find Mary Elizabeth, wondering if she might not have vanished, if she could possibly be there in the flesh and not a figment of his imagination. He met her eyes again and found her broadcasting that keen delight in what they were doing, found himself responding to that glint in her eyes, that bit of a smile in the corner of her lovely mouth. It was as if they had known one another for a long time. It couldn't be true that he had only just now seen her and for the first time felt that start of his heart at the vision of her! It couldn't be true that he had never been introduced to her!

John Saxon had arrived but the day before the wedding and spent the most of his time since in acquiring the necessary details of raiment in which to appear as best man.

Quite casually he had asked when he first met Jeff at the train, and as he pocketed the directions Jeff had given him to find the right tailor and haberdashery shops:

"And who is this person, this maid of honor I'm supposed to take on as we go back up the aisle after the ceremony? Some flat tire I suppose, since you've picked the one and only out of all the women of the earth," and he gave Jeff a loving slap on the shoulder.

"Why, she's quite all right, I guess. I haven't seen her yet, but she's an old schoolmate of Camilla's. She's on her way back from California just to attend the wedding. Camilla says she's a great Christian worker, and interested in Bible study, so I guess you'll hit it off. Anyway I hope she won't be too much of a bore. She's expected to arrive to-morrow afternoon sometime. Somebody takes her place to-night at the rehearsal I believe, so she won't be around long enough to matter anyway. Her name is—Foster—I think that's it. Yes, Helen Foster."

Nobody had told John Saxon about a washout on the road half-way across the continent, a wreck ahead of Helen Foster's train and a delay of twenty-four hours. He had not heard that in spite of frantic attempts to reach an airport from the isolated place of the wreck, in time to arrive for the ceremony, the maid of honor had telegraphed only two hours before the wedding that she could not possibly get there. John Saxon had spent most of the day in shops perplexing his mind over the respective values of this and that article of evening wear, and arrived at the hotel only in time to get into his new garments in a leisurely manner and repair to the church at the hour appointed. In fact he was there even a few minutes before Jeff. And so he had escaped the excitement and anxiety consequent on the news of the missing maid of honor. He did not know how hurriedly and anxiously the troublesome question of whether or how to supply her place at this last minute had been discussed and rediscussed, nor how impossible at this last minute it had seemed to get even a close friend to come in and act in a formal wedding without the necessary maid of honor outfit.

Excitement had run high and Camilla had just escaped tears as she thought of the Warren Wainwrights, and the Seawells of Boston, and the Blackburns and Starrs of Chicago and New York, all new unknown to-be-relations. She went down the list of all the girls she knew who would be at all eligible for the position of maid of honor and shook her head in despair. There wouldn't be one who could take the place at a moment's notice that way and fit right in, and if there were one what would she do for a dress?

Dresses could be bought of course, even as late as that,

but no ordinary dress would be able to enter the simple yet lovely scheme of the wedding without seeming to introduce a wrong note in an otherwise perfect harmony. Oh, of course it might be bought in New York if one had the time to shop around, but the home town wasn't New York, and no one had the time. Camilla stood in the sitting room of the hotel suite she and her mother were occupying together, and drew her brows together in perplexity, trying to think of some dress she had herself that would do, that she could lend to someone, no matter who, so that the wedding procession should not be lacking a maid of honor, trying to decide to do without a maid of honor, when Jeffrey Wainwright walked in and wanted to know why Camilla's eyes didn't light at his coming as they had lighted all day whenever he had appeared on the scene.

Camilla told him anxiously what was the matter, but he met it with a smile.

"That's all right," he said gaily when he had listened to the tale, and stood looking at the telegram over Camilla's shoulder, "get Mary Beth! That is if you don't mind having one of my cousins instead of one of your own friends. Mary Beth always has oodles of clothes along of every kind. She'll find something that will do. She's just arrived, and she'll just love to do it. You haven't met Mary Beth yet, have you? She's my very best cousin just got back from abroad. Shall I go get her? She's only down the hall a little way. Just show her what you want and she'll manage it somehow, she always can."

And so Mary Elizabeth had come smiling at Jeff's summons, had kissed Camilla and her mother, had looked over the bridal array, including the bridesmaids' crisp pale organdies, and then had departed with a confident smile and a lift of her happy chin as she said:

"Leave it to me! I'll love to do it. I've got just the right thing, a pale rose chiffon I picked up in Paris—a little confection and just as simple as a baby!"

And when Camilla saw her an hour later as she slipped in for inspection, she forgot her worries, knowing that the simple little dress from the exclusive Paris shop knew how to keep its distinguished lines in their place and would never stand out as being too fine for its associates.

And so quite unexpectedly, Camilla came to know and love Mary Elizabeth. But of this John Saxon knew nothing at all.

And now though John Saxon was sorely tempted to study the face across from him to the exclusion of everything else, he was a dependable person, and he knew his responsibility as a best man. He had a ring to deliver at just the right moment, and he was not a man to forget his duty. So he held his eyes and his thoughts in leash until the ring was safely given to Jeff and Jeff had placed it on Camilla's finger, and then his glance lifted and met the glance of Mary Elizabeth full, and both of them smiled with their eyes, though their lips were perfectly decorous, but each of them knew that they had been enjoying that little ceremony of the ring together. Mary Elizabeth was now holding the great bouquet of orchids, along with her own green and white and blush-rose sheaf. Sweet, fine Mary Elizabeth! John Saxon thought how sweet and unspoiled she looked, and stood there watching her with his eyes alight, thinking quick eager thoughts, his mind leaping ahead. In a few minutes now, or it might be even seconds, it would be his duty to turn and march down that aisle by her side, and he could actually speak to her. They had not been introduced, but that was a mere formality. They were set in this wedding picture to march together and they could not go like dummies because they had not been introduced. He thrilled at the thought of speaking to her.

The prayer was over, the solemn final sentences said that made Camilla Chrystie and Jeffrey Wainwright man and wife, the tender consummating kiss given, Mary Elizabeth handed Camilla her lovely white orchids, adjusted the veil and the quaint old-fashioned train and Jeffrey and Camilla started down the way of life together. Then Mary Elizabeth adjusted her own flowers and turned smiling to greet the best man who stood there breathless above her.

John Saxon laid her hand on his arm as if it had been something breakable. The thrill of it gave his face a radiance even through the Florida bronze. He looked down at her eagerly, just as though they were long-lost friends who had by some miracle come together again.

"I've been looking for you for a long time!" said John Saxon, as they wheeled into step and Mary Elizabeth looked up and saw something arresting and almost disturbing in his glance.

"Yes?" she said brightly. "I have been running around a good deal to-day. I guess I was hard to find."

"Oh, not just to-day!" said John Saxon, conscious that the next measure was the one they should start on to follow the bride and groom. "A long time! Years! In fact I guess I always knew there would be you sometime! But will you mind if I'm abrupt? We've only got from here to the door to talk and then the mob will snatch us apart and I've got to leave on the midnight train!"

"Oh!" breathed Mary Elizabeth looking up wonderingly into his eyes, a sparkle in her own.

They were off in perfect time with the stately old march now, quite unconscious of the eager audience watching them with keen eyes, not realizing that they were the next most interesting pair in the whole show, after the bride and groom who had now passed out of sight of all except a few who deliberately turned around and stared at their backs.

"Who is she?" whispered Sallie Lane to Mrs. Sampson.

"Some relative of the groom I heard."

"But I thought it was to be Helen Foster!"

"Oh, hadn't you heard? There was an accident and Helen's train was late. They had to get somebody at the last minute. Don't you see her dress is different? It isn't the same stuff, doesn't stand out so stiff and crisp, and it's terribly plain. Too bad! I heard the bridal party all had their dresses made off the same pattern."

"I like it. It kind of fits her. Say, don't they look wonderful together? I shouldn't wonder if they're engaged or something. Look at the way he looks at her! They certainly know each other well."

"I love you," John Saxon was saying in a low thrilling voice, a voice that was almost like a prayer.

And Mary Elizabeth, quite conscious now of the many eyes upon her, kept that radiant smile upon her lips and the sparkle in her eyes as she looked up to catch the low words from his lips.

"But you couldn't, of course, all at once like that!" she said smiling as if it were a good joke. "Is this supposed to be the newest thing in proposals of marriage? I've never had one going down a wedding aisle, though I've been maid of honor several times before."

She looked up at him archly with her sparkling smile to cover the trembling of her lips, the strange thrilling of her heart over this stranger's words.

"Is there any reason why it shouldn't be that?" he breathed as they neared the door and the wedding party began to mull about them in the vestibule. It seemed to him they had fairly galloped down that aisle.

"If my gloves had been off I suppose you might have thought there was," said Mary Elizabeth with a sudden memory in her eyes.

"Your gloves?" said John Saxon, looking down at the little white scrap of a hand that lay there like a white leaf on his arm.

Then suddenly he laid his other hand upon hers with a quick investigating pressure, and looked at her aghast.

"Then,—you mean—that I am too late?" he asked, caring not that they were now in the midst of the giggling bridesmaids, whispering what mistakes they had made, and how this one and that one had looked.

"Oh,—not necessarily!" said Mary Elizabeth now with a wicked twinkle in her eyes. "It was only an experiment, wearing it to-night. It came in the mail a few days ago with an importunate letter and I thought I might try it out. But there's nothing final about it!"

And Mary Elizabeth gave him a ravishing childlike smile that left him bewildered and utterly routed. He didn't know whether she was trying to be flippant, or merely making talk to cover any possible embarrassment, for they were right in the thick of the crowd now, with someone outside directing traffic loudly, and suddenly John Saxon realized that he was still best man and had duties about putting the bride and groom in the right car. He fled into the street precipitately.

He was a fool of course, he told himself. He had gone off on a tangent and no girl in her senses would take sudden words spoken like that seriously. Oh, he had probably messed the whole thing now. She wouldn't even recognize him when she got to the hotel, or would call a lot of her friends to protect her. What a fool! What a fool he had been! He hadn't thought that he could ever be impulsive like that!

But when he had slammed the door on Jeff and his

bride and turned about with his miserable eyes to see what he could see, and whether she was still in sight, someone caught him and whirled him into a car.

"Here, Saxon," the unknown voice said, "get in quick! Jeff wants you there as soon as he is!" and the car whirled away before he was fairly seated. In fact he almost sat down on someone who was already there in the dark, sitting in the far corner.

He turned to apologize and she laughed, a soft little silvery laugh.

"I bribed the traffic man to give us a whole car to ourselves," she said gaily, "so that you could finish what you had to say."

He caught his breath and his heart leaped up.

"Do you mean that you are going to forgive me for being so—so—so presumptuous?" he asked.

"Do you mean you didn't mean what you said?" rippled out Mary Elizabeth's laughing voice, the kind of a laugh that sometimes covers tears.

"Mean what I said?" said John Saxon, in the tone he often used to rebuke a boy whom he was coaching when he was scout master in Florida. "I certainly did mean what I said!" he repeated doggedly, "and I'll always mean it. But I know I ought not to have flung it out at you that way in public, only I didn't see that I would ever get another chance if I didn't do something about it right away."

"Why, I didn't mind that," said Mary Elizabeth gravely, "it was quite original and interesting. It made the walk down the aisle unique. Something to remember!" There was a lilt in her voice that might be suppressed mirth. John eyed her suspiciously through the dark, but she sat there demurely in her corner, and he felt awed before her. Perhaps he had been mistaken and she was one of those modern girls after all.

But no! He remembered the haloed face, the lovely unpainted smile. He would never think that! She might not be for him, but she was what she seemed. She could not be otherwise.

"Yes," he said with a tinge of bitterness in his nice voice, "something for you to laugh about afterward! A country hick come to town to make a fool of himself, putting a girl in an embarrassing position in public!"

"No!" she said sharply. "Don't say that! You didn't! I wasn't embarrassed! I liked it! I really did! I—felt—honored!"

And suddenly one of the little white hands stole out of the darkness and crept into his hand with a gentle reassurance, and—it was ungloved!

Awesomely he folded his hand about it marveling at its delicacy, its softness, the way it lay relaxed within his own strong hand. It was then he remembered the ring under the glove.

"But—you are already engaged!" he reminded himself aloud sternly. And then he felt for the ring again. This was the same left hand that had lain upon his arm as they went down the aisle together,—galloped down!

Then he sat up sharply, felt the little hand all over, and then reached over to the other hand that lay in her lap. It still wore a glove!

He sat back again and drew a breath of relief.

"Where is that ring?" he said.

"Here, in my handbag," she said, sweetly offering him a tiny scrap made of white beads and gilt, "did you want it?"

"Was it a joke you were playing?" he accused sternly.

"Oh, no," she answered lightly, "I told you it wasn't at all final. I've had that ring several days, and I just thought I'd try it out to-night and see if I cared to keep it."

He hesitated a moment still holding the little ungloved hand that lay so yielded in his own.

"Then—there—is no reason—why—I may not—tell you of my love!"

"Well, I would have to consider that," said Mary Elizabeth gravely. "It was rather unexpected, you know. But here we are at the hotel, don't you think perhaps we'd better get out now?"

John Saxon helped her out, thrilling with the thought of touching even the hem of her garment, guarding her flowers, picking up her glove from the cushion, touching her belovedly, his heart pounding away with an embarrassment and trepidation that was quite new to him. John was usually at his ease anywhere, and he had been in the world enough not to feel strange. But he felt a perfect gawk when he thought what he had been saying, and recalled the keen, gay retaliations.

They hurried through the hall and up in the elevator to the big room set aside for the wedding reception, and John blessed the fate that gave him even this silent bit of time more before they had to face the others. He looked down upon her, in her lovely halo hat, and she looked up and smiled, and there was no scorn in her smile as he had feared. Yet she had in no way put herself in his debt. She had held her own. His eyes drank in her delicate beauty hungrily against a time of famine he feared might be swiftly coming. He would never forget her nearness, the soft fragrance that came from her garments, the natural loveliness of her. He tried to summon her name from his memory, where it hovered on the edge of things and evaded him. Was it Helen? But that was not the type of name for such a girl as this.

Then the elevator door clanged back and they stepped into the big room smothered in ferns and palms and flowers, and there in a distant bower that seemed almost like an orchid-hung hammock in one of his own Florida forests, the bride and groom were taking their places, Camilla smiling up at Jeff so joyously that John Saxon's heart gave another leap. Would such joy ever come to him?

He looked down at the girl by his side and their eyes met and something flashed from one to the other, a gleam that thrilled them both.

2

"COME," said the girl with a certain possessiveness in
her voice, "we must go over and stand by them, you
know," and she put her still ungloved hand on his and
led him across the room. Behind them the elevator
clanged again and opened its doors to let the green
bridesmaids surge in with the ushers, and the reception
was upon them in full blast. But somehow John Saxon
didn't mind. His heart was leaping in new rhythm, and
a song was in his heart.

"Hold this for me, please, while I put on my glove,"
said Mary Elizabeth handing over her little pearl purse as
if she had been used to having him all her life for an
escort.

He took the purse shyly in his bronzed hands. He had
not been accustomed to hold such trinkets for ladies.
Not that he didn't know plenty of ladies, but he had
always shied out of paying them much attention. But he
liked the feel of it when it was in his hand, and while he
watched her putting on the glove so expertly, he grew
bold enough to gently prod the purse till he had located
the ring, a great ox of a stone, he told himself as he

carefully appraised its value. He could never get her a ring like that, he thought to himself dismally in one of the intervals of the passing throng of guests. Even if he succeeded beyond his hopes he couldn't. That ring had been bestowed by some millionaire of course, and she had been weighing its worth, and perhaps its owner. He frowned so hard that Uncle Warren Wainwright asked his wife afterward if that best man wasn't a rather stern-looking fellow. But his wife said, no, she thought he was splendid-looking, so nice and tanned and well built, so he said he guessed he must have been mistaken. Uncle Warren was like that, always ready to concede to his wife's opinion. He had made his money in spite of doing that.

The long procession of gushing or shy friends had surged by at last and the bridal party were seated around the bride's table in the "throne end" as Jeffrey called it, of the banquet hall.

"There," said Mary Elizabeth as John Saxon seated her, "isn't this nice and cozy? You didn't know we were going to sit together, did you?" John sat down beside her feeling like a prisoner on parole.

There was comparative privacy where they were, amid the gay laughter and talk of the rest of the wedding party. The wedding roses, the tall candles, all made it a fairyland and they carried on their little private conversation there between themselves, the girl continually ready with her sparkle and smiles. And nobody wondered that the attractive best man was absorbed in the lovely maid of honor.

Quite suddenly, it seemed, the wedding supper was over. He found his heart sinking. Soon the beautiful links would be broken and when would he ever see her again? He tried to make some plans, say something to her about it, but the glamour of her presence somehow dazed him. He ought to tell her that he was a poor man. That it would be some time before he could claim her. He ought to let her know about his one year more of graduate work in the medical college. She ought to know that his wedding could never be the grand affair that this was. He was not a Wainwright. There were things he ought to say to arrange what they should do in the future, but to save his life he could not say them, could not put them into the words that ought to frame them. Not with all these gay kindly people around them, shouting pleasant nothings across the table, mixing together for that one night, strangers, but with a common interest in the bride and groom. His tongue was tied! And perhaps there would be no other time!

"And I don't even know your address," he wailed, as suddenly the bride arose and everybody got up with her.

"I'll write it for you and give it to you before you leave," she assured him with a smile. "Where is my little bag? I have a pencil and card in it."

He handed it forth reluctantly. It seemed he was giving up one of the slender links that bound them.

"I'll have it ready for you when you come down." Her smile was bright. "You have to go upstairs with Jeff, don't you? Well, I'll be waiting over there by the alcove, and—you know I'm driving you to the station afterwards, so don't go and order a taxi or anything. That's the business of the maid of honor after her duties for the bride are done. She has to look after the best man, you know. That is—when he needs looking after."

She slipped away up the stairs with one of her sparkling glances, and looking after her he had to own to himself that he actually wasn't sure yet, whether she was only playing a game with him, or had taken his words seriously. Nevertheless he went to Jeff's room with something singing down in his heart.

So while the guests waited below to play the usual bridal tricks on the departing couple, with a sentinel stationed at every hotel exit, Camilla with the help of her mother and Miss York, their friend, got out of her bridal array and into the lovely simple going-away outfit and calmly kissed them good bye, including Mary Elizabeth who had slipped in a minute before and now stood holding the precious orchids.

"But what are you going to do with your bouquet, Camilla?" she asked. "You can't go away without the time-honored ceremony of throwing your flowers for the bridesmaids to catch."

"You'll have to do it for me, new cousin," said Camilla smiling. "Or perhaps you'll prefer to keep them yourself. If they bring any potent virtue I'd rather you'd have them, Mary Elizabeth, dear! I'm going to love you a lot."

Then Camilla put on a stiff white starched nurse's uniform and a tricky little cap, tucking her own soft hat under the big blue nurse's cape. She stepped to a door connecting with another suite of rooms, unlocked it, and stood a moment looking at them all with happy eyes.

"Good night!" she said sweeping them a courtsey.

"But, Camilla, where are your bags?" said Mary Elizabeth.

"Safe in our car and waiting for us in a little village three miles from town. Jeff saw to all that. Goodbye, and it's up to you, Mary Elizabeth, to go down and announce that I've fled and you've found nothing but my bouquet, and therefore it's yours because you found it first."

And with another smile and a kiss blown at them all, she turned and went into the other room closing the door. Nurse York swiftly locked it after her, and the three conspirators hurried downstairs by devious ways looking most innocent.

No one noticed a nurse with a tray of dishes slip out of the end room and hurry down the servants' stairs.

Down at the back of the building the caterer's car was drawn up for hampers of silver and dishes to be stowed away, and two young men in chefs' linen coats and aprons stole through the basement kitchens with the nurse behind them. They slipped into the back of the caterer's car, that is, one young chef and the nurse slipped in, and one chef stayed behind. And not even the careful watchers in the yard had a suspicion. The back door of the car was slammed, and a driver got into the front seat and put his foot on the starter.

"Oh, by the way," said John Saxon slipping up again to the little window at the back of the car. "I liked your Miss Foster a lot. Thanks for helping me to meet her!"

"But you didn't meet her," giggled the young woman in nurse's uniform.

"Oh, but I did," said John Saxon heartily, "we didn't mind a little thing like that. We introduced ourselves!"

"Oh, but you didn't," cried the soft voice again. "She wasn't there at all!"

But the driver had put his foot on the starter and the car clattered away and John Saxon was none the wiser for that last sentence.

He stole back through the servants' corridors, rid himself of his disguise, and mingled again with the guests unobtrusively.

"Oh, hello!" said someone presently. "Here's the best man! Where are they, Mr. Saxon? Which way are they coming down?"

"Why, there isn't any way but the elevator, is there?" said John Saxon innocently. "Jeff was all ready when I left him."

There was excited gathering of guests in little groups, then the appearance of the bride's mother, smiling and a bit teary about the lashes, brought about a state of eager intensity. The elevators came and went, and there was a dead silence every time one opened its noisy doors to let out some guest of the house. They all stood in the big entrance hall clutching their handfuls of paper rose leaves and rice and confetti. Outside the door stood a big car belonging to Mr. Warren Wainwright, understood to be the going-away car, well decorated in white satin ribbons and old shoes and appropriate sentiments, but time went on and nothing happened!

"I'm going up to see what has happened!" announced Mary Elizabeth when excitement grew to white heat and suspicion began to grow into a low rumble of anxiety.

Mary Elizabeth stepped into the elevator and disappeared, and a breath of relief went up from the guests.

Then Mary Elizabeth descended again with the great bouquet of white orchids in her hand! The bouquet that every one of those four bridesmaids had so longed to be able to catch for herself!

And when they saw the orchids it did not need Mary Elizabeth's dramatic announcement: "She's gone! And I've got the orchids!" to tell what had happened.

A howl went up from the disappointed tricksters and if it had been anybody else but Mary Elizabeth with her gay friendly smile, she might have been mobbed.

But Mary Elizabeth had disappeared in the excitement, slipped up to her room, and by the time the guests had begun to drift away, she appeared with a long dark wrap over her arm, jingling her key ring placidly, with no offending orchids in sight, and when John Saxon came back after seeing Camilla's mother to her room as he had promised Jeff he would do, there she was sitting demurely in the alcove, the long satin cloak covering her delicate dress, and her eyes like two stars, waiting for him.

It thrilled him anew to see her there, and meet her welcoming smile, just as if they had been belonging to one another for a long time. Even in the brief interval of his absence he had been doubting that it could be true that he had found a girl like that. Surely the glamour would have faded when he got back to her.

But there she was, a real flesh and blood girl, as lovely in the simple lines of the soft black satin cloak as she had been in the radiant rosy chiffons.

She had taken off her gloves, and he thrilled again to draw her hand within his arm as they went out to the car.

The doorman put his bags in the back of the car and Mary Elizabeth drove away from the blaze of light that enveloped the whole front of the hotel. They were alone. Really alone for the first time since he had seen her! And suddenly he was tongue-tied!

He wanted to take her in his arms, but a great shyness had come upon him. He wanted to tell her what was in his heart for her, but there were no words adequate. Each one as he selected it and cast it aside as unfit, seemed presumption.

John Saxon had a deep reverence for womanhood. He had acquired that from the teaching of his little plain, quiet mother. He had a deep scorn for modern progressive girls with bloody-looking lips, plucked eyebrows and applied eyelashes. Girls who acquired men as so many scalps to hang at their belts, who smoked insolently and strutted around in trousers long or short. He turned away from such in disgust. He hated their cocksure ways, their arrogance, their assumption of rights, their insolence against all things sacred. He had had a great doubt in his mind about even Camilla until he had seen her, watched her, talked with her, proved her to be utterly unspoiled in spite of her wonderful golden head and her smartly plain attire.

And now to find another girl with beauty, and brightness, and culture, who assumed none of the manners he hated, almost brought back his faith in true womanhood. Certainly he reverenced this girl beside him as if God had just handed her to him fresh out of heaven.

"Well," said Mary Elizabeth presently as she whirled the car around a corner and glided down a wide street overarched with elm trees, "aren't you wasting a great deal of time? Where are all those things you were going to say and didn't have time for while we walked down that aisle?"

"Forgive me," he said, "it seemed enough just to be sitting by your side. I was trying to make it seem real. I wasn't quite sure but I might be in a dream. Because you see I was never sure whether my dream of you through the years would be like this when I found you—*if* I found you!"

"That's one of the nicest things anybody ever said to me," said Mary Elizabeth softly, guiding her car slowly under the shadow of the elms.

"I suppose scores of men have said nice things to you," John Saxon remarked dismally.

"Yes," said the girl thoughtfully, "a great many. But I'm not sure they were always sincere. They didn't always please me. Yours do. You know it's rather wonderful to find someone that doesn't have to be chattered to in order to feel the pleasant comfort of companionship. Even if I never see you again we've had a lovely evening, haven't we? I would never forget you."

John Saxon started forward and closer to her, looking in her face.

"Is that *all* it means to you?" he asked searchingly.

"I didn't say it was," said Mary Elizabeth with a dancing in her eyes that gleamed naughtily even in the dark as she turned toward him. "I shouldn't prevent your seeing me again, of course, if you want to. I only said, even if I never saw you again, I wouldn't forget that we've had a most unique and wonderful evening. You must remember that I have no data by which to judge you, except that presumably you are one of Jeff's friends. Remember I've just arrived on the scene this morning and not a blessed soul had time enough to gossip about you!"

"They wouldn't," said John Saxon ruefully. "There wasn't enough to say. But I was presumptuous of course to dare say what I did right out of the blue. I'm only a plain man, and you may be bound irrevocably to someone else."

"I told you it was not final!" said Mary Elizabeth driving smoothly up to the station and stopping her car.

"Yes," said the man giving a quick startled look out at the station. "Yes, you said it was not final, but you gave me no hope that you would listen to me."

"But I listened to you!"

"But you didn't give me an answer."

"Did you expect an answer?"

"I don't know," said John in a low tone, "I wanted one."

"Just what did you say that needed answering?" Mary Elizabeth's tone was sweet and courteous, and also the tiniest bit reserved.

"Why, I told you that I love you, and—I asked you to marry me!"

"Did you?" said Mary Elizabeth, still sweetly and innocently. "I wasn't sure. I thought I sort of dragged that out of you!"

He looked up quickly at her and caught that starry look in her eyes, and yet was there a twinkle of mischief too? Could it be that she was still making fun of him, able to hold her own until the end?

"You surely didn't expect me to tell you that I loved you, going down a church aisle at another girl's wedding, did you?"

There was still the twinkle in her eyes, but there was something dear and tender in her voice, as if she were talking to the little boy he used to be long years ago when he dreamed her into his life some day in the far, far future.

"You couldn't, of course. I wouldn't expect you to feel the way I did," said John Saxon humbly.

"I'm not saying how I felt," said Mary Elizabeth with her head held high, "but even if I felt it you surely wouldn't expect me to blurt it out that way right before the assembled multitude, would you?"

"No, I suppose not!" said John Saxon in a very dejected tone.

"And as for marrying, people always have to have time to think that over, don't they?"

"I suppose—some people—do. I didn't!"

"But you should have, you know," said Mary Elizabeth still in that sweet tone in which one imparts knowledge to a small boy, very gently.

"I'm glad I didn't!" said John Saxon quite suddenly, with a firm set of his jaw in the dark, that Mary Elizabeth could see because his profile was perfectly outlined against the bright light of the station platform.

"Yes,—and so—am I!" said Mary Elizabeth with an upward fling of her chin, ending in a little trill of a laugh with a lilting sound in it. "John Saxon, there comes your train, and you have to get your bags out! Do you really *have* to go to-night?"

"Yes, I really have to go!" said John Saxon through set teeth, giving Mary Elizabeth one wild look and springing out of the car.

He dashed to the back of the car, opened it, slung his bags down, gave a furtive glance down the track at the great yellow eye of light that was rushing toward them, so speedily to part them, and before he could look into the car for a hasty farewell he found Mary Elizabeth beside him.

"You haven't given me your address," he said breathlessly, measuring the distance of the track with another glance. "Tell me quick!"

"Here it is," she said, slipping a small white envelope into his hand. "When am I—? When—are—you? I mean—you'll let me hear from you—sometime?"

Her voice had a little shake in it, but she was looking steadily up with that brave smile on her lips—no, it wasn't a mocking smile, he decided. His eyes lighted.

"I'll write you to-night, at once!" he said. "Oh, I'd give anything if I only had another hour. How I have wasted my time!" He looked down at her tenderly.

"Yes," she said sweetly, "you have, perhaps, but it was nice anyway, wasn't it?"

He caught his breath at the sweetness of her voice and longed to catch her and hold her close, but dared he, now, without knowing how she would take it? His own reverence held him from it. And the train was slowing down a few steps away.

"Oh!" he breathed, "I love you!"

"But—" said Mary Elizabeth with a wistful little lifting of her lashes, and that twinkle of a glance, "aren't you even going to kiss me good bye? Just friends often do that you know!"

But the words were scarcely out of her mouth before

his arms went eagerly round her and he laid his lips on hers.

"My darling!" he said. "Oh, my darling!"

Into the tenderness of his whispered words stabbed the sharpness of the conductor's call:

"All aboard!"

John Saxon released her suddenly as if he were coming awake, seized his bags and took three strides to the step of the nearest car which was already beginning to move slowly. But when he turned about, there was Mary Elizabeth beside him walking composedly along the platform, her cheeks very rosy, and she did not look angry. In fact her eyes were still starry and there was a twinkle of a smile about her lips. Her chin was tip-tilted a bit as if she were proud of it.

Then did John Saxon's heart leap with joy.

"That was final, dear!" he shouted down to her through the noise of the train.

"Yes?" said Mary Elizabeth. "You certainly did it thoroughly."

And then the train got alive to its duty and swept them apart like a breath that is gone, and Mary Elizabeth stood alone on the long empty platform gazing after a fast disappearing red light at the end of the train.

Gone!

She put up the back of her hand to her hot cheeks, she touched her lips softly, sacredly, and smiled.

Had it been real?

Finally she turned, got into her car, and drove away.

When she reached her hotel the doorman summoned a man to take her car to the garage, and Mary Elizabeth went up to her room, turned on all her lights, and went and faced her mirror to look straight into her own eyes and find out what she thought of herself.

3

MEANTIME out in the silence of a smooth dark road in their own luxurious car, the bride and groom drove happily through the night to a destination that Jeffrey Wainwright had picked out, and not even Camilla knew.

They had completed their exciting trip in the caterer's car, had made a quiet transfer to their own in the haven of the back yard of an old farm house where a friend of Camilla's mother lived. Not even the farmer and his wife were there to interfere though they did stand a-tiptoe behind a sheltering curtain and watch the car move smoothly out of their drive and down the road, and they felt the thrill of their own first journey as man and wife.

There had not been opportunity to talk in the caterer's car, nor safety, lest they be followed, and by the time they were launched on their own way there were so many other thrilling things to say that they forgot that last encounter with John Saxon. But an hour later as they swept over a hill and looked down across a valley to where the lights of another small city blazed, the memory of John Saxon recurred to them.

"What did he mean, Jeff, about Helen Foster? Did no one tell him she wasn't there?"

"Evidently not from what he said. You see we didn't really have much time to talk. He probably confused Mary Beth with her. But what's the difference?"

"A great deal, I should say," said the bride in a wise tone. "If you'd noticed his eyes when he looked at her!"

"Now, Camilla, don't go to being a matchmaker!" laughed Jeff. "Because if you do you'll be disappointed. Those two will never get together. They're as wide apart as the poles."

"Any wider apart than we were, Jeff?"

She laid a caressing hand on her new husband's arm and he looked down on her tenderly, and then leaned over and gave her another kiss.

"I insist," he said and kissed her again, "that we were never far apart. If we were I never could have made the grade."

Then they floated off to reminiscing again, but eventually got back to John Saxon.

"What did he mean by saying they had introduced themselves? Can it be that nobody looked after that little matter?"

"It must have been. But it strikes me that John Saxon is able to get around and look after himself pretty well. It looked that way to me. They seemed to be having an awfully good time together."

"Well, they would," said Jeff thoughtfully. "They're both unusual. But I'd hate like sixty to have John get interested in Mary Beth. She's always been my favorite cousin, but I'll have to own she's a bit of a flirt. I don't know how many men she's kept on the string for a number of years now, and they're all deeply devoted, but Mary Beth goes smiling on her way and takes none of them. I wouldn't like John to get himself a heart and have it broken. He's a constant old fellow, and he doesn't care much for women, doesn't have much opinion of the modern ones, and wouldn't understand it. It might go hard with him."

"But she seemed so sweet and genuine," protested Camilla, perplexed.

"Yes, she is," said Jeff, "but she's always had her own way. Her father spoiled her, and her mother spoiled her, and then when her mother died and she inherited all that money besides what her father will leave her some day, she did more and more what she wanted to. Oh, I'll admit she usually wanted to do nice things. She wasn't bold and arrogant like the modern girl. She had ideals of her own and she stuck to them. And that's remarkable too, since she's traveled the world over a lot, and had plenty of chances to go modern. She's kept her smile and her natural face and hasn't taken on rowdy airs and habits. She's a great sport and I admire her a lot. But she does let a lot of men trail after her, and just smiles and plays with them a while and then lets them go. They are just a lot of toys to her it seems. And I'd hate to have John Saxon treated that way. He's too genuine to be played with. And I'm not sure whether she could understand a man like John. I guess it's a good thing that they're not likely ever to meet again. I wouldn't have John hurt for the world."

"He looks to me as if he could take care of himself," said Camilla.

And then they turned to the right and swept down into the heart of the little city, and drove to their hotel, forgetting all about John Saxon and his affairs.

Back in the hotel where Camilla's mother and Miss York were preparing for rest Miss York was saying:

"What kind of girl is that Miss Wainwright who took the place of maid of honor to-night?"

"Why, I think she's very sweet," said Camilla's mother. "It was so nice of her at the last minute that way to be willing to fill in, not having the regular dress or anything."

"She had a stunning dress!" said Miss York, "and she certainly was agreeable. Of course most girls love a thing like that, and she certainly did the part well."

"A great deal better than Helen Foster would have done," said Camilla's mother. "Poor Helen isn't very pretty and never has known how to dress, but she's a lovely girl and Camilla was very fond of her. But Miss Wainwright was sweet. I liked her very much. She seemed a good deal like Jeffrey, didn't you think? The same blue eyes and clear complexion with dark hair. He's always been very fond of her. She seems almost as if she might have been a sister."

"Yes," said Miss York reluctantly, "if she's like him in spirit she couldn't be improved upon. I was just wondering whether a girl *could* be as beautiful, and as rich as they say she is, and not be spoiled."

"Jeffrey wasn't spoiled," said Jeffrey's new mother-in-law.

"Jeffrey is unusual," owned Miss York. "You know he's unusual. You said so yourself!"

"Well, couldn't his cousin be unusual too?"

"She *could*," said the nurse. "I was wondering whether she *is*. I've been watching her all the evening. That friend of Jeffrey's is a very fine young man."

"Yes, he is," agreed the mother. "He is very wonderful! Camilla has been telling me about him."

"That's it," said Miss York, brushing out her long old-fashioned hair that still had a pleasant natural wave in spite of the threads of silver here and there. "That's just what I mean. He's fine. He's rare! And is that girl good enough for him? I watched them all the evening, and sometimes I thought she was and sometimes I wasn't sure."

"Well," said Camilla's mother smiling, "isn't it good that we don't have to settle that? I suppose our heavenly Father can look out for those two as well as He has looked out for my child. My, how strange it is to think that Camilla is married! And how glad I am it is Jeffrey she married instead of that other man I was so afraid she would take. Oh, God is good!"

And so the discussion ended, and presently the light was out and the two women lay quiet with their own thoughts.

Down the hall a few doors Warren Wainwright was struggling with the collar button of his dress shirt.

"Who's that chap Mary Liz was running round with to-night, Fannie? What do you know about him?" he said as he conquered the button at last and flung his collar down upon the bureau, drawing a relieved breath as his constricted flesh relaxed in his puffy pink neck.

"Why," said Mrs. Warren Wainwright placidly as she unwound the heavy ropes of pearls from her own ample neck and took a satisfied look at the set of the frock she had been wearing all the evening, noting that it was exceedingly becoming, "why, he's one of Jeff's friends. Jeff speaks very highly of him. He told me he's very scholarly and very keen. He's going to be some special kind of doctor I think, though I believe he hasn't much money at present."

"Mary Liz has enough money of her own of course," growled the uncle, "but I'd like to see her happy. I wouldn't like to see Mary Liz get some puppy she'd have to divorce in a few months, or years. I'm very fond of Mary Liz. She's a fine girl!"

"Yes, of course," said Mary Elizabeth's aunt yawning

delicately and placidly, "but you know Mary Elizabeth can look out for herself, and she always would."

"Yes, and that's the very reason we ought to find out about that chap and manage somehow to get her away from his vicinity if necessary till he lays off her, if he isn't all right. Where is he staying anyway? I saw how he looked at her when they came down the aisle. I'm not so old I don't know what a look like that in a man's eyes means."

"Why, he's left already," said Aunt Fannie beginning to take down her hair, and wishing she hadn't sent her maid to bed.

"What?" said Uncle Warren Wainwright sharply. "He's left already? I don't think much of him for that!"

"Why, you were just worrying about him staying around," laughed Aunt Fannie. "And very likely Mary Elizabeth turned him down anyway. You know her! Besides, I saw her wearing a perfectly gorgeous diamond on her left hand just before she went down to the church. I think it came from Boothby Farwell, I really do. I saw the white case it came in lying on her bureau and it came from Tiffany's. There's been a rumor around about them for months and I suppose it's settled at last."

"H'm!" said Uncle Warren relieving himself of his dress shirt. "He's too old for her! And by the way, he wasn't here, was he?"

"Jeff doesn't like him!" said Aunt Fannie in her placid tone.

"H'm!" said Uncle Warren. "The little jade! Well, he's bound to have a good time wherever she goes, isn't she?" and he laughed grimly. "Even if she is engaged she'll have her little fling!"

"Now, Warren," said Aunt Fannie, "I don't think you're fair to Mary Elizabeth. She isn't a flirt. She really isn't. She's just friends with them all."

"Yes, I know," said Uncle Warren. "I'm not blaming her. But I hope she keeps 'em all just friends till one comes along fine enough for her. She's a sweet girl."

"Yes, she is!" agreed the aunt.

"That's what I'm saying about this chap, Saxon, is that the name? Queer name. We must look him up. Get Jeff to give us his credentials when he gets back. That is if she hasn't forgotten him by that time! But somehow I don't think she'll forget him so soon. I shouldn't if I were a girl."

"You don't know what you'd do if you were a girl, Warren. Now do get to bed. You know we've got to take a journey in the morning," soothed Aunt Fannie.

And very soon in that room also all was quiet.

But Mary Elizabeth lay in her bed with her eyes wide, her cheeks burning and a thrill upon her lips, thinking over every instant from the moment she entered the church door and caught that look of John Saxon as he stood there beside her cousin Jeff, down through the unprecedented events of the evening until she saw him swept away from her by the train in the darkness, with only a little red light winking back at her.

Would she ever see him again? Would she ever hear his voice again thrilling into her soul? Was that little red winking light at the end of the train that took him away by any possibility a warning, a danger signal to her, to stop right here and not carry it any farther?

Well, in the morning she would wire to Jeff to tell her all about him. No, she couldn't do that. She didn't know where Jeff was going. And there was Camilla. She didn't want Camilla to know that she was interested. That was the trouble when your favorite cousin got married, there was always his wife, no matter how nice she was.

And she didn't want Jeff to know either that she was interested. Any question would have to be oh so casual, and that couldn't be accomplished as things were now. No telling when she would see Jeff alone again.

And besides, of course she must wait to see if John Saxon ever came again or wrote. Oh, strange sweet perilous situation!

Then she thought of his voice whispering, "my darling!" and fell asleep with her cheek against his.

To-morrow she would have to see about sending back that ring, but to-night was hers and John Saxon's.

4

JOHN Saxon made his way to the club car and sat down at the desk to write his letter. It seemed the most momentous thing of his life. In his hand he still clutched the tiny envelope Mary Elizabeth had given him at parting. He hadn't as yet looked at it. But he glared around on the other inhabitants of the car sternly. They were not his kind. Three men at a table were playing cards and drinking, had been drinking for some time if one might judge from their loud, excited voices. A highly illuminated girl was smoking in the far corner and watching the men sleepily. An old man with cigar ashes sprinkled over his ample vest front was audibly sleeping in the chair next to the desk, his rank cigar smoldering in his limp hand.

Saxon turned away in disgust. It seemed a desecration to write to her in such surroundings. Such thoughts as he wished to pen to her were not fitting here.

He arose and went back to his section. It would not be comfortable to write there, but at least he would not be annoyed by others talking. John Saxon had not spent a large part of his life roughing it for nothing. He could make the best of circumstances. So he disposed of his baggage as best he could, got out his writing materials, folded his length up in as comfortable a position as he could beside the tiny light of his berth, and started to pour out his heart to the girl he had just left. He had promised her a letter at once and she should have it.

"My dear—" he began. He did not want any names interfering in this first letter. He wanted to tell her all that was in his heart before his thoughts would be entangled with the things of this world, including even a name. As he remembered it she didn't have a very pretty name anyway, but what was in a name? So, "My dear—" he wrote and lingered over the writing of it pleasantly.

I want to tell you what you seemed like to me when I first saw you, to tell you all the things I wanted to say going down that aisle and couldn't because there wasn't time, to let you know what you seemed to me all the blessed evening while we were together. They are things of course that I should have said on the way to the station when I was tongue-tied with the thought of your nearness and my privilege. Yet the time was not wasted for I learned that just to be quietly near you was enough to bring great joy and peace and preciousness.

And now, I find there are no words that will express the depth of my thoughts about you—as if I were a painter and, getting out my pigments, I find none of sufficient clearness and depth of color to paint you as you are. I should have to mix the colors from my heart. That's how I feel about you.—As if I were a poet and could find no new phrases not worn dull and shabby by other men's thoughts about other girls down the ages. You are too lovely to be described by worn out words.

If I could summon all the lovely descriptions by poets of all ages, all the wonderful portraits ever painted, and select the best and put them together, they could never equal you. There hover in my mind phrases I have read and admired, loved indeed sometimes, one that likens hair to a glossy raven's wing, but it seems stale when I think of the beautiful crowning of your dark hair, and the way it waves away from your white forehead.

There are lines that stand out in literature likening a beloved one's eyes to stars, and there is a starriness in your eyes, but there is something more. None of the words I find cluttering about in my mind quite satisfy. It must be because my love for you goes deeper than the mere outer look of you. It recognizes a spiritual glow from within, a radiance that does not come just from feature or form or color, though you have those to perfection.

But words, mere words fail to help me tell you what you are to me. I would have to lay my lips again upon yours, to hold your face close to mine once more, and to fold you close in my arms to make you understand what I mean. And you will readily understand that I could not have done that coming down the church aisle.

When I looked down toward the church door and saw you coming with your lifted face and that inner glow lightening your eyes I cannot express to you what it meant to me. The years will have to tell you that, if in the kindness of God He gives us years together. I only know your face is like a flower, lovely and full of sacredness, and I thought your eyes spoke to my eyes, an understanding look, and told me I might dare.

These things seem hard and cold when written down upon paper, and the thought that you may laugh at them makes me quiver, for although your laugh is very lovely, these feelings I here hand over to you are delicately sensitive, for I love you, love you, love you. And that after all is the most satisfactory thing I can write, for it is true and deep and will reach out to eternity.

And now there are things I must tell you, though I can tell them better and more in detail when I get to a quiet room and a desk. But they are things you should know at once.

I am just a plain, poor, young man with a lot of hard work behind me, and probably a lot still ahead. I finished my course in medicine a year ago and have been working since to get together enough for a special graduate course which I need for what I want to do. This has been arranged for, and it was to meet by appointment the great man with whom I am to study that I had to tear myself away from you to-night. If I had missed the meeting it might not have come my way again. As I look back on the possibilities of the evening I find that in case I had had no opportunity to talk with you I would certainly have missed my appointment, much as it meant to me, and difficult as it was to arrange, rather than run the risk of losing you. As it was I found it by far the hardest thing I ever had to do to leave you. And after I was under motion and it was too late to go back it came to me what I had done, and I was appalled that I had let you bring me to the station, much as I delighted in having you to myself, and that I had left you at that hour of the night to go back alone! Oh, I realize that it was but a short distance in a well-traveled district and that you are probably quite used to being out that way alone. But it is not my idea of the way to take care of a girl, and it is not the way I shall want to take care of you if the precious privilege is ever mine.

I want you to understand that my people, though educated and cultured to a wide degree, are very plain, and not well off. I go from my appointment in New York back to our Florida orange grove where I have duties to that grove that mean hard work and plenty of it if the grove is to bear our fortune's worth this next season.

Be sure I would be planning to return straight to you, wherever that might be, before going south, but that the simple fact is, I cannot afford to be away from my work another day just now. The wind and the sun and the weather are doing things every day to my grove and my garden that will hopelessly tie my hands for the immediate future if I do nòt get right back to my work there. Even a day more makes a difference.

But know this, beloved, the moment I am free I shall come to you if you will let me, even if I have to walk to get there.

Now there is just one more thing, and perhaps it should come first instead of last, for after all it is paramount to everything else in my life. I want you to know that the first, foremost, and highest thought in my life, is of my Lord and Master, Jesus Christ, the Saviour of my soul. What He says I must do, where He leads I must follow. To study His Word is my greatest delight, and to witness of Him my highest joy.

Your place in my life, if you grant me your love, will be second only to my Lord.

I have been trusting that these standards are yours also, and surely, if that is so, we should have great joy in living our life together in Him.

Earnestly wishing that I might give you good night face to face instead of on paper, and eagerly awaiting some word from you, at the above address,

Your lover,
John Saxon.

John folded the letter carefully, and put it in an envelope. Then he drew the little missive she had given him from his pocket and read it.

"Miss Mary Elizabeth Wainwright."

He stared at it in dismay! Wainwright! Was she a Wainwright? What could it mean? Had some one played a joke on him? Had she put some one else's card in the envelope? Hadn't Jeff said that the maid of honor was named Helen Foster? Surely his memory had not played him false.

Carefully he went back over the time since he had arrived from the south. He recalled distinctly that Jeff had said he would like the maid of honor, that she was his kind, or something of the sort, a great church-worker. He had said that positively. He had certainly conveyed the idea that the girl was a Christian, in sympathy with his own beliefs and standards.

And now he recalled the bride's words from the back of the caterer's car, "But you haven't met her!" It hadn't meant a thing then but that nobody had introduced him, and he had to perform that function for himself. But now he began to see that something must have happened to the original maid of honor, and this girl had been substituted.

Wainwright! Now what would that mean? Wealth, honor, sophistication, all that made up a different world from his, and no guarantee whatever about her being a Christian! His heart began to sink.

And he, what had he done? Rushed ahead and committed himself without so much as an upward glance to see what had been his Lord's will in the matter! He had been so sure that she was all right. Her face had been so wonderful, her whole manner so lovely, so in keeping with what a servant of the Lord should rightly be, that it had never entered his mind to question, to hesitate. And now here she was a *Wainwright,* and he knew what the Wainwright tradition would be. He had come close enough to Jeffrey Wainwright before he had been born again, and closer still afterwards, to know that the family were utterly worldly. Jeff had mentioned no exception in his family, and he most certainly would have done so if there were one. They had had many a heart to heart talk about what Jeff's new life was to be after he took the Lord for his Saviour and Master. Jeff had known that he would meet with opposition on every hand. He had said that his family, though tacitly connected with church life, had no understanding whatever of the truth of the Gospel, nor of true Christian life. They had only a feeling that it was the respectable thing to do to belong to a church and might perhaps pave the steps to heaven by and by. Oh, God! Could she be like that? And he, pledged to give his life to the service of Christ! There was no turning back for him. There was no possibility of compromise.

Into his mind surged verse after verse of scripture. "Be not unequally yoked together with unbelievers!" "Can two walk together except they be agreed?" If his earthly love and his heavenly service did not agree his love would have to go. There was no question about that. His

Lord came first. And he was glad that before he knew who she was he had made that plain in his letter. But oh, what pain this might bring!—Certain pain to himself. Would it also perhaps bring pain to her, to whom his soul clave already?

John Saxon buried his face in the pillow beside him and began to talk to God, letting God search his heart, owning his own impetuous fault, asking for guidance and strength.

Gradually a number of things became plain as he prayed. For one thing he realized that a Wainwright was a very different proposition from a quiet, plain, village girl who had been a friend of Camilla's. He knew that Camilla had worked for her living. Likely her friends were of her status socially. A Wainwright would expect larger things in the way of wealth and position. A Wainwright would laugh at his presumption. He writhed as he thought of these things, as he remembered the mocking light in her eyes sometimes, the twinkle of fun at the corner of her mouth. Could it be that she was not what she seemed to be?

He remembered her lips on his, remembered her hand nestling in his. Was she only playing with him? Did she practise this sort of thing? No! His soul recoiled from the thought. He had given her his love, whether right or wrong, impetuous or wise, it was done, and he must trust her until she had been proved false. That was the first exaction of such love as his. And yet it must be in obedience to his Lord, or it could never be blest.

"Lord, Thou canst make her a child of God. Thou canst send Thy Holy Spirit to draw her to Thee if she is not already Thine. I do not deserve that Thou shouldst do this for me, but I ask it in the name of the Lord Jesus, for Thy glory, if it be Thy will. Nevertheless, not my will but Thine!"

Somewhat refreshed from contact with his God John Saxon sat up and read over his letter. After due deliberation he decided to send it. It was all true. It was no more than he had told her before he left her, and it was her due after what had passed. But there was a little more that he should say. So after some thought he wrote again.

The foregoing letter was finished and signed before I opened the envelope you gave me. I find now to my consternation that you are not the girl I was told I was to partner with. She was an utter stranger to me as much as you were. I knew nothing of her family or station in life. Her name, they told me, was Helen Foster, and I was not greatly curious about her, till I saw you coming up the aisle and knew that you must be the maid of honor, and my heart went out to you. I felt I must not run the risk of losing you.

Now, when I see your name, and know you are a Wainwright, my heart is turned to water and my hope sinks low. You come from a family of fabulous wealth and station, and I am a plain man with my way to make. I had no right to presume without knowing all about you. You must have laughed quietly to yourself over my presumption, for doubtless you knew more of me than I did of you. Also, I see another cause for blame in me. What right had I to assume that that other girl, whoever she was, would not be wealthy and socially prominent and resent an impetuous courtship as well as yourself? Oh, the whole thing has made me despise myself. I never knew I was impetuous before. Yet like any school boy I have confessed my love for you before you had a chance to judge me. It wasn't fair to you.

And yet, I love you, O I love you, Mary Elizabeth! I write your beautiful name reverently. Mary Elizabeth. How wonderful if I might some day say, *my* Mary Elizabeth!

I shall love you and pray for you. John Saxon.

Having addressed and sealed this letter John Saxon lay down to sleep. He was more weary than he remembered to have felt ever in his life, and as he sank off to sleep he had the feeling that something so fine and lovely that he was almost willing to give his life for it, had touched him and glanced away.

It wasn't a long night. The porter awakened him before they reached New York. He had time to get himself garbed for the day and pack away his evening clothes smoothly for the journey south. He would not be needing them again. At least not till he came back in the fall,—*if* he was accepted, and *if* he came back.

The morning light had not taken away his submission, but it had brought sober second thoughts. It had made him grave and almost sad. It had made him see his own act of proposing to a stranger, and such a stranger, as almost unforgivable. It had made him judge himself most severely. It would seem that he had entered this race with several handicaps that he was not even aware of until it was too late. His judgment had been on a debauch, and had landed him in a situation out of which there seemed no possible escape.

Now and then there would return to him a swift vision of the girl, and his heart would thrill to it instantly. Whatever she was she was not false, not mocking. He was sure of that. That clinging form, those yielded lips were not merely playing a part. The fact that they were not painted lips bespoke in part an inner cleanness of mind that would not yield to falseness of this sort. He found that most of all he wanted to find her true. Even if it meant a parting from her forever, he kept praying that she might be clean, might be true, as she had seemed to him.

Ordinarily the errand upon which he was bound that morning, the meeting of a world-renowned scientist who chose his associates from among the greatest scholars, and refused students at the slightest whim, would have kept him on the *qui vive*. He had so longed, so prayed for this opportunity, yet now that it had arrived it seemed small in comparison with what was occupying his mind.

He ate a meager breakfast sitting on a stool in a cheap restaurant, and thought in humiliation as he lifted the thick coffee cup and put it to his lips, that the girl whom he had dared to kiss last night might even now be driving in a great limousine up Fifth Avenue, or Riverside Drive or wherever the Wainwrights of the world took their morning airings.

Fool that he was, he might have known when he saw the make of her luxurious little car, and heard its costly purring, that she was not of his class at all. The very size of the stone she had worn under her glove, which he had touched there on his arm, might have taught him that a girl who could command gifts like that was not the girl for him to dare aspire to. Fool, fool, fool!

And presently, after she had gently and kindly told him where he belonged, she would tell her cousin Jeff, and he would have to go through all his life knowing that Jeff, whom he loved like a brother, despised his good sense, and regarded him less because of his impulsive act.

Lower in spirit John Saxon could not possibly have been, as he started out that morning to meet his appointment with the great man. He had borne poverty, toil, sickness, even sorrow like a man, sometimes almost like an angel, but this new form of trial, that was thrillingly sweet, and bitterly tender, and gallingly humiliating, really got him down and out. For a few hours a little demon sat on his throat and laughed to his fellows about how John Saxon, Christian, had surrendered to the common passion of love, and compromised with his good sense as well as his trust in God.

"I told you so!" the little demon cried to the others gathered round to gloat. "I told you his trust wasn't so great! I told you he'd forget his Guide and go the way his feelings led him when it came to something he really wanted!"

But John Saxon had not his trust in God for naught. The habit of prayer was too firmly fixed upon him to be long intermitted, and in his despair he turned to God. He prayed on the street as he went, threading his way among traffic and pedestrians. His heart was in touch with heaven, and his soul was crying out for help, for confidence, not in himself, but in the God Whose he was.

By the time he reached the place of his appointment he was steady and calm. His natural gravity sat well upon him, and there was none of the trepidation he might have felt at another time.

It was good to get in touch with every day affairs again, to be planning his life's work, to look into the face of the great man and read the genius that made him eminent among his peers. Saxon felt again the enthusiasm for his profession, the zest to do his best, and although he did not realize it, he made a fine impression upon the man who was accounted to be hard to interest.

The interview was not long. Dr. Hughes asked him a few crisp questions about his work so far, about his interests, and where he had pursued his studies, about his financial state, and how he had earned his way. He seemed pleased with the answers, and then, just as if it had been a foregone conclusion that he would be accepted, John Saxon found himself accepted and approved, was told briefly when and where and how to present himself in the fall, and with a brief handshake was dismissed.

He carried with him a glow from the last smile the great man had given him. Now, at least, he had something to say for his own prospects that needn't make him feel ashamed. It was not everybody who could claim to be this great man's special student. If all went well his professional future was assured.

And then his heart sprang back to last night. Sharp as a sword thrust through his heart went the thought that he ought not to think about Mary Elizabeth any more. And yet his human heart went throbbing on and loving her in spite of all.

How he longed to jump on a train and go back to the place where he had left her. Of course she wouldn't still be there. She didn't live there and she would have started home by this time. Finally he could stand it no longer and he got Long Distance and called the hotel, asking for Miss Wainwright. He had decided that he would tell her he had been anxious lest she had not reached the hotel safely alone last night. That was a poor excuse of course, she would laugh at it, but it would be so good just to hear her voice, even in a bit of laughter.

But he was promptly told that Miss Wainwright had checked out early that morning, and he hung up with a dreary, desolate feeling that his dream had turned into practical every day living and wouldn't ever come back. He had mailed his letter early that morning, against his better judgment. His judgment said it ought to be revised and less revelation of his own foolish heart and its deep feeling made known. But judgment had been set aside and he had sternly mailed the letter. He told himself that he had promised to write that letter and now that was done and it was up to her.

He wandered up to the shopping district which he knew well from his college days, and bought his mother a lovely little soft gray dress. It wasn't the kind of dress she usually wore, and she wouldn't likely have much place to wear it, but something in him yearned to bring into the life of his sweet little patient mother a bit of the beauty he had seen in other women last night. He got his father some shirts and ties, things he knew he needed, and his heart went out to them in a deeper love than he often took time to realize. They might be plain and unsophisticated, and many people might despise them, yet so all the more he would love and be loyal to them.

When he had finished his purchases, spending more than he really could afford, he idled past Tiffany's, lingered, went back, and finally went in. He wanted to find out just what really nice diamonds cost. Not as large and wonderful perhaps as that diamond must have been that she wore last night. He knew that there were rings of comparatively small dimensions that cost fabulous sums, but he wanted to see for himself just what one ought to spend for a reasonable ring, if ever he should see his way clear to get one—and if he should have anyone to get it for.

He came away from Tiffany's a sadder and wiser man, and went thoughtfully to the Museum to use the remaining hours before his train left in something more profitable than dreams.

DESPITE the fact that Mary Elizabeth had slept very little the night before, she was up and around quite early the morning after the wedding. She had several fish to catch and fry before she left the town, and she didn't intend to miss one of them.

She had her door a tiny crack ajar and kept watch as the different members of the wedding party came from their rooms, and it wasn't an easy thing to do either, because she wasn't sure how early they were going to start.

The bride's mother was the first to come out, with Miss York in trim traveling suit of sheer brown and a becoming brown hat.

Mary Elizabeth was on hand, fresh as a rose, as the elevator clanged its doors open to take them down. She had a letter in her hand to mail and she greeted Mrs. Chrystie enthusiastically. Mary Elizabeth liked the bride's shy sweet little mother, and looked her over approvingly. Her dress of soft black and white silk was most becoming, and there was a faintly haunting memory of Camilla in her eyes. Mary Elizabeth had fallen very much in love with her cousin's new bride, although she had had such a brief fleeting acquaintance on the wedding day.

"My dear!" said Mrs. Chrystie, "I'm glad you are here yet. I was so troubled last night when I couldn't find you. I wanted to thank you personally for coming in at the last minute and taking that important place in the wedding party. So many girls wouldn't have been willing. It was most gracious and lovely of you. And you did your part so perfectly without having to be told a thing. Of course you've been in so many such functions before it wouldn't seem the bugbear to you that it would be to a lot of girls."

"Oh, I just enjoyed it, Mrs. Chrystie. Jeff has always been like a brother to me and it was lovely to have an intimate part like that in his wedding," said Mary Elizabeth.

"Well, Camilla appreciated it more than she had time to tell you. The last word she said to me was to ask me to please hunt you up and tell you that you were just wonderful. She'll write you of course but she wanted me to tell you especially."

"Oh, I'm so glad she was pleased. She's lovely, Mrs. Chrystie. I was afraid I was going to be horribly jealous of anybody who married Jeff, we've always been so close. He couldn't have been dearer to me if I had been his own sister, though of course we haven't seen so much of each other the last five years while I've been abroad. But he's a dear! And I'm just crazy about Camilla. She just suits him. She's perfect. I couldn't have dreamed a girl for him any better. I'm so pleased. I do hope we're going to be so situated that we can see a good deal of each other. I never had a sister, and I've always wanted one. She looks like the sister I've always imagined."

"Why, how sweet of you, dear. I know Camilla will enjoy you. And by the way, she wanted me to tell you that Jeff was so pleased that you made his friend Mr. Saxon have such a pleasant evening. He said Mr. Saxon was usually rather quiet and reticent, especially with ladies, and he had been afraid he wouldn't have a good time. He had asked Camilla to be sure to introduce her old friends to him, but really, Camilla's old friends all seemed to have so many of their own friends around them that there wasn't any chance. And you took the whole responsibility and made Mr. Saxon feel at home. Camilla said she watched him and she was sure he had a good time."

Mary Elizabeth was not pale, even after her night's vigil, but the quick eyes of Miss York saw the color rise a little warmer in her smooth cheeks and a softened light come into her eyes.

"Yes?" said Mary Elizabeth quickly, her voice in perfect control. "Why, anybody would be honored to have the privilege of entertaining Mr. Saxon. He is—a most interesting—person, don't you think, Mrs. Chrystie? I certainly enjoyed every minute of the evening. I thought Jeff ought to be proud that he came so far to be best man. And I understand he is a very busy person indeed. Science of some sort, isn't that his line? He was—very—versatile. I—didn't find him reticent at all!"

Mary Elizabeth's eyes were dancing now with subdued lights and Miss York didn't miss a glint, but there was a little upward curve to her lips that had not been there last night when she had discussed Miss Wainwright with Mrs. Chrystie. She was beginning to feel that there was more to Mary Elizabeth than she had at first thought.

"Well, then, you must have interested him," laughed

Mrs. Chrystie. "And now, I do hope we shall see more of you. Are you leaving for—where?—this morning?"

"Yes, I suppose so," said Mary Elizabeth. "It all depends on Aunt Clarice. They're driving home and I promised to drive in their wake, and there's no telling what time they will appear on the scene. Aunt Clarice likes her morning rest. You know I drove Dad down yesterday afternoon, but he took the midnight train back home. He had some business this morning that he couldn't be away from, so I'll just take in some other member of the family I suppose. Are you leaving?"

"Yes, Miss York and I are driving up in Camilla's old car. She's willed it to me though Miss York is the driver. You met Miss York last night didn't you? She's our good angel, you know."

"I didn't meet her," said Mary Elizabeth with a warm little smile, "but I wondered who she was last night, and I'm glad to know her. I often need angels myself, guardian ones, and I might want to borrow her."

She put out her soft shapely hand and gave Miss York a warm grip, and that woman was heartily won over. She noticed too, as Mary Elizabeth turned away that the big glowing diamond she had glimpsed on her hand last night wasn't there this morning. Perhaps she had been mistaken in her judgment.

Mary Elizabeth went over to the desk and mailed a letter she had written about some trivial matter, and buying a morning paper sat herself down to watch the elevators for the next one of her victims. While she pretended to read the news in which she wasn't in the least interested, she reflected that she hadn't got much information so far concerning John Saxon. And yet, as she held the paper before her eyes her lips were smiling. John Saxon was reticent, was he? He hadn't sounded especially so as they came down the aisle together last night!

It was Uncle Warren and Aunt Fan who came down next to breakfast, and paused in the lobby to greet her.

"What, up so early, Mary Liz?" greeted Uncle Warren playfully. "I thought you'd have to take your beauty sleep this morning after being up so late last night."

"I wasn't up so very late last night, Uncle War," protested Mary Elizabeth quickly. "I wasn't up much later than you, I'll dare to say. I'm sure I saw your evening coat disappearing into the elevator just as I was about to go up myself."

"You don't say!" said Uncle Warren. "And what did you do with the big bronze giant? Or are you waiting now for him to come down and play golf or something? I saw you took quite a shine to each other last night. But look out, Mary Liz! He's a poor man. Jeff told me that yesterday. A poor man and a genius! You should never break the heart of a genius, Mary Liz. It unfits him to be a public benefactor. And besides, Mary Liz, I understand Jeff picked him up in a Florida swamp somewhere, and he wouldn't be your style nor able to go your gait, so I suppose you're wise to take up with that nice, settled, staid Grandpa Farwell. He can give you quarts of diamonds, and take you to all the horse shows in the world, and keep a general eye on your behavior. For you must own, Mary Liz, that you're an awful flirt, and I don't want any of Jeff's protégés trifled with!"

"Oh, Uncle Warren, aren't you complimentary!" said Mary Elizabeth with a gay little ripple of a laugh. "As if you didn't know that it was part of my duties last night to entertain the best man and make sure he had a good time! But you needn't worry about him, you gorgeous old fraud you, I understand he's left for parts unknown and he probably won't appear on the scene again."

"You understand! H'm! You understand!" grinned Uncle Warren.

"And as for Boothby Farwell," said Mary Elizabeth coolly, "I'm not looking for an overseer just now, thank you, though I suppose from your point of view I need one badly."

"Well, forget it, Mary Liz!" said her old uncle patting her cheek. "Had your breakfast? Why don't you come on in with us? Or are you waiting for some younger man to stroll by and ask you, my dear?"

"I'm waiting for Aunt Clarice to come down. I promised I'd take some of their party in my car, and I've got to find out just what she wants of me."

Aunt Fan patted her hand lovingly, and passed on to the dining room with her jocular old husband, and Mary Elizabeth settled down to her paper again.

But she had time to read the paper several times through before the other Uncle and Aunt appeared for they were having a discussion while they dressed.

"I liked that best man Jeff selected," the bridegroom's father was saying as he stretched his chin to give the last jerk to his tie.

"He was all right," said Jeffrey's mother, "only I did think it was such a pity he couldn't have chosen one of his own classmates, or some one in our set. It really isn't worth while to go out of your way to hurt people's feelings. There is Gerry Appleton, Jeff knows his mother is one of my very dearest friends."

"I don't see what that has to do with it. Jeff only gets married once—I hope—and why in Sam Hill can't he choose whoever he wants to be his best man? I can't think of Jeff ever choosing that little sissy of a Gerry, anyway."

"Really, Robert!" said his wife with dignity, "I don't understand your speaking that way of a son of an old family. It's bad enough for Jeff to have chosen a wife from an obscure family, a wife who had to work to earn her living, without having him go to the ends of the earth to haul up a nobody for his chief attendant at the wedding."

"Now look here, Clarice, it's time you got this thing straight," said her husband, facing her firmly with a glance of intensity from under his shaggy white eyebrows. "I told you very clearly that Camilla's family is just as fine and old as our own, and there have been several men of note in both her father's and mother's lines. I think you ought to put that idea out of your head once and for all. She is good and beautiful, and she loves Jeff and he loves her, and that is enough anyway. It was noble of her to go to work to support her mother when her father's fortune was destroyed through the wrong doing of their bankers. Would you have admired her any more if she had settled down on some of her distant relatives to be supported, or let her mother go to a Home? Now for Jeff's sake and for her sake and for all our sakes, you've got to put that snobbery away forever. Camilla is just as good as we are. And I'm saying that I liked that best man very much, and I thought you did too. You said so last night when you told me how much Jeff admired him."

"Oh, yes," said Mrs. Robert Wainwright. "He was all right. He is very good-looking of course, and appeared quite impressive standing up there by Jeffrey. But I am annoyed at Betty Wainwright that she should have made herself so prominent in his company all the evening. It wasn't required of her at all. She could have been polite without fairly falling in his arms. We certainly don't want two of our family going into obscurity for life, do we? Really I am worried about Betty. Her father lets her have her own way too much. Your brother Samuel always was too easy! You know I said that long ago."

"I wish you wouldn't call Mary Elizabeth 'Betty'!" said Uncle Robert in an irritated tone. "'Betty!'" he snorted. "It undignifies her good old-fashioned name. And as for the way she treated Saxon, I thought it was modesty itself!"

"Oh, yes, you always think everything that girl does is all right. You're just like Samuel. You haven't an idea how careful a girl has to be in these days. It's a good thing we didn't have any daughters, for you would have spoiled them terribly. I shall have to speak to my niece I'm afraid. She needs a woman's advice."

"You let Mary Elizabeth alone!" said her husband. "She's nice and sweet and good, and she doesn't need any advice. She's doing well enough bringing herself up. Now, are you ready at last? Where is Sam? Talk about spoiling, I don't see why you can't understand you are spoiling Sam, letting him sleep every morning as late as he pleases. He'll never amount to shucks if he doesn't learn to get up early in the morning. I've threatened him with cutting his allowance, but you always manage to excuse him somehow."

So they went down to meet their niece, who arose with a smile to welcome them and did seem to justify all that her doting uncle had said of her.

Aunt Clarice gave her an indulgent kiss and surveyed her critically.

"You're looking a little pale, Betty dear," she said as they walked together to the dining room. "I do hope your duties last evening as maid of honor were not too strenuous. It was hardly fair of Camilla to ask you that way at the last minute, you having no chance to prepare a special dress or anything. You did very well of course, but it must have been trying, dear."

"Oh, not at all, Aunt Clarice," twinkled Mary Elizabeth slipping on the armor that she always used in conversation with this aunt. "I had the time of my life. I enjoyed every minute of the evening."

"Well, that was good of you, but I think, if you ask me, that they might have raked up somebody from their own friends, if they had to have a maid of honor at all, since they didn't ask you at first. They really should have asked you in the first place you know, Betty Wainwright! It was quite the proper thing, since Camilla hadn't seen her own friends in a long time. It is certainly a wonder it all went off as well as it did."

"Oh, I thought it was beautiful!" said Mary Elizabeth. "And Camilla made such a precious bride. I'm just going to love her, Aunt Clarice!"

"Yes, she did very well," admitted the bride's new mother-in-law with a sigh. "It wasn't what I'd planned for my son, but I think she'll be all right. Of course it's a satisfaction that he's settled down at last and didn't do any worse. Jeff always was erratic you know. But—I'm very well satisfied."

"I thought it was a perfect wedding, Aunt Clarice, with not a thing to be criticized. Those bridesmaids were sweet, and the ushers were all Jeff's friends, and the best man was a peach! I'd never met him before, you know. How long has Jeff known him?"

"Only just this winter!" said Aunt Clarice with a resigned sigh. "And that was another regrettable thing of course, though it went off quite smoothly thanks to your kind offices. He's only a passing acquaintance that Jeff took an interest in. He's really nothing but a sort of teacher, or coach, scout master I believe they called him. He took Sam out with a crowd of boys for a camping trip. Jeff went along to see that all was right, and this is the result! But then Jeff always was so democratic! And

Sam just simply lost his head over him. I can't quite make it out, though I suppose it's all right, now it's over anyway, and we'll likely never see him again. Are you going to have grapefruit or melon, Betty dear? They do have such a limited menu in this rural hotel, though it's very good what they have, of course, and it did turn out to be quite convenient."

Mary Elizabeth's eyes danced. She had found out something more about John Saxon. So Sam was crazy over him! Then perhaps Sam could be made the key to her situation.

"Melon, please!" said Mary Elizabeth, and then turned a glowing face to her aunt.

"Aunt Clarice, you said your car was rather full. Why can't I take Sam with me? I haven't seen him much since he is growing up and I'd like to renew my acquaintance with him."

"Oh, would you want to bother?" asked her aunt thoughtfully. "I don't know but that might be as good a solution of the problem as any. Sam is always so restless in a car that he makes me nervous. He is always teasing to drive, and of course he can't. I certainly shall be glad when Sam grows up."

So Mary Elizabeth finished her breakfast hastily and went in search of her young cousin Sam.

6

JOHN Saxon in his upper berth—because it was cheaper and he felt that he should save every penny— tossed about uncomfortably, trying to keep his thoughts on something he had read in a medical journal during his long evening in the railroad station. Finally he threw discretion to the winds and let his thoughts drift back as they would to last evening. Was that perfume, borne to his mind above the stuffiness of sleeper curtains and the rank tobacco fumes from the smoking room? Perfume! Yes, the perfume of her hair as he held her in his arms when they said good bye. It didn't assert itself as perfume, just the fragrance of flowers. She seemed a lovely flower herself.

And there he was off thinking about her again! Fool that he was. A rich worldly Wainwright. Well, at least a Wainwright, and likely worldly too in spite of her delicacy and sweetness. And who was he to have presumed? He ought never to have mailed that letter of course. Very likely she didn't expect him to write any of the time. Very likely it was just a game with her for the evening, and she would think him an innocent that he kept it up.

Well, the letter was gone, he told his persistent soul that would keep defending her, and hurling the lovely thrills of memory at him to prove it. The letter could not be recalled, and he would have had to send one eventually. It was gone and if she never answered it, it would serve him right of course, and would probably be the best dose of medicine to cure his madness that he could take.

And then he went to calculating how long it would be at the shortest that he could possibly expect an answer. Inconsistency was in the ascendancy. Well, probably when he got home and got down to good hard work again he would settle down to sanity as well, and he would take good care never to let himself get caught in social life again. Here he had been always sneering at the follies of the social set, and then had fallen as far and as hard as anybody he knew. Fallen in love at first sight, committed himself without knowing a thing about her except her lovely face and manner!

He would get so far and then falter. The memory of that face and manner, even if there had been no words, even if she had not yielded those exquisite lips to his, disarmed every one of his efforts to put her away from his thoughts. She hovered quietly about him, like a lovely precious atmosphere that breathed balm and healing. And here was he who had always controlled himself, body, soul and spirit, utterly unable to keep his thoughts away from the dear memory of her!

Well, perhaps in the future years the time would come when he could think of her calmly, remember the sweetness of her, without that hungry longing for her, without that fierce desire to possess her for his own. It might be that in the ages to come he would even be glad that he had her safe in his memory, a lovely picture to look back upon, a picture that could never be sullied by human faults and frailties because he had known her only one brief evening. Even that was more than some men had, an eternal ideal never shattered by everyday living. At least, that much was his if nothing else ever came. Almost he felt like praying that nothing would, that she would somehow be prevented from destroying his beautiful vision of her, that she might never answer his letter rather than answer it with mockery, or worse still with gentle pity and kind refusal.

He groaned aloud and rejoiced that the train made so much noise that he might groan again and again and nobody hear but God.

And then suddenly he remembered that he was God's child in God's care, and this affair belonged to God—he had put it in the will of God to do with as was best and right. He must not meddle further.

Then softly there came a peace upon him, and he sank to sleep with that breath of fragrance drifting about him, soft arms clinging about his neck, soft lips, sweet lips on his. The memory of her smile! God, how lovely she had been! How wonderful that it had fallen to his lot to know her even for one brief evening!

Young Sam Wainwright when approached by his cousin Mary Elizabeth scowled. He did not take kindly at all to the idea of being shunted off from the general party. He had hoped to ride with his father and bully him into letting him drive perhaps, or into giving him money for a motor cycle in case the driving was beyond a possibility.

"You're riding with me, did you know it, Mr. Wainwright!" said Mary Elizabeth.

Sam's experience with older cousins, any older relatives, especially of the weaker sex, was that if they noticed him at all they wanted something of him.

"Aw, heck!" he answered ungraciously. "What's that for?"

"Well, you see," confided Mary Elizabeth in a low tone, with a furtive glance about, as if the family *en masse* were spying about to hear what she was saying, "I was just thinking there might be a bit of a crowd, and I was afraid they'd expect me to take Cousin Eliza Froud, so I thought I'd forestall that. I'd so much rather have you to buddy with. You know I haven't seen you for so long I'd just like to get acquainted with you over again, and have you tell me all about your school and your sports. They tell me you're a great sportsman."

"Aw, they're kidding you," said Sam, still with his unbending frown. "You can't get anywhere in sports with the family I've got. Mother thinks I'm a kid, and she puts her foot down on every blessed thing I want to do."

"Say, that's a shame!" said Mary Elizabeth sympathetically. "I wonder if she couldn't be made to understand? Suppose you tell me all about it and I'll use my influence."

Sam eyed her doubtfully.

"Nothing can influence my mother," he said sadly, shaking his head, "she thinks for herself."

"Yes," said Mary Elizabeth crisply, "but there are ways. We'll see what can be done. In the meantime you're going to help me."

"Oh, yeah?" said the incredulous youth. He thought the crux of the matter had arrived, and he didn't intend to be tricked into anything by a smooth-tongued cousin if she had been round the world.

"Yes," said Mary Elizabeth, "I need a man to-day to travel with me. A girl doesn't like to travel alone. Beside my car has been behaving badly. I might need you. Can you help change a tire?"

"I can change a tire all by myself!" said Sam with contempt. "I've done it in our garage when the chauffeur was out for the day, and he never knew it."

"Did you really?" chanted Mary Elizabeth like a fellow-conspirator. "How perfectly spiffy! Didn't he ever find it out?"

"Not yet. It was last week and he was too busy going on errands before the wedding to notice. He will though. He has eyes like ferrets."

"Well, he certainly won't know who did it, will he? You were careful to wipe off the finger prints I suppose?"

Sam laughed. He exploded first as if it came unexpectedly, and then he looked at her a minute and bent double laughing.

"Okay!" he said when he'd recovered, "I'll go with you. I wasn't going to, but you've got a sense of humor. So many relatives haven't. Jeff's the only other one that has and now he's gone."

"Oh, no, he's not gone. He'll be back sound as a nut pretty soon, and you'll like your new sister Camilla, too. She's a peach!"

"Oh, she's awright I guess," said Sam with a grimace. "But I don't see Jeff's getting married. Why couldn't he have stayed at home?"

"Well, it is strange, isn't it?" said Mary Elizabeth. "However I guess we can't do anything about that now. Now, partner, how much baggage have you got? Is it all packed? When do we get started? Or do we have to wait for the rest of the crowd? Because you know we might have some of our plans upset if we did."

"That's right," said Sam with another frown.

"Had your breakfast?" asked Mary Elizabeth.

"Sure thing!" said Sam contemptuously. "Had my breakfast an hour ago and been down to the wharf watching the boats. You didn't think I was going ta stick around till the family got up and then go in the dining room and have 'em all telling me what I was to eat, did you? It makes me sick the way they treat me, just like a baby."

"Well, that is hard lines, isn't it? Then suppose you hustle up and get your bags and bring them down to that side door over there, and I'll go and tell your mother we're starting ahead because I have a place I want to stop a few minutes on the way. There's a place I saw on the way down where they have the darlingest wire-haired terriers for sale, puppies, the cutest ever. Like wire-haired terriers?"

"Betcher life I do," said Sam, now wholly won over, his eyes shining with a great relief. "Gee, we're gonta have fun, aren't we?"

"Sure thing!" said Mary Elizabeth boyishly, giving him a real boy grin that endeared him to her, even as many an older youth had been endeared in the past.

So Mary Elizabeth ordered the porter to bring down her luggage, and went on her way to the dining room to let the uncles and aunts, principally the aunts, knov' that she was starting.

"But we wanted you to go along with us," said Aunt Fannie buttering and syruping her waffles.

"Sorry, Aunt Fan," said Mary Elizabeth sweetly, "I've promised to get home as soon as possible. I'm expecting some mail that is very important. And we couldn't see each other very much anyway on the road. You know it's terribly hard to follow a car and try to keep together in traffic."

"You'll drive carefully, won't you, Betty dear?" said Aunt Clarice.

"Oh, I'm the world's best, Aunt Clarrie, don't you know that?" smiled the girl.

"Well, be sure to see that Sam washes his hands and combs his hair before he leaves. I declare that child can acquire more dirt in a given time than any other of the human species I believe. Where he's been this morning I can't think! I went in to wake him up and found him gone. I don't know what he's going to grow up to! A tramp, I'm afraid. Well, I hope you won't regret your bargain taking him along, but it's a real charity, he makes us all so nervous. He gets restless you know, wants to get out and chase butterflies and dig up plants. Since he went on that camping trip in the winter he's simply impossible! You don't know what you're letting yourself in for, Betty dear!"

"Oh, I don't mind," said the girl with a happy smile. "We'll have a good time. Good bye. See you tonight sometime."

"Well, if you get tired of Sam just stop at that place where we took lunch on the way here and wait for us. We'll take him over and let you have Miss Petty, or Cousin Eliza Froud, you know."

"All right," said Mary Elizabeth, "I'll remember, but I won't get tired of my bargain so don't look for us." And Mary Elizabeth hurried out of the dining room.

She found young Sam with a suitcase, standing uncertainly by the door, an anxious eye on the dining room entrance.

"Didn't they can it?" he asked eagerly. "There must be some reason then. They likely wantta talk over the wedding and say how they hate somebody or they would."

"You uncanny child!" laughed Mary Elizabeth. "What made you think of that?"

"Oh, I've heard 'em when they didn't know I was

listening. They've made me like a lot of folks different times, talking against 'em."

"You're a scream!" said Mary Elizabeth. "I foresee we're going to have the time of our lives. Now, put your baggage in behind and hop in. Let's get started or somebody will try to go along with us."

"You said it!" said Sam, jamming his suitcase into the back of the car and letting down the cover carefully. "This is a peach of a car, isn't it?"

"It is rather nice," said his cousin settling down to her wheel as Sam sprang in slamming the door proudly as if he were the owner.

They rolled away from the hotel and around the little circle park in front and two blocks further on came to a halt before a candy shop.

"Like chocolates?" asked Mary Elizabeth fishing around in her hand bag for her purse.

"Sure thing!" said Sam with shining eyes.

She handed him a five dollar bill.

"Well, slide in there and buy as much as you want of anything that appeals to you. Get several kinds."

Sam took the money and crammed it into his side pocket with the studied indifference toward money he had noticed in all male persons when they were attending a young lady.

He came out so eager that he had almost lost his grown-up manner.

"I got several kinds because I wasn't sure which you'd like best," he explained as he climbed in and shut the door importantly again. He felt it was great, her using him this way, as any lady would send a young man on her errands. And she hadn't limited him as to how much to buy. He almost forgot that he wasn't driving the car.

"That's fine," said the lady curving smoothly into

traffic again. "I like them all. We're going to have a good time!"

"I'll say!" said the young cavalier. "Here's yer change!"

He almost felt that she was another boy and dropped easily into the boy vernacular.

"Oh, you'd better keep the change for any expenses we have. There is at least one ferry to cross if I remember rightly, and there'll be gas. You'll need more than that. Just put it into your pocket and look after things for me, won't you? It's such a relief not to have to bother. It's so nice to have a man along."

He gave her an appreciative grin, and after a minute said:

"Say, d'ya know, you remind me an awful lot of my scout master, Mary Beth?"

"Your scout master?" said Mary Beth with keen interest in her eyes. "Who is he? I hope he's nice."

"He is! He's a peach of a man. Why, he's Mr. Saxon, the one that was the best man last night at the wedding. You know him. You were talking to him a lot last night. Only he didn't look a bit like himself in those glad rags."

"Glad rags?" said Mary Elizabeth. "Doesn't he usually wear glad rags?"

"Naw, he wears khaki mostly, and flannel shirts and leggings. He's a crackerjack in the woods."

"He was rather nice, wasn't he?" said Mary Elizabeth with dreamy eyes as she guided her car out of traffic into a lovely country road. "I should think he would be good company in the woods. Tell me about it."

The boy's eyes grew dreamy too, and he stared off into a maple grove and saw live oak trees and palms instead. His thoughts were back in Florida with his idol.

"I don't know as it'll tell," he murmured. "You'd have to be there."

"I'll try," said Mary Elizabeth. "How does it look, the morning we start, or do we start at all? Do we just be there?"

Sam grinned.

"We start!" he said, entering into the game that his cousin was making. "We get up very early before it's light."

"I see," said the girl, her eyes half closed, "it gets light all of a sudden in Florida just as it gets dark all of a sudden at night. I know. I've been there. I only wish I could have been along with you. We wear old clothes, don't we, and don't take along a trunk, nor even a suitcase?"

The boy chuckled again.

"That's right. Just a pack. And we meet on the beach when the sky and the sea are altogether and look like mother's big opal."

"But that's very pretty," said Mary Elizabeth looking at him appreciatively. "Did anybody else notice it?"

"Aw, no, I don't even know as I did, but it was there if you wanted ta notice it. Mr. Saxon looked off at it a good deal. But he didn't say anything much. He doesn't. He only talks when it's necessary, except sometimes."

"What times?"

"Well, at night when we're sitting round the fire."

Mary Elizabeth thought that over while they were passing a series of trucks carrying a lot of new automobiles fresh from the factory.

"Well," she said, "what comes next? We don't just walk by the sea all the time."

Sam grinned.

"Next we have lunch. We boys rustle a fire. We were divided into squads you know, and each man had his duty. Jeff cut the bread and handed out butter. Mr. Saxon did most of the cooking at first, but afterwards we boys learned how."

Mary Elizabeth took in the picture.

"I certainly would have liked to be there. So Jeff was along too. That must have been grand."

"He was all right," boasted the proud brother. "He took care of the little kids. You know Mother had him go along because she didn't know Mr. Saxon, and I don't think Mr. Saxon liked it much at first, but afterwards they got to be buddies. And Jeff was fine, especially when the kids got scared of the snakes and things. There was one little kid hadn't any father and mother, or at least they didn't have any home together, and he was scared of snakes something awful. He just froze on to Jeff for a while till he got more brave."

"Snakes?" said Mary Elizabeth. "I don't know that I should care for them myself. *You* weren't afraid of them of course?"

"Naw, I don't mind snakes. There's nothing in snakes! Mr. Saxon told us a lot about their habits and things. He knows a lot about them. He isn't afraid of them. When he was a boy he used to have them for pets sometimes. His mother let him. He's got a swell mother! Mine would never stand for that! And once on the way we found a big red moccasin as big around as his arm and more than two yards long, and Mr. Saxon just picked him up by the tail quick and swung him around his head several times and flung him off, just like that!"—Sam demonstrated the manner vividly with his arms—"and Mister Snake he just lay still for a second and then he wabbled off all crooked, as if he was drunk. Mr. Saxon said it made him dizzy."

Mary Elizabeth considered this phase of her new friend several minutes. At last she said:

"He's not afraid of *anything*, is he?"

"I'll say he isn't!" said Sam.

"And what was it like when you got there?" she asked. "You finally got somewhere, didn't you?"

"Sure thing!" said the boy his eyes gleaming at the memory. *"And were we tired? And hungry!* We could have eaten nails. Sure, we got there. Why, it was all water, not the sea, just smooth water. First a little stream, and there were two Indians there with canoes, and we paddled till we came to a big lake with palms and tall pines around it, and across the lake was the camp. We got supper and sat around the fire on the sand to eat it. The sun went down before we were done, and the lake got all black like velvet, and then pretty soon the moon came up and made bright splashes like silver, and the rest of the lake was all like it had been lacquered. And then Mr. Saxon read—"

"How could he read if it was dark? You didn't have electric light in the camp did you?"

Sam threw back his head and laughed.

"I'll say we didn't. We had pine knots lighted and stuck in trays of sand, big wooden trays up on a post, and they flared like torches. They burned all night."

"And he could read by that light?"

"Sure, he read to us every night before we went to bed. Just read, and sometimes told us what it meant, just a word."

"What did he read?"

"Oh, the Bible," said Sam as if he was surprised that she didn't know. "He reads that all the while anyway, when he isn't doing anything else. You come on him lying in the hammock with his little Bible. He carries it in his pocket everywhere and gets it out any time when he's resting or anything. And he sure does make it plain when he reads it, just the way he says the words, without any talk at all, just reading. We fellas all liked it a lot. We wished he'd read longer, but he never did. It was always short. And then he'd sing."

"Oh, he sings, does he?"

"I'll say he sings! He's got a peach of a voice. And when he sings out in the open like that it's great! It just rolls out and echoes all across the lake. And then he made us sing too."

"What did you sing?" Mary Elizabeth's voice was filled with a kind of wonder. This Bible-slant on the man was something unexpected. Was it a part of his duty as a scout master? Was he under some kind of religious organization and had to read to the boys? She was considering this as she asked about the singing.

"Why, that first night we sang a chorus. He sang it first and then he taught it to us. Even Jeff sang. You know Jeff can *sing!*"

"Yes, he's got a wonderful voice," assented the audience.

"Well, when the two sang it was great. They took different parts, and say, it was silky!"

"What was the chorus?"

"Why, it was just a chorus. We learned a lot of them. Want me to sing it for you?"

"Oh yes, that would be great!"

Sam's clear treble piped out sweetly, every word distinct:

> *"I know a fount where sins are washed away!*
> *I know a place where night is turned to day!*
> > *Burdens are lifted, blind eyes made to see,*
> *There's a wonder-working power*
> *In the Blood of Calvary."*

"That's good!" said Mary Elizabeth hiding her astonishment. "Sing it again!"

Sam sang it again.

"It's very catchy. Try it once more and I'll hum it with you."

They sang it together several times and Mary Elizabeth saw it gave the boy pleasure.

"Gee, we had a good time down there!" he said, his face kindling with memory. "We useta sing till the old palm trees would rattle. We learned a lot of those choruses. I got a book home full of 'em. I'll show it to you sometime when you come around."

"I'd like to see it."

"Here's another. We useta sing this for a sort of grace sometimes before we ate.

"Everything's all right in my Father's house,
In my Father's house, in my Father's house,
Everything's all right in my Father's house,
There'll be joy, joy, joy all the while!"

"That's rather rousing, but wasn't it a bit hard on the little kid who hadn't any house because his father and mother were separated?"

"No, he just loved it. He useta go around singing it. It doesn't mean this earthly house down here, you know. It means heaven, and God's your Father."

"Oh!" said Mary Elizabeth in a small rebuked voice, marveling at the freedom of childhood. There was no embarrassment in Sam's voice. And yet she was positive most boys wouldn't speak like this of religious matters. Probably it was just this camp experience that had given him a different slant on such things. And that, of course, would be due to John Saxon! Amazing John Saxon!

She gave a little nervous shiver, warm though the day was. Serpents and gods! Her new friend and lover was as familiar with one as with the other. No wonder he had dared propose to a stranger going down a wedding aisle! Was she sure she wanted a lover like that, even though he could make love in a deeper strain than any who had ever come courting her before? Even though every new thing she heard about him but thrilled her the more? Gods and serpents!

Sam was singing over again that everything was all right in his Father's house and presently Mary Elizabeth was singing it too, taking the alto and delighting the boy with the blending of harmony.

"Say, that's great! I wish you had been down there, Mary Beth, you'd have just fitted!"

"H'm!" said Mary Elizabeth. "I don't know what your Mr. Saxon might have thought about it. By the way, Sam, why did you say I was like him? I'm curious about that."

Sam grinned.

"It was you sending me for those chocolates. And, gee! Isn't it about time we ate some?"

Mary Elizabeth handed over the chocolates with a smile and Sam crammed in a big chocolate peppermint and went on.

"Gee, you were nice, just handing over a lotta money and not saying how much to spend. If my family had sent me they'd have counted out the money and told me just what kind I hadta buy because it was 'wholesome.' Gosh! I hate that word wholesome! But you just let me have the fun of choosing. And that's the way Mr. Saxon does. He makes even work, fun, and he's always doing something for somebody, no matter whether he can afford it or not. Why he hocked his watch and some of his best medical books to send a little kid up north to a special hospital where he needed to go."

"He did?" said Mary Elizabeth, soft color stealing into

her face. "How kind of him! But—hasn't he got any watch now?"

"Oh, yes, Jeff found it out and bought his things in and managed to get 'em back to him so he didn't know who did it."

"That was nice of Jeff!" said Mary Elizabeth drawing a long breath and wondering why she was so glad that John Saxon did not have to go without his watch and valued medical books. "Sing that first song again, Sam, it kind of haunts me. There's something catchy in the tune."

So they sang it again and again, till Mary Elizabeth knew the words by heart.

"I'll sing ya another!" volunteered Sam. "Here's one we useta sing for morning prayers. It's to the tune of 'The Bells of Saint Mary's.' You know that one, don't ya?"

Mary Elizabeth hummed a little experimental bar or two.

"That's it. Only ya don't know the right words. You just haveta remember four kinds of songs and you have it. This is it:

"We'll sing in the morning the songs of salvation,
We'll sing in the noontime the songs of His love,
We'll sing in the evening the songs of His glory,
We'll sing the songs of Jesus in our Home above!"

They sang that several times together and Sam settled back replete with chocolates and happy as a boy of thirteen could be.

"Gee! Aren't we having a good time?" he said with a sigh of joy. "Gosh! I'm glad I came with you instead of the family."

"Well, that's nice," said Mary Elizabeth feeling a new

kind of joy in the boy's pleasure. She wondered if she hadn't been missing something in life by not cultivating children before. Then she remembered Aunt Clarice's words.

"By the way," she said quite casually, "how would you like to get out and stretch your legs a few minutes? See those three butterflies out there over that patch of buttercups? How about seeing if you can catch one of them."

Sam looked at her awesomely.

"You don't mean you'd stop on the way and let me chase butterflies?"

"Why not, if you'd like to?"

"But I thought you were in an awful hurry to get home?"

"Well, I thought I was," said Mary Elizabeth slowly, "but I don't know as it makes so much difference as that. I'd like to see you chase butterflies. If I didn't have my good shoes on I'd come and try my own hand at it."

Sam gave her a glowing look and started out of the car with a bound, but when he reached the fence rail and was about to spring over he suddenly turned back and hurried to where the car was parked.

"Say, I don't know as we'd better stop," he said cautiously casting a furtive eye back on the road. "The folks might catch up with us and Mother'd give me the dickens for holding you up when you are in such a hurry."

"Oh, that's all right," said Mary Elizabeth with a grin, "we're not on the regular highroad that they will take. I thought it would be more fun to be by ourselves."

The boy's eyes were filled with comprehension of her complicity, and with the deepest admiration that the eyes of a boy can hold.

"Say, you're swell!" he said eagerly. "You're just like

Mr. Saxon! I didn't know there were two folks in the whole world like that! You and he oughtta—oughtta—"

"Oh, that's all right, Sam," laughed the girl hastily, "don't worry about that. Run off and catch your butterflies before they are gone. I'll just sit here and think of something else nice to do."

Then Mary Elizabeth lay back on the cushions, with her cheek against the fine leather of the upholstery, and her eyes upon the dreamy, lazy, little June clouds that floated across a faultless blue, and thought of the new things she had been hearing about John Saxon. And then she closed her eyes and felt again his lips upon hers, thrilled again at the memory of his arms about her, at the words he had whispered in her ear. John Saxon! Oh, John Saxon! Why did you come marching down the aisle disturbing all Mary Elizabeth's well-ordered conventional life, and stirring up all sorts of longings that had never wakened before in her heart? Why did you make yourself the answer to every yearning of her heart, and yet be a new kind of person who would not fit at all into life as she knew it?

7

SAM came back eagerly with two butterflies, one pinioned in his cap, the other in his handkerchief. His face was dirty, and wet with perspiration, his hands were grimy, and his hair stood on end, but he was happy and his eyes were dancing.

"Gosh! That was fun!" he said as he climbed into the car.

Mary Elizabeth made him mop up to a certain extent at a brookside before they stopped for lunch, gave him an extra handkerchief for a towel, loaned him a little gold-mounted comb she carried in her hand bag to comb his recalcitrant hair. By this time he was as wax in her hands, and she felt another thrill of having captured his heart.

They had a wonderful lunch at a wayside dairy with milk in tall foaming goblets and ice cream made from rich cream, a few cakes and crackers for foundation, and they both decided it was the best lunch they had tasted in a long time.

Resting back on the cushions after lunch, Mary Elizabeth driving along through a bit of woodland, and Sam with the map on his lap, pointing out the turns to take in the road, the boy fell to singing again.

"I know a fount where sins are washed away!"

"Sam, why do you like that song so much?" she asked. "What have you to do with sins? You never did any very great sinning yet. You're only a kid."

"Oh, that doesn't make any difference," said Sam soberly. "Mr. Saxon said there was only one sin God judges people for anyway. All the others come outa that."

"What's that?" asked Mary Elizabeth sharply, wondering what new revelation was to come.

"Unbelieving," said Sam.

"Unbelieving?" said the girl in surprise.

"Yep! That's the big sin. That's sin. The others are only sins, and they're the result of it."

"What on earth do you mean, child?"

"Well, it's right!" said Sam with conviction. "It's all in the Bible. Mr. Saxon read it to us, and made us say it over and over and over. There isn't one of us will ever forget it."

"Well, explain, Sam. I don't understand."

"Why, you see, sin began in heaven," said Sam.

"In heaven? How could it? I thought heaven was perfect and everybody there was supposed to be sinless!"

"It was till Lucifer got stuck on himself," said Sam earnestly. "He thought he was It and wanted to be like God. He really wanted to be God and have everybody worship him and so he had to be thrown out of heaven."

Mary Elizabeth looked down at him in amazement.

"Go on," she said.

"Well, then Lucifer—he was called Satan by that time—came down to the Garden of Eden after God made Adam and Eve, and got in a snake and told 'em it wasn't so what God had said. You see God said they'd die if they ate any fruit off that forbidden tree, and they believed him instead of God, and did what God told them not to, and that's how sin got on earth. And death. That's why death hadta come. 'Cause God hadta keep His word."

Mary Elizabeth stared at the boy astounded. This was extraordinary talk for a boy. Also it was a story Mary Elizabeth had never heard before. She wasn't very familiar with the Bible, and Satan to her had always been something to joke about. It had never occurred to her that he was a literal person. Could it be that Sam had this right?

"Where did you get all this?" she asked after a moment's thought.

"Oh, it's in the Bible! Mr. Saxon read it to us. We studied Genesis an hour every morning while we were off on that trip. It was great. We liked it. Everybody liked it. Jeff did too. We had an examination on it the last day, and I had ninety-eight. I passed all right. And Mr. Saxon is sending us lessons this summer to do by correspondence."

"He is?" said his astounded audience. Then after an instant's hesitation, "Do you—*pay* him for that?"

"Pay him? Not on yer life. He does that just because he's interested. He wants us to get on. He wants everybody ta be saved. That's the most he cares about."

"Saved?" said Mary Elizabeth with puzzled expression. "Just what do you mean by that?"

"Why, saved! Eternal life and all that! 'God so loved the world that He gave His only begotten Son that whosoever believeth in Him should not perish, but have everlasting life.' Doncha know that? Everybody knows that. That's John 3:16 ya know."

"Why—it seems to me I've heard it somewhere," said

Mary Elizabeth uncertainly, perceiving that she was losing caste fast with her young companion.

"Well, that's about the most important verse there is, I guess. People can be saved just knowing that and nothing else."

Mary Elizabeth looked at him as if he had suddenly begun to speak in an unknown tongue.

"Just what do you mean by being saved?" she asked at length.

"Why, saved from punishment from yer sin. That's eternal separation from God ya know. I'm saved!"

He said it with an air of quiet conviction that was startling.

"How do you know?" asked Mary Elizabeth.

"Because Christ said so," said the boy. "He said: 'He that heareth my words, and believeth on Him that sent me, *hath* everlasting life, and *shall not* come into condemnation, but *is passed* from death unto life.' Mr. Saxon drilled us a lot on that. He said we might havta tell someone someday that was dying and afraid."

"And aren't you afraid to die?" There was awe in her voice now as she studied her young cousin's face.

"Not any more. Not since I was saved."

"How do you get 'saved' as you call it?"

"You just believe Christ died in place of you. Not just believe it with yer head ya know, but with yer heart. You just accept Him as yer personal Saviour. Then He sends His Holy Spirit to live in ya, and tell ya what's right and wrong, and help ya ta be pleasing ta Him. That's all there is to it. He does the rest."

Mary Elizabeth was quiet a long time and then she asked:

"Did all the boys in the camp get saved?"

"No," said Sam thoughtfully, "not all. There was Flinty Robison. He just listened. He seemed interested enough but he wouldn't ever give in and say he'd take Christ fer his Saviour. And he wouldn't pray. He said it was nobody's business what he did. And there was Stew Fuller and Corky Mansfield. They really didn't pay much attention. They snickered a lot. They haven't got much head, thóse guys, anyway. But we all are praying for 'em. I somehow think Flinty'll come sometime."

"Oh, you pray?"

"Sure thing! We got a prayer league. We write and tell each other who ta pray for. And Mr. Saxon writes ta us about it!"

They drew up just then at a filling station and no more was said about it. After they started on Mary Elizabeth seemed very quiet, and Sam was occupied in counting the different makes of cars they passed. He got out a pencil and paper and jotted them down. It seemed quite important to him. Mary Elizabeth was in deep thought adjusting this new light on her amazing lover.

She was realizing that the impetuous stranger had taken a deep hold on her inner life, and that everything she heard about him but filled her with more wonder, but this religious slant frightened her. Here was something in which she could not follow him. She wasn't sure she wanted to follow him even if she could. It would be almost like living with God to live with a man who thought about Him that way and was interested in the things of the Spirit. Mary Elizabeth realized that it would be wonderful to be loved by a man like that but wouldn't it be more than one like herself could ever live up to?

She thought of her other lovers in contrast. Rathbone Royce, steeped in art and literature, sophisticated to the last degree, adoring her languidly, critically, half sarcastically, bringing her gifts of rare editions of musty old volumes in which she had no interest, discoursing on modern philosophy. Herbert MacLain, gay, irresponsible, handsome, a bit given to drinking which he had promised to give up entirely if she would marry him. He was a dear and she was fond of him, but did she want to devote her life to keeping him straight? She wasn't fool enough to think that merely marrying the woman he wanted was going to change his habits. There was Raymon Vincente, a musician of real worth, successful, devoted, urging her at intervals to link her life with his. Last year she had almost thought at one time she would. But time had gone on, and the lure of his music, while still enchanting, had ceased to cover the multitude of his sins, till at last she saw the real man, a weak selfish character. There was Harry Kincaid. They had been going together more or less since their kindergarten days. There was nothing wrong with him. He was part of her everyday life, and often she had thought that fate had set them apart for one another, yet she continued to laugh him off. There was nothing thrilling in the thought of marrying Harry.

And lastly there was Boothby Farwell, he of the great square diamond, which last night she had been fully persuaded she was going to return as soon as she reached home. Was she?

Boothby represented perhaps the cream of all her lovers, not excepting a couple of men in Europe who had been quite attentive. Boothby was handsome, cultured, successful, prominent, popular, so rich that one didn't stop to think of a limit to his wealth, perfect in his manners, interested in science, art, music and literature, owning several city residences of royal dimensions and charm, and as many country estates, in addition to a castle in Scotland. She might live in a palace if she chose, if she were his wife. Horses and chariots and yachts, even airplanes would be at her command at any hour of the day. He could give her diamonds galore, and pearls; he was wanting now to buy her a rope of pearls and an emerald bracelet. His flowers were the costliest that came to her. He had intimate friends among royalty, an *entre* everywhere. His entertainments were always in good taste. Private views of pictures and plays, paintings and statuary, private hearings of great music performed by greater musicians, these were among the attentions he lavished. If she married him there would be practically nothing that money could buy that she could not have for the wishing. And he was only ten years older than herself, splendidly set up, with just a distinguished gleam of silver on the edges of his hair. He was not tied down by business, for his business had reached the pinnacle where it could take care of itself, and he would be free to take her where she would!

All this and yet she had let a poor young doctor make violent love to her going down a church aisle in the presence of an assembled multitude. All these other desirable lovers and yet she was still thrilling to the clasp of his arms at the station, the touch of his reverent lips at parting, the vibrant voice that told her he loved her!

And he was poor, and a stranger, a man who had to work for his living, and religious! Could any more incongruous set of descriptions be imagined for a possible aspirant to the hand of a Wainwright heiress?

It was late in the afternoon that they stopped again to let Sam forage in a great open space toward which he had turned wistful eyes. He came back this time with a big bunch of swamp lilies, like lovely flames, and Mary Elizabeth helped him to bank them up back of the seat where they would get the air and be out of the way. She noticed as she turned back to smile at Sam that his whole face was aglow with joy, and a certain interesting beauty had begun to dawn in it. For the first time she saw a slight likeness to her cousin Jeff in its happy lines.

"This is a great day!" he said reminiscently. "Gosh! I wish it could last! When I get home there's no one cares a rap if I have what I want or not. They don't pay the slightest attention to me except to tell me to stop whatever I wantta do!"

"Well, why don't we do this again?" asked Mary Elizabeth. "I'm thinking of going down to look over our shore cottage and see if I want to open it a while this season. How would you like to go with me?"

"Gosh, I'd like it!" he said earnestly. "I'd like it a lot. When ya going?"

"Why, I'm not sure," said the girl thoughtfully, "soon, perhaps."

"Gee! I wish I could go!" he said plaintively. "But I suppose they'll begin ta talk camp again as soon as I get in the house."

"And don't you like camp?"

"I'll say I don't!" said the boy with bitter emphasis. "Not the camp I'm supposed ta go to summers. I don't like the man that runs it, but his mother belongs to my mother's bridge club so she thinks I havta go. He's the biggest fake I ever saw. He isn't fair to anybody. And he's a coward too. He was afraid of a snake last summer. I hadta kill it myself!"

"Really?"

"Yep! And then he had the nerve to say 'we' killed it when we got back ta camp and he was telling about it. Just because there wasn't any other fella along who saw what happened, and he knew I wouldn't dare tell 'cause he could mark me down for insolence if I did!"

"Well," said Mary Elizabeth, "he can't be much like your Mr. Saxon then?"

"I'll say he isn't!"

"But don't you have a lot of fun at camp?"

"Naw! They're a lotta Miss Nancys! They aren't my crowd! They all live up on Bleecker Hill and go to the Prep School. I suppose I'd be there too if it weren't fer Dad and Jeff. They don't like that school a little bit. Mother's tried to work it several times, but they just told her I'd gotta have a real he-man school."

"Of course!" said his cousin. "You go to the same one where Jeff went?"

"Yep! And Mother thinks it's old-fashioned, but Dad says it has the best English department in the whole city. So at least my school's safe. I got on the right side of Dad about that. And Jeff was with me. I'm gonta miss Jeff a lot!"

He sighed a deep boy-sigh.

"But he's not going so far away!"

"No, but it won't ever be the same of course!"

"Don't you like Camilla?"

"I sure do! She's a peach! I've always wanted a sister. Course I'd rather have you, if you just lived at our house."

"Thank you!" Mary Elizabeth smiled. "I'll be a sister to you, Buddie, and I'll see what can be done about that camp, too. It's a shame when you know what a good camp is to have to stand a poor one."

"Oh, gee! I wish you would!" said the boy. "I just wish Mr. Saxon would start a camp up north!"

Then he suddenly put his head back on the cushion and began to sing:

> *"Calvary covers it all!*
> *My past with its sin and shame,*
> *My guilt and despair*
> *Jesus took on Him there,*
> *And Calvary covers it all!"*

Again and again he sang it, till Mary Elizabeth joined in. Then they went back over some of the songs of the morning, but came again to the "Calvary" one.

"I don't understand, Sam," said his cousin looking at her young companion through the dusky shadows that were beginning to settle down over the world as evening drew on, "a lot of your songs talk about how bad you feel that you're a sinner. That doesn't seem real. You haven't got any 'past with its sin and shame,' have you? You never felt you were much of a sinner, did you?"

"Sure!" said the boy in a diffident tone. "Sure thing, I'm a sinner! You see it's this way, you don't feel it so much till you're saved. You think you're pretty good till you know Christ, and get ta talking to Him, and reading about Him, and thinking about Him. Then ya begin ta see yerself. That's how 'tis. I can't tell you how 'tis, but it's so!"

"Oh!" said Mary Elizabeth in a small voice as if she were once more filled with awe over the knowledge of this scarcely more than a child.

Very soon after that the lights of the home city began to appear through the evening and the boy watched them grow nearer with gloom deepening in his face and voice, gloom that settled into silence.

"Oh, gosh!" he breathed as they turned into his own street.

"Don't despair, Buddie," smiled Mary Elizabeth. "This isn't the end, I promise you. You and I have found each other and I at least don't intend to lose you again."

"You're some peach!" murmured young Sam shyly, and then sprang out of the car and gathered up his things. "Can't-cha come in?" he asked wistfully. "Just a minute?"

"Sure!" said Mary Elizabeth, "I'm coming in!"

The family had arrived only a few minutes before and

there was a bustle of getting settled at home, but they pressed Mary Elizabeth to stay. Answering the wistful gaze of the boy she assented.

"I'll just telephone Dad that I'm back safe," she said, "and unless he's waited dinner for me I'll stay."

Sam waited anxiously outside the telephone booth, and was radiant when she told him that her father had a directors' meeting and hadn't been able to wait for her.

"You must be all worn out, Betty dear!" said Aunt Clarice as they sat down to the table. "I declare you certainly were a godsend to-day, taking Sam. I just couldn't have stood his restlessness."

"Why, we had a beautiful time!" said the girl with a quick look of sympathy for Sam. Poor kid! Was this the thing he had to stand continually?

"Well, you certainly are a wonder, Betty!" said Sam's mother. "He's the most restless creature! Now Jeff was different. Jeff never wriggled."

"You weren't quite so old then, Mamma," said Robert Wainwright bluntly, "your nerves can't stand as much as they could when you were young. As I remember Jeff he had a lot of spirit in him too."

"Now Robert, I'm not talking about spirit, I'm talking about wriggling and sighing and wanting to get out and run, and things like that!"

"Mary Beth doesn't mind that, Muth!" growled Sam protestingly.

"Your cousin Betty is very kind, Samuel!" said his mother firmly. "She probably minds it as much as I do but she doesn't let you know it!"

Sam cast a quick suspicious look at Mary Elizabeth and met the disarming steady look in her eyes, and the wide understanding smile.

"No, Aunt Clarice, I don't mind restlessness, I get restless myself. I like to stop and do things too, and Sam and I had a wonderful time. Butterflies, and lilies,—by the way, Buddie, did you put the lilies in water?"

"I sure did!"

"Yes," said his mother ruefully. "He took one of my priceless jardinieres and filled it full of weeds!"

"Oh, but they were wonderful in the swamp, Aunt Clarice," said Mary Elizabeth enthusiastically. "But say, Aunt Clarice, why can't you lend Sam to me this summer? I'm thinking of opening the shore cottage, and if I do I'd love to have him there. We could practise tennis together, and go swimming and sailing. Of course if we open the cottage at all Dad would come down every night, or week ends anyway, and I'd take Roger and his wife, and some other servants. It wouldn't be lonely for him even if I were away a day now and then. You know Roger just adores boys, and he would look after him."

"That's awfully kind of you, Betty dear, and I must say you are brave after having him all day long, but we couldn't think of taxing you that way, especially this summer. You'll be having a lot of guests, and you couldn't depend on Sam. He'd come down to meals with his face dirty and his hair sticking every which way. And that nice particular Boothby Farwell there so much! Sam would disgrace you."

"I'll take the risk on Sam," laughed Mary Elizabeth. "Besides Boothby Farwell won't probably be there very much. If I remember rightly he said he was going abroad this summer."

Mary Elizabeth's voice was very blithe. She didn't say that he had asked her to go along with him, but she was jubilantly remembering that she had decided not to go.

"Oh, but Betty! Europe?" said Aunt Clarice in dismay. "Surely you don't mean he's going this summer!

Why, I thought he—I was sure you—that is—why, I supposed you were engaged!"

"Nothing of the sort!" said Mary Elizabeth in a ringing tone. "He's just one of my friends, and as such if he were to object to my cousin Sam he wouldn't be any friend of mine any more. Really, Aunt Clarice, I mean it seriously. I'd love to have Sam stay with us this summer, and I know Dad would just be delighted."

"Let him go," said Sam's father suddenly. "That is, if he wants to. Do you want to go with your cousin, Sam?"

"I sure do!" growled Sam dropping his long lashes over his big eager eyes to hide their eagerness.

"Then let him go, Clarice. It'll be a change for him, and you know you don't want to bother with him up in the mountains!"

"Of course not!" said his wife firmly. "But Robert, I've already written and registered him at the camp where he was last summer. It's quite too late to make a change. You know they have a long line on their waiting list and it's a great honor to get in."

"That's all right! Let somebody else take the honor then. I'd like Sam to go where he wants to this summer. And it will do him good to be with Mary Elizabeth. She's a good girl to want him, Mother!"

"Oh, certainly," said Aunt Clarice severely. "Betty is very good. But it's really too late, Robert, I've already paid the registration fee!"

"Well, lose it then, if they aren't honest enough to refund it. I don't see making Sam a martyr for the summer if he doesn't enjoy the camp. You know he didn't like it last summer."

"But Robert, it's so good for him. They are such a refined set of boys that go there."

"Refined *nothing!*" murmured Sam under his breath.

"And the young man who has charge is such a marvelous person!" said his mother waxing earnest. "His mother is one of my dearest friends! I really couldn't go back on it now, the matter has gone too far."

"Nonsense!" said her husband. "Sam is old enough to choose where he wants to spend his summer, at least within limits. We always allowed Jeff to do that and it seemed to work well. Look how he turned out!"

"Now, Papa," protested his wife, "you know I always felt that that one summer he spent with those quite common friends of his in Canada did more harm—! He got notions about being democratic. He seemed to think that all people were alike and one was as good as another."

"Well, aren't they?" snorted Papa, who always grew exasperated right at the start. "I'm sure Jeff turned out all right anyway."

"Well, of course," said his wife elevating her eyebrows, "but look at all the worry I had about him while he was going with that impertinent presuming movie star, expecting him every day to announce that he was going to marry her."

"Well, he didn't, did he?"

"Well—Papa,—you certainly don't think he looked very high when he did marry, do you?"

"I certainly do!" snorted Papa. "Camilla is a good girl. What more could you want?"

"Oh, yes, she's *good!* Of course she's a good girl. I have nothing to say against her."

"Well, you'd better not have since she's your son's wife. And she's beautiful! You couldn't find a more beautiful girl than Camilla if you searched the earth over."

"Oh, yes, she's beautiful; I admit that! She's good and beautiful!"

"And she loves him, doesn't she?"

"Obviously."

"And he loves her?"

"Quite obviously, of course. Still, you must own she hasn't anything to boast of in money or family."

Aunt Clarice was in her most disagreeable form, with cold steady gaze down into her plate, and impenetrable front.

"No, she is only the daughter of a highly respected man who lost a good fortune through the fault of others, just as nine out of ten business men have been doing to-day. And honorably, too, which isn't the case with many of them. And as for money, hasn't Jeff got enough for both of them?"

"Oh, yes, you Wainwrights are so open-handed about money," sneered his wife.

"And if I mistake not," roared the head of the house, now thoroughly aroused, "the girl that you most highly favored as eligible for Jeff was the daughter of a scoundrel who was convicted of graft and crime of the most flagrant sort, and is outside of jail only because he was able to pay three hundred and fifty thousand dollars to get free. Yet you shut your eyes to all that! You wanted our son to marry her and partake in the money gained through crime. I'm thoroughly ashamed of you, Mamma, and I don't want another word ever said reflecting on Camilla. She is our daughter now, and as such her name and antecedents are irreproachable, in my presence at least. And I'm surprised that you will cast such insinuations on her before Sam."

"That's all right, Dad," said Sam, "I think Camilla is a peach!"

"Certainly, Son," said Robert Wainwright, "of course she is. And that's what your mother really means, only she has got herself all wrought up over this camp business. But I'm putting my foot down, now, Clarice. Sam goes to no camp this summer, unless he wants to, and he will never go to that special camp again, no matter how much money has been paid. If Mary Beth wants him, he can go with her."

Sam drew a breath of relief and grinned across at his cousin.

"I think you are very unwise to discuss such matters before Sam," said his mother offendedly. "And as for aspersions, I certainly didn't cast any aspersions on Camilla. I'm exactly as fond of her as you are, and I don't know what Betty dear will think of you."

"That's all right, Aunt Clarice," smiled Mary Elizabeth with a sly twinkly-wink at Sam, "I'm so glad you're going to let me have Sam. I'll try to look after him and make him have a good time, and we're going to get really acquainted this summer, aren't we, Buddie."

"Sure thing!" said Sam, and arose gallantly to help her pull back her chair as they were leaving the table. Mary Elizabeth soon went home, wondering if it would be possible for that promised letter to have arrived yet?

8

MEANTIME, down in Florida, a little light twinkled in the inner recesses of a small neat house deep in an orange grove, and two people sat outside on the porch watching the great June moon come slowly up.

"Well, Mother," said the man, "I suppose the festivities must be about over now. John's probably marching down that church aisle with some high and mighty flibberty-jib of a bridesmaid, now."

"The maid of honor," corrected the sweet old wife. "Yes, I've thought about her, too. Oh, I do hope John won't fall in love with somebody utterly unsuitable. He's such a wonderful boy."

"And being a wonderful boy of course he won't!" said the father decidedly. "I'm sure I don't see what you find to worry about, Mother. He's steered himself safely through all kinds of groups of girls, and isn't scathed yet. You don't suppose he's going to lose his head just because he's best man at a wealthy wedding, do you?"

"No," said the mother with a slow little trembly sort of sigh. "I suppose not. But—life is so full of pitfalls."

"Meaning girls," said Father.

"Yes, meaning girls. You know that yellow-haired girl that came out here one day last winter hunting for Jeffrey Wainwright after he had gone home to his Camilla. She was—unspeakable!"

"Yes," said the father, "she was, but don't you know John would have thought her unspeakable too? And besides, Margaret, have you forgotten that John is under guidance. Our Father isn't going to let our John go through anything that He doesn't want him to meet and pass safely through!"

"I know." The voice was very sweet and low. There was strength and sweetness in the dim outline of her cameo face, a hint of John Saxon's seriousness and depth of character in the soft brown eyes she lifted to gaze at the moon. Her hair was soft and white. She reminded one of a delicate flower, fragile and sweet.

They were silent for a long time watching the moon march up the heavens. At last the old man spoke. He was fine and strong himself, though a bit bent with hard work, but there was still the ring of the conqueror left in his voice.

"Isn't it time you went in, Margaret?" he asked at last. "You know these nights are really chilly even in June, after the terrible heat of the day."

"Oh, Elam, it's such a relief after the heat of the day. I can't bear to leave it, this sweet coolness. I love to watch the dark shadows among the orange trees, and I love the perfume in the air. I sort of dread to-morrow again. That intermittent rain, and steamy sunshine are almost unbearable sometimes."

"You poor child!" said the man regarding her anxiously. "I'm almost afraid this is going to be too much for you. It will likely be only another year or two before we can afford to go north for the summers. The grove is coming into bearing so nicely now, and if we just don't have another freeze we'll be on our feet. But Margaret, we could have borrowed money on the grove and sent you north this summer. You ought to have gone with John. Even a few days in another climate would have done you good. You've been down here too long."

"And what about you, Elam?" said the sweet old voice.

"Oh, I—I am all right! You know I like this hot weather! I just thrive under it. It's you I'm thinking about. You've been down here too long. You ought to have gone with John. He would have found a nice quiet place for you to board cheaply—"

"I? All alone? Oh, father! I couldn't stand it alone. I'd just mourn for you. Nonsense! Don't talk like that! I can't even bear to think about it!"

"Well, I'm not so sure John won't say something more about it when he gets back. If he gets the chance to study with that wonderful doctor he's talked so much about, there's no reason why he couldn't take you with him and let you mend his socks and cook his breakfast at least."

"No, Elam! I'd never consent to go and leave you! Never! And as for John he needs every cent he has saved. He's got to have these advantages he's worked so hard for, and we ought to save everything we have to help him out."

"Oh, John'll do all right. Don't you worry about him, Mother. He's young and strong. Mother, do you realize how late it is getting? That wedding must be about over. They've eaten the ice cream and cut the wedding cake, and maybe thrown rice, or is it old shoes they throw at the bride? And it's time you and I went to bed."

"We don't go to a wedding every night, Elam," said the old wife wistfully. "I've been looking down that aisle in the orange grove watching the bride walk away from the altar and thinking about our wedding, Elam. We had a nice wedding too."

"We certainly did, Margaret, and you were the most beautiful bride a man ever had. And you're beautiful to-day, Margaret. Your hair was brown then and it's silver now, but it's just as lovely. In fact I don't know but you look even more beautiful to me to-night than you looked then. You were almost a child then, a bonny child, but untried. But now I can see the dear lines that time and care and pain and sickness and trouble and poverty have graven on your face, and they have only made you more lovely. I think it'll be like that in heaven, Margaret, we'll see the graving that life has put upon us; in some it will have cut away all the faults and mistakes and follies and there will be little left, but with those who have been faithful in the testings it will show up a wonderful beauty!"

"You're a foolish old flatterer, Elam Saxon, and you always were, but I like it of course, and I could say a great deal more about the way you've been true as steel, and strong and courageous and always borne me up. You've been a tower of strength!"

"That's it, Margaret, that's it! Keep it up! I know it's overdrawn, but I like it too. And just to think all those years have passed since you and I walked down that aisle together into life, and now our boy is attending a grand wedding and taking part in it. I'd like to see it, wouldn't you? He'll tell us all about it when he comes back."

"Yes," said John Saxon's mother, and drew a little fleeting sigh. "And then, some day, he'll probably be walking down an aisle on his own account. And oh, I hope he'll get the right girl—!"

"Of course he will!"

"And that you and I can go to the wedding," finished the sweet old breathless voice hurriedly.

"We'd go to John's wedding if we had to cut down the orange trees and sell them bit by bit for kindling wood. We'd go if we had to *walk!*" said the father rising and reaching out his hand to her. "Come, Mother, it's time for you to be in bed. John's finished this wedding and gone to his train. It's midnight, and to-morrow he's going to see the great doctor man. We'll go in now and pray for John!"

Mary Elizabeth arrived at her own home, looked eagerly among the mail lying on her desk and felt a distinct pang that there was nothing there that she could not immediately identify. It seemed reasonable to suppose that if he wrote a letter as soon as he got on the train it might have reached here by the time she did, and her heart went down with a dull thud and seemed to touch the foundations of things.

Maybe he wouldn't write at all. Maybe this had been after all only an incident with him, and now it was a closed incident although her heart bounded up once more and told her firmly that that couldn't be so! After all she had been hearing from Sam about him, he just couldn't be that way. It was impossible!

With her heart on the rebound again she sat down and gathered up the rest of her discarded mail and went through it. Nine invitations. She threw them down on the desk. They didn't seem to interest her, no matter what they were. Several bills, those didn't bother her. Bills never had. Yet it did come to her with a strange pang that there were people in the world who had hard work to meet bills when they arrived. John Saxon was a man who had always had to be careful. To think of his pawning his watch and precious books to send that little child to be cured. How wonderful of him!

There were racy letters from several of her girl friends

telling of their social engagements, of their triumphs and disappointments. They all seemed flat to her just now. Perhaps by and by she would be interested in them again, but now her heart was on the *qui vive*. Was it possible that a few hours in the company of one stranger had entirely queered the flavor of other life for her? Ridiculous!

She reached for the last letter in the pile, Boothby Farwell's. She recognized the handwriting at once of course. He had a pride in doing everything he did precisely, and perfectly. His handwriting was no exception. It was almost like copperplate. The address on his letters was always intriguing because of that perfect writing. Yet she found herself drawing a weary sigh that she must read that letter and face the problems that it would inevitably bring to light.

She still had that gorgeous ring in her possession. She had promised, half reluctantly, to wear it while she was away, and test herself out. He had hoped, she knew, that it would help her to a decision. He had thought, she was sure, that she was merely playing with him, and that she certainly meant to marry him in the end, and she felt he was growing weary of the delay.

She had gone away to Europe twice to get away from his insistence and his persistence had almost brought her to think that perhaps she might yield in the end. If she had not felt so she would never have consented to take the diamond away with her. She had taken it more to please him than with any real idea of keeping it. He had counted greatly on the beauty of that stone, she knew. He was proud of it. And indeed no man could show his devotion more flatteringly than by presenting the woman of his heart with a remarkable stone like that. Perhaps she had even been a little pleased herself at the thought of wearing it, of trying out the idea that it belonged to her.

And she had worn it but one short hour! What would he say if he knew?

Then she opened the letter and read.

There was a smug assurance about his sentences that had never struck her before. Perhaps she had never really taken him seriously until now. Perhaps the wearing of his ring for that one brief hour had given her a new vision of what he was and what it might be to live out the rest of her days by his side.

He seemed to take it for granted that all was settled between them, now that she had consented to wear his ring, at least to receive it for consideration, for that was all he had at last persuaded her to say. And now he wrote as if she had actually become engaged to him! She was astonished how it annoyed her.

The letter was about their plans for the future. That is, he was announcing to her when they would be married, and what they would do, where they would go, and how they would live. It would seem that he had thought out every detail and had no idea of asking her to suggest what she would like. His was the last word in everything, his taste, his wishes, his likes and dislikes.

And then she suddenly saw something that had not been plain to her before because she had not been thinking much about such things, and that was that she did not, could not, never had loved him at all. She hadn't even been considering him from that standpoint. In fact, love had not figured in her thoughts with regard to him. It had all been a question of whether he would be pleasant to get along with, and one whom she could rely on to act according to the code of her upbringing. She hadn't been very sure a few days ago that there was such a thing as love, and that if there was, whether it was something to be seriously considered when one was thinking of marrying. Very young uncontrolled natures might indeed fall into what they called love, a sort of wild idealism that took hold of unanchored souls, but never of well-trained sane people who could look ahead and plan for the future.

Now she saw that she had reckoned without knowledge, and that new knowledge had come to her hitherto untried soul and given it a vision that changed everything.

That one brief walk down a church aisle, those few, sweet, deep sentences, red hot from a strong true heart, had changed her whole outlook on life. She suddenly saw that it made all the difference in the world whether you loved a man or not if you were going to marry him. There might be other weighty matters to consider, but that was the first, and must be paramount to all others. And she saw that if she loved Boothby Farwell this letter would thrill her—or would it? She read some of the smug dictatorial sentences over and considered them in the light of possible love between them and they still sounded almost selfish and utterly conceited. Oh, he told her in very fine English that he loved her, that she had been his ideal woman for a long time, that it was a great satisfaction to have the matter settled at last, and that now he might begin to put his mark upon her, and enjoy her.

It seemed as if she were a new car, or an exceptional kind of yacht that he had been purchasing, and that he were setting forth the price that he was to pay. She was to be taken to the ends of the earth to see all the things he enjoyed seeing, and then they were to settle down where *he* had always wanted to live, and do the things *he* liked to do, and *she* was to *like* them.

Then her mind ran away from the words her eyes

were reading, back to last night, to precious words that had been spoken in her ear in desperate haste, the dear feel of arms about her that hungered for her, the look that she had felt meant lovely deference to her in all ways possible!

Then there was another thing she began to understand, and that was that when a man loved her that way and she loved him, her utmost desire would be to please him and not herself, and that any true marriage would be that way, each desiring most the will of the other. Strange that one brief evening with a stranger had taught her all that!

At last she cast Boothby Farwell's letter aside, carelessly, gathering it up with her other letters and stuffing it in a drawer. In the morning she would send back his ring. That was a foregone conclusion!

Stay! What had his letter said? That he was calling at eleven in the morning to go with her to look at an estate he had thought of purchasing, and they would lunch in town together afterwards.

Well, then, the ring must go back to him earlier. She did not want to look at estates, and she did not want to argue questions of matrimony with him any more.

So she seized her pen and a sheet of paper and wrote large:

> *Dear Boothby:*
> *I tried your ring for a little while, but I found it far too heavy for my hand. I couldn't live up to it. And the truth is, Boothby, I find I don't really love you enough to marry you, and so we'll just call the whole thing off if you please.*
> *Sorry I can't ride with you in the morning but I have another pressing duty which includes lunch, but thank you for the kind thought of me. And I hope you won't*

hold it against me that I hadn't thought about this matter of love before, for it really seems quite important you know. So I'm returning your ring by Thomas who has instructions to give it into your hand direct.

Always your friend and sincere well-wisher,
Mary Elizabeth Wainwright.

Then Mary Elizabeth sealed her letter, put the ring in a lovely white kid box, enclosed both letter and ring in another worthy box, addressed her package in that same firm large writing, set her alarm clock for an early hour, and went to bed to dream she was walking down that church aisle with John Saxon.

9

SAM Wainwright woke early the next morning and began to consider his prospects for the summer. He felt very sure that something more must be done, and done quickly, or his mother would manage it somehow that he would go to the sissy-camp after all. He had had one-night victories before that had turned out the wrong way next day. But what to do was the question?

Of course he might write to Jeff, but Jeff was a long way off by this time, in fact no one knew yet where Jeff had gone. Silly thing, that, going off from everybody just because you had got married. He wouldn't do that when he got married, if he ever did, he'd stick around and have a good time.

And like as not Jeff would be too busy getting acquainted with Camilla to answer him right away, even if he knew where to write, though Jeff was always pretty good about knowing when things were important. Well, he'd write. He'd get up pretty soon and write just a line or two anyway, and likely Dad would know where was a good place to send it. Jeff would tell Dad. Dad knew how to keep his mouth shut.

His next best bet, he decided, was Dad. He would get Dad off by himself and tell him some more about that camp. Tell him plenty. Tell about the gambling that went on there, that would get Dad's goat. Tell him about some of the songs they sang and the stories they told. Tell him how that poor fish that thought he was the camp manager was off with a lot of fool girls all the time and didn't pay any attention to what the fellas were doing. Tell him you could get by with anything. Those things would open Dad's eyes.

And then he'd tell Dad about Mr. Saxon's camp, how different it was. He'd tell him to ask Jeff about it.

He lay still a long time thinking what he would say to Dad, thinking how the Florida camp had cemented the boys together in a bond of friendship that never could be broken, thinking about the camp fires and the singing, and the prayers, and suddenly his eyes grew large and thoughtful and he arose from his bed, and went down on his knees. God knew about the camps, both of them, and if God wanted him to go to the sissy-camp of course he had to go, but personally he felt sure God wouldn't approve that camp at all. So he put the matter before God in his most earnest way, and then, with a cheerful face he arose and began to dress rapidly. He was no longer worried about his summer. He felt sure that his prayer would be answered. He meant of course to do all he could to help answer it himself, but he had confidence that God would look after the rest for him, and he went down the stairs whistling softly, knowing that his father usually ate breakfast early and went to town before the rest of the household was even awake.

His father looked surprised when he walked into the dining room. He lowered his paper and greeted him with a smile.

"Thought mebbe I'd go down ta the office with ya,

Dad," he said genially. "Thought mebbe ya might miss Jeff a little, and I could take his place, run errands ur something for ya."

"Why,—ur—yes, Son, that's a fine idea!" said Mr. Wainwright pleasantly. "But—aren't you afraid you'll be bored to death by business?" He regarded his son with a puzzled grin of surprise.

"Well, I guess it bores you sometimes too, doesn't it?" said Sam accepting hot biscuits from the waitress. "I suppose ya can't stop doing things just because they bore ya! I think it's time I began ta learn some things about the business, don't you?"

"Well, Son, I hadn't thought of it in just that way yet. I thought at your age you might take a little more time at doing what you pleased before you got into the grind of business."

"Aw, you can't begin too young," quoth Sam. "I'd like it if you'll give me a job down there for a while, that is, till Mary Beth needs me. I could go with her for a little vacation p'raps and then come back and work again till school. I can't see just hanging round."

"Well, Son, suppose you come along down with me this morning anyway and we'll talk it over. I like your spirit at least."

"All right, Dad. Thank you. I'll like that a lot," and Sam ate his breakfast in grave silence letting his father finish the paper, and then together they went out to the car and drove to the city.

It was a pleasant ride for both of them and Sam managed adroitly to put a picture of both camps before his father which opened his eyes not only to the camps and their respective managers, but also to the fact that this boy Sam was no longer a wriggling writhing youngster with no thought for anything but play. He had thoughts, good original ones, and wanted to do things with his hands. His father realized that there was a wistfulness in his funny off-hand casual remarks that held a hidden appeal for a new kind of sympathy, a yearning for understanding that he could not get from only women.

Sam talked a little about Mary Elizabeth too, and how she had been "such a good scout" and was interested in boy things, and finally his father said:

"So you'd like to go down to the shore with your uncle's household a while when your mother goes to the mountains, would you?"

"Sure I would!"

"All right, we'll fix it that way if your cousin really wants you. But, Son, don't get up an argument with your mother. Just you hold your tongue and grin, and we'll fix it."

"Okay!" said Sam with satisfaction, and followed his father up to the office.

All that morning he stuck to his father gravely, sitting silently without wriggling, and doing eagerly any little errand his father found for him. He proved himself keen and attentive when he was allowed to look through the files for some papers. Of course he didn't know that they were not important papers, and that his father was merely trying him out, but perhaps he was just as careful as if he had known. Somehow Sam had a new motive in his life, a motive that made it seem worth while to do everything you had to do in the very best way you knew how.

During the whole morning while Mr. Robert Wainwright was engaged in important affairs, there was an undercurrent of interest in that quiet stubby boy over there, his freckled face so earnest over the filing cards he was working with, his brow drawn in a puckered frown as he laboriously copied names and addresses from the filing cards into a neat list. When he brought it at last for inspection his father was surprised at the neatness of the work, and the clear legible writing. There was going to be character in that hand a little later. There was character and strength of purpose in the freckled tip-tilted nose and clear brown eyes. There was something else, too, his father saw. A clear vision and balance that he was sure had not been there a short time before. Could it be the result of that Florida camp? He must look into that. He must cultivate this son. It would help to ease his loneliness about losing the other son.

And yet he had not lost Jeff! He was going into business with him as soon as he returned from his wedding trip, and they would see each other every day. Well, he would take both sons into business. He would gradually work Sam in little by little whenever he felt the urge for work. And as for that camp the boy disliked, he must see that Clarice didn't try to press that any more. The boy was old enough to choose a few things for himself.

"We'll go to lunch together, Son," he said to Sam in a low tone and together they walked out of the office, Sam swelling proudly and holding his shoulders up squarely. His father eyed him proudly too. He was a well set-up lad, and would be as tall as Jeff when he reached his age. He watched the light play across the speaking face of the boy, and a tender mist spread over his eyes. Sam, little Sam, growing up!

For a week Sam stuck close to his father, and his mother almost forgot she had to worry about him. He hung around the office making long lists of names from old files. The lists were unnecessary to the business of Wainwright and Company, though he did not know that. But his father felt they were necessary to the study and development of his youngest son, and the lists went on, each one written a little better than the last, and bringing a quiet word of praise to the writer, and Sam was content.

When there was nothing to do Sam fell into the habit of pulling out a little book from his pocket and sitting engrossed in it until there was need for him.

One day his father asked him what he was reading and he said he was learning some scout stuff, and when his father looked over his shoulder he saw he was studying the third chapter of John's Gospel.

"It's just some stuff we all promised Mr. Saxon we'd learn," he explained.

When Robert Wainwright went home that night he delved into the bookcase and finally brought out a rusty little old Bible in very fine print and retiring to his own private room read the third chapter of John's Gospel through considerately.

"It's extraordinary!" he said aloud to himself as he closed the book. "Something's got hold of that boy. I wonder if it's the same thing that struck Jeff? That Saxon must be unusual."

10

THE mail that brought John Saxon's letter to Mary
Elizabeth arrived at eleven o'clock, but Boothby Farwell
arrived at ten. The matter of the returned diamond had
not deterred him in the least from his purpose of taking
Miss Wainwright out to see the estate he wanted to buy.
The fact that she had declined he did not take into
consideration.

When he was announced Mary Elizabeth paused,
turned from her mirror where she was putting on her
hat and looked dismayed. Then a determined look came
into her eyes.

"Tell him I am dressing for an engagement, and I can
spare him only a moment, but I will be down as soon as
possible," she said to the maid. Then she turned about
and faced herself in the mirror again.

Since she had wakened very early that morning she
had been trying to convince herself that she was done
with the incident of the wedding night. She would
probably see no more nor hear no more of the strange
ardent lover whose impetuous courting had so swept her
off her feet, and the accounts of whom since had been

so intriguing. She must get him out of her mind, and to that end she must fill her mind full of something else absorbing. But a firm conviction had been growing that Boothby Farwell was not what she wished to fill her mind with.

She had hoped that the return of the ring, and the accompanying note would have kept him away. Failing in this she had hoped to get away before he could possibly arrive, but details of the household had delayed her, and now that he was come she was too frank and honest a nature to slip down the backstairs and leave word that she was gone. She must go down and face him.

Since she had to go down it would have been so much easier to have gone with her mind filled with the thought of another man. But having convinced herself that there was no other man for her, she must be consistent. So she faced herself in the mirror a moment, made a little wry face at herself, then hurriedly hunted out her gloves and purse and went downstairs.

She entered the room where her would-be lover waited and essayed to take the initiative in the situation, to get the upper hand from the start.

"Good morning!" she said breezily. "I'm sorry to have to disappoint you. You got my note in time to save your coming, didn't you? Thomas said he delivered it."

"I did," he said stiffly rising and standing before her with a judicial air, "but of course I couldn't accept any such decision as that and I came at once. I feel that you do not understand the gravity of the situation. You are no longer a child to play fast and loose in this way. Of course I know you did not mean that sweeping declaration, and I came at once. I feel that I have a right to demand that you put aside all other duties and engagements and talk this thing over with me. It is a matter that concerns both your happiness and mine, and you have no right to trifle with it, flippantly telling me that the ring was too heavy. What nonsense! A stone that cost a fabulous sum! A ring that a queen might be proud to own!"

His eyes were hard and cold. Mary Elizabeth suddenly had a revelation of what it would be to be tied to him for life and be under his condemnation. A spot of color flashed out on either cheek and there was battle in her eyes. She drew herself up to her full height and regarded him coldly but sweetly.

"That's exactly it, Boothby, I didn't feel up to the stone. I had no intention of being flippant about it. The ring is perfectly gorgeous of course, and I am duly honored that you had the thought of placing it with me. You will recall that when you handed it to me you said that you wanted me to take it and try it out. Were you being flippant when you said that? I was but answering you in the same vein. But indeed, Boothby, I was most serious when I returned it. I wore it but one hour and it gave me some very serious thoughts, and I found it stood for more than I was able to give."

"Nonsense!" said the man sharply.

"No, it is not nonsense," said Mary Elizabeth, "it is fact. I looked the matter quite frankly in the face and I've told you the truth."

"How ridiculous, Elizabeth,"—Boothby Farwell had always called her Elizabeth. He said it was more distinguished than Mary Elizabeth—"You have always liked me, you know you have. You have shown by your manner that you were very fond of me."

"Yes," said Mary Elizabeth with a dreamy look in her eyes, "I've been very fond of you. I still am. But that's not enough when you are talking about marriage. I don't know that I shall ever marry."

"That's absurd of course," said the man with great annoyance in his tone, "I'm sure I don't know what you're holding off for. If you've anything in mind suppose you state it."

"Why, I hadn't anything in mind," said Mary Elizabeth innocently, "I'm not trying to play a game."

"But you've never talked this way before, Elizabeth."

"Perhaps not," said the girl dreamily, realizing that a new door of experience had opened during the last two days and given her a vision of what love and marriage might mean under the right circumstances, "but you must remember I've never promised to really think it over seriously before. That was all you asked me to do when I accepted the ring on trial, and I kept my promise. I thought it over very carefully, and—well, I knew I couldn't. I knew you were just a friend—a very nice friend of course, but just a friend—and you couldn't be anything more."

She lifted sweet earnest eyes to the cold annoyed ones that were searching her face, and the man of the world found something baffling in her.

"Sit down," he said, a harsh note coming into his voice that was usually so smooth and oily and satisfied. "We've got to talk this thing over seriously."

"I'm sorry," said Mary Elizabeth, "I told you I had other duties to-day!"

"Sit down!" he said imperiously. "This is a matter of life and death!"

"That's it," said Mary Elizabeth, "it isn't to me, you know. I just couldn't feel that way about it!"

He bit his lip vexedly and let his eyes be gimlet-wise, boring down into her half contemptuously, most impatiently, to see if he could discover the cause of the sudden defection in this girl who heretofore had merely laughed his gravity away, and gaily introduced other themes. He had always felt sure of her. Could it be that there was really something coming between them? He quickly reviewed the men who were her friends.

"What do you find wrong with me, Elizabeth?" he asked at last in the tone one uses to a naughty little child who has to be soothed to bring it to reason. "What do I lack that you find elsewhere? Whom else do you know who is better prepared to make life one long delight? I can buy you anything in reason, and can gratify your every wish."

"I'm not sure that you could," said Mary Elizabeth earnestly.

He stared at her astonished.

"What—just what do you mean?"

"I'm not sure that I know what I mean," she looked at him speculatively.

"What have you in mind that you want that you think I wouldn't give you? I have yachts, two of them, considered by many to be superior to most boats of their kind now in existence. I can build you a home anywhere we like." (Mary Elizabeth noted the "we.") "I'm even considering a plane—"

"Yes," said Mary Elizabeth, pleasantly, "but you see I have more or less of those things now, or could have them if I chose, why should I get married to get them? Besides, I understood it was you that I was being asked to marry and not things."

"Then what is it, Elizabeth?"

"It's just that I can get along all right without you. I've tried it twice now, going off to Europe for months, and it didn't bother me a bit. I don't see why one should get married unless there's something more than just that. Of course there might be people who felt they had to marry, or were justified in marrying, for other reasons, say, if they were lonely, or needed someone to take care of them, for instance. But I'm never lonely, and I could take care of myself very well, even if I didn't have Dad and a host of loving family. It's just that I don't see marrying unless there's something more than that."

"Are you trying to make me sentimental?" he asked half savagely. "I'm sure you're not a child! And I've already told you that I have the very highest admiration and regard for you, and you certainly know that when I have attempted to caress you you have always held aloof."

Mary Elizabeth suddenly rose with her cheeks flaming and a firm little set of her lips and chin, but behind her hazel eyes there was a flood of light that made her seem suddenly illuminated. Boothby Farwell watched her half startled. She was more serious than he ever remembered her to have been before.

"Please, Boothby," she said gravely, "we won't discuss this any more, either now or at any other time. I have given you my answer."

He stood with his eyes upon her, almost savagely. It seemed incredible that she was actually refusing him. This must be just a whim. He had a high estimate of himself. Also, many women had spoiled him.

He lifted his chin haughtily.

"You can't keep this up interminably," he reminded her. "You must make a final decision! I won't stand for everything!"

She looked at him astonished.

"This *is* final!" she said, and then her eyes alight again she added, remembering when those words had been spoken to her, "This *is final!*"

He turned away from her with an offended air.

"Very well!" he said and his voice was like icicles.

He walked to the door, and then turning toward her again said,

"You can let me know when you return to sanity again! Good morning!"

"But," she said, and there was almost a lilt in her voice, "this is *final*, and I'm sorry if I ever made you think it would be otherwise. I just didn't understand myself before!"

He went away then without another word, his eyes averted from her. He wanted her to understand what his scorn would be for one who turned from the advantages he could offer the woman he married.

She felt it. She understood. But in her heart were ringing those words she had just said, those words another had said before her.

Final! Was anything ever final? Were John Saxon's words, his kiss, a final thing that was to change her life and make her thoughts belong to another?

She stood there where Boothby Farwell had left her, with a wondering light in her eyes and a glorious color in her cheeks, and it was well that he did not return to further question her for he would surely have asked her if there was someone else for whom she cared. But he did not return and she presently heard the dull thud of the front door letting out an outraged caller, who yet had by no means given up.

A moment more and Mary Elizabeth realized that the maid was coming down the hall. Quickly she closed the shutters to her soul and put on her gay accustomed manner.

"The mail has come, Miss Wainwright. I thought perhaps you'd like to look it over before you go out."

"Thank you, Tilly," said Mary Elizabeth swinging around with her heart in a sweet tumult and taking the handful of mail.

Tilly disappeared discreetly, and Mary Elizabeth tripped up the stairs to her room and fastened her door before she sat down to examine those letters. Oh, if it should be here! Oh, if it shouldn't! Of course it wouldn't be. She had settled that in the small hours of the night. That was merely a closed incident!

It was there! Right on the top! She knew it at once even though it was a plain envelope and she had never laid eyes on his handwriting before. It was there, and the very handwriting shouted at her soul as she touched it and gazed upon it!

MARY Elizabeth drew a deep breath and settled down to read her letter. Her eyes were very bright, she felt her lips were trembling. Her hands were trembling too as she held the pages of the letter, and devoured the words with her eyes.

There was something about his handwriting that seemed strong and satisfying, like himself, and her heart leaped up and rejoiced as, the words of the letter fitting with her memory of him, her vision of him ran true to form.

How that "My dear—!" thrilled her, as if she were again in his arms, his lips on hers. And then her heart began a song that lasted all through the letter, lilting on its lovely way through the precious sentences.

In all her favored life Mary Elizabeth had never received a love letter like that. Such delicate admiration, expressed in phrases that a poet might have used! Such exquisite melody of love! What a man this was who had crossed her path and flung his heart down at her feet without warning! Who or what was she, to have won this great prize from life? But no, it was nothing she had won, it was a gift come straight out of the blue and her heart stood still with the glory and the wonder of it.

But it was a mistake, of course, she told herself as she paused to look up and blink away the happy tears that came and interfered with her vision. He did not realize how superficial she was, how small and trifling, how gay and earthly. He never would have picked her out if he had known. Already her love was humble and she had put him high upon a pedestal. She had never met a man like this one before. Her men friends were all among the class who had no set purpose in life. They were rich, they had no need to work. They did not need to worry even about amassing more wealth, but only how to spend what they had. Their interests were to acquire better polo ponies, to race their yachts for more silver cups, to ride higher in the air, or drive a better ball over a fairway, or across a net; their only cares were to escape the cold in winter, the heat in summer, and to buy their way out of all labor or waiting or unpleasantness of any sort. Even to acquire the woman of his choice none of them would humble himself, or go seeking through literature or art or music for the words and colors and lilt to tell of it. Therefore she thrilled and thrilled to his words, and bright tears dimmed her eyes.

Perhaps though, she thought, this was the only real love that had ever come her way. Perhaps real love was always humble, always thinking more of the other than of self? She put that by to consider later and went on with her letter.

But when she came to that bit about laying his lips upon hers and holding her close she had to close her eyes and rest her head back in her chair, and let the joy and wonder of the thought flow over her like strong gentle waves of water that bore her spirit up and floated it away into a bliss she had never known before. His lips upon hers! His arms about her! Ah! But this was too beautiful, too wonderful to last!

The telephone interrupted. She looked at it like an intruder and let it ring on. She could not be interrupted now, and presently it hushed its clatter and let her go on.

There were words and phrases that stood out as she read slowly, "Years together!" Could it be possible that anything so heavenly could come to her as to have years together with a spirit like his? "Your eyes spoke to my eyes!" Was that true? Did she answer the look she had seen in his eyes when she first lifted her own and saw that strong bronzed man standing like a young god beside her cousin Jeff? The color deepened in her cheek as she acknowledged to herself that an involuntary message had gone forth in her glance and the acknowledgement made her heart beat the faster.

"I love you, love you, love you!"

She bent her head almost reverently and laid her lips on the words, as if she were drinking in the sweetness of their meaning.

"Eternity"! How long was that? She had never before had occasion to think in terms of the ages, but now it seemed good to do so, even necessary. For a thing as precious as this must last forever!

But when she came to the sentence that said there were things that she should know at once her heart stood still with fear, and she hesitated to turn over the next page lest a spectre should await her there which would destroy this new found joy. So near to that word "eternity" she could not bear it.

But when at last she turned that page and found him telling of his poverty and struggle she drew a breath of relief and a tender smile came upon her lips. Why, these were all things she knew already, through Sam's boyish tale, and they were precious. They only made him more dear. And his people! Why it wouldn't matter, would it, about his people? He was the one that mattered. And she would love his people no matter what they were just for his sake, wouldn't she?

She drew in her breath as if it hurt when she read of the idea of his coming to her, and again sharply when she thought of him struggling away in sun-drenched Florida, alone in an orange grove battling against such enemies as belonged to orange groves. Struggling alone. A wild, sweet, futile thought came that she would like to go and help him.

There was another page to turn when she came to that last thought which should have come first because it was paramount to everything else in his life. She drew in a long, slow, sore breath of pain before she turned the page and came upon God! God, standing there in her room looking down upon that letter, knowing what was in it, having a right to know, and to come between her and this marvelous lover of hers! God, watching her! And she *didn't know God!*

It was not that she resented His being there, or that it astonished her, what John Saxon said, for she had heard all about it from young Sam, and it had rather pleased her. It seemed a unique part of this winsome man who was so strong and so sweet and so tender, and yet so true. It was not entirely that it frightened her, to have this Christ of John Saxon's standing there in her room, judging her, whether she were fit for His man. It was that she had suddenly become so small in her own eyes, and so useless, so far away and utterly worthless. It was as if His presence there watching her quietly as she read that letter, were judging her and setting her away back where she belonged, so far away from John Saxon that she could never, never catch up with him, and she found herself wondering pitifully about his disappointment in her when he found she was not what he had thought. All those lovely things he had said in the letter about her, how she wanted to live up to them! How she longed to be his equal mate. And yet she felt she could not be because she did not know his God.

A long time she sat there staring at his name as signed to that first part of his letter, unable to go on because she had to stop and let his Christ search her life from beginning to end and show her how very small and useless it was. Full of just nothing but trying to please herself, that was all!

At last she roused to see what was after his name.

Then suddenly her heart which had felt small, but happy in spite of its smallness, went down, down, down, with a thump till it seemed that it could go no farther. What was this he was saying? That he had thought her another girl! That he was blaming himself for having made love to her? Oh, the bitterness of humiliation that she had come to this, had grasped for this bright bubble of a dream and now saw it melt and fade away because it belonged to another!

For at first she did not see that it was her name, her honorable name, her wealth and position that had frightened him. She only saw that name of Camilla's little absent friend whose place she had taken. Helen Foster! All that priceless love belonged to another? She sat speechless, humiliated, and stared!

Well, hadn't she known that it wasn't the thing to pick up a strange man that way? She had realized at the time that a Wainwright couldn't do a thing like that! That a Wainwright according to tradition must meet a man formally, must know him well, and his position and eligibility, before she allowed him to speak of love to her. Yet she had not only listened, but had taken a part in it actually asking him if he wasn't going to kiss her good-bye! How her cheeks burned with shame. How the kiss that he had given, and—yes,—she had more than just *received*, scorched sweetly, bitterly on her lips, and she buried her face in the beloved letter and let hot tears flow down and wash away the sting. How that Helen Foster whom she had never seen had come and taken away her joy!

But it came to her that she had not yet finished reading the letter, and she lifted her face and read on, till she came to the place where he said: "I love you, Mary Elizabeth! I write your beautiful name reverently, Mary Elizabeth! How wonderful if I might someday say, 'My Mary Elizabeth'!"

Then suddenly the joy bloomed out again and her heart began to leap. His love was hers, after all, not that other unknown girl's. He had never seen her. He did not want to see her. He had set his love upon herself, Mary Elizabeth, as soon as he had seen her, even before he had spoken to her! And all that was worrying him was her wealth and position! What foolishness! Wealth and position! What were they? She arose to her feet. She broke into smiles! She felt like singing.

She lifted shy eyes to where the vision of John Saxon's Christ had seemed to stand, as if she would question whether she might rejoice, she, Mary Elizabeth, pampered daughter of wealth, who had wasted her bright days on nothings instead of getting ready to mate this wonderful man of God. Would John Saxon's Christ let her have this precious jewel of love for hers? Could she ever walk softly enough before Him to be half good enough for a man like that?

She laughed out gently, a little apologetic laugh. She, Mary Elizabeth, seeking to be religious! She didn't even know how!

Presently she sat down again and read the letter over

slowly, this time taking in every precious turn of sentence, till she felt as if her lover were beside her. He loved her, yes, he loved her! She had to get used to it. She had to let it sing itself into her heart and her life. She couldn't sit right down and answer that letter. It was too sacred a thing to do. It would take time to think out the answer. Could she ever put upon paper what she felt toward him? She had no poetry at her command that could fittingly reply to his.

The telephone broke in upon her meditations again, and with sudden premonition that Boothby Farwell might be asking if she were yet returned, she gathered her precious letter into her handbag and fled, sending the maid up to answer the telephone and say that she was out. By the time the maid reached the telephone she was out at the garage starting her car, joy singing a high paean in her heart, joy smiling on her pleasant lips. She wasn't just sure where she was going now, or what she wanted to do, but she felt that somehow she had got to get away where Boothby Farwell could not reach her until life had taken on a more definite outline. Perhaps she *had* been laughing down a sunlit way ever since she had begun to grow up. Perhaps she *had* let people take too many things for granted. Could it be that she had unintentionally allowed Boothby to take too much for granted? He seemed to think she had. Perhaps she would have to write him a note pretty soon and ask his pardon for playing around so long when she was not serious. But that, too, would require thought, and she was too much shaken by her own new joy to think out what to say just now.

She decided to wheedle her father out to lunch with her some day soon and talk over the possibility of opening the old shore cottage.

She turned her car downtown, and went singing on

her way. And presently she laughed out loud at herself again, for the words she was singing were:

> *I know a fount where sins are washed away,*
> *I know a place where night is turned to day!*

Mightn't that be a reminder to her that even she might find that place some day and get her life changed so that it would more possibly fit into the life of the man who loved her, and who yet was bound to put his Christ first?

Second to Christ, only! In a way, a rather wonderful way, that was probably a great honor!

12

"WHY, no," said Mary Elizabeth, over the very delicious luncheon she and her father were eating together a few days later in the quiet old-fashioned restaurant on a back street where he usually went at noon, "no, I don't see why it would need doing over. I want to open the house just as it is. I thought I'd like to be there, where I can remember Mother. I'd like to have the same furniture and the same arrangement and everything. I thought maybe you'd enjoy coming down nights, or at least week-ends. You always liked the sea."

Her father looked at her quizzically.

"You don't realize," he said half sadly, "that things deteriorate, especially by the sea, and that they get very old-fashioned. What do you think your fancy friends that you will gather about you will think of being invited to a shabby old place like that?"

"Well, in the first place," said Mary Elizabeth, "I don't intend to have any fancy friends down there. That's the very thing I want to get away from. I don't want week-end parties, nor a mob of people. I want to have a quiet homey time. I thought maybe you'd like it."

Her father's face softened.

"I should," he said his eyes resting tenderly on her bright face, "but you wouldn't like that long you know, and what's the use fixing up an old seashore cottage for a few days' experiment?"

"I don't mean a few days, I mean all summer," said the girl eagerly, "and I don't want to fix much. Don't you keep it in repair?"

"Oh, somewhat," said the father thoughtfully. "The roof doesn't leak, and I had it painted last fall. There's a man of course who keeps up the grounds to a certain extent, too, but you've forgotten how utterly out of date the old ark is."

"No, I'm sure I haven't forgotten," she said, "I always loved it, that white, white building with the lovely fluted columns standing among the pines with the sea at its foot."

"Yes, it was considered very fine when I built it, when you were a baby and your mother was with us!" He sighed heavily, and looked thoughtfully down at his salad without attempting to eat it. "But you've forgotten, Mary Elizabeth, that none of your friends go to Seacrest any more. It isn't the thing to do. They will laugh you to scorn when they hear of it."

"Let them laugh!" gurgled Mary Elizabeth gleefully— "Why tell them about it? We'll just casually disappear, and when it leaks out where we are the summer will be nearly over. Don't you see it will be fun?"

"It sounds that way," said her father cautiously, "but I'm sorely afraid you'll be lonely and wish you hadn't tried it. However, I suppose we can leave if you don't like it."

"We?" said Mary Elizabeth eagerly. "Then you'll go, too?"

"Why yes, of course, if you want me. I wouldn't miss

an opportunity like that. But remember I may not be able to come down every night, though I'd enjoy it sometimes. It would be like the old days."

Mary Elizabeth looked as if she wanted to jump right up from her chair and embrace him though she didn't. She only sat eagerly and outlined her plans.

"Better take some of your friends down with you, first, and see how the old house looks. That will probably cure you," said her father with another sad little smile.

"No," said the girl, her eyes shining. "I'm only taking Sam. He and I get along famously, and when we've looked things over I'll report. Do I need to take a carpenter and a plumber and an electrician down or can I find them there?"

"Find them there, of course. That's the fair way to treat a place where you own property anyway, employ local men. But I should say you'd better take some servants along."

"Not till I've seen it," said the girl firmly. "Just Sam and I are going first to look things over. Uncle Rob said he might go, though I don't think Aunt Clarice liked it very much. She has a pet camp where she wants him to go, and he hates it."

"I see. Well, if you think Sam would be happy going with you I'll call your uncle up and ask him to see that he goes to take care of you. How is that?"

"Fine," said the daughter, giving him a loving look. "I think we'll start to-morrow morning. It's only a two-hour drive isn't it? I've almost forgotten."

"About that!" said her father. "Better have the car gone over before you leave, and don't run any risks."

"I won't," said the girl with shining eyes, "and Dad, please don't inform anybody where I've gone or what we're going to do. I've got a special reason for asking."

He looked at her keenly an instant.

"Of course not," he said. "You're not running away from anybody, are you?"

"Not anybody that matters," said Mary Elizabeth with a comforting smile, "not now that you've promised to go along."

"All right, little girl. And if you decide to really carry out this scheme you'd better leave an order for the telephone to be connected."

Mary Elizabeth's next move was to call her uncle's house on the telephone and ask for Sam.

Fortunately Aunt Clarice was not at home. The housekeeper answered.

"Mr. Sam's went down co the office with his father this morning, Miss Mary," said the woman. "He mostly goes with his father, lately."

So Mary Elizabeth with a question in her eyes called up her uncle's office.

"Uncle Rob," she asked crisply, "is Sam there? And if I come down to the office could I see you and him for five minutes? I'll promise not to stay longer."

"You'll be welcome, Mary Beth," said her uncle, "and you can stay as long as you like. You always had good sense."

So Mary Elizabeth went to her uncle's office, and was welcomed eagerly by both the old and young Wainwright.

"It's about Sam," she said with a gleam in her eye for both relatives. "Is Sam working regularly in the office now?"

"Well, he's been helping me out the last few days," said his father looking at the boy with a twinkle and a grin, "because why, Mary Beth? Did you wish to offer him another position?"

Sam grinned at his father's grave tone.

"Well, I wanted him to help me out for a few days," said the girl, "but I wouldn't want to take him away from a regular job."

"Well, I don't know but I could spare him a while if it's anything important. How about it, Sam? Can you help your cousin out?"

"Sure thing!" said the boy with embarrassed eyes.

"Well, I'm driving down to the shore to look the old cottage over for Dad, and I'd like a man along," said Mary Elizabeth.

"H'm!" said her uncle comically. "This is the first time I've ever known you to be short a man, Mary Beth, and I wouldn't want to see you in a situation like that. But are you sure there isn't some more eligible man?"

"I'd rather have Sam, Uncle Rob, if you can spare him."

"Of course I can spare him if you really need him. When do you want to start?"

"To-morrow morning early, if that's not too soon."

"Well, Son, speak up, will you go?"

"Gosh, yes!" said Sam with a look of delight in his face.

"Then I would advise you to go home early, boy, and get your fishing tackle and your bathing suit together. You might need them in between helping." Uncle Robert gave a wink toward Mary Elizabeth. "How long are you staying, Mary Beth?"

"Probably only two or three days now. It depends on how I find things, and what needs to be done. Are you still willing I should take Sam down with me if we decide to stay there this summer? Dad thinks he'd like it. He'll come down week-ends anyway. Perhaps you'd come with him sometimes?"

"Sure, I'll come. I'd love to. It gets rather dull here in the city when your aunt is in the mountains. Yes, Sam can come if he likes. There won't be so much for him to do here in the office during the hot weather. I think he can finish the lists he's making between trips," and he gave his niece another broad wink and a curious twist of his kind pleasant mouth that looked sometimes so much like his son Jeffrey's mouth.

"That's great! Then he doesn't have to go to camp?"

"No!" said his father. "I've put my foot down on that."

So Mary Elizabeth carried Sam off in her car and landed him at home to pack, and went back to her own preparations as gleeful as if she were only thirteen herself.

The next morning they started like two children on a picnic, Mary Elizabeth reflecting wickedly that she would be away when Boothby Farwell called that morning according to a note she had received the night before, and her maid was instructed to say only that she was away for a few days. So she would not be followed, and she would have time to examine herself and find out just where she stood. For Mary Elizabeth had not yet answered John Saxon's letter, and that was one of the things she meant to do when she got to the shore. It had seemed to her that there in the stillness and beauty and freedom from her world she could more properly answer that letter, and her soul was impatient to find out just what she was going to allow it to say.

The day was fair and lovely, neither too cool nor too hot, a rare day, a June day at its best. The roads were good, and the way open with little traffic.

By common consent the two travelers talked but little till they were out in the open country, with only a little clean village by the way now and then.

"I had a letter from Mr. Saxon," volunteered Sam at last, settling comfortably back with his eyes ahead for a startled rabbit that might spring out of the scrub oak along the way.

"Did you?" answered Mary Elizabeth coolly with no sign of the start the announcement had given her senses. "How is he? Did he say?"

"Naw! He doesn't talk about things like that. He doesn't talk about himself. He was talking about us fellas. He's writing to us every little while, every week, maybe. If we do the work he sends us and answer him, then we get another letter."

"Work? What work are you doing for him?"

"Why the Bible lessons he sends. We're taking a course, see? He sends us a new one as soon as we get the first one worked out."

"That sounds interesting," chirruped Mary Elizabeth. "I'd like to see them. Has he sent you any yet?"

"Oh, sure! This is the second one I have."

"Did you bring them along?"

"Course! I expect to do a lotta studying while I'm down here, that is if you think I'll have time."

"Why, of course," said Mary Elizabeth. "There'll be heaps of time. We just have to give orders to men and things like that, and then wait around and see that they do it. I'd like to do some studying myself if you think I'm not too stupid. I never knew much about the Bible."

"Aw, quit your kidding!" said the boy.

"I mean it," said Mary Elizabeth. "I never studied Bible at all. I'd like to see if I could understand it. You see I've never had a scout master to teach me."

"Well, ya can read my papers. I guess you can understand 'em if I can."

"All right, we'll try. Now, how soon do you think we'd better stop for lunch? I asked the cook to put us up a lunch. I didn't seem to remember any very inviting place to stop along this road. She put some lemonade in one thermos bottle and some milk in the other so we can have cold drinks without stopping, and Father says there's a nice place to eat when we get there, so we're sure of a good dinner tonight."

"Gee! Aren't we having fun?" said Sam.

The old Wainwright summer place stood up a little from the shore, a fine old colonial house, spacious yet simple and lovely of line. Its lawn ran down incredibly near to the sea, and its outlook was clear to the skyline, though it was partly surrounded by great pines, and other imported trees, which in the time of the house's greatness had been the wonder of the resort. The white fluted columns which had been kept painted every year, still gleamed out among the dark pines, almost like marble, and the stately piazza across the front, the lovely fantail window over the front door, the high iron grille that surrounded the place were in perfect repair, and the lawn kept trimmed as if it were in use. The place stood out among the quieter, smaller homes as a great estate of a bygone day, quaint and restful and almost awe-inspiring in contrast to its rows of bungalow neighbors, which had crept up nearer and nearer to its greatness as fashion receded from the resort, and tales of its wealthy owner became a mere tradition in a quiet, comfortable, but unsmart straggling town. Thus early in the season, there were few summer residents, only the winter inhabitants who stayed there because they had no other place to go, and because it was cheaper to stay there and vegetate than to migrate. It was almost like visiting a deserted village, as they drove down the wide main highway that wound around behind the Wainwright estate, locked in behind its massive iron grill.

"Oh, Boy! Isn't this great!" sighed Sam in delight. "No boardwalk! No dolled-up people cluttering the beach. We gotta beach all to ourselves! I was never down here. Why didn't we come before? Why don't all of our family come down ta this place and stay all summer?"

"Well, I'll bite, why?" asked Mary Elizabeth boyishly, her eyes taking in the beauty of the sea spread before her, the plumy pines, the gleaming of the white, white mansion set up on a slight eminence.

"I guess it's because there wouldn't be any chance ta dress up and show off!" said Sam thoughtfully, studying the scattered humble cottages in the near distance.

"Well," said Mary Elizabeth, "perhaps you may have hit the nail on the head. But how would you like to get out, Sam, and see if you can open our gate with this great, big, old, funny key?"

Sam accepted the key with delight and scrambled out to try the well-oiled lock which the caretaker kept always in order, and presently they were driving in along the graveled winding way, skirting the house till they came to the front, where the trees were cut away to show the sea in all its broad blue and gold beauty, under a perfect sky.

Mary Elizabeth stopped the car and sat looking off at the wonder of it all, and even Sam kept still and took it all in.

"Gosh, I don't know what they'd want of any prettier place than this!" he said at last with a sigh, "they" meaning his mother who was the general that managed all their family migrations.

"Yes," said Mary Elizabeth, "I've been almost around the world, Sam, and I don't remember anything prettier than this. And listen to those pines, boy, they are whispering in perfect rhythm with the waves down on the shore! I suppose they've got used to it, being together so much all these years. Especially in winter they've nothing else to do but practise, and it must be magnificent to listen to their harmony. There must be some grand music in a storm. Sometime I'm coming here in a storm just to hear it!"

"Oh, Boy! Say, I'll come too, then!"

"All right! That'll be a compact. Now, shall we go in?"

But just then there appeared a man walking around the path that skirted the house, his cap in his hand deferentially.

"Is this Miss Wainwright?" he asked. "I had a wire this morning from Mr. Wainwright saying you was coming. I hope you'll find everything in order, Miss. We've always tried to keep it as though the family might come in any minute!"

"Why, that's wonderful!" said Mary Elizabeth beaming at him. "I wish we had come before! You're Mr. Bateman, aren't you? Father said you would be here. You have the keys?"

"Yes, Miss, and you can call me Frank. It's easier to remember."

"All right, Frank, and this is Sam Wainwright, my cousin. You'll be showing him all around and telling him about everything, I know."

"I had the windows open, Miss, all morning. And you'll find everything all right. My wife Susan was over getting out fresh linen. She thought you might want her to get you a bit of dinner to-night. She's a fine cook, if you think she can please you?"

"Why, that would be lovely," said Mary Elizabeth interested at once, "if you think she would. Sam and I had our lunch by the way, so we wouldn't want anything before six I should think." She glanced at her watch. "Tell her just something simple will do. We don't want anything elaborate. And how about a place to stay to-night? Is there a hotel open yet?"

"Not any hotel in Seacrest, not yet. We haven't but

one in the town left now, and it went broke last fall. I don't know if it will open at all. The rest are all standing idle, with their shutters down like so many of the dead. But we thought, Susan and I, that perhaps you'd be staying here in the house. We could make you comfortable. We've been using the servant's quarters ourselves you know, so the house isn't to say closed, nor damp. We've had some part open to air most every day."

"Well, I should say there wouldn't be anything better than that," said Mary Elizabeth looking around with delighted eyes. "I would rather stay here than anywhere else, wouldn't you, Sam?"

"Sure thing!" said the boy, grinning his delight.

"Well, we thought you might, so Susan made up two of the rooms, and she'll be glad to be of service in any way. She used ta be lady's maid to a senator's wife before I married her, so she ain't to say ignorant exactly."

"Well, that's wonderful," said Mary Elizabeth, her eyes dancing, "but I don't need a maid. We're going to live simply here. But I'm quite sure everything is going to be lovely. Father said you would tell me about things, and whether any repairs were needed."

"I shouldn't say so, Miss, I've tinkered up anything that was out of the way myself. But you can see when you look around."

So Mary Elizabeth entered the large, old rooms shrouded in memories of a bygone generation.

Big, wide rooms with fine white matting on the floors, and many comfortable willow chairs and couches, with cushions of faded but fine texture. Quaint, old pictures on the walls, some of them very fine, done by artists of renown. Long, sheer curtains at the windows, floating in the breeze. Mary Elizabeth looked at them in wonder.

"Are these the old curtains? I would have thought they would have dropped to pieces."

"Yes, they are the original curtains that were up when we came here to take care o' the place. But Susan she took care o' the curtains. She kept them washed and folded away where they wouldn't mold nor rot, and now and again she's done them up to have them ready in case some o' the family came back. She wanted it to look like home for them."

"And now we've come," said Mary Elizabeth. "I'm glad! And it looks so nice. It seems just as it was when I was a child."

"Well, we figured you might like it," said the man with a pleased grin. "We didn't get all the curtains hung yet, of course, but we went to work as soon as the wire came this morning, and we got all downstairs, and two bedrooms done. I'm glad you like it. Now I'll call Susan."

Susan came in a clean blue gingham dress, with her hands wrapped embarrassedly in her white apron, and her face shining with welcome.

"It's wonderful, Susan," said Mary Elizabeth. "I came down here expecting to find things all run down and needing a lot of repairs before we could be comfortable here, but it seems everything is perfectly all right and doesn't need a thing done to it."

"I'm glad yer pleased!" said Susan, her face shining with pleasure. "I been hoping ye'd come some summer. It seems such a nice pretty old house."

"It is!" said the girl looking around with loving eyes. "I love it here! I don't know why we never came before. But we're staying here this summer. My father will be down week-ends sometimes, and as often between as he can spare the time."

They went over the house eagerly, Sam as interested as anybody.

"Say, this is a swell joint!" he said.

But Sam didn't waste much time in the house. He took possession of the room allotted to him, hung up the things he had brought with him, jammed himself into his bathing suit and was off down to the beach.

Mary Elizabeth went about in a daze of bliss. It seemed somehow as she trod the old halls and went into the rooms that had once been dear and familiar, as if her own mother had left the impress of her sweet spirit there, and by and by when Susan left to prepare the evening meal she took out the letter of her stranger-lover and went to her mother's own room to read it over again. It gave her a sense of confiding in her mother, reading it there where she could remember sitting on a little footstool beside her mother, playing with her dolls.

Somehow the letter took on new sanctity, read there. She could fancy telling her mother all about it, what the stranger-best-man had said going down that aisle, what had happened all the evening, and his farewell at the station. It seemed, read in the light of a mother's eyes, as if John Saxon would bear the scrutiny, and have a loving mother's approval.

Sometime she would tell her father all about him, but not yet. Not just yet!

The summons to dinner came while she was still sitting in her mother's big chair by the window looking out between the pines to the sea, dreaming.

She had seen Sam come dripping up from the sea and vanish into the house, and now she could hear him clattering down the stairs, hungry from his swim. So she tucked her letter away into safety and went down. To-morrow, or perhaps the next day, she must answer that letter. She hadn't yet felt ready to answer a letter like that. There were so many things to be considered about it. But soon she must answer it. She must not wait too long! It was as if the content and wonder into which his letter had led her were a spell too precious to be broken, a dream from which she was not ready yet to wake. And she felt instinctively that to answer that letter was to make more definite one way or the other this marvelous thing that had come so unexpectedly into her life. For the time she was so lifted out of the conventions of life that she feared to get back into them by the formalities of correspondence, lest she might lose some part of the wonder that had touched her soul. Afraid lest facing facts, Wisdom might step in and forbid the joy that was welling up inside her.

So she put it off, the writing of that letter, from day to day for three days more, going about as in a lovely dream, allowing her mind to frame tender phrases that hovered on her lips in a smile and made her so lovely that even Sam looked at her and wondered.

The second morning there came a letter for Sam, forwarded from home. And there were also letters from her father and uncle for Mary Elizabeth, her father giving directions for certain modern improvements in the way of plumbing to be installed in the house, for renovation of the old stable into a garage, and for several minor repairs and changes to be made in the house before he came down.

From her uncle came a brief note telling Mary Elizabeth that her Aunt Clarice had gone to the mountains with a friend, and that therefore Sam was at her service as long as she wanted him, but that she was to return him to his home whenever she grew tired of his company. Sam could be in the office with him a good deal, and would get along well enough, if he grew troublesome to her, or she was bored with having a child about.

She looked up from these letters to find Sam at her feet sprawled on the upper step of the piazza, absorbed in a letter of his own. She watched him for a moment for there was an eagerness in his quietness that interested her.

"Did you get a letter from your mother?" she asked, wondering if the matter of the camp were still hovering in the offing.

Sam looked up with a bright face.

"Gosh, no!" he said. "It's from Mr. Saxon! He's sent the new Bible lesson for this week! Gee! I gotta get ta work!"

"Oh," said Mary Elizabeth with a heightened color in her cheeks, "is he—back at home—again—yet?"

"Oh, sure!" said Sam. "He's back. He's been working in the orange grove all day the night he wrote this. Wantta read it?" And Sam handed up the letter into her hungry hand.

It was just a brief simple letter, as if an older brother were writing to a beloved younger one, yet the girl's eyes lingered on every pleasant word.

> *Dear Sam:*
>
> *I got back home last night late and have been working in the grove all day, so haven't had much time to write, but I made out the lesson for this week on the way down and enclose it. Am anxious to know how you got on with the first lesson, and shall hope to hear from you soon. If you find the work too hard let me know. I'm hoping it interests you as much as it has me to get it ready for you.*
>
> *Your friend in Christ,*
> *John Saxon.*

What a friend for a boy to have! What a tie to claim, "in Christ"! Mary Elizabeth felt a passing pang at the sure strong bond that bound them, and gave a half envious smile at the boy as she handed it back. There was no disturbing separation between those two, it was all settled. It was a friendship, a fellowship, that nothing could break. There were no disturbing questions to settle.

"This looks like a corker!" said the boy lifting his eyes from the other paper he held. "Wantta see it?"

Mary Elizabeth accepted the other sheet and ran her eyes down at the startling questions, the strange symbolic abbreviations, and her eyes grew large with earnestness.

"It looks—" said Mary Elizabeth searching for the right word, "it looks—rather—startling! I'm afraid I wouldn't know how to go to work to answer those questions."

"Aw, the references'll answer those," said Sam easily, "only sometimes ya do havta use yer head. How'd it be if I get my Bible and show ya?"

"I'd love it," said Mary Elizabeth fervently. "But— have you a Bible with you? I don't know whether there would be such a thing about this house or not."

"Oh, sure! That's part of it. We fellas always carry our Bibles wherever we go. We all got small ones that don't take up much room fer traveling!"

Sam tore up the stairs three steps at a time and returned with a small limp Bible of surprisingly supple and diminutive proportions, and sat himself down on the upper step again.

"Now, Mary Beth," he commanded, "you read out the questions and references and I'll look 'em up and read 'em!"

So for nearly two hours through that long bright morning the two sat on the piazza and studied the Bible together. Questions grew out of the first question, and Sam found he had to go back to foundation principles and give some of the instruction that had been given to him during his winter in the Florida scout camp with John Saxon, but both the young teacher and the learner were deeply engaged in the study, so that they were surprised when the lunch bell rang to discover that the morning had fled.

Bright-faced, the boy got up from the step and tossed back his sandy hair that matched his golden freckles and grinned at her.

"Gee! I was going crabbing this morning, but I guess it doesn't matter. Anyhow I'm glad I got this lesson worked out. It's lots more fun having you do it with me. I wish I had somebody all the time. I hope I didn't bore you."

"Why, I think it's wonderful!" said Mary Elizabeth. "If you don't mind I'd like to study it every week with you,—unless—you think Mr. Saxon—might mind. This isn't a secret organization, is it? This Fellowship of yours?"

"Not on yer life!" said Sam. "We're out ta get everybody studying we can. I'll tell Mr. Saxon I got a new recruit."

Mary Elizabeth's cheeks flamed.

"Well, perhaps you'd better not, just yet, Sam. It might make me sort of embarrassed, you know. I'd rather wait till I learn a little more. You see I don't know so much about it yet. Just keep it to yourself awhile, Buddie."

"Okay!" agreed Sam cheerfully and grinned as if he understood. And so they went out to lunch.

After lunch Sam went with Frank Bateman out in his boat for a little crabbing and later to watch the hauling in of the deep sea nets.

But Mary Elizabeth sat on the porch and faced her future.

13

THE day that Mary Elizabeth finally wrote her first
letter to John Saxon, Sam had gone off to the Inlet with
Frank Bateman. They had taken a lunch and Mary
Elizabeth had the day before her uninterrupted.

She had been invited to go along, but had declined
on the plea that she had letters to write and would go
another time. So quite early in the middle morning
she took her writing materials and established herself
in a great steamer chair where she could look out
across the vista of pines and lawn and see the wide,
blue sea and sometimes catch a glimpse of a great wave
curling high and breaking in foam on the white sand
through the lacework of the iron grille that surrounded the estate.

A long time she sat with pen in hand, gazing afar
where a little white toy of a boat tossed on the blue
horizon, trying to decide how to begin. She wasn't just
sure how much of her heart she was willing to reveal in
that first word she would put upon the paper, but at last
she began to write:

Dear Breath-taking One:

I have been waiting a few days since receiving your letter, trying to get my feet down to earth again after being up in the clouds with you! For you must own you were unexpected to say the least.

You see you had the advantage of me, you having been looking for me a long time, you see I am afraid the traditions of my family had prepared me for a more conventional form of prince, less interesting, less eager, more calculating! That was what I was brought up to expect in a lover. My highest dreams had not dared snatch at such a romance as you flung to me so unexpectedly coming down that aisle.

And so I've had to get my bearings, and my breath, before I answered you.

Not because your letter did not also carry me away again, but because I sensed that this was the gravest, most serious thing that would ever come into my life, and I must not write this lightly, gaily, as I have always taken all things in life so far. I wanted to weigh every word of my reply, and be sure I answered you as you had a right to be answered. Your letter meant too much to me, to be answered on the spur of the moment.

So, I have come down to Seacrest, to an old summer home we have had a good many years, where we used to come when I was a child, when my mother was living. It seems more like home than any other place on earth now, with memories in every corner, and the blue sea stretched out before me. It seemed to me a place where I could be still enough to think, and alone enough to talk with you.

I brought my young cousin Sam along, whom

you know. But he is away crabbing for the day, and I am alone with you.

If I were a painter I could make you see where I am sitting looking over toward the sea. If I were a musician I could make you hear the melody the waves and pines are making in such perfect rhythm. If I were a poet, like you, I could tell you how the sea and sky and pines, and the perfume of the roses growing over the porch, and the quiet of the big old house behind me, full of dear memories of the past, are combining to make a haven for me where I can talk to you, this first time, as I did not feel I could back in the city.

But I am neither poet nor painter nor musician, only a gay girl who has gone about like a butterfly tasting of this flower and that all over the earth wherever a bright bloom called me. Never before have I come face to face with a great love and a great wonder and been able to call them mine. Therefore I approach the matter with deep reverence and heart-searching.

And now, *I* have the advantage of you! For you seem only to have found out about my financial and social position and the possible traditions that belong to the family of Wainwright; while I have been learning much of your inner life from one of your most devoted admirers, my young cousin Sam, who seems to be remodeling his life after the pattern which you have given him.

You cannot know what it has been to me to learn of you in this way, out of the mouth of a guileless child who adores you. And the more I have learned the more I am filled with humility and awe to know that you should have put your love upon such a one as I.

You have been blaming yourself for the beautiful thing which you did, in confessing your love, because you think that perhaps I have more money than you, or a higher social rank in this world!

But don't you know that such great love as you have to offer far outweighs any such differences as those? Just material differences! And anyway, if I give you my love wouldn't any wealth and position I might have be yours also, just as any other asset I might have, such as hair and eyes and smiles and the like?

And you have tried to humble yourself for matters of that sort! But I, far more, for another reason!

Why, John Saxon, you made me feel for a few paragraphs that you were sorry for what you had done, that you repented having told me of your love. You made me jealous of that poor other girl—Helen Foster, whom neither of us has ever seen—until I read on farther, and found your love again, and that healed the hurt. But it made me know as I read on, that it was my place to be humble, not yours.

Because you have something that makes a far greater difference between us than wealth or station. You have a God, and I don't know Him! And I'm afraid He doesn't approve of me!

It is not that I mind being second to your God. I would count it a great honor to be so near to God as that. But John Saxon, beloved stranger, I'm afraid He wouldn't want me there! He wouldn't think that I was worthy to be near to you.

In fact, ever since your letter came, I have felt your God standing near me, looking through my soul, and I feel so small and shamed and utterly undone, I need to hide somewhere. I never knew a God before, not so near. I never thought about God before at all! And *you* are *His!*

You see now, don't you, that it is not money, nor family, nor position that should separate us, but your God!

I feel that perhaps you know this already.

But I love you, oh I love you, John Saxon, beloved stranger! I never loved anyone this way before. I never knew there was such love!

And you have said that you will pray for me!

It seems to me that I shall go reverently all my days, just because you have made mention of my name to God.

Mary Elizabeth

14

ONE morning a couple of days after Mary Elizabeth sent off her letter to Florida, she and Sam were sitting on the piazza deep in their Bible study. It was nearly eleven o'clock and they had been down to the beach since breakfast having a good long swim and a run up the beach to the lighthouse and back, with another dip for a finish. They were feeling tired and quiet and ready to sit down in the coolness of the piazza and rest.

They had been doing this intensive study for three days now and it was a question which of the two enjoyed it most, for it had developed that Mary Elizabeth asked just the questions that the boy needed to bring back to him knowledge acquired the last winter in the Florida camping class, and he brought it forth in his most original boy manner, yet clearly, so that it was like a revelation to the girl to whom heretofore the Bible had been a sealed book full of dead sayings that meant nothing.

Mary Elizabeth had ransacked the house for a Bible, and had found one most unexpectedly in possession of Susan, the caretaker's wife. Susan had two, one that she had earned in Sunday School as a child, reciting certain Psalms, and another with big print. She loaned the one with big print to her young mistress with great delight that she had something worthy to lend. So Mary Elizabeth was equipped with a Bible if not with the knowledge to enable her to find its different books. Sam had to put her through a course in the books of the Bible before she was able to hunt out references. It was amusing to see how patient and eager Sam was as a teacher. He felt it was great of Mary Beth to companion with him this way. She was as good as a boy, any day, and a "lot better than some fellas!" he told her gallantly.

This exclusive feminine fellowship might not satisfy indefinitely. Doubtless there would come a time when he would hunger and thirst for a good rousing game of baseball. But for the present to the lad who was accustomed to frustration of his many plans by a too-anxious parent, and ensuing loneliness, it seemed for the time being bliss.

They were deep in the mysteries of a perplexing question on John Saxon's lesson list, the answer to which was to be found among half a dozen Bible references, and required careful thought and consideration of various phases of the subject, when suddenly the honk of a loud and arrogant automobile horn close at hand broke the stillness startlingly, and around the curve of the graveled drive which circled the house there swept two costly sport cars gleaming smugly in chromium wherever chromium could find an excuse to be, and filled with a noisy company of young people in smart costumes. The foremost car was driven by Boothby Farwell!

"Oh heck! What's this?" exclaimed Sam half rising from the step and dropping his Bible on the piazza. One could almost see his hair bristling like a cat's at sight of a dog in the offing.

Mary Elizabeth looked up in dismay with a blankness in her gaze as she stared unbelievingly at her unwelcome guests. Now, who had invaded her quiet when she had taken so much pains to hide her going? Boothby Farwell, of all people!

And he had dared to bring the whole gay bunch of her old associates from home! Cissy Ward, Tally Randall, Jane Reefer, Rita Bowers, Anne and Maude and Whitty Gensemer! She recognized them one by one, the dismay growing in her heart and face as she rose hastily from the steamer chair leaving her open Bible where she had been sitting, and came forward to greet her uninvited guests.

How in the world did they find out where she was? Surely her father had not given her secret away!

But here they were and there was nothing to do but receive them, though she felt like a child whose doll had been broken and her tea party shattered.

"Well, isn't this unexpected!" she said as she tried to summon her inbred courtesy, and some degree of welcome into her face.

"How in the world did you find out where I was?"

This last question to Boothby who took her hand severely, possessively and gave her a look of reproof.

"Bribed old Tilly to tell where they forwarded your letters," answered Boothby promptly and a little curtly. "Just what was the idea in running away like that? A game of hide and seek, or some similar child's play?"

"I came down to look the old house over and see what repairs it needed," answered Mary Elizabeth coolly, with a steady impersonal look at her former lover and no heightening of her color.

"Well, it's about time you came back again then," he said with a contemptuous glance at the house of other days. "What's the idea of repairing this old barracks anyway? It's a waste of money, I should say."

"It happens that we don't feel that way," laughed Mary Elizabeth. "Won't you come up on the piazza? I think we can make you fairly comfortable, even if we are a bit antiquated. Sam, can't you bring out a few chairs?"

Sam greatly resembled a cat up a tree with its back arched, but he slowly unbristled and went into the house after chairs, giving a baleful glance backward at Boothby Farwell, the perpetrator of this intrusion into his Eden.

"Oh, don't bothah!" said Boothby Farwell, looking about contemptuously, "we're not going to stay here of course. We came to get you and take you up the coast to lunch. Get your hat and come on. Or perhaps you don't need a hat?"

"Sorry to disappoint you," said Mary Elizabeth sweetly, "I couldn't possibly leave. I have a man coming to do some electrical work and I have to be here all the afternoon. He may come any minute now."

"Send word to him not to come then, you simply must go with us! We've come all this way to get you and you can't disappoint us that way."

Then the girls began to clamor, and the other men.

"Oh, come on, Elizabeth! Don't be a flat tire!"

But Mary Elizabeth stood her ground firmly.

"I can't possibly go," she said. "You'll have to get out and take lunch with me. I have a maid here who will be delighted to have some one to serve. Come up and sit down and cool off. There's really a wonderful view of the sea here, and we'll have a pitcher of lemonade at once. Sam, dear," she gave her young cousin a ravishing smile that reduced him to her abject slave again, "could you ask Susan to make us some lemonade?"

"We've something better than lemonade, in the car,"

said Boothby coolly, "and none of us are thirsty! We've just been drinking. We came to get you."

"Oh, I didn't know!" said Mary Elizabeth with a twinkle at Sam. "No lemonade, then, Sam. We don't need it!"

Sam grinned and took his seat on the step again, gathering up his Bible as calmly as if it were a spelling book.

"What on earth are you doing?" asked one of the girls coming up the steps and looking at the Bible curiously.

Mary Elizabeth looked at her guest as if she had not noticed her before, she caught also a glimpse of Sam's lowering countenance, and then she said brightly:

"Why, my cousin and I were doing a little studying together."

Cissy Ward flung a curious glance at her in turn and then picked up the Bible from Sam's knees and gave it a comprehensive scrutiny.

"Oh," she said lightly, "is this your spelling book? Tally, can you spell Methuselah?"

"Not me!" shrugged Tally lightly with a wicked little gleam in his handsome reckless eyes. "I couldn't even pronounce it."

"You're mistaken," said Mary Elizabeth in a clear voice that they all could hear, "that isn't my speller, it's my A B C book. I've only just begun on my alphabet, but if I live long enough I mean to get so I can read it and understand it. I never took a course in the Bible and I thought it was about time."

They all focused their eyes on her. Cissy was flicking the leaves of Sam's Bible through carelessly. Tally had picked up the Bible that Mary Elizabeth had left lying in her chair, examining it comically as if he meant to analyze it and dissect it. The other young folks were climbing out of the car and coming up the steps. They sensed that there was a distinct situation and that Mary Elizabeth was dominating it. They had wondered a little why Boothby who was usually so exclusive in his invitations had invited them all to come along after Mary Elizabeth. Now they were sure that something had gone awry between him and Mary Elizabeth, and she most unusually was holding out against him. They were not quite sure what part they were to play in this one-act drama but they entered gaily into it, determined to get as much fun out of it as possible, and incidentally stir up the chief actors in the plot to reveal the point of the whole matter. So Cissy, who stopped at nothing when she was out on a riot, suddenly held Sam's precious Bible aloft in her thumb and finger, and shouted in a high shrieking voice:

"Listen, boys and girls, I've found out what's the matter with 'Liz'beth! She's turning religious and we'll have to snap her out of it. This book's evidently at the bottom of it, and we'll have to burn the book! Who'll build the bonfire, boys and girls? Here goes the book! Catch it!"

But just as Cissy Ward was about to fling the offending Bible out over the steps Sam sprang into the air catching his precious Bible in one hand and Cissy Ward's extended arm in the other, setting her down hard on one of the porch rockers.

Sam looked almost grown up as he turned angrily upon the astonished girl.

"That's my Bible!" he declared in a clear ringing voice that had lost its boyish treble and seemed almost manly in its accent. "If you wantta play horse with Bibles go getcherself one of yer own ta use, and don't take mine. I guess they have some back in the city stores!"

Mary Elizabeth looked at her young cousin startled. She opened her mouth to say something to him about his behavior and then closed it again. Instead she quietly stepped to Tally's side and took her own borrowed Bible firmly away from Tally's careless hand. Then turning to Sam she smiled and handed him the other Bible.

"Buddie, will you just take these in and put them away? They wouldn't be understood here," she said calmly, and then turned back to her surprised guests.

"Won't you all be seated?" she said with grave courtesy. "We have plenty of room and lunch will be at half past one. What can we do to pass the time? Would you like to take a swim? I think I can rustle up enough bathing suits. They may be a little out of date, but I'm sure that won't matter for once."

Sam disappeared with the Bibles and then reappeared quietly and kept in the background, ready to do his cousin's bidding. She noticed him several times, sitting easily on the railing of the piazza with one foot swinging lightly back and forth, his eyes gravely off on the distant sea where a little boat went curtsying across the horizon. Once his eyes met hers and a look flashed between them of perfect understanding, and she was sure that unless something outrageous happened Sam would keep further words to himself. He was angry, but he was under control. She pondered this the while she tried to play the part of courteous hostess, greeting her guests as if nothing unpleasant had happened, getting the right seat for each, giving a gay little word here and there in answer to their own protests that she would not go with them up the shore. Sam and she understood each other and Sam would stay by and help her out in everything even though he fairly hated every one of the guests.

Presently she excused herself to speak with Susan, and Sam appeared at her side suddenly as she arrived in the butler's pantry.

"They're only a bunch of unbelievers!" said Sam in a low tone. "You don't need ta mind!"

She gave him an astonished look, and then her face broke into smiles.

"That's right, Sam," she said, "let's try to remember that. I don't really know just what you mean by unbelievers, but we'll take that up when we have more time. And meantime, if Susan needs anything could you take Frank's bicycle and go for it?"

"Sure thing!" said Sam eagerly. "Watcha want?"

"Well, I thought maybe some of those lovely big strawberries with white insides. And some fresh fish. I'll see what Susan says."

"I'm right here, Miss Wainwright," said Susan appearing excitedly from the kitchen, a long streak of flour on her rosy cheek. "It's all right whatever you want. I mixed up some soda biscuits as soon as I saw the cars drive in. I thought maybe you would want to ask 'em to stay."

"Oh, that's nice, Susan. I'm sorry it will make you so much extra work. Couldn't Sam get that little Ivy girl you had over here the other night to help you?"

"I already sent Frank to tell her, and he's bringing the fish. If Mister Sam would get me the strawberries and cream? There's sponge cake. That'll do for dessert. Will fried fish and hot biscuits and a tomato and cucumber salad do for the main course, and iced coffee for the drink?"

"Wonderful, Susan! That will be great. Isn't that going to be too much for you to accomplish?"

"No indeed, Miss Wainwright! I love to have company. And how about the table?"

"We won't set the table," said Mary Elizabeth. "We'll serve lunch on the porch. When Sam gets back with the berries he can bring out the two nests of little tables, and you can show him where to find the linen doilies to put on them. Then you get out the knives and forks and spoons, and glasses and napkins and put them on a tray and he'll look after fixing them on the tables, won't you, Buddie?" She gave her cousin a loving look, and Sam's eyes were full of devotion.

"Sure!" he growled hoarsely.

"Then, Susan, you can bring the fish in right on the plates. Pass the rolls and butter. Fix your salad on little plates that won't take too much room, and will Ivy help serve? Then I think that'll be all right. Fine! Call me if you want me. Sorry I can't come out and help."

"Oh, Miss Wainwright my dear!" protested Susan smiling. "We don't need more help. That Mister Sam is a perfect angel."

So Mary Elizabeth went back to her guests and Sam departed on the borrowed bicycle, thinking scornful thoughts of the interlopers, and in particular despising the man Boothby Farwell. Now what did Mary Beth want with a chump like that when there were men in the world like John Saxon?

"Now," said Mary Elizabeth arriving back on the piazza with all the gaiety and most of the zest of former days, "we're going down and take a swim before lunch. Girls, come upstairs with me. Boys, go down those steps at the end of the piazza, turn to your left and open the door under the back piazza. You'll find a row of bath houses and plenty of men's suits in the chest near the shower. Make your own choice. We girls will meet you at the beach in ten minutes. See who'll be there first!"

The girls trooped off gaily and Mary Elizabeth led them to an upper row of bath houses off the upper back piazza, and there was much fun and laughter getting arrayed in the old-fashioned bathing costumes.

"Girls, I've found a peach!" cried out Cissy Ward.

"Black with sleeves to the wrist and a full kilted skirt. And stockings to wear with it, black stockings, as I live! Bloomers, too, that come to the knee. I'm wearing this one, girls, and I'll be sure to drown, and all the rest of the crowd will have to dive for me and bring me up. Just wait till you see me. Here's a sunbonnet too! What luck. The vintage of eighteen seventy-five!"

The morning passed quickly, Mary Elizabeth having a time of her own, which became almost a race, trying to keep herself in a crowd so as not to let Boothby Farwell isolate her for a private lecture.

She was relieved indeed when the bell rang loud and clear from the front porch as a signal to them to come back and dress, and they swarmed back through the hot sand, laughing and shaking briny drops from their voluminous garments, all talking at once, all except Boothby Farwell, who was trying to show Mary Elizabeth how hurt and angry he was.

BOOTHBY Farwell tried to walk back with Mary Elizabeth but she eluded him three times and dashed ahead to speak to somebody else and at last he gave up and sulked behind the crowd.

When they all were dressed and back on the piazza again they found there were little tables scattered about and pleasant chairs beside them, enough for everybody. The tables were set with spotless white linen squares, and everything needful in the way of dishes and silver. There was a plate of salad, cool and inviting, at every place. Mary Elizabeth gave a sigh of relief. Susan and Sam had done wonders.

They were no sooner seated than Sam marched in with a tray of plates, the appetizing odor of fried fish spicing the air and whetting appetites already keen by the plunge into the sea.

Big reserve platters of fish and quaint linen-lined baskets of hot biscuits appeared as soon as there was need of them. Pickles and cheese went the rounds, and approval ran high.

"Say, this is great! You can't take Elizabeth off her

guard! She's always prepared for an unexpected crowd!" They called out for more butter, and to have their glasses of iced coffee replenished again and again.

Sam, going about with trays and pitchers, waiting gravely upon the guests, had the air of an elderly host who disapproved of the company but nevertheless desired to stuff them to their capacity. After the super-strawberries and cream and sponge cake were finished with more iced coffee, the little tables disappeared as if by magic, and Sam was seen to saunter by in a brilliant red bathing suit going in the direction of the beach.

"What about a little drink, Tally?" called out Boothby Farwell as Sam stepped noiselessly by the piazza on the thick turf of the lawn. Sam grinned on the off-side of his mouth. Only Sam knew that there was no drink. He had carefully investigated while the crowd were in bathing in the morning, had dextrously opened each bottle stowed in the cars, and sent the contents gurgling harmlessly down the drain behind the house, filled the bottles with good honest water from the hose faucet, cleverly replaced the stoppers, and gone on his way rejoicing in silent revenge for a lost morning. He had silenced his conscience by telling it that he did it so there wouldn't be any funny business to annoy his cousin, in case Tally Randall took a little too much. Sam was a canny lad. And so he stalked sternly down to the water, dived out into the waves and planned to be a good way from shore and duck under if anybody came after him to visit a just punishment upon him.

But it happened that Tally and Boothby returned from their visit to the car with empty hands.

"There's been a mistake in that case of liquor," announced Boothby in annoyance. "They must have given us a case of bottles that were not properly inspected. I can't understand it. There's nothing but water in the rest of them. I can't understand it. The bottles we opened on the way down seemed all right, didn't they, girls?"

"They certainly did!" clamored the girls. "Hasn't somebody been tampering with them?" They looked at Mary Elizabeth. "How about it, Mary Beth? What kind of servants do you keep about the place?"

Mary Elizabeth hid a startled look in her eyes with a smile.

"Absolutely impossible!" she said. "Frank and Susan are ardent prohibitionists. And nobody from outside could get in the gate without ringing the servant's bell." But Mary Elizabeth's eyes rested meditatively on a bright spot of red darting among the white-crested waves.

"Well, we'll have to report this when we get back to the city," said Boothby with annoyance. "They certainly must have made a mistake and given us a broken case. That makes it very awkward. We can't get anything worth drinking this side of Allenby's Lodge, and that's quite out of our way. We'll have to be starting pretty soon if we must go that far. Come, Elizabeth, change into something for evening and come with us. We're not going to let you off. We've had a royal time and a delicious lunch, but we came down to get you and we don't mean to leave you behind! Get down to the basement and give your orders to your electrician if you must, but make it snappy! We ought to be moving out of here in half an hour if we mean to make the Crestmont Inn in time for an eight o'clock dinner, and we oughtn't to be later than that for there are special attractions there all the latter part of the evening that we don't want to miss."

Mary Elizabeth recalled her eyes from the bobbing red bathing suit and set her lips sweetly but firmly.

"Sorry to disappoint you," she said, "but it is absolutely impossible. I have other plans!"

Boothby Farwell flashed her a look of displeasure, but his firmly set lips showed he had no intention of giving up, and presently he asked her to show him about the house and grounds. The whole company started out together to wander about the lovely grounds, which though not extensive, had a sweet quaintness about the shaded walks and neatly kept drives and garden groups of perennials that at least made it an excuse for a walk.

Mary Elizabeth tried to make this an affair of the whole company, but in spite of her Boothby Farwell drew her away from the rest and made her sit down on an old rustic seat which had a view straight to the sea. He began to urge her once more to marry him, even taking out that gorgeous diamond and begging her to let him place it upon her finger. But something seemed to have changed within Mary Elizabeth's mind. The ring no longer drew her. The prospect of a leisurely life of pleasure in Boothby Farwell's company, drifting about the world wherever an attraction was offered, no longer seemed to her possible even of consideration. Finally she looked at him steadily, giving him that clear, frank gaze that she so seldom gave to any but those who knew her well.

"I can't marry you, Boothby, not *ever,*" she said. "I'm sorry you feel the way you do about it. I'm sorry I didn't know sooner myself, although you'll have to own that I never gave you encouragement. But I know that I shall never change about this and I wish that you would promise me to put the whole thing out of your mind finally and never speak to me about it again."

The man looked at her sternly, deeply offended.

"You are going a little too far, Elizabeth," he said sternly. "I have come a long way to-day to get you, and you refuse to go with me. Now you are trying to put off our marriage again and the time has come when I must refuse you. I insist that you come out in the open and acknowledge our engagement, and that you set a near date for our marriage. I am not willing to be played with any longer."

Mary Elizabeth was white with annoyance, and there were dangerous lights in her eyes.

"Engagement?" she said in astonishment. "There has never been any engagement between us."

"You wore my ring!" challenged the man.

"For one brief hour," said the girl. "I am not sure it was even so long. I put it on as you asked in the letter you sent with the ring, as an experiment to see how it would feel to wear it. That was what you asked. I never really expected to wear it longer than that evening, but I did as you requested, put it on and tried honestly in my heart to think how it would seem to have it belong to me, with all that it would mean if I should accept it. And I found—" Mary Elizabeth's eyes softened with a memory that still seemed like a fairy dream—"I found that it was quite impossible. As soon as I was back in the car I pulled off my glove and removed it. Boothby, you and I were never engaged and you know it perfectly well. You know that I have always refused to even consider such a thing. We have been friends. Just good friends. But if you will not put this thing out of your mind, if you still go on insisting that I shall marry you,—well, we shall have to cease to be even friends."

"Nonsense!" said the man with a sneer on his lips. "You don't mean that! You don't suppose for a minute that I am going to take this seriously!"

Mary Elizabeth lifted her chin a little and looked at him haughtily, her lips closed in a thin, firm line. She said no word but there was battle in her eyes. Before her steady gaze the man's cold eyes shifted almost uneasily at last and he said, his tone still angry:

"You act exactly like a kitten playing with a costly crystal ball."

"You being the ball?" asked Mary Elizabeth, and suddenly laughed, uncontrollably.

The man's face flushed angrily.

"Or else," he added with a sneer on his lips, "like a naughty woman who is playing with another man!"

At that Mary Elizabeth flashed him a cutting glance of scorn.

"That will be about all!" she said coldly, and got up to go.

"No, that is not all, Elizabeth!" said the man as if he had the right to rule over her. "I do not propose to give you up to any other man, no matter who he is, whether lover, friend or husband. I always get what I want and I never give up what I choose to keep. You will find it will not be easy to get away from me. And there are more ways than one to carry out that promise. Everyone has a weak spot somewhere."

Mary Elizabeth looked at him for a moment and a procession of emotions swept over her speaking face, the final look being utter contempt. And she said, in a clear cold voice:

"If I had needed anything further to make me know that I would rather be lying dead than marry you, you have furnished it in that remark!" And Mary Elizabeth marched definitely away from him and went into the house.

The other guests were gathering again to the piazza, sitting about smoking, laughing, beginning to be a little bored and quite thirsty, but Mary Elizabeth was in the house telephoning to a carpenter. They could hear her quite distinctly from the booth in the hall, where she had purposely left the door open a crack. She was arranging with the carpenter to come and adjust the garage door, and to be there early the next morning. They ceased their indifference and looked at one another inquiringly. They looked out toward the rustic pergola where their hostess had been seated but a moment since with Boothby Farwell and found nothing but a rustic seat smothered with summer roses. Boothby Farwell was not in sight. He presently came around the corner of the house from the direction of where the cars had been parked. He was frowning, his eyes still filled with fury.

"What has become of Elizabeth?" he asked one of the girls.

"She just went into the house," said Cissy watching him curiously. "She seems to be talking to a carpenter. Isn't she going with us?"

But just then Mary Elizabeth came out, a cool little smile on her lips and in her eyes. She had gained control of herself again, but she did not look at Boothby Farwell as he stood there cold and forbidding, eyeing her with retribution plainly written on his handsome face.

"It is time we left," he said haughtily to his party. "Get your belongings. Tally and I'll have the cars around here at once! We haven't any time to waste if we want to be up the coast in time for the performance!"

He turned on his heel and marched around the house out of sight.

"Of all the grouches!" cried out Cissy. "Do let's hurry and get the dear baby a drink! That's what's the matter, of course! He won't rest till he's had all he wants! Liz'buth, aren't you really going with us? Oh, why not? You'll miss the time of your life. Come on and be a sport! I've got two evening frocks along, if you haven't your togs down here. I didn't know which I liked best so I brought both. You can have your choice! Come on and play the game!"

Mary Elizabeth gave them a bright little enigmatical smile and shook her head.

"I really couldn't," she said cheerfully, "though it's darling of you to be so generous."

"You better run along, Cis, and get your hat or Farwell will bite when he sees you're not ready!" admonished Tally, whirling his car around the corner of the house and coming to a noisy stop.

There was a scurrying of feet up the stairs, a quick powdering of noses and adjusting of smart, silly, little hats, all the girls talking at once, pitying Mary Elizabeth, gushing over the nice lunch and the swim, and then a fluttering downstairs again, a clamoring and laughter as they adjusted themselves in the cars.

But Boothby Farwell did not come up on the porch again. He did not bid his hostess good bye, nor say he had had a good time, not even in the modern patter of the day did he do the courteous thing. He stood dourly in the driveway assisting the ladies into the cars, but he did not once turn his eyes toward Mary Elizabeth until they were driving away and then he turned and gave her such a look of menace and hate as she would not soon forget. It was like a threat.

But Mary Elizabeth kept her lovely color, the shine of her eyes, the serene smile of her lips, until the cars had swept away around the curve of the drive, out the big iron gate, up the coast road, and disappeared like two wild specks in the distance. Then she suddenly dropped limply in one of the porch rockers, put her burning face down in her cold hands and began to laugh.

She laughed until the tears began to come, and then, lifting her face to brush them away she became aware of a stubby young figure in a wet, red bathing suit, with dripping hair and a look of terror on his face.

Sam was standing on the grass beside the path and regarding her with deep anxiety. Mary Elizabeth looked at him and began to laugh again.

"Sam," she said when she could speak, *"what* did you do with the gentleman's liquor?"

Sam looked sheepish and slowly began to grin.

"Put it where it can't do any harm!" he said laconically.

"Where, Sam? Where did you put it?"

"Down the drain!" he said, eyeing his cousin keenly to see if she was going to make him confess and apologize.

But Mary Elizabeth was laughing again. Somehow she had to laugh or cry and she chose laughing. For Boothby Farwell had managed to unnerve her, as she knew he knew he would.

Sam stood still and regarded her with a half fearful little grin. He wasn't just sure of this cousin since those "city bums" as he chose to call their recent guests, had been here. He couldn't tell just how much Mary Beth thought of that poor fish Farwell. Maybe she was engaged to him after all, as his mother had once intimated, and if that was so he was done with her. A girl who could have Mr. Saxon for a friend to go and get engaged to a rotten egg like that Boothby Farwell, well, if she was he would go back to the city to-morrow. He wouldn't stand for it, not a minute!

But he had seen a look of weariness and defeat in her eyes when she looked up through her laughter, and he sensed that something had happened more than he knew. He felt troubled for Mary Elizabeth. He was there to protect her, and what could he do?

So he stood on one cold foot after the other, beginning to shiver a little now. A strong sea breeze was coming up and he was turning blue around his mouth and his teeth were chattering, but he stood there puzzling what to do.

Then Mary Elizabeth looked up again, saw him there and stopped laughing.

"You're a dear!" she suddenly said earnestly. "But you are catching cold, Buddie, run up and change quickly and you and I will take a run together on the sand and get the day out of our system!"

So Sam hurried off to his room, and in a very short time appeared reasonably attired, his hair giving evidence of having received what is known as a lick-and-a-promise, but his face full of eagerness.

They had quite a run on the sand and came back shining and a bit breathless.

"Did you get the afternoon mail from the box, Buddie?" asked Mary Elizabeth. "Dad said he was going to write me about that electrical work."

"Why, no," said the boy, and sprang away to get it.

He came back with several letters in his hand and eagerness written all over him.

"Oh, gee!" he said. "There's one for me from Mr. Saxon. That'll be the new lesson. Won't that be great! Now we can do some of it this evening, can't we?"

"We surely can," said Mary Elizabeth looking up from her own handful of mail and giving a wistful glance at the address on Sam's letter, then turning back to her own and sorting it over, hoping there might be one for her also, though she knew there had been scarcely time since she had written.

They settled down on the piazza to read their letters, Mary Elizabeth lifting a furtive glance to the boy at her feet in his usual place on the top step. She watched his face change from bright eagerness to dismay. Then he suddenly exclaimed:

"Oh Gosh! *Good night!* Read that, Mary Beth!" and springing up he cast his letter in her lap and dashed away up to his room.

16

WITH consternation in her eyes and a great fear clutching at her heart Mary Elizabeth stared after the excited boy. He leaped up the stairs three steps to a bound and banged his door after him. Then she picked up the letter and began to read:

Dear Prayer-Partner:

I am writing in great haste to ask you to help me pray for my dear mother who is very critically ill. There are no doctors left in our vicinity whom I can trust, all the specialists have gone north, and not a nurse to be had. I have to be doctor and nurse and housemaid, for Father has broken his ankle and is able to do very little to help.

Humanly speaking there is no hope for Mother, though if I had my old doctor-teacher here from New York, of whom I have told you, I feel certain he could save her for us, for I saw him perform just such an operation as she needs and save a woman's life.

But I know that with God all things are possible, so I am calling on all you boys to pray with me that if it be God's will He will let her live a little while longer.

You will understand, I am sure, why I cannot send you the lesson just now.

Feeling comforted because I know you will be praying with me,

Your friend,
John Saxon.

Mary Elizabeth read the letter through twice that she might not miss anything. Then she put it in her lap and sat looking off at the sea, but seeing a little house in a Florida grove, and a man carrying a heavy burden of sorrow and doing everything alone.

No, he wasn't alone, either! There was God! His God!

Mary Elizabeth wished she knew God. How she would pray!

But not knowing God, what was there else that she could do? John Saxon had not yet had her letter when he wrote this one to Sam. It might not reach him till to-day. If he had to go to the post office for it he might not get it even then. He had not asked her to pray. Perhaps he suspected she did not know how. And anyhow, until he got her letter he would not know whether he had the right to call upon her. His letter to her had made it plain that he was not counting on her now that he knew who she was.

But, oh, there must be some way she could help! Doctors and nurses were what he needed! Money could bring them to him in a few hours by airplane! Perhaps he would not like her to help that way, but one could not stop on a matter of that sort when a life was at stake! She sat several minutes thinking rapid thoughts, making quick plans, unhampered by any question of cost. Then she got up and tiptoed upstairs to Sam's door, intending to tap and ask him to come out, but when she reached the door she found he had banged it so hard after him that it had not latched and had sprung back again. It was open several inches and she could see Sam kneeling beside his bed, burrowing his nose into the pillow and praying in a half-audible murmur. He evidently thought himself shut in alone with God.

"Oh, God! You promised! Anybody who abides could ask what he would and you'd do it. Mr. Saxon does that. You know he does! I'm not much at it, but I'm reminding you of your promise. Do it for him won't you? Make his mother well! And you said if we ask in Christ's name you would do it for His sake! I'm reminding you! I'm not much good to you myself. I snitched those bottles and threw out that stuff. I hated those folks too! But do it for Christ's sake, please—!"

The pleading voice was smothered in the pillows again and Mary Elizabeth tiptoed away to her own room with a mistiness in her eyes.

Mary Elizabeth sat a long time listening to the stillness in the house and thinking out a plan that had come to her with breath-taking vividness. Dared she?

She leaned her head back and closed her eyes thinking out the details, weighing possibilities. Perhaps he would not like her to meddle. Perhaps the plan was on too large a scale. And yet, if God were going to answer that prayer He would have to do it through some individual, wouldn't he? But she! She was in a rather anomalous position. It might hurt John Saxon unnecessarily, as if she were flaunting her wealth and influence. Could it be done without her? She turned the question this way and that, all the time feeling more and more that the time was short, and knowing that somehow she was going to do it. And then she thought of the boy, and after a moment called him softly.

There was silence for a moment and then she heard a

stirring, and presently he came in the dusk of the hall and stood by her door.

"Did you call, Mary Beth?" he asked in a subdued tone.

"Yes, Buddie! I've been thinking. How would you like to help answer those prayers?"

"Oh—Boyyy!" came the answer in a long-drawn-out wistful voice.

"Come here and sit down." She drew a low hassock near the window and he came and sat in the shadow, but his whole attitude was eagerness.

"I think we ought to get a doctor and a nurse down there just as quickly as possible, don't you?"

"Sure! But how could we?"

She was still a minute and then she said,

"Sam, if you had a lot of money what would you do with it?"

"Why, take a doctor and a nurse down there in an airplane," answered the boy without an instant's hesitation.

"Exactly!" said Mary Elizabeth with a quick breath of satisfaction. "Well, I'm going to give you the money. He wouldn't probably take it from me. I'm—rather—a stranger—you know, but if you did it that would be different. You could say when it came to the questioning that you had some money that you were free to use, see?"

"I see! Oh gee! Mary Beth, you're a peacherine! Oh gee!"

"Well, Buddie, we've got to work fast! Sickness doesn't wait on time. The first thing is to get the right doctor. I don't suppose you know who that doctor was that he mentions, do you?"

"Sure I do!" said Sam, on the alert at once. "He told us a lot about him down at camp. Told about his operations and all that, and how he had learned more from him than any other teacher in medical college. His name is MacKelvie, Martin MacKelvie. But the college would be closed now, it's vacation time."

"Still, it oughtn't to be so hard to trace him if he hasn't gone abroad. That's a rather unusual name."

Mary Elizabeth was writing the name on a pad from her bedside table.

"Now, Bud, do you know the directions for getting there? Were you ever at Mr. Saxon's house?"

"Sure thing," said Sam eagerly, "so was Jeff! He stayed down and worked with Mr. Saxon after camp a lot."

"Well, write out the directions and everything you know while I go telephone New York."

Mary Elizabeth hurried down to the telephone booth and did some pretty good detective work for the next half hour. She was rewarded by discovering that Dr. Martin MacKelvie was at his summer cottage on Lake George. A little more clever work assisted ably by the telephone operator, and Dr. Martin MacKelvie was on the wire.

Sam was just outside the booth listening, his heart in his eyes, and Mary Elizabeth will perhaps never feel a thrill more triumphant than when the doctor's vibrant voice spoke, "Dr. MacKelvie speaking."

Mary Elizabeth caught her breath and tried to steady her voice.

"Dr. MacKelvie, I'm a friend of John Saxon who once was in your class at medical college. Do you remember him?"

"I certainly do!" came the ringing answer. "One of the best men I ever had the honor of instructing."

Mary Elizabeth drew another breath tinged with relief and went on eagerly:

"John Saxon's mother is very critically ill in Florida.

He feels that you could save her life. We're taking you and a nurse down in an airplane to-night if you'll go, and we'll gladly pay whatever fee you ask. Will you go?"

"What's the matter with her?" came the crisp keen question.

"We don't know. He spoke of an operation he had seen you perform. That's all we know about it. He is out in the country on his own, and the best doctors have all gone north. He said there was no one near whom he could trust."

"Yes, I'll go!" came the answer after an instant's deliberation. "If John Saxon wants me I'll have to go, but I won't charge him a cent."

"That's all right, Doctor," said Mary Elizabeth with a ring in her voice, "we want to pay it for him."

"We'll talk about that later. How soon do we start and where do I meet you?"

"As soon as we can get a plane. I'll telephone at once and make arrangements. Wouldn't it be better for the plane to pick you up? Where shall I tell them to come?"

A few minutes more of careful directions, telephone numbers exchanged, and the matter was arranged.

"Will you get a nurse, or shall I?" she asked.

"I'll look after that! I'll be ready inside of an hour. Let me know if you can't secure a plane and I'll see what I can do."

"Oh, I'll get a plane," said Mary Elizabeth with a lilt in her voice. "I know a pilot in New York. I'll call you again as soon as I get him."

"Oh, Boy!" said Sam softly, out in the hall. Then he tip-toed into the dining room and suppressed the dinner bell that Susan was about to ring, while Mary Elizabeth called up the flying field. Now, if her man was only there!

Fifteen minutes later she came out of the telephone booth triumphant.

"He says he'll go. He gave orders to have his plane ready inside half an hour. I heard him. Now, Sam, we've got to work fast. I'll have to call Dad and Uncle. Do you want to go? Will Uncle Robert stand for it?"

"Do I wantta go?" echoed the boy. "Do I *wantta* go? But I don't know about Dad. Do we havta tell him?"

"Yes, we have to tell him, Buddie. I couldn't take that responsibility. Perhaps we'd better get it over with before we eat."

So Mary Elizabeth went into the booth again and called her home, getting her father on the wire.

"Dad, I'm taking a doctor and a nurse in an airplane down to Florida to-night to a very sick friend. You don't mind, do you?"

"Why can't the doctor and nurse go by themselves?" asked her father.

"Because, they can't! There are circumstances that make it impossible. The sick friend is poor and might not accept the help if—I—didn't go and engineer it. Dad, I haven't time to explain. It's a matter of life and death and I *must* go. The woman will die! I'll write you all about it."

"Whose plane are you going in?"

"Cousin Richie Wainwright's."

"Oh, well, that's different. Why didn't you tell me that before? All right, but wire me the minute you land?"

"Yes, Dad. And Dad, I'd like to take Sam. Do you think Uncle would mind? He's crazy to go."

"Well, ask him. I don't know what he'll say. You say there's a nurse going along? And who's your doctor?"

Mary Elizabeth answered his questions and then called her uncle.

"Uncle Robert, I want to ask you something very particular. I hope you'll say yes. I'm taking a doctor and nurse down to Florida to a sick friend to-night. Cousin Richie is taking us in his big plane. I'd like to take Sam with me for company if you are willing and he's just crazy to go."

Sam held his breath for the answer as he stood by the open door of the booth and waited for his father to consider. After a moment's hesitation he answered:

"Why, yes, I guess he can go, Mary Beth. A boy loves that sort of thing, I know. But Mary Beth, tell him if he wants to write to his mother—she's in the mountains, you know—tell him to address his letter all right and then send it to me to mail. She's rather shy about airplanes you know, and there's no need to stir her up. And Mary Beth, wire me when you get there. Let me speak to Sam a minute!"

Sam with a trembling hand took the receiver and spoke in a serious grown-up voice.

"Yes sir?"

His father gave him a few general directions, bade him take care of his cousin and do just as she told him. He answered "Yes sir!" "Yes sir!" "Yes sir!" in that grave, awed tone, and the matter was settled.

They hurried through their dinner, packed their suit-cases, and drove to the nearest flying field to await Cousin Richie and his plane. After arranging about the care of the car during their absence they sat in it and talked in low tones, Sam going back over John Saxon's stories about his wonderful doctor-teacher and friend, and Mary Elizabeth listening eagerly.

The moon rose and touched the flying field with silver sheen, filling the heavens with glory, and Sam sat quietly looking up into the sky trying to realize that in a few minutes now he would be sailing along above in that sea of silver.

And at last, sooner than they had dared to hope, they saw the lights, and heard the humming of the great bird that was to carry them away on their errand of mercy. As Mary Elizabeth sat there watching it arrive she marveled that the intricate arrangements for this journey had been made so quickly and so easily. There were a thousand and one little things that might have happened to spoil it all. The doctor might not have been found, he might not have been willing to go, Sam might not have remembered his name. Some other doctor might have been difficult in more senses than one, and might not have been acceptable. It was just a miracle that all had worked out as it had. That was it, a miracle, an answer to prayer! Then there were such things as answers to prayer! She would never again doubt that.

Mary Elizabeth liked the doctor's face at once, and the nurse was a quiet elderly woman, who, it developed, often went with the doctor when he was called to very critical cases. She had gentleness and tenderness, and strength and firmness written in her face, and the very look in her gray eyes gave Mary Elizabeth confidence.

The doctor asked a few questions, some of which Sam had to answer because he knew more about John Saxon's affairs than any of them. Then at the doctor's advice they settled down to rest.

But Mary Elizabeth, as she gave a look at the world below sailing in its silver sea, and then closed her eyes, turned the page into the next day and the problems she would have to meet when she reached Florida.

And Sam, though ostensibly resting, did not take his eager wondering eyes off that silver world below him until they actually dropped shut with sleep, and then as he slipped off into slumber there was a prayer upon his young lips.

"Oh, God, keep her alive till we get there. Oh, God, show the doctor what to do, and save her life if it be Your will—!"

17

IT was after one o'clock when Mr. Robert Wainwright turned over for the thousandth time in his bed and stretched out his hand for the telephone, calling a familiar number with a sort of sheepish sound in his voice.

"That you, Sam? Well, I couldn't sleep. Sorry to wake you up but I thought it would be better now than to wait another hour or so. I was bound to do it before the night was over."

"Yes, all right, Bob," came the sleepy voice of Mary Elizabeth's father, "I got used to that long ago. As I remember, the night you were born you began waking me in the night—!"

"Shut up!" said Robert Wainwright. "You couldn't remember that far back. You know I'm only a year younger than you are. And besides I shall wake you if I like. I intend to keep on waking you up whenever I please the rest of my life."

"Yes, Bob, I know I couldn't expect anything else. What is it this time?"

"Well, it's that pest of a Mary Elizabeth of yours. Whatever is this mad scheme she's got up now, and pulled my Sam in with her? Where has she gone anyway?"

"Why, Florida! Didn't she ask your permission? She said she was going to."

"Yes, she asked it and I said yes, he might go, but somehow since I got to bed I got to thinking how Clarice would feel about it. She'd think of that awful wide sky and so many mountains to fall on and die, and all that bunk you know, and I decided he'd better take the morning train back to the city and stay with me till she got back."

"Too late, Bob, they left half an hour ago. Mary 'Liz'beth phoned me just before they started."

"Yes, I found that out!" snapped his brother, "at least I was afraid I had. I called up that shore cottage of yours where they were supposed to be stopping and nobody answered. Don't you keep any servants down there to answer the phone?"

"Why, yes, there's the caretaker and his wife, but they likely sleep in the far corner of the house, and there isn't any extension. But it's too late, Bob. They've gone, and I wouldn't worry. Mary Elizabeth promised to wire as soon as they arrived. And if you just turn over and snatch a nap or two the wire will be here and the thing will be over. You can write Clarice he's gone to Florida. She doesn't need to know how he went. In fact you don't need to say anything about it for a few days, she knows he's at the shore, why not let it go at that? Go to sleep, old man. It's only a few hours now till they arrive."

"Yes, but a lot of things could happen in a few hours!"

"There always could. Even if he was at home things could happen."

"Yes, but Clarice would blame me!"

"I don't see that. He's half your son. Haven't you a

right to let your half go planing? He's old enough to enjoy it. That's the kind of things boys like."

"Yes, that's what I figured when I said yes," moaned Sam's father.

"Well, figure it again. Richie's along. No flier has a better record than Richie. He'll look after them."

"You're sure he went?"

"Absolutely. He called me up and said he'd look out for them."

"Well, that's different. But all the same that Mary Elizabeth of yours is a wild, erratic child and ought to be spanked."

"Absolutely! Try and do it!"

"What started her off on this wild goose trip?"

"Some old lady dying for want of a special operation, and Mary Elizabeth seemed to think the people wouldn't let the doctor in or something unless she went along. Sam seemed to be mixed in it too, somehow, some friend of his. Saxon's the name."

"Saxon? Not anyone belonging to that friend of Jeff's? Not the best man of Jeff's wedding?"

"Might be. How should I know? Mary 'Liz'beth didn't have time for details. She seemed to think your Sam was even more essential than the noted doctor they raked up."

"H'm! If it's John Saxon then I guess it's *my* child that needs spanking, though yours was a party to it. She humors Sammy too much. He seems to be able to get anything out of her he wants. Look at the way he wheedled her into keeping him away from that lady-camp his mother wanted to send him to! But Sammy is just gone daffy about John Saxon!"

"*John* Saxon!" said Mary Elizabeth's father. "She said it was a woman!"

"Perhaps it's Saxon's sister," said the brother Robert.

"Likely somebody she knew in college. This Saxon is an intellectual fellow I believe."

"What kind of man is this Saxon, anyway? Is he down there *now*, do you suppose?"

"I wouldn't be expected to know that," said Robert, "but he's an A number one lad all right according to Jeff. Jeff thinks he's the finest fellow he knows. That's why he chose him for best man."

"H'm!" said Mary Elizabeth's father thoughtfully. "Rich and conceited like all the rest I suppose. I declare I wish I could hide Mary Elizabeth away from them all. I haven't liked any of 'em so far, but I suppose a mere father is not expected to interfere in such matters any more. There's that Farwell, I can't stay in the room with him he irritates me so. Thinks he's the only authority on any subject you happen to mention, has a way of looking at you as if you hadn't a right to exist, thinks all people over his own age are in their dotage."

"Just so!" assented Uncle Robert. "I wondered what you were thinking about to tolerate that intimacy. If it were my affair I'd read the riot act to Mary Beth, even if she *is* twenty-one. I wouldn't have it! That fellow is a puppy! I could tell you some things—well—not over the phone, but I will when I see you!"

"Oh, yeah? Think I don't know a few myself? But the thing is how to get rid of him? I've taken her to Europe with me twice hoping to shed him, and what does he do but trot along, or come afterwards!"

"Why don't you talk to her?"

"Well, you know Mary Elizabeth's a chip off the old block. She's like the rest of us. She likes to run her own affairs. I was afraid I might only make her stronger for him if I said anything against him, although she knows I don't like him. At least—she ought to know. Man! I wish I knew where there were some real men. I'd like her to meet a few. I begin to think your Jeff is the only one left I know, and I wasn't so sure of him a while ago. But he seems to have settled down for sure now. What's he going to do? Going to take him in with you?"

"That's what I've planned to do, and he seems to think it's about the best thing he knows."

"Well, that's great, Bob! I wish I had a son to come in and lift the burden off my shoulders. But now, how about this Saxon fellow? If he's down there and my girl's gone down, I suppose I'll have to begin to worry about him. What's he doing down there this time of year anyway? Did the sister or whoever she is get sick and they couldn't come back north when everybody else did, or what?"

"Oh, they live down there I understand. They have an orange grove."

"You don't say? I don't see why anyone would stay so far south in the summer. What's the idea?"

"Well, I don't really know much about it, but I've surmised they couldn't afford to travel around and they've just settled there."

"What's the matter? Lost their money? What was it? Investment or Real Estate? Don't tell me they were Florida boom people!"

"Nothing of the kind, Sam, they never had any money to lose. As I understand it Saxon's father is a retired minister or doctor or something professional, I'm not sure just what. They're nice people, Jeff says. But you needn't worry about Mary Elizabeth. This young Saxon's poor as a church mouse and has his own way to make yet so he's out of the running so far as Mary Beth is concerned."

"I don't see why," said Mary Elizabeth's father, "not if she took a liking to him. She's not a gold digger, and after all she's got plenty of her own. But I'm not so sure

I wouldn't like him all the better for being poor.
Money's what's spoiled most of the young men to-day.
They've had too much of it, and they don't know what
it means to have to get down to hard work and earn it
the way you and I did. I guess it's a mistake to hand over
a lot of money to your children before they've cut their
eyeteeth. Your Jeff was an exception."

"Yes, Sam, our children are always exceptions. However, you're bearing me out in what I used to say long
ago. Clarice always thought I kept Jeff on too small an
allowance, but I felt with all that money coming to him
from her father when Jeff would come of age, and all I
would naturally leave him, he needed to get a little
experience before he had the chance to handle it."

"Well, you certainly did a good job of bringing him
up," said Jeff's uncle heartily, "and I guess I can trust
Mary Elizabeth, too, to use good common sense. And
don't you worry about Sammy. It'll do him good to be
on his own a while. Anyway, you were going to send
him to camp, what's the difference?"

"Yes, I suppose so," said the troubled father, "only
Clarice makes such a fuss about airplanes, and if anything
should happen she'd never let me hear the last of it."

"Well, nothing's going to happen. Just make up your
mind to that, Brother. Get to sleep now and get a little
rest and by the time you wake up it won't be long till a
telegram comes. I suppose we're a couple of old fools!"

"What! Couldn't you sleep either?"

"No, blame it!" laughed Mary Elizabeth's father, "but
I'm going to now. Good night!"

18

BOOTHBY Farwell was exceedingly gloomy and silent as his party went on its way in search of amusement. When he spoke at all he was so disagreeable that presently the rest refrained from speaking to him any more than they could help.

At the first opportunity to quench their thirst, which by the time they had driven for an hour had become almost unbearable, the entire party indulged freely, Farwell drinking more deeply than the rest. When they arrived at the fashionable hotel a hundred miles up the coast which was their rendezvous he drank again and often during the evening. Also, he annexed a young woman of his acquaintance, Stephanie Varrell by name, whose startling artificial beauty was only rivaled by her daring conduct, and the whole party had a very gay time indeed. But during it all, and while he paid for most of it, and was a participant in all their hilarity, he was morosely silent, glowering at them and answering only when he had to do so with caustic sentences that might have been written with a pen dipped in vitriol.

Now Boothby Farwell was not a man who easily gave

up. He had been wont to boast that he always got whatever he really went after. The only question in his mind was whether he really wanted to go after Mary Elizabeth enough to make the effort. There would be ways to get her, of course. He considered several, as he sat at tables with the gay group he was entertaining. There would be weak places in Mary Elizabeth's armor. If money would not buy her there were other ways. Her family was a great weakness of hers, the pride of race. Just how to get her through her family was not quite plain.

But the family standards—ah—conventions! Even though she was fairly broad-minded for the times, her family were great sticklers for the conventions. They were almost Victorian in some things. Suppose, now, that one could plan to get Mary Elizabeth off somewhere in a lonely situation where she would be compelled to stay all night in his company? Would it not be likely that Mary Elizabeth's father would urge immediate marriage?

But how to get her away, even after the plan was made? Mary Elizabeth was a young woman who knew her own mind and who did what she wished to do.

He drank a great deal that night, and when he finally piloted his gay and irresponsible party back to their homes again he was keyed up to almost any measure that would reduce Mary Elizabeth to his terms. The next day he studied his plan again and finally got into his high-powered car and drove back to Seacrest alone.

It wasn't conceivable that Elizabeth would refuse to see him, nor that she would not accept his apologies for anything that might have been done to annoy her yesterday. It could easily be blamed on some one else in his party. He would have no trouble in persuading her that everything disagreeable he had done had been because

184

of his state of mind, because of his frustrated love for her. For after all Mary Elizabeth Wainwright was a gentle, kindly soul and did not like to hurt people. Perhaps he might even come to confessing a weakness or two, a little sentiment, which wasn't his natural line. It might even be that she was holding him off playing for something of this sort. He had been going with her for so long that perhaps she felt he had come to take things too much for granted. Well, he could give her sentiment, romance, if that was what she wanted. He knew how. He had had large practice in the past, before sentiment and romance walked hand in hand out of the picture of modern times.

As he drove along in the brightness of the morning he was making shrewd sinister plans. He would try romance, make violent, desperate love to her, and if that failed then he would be abject before her, touch her pity, until she would finally promise to go and take a last ride with him before he left for parts unknown to solace his broken heart.

Once get her in his car, and out of the town where people knew her, and his car would do the rest. He knew a lonely place where they could be stranded for the night while he pretended to work on his car.

The devilish scheme grew in his mind as he tore along the highway, bearing south and east, arriving at Seacrest an hour sooner than he had expected.

As he came in sight of the Wainwright estate, its tall plumy pines shut in by the handsome iron grille, he was reminded of the last time he had seen it, when he had had a vision of an imp of a boy in a bright red bathing suit striding down to the beach.

He was instantly on his guard, instinctively slowed down his speed, and considered. He must reconnoiter.

It would not do to come on that kid. He was uncanny. He would suspect something perhaps and make trouble!

So he traveled cautiously about the town, approaching the Wainwright place from different angles, but saw no sign of anybody about and the vista of the beach was free from bathers. No red bathing suit loomed on the prospect.

He had to ring at the entrance gate, however, as all the approaches to the house were firmly locked with formidable chains. It annoyed him to have to ring for entrance. He was full of impatience. Now that he was here he was anxious to carry out his plan at once. As he sat in his car awaiting admission he told himself he must proceed cautiously, with a friendly attitude as if nothing had annoyed him at their last meeting. Elizabeth had always been friendly enough if approached diplomatically. He must remember that and not lose his temper. But once get her married to him and he would break her will and stop her gay independence! He set his lips together in a thin, hard line, and a glitter came into his eyes. He was certainly going to enjoy breaking Elizabeth's will, and putting her through training, once he really had her fast!

But when Susan arrived a little hurriedly because of having waited to put on a clean apron, he learned that Elizabeth was not there.

"They've gone!" said Susan with perhaps a bit of satisfaction in her voice, for she recognized the man and the car, and she had not liked the man. She thought he was not a gentleman.

"Gone?" said Farwell blankly. "You mean she is out? When will she return?"

"No, sir, she's gone away. I couldn't say when she's coming back. She said she'd let me know."

"When did she go?"

"Night before last."

"Oh! You mean she has gone back to the city, to her home?" What a fool he had been not to try her home first. Of course she wouldn't be likely to stay long in a little backwoods place like this.

"I couldn't say, sir," said the well-trained servant. "She didn't tell me her plans. She just went away and said she would let me know when she was coming back."

"Well, surely you know whether she is likely to come soon."

"She might and then again she mightn't, she didn't say."

"That seems very strange," said the man giving her an ugly look. "I suppose you are holding out for money, but I'd have you to understand that I shall report this to Miss Wainwright. Perhaps you do not know that I am going to marry her. But here, take this, and give me her present whereabouts, or her address or something, or it will go hard with you later."

Susan drew back from the offered bill, and her chin went up angrily. She stepped back inside the gate and closed it with a click, letting down the bar that held it from intruders.

"I've no address to give you, and I don't want your money, no matter who you are. I know my duty and I'm doing it. I'm earning my money. I don't take it in bribes. I have nothing more to tell you!" And Susan, tossing her head, walked indignantly away from the gate, and no amount of subsequent ringing of the gate bell could induce her to make her appearance again.

At last the man who always got his way turned his car toward the microscopic town of Seacrest and invaded the post office, confident that money would give him the lady's present address. She must have left word to have her mail forwarded.

But he discovered to his amazement that here was at least one honest servant of the government, for the little, round, sturdy postmaster shook his head.

"Can't do it, sir, it's against the law. If you wantta leave a letter here with her name on it I'll address it and forward it to her, but the law says I can't give out addresses."

He tried more money but the government official remained obdurate and at last Boothby Farwell shook the dust of Seacrest from his feet and departed at high speed for the city.

In the early evening, having attired himself for an evening call he arrived at the Wainwright home. But the butler said Mr. Wainwright had gone to New York and Miss Wainwright was away somewhere. When he pressed the old servant for more explicit directions, the old housekeeper was called upon and vouchsafed her young lady was spending the summer at Seacrest.

When Farwell said he had been to Seacrest and that she had left there, she shook her head.

"She's down in Florida somewhere visiting a sick friend," she said, "but I don't know the address. She had her cousin Sammy with her. Mebbe Mr. Robert Wainwright would know."

So, growing angrier and angrier, Boothby Farwell drove over to Robert Wainwright's home and rang the bell with vigor.

The second maid who answered the bell didn't know anything about the young master Sam's whereabouts and while she went to ask, Farwell lingered in the hall tramping impatiently up and down. Suddenly his eye was caught by a pile of letters on the hall table and right on the top was one addressed to Master Samuel Wainwright care of Dr. John Saxon, with a Florida address.

Farwell whipped out his note book and jotted it down before the maid's tardy return with word that nobody knew anything about young Sam, and got himself out of the house with brief courtesy.

His car shot out down the street toward his own apartments. Arrived there he sent for his chauffeur and gave orders that the car should be looked over and conditioned for a long drive, sent for his man, and finding him gone for the evening, himself filled a bag with a few necessities, scribbled a few directions, called up a few people and excused himself from a few engagements, and inside of two hours was on his way on the highway, under a brilliant moon, his car headed toward the south. As he rode he made his plans, definite, detailed and devilish. Little gadabout! Playing fast and loose with him! She needn't think she could escape him this way! He would get her, and get her good and fast.

He thought of her happy eyes with that starry look in them in which he had no part. It galled him to think that she could exist so easily without him. She was playing with a high hand, and thinking likely to bring him to her feet in utter subjection at last, but she would never do that! He would conquer her. And when he did he would take it out of her for every bit of trouble he had taken to find her and bind her.

Bind her! That's what he would do! Bind her and show her who was her master!

In the night, in the moonlight, as he shot southward, his eyes glittered with a baleful light. He was planning how he would woo her with something more deadly than diamonds. He would woo her and make her pay an hundred fold for all she was doing to him now. She had dared to put some other one's trifling interests above his, running away again from the honor he would have put upon her. No girl in her senses would really intend to do that permanently of course. She was just enjoying the game of tantalizing him. And this was now the third time she had done it. Once she had run to Paris with her father, once to Egypt with a party of friends. Now she was running to Florida in summer time on pretense of seeking a friend! A friend in Florida in summertime! How absurd!

And he would catch her, and carry her off, and make her pay, pay, pay!

And so, a Nemesis, he rushed on through the night!

19

A HOT, hot morning in Florida with a burning blue serene sky, relentlessly bright and hot after the blessed coolness of the night.

The sun looked down unflinchingly upon its ally the white, white sand, that burned back smilingly from every white hot particle of sharpness and radiated the shimmering heat waves which rose from the earth in visible quavering wreaths.

The long, gray moss hung straight and limp like an outworn, ancient garment, not a quiver of breeze to disturb its ghostly draperies. The orange trees only stood shining and bright in their glossy foliage, a few golden discs left from the winter work, a stray gracious blossom here and there filling the air with heavy musky sweetness, the hot, shimmering, still air.

Out in the town that in winter had been so gay and sumptuous, tall palatial buildings with hot red tiled roofs and picture palms towering above them stood with closed eyes, a dead place with all its gaiety fled. A wide, bright, lonely ocean stretching away to emptiness lay beyond.

Out in the empty streets where few humans remained to walk, little shadowy lizards slithered, and paused at the approach of any, to turn to background, motionless till the interloper passed. Out beyond the town to isolated little bungalows among the orange groves, narrow board walks, hot and strangely resonant, spanned the sand, and more little lizards scuttled in and out the wide cracks between the narrow boards so much like ladders set on stilts. Little blue chameleons lay basking on hot fences or neatly stacked piles of wood, their little white vests palpitating as they surveyed an interloper with their mild, intelligent, bright eyes, pretending by their very stillness to be only a bit of the fence, or the woodpile, changing their color imperceptibly to that of their resting place.

Not a cloud in the sky and yet before an hour it might rain a downpour, as if the very floor of heaven were drawn out to let fall a solid chunk of water that would cease as suddenly as it came and cause the steam to arise from all the blazing points of hot, white sand and hurry back to the clouds again, to get ready for the next downpour. It is a game they play, the clouds and the sun, in this hot, bright, intermittent, rainy season. Another hot, hot day like those intolerable ones that have preceded it! If it were not for the blessed coolness of the night it would be unbearable.

John Saxon came to the door and stared out at the bright shimmer of the world. His face looked old with anxiety, worn with weariness. It somehow seemed that strong and young though he was he had reached the limit. His eyes were too heavy to stay open. He turned and stepped back into the room and dropped into a chair, his head in his hands, his elbows on his knees. Tears stung into his eyes. Must he give up the fight with death, give up because he was not able of himself to cope with the disease? He groaned within himself.

"God, it is not that I will not give her up if You want to take her. It is that I must see her suffer when I know that she could be relieved if I only had the skill. Oh, God! Must she go this way?"

His soul was filled with anguish! Father, too, suffering deeply and unable to get about and help! It seemed as if everything had come upon them at once. The hard winter and the small crop of oranges, smaller of course because they had not had the money to put into fertilizers and cultivation for the grove. His father working too hard always! He recalled how he had found his father in the grove, nearly fainting with the pain of his broken ankle; how he discovered that the laborer who had been hired had failed them, and there seemed no other available, so his father had been going out as soon as it was light, and working without breakfast, because he feared to wake Mother if he stopped to eat, also Mother would have protested against his hard work. Mother and Father, saving and scrimping without his knowledge that he might have the more to pursue his studies! Oh, it was all a confused tangle! Perhaps he ought never to have tried to study medicine. Perhaps he should have stayed at home and cared for them and spent his days in cultivating oranges.

Yet they had wanted him to go into a profession, had urged and begged him to go! And everything had seemed so well planned. To make good with the great specialist would mean that in another year or so he would be earning enough to give his Father and Mother luxuries!

Ah! but he had not reckoned with sickness, and threatened Death.

All night long he had sat by his mother's bedside

giving her medicine faithfully, watching her pulse, her temperature, seeing the frail, delicate features drawn with terrible pain at increasingly frequent intervals. Frantically he had telephoned to doctors he knew in the north, not even counting the expense of long distance, searching here and there to locate someone to advise with him, and failure had been written on every attempt but one, and that one a fading hope, a last resort. All the others he had tried had been away where he could not trace them. This one he had little faith in, yet he dared not go another night through without advice. And this doctor had given him little hope, corroborating his own fears, suggesting a remedy that might ease the pain, but giving an impression of indifference toward the case, as if he had said, "Oh, well, she's old. It's time she died. Why bother?"

Yet John Saxon had telephoned for the medicine and when it came had given it faithfully, hanging on to the last shred of hope, yet knowing that the frail sweet mother was growing momently weaker. He suspected that the medicine was merely doping the patient, dulling her pain somewhat. He was fearful that she might slip away from them in a stupor now at any moment.

His father was still asleep, worn out with anxiety and pain. John Saxon had come away from his vigil by his mother's bed to get a breath of air, lest he fall asleep at his post, and now here he was sinking down in his chair, too tired for even the tears to heal the smarting of his eyes. Too tired and sore-hearted to even think.

Into the open doorway stole the sweet spicy odor of the orange blossoms from the trees about the house, just a faint little breeze stirring the hotness of their waxen petals, lifting a burnished leaf or two here and there, rustling the great banana leaves at the back of the house like the sound of silken skirts on ladies near at hand.

Silken skirts and orange blossoms! How that brought back the sweet, sharp memory of the wedding, and the girl coming with graceful tread up the aisle, looking at him with that glad, clean look in her eyes, the girl of his dreams! And how like a fool he had rushed out to secure her at once without even lifting a questioning eye to his Guide. He had dared to tell her of his love, without guidance, so sure he knew she was a Christian girl! And now—to find her a woman of the world, the world from which he stood pledged to live a separated life!

Ah! God! Was all this trouble, this fight with death for the saving of his precious mother, to show him that he must not try to walk alone and guide himself?

The heavy delicacy of the perfume stole upon his weary senses and brought a dream, flung it about him as if it were her arms, the perfume of her hair, the beauty of her features, her face against him. The thrill of her lips on his came over him with crushing sweetness. In fancy he let his face lie there against her sweet breast an instant, resting from his fearful weariness, drifting unconsciously into momentary sleep.

Outside the perfume drifted back stirred by honey seekers, and the drone of bees mingled with the distant caw of vultures hurrying in search of prey. The gray moss waved majestically, now and then a mocking bird struck a raucous note, the little chameleons skittered under and over the narrow resonant board walk, and John Saxon slept.

Slept and dreamed of walking down a church aisle with a wonderful girl beside him, breathed words of love hot from his heart into her listening ear, felt her small hand tremble on his arm, saw again the starry look she gave him, the breath of the orange blossoms, oh, how sweet it was, the drone of the bees like a lullaby! Her arms were about him, and he murmured in his sleep, "Mary Elizabeth! *My* darling!" and that woke him up!

Startled he lifted his bloodshot eyes and looked about the familiar plain little room so eloquent of home and mother and father. He rubbed the sleep out of his eyes and tried to get his feet down to earth. Then all his burdens descended upon him again. His mother! How long had he been asleep?

He sprang to his feet and stepped softly into the bedroom. There was no change! He turned from the precious fragile face, so like to a fading flower, and felt again the stab of pain. A glance at his watch showed it to have been but a very few minutes since he had come out to get a breath of air, and yet in that time she seemed to have drifted farther away. It was no use! He had tried everything and nothing helped!

He glanced over at his father, still asleep, and thought pityingly of how it was going to be for him if Mother went. He too was frail. Yet always so gallant! Such a pair of saints for parents! How blest he had been! What was poverty and sickness beside the loss of these dear souls? And he could do no more! If only there had been time for him to order medicines! His stock was so small and did not contain many drugs that might have at least helped! Oh, why had he run this risk for his precious mother? Why hadn't he been sure to have everything on hand that might be needed, here in this wilderness home, when everything within hailing distance was closed for the summer.

Ah, that was the trouble with his mother. She had spent too many long hot summers in this forsaken place. She had been happy, yes, and had never complained, but she ought to have gone north and had a change of climate, at least every other year. This tropical climate invariably got every northerner who did not have a change now and then.

He had seen it coming. He had noticed her growing frailer, saw how easily she tired, and he had said more than once that she ought to go north for a change, but she had always smiled and shaken her head and declared she was all right. She had always said she would wait till he was done with his studies, and then they would save money and go north for a summer together. Lately, just since he had come back from the wedding and had been telling them all about it, she had said:

"We'll go north for your wedding perhaps!"

And now—*and now*—*!*

His thoughts trailed off into sorrow, and tears filled his eyes again. He was all in! He must get another wink of sleep somehow or he wouldn't be fit to go on nursing. A glance at his watch showed there was still fifteen minutes before he must give the medicine again. Now while they were both sleeping he would just stretch out for a minute.

The couch had been put in the bedroom for his father, so that he and his dear companion need not be separated. John's own room was in the second story. He would not go so far away. He flung the cushion from a chair on the floor and lay down there. The perfume of the orange blossoms drifted in and wove their spell again, and the droning of the bees in the blossoms hummed with the music of his dreams. He slept instantly and profoundly, tired brain and weary body refusing even the golden walk down the aisle with Mary Elizabeth. Some severe sub-conscious conscience told him this was no time to dream dreams, while his mother lay a-dying! He had need for every faculty, and he must rest if only for a minute.

Yet perhaps the perfume and the memories were still

at work within that sleeping mind, for sharply he came
to himself a little later, aware that the bees' humming
was extraordinarily loud, they seemed to be coming
toward the house in a body, they were almost at the
door.

He sprang into action. It was time to give that medicine! Alertly he paused to listen. Those bees! He had
never heard such humming! Was he still dreaming? He
must not go to the sickroom until he was wide awake.
He might make some mistake.

He stepped to the door and the humming increased
and drew nearer. Lifting his heavy eyes he stared in
amazement. Was he seeing things? Was he losing his
mind? Surely just loss of sleep wouldn't do that!

He pressed his hands on his eyeballs and looked again.
It seemed a great bird was flying low and coming straight
toward him, and the sound was like the droning of
millions of great bees.

And then all at once he was thoroughly awake and
saw what it was, a great plane, flying low and evidently
going to land on that big open space across the road that
he had just finished clearing of stumps for his new grove
before he went north to the wedding.

What in the world were they trying to land there for?
Were they in trouble, had something gone wrong with
the motor? He frowned. He couldn't go out and help
them now. He couldn't leave the house. And they
would make a noise and disturb his mother! Even just
coming to the door to telephone for help they would
make a noise. What should he do? He couldn't refuse
help—yet—he couldn't have his patient disturbed.
There was scarcely a shred of hope left, yet he couldn't
give up that shred!

Mutely, anxiously he watched the plane, hoping
against hope that it would go on. There really wasn't any

place nearby where they could get a mechanic, if they didn't have one of their own. There were no supply shops. There wasn't even a gas station if they were out of gas.

Yet against his wish the plane came on, nearer and nearer, lower and lower, and now he could see that it was as big as the passenger planes that went overhead in the winter when the town was full of tourists. What could such a plane be doing here? Surely a man who could operate a plane like that would realize at this time of year that this locality was as barren of help as a wilderness! He must be in terrible straits to land here! Yes, he was unmistakably trying to land, circling about, reconnoitering, and the roar of the powerful engine was terrible in the hot bright stillness. It might frighten his mother if she woke from her stupor! If there were only some signal he could give them to go on! If he could only prevent them from landing there! He was frantic and helpless! It was not like the calm strength of John Saxon to be so unnerved, but the truth was he had had only snatches of sleep for the last four days, and he was appalled at the new danger that seemed threatening his patient.

Suddenly the engine was shut off and the plane drifted to a standstill exactly opposite the little house in the orange grove, in a direct line with the front door and the neat path of Bermuda grass that went down like a carpet to the white wooden gate. And then, as he watched, a person detached himself from the plane and came on a run toward the house, and he had a dim impression of others disembarking. He must do something about this at once. They must not be allowed to come to the house and make a lot of noise. Several people talking! It must not be! He would tell them there was critical illness here, and they must go on, even if he had to lend them his old flivver to go in.

He tried to think where to send them. It was five miles to a garage where any sort of mechanic could be found, or even makeshift parts of machinery. There was a new man over at the Lake, but he knew nothing of his ability. Still it was only a mile and a half away. Perhaps they could telephone for help. No, he must not let a lot of people come in to telephone. His mother would be startled.

He started down the path to meet the approaching boy, his hand up to hush him to silence should he start explaining in a shout.

But this boy did not shout. He came silently, with shining eyes and a solemn face as if he were performing angels' duty. And he came as if he were answering a far desperate call.

It was when John Saxon reached the little white gate and swung it open to stop the progress of his unexpected guest that he recognized the boy, and stopped short in wonder and astonishment and a growing relief. Here at last was someone he knew, someone who would understand, even though he was but a boy. Someone who could run errands if he could not do anything else! And John Saxon swung out into the road and grasped the hand of the prayer partner who had arrived so suddenly out of the blue.

"Sam! Dear lad!" he managed to say in a husky voice, and with a tone that one man might use to another deeply beloved.

"How is she?" Sam asked breathlessly. "Is she alive yet? 'Cause I got yer doctor and a nurse! They're right behind me! Did we get here in time? We started as soon as we could after the letter came."

"You've got a doctor?" John Saxon eyed the boy in

joyful wonder. Almost any doctor would be a help when he had had to go on his own so long, tortured with uncertainty, and mortally aware of his own inexperience.

"Yer own doctor! Doctor MacKelvie! Dr. Martin MacKelvie!" said Sam proudly, mindful not to let his voice rise. Both the doctor and the nurse and the two cousins had warned Sam about this. He must be utterly aware that he was in the presence of great danger. He must not startle a sick person.

John Saxon put his hands on the shoulders of the boy and looked deeply into the young eyes, and his own eyes were full of tears.

"Kid!" he said. "Oh, *kid!* I'll never forget this! It's a miracle! How you ever did it I can't understand, but thank God you've come!"

WHEN Mary Elizabeth awoke the morning after they set sail in the air all the world was roseate with an opal sea. Clouds like lovely pastel draperies were floating intimately and the earth showed below quite empty of human life.

And then it all came over Mary Elizabeth just what she was doing and she was appalled at herself. How did she know that her ministrations would be welcome? How did she know that they would not be resented as unwarranted interference? Just because the doctor and the nurse had assented to going, even a great doctor like the one she had secured, just because her father and her uncle had made no serious objection, and her cousin Richie was piloting his most commodious plane in his best and swiftest style was no warrant that John Saxon might not be angry at what she was doing.

After all, John Saxon was a stranger, an utter stranger, and the letter he had written her days and days ago, the contact she had had from him, might be repented of by this time, or forgotten. He might be angry that she had not replied to it sooner.

And now she was sorry that she had written so soon. It would be easier to face him, not having replied so frankly to him yet, than to go down there nosing into his affairs, daring to bring a nurse and doctor without his knowing it, and remember that she had told him baldly that she loved him. Him! An utter stranger! She must have lost her head!

She remembered how jubilant she had been last night when each step of the way had been accomplished so easily. She might have known it was all too easy. There would be a hitch in her plans somewhere. Either John Saxon would have telegraphed for another doctor and he was already there, and his mother better, or she might have passed away even before their expedition of relief had started. In either case how flat she would feel to arrive under such circumstances.

How clearly she saw that she should have wired her intention, or asked for permission, or at least sent him word they were on the way! Yet just as clearly she had thought last night that it would be better to come as an entire surprise. She had instinctively felt that he would never allow her to come if he knew beforehand, and she would never forgive herself if his mother died and she had done nothing to save her.

She went through an embarrassing dialogue between Dr. MacKelvie and the possible other doctor John Saxon might have secured. She met a withering glance from the keen MacKelvie Scotch blue eyes that she knew by instinct could glitter like steel when reproving. And how she would hate being disapproved of by him whom she had already begun to like, possibly just because she knew John Saxon liked him.

Then she took up that other possibility of Death having arrived before them. In that event she would be questioned. There had been little time so far, and she had to remember that the approval of doctor, father, uncle and cousin had all been given without a sufficient knowledge of the facts. She fairly cringed when she remembered that.

Suppose for instance that they knew that her sole connection with the sick woman whom she had turned heaven and earth to rescue was through a son whom she had never seen but once and who had proposed marriage on the way down the aisle at a church wedding? "Unwarranted interference" that is what her father would say, and her uncle would ask "What is HE to Mary Beth?" She could hear him now. She could almost hear the disapproval of Aunt Clarice's tone even from the mountains afar, when she heard about it. Not that anybody who knew would mean to tell her, but Aunt Clarice always heard about everything.

Suppose they knew she had written him a shameless letter telling him she loved him, when she hadn't known him but a few hours? Suppose they knew that she'd never even laid eyes on the sick woman for whom she was taking this wild extravagant trip?

Mary Elizabeth shut her eyes on the roseate and opal world below her and let these things roll over her. Yielded her thoughts to the prospect of the morning when she should arrive before this unknown lover not knowing how he had taken her letter. This lover who knew God so well, and lived in a world of spiritual things that she could not even understand.

And then panic took her. She could never, never be present at that arrival. She must not be part of the picture. Her presence would only bring mortification and misunderstanding to John Saxon. And certainly to herself! Before this strange doctor who knew John Saxon, and who thought of her—what did he think?

Before this unfamiliar nurse with her gray hair and keen eyes who doubtless had her thoughts also.

She arose precipitately and went forth to prepare her plans. She must get hold of Sam and wake him up and have a talk with him. Sam was her biggest asset. Sam believed in her and would do as she said. He would be true and keep his mouth shut. A pity to wake him up so soon but better to get the matter settled between them before others awoke and took a hand in making plans. This was her party and she meant to manage it.

But she discovered that Sam was up and wide awake, as perky as a robin. Sam was not missing a single rose nor opal of the world below him. Sam was looking down and his eyes were full of wonder and deep satisfaction, and also a kind of queer boy peace. But when she thought about it a second time she thought his eyes seemed as if he were praying, right out there in the clouds, watching God's wonderful waking world below him!

She conveyed to the boy her idea of arrival, that he should be the first to announce their approach. His eyes assented understandingly.

"And you'll make it appear that this was your expedition, because it would hurt him otherwise?"

"Oh, sure!" said the boy, like an experienced accomplice.

"And you won't say a word about me?"

Sam gave her a quick, startled look.

"Aren't you going to be there? Aren't you coming with us? I thought you were coming with us, Mary Beth! You *are* with us! You can't go back on that!"

"Oh, of course, but I'm going to keep in the background. It may not be necessary for me to go to the house. The more people there are the more embarrassing it will be for your Mr. Saxon."

He thought about this a minute and then he said, fixing her with troubled searching eyes:

"You'll come when it is necessary. You'd come then right away, Mary Beth?"

"Oh, of course," she promised easily. "If I am needed for anything."

"You'll be needed."

"Well, you'll remember what I said and keep me out of it if possible? I did this—for you—you know."

"Okay!" said Sam sturdily, and she knew he would.

And afterwards she had a talk with her grave gray-haired cousin Richie.

"I think it would be better if you were just to stop in the town and drop me off, Cousin Richie," she said. "I can be looking up accommodations for us all and hire a taxi or car to drive back and forth with."

Her cousin studied her silently a minute.

"What's the idea, Bess? Somebody you're afraid of? It isn't like you to get up an expedition and then cut and run and leave the whole business on your poor henchmen."

Mary Elizabeth colored up rosily in spite of herself and then was vexed.

"Not at all, Cousin Richie. I thought you would think that plan eminently sensible and showing foresight."

"On the contrary, it looks to me as if you were losing your perspective, and forgetting the main object of the flight, which is to save a life as I understand it. I've just been talking with your eminent doctor and I find he is anxious to lose not one more minute than is necessary. He evidently has some suspicions as to the nature of the trouble and he feels that time is a big factor. I think we'll just drop down there by the house as quick as we can."

"Oh!" said Mary Elizabeth with a sudden fright in her eyes. "Of course! I didn't realize!"

"And besides, Mary Bess, we've slept in this old ship one night, can't we stand a few more nights if necessary, to save a life? Speaking of foresight, I stocked up with eatables to last several days. We carry our hotel with us, remember, and if you ask me, I think you'll find it about the only stopping place open around our destination. This is summer, lady, and hotels have mostly moved north."

"Oh!" said Mary Elizabeth a trifle appalled. "Of course!"

Then she was still for some time trying to adjust her mind and her plans and her panicky state to this new point of view.

"I've been talking with the kid," went on her cousin. "He says there's a vacant field across the road from the house large enough he thinks for landing. I think we'll make for that."

"Yes!" said Mary Elizabeth, wondering what had become of her poise.

She looked up and assented to her cousin's plans, and managed her usual smile, but the fact remained that she was just plain scared at the whole thing.

It was not until the doctor came to her and began to ask questions again about how much she knew of the case and the circumstances, that she got her self-control back, and forced her thoughts into sensible every day grooves. This was just an emergency in which she was trying to save a life and she must not think of anything else. Romance and all that must be put aside. She must strain every nerve to help answer the prayer that Sam had made for John Saxon's mother!

Then the doctor looked her in the eye.

"If this is a case for operating," he said, searching her

face, "have you the nerve to help the nurse? I may need several hands to work quickly. Our pilot here has already offered himself. It may not be necessary, but can I rely on you if I have to?"

"Of course," she said simply.

"Ever present at an operation?" He was still searching her face.

"No," she said, feeling very ignorant and useless.

"Lose your nerve easily? Faint at the sight of blood?"

"Oh, no!" said Mary Elizabeth earnestly, realizing that it was only the sight of a certain young man who could make her lose her nerve. And she never remembered to have felt this panicky way before.

"All right, you be ready then if I call on you," he said, and began to instruct her in the common rudiments of being sanitarily ready to enter an operating room.

Then Mary Elizabeth ceased thinking about herself and her own emotions, and was filled with awe over the courage it must take to cut into a human life, even in order to try and save it. All the rest of the way she was thinking about that mother lying there dying with her desperate doctor-son doing his best to save her, until she wanted to cry out to the plane to go faster, and she tried to look down and count the miles as they sped on.

It was Mary Elizabeth who first began to notice the tropical trees, the tall pines with their draperies of moss, the palmettos turning their fanned spikes to heaven, the groves of dark glossy orange and grapefruit trees.

But it was Sam who finally guided the pilot to that wide vacant space, cleared of logs and stumps and offering no hindrance to landing.

The nurse had not spoken often. She was old in experience. Many words were not needed to adjust her to a given set of circumstances. That was why Dr. MacKelvie brought her on emergency cases, instead of a younger nurse. She asked Mary Elizabeth a few questions about the case, and when she found how little she really knew she just smiled gravely and said, "Oh, well, we'll find out when we get there."

But she was a woman of skill and courage and adaptability, one could easily see at a glance, and Mary Elizabeth liked her. She gave one a restful feeling of trust and assurance.

Sam recognized landmarks long before Mary Elizabeth did, though she had often been to that same beach, but never out in the direction of the Saxon home.

Gravely the boy sat beside the pilot and pointed out the way to go, and at last the great bird glided down and came to rest.

Sam did not need to be told when to get out. At the first possible moment his feet touched the ground and he started on a run. The doctor was not far behind, with his leather case, leaving the nurse to follow. These two, the nurse and doctor, were intent only on the case for which they had come. They did not look about them, nor apparently have a thought beyond the immediate danger they had come to meet, the life they had come, if possible, to save, and they hurried to the house exactly as if they had been there before and knew every inch of the way.

But Mary Elizabeth lingered, for she suddenly saw John Saxon standing by his gate, the crisp curls of his hair standing awry, his shirt open at the neck, his sleeves rolled up, a rumpled look about his garments and a haggard look upon his dear face so different from the handsome lover who had walked beside her down that aisle.

But suddenly she knew she was glad that she had come. She would not have stayed away for anything in life, not for fear of shame nor scorning. She would have come just to help him whether he wanted it or not. The fact that he needed it justified anything she had done.

Cousin Richie came behind her as she hesitated and helped her from the plane and together they walked over to the house, gravely, in silence. She was glad he did not talk to her. She thought that after this was over if there was anything left of her, she would make him know how wonderful he had been. But now her eyes were on the tall man standing at the gate, the man with weary eyes and lines about his mouth, lines of suffering. How dear, preciously dear he was to her! It was almost unbelievable that a stranger could in such a short time have become so dear.

He had not seen her yet. He was all taken up with the surprise of meeting his old professor. She could hear the ring of his voice, the very eagerness in this clear, silent atmosphere, even though she could tell his voice was hushed for the sick room near at hand. Yet in spite of that she could hear his words.

"This is great of you to come, Dr. Mac! If I had known where to find you at this time of year I wouldn't have dared ask!—" and then the two turned and took great strides across the road and into the house, their voices dropping lower, gravely speaking of the case, but the words could no longer be heard.

She was almost glad he had not seen her, though her heart was crying out hungrily for just one glance. She continued to walk slowly across the road beside her cousin, aware that he was watching her keenly and wondering about the good-looking giant who hadn't even seen her. She struggled to regain what she called her poise, looking with tender eyes toward the plain little house, that had yet so much atmosphere of home about it. She was taking in the beauty of the setting among the glossy dark trees, breathing the perfume of the hidden blossoms, getting glimpses of golden fruit. But most of all she was feeling the peace that seemed to hover over the place, even though the shadow of death might be approaching. She had a feeling that the inmates of that home were all ready for it if it should come, and would accept the sorrow that it might bring in sweetness and courage. How was it that she seemed to know so much about this stranger-lover and his family? Did love give one new perceptions?

They had reached the open door of the house now and were glancing hesitantly within.

The big cool room with its cheap, white muslin curtains, its comfortable but shabby chairs, its home-made book shelves filled with rows and rows of books, running all about the room wherever there was space, was most inviting, everything in perfect order, though the mistress of the house was laid low. John had kept it that way. There could not be many servants available, she knew, even if he had not stated in his letter that he was housemaid, nurse and doctor in one, for Mary Elizabeth had noticed as they were coming down that there were no houses, nor even shanties for any servant to come from, any nearer than the village. With appreciative eyes she took in the few bits of ornaments, the one fine picture, the photographs. There was culture and taste here. But of course she had known there would be. Her eyes were only corroborating what her heart had told her.

Hesitantly they lingered at the doorway, Mary Elizabeth and her cousin Richie, anxious eyes fixed on the open door where they could dimly see the outlines of a white bed. The doctor and nurse and John Saxon had gone in there and were consulting.

Cousin Richie had dropped upon a chair by the door, a straight chair, alertly as if he were ready for immediate action if it were needed. Mary Elizabeth gave him a grateful glance. It was as if he were an old friend of the family and understood. She noticed suddenly the dependable dear look about Cousin Richie. Of course he was a noted flier and had his name and picture in the papers all the time, and she was entirely familiar with his genial smile and his keen eyes and weathered face, but she hadn't noticed before that dependable look, that tenderness about his lips, that was usually masked in his merry smile. She was used to him probably, and of course it must have been there all the time and that was why she had turned to him instinctively when she needed the plane. Sometime she would tell him how he had made her feel. But now she was just grateful. She felt as if this was a sacred moment, while she was looking about for the first time upon the home of her stranger-lover.

Sam was standing out at the back door, having gone around the house to the pump he knew so well of old, to get himself a drink of "real water," he told her afterwards, but in reality to recover from his own emotions, and to get through the period of waiting for the doctor's verdict, into the time of action that would be sure to come afterwards. He stood there in front of a big banana tree, his profile outlined clearly against it, his eyes so grown-up and serious and his lips set in trembling determination, as if he had suddenly been required to take his place as a man, and he wasn't quite equal to it. As if this time of anxiety for his beloved friend were just too much for him.

Behind him the great banana leaves rustled and flapped like softly rustling taffeta skirts. Beyond him the long gray moss on a tall pine stirred slowly in the still air.

Mary Elizabeth, sitting in the same chair where John Saxon had dreamed of her but a few minutes before, felt the spicy air, heard the drone of the bees, and heard the marvelous stillness, such stillness as she had never experienced before, but kept her ears attuned to what might be going on in that inner room. Had they arrived too late, and was she already gone? It was strange that so many people could be in a room together and be so quiet about it. Her heart stood still with fear.

Then after a long, long waiting, when it seemed as if even the moss on the pine out beyond the window did not move, nor the banana leaves in the hot morning, when Sam's profile seemed a bronze statue, and even the bees ceased humming, the nurse came forth from the room as silently as a moving picture might have done and stood before them looking at them uncertainly.

"She's still living, but she's a very sick woman!" she said in her lowest professional tone, a tone that gave the words distinctly, yet left no sound over to echo beyond their own ears. "The doctor's going to try to operate, I think. The difficulty is the lack of proper light of course. But we've got to bring her husband out. He mustn't be in there of course. He's very frail! I'll get him into a dressing gown. He can walk with help. He just has a broken bone in his ankle. I wonder which chair we'd better put him in?" She gave the room a quick survey.

"I guess that's my job," said Cousin Richie smiling. "You fix him up and I'll bring him out. How about this chair? And those cushions will help prop up the foot. I know. I've had one. And I guess I can rig up a light. I have plenty of equipment in the plane."

"Oh, that's right," said the nurse relieved. "I'll tell them."

Then she paused before Mary Elizabeth who was listening mutely for something she could do. She felt so utterly left out.

"I wonder if you could fix a tray for the old man? Can

you make coffee?" She spoke as if she did not expect her to say she could. But Mary Elizabeth brightened.

"Oh, yes," she answered. "I used to make it a great deal in college. I had a percolator with me."

"There may not be any percolator!" remarked the nurse dryly. She had an idea that this daughter of a millionaire knew very little about real life. "Well, do your best. The doctor needs me. I must get some hot water going at once!"

Mary Elizabeth vanished softly through the door that obviously opened into the kitchen.

"Sam," she called softly, taking pity on the boy's dejected attitude, "come and help me, but don't make any noise."

The bronze statue came promptly and gratefully to life. He slipped off his shoes and entered the kitchen.

"What to do?" he asked alertly.

"We're getting a tray for Mr. Saxon's father. You'll have to help me find things."

"Okay!" said the boy, "I know where everything is. I been here a lot, ya know. Whatcha want?"

"Well, a coffee percolator if there is one."

"Sure there is. A toaster, too. They keep 'em here on this cabinet shelf."

He swung open a door and produced an up-to-date electric percolator. Mary Elizabeth seized upon it eagerly. She was exceedingly doubtful about her ability to make good coffee in any other utensil than an electric percolator. To achieve a tray for that cold-eyed nurse to pass upon was another thing that troubled her.

But she was reckoning without the knowledge of what an experienced helper she had called to her aid. She did not realize that her young cousin Sam was a far more seasoned cook than herself.

"The coffee's in that stone jar!" announced the assistant cook. "Ya put a heaper ta each cup, dontcha? And one fer the pot. That's what we did on the scout camp trip. The measuring spoon is in that drawer. There's the tray on that shelf. Better make enough fer our Mr. Saxon too, hadn't we? He looked as if he needed it. Though it's a gamble if he stops ta drink it if there's anything else he oughtta do."

Mary Elizabeth's cheeks flamed at the pronoun "our" but she assented.

"The napkins and the silver are in the dresser drawer in the other room. I'll get 'em!"

Sam dashed silently into the front room and returned with everything needful for a tray, and Mary Elizabeth's opinion of her own ability shrank perceptibly. How her education had been neglected!

Sam got out the toaster, produced two slices of bread, also the eggs. He volunteered to poach an egg for Father Saxon.

Between them in a very short time a tray was ready.

The nurse coming in to see if her big kettles of water were hot looked askance at the boy, and then gave an admiring glance at the tray. She couldn't have done it better herself, though she couldn't conceive why the young woman let a kid like that bother around her in the kitchen at a time like this. But when Sam, keeping a weather eye out for affairs in the other room, came silently in with the tray, carrying it carefully as any woman could, her grim disapproval relaxed. Sam could be quiet even if he was a boy, and he could carry a tray without slopping the coffee into the saucer. Neither was anything missing from that tray, salt, pepper, sugar, cream, spoons, butter, delicate toast. She gave up the idea of keeping half her mind in the kitchen during this campaign and put it on the operation. Perhaps this wasn't going to be so bad after all.

So Mary Elizabeth remained in the kitchen looking over her own possibilities and the supplies with a view to getting more meals later when they should be needed. Of course it had been arranged that the guests should eat and sleep in the plane, so far as possible, but there would be individual meals here at times, and she was the obvious one to look after them. How she wished she knew more about cooking! She could make delectable fudge over a gas hot plate, could brew a cup of delicious chocolate, fluffy with whipped cream, or coffee of just the right shade of amber, and she could scramble eggs to perfection on an electric grill, or mix a salad that a famous chef might have envied. But after that her culinary knowledge failed.

A glance into the bread box showed little more than half a loaf, and that of a texture which she judged to be homemade, for it looked wonderful, even if it was a trifle dry. Didn't they have baker's bread delivered daily out here? She stood aghast. How did people live afar from civilization?

Suddenly she perceived another wide gulf of separation between herself and the man she had so unwittingly come to love. She simply did not know anything of the life in which he had always lived. Neither spiritually nor materially was she in the least fitted to be his mate. For dimly she perceived that a man like this would go anywhere, do anything, answer any call that Duty made, unhampered by the limits of civilization. Could she adjust herself to that way of life? Could she ever learn all the things she would need to know in order to be fitted for any environment? The idea appalled her, yet intrigued.

Quietly she went about planning some kind of lunch for whoever would eat lunch in the disorganized household. Investigation of the store closet showed several rows of cans, canned vegetables and soups. A large porous earthenware covered tureen wrapped in a wet cloth, standing on a shelf in the open window, revealed a head of crisp lettuce, a few stalks of celery, a couple of ripe tomatoes, three green peppers and a little nest of raspberries in a lettuce leaf. They were all fresh and crisp. Was this strange dish a sort of refrigerator? Three curious looking objects also attired in wet cloths and hanging from cords in the open windows proved to be bottles of water, of milk, and of some kind of broth, probably for the invalid. And they were astonishingly cold! Could it be that people had to exist through hot days indefinitely without ice? Couldn't they *get* any ice at this time of year?

She stood appalled and looked at the bottles as if they were some strange magic, taking in what it must have been to live in primitive times, and what all her forefathers and mothers had gone through for mere existence. She was still looking thoughtfully at the bottles when Sam returned and explained them.

"Sure, that's the way they keep things down here. Ice is awful expensive to haul way out here, even when they have ice, and of course they don't have any even in the village this time of year. That's evaporation you know. You just havta wet the cloths every little while when they get dry. That useta be my job when I was out here visiting, that time when Jeff stayed here and worked."

"Jeff?"

"Sure! Didn't ya know Jeff came out here and helped Mr. Saxon in the grove, all spring?"

"No," said Mary Elizabeth thoughtfully, "I didn't know it. I'm glad he did." Then she turned away and looked out of the window at the flapping silken leaves of the bananas.

Sam presently brought her word of what was going

on in the other part of the house. Cousin Richie was rigging up a big light with a reflector. The doctor was getting out his case of instruments. Mr. Saxon was hollowing out holes in four blocks of wood to put under the feet of the bedstand to lift it high enough for an operating table. The nurse came in with a grave face and took the pans of hot water she had been heating. Everything was carried on in silence. It filled Mary Elizabeth and Sam with the utmost apprehension.

"How about Mr. Saxon's father?" whispered Mary Elizabeth to Sam in one of the awful intervals filled with silence.

"He's okay!" answered the boy. "The doctor told him he could help in the operation by eating his breakfast, so he ate it like a good child, and he's sitting there in the big chair now with his eyes shut and a smile on his lips. You oughtta see him. He's a prince! I guess he's praying! He's awful keen, you know, on Mrs. Saxon. 'Mother' he calls her, just like that. And she's a peach, too. Wait till you see her. Looks just like a piece of lace Mother has that she wears with a pearl pin. Her hair is white and her eyes are, well,—wait till you see her!"

Mary Elizabeth went on with hunting her condiments for the salad, her thoughts deeply occupied.

When the salad was finished she put it in a covered dish from the closet, wet a napkin and tucked it about and set it in the window, wondering if her crude arrangement would work as well as the other big tureen.

The nurse came out to put more water to heat and told them that the operation was about to begin. Mary Elizabeth asked if there wasn't something else she could do and the nurse gave directions about heating more water.

So there she sat with her thoughts, and nothing to do but put on more water when it was needed. Sam went and sat on the back steps under a big lime tree with the banana leaves rustling a melancholy tune. He had his elbows on his knees and his head bowed in his hands. She remembered his words about John Saxon's father, "He looks as if he is praying." What an extraordinary thing to have got hold of Sam, the wild young boy. And all from John Saxon's influence! Jeff, too! Jeff the easy-going, happy-hearted gay youth! Herself too!

And then Mary Elizabeth put her head down over her folded arms on the kitchen table. Perhaps she too was praying!

MEANTIME Mrs. Robert Wainwright had gone on the warpath.

She called up her home first, hoping that by this time her youngest son had returned from the shore and that she might be able to speak to him. She knew her power over him when she could get him to himself without his fond father by to alter her authority.

It was Rebecca, one of the oldest and most faithful of the Wainwright servants who answered the telephone.

"Is Sam there, Rebecca?" asked Sam's mother.

"No ma'am. He hasn't got back yet."

"You don't mean he's still down at Seacrest with his cousin, Rebecca?"

"Why, I couldn't say, ma'am," answered Rebecca with some hesitation.

Now Rebecca was one of the most honest of persons, and never had been known to tell an out-and-out lie, but she had figured it out with her conscience, or what she used for a conscience, long ago, that when she was asked a question that loyalty forbade her to answer, and she replied, "I couldn't say," she did not mean that she didn't *know* and therefore was unable to state; she meant that loyalty, or wisdom made it impossible to give an answer. In this case of course there was loyalty demanded either side of the question, for she knew quite well where young Master Sam was, but the old master had told her not to let *any*one know where he was gone, especially his mother, and particularly *how* he had gone. And in a case like this Rebecca's conscience always dictated that she should be loyal to the one whom she liked best to please. Rebecca's loyalty without question, was first to Mr. Robert Wainwright, for not only did he appeal to her as the one of the two most likely to be right and just to every one in everything, but also he was the one who paid the servants, and who slipped them a little extra sometimes, when there had been a special request of some kind, such as was now the case. Therefore Rebecca answered firmly a second time.

"Really, I couldn't say, Ma'am."

"No, I suppose you wouldn't know," said her mistress thoughtfully. "Well, has Mr. Wainwright come home from the office yet?"

"No, ma'am," said Rebecca briskly, "he told me he had extra work to-night and might be late for dinner. He said to have it a half hour later."

"Oh, then I suppose I can get him at the office. Tell the cook not to give Mr. Wainwright too many greasy things. I know he likes them but they aren't good for him this warm weather! Everything going all right? If Sam comes home soon you might tell him to call me up at once. Well, Good bye, Rebecca," and she hung up.

With a smile of relief on her lips and a glitter of triumph in her eyes Rebecca walked away from the telephone, well content. She had not betrayed her master's secret, and she had not told what she called a lie. Her answer had been discretion itself.

Then Sam's mother called up Mary Elizabeth's cottage by the sea, but it happened that the caretakers were off to a Sunday School picnic and she got no answer. As a last resort she called up her husband. As a matter of fact she didn't want to talk to him, because if she had anything to put over on the family he generally frustrated her efforts if he found it out in time. But time was a factor in what she wanted now, and there was nothing else to do. So she set her lips firmly and called him.

He was just about to go out to an important conference of some business associates, but he came obediently to the telephone and answered her fondly:

"Hello, Clarrie, is that you? I hope you're nice and cool up there in the mountains. It's hot as cotton down here in the city."

Mrs. Wainwright made a few caustic remarks about people who "preferred" to stay down where it was hot when they had plenty of money to go off for the whole summer and escape the heat, and then she came to the point.

"Where is Sam, Papa?"

"Why, Clarice, you knew he went down to the shore with his cousin!" said Papa Wainwright guardedly.

"Yes, but don't try to make me believe he's there yet! I know better!"

Papa Wainwright's heart took a flop. Had she found out where Sam really was? Had she found out *how* he went? *How* had she found out? This was going to be uncanny!

But he answered in a bland tone.

"Why, Sam loves it down there, Mamma! Hasn't he written you about it? He's been hobnobbing with the Life Savers, and he's been helping haul in the deep-sea nets, and learning all about the fish, and—and—"

Papa Wainwright tried to think of some of the other

things that Sam might be doing that his mother would think were perfectly harmless, but words were failing him. It wouldn't do to mention fishing or boating for she had always been afraid he would drown. But he didn't need to think of anything else just then for he was interrupted.

"But he would soon tire of those things, I'm sure, Papa, with no companions but Betty, and by this time she's got the house full of her crowd and wouldn't have any time for Sam."

"I think not," said Papa Wainwright gathering courage. "I happen to know that she didn't intend having any young folks down, at least not at present. She's just—*resting* you know!"

"What from?" snapped Aunt Clarice sarcastically. "She never *did* anything that I know of. She can't even *knit!* And as for contract bridge she can't keep her mind on it!"

"Well, at any rate," said her husband evasively, "Sam's all right. I just had word from him last night. I think you'll get a letter soon. I told him to write."

As a matter of fact Sam had written and enclosed it to his father to mail, and the father had mailed it that very morning. Now he regretted the home post mark that she would be sure to notice. She would think he was back at home again.

"That is, you see," he began again, "I told him to write you a letter at once and mail it to me, so I would know he had written, and I would forward it to you."

"Oh!" said the boy's mother graciously, knowing her offspring's dislike of correspondence. "Well, I'm sure I hope he does. It's very rude of him not to. But what I want to say is, that I've already tried to get him on the phone down at the shore and failed! So he must have gone somewhere." Her tone was suspicion itself.

"Oh, well," began the weary husband blandly, "I suppose then they've just gone off on some little trip or other. Mary Beth drives around a lot you know. Come to think of it they spoke of visiting some friend of hers sometime soon. They won't be gone long. I wouldn't worry. Mary Elizabeth is very careful."

"I'm not worrying, Papa!" snapped his wife annoyedly. "I wish you wouldn't always think I am worrying! Though it's a pity if you wouldn't do a little worrying yourself sometimes. But I want Sam. I want him to come up here at once. If he won't go to that perfectly wonderful camp where I wanted to send him, at least he's got to have some cultural influence about him before the summer is over. And I want you to find him by telephone or telegraph or something and send him right up here. There's a perfectly marvelous man up here teaching dancing and all the young fellows and girls are taking lessons, and it's high time that Sam had a little of that under circumstances that he can't help liking. You know I simply couldn't compel him to attend dancing classes last winter. He said it was 'sissy.' That's the answer he gives to everything I want to do for his education. And it's all your fault, Robert. You encourage him in that. And he's going to grow up a perfect gawk if something isn't done about it. You know Jeff used to dance so divinely, the girls were all just crazy about his dancing, and it's high time that Sam began to get into some shape. Next winter there will be the Junior dances in the schools, and it's time he went around and got to be a little civilized. There are some charming young fellows here at the hotel, just his age, two brothers from England among them, and they are so well trained, and so courteous! Just perfect little gentlemen! They wait on the girls so delightfully. It's really quite cunning, Robert. You would love to see them. And Sam has just got to come up here and get a little of this atmosphere or he'll grow perfectly wild!"

"Well, I'll risk it," said Sam's father shutting his lips firmly after his words so he couldn't be forced to swallow them. "I'd rather see Sam a fine strong boy with a little horse sense than have him made into one of your imitation little gentlemen, at his age. Clarice, you let Sam alone this summer and let him grow! You'll be surprised how much sense he's getting. He's going to be a lad to be proud of. And I'd rather see him with his cousin Mary Elizabeth for a little while longer before he gets to being so polite to the nice little modern imps that pass for girls to-day. Say, Mamma, where did you put those thin old Palm Beach suits I like so much for hot days?"

"Now, Robert! I told you I gave those away last summer! They weren't fit for you to wear. You looked like a rag-picker in them. They never had any shape anyway. I got you some nice light gray suits, why don't you wear them?"

"Because they're too hot, Clarice, and because I don't like 'em! Anyway, I've given them away. I didn't want 'em!"

"Robert! You didn't give away those lovely suits! Why, I paid—"

"Never mind how much you paid for them, Clarice, I'd rather not know. I've given them away and that's that! And I've got a conference right now, Clarice, and I've got to go! Good bye!"

"But Robert, wait! I want you to promise me that you'll telephone to Sam right away to-night and send him up to me by the first train in the morning!"

But Robert Wainwright had hung up and gone to his conference!

There was nothing for his wife to do but pour her

heart out on paper to her youngest son, and send it special delivery care of his cousin.

Boothby Farwell, on his way southward, having tested out the different kinds of liquors offered by the way, and evaded several detours that seemed more or less casual, finally shook his fist at a perfectly plain detour, about halfway down to Florida and plunged into forbidden roads.

"I'm doing this at my own risk!" he snarled at a workman who rushed up to him with a red flag trying to persuade him otherwise, and then put his foot on the gas and dashed on, bumping up and down over ruts unspeakable, getting all messed up in some fresh cement, and arriving with a dash just in time for a nasty bit of blasting through some rocks in the road bed, to avoid which he swerved to the side and brought up with his car in the embrace, as it were, of a great doughty truck of the working class.

Boothby Farwell himself was thrown forward on his knees and cut and bruised about the face and hands annoyingly but not dangerously.

When he recovered his wind and his senses he said a great many uncomplimentary things to the workmen who were doing their best to extricate his car from the clutches of the truck and to wash his wounds and bind them up. Silent workmen they were, angry at his bull-headedness, men who could say such things as he was expressing much better than he could, gazing at him in a kind of disgusted pity.

They pulled him out of his trouble, sent him in a little old rusty flivver, with one of their best linguists to tell him on the way to the hospital some ten miles away just what the whole gang thought of him, and to get a wrecking machine to bring what was left of his car after him, and then they dismissed him with contempt and washed their hands of him.

Farwell stayed in the hospital annoying the whole staff of nurses and doctors with his complaints, until parts could be sent for by telephone for his mutilated car. And at last, when it was patched up, he headed south again a sadder but no wiser man. He felt that everyone he met was against him and declared the liquor was growing worse and worse the farther south he went. Of course he could only judge by wayside inns, because he had no time to hunt hotels of distinction. He was already behind his schedule and his bird would perhaps have flown before he got there.

This thought annoyed him more and more until he reached the next large city and found a hotel. There he telephoned to Seacrest and tried to get the caretaker. But the telephone at Seacrest did not answer. Frank and his wife had gone to prayer meeting.

Somewhat reassured by the fact that there was no answer, but not yet relieved, he finally called up Sam's mother whom he happened to know was at the Mountain House where he wished himself at that moment,— but only if Mary Elizabeth could be there also.

"Good evening, Mrs. Wainwright," he said suavely, "this is Boothby Farwell. I wonder if you could tell me just when Mary Elizabeth and your son Sam are coming back from Florida?"

"Florida!" snorted Aunt Clarice. "What in the world do you mean? Who would go to Florida this time of year?"

"Well, I thoroughly agree with you, but that's where your son and Mary Elizabeth are, and I'm trying to find out how soon they are coming back!"

"Well, they certainly will return at once if I have anything to do with it, that is, if they are really there. I doubt it. Where did you get your information? I shall telegraph her immediately to bring Sam back."

"Don't worry, Mrs. Wainwright, I'm on my way down after them now. I'll have them back within a few days. I only called you to make sure that I should not pass them on my way. You see I have been delayed a little for repairs on my car. But all is right again and I am on my way. I hope to make Florida to-morrow sometime. But I was afraid they might already have left. You see I came down as a surprise, but I suppose I should have wired them I was coming."

"But I don't understand!" said Sam's mother now thoroughly aroused. "Did Betty tell you they were going?"

"No," said Farwell, "you see I was away for a few days. But it's quite like her, don't you think? She's so impulsive. However, she'll be all right, I'm sure. Don't worry. I'll let you know when we are starting back."

"Oh, that's so sweet of you, Boothby dear. I shall feel so comfortable about Sammy in your care. And I'm certainly ashamed of Betty running off like that without telling anybody."

"But she's quite used to doing what she likes, you know," said Mary Elizabeth's would-be lover. "What she really needs is some one to look after her."

"She certainly does," agreed Mary Elizabeth's aunt. "I've been hoping—"

"Yes, so have I!" said the man gallantly. "Well, I won't keep you, Mrs. Wainwright. I just wanted to make sure they hadn't started home. I thought you would be sure to know."

"But where are you, Boothby?" asked Mrs. Wainwright coming to her senses.

"Oh, just in a little town in Georgia. I'm on the regular highroad you know, and I'm bound to meet them if they start before I get there. I know Elizabeth's car, you know."

"Of course," said the agitated lady. "And please tell Betty that I want her to send Sammy up by the very first train after she gets home. I need him up here now. Tell her that."

"I will indeed, Mrs. Wainwright. In fact if you like I'll put him on the train myself when I get there and see that he goes directly up to you."

"Oh, that's so good of you, Boothby dear. And if there's any expense connected with it his father will of course take care of it."

"Oh, that's all right!" said Boothby Farwell, impatient to be done with the voluble lady. "I'll wire you when I find them. Good bye!"

"Thank you so much! But Boothby, you didn't tell me how you found out they were in Florida!"

But Boothby Farwell frowned and hung up. He didn't care to enter into that question.

Mrs. Wainwright, however, was greatly disturbed. She went and sat down to her delicate knitting again, but her mind was on the matter of her young son, and her niece. How had Betty dared take Sam off without permission? Finally she arose and sallied forth to a telephone booth and spent most of the rest of the evening trying to get her husband on the wire. Failing to get him, and being told that he was still in New York, she called as a last resort Mary Elizabeth's father, and after some delay got a servant who told her that Mr. Samuel Wainwright had gone to New York with Mr. Robert Wainwright.

Much vexed she hung up and went to bed early to consider how she might visit retribution on all the delinquents. Her husband was not at home looking after things as he ought to be. Her brother-in-law never did look after his daughter as she thought he ought to do and Mary Elizabeth had probably taken advantage of their absence and gone off on some wild tangent of her own. No telling but she would bring them up in Egypt with Sam yet. This really must be stopped. If there was no other way to do it she would have to go home in the heat and stop it herself, much as she hated to do so. She certainly would make her Robert understand a thing or two when she once got his ear again!

To make matters worse the next morning she received a loving letter from her husband postmarked New York, crisp and brief, telling of his sudden business call and saying he wasn't just sure how soon he could get home, but when she called up the hotel where the letter was written they said both Mr. Wainwrights had checked out.

Nothing daunted she tried home again, but received the same answer as the night before. Rebecca played off two stock phrases in her replies and got by nicely. "You don't tell me?" when her mistress announced she had heard that Sam was in Florida, and "I couldn't say, indeed ma'am!" when asked if she had heard anything about it.

Baffled but not discouraged Mrs. Wainwright retired to her room and missed a morning of bridge to write letters to her husband and brother-in-law, setting forth her ideas of bringing up children, and what she would and would not stand. But the Brothers Wainwright were taking a holiday. They were up in Maine on a rugged old farm, most of the time sitting on a rock in the shelter of great old hemlocks, where they used to sit as barefoot boys, fishing by the hour. They had stopped in Boston and bought new-fangled fishing tackle, and brought it along as an excuse for sitting there, but most of the time they were reminiscing, much to the annoyance of the fish who would have liked to be biting that lovely modern bait.

Mr. Robert Wainwright had dutifully written a nice loving letter to his wife and mailed it from Boston, and another from Portland, vaguely mentioning a business trip, and giving the impression of a swift return home. His wife's letter did not reach him for several days, and that not until he was actually back in his home city but his own letters had kept his wife from further attempt to create a campaign against Mary Elizabeth and Sam in Florida, if that was where they were.

Mrs. Robert Wainwright, realizing that she was wasting ammunition, went back to her bridge and awaited a telegram from Boothby Farwell which was so long in coming that one morning she awoke in genuine alarm and began to telephone again.

But that was days later.

MARY Elizabeth was startled from her position bowed over the kitchen table, by a sudden sense of someone standing by her side, though there had been no sound.

She looked up and there stood Miss Noble, the nurse.

"The doctor wants you," she said, in that almost inaudible voice that yet could be heard so distinctly by one close at hand. "Put these on!" She handed forth a long white gown and a white cap that would cover the hair entirely. "Make a solution of this tablet in water and wash your hands. Be as quick as you can, and *come!*"

The nurse vanished and Mary Elizabeth arose feeling her heart beating so hard that it seemed as if it would choke her. It was not assisting at a solemn operation that frightened her. It was that she knew she must be going into the presence of John Saxon.

She looked up and there stood Sam, wide-eyed, white-lipped, watching.

She put on the garments instantly. She took the tablet the nurse had left and washed in the solution carefully as the doctor had directed. Then she gave Sam a radiant smile. There was fright in her eyes, but there was a gallant light also. She went swiftly and silently into the sick room and stood beside the doctor. She did not look up. She did not see John Saxon, but she knew he must be there. She fixed her attention on the doctor and did exactly according to his low-voiced directions, and whether she was receiving a bloody instrument, and placing it in its antiseptic bath, or whether she was handing him another for which he asked, she kept her eyes directly on her work. She did not look up nor allow her thoughts to do so. And presently her thumping heart quieted and she was able to draw a long, still breath and go on with her little part in this tremendous business of life and death.

She did not trust herself to look at the patient lying there so white and still, she did not let her eyes wander to the details of the work that was going on, nor to think of who was in the room and what part each was taking in this solemn scene. John Saxon might be standing close beside her for aught she knew, but she would not let her mind wander to him. There was just one person of whom she was conscious in that room, and that was John Saxon's Christ, who seemed to be standing across from her on the other side of the bed close beside the sick woman, as if she were very dear to Him, and somehow Mary Elizabeth knew that He had been very close to this woman all her life, and in the event of her death it would be only going with One she loved. Somehow she knew suddenly that this mother had been part of the reason of John Saxon, why he was so different from all other men she knew.

Humbly she stood there and held the instruments, giving thanks that she was counted worthy for even that.

She heard the low spoken directions of the doctor to the nurse, she heard sometimes a word of explanation, which might have been given to John Saxon, but she would not let them lodge in her mind. She was intent on only one thing, doing what she was told to do, and doing it under the eyes of John Saxon's Christ.

As a matter of fact John Saxon hadn't seen Mary Elizabeth at all. It hadn't entered his mind that she was there, or could be there. He was just at the other side of the doctor, helping now and then. He might have seen the other white-robed, white-capped woman enter and take her place to serve, but it had not entered into his realization at all. The white figure on the other side there was just a shadowy helper whom the doctor had brought along. He did not look up nor see her face and she did not look at his. For the time she was set apart from thoughts of him. And John Saxon's eyes were on his precious mother, watching the hand of skill that was guiding the knife.

Now and again there would be almost inaudible sounds spoken between the two doctors, but it was as if they were in another sphere. Mary Elizabeth stood serving as if she were passing the first test under the eyes of John Saxon's Christ.

It might have been years that she stood there. Time seemed to have stood still. But there came an end at last. And still following directions she found herself out in the kitchen again washing her hands, taking off the white garments and folding them up, facing Sam white-lipped and anxious, and somehow she managed a little trembling smile for him.

"Is it over?" his eyes asked, and her own nodded.

Mary Elizabeth felt as if she wanted to cry, and yet there was a kind of exultation in her heart.

The door swung open silently from the front room and the nurse came in, a clinical thermometer in her hand.

"You'd better go over to the plane and lie down, Miss

Wainwright, you look white," she said in her professional tone.

Mary Elizabeth took a long breath and shook her head.

"I'm quite all right," she said proudly. "What can I do next?"

"Nothing, just now, except to be on hand. I've made her as comfortable as it's possible for her to be at present. Young Mr. Saxon is driving somewhere to bring ice and other things the doctor wants. Your cousin is with Mr. Saxon senior. If there were only something for you to lie on it would be good for you to get a little rest now so you would be better able to help when you are needed."

"I know where there's a cot," said Sam eagerly, and opening a door over in the corner vanished up a sort of ladder into a loft, presently descending with an army cot coming on ahead of him.

"That's fine!" commented Miss Noble. "I believe you're going to be a big help!" and she eyed Sam with surprise.

He lifted his eyebrows in a comical way behind her back, and then with his tongue in his cheek vanished out toward John Saxon's old flivver which was beginning to send forth a subdued clatter preparatory to starting.

"I've made some salad," said Mary Elizabeth to the nurse, and then thought how flat that sounded.

"You did?" said the nurse. "When did you manage that? That sounds good. I think it will be needed when everything settles down to quietness."

"Were we in time?" asked Mary Elizabeth suddenly, as if the words were wrenched from the aching of her heart. As if she could not wait any longer to ask.

"It's hard to tell that yet," said Miss Noble. "Her pulse is very weak. She may rally. I don't know. I don't think the doctor is very hopeful, but at least we've done all we could. It's a pity we couldn't have come a week sooner. She was almost gone when we arrived."

"Yes," said Mary Elizabeth sadly, "if we only had known!"

Mary Elizabeth stretched out for a few minutes on the cot until her frightened trembling limbs had ceased to shake, but her mind was on the jump now. She could not lie still.

It must have been two hours at least that John Saxon was gone but when he came back Mary Elizabeth had vanished from the kitchen leaving a pleasant meal set forth on the white kitchen table ready for any one who wanted it.

It was Sam who came after her, flying excitedly across the sand and mounting into the plane.

"Mary Beth! Where are you?" he called in a loud whisper. "Come on over! The doctor wants you!"

Mary Elizabeth was on her feet at once, her eyes filled with premonition.

"Is she worse?" she asked hurrying after the boy.

"Naw, she's just the same yet I guess. But they want you. The doctor says you can sit in the room a while and let the nurse rest a couple hours, and he and John'll rest too. He says to-night'll be the time they wantta watch her through, so they better get rested now."

Mary Elizabeth's eyes shone. She was to be allowed to help again! That seemed a great honor. And John Saxon would be resting and wouldn't be there. She wouldn't have to worry about what he thought of her coming.

"All right, Buddie, I'll just put on something suitable. I'll be ready in a second. You can run along. Maybe there's something you can do."

"Naw, I'll wait for you. I told them I'd bring you."

Mary Elizabeth slipped into a little white linen dress

and a pair of white tennis shoes and was ready. Sam regarded her with admiration.

"You look almost like a real nurse!" he said.

"Thanks! Is that a compliment?"

"Sure! They look awful neat!"

"So they do! But, Buddie, you didn't tell Mr. Saxon I was here did you?"

"Absolutely not!" said the boy. "He said a lot about how great it was and all that while we went after ice, and I wanted like the dickens to tell him, but I didn't. I let him think I had a legacy. I didn't say so, but I guess he thought that. Anyway he said sometime he'd be able to pay me back, but he couldn't ever pay what it was worth to him, and he told me a lot how he felt before we came, hopeless and helpless and all that. Gee, I guess we got there just in time. The doc told me he thought there was a *little* hope she might get over it!"

"Did he? Oh, how wonderful!"

"He said it wasn't sure yet, but he thought there was a chance. He told Mr. Saxon that! And he told Father Saxon that, too. But say, you'll never know how much our Mr. Saxon needed us. I wish you could have heard him!"

Mary Elizabeth's eyes were shining and something lifted her heavy frightened heart and bore her up. She looked about on the sand she was walking over and noticed for the first time the little wild pea vines with their cute little blossoms of white and pink and crimson like little imitation sweat peas, rambling all over the sand, a lacy carpet.

"Where is Mr. Saxon now?"

"He's gone up to his room to lie down. The doctor made him. He said they would have three patients instead of two if he didn't!"

"Oh," said Mary Elizabeth drawing a breath of relief, "that's good! That's a wonderful doctor!"

"He sure is!" said Sam. "Say, you oughtta hear how great he is. Mr. Saxon's been telling me about what wonderful things he's done, just like miracles!"

Mary Elizabeth entered the house shyly, relieved that John Saxon would not meet her just now, stepping softly through the front room where Mr. Saxon senior lay on an improvised couch apparently asleep, slipping into the dimness of the sick room like a wraith.

Nurse Noble came over and gave her directions, what to do, what to watch for, when to call for her if she didn't know what to do, and then Nurse Noble went into the kitchen and lay down on the cot.

It was very quiet in the house as Mary Elizabeth sat alone in a big quilt-lined rocker and heard the soft breathing of the sick woman.

For the first time she could see the outline of her sweet cameo face, the soft white hair curling into waves about her forehead. There was something fine and gentle and lovely in the face, something that made her understand John Saxon in his strength and sweetness better than she had done.

And presently, over there in the shadowy part of the room she seemed to feel again the Presence that had been there during the operation, and it was as if she sat there in that Presence and had her heart searched. She seemed to see that life had not been the gay, bright trifle she had always supposed it. It had a deep, true, serious meaning and there was a reason for everything that came if one could only get near to the Source of understanding.

She had heretofore classed people as rich and poor, good and bad, ignorant and cultured. But here was a different quality. Not just goodness, nor even culture and refinement, but something deeper, far more valuable. These people were set apart from all people of earth, it seemed. There might be others like them, but she had not come in their way. It might be possible for others, just common ones, to become this way, she wasn't sure. But with all her heart she wished she might belong in a class with them.

It seemed as she sat in the room with that Presence of John Saxon's Christ that she sensed that what made the difference between these people and all others was that they walked daily as in the Presence of this Christ.

The afternoon droned on in that wonderful quiet, with only the distant hum of the bees, the note of a bird high and faraway, and the perfume of the orange blossoms coming in the window as a little breeze stirred the thin, white curtain.

The patient was coming out of the ether and moaning now and then, speaking hazy little sentences that were almost inaudible. The gentleness of her tone drew Mary Elizabeth. She longed to be able to comfort her in the physical distress she knew she must be feeling. The little services she could render were so exceedingly small and inadequate to the pain she was bearing. Just moistening her lips occasionally, or wiping her forehead with a soft cloth.

But as the afternoon waned the patient's voice grew stronger, the accents more natural. She was coming more and more to herself, and the words she spoke were sane. It would not be long before she was back among them, if all went well, an individual again, understanding what was going on. Of course she was very weak, but she would presently be wondering who they all were who had arrived during her unconsciousness. There would be that to be reckoned with. And the father too! Mary Elizabeth had not met him yet. They would wonder who she was. They would not understand her coming, perhaps!

Her cheeks burned at the thought. How could she explain herself? She could not pass for long as just another nurse. There would surely come a time of reckoning, and what was she to say, to do? She realized that she had not foreseen this side of the matter at all. And she furthermore realized that it mattered very much indeed to her what these two thought of her, these gentle people who were the parents of her lover! So far, they probably knew nothing of her existence!

John Saxon didn't know she was here, either. She was sure he didn't. If he had caught a glimpse of her at all he had probably just thought of her as another nurse whom they had brought along! Was there any way she could just keep out of it entirely? If she went to Cousin Richie, perhaps, and told him a little bit about things—could she bring herself to confide the preciousness of it all to him? Would he understand? Would he help her to get away into the village till the patient was well and they could go back north, and she could meet John Saxon's parents in a regular way as such matters should be conducted? Would it take away from the sacredness of what had happened if she told it to Cousin Richie?

She sat considering, weighing one situation over against the other. Whether it were better to do that and keep out of it all, or just to face things as they might come? If she went away how could she explain it to the doctor, and that keen-eyed nurse?

And yet, how could she stay here and meet the questioning eyes of these dear people, the alien eyes, perhaps, of John Saxon, if he had already found out what a mistake he had made?

And then the little mother on the bed spoke out clearly in a new love-tone.

"John," she said looking up and away as if she saw him, "you're not to worry. I'll be all right. We'll just stay here in Florida till you're through with your studies. And when you're married, Father and I will come to the wedding! Father's promised me that! We'll save up our money and come!"

Mary Elizabeth held her breath. Had John told them about her? Or could it be that there was another girl? Perhaps someone he was engaged to? Oh, not that, not that! God, don't let him be unworthy, untrue! Don't let it be that he made love to me when he had no right!

Then instantly she knew that could not be. Of course there was no other girl! She would not harbor a thought unworthy of him! Whether she ever came to know him better or not she would always trust him utterly!

But the gentle voice from the bed was speaking again.

"John, you'll be careful to get the right girl! You won't take up with anybody who isn't worthy? I couldn't bear that, dear! Father was afraid you might be dazzled by some modern girl!"

Mary Elizabeth sat petrified, feeling that she had no right to be hearing this, yet unable to move. And it was just then she suddenly realized the presence of John Saxon in the doorway the other side of the bed.

He was not looking at her. He was looking down at his mother tenderly, oh, so tenderly! Mary Elizabeth caught a glimpse of his face and lowered her lashes before that sacred look. He had not seen her. If he had she realized that she was nothing but a nurse to him anyway. He came forward as silently as a shadow might have moved and bent over his mother.

"It's all right, Mother dear!" he said as gently as she herself had spoken. "I'll get the right girl or I'll get none! I promised you that long ago. Don't you worry!"

The sick woman brought her wandering gaze to rest

upon her boy's beloved features, and she seemed to recognize him and smiled, such a radiant look, showing the precious relationship between the two.

She put up her frail little hands gropingly and caught his hands.

"Dear boy!" she said, and closing her eyes slipped sweetly off to sleep again.

He stood there for some time holding her hands, not stirring lest he disturb her. Then softly laying her hands down, he stepped back and lifted his head, a tenderness in his face, a light of hope in his eyes. He looked toward Mary Elizabeth then for the first time, a smile on his lips that asked her indulgence, her understanding.

But the smile stopped midway in a look of utter surprise as he met the eyes of Mary Elizabeth, and he just stood there gazing at her in amaze, wonder and delight coming slowly into his face, yet with it a look of reserve that she could not quite understand.

Suddenly he came swiftly round the bed and stood beside her. She rose precipitately catching her breath in apprehension for what might be coming, longing for his nearness, yet fearing to meet all the questions and his possible disapproval. Fearing it more after the dialogue between himself and his mother to which she had just been a forced listener.

He reached down and took her two fluttering hands that were clasped on their way up to her heart, and he held them together in both of his, tenderly, like something precious, yet he did not take her in his arms.

"You!" he whispered looking down into her eyes with an unfathomable look, "so it was you all the while! You did this lovely thing! Oh, *my dear!*"

And then he suddenly dropped his head down upon her shoulder and stood so, his face against her soft neck.

She could feel his eyelashes and they were wet with sudden tears.

Then, without premeditation, just as a flower turns to the sun, just as a mother comforts her child, she bent her own head and touched her warm lips to his wet eyelids. There was something so precious about it that Mary Elizabeth felt almost as if it were a holy sacrament. It seemed entirely apart from the flesh, a thing of the spirit, and it seemed as if God were there, standing just a little apart from them.

Into the hush of that precious moment came the subdued sound of footsteps outside on the grassy velvet of the path. They entered the front room quietly, and were coming straight toward the sick room.

John Saxon lifted his head, looked deep into her eyes, then with a quick pressure released her hands and was on the other side of the bed looking down on his mother sleeping there so peacefully when the doctor and Nurse Noble entered the room.

23

MARY Elizabeth sped out of that room like a wraith, her cheeks fairly blazing, her eyes so bright that they would have blinded the eyes of any but a casual observer, though no one was looking at her. She fled to the kitchen, glad that Mr. Saxon senior was sitting with his back toward the bedroom door reading.

She was tidying up Father Saxon's tray that had been brought out after his noon meal when Nurse Noble came out to prepare a little cracked ice in a linen cloth for the patient to suck when she moaned for water.

"You're to go over to the plane and get something to eat," said the nurse. "Mr. Wainwright has it all ready waiting for you. The doctor and I have eaten. You'd better stay there and take a good long nap now. You seem to be a pretty good nurse. We'll likely need you in the night so you had better be prepared by some really refreshing sleep."

"How do you think Mrs. Saxon looks?" asked Mary Elizabeth.

"Why, she seems to be holding her own pretty well!" said the nurse briskly. "Of course I haven't talked with the doctor yet since he came back, but I could tell pretty well by his expression he felt well satisfied. Now you run along!"

Mary Elizabeth ran along. In fact she went out the back door, not to encounter anyone, and literally ran all the way over to the plane with a happy little song in her heart.

All through the ensuing hours, and in fact the first two days after the operation the little party of rescuers waited, tense and anxious, watching the fight between life and death. Hoping, praying, fearing and hoping again. But at last the doctor came out of the sick room and told them he thought the worst danger was over, and a great burden was lifted from their hearts. Later that morning Mary Elizabeth went over to the plane for something and Cousin Richie looked up with a smile.

"Pretty well satisfied with what you've done, aren't you?" he said with a grin. "Your doctor says he thinks the patient is going to pull through after all. He says when he got here he didn't think it was possible she would live through the operation, but she seems to have marvelous vitality."

"Oh, isn't that wonderful?"

"Yes," said Richie Wainwright, "it is! There's some satisfaction in having things turn out right. I'm glad you let me in on this."

"Oh, but, Cousin Richie, I think it is so wonderful that you were willing. I was so afraid to ask. I thought everybody would think me crazy. And I think it's great of you to hang around this way and help. I was afraid you'd have to go right back and take the doctor with you, and then what would we do if anything went wrong?"

"What do you think I am, Betchen, a quitter? No, I intend to see this thing through. And I guess the doctor does, too. He talked that way. You see it's fortunate that this is his vacation time and he doesn't have to hurry back to his classes. His patients, too, are mostly away on vacations, and he's got a young graduate doctor or something in the city taking his place. He means to see the little lady through to safety, I think. He told me if for nothing else than John Saxon he would do it. He thinks John Saxon is great. Says he's going to be a coming man, is as brilliant as they make 'em and good as gold into the bargain, and you don't get that combination in the medical profession any too often."

Mary Elizabeth's cheeks flamed annoyingly, and Cousin Richie watched her lovely face furtively, quite confirmed in his own surmises.

"How long have you known John Saxon, Bess?"

Mary Elizabeth dropped her eyes and busied herself with a handful of wild pea blossoms she had picked on her way over to the plane, picked them just out of sheer relief and gladness.

"Why, not so long," she said with a steady tone, aware that Cousin Richie was watching her searchingly. "He's a friend of Jeff's, you know."

"Yes, I know, but I was wondering—. How about the old lady? Know her well?"

"No," said Mary Elizabeth letting her voice trail off, "no, but I've heard a lot about her. Sam has been here before. He liked her a lot and he told me what a wonderful old couple they were."

"I see! Well, Bess, it was a good thought. It certainly was a good thought, and I'm glad you let me in on it."

"I couldn't have done it without you, Cousin Richie, and I don't know how I can ever thank you enough."

"I'll tell you," said the man of the world, "ask me again when you have some more angel's work to do. I'm no angel, but I can fly a plane, and sometimes that'll be worth while."

"I should *say!*" said Mary Elizabeth. "And I certainly will ask you again. I'll know who to depend upon. Oh, it's so wonderful that the doctor thinks she may get well!"

"Yes, it is! He says the only thing that's really against her is staying down here in the heat. He says if he could get her north into more bracing air it would do wonders. He says if she were up north in the right place we'd see a difference in her in a few days."

Mary Elizabeth turned a thoughtful look at him.

"I suppose it would be a long time before he would dare move her," she said speculatively.

"No, he seemed to think not," said Cousin Richie. "He seemed to think it might be only a matter of a few days before it would be safe to move her, provided we'd fly carefully and avoid rough weather. The trouble is, though, he thinks they haven't much money, and there seems to be no place where they could afford to take her. The doctor felt it out with young Saxon this afternoon, I believe. And then he says, too, she wouldn't go and leave her old husband behind."

"But why couldn't I take them all down to Seacrest?" said Mary Elizabeth breathlessly, her eyes shining. "Why that would be wonderful! I'm sure Dad would like it. He's always willing for anything I want, and the house is big enough to make two or three private hospitals out of it. There's a great big room on the first floor opening off at the left of the front door. Do you remember? And there's a bath connected with it, and then a little room back of it that we used to call the library. That would make a splendid suite for them. The back room would do for Mr. Saxon, or the nurse if she didn't have to sleep in the room with Mrs. Saxon when she got better. And there are rooms and rooms upstairs. Don't you think that would do?"

Cousin Richie did. He smiled. His words were having exactly the effect on Mary Elizabeth that he had hoped they would have.

"Go talk to the doctor, Bess, and then get the consent of that big bronze giant that rules things around here. If you can I'll stick around till your party's ready to return."

"Oh, Cousin Richie! You certainly are a peach!"

"He's a whole basket of fruit!" said Sam suddenly appearing on the scene. "Got any food, Mary Beth? I'm starved!"

But that was not the last time they talked over a possible transfer of the patient to a cooler climate for the summer. Mary Elizabeth met the doctor as she started back to the house a couple of hours later. He wheeled in the path and walked back with her.

"Your cousin Mr. Wainwright says you've got a house by the sea," he said. "Tell me about it."

Mary Elizabeth told, not forgetting the whispering pines and the rhythmic waves. The doctor listened and his eyes took on a faraway look.

"That sounds good," he said. "Where is this?"

Mary Elizabeth told him.

"I could come down there and look her over now and then," he said meditatively. "That looks good to me. We'll see how things go the next few days. I'd like to take her up with us. I don't see leaving her down here any longer than possible. She needs a change of climate at once. She's as frail as a breath of air, although she must have a marvelous constitution or she never would have got through the operation. But I have great hopes now."

"That's wonderful!" said Mary Elizabeth. "I can't ever tell you how splendid I think it is that you're willing to stay here a few days and look after her. I was so afraid you would have to hurry right back the next day."

"Child, I wouldn't do that!" said the doctor looking kindly at her. "I wouldn't do that to John. John's the best young man I know. I love John Saxon like my own son. If I had a daughter I couldn't think of any better future for her than to know she was going to marry John Saxon. Young lady, I don't know how well you know him, or whether you have other plans for your future, but if you haven't, just take my advice and get acquainted with John Saxon. You couldn't do better for yourself."

There was a twinkle in the doctor's eye and a grin on his wry old lips as he said it, but he gave Mary Elizabeth a searching look and she turned as red as a peony.

"Well, all right, Miss Wainwright," he went on returning to his formal voice, "you've relieved my anxiety very much. We'll try to work it in a few days. I'll have a little talk with Saxon as soon as the worst danger is over, and we'll plan to go north as soon as we can."

For the next two days the little group of people centering round that sick bed were busy and a bit breathless. Anxiety was still in all their hearts, fear lurked not far away, and there were constant ups and downs. Mary Elizabeth marveled that the nurse could stand it. For each set-back brought Mary Elizabeth to the point of utter discouragement. But the nurse went steadily on from hour to hour taking whatever came and never seemed to lose hope.

But there was one thing which troubled Mary Elizabeth, and that was a sort of veil, or wall, that seemed to have come between herself and John Saxon. She couldn't understand it.

All night long that first night after he had seen her, her heart kept waking up and singing with the thought of his head down on her shoulder, his wet lashes against her face. But when morning came and she saw him, while his face lighted with greeting, it still had an aloof look, as though he were glad that she was there, but he must not come nearer than a look.

At first it did not worry her because she thought that while his mother was so ill he could not take time nor thought for anything else, but when it went on all day, and all the next day, even though the doctor's word had gone forth that Mrs. Saxon was practically out of danger, his aloofness began to trouble her deeply. She could not forget it, no matter what she was doing, for almost it seemed that he was avoiding her, and what could be the cause of that? Certainly he had shown great delight that she was here! She just could not make it out.

Sam seemed to be a bit puzzled about their relation, too, for several times he made an effort to throw them together, all to no avail.

It was the morning that Mrs. Saxon seemed so decidedly better that John Saxon announced his intention of driving down to the village. But he did not ask Mary Elizabeth to go along. In fact Mary Elizabeth took particular pains not to be in evidence when he was starting so that he would not think he had to ask her, for by this time she was getting most sensitive and keeping as much out of his way as possible.

All this worried Sam who adored them both and wanted nothing better in life than to see them delight in one another's society.

Mary Elizabeth slipped away over to the plane until Sam and John Saxon should be done. There were things she could do over there to tidy up a bit, and when she saw them drive away she could go back and fix up the beds and the kitchen.

She got everything in order and was just starting back,

but she had gone only a few steps when John Saxon came across the road and confronted her. He was looking almost haughty, with his nice chin raised a little, the way he had been doing lately. Mary Elizabeth felt that he was hurt at her for having forced so much assistance upon him, but his eyes were looking straight into hers now as if he would see deeper than just eyes were supposed to see.

"Mary Elizabeth," he said, and his voice had a quality of demand in it that small boys' voices have sometimes when they are half puzzled, half angry, wholly worried, "did you ever get my letter?"

Mary Elizabeth's eyes opened wide in astonishment and the bright color flew into her face.

"Oh, yes," she said eagerly, "why of course I did! What do you mean? Didn't I tell you in my answer that I got it? You didn't think I would have written all that if I had never got it, did you?"

"Mary Elizabeth! Did you write me an answer?"

"Certainly!" said Mary Elizabeth a bit formally, remembering some of the things she had said in that letter, her eyes very starry, though her chin was lifted now a bit haughtily. If John Saxon didn't like what she had said she couldn't help it now, could she? But there must be some way to keep tears from coming into her eyes just at this critical moment.

"When did you write?" demanded the small boy in John Saxon, almost as if he had shaken her and told her to divulge the secret at once or she would have to suffer for it.

"A few days before we started down here," she told him shamefacedly, knowing now, quite suddenly, that she had waited far too long to answer a love-letter like that. "I couldn't write you sooner," she faltered. "I had to think things out—"

But John Saxon was gone.

Like a whirlwind he had dashed away again back to the house, leaving Mary Elizabeth standing there in the sand with the little pink and white and crimson pea blossoms creeping all about her feet on their lacy vines. and a great hawk over her head circling and looking down, wheeling, slanting, a big menacing shadow at her feet whenever he came between her and the sun.

There she stood and looked after him with sinking heart. He was angry then that she had kept him waiting so long for an answer! Angry! And she hadn't thought John Saxon could get angry. But now she saw that he had a right to be angry, and the tears welled up and rolled down her cheeks which had been so pink a moment before and had suddenly gone white. Would she ever, ever be able to atone for having waited so long before she answered that letter? For now she saw how her heart had really wanted to write that letter at once, and she had been holding back because the conventionality with which she had been born told her not to be too precipitate. And now he was angry, and her heart had told her all the time that he would be! What should she do?

Then while she was still standing there John Saxon's old flivver came racketing out the drive and down the road past her, and John Saxon, driving like a wild man, did not even look her way.

Right down there in the sand among the pink and white and crimson blossoms she dropped and putting her face into her hands began to weep, right where anybody might have seen her from the house if they all hadn't been much too busy to watch.

And when she had wept the tears all away, she suddenly lifted up her face and began to laugh. She had just remembered how like an angry little boy John Saxon had looked as he drove away, and he wouldn't be angry like that, would he, if he didn't *care?* And besides what did he mean, asking her when she wrote? Didn't he get her letter yet?

And now she understood and laughed the more.

Afterward when she had laughed a good deal of her worry away and got a bit of hope hung out in her eyes she laughed again at the puzzled glance there had been on Sam's good honest freckled face.

Then Mary Elizabeth got up and went back to the house to work.

John Saxon drove with all his might down to the village to the post office.

"I haven't been to the post office since I mailed that letter to you, kid!" he said to Sam who was with him, like a faithful dog, never speaking unless he saw the time was propitious, just sitting there waiting for him. "I haven't had time, I haven't had a chance to get away from the house!"

Sam looked at him with a puzzled frown, and wondered why that was so important. He kept on wondering while John Saxon went in to the post office and then he wondered some more when his friend came out with a handful of mail in his hand and his eyes happy as he looked down at the pile of letters he was carrying.

John Saxon handed Sam a bill.

"Run over to the store and pick out anything you think they need at the house. You know what is wanting better than I do just now. I'll stay here and read my letters," he said as he sprang into his seat already tearing the end off of one particular letter.

Sam caught sight of the writing on that envelope and knew his cousin had written it. Now, when had Mary Beth written to John Saxon? What did it all mean?

And what would Mary Beth write to John Saxon for? She hadn't known much about him till he told her!

Of course she had met him at the wedding, and likely it was something about that. Perhaps he had carried off her handkerchief or something by mistake that night and had sent it to her and she had written to thank him. That might be it. Probably it was something like that. Or else he was mistaken and that was just some writing that looked like Mary Beth's, some other girl perhaps. But that in turn made him uneasy. He didn't want any other girl but Mary Beth in John Saxon's life! It troubled him a lot as he walked through the hot sand to the grocery store and looked around for things he remembered they had needed. Cereal and sugar and butter. Raisins. Mary Beth had said she'd found a cook book and could make a rice pudding if she only had some raisins. Sam bought the raisins and a few other things that appealed to him, and sauntered slowly over toward the car where John Saxon was still absorbedly reading his letter. Sam stepped back into the store and selected a few more simple articles they could use, and kept a weather eye out toward the car till he saw John Saxon fold that letter and put it in his breast pocket. Then he came hurrying with his packages. Sam was discreet at times, almost uncannily so.

There was no mistaking the look of relief and exaltation on John Saxon's face on the way back to the house. Sam wondered and wondered. Perhaps after all the letter was from that new doctor he was going to study with. Still, no, his friend would tell him if it was anything like that.

Sam cudgeled his brains all the way home, but he kept his mouth shut, and when they arrived at the house, just as if he had been telling Sam all about it, John Saxon turned to him with a bright look and asked:

"Sam, where do you suppose Mary Elizabeth is? Would she be in the house or over at the plane? Would you mind finding her and telling her that I'd like to see her a few minutes if she can spare the time? Tell her I'll sit right here in the car till she comes."

Sam gave him one astonished look and then got out with a respectful "Yessir!" instead of his usual "Okay." *"Mary Elizabeth"* of all things! When had *he* ever called her that before? It was always a formal "Miss Wainwright" when he mentioned her at all, which had been but seldom.

Mary Elizabeth had been washing lettuce that she had picked in the shaded little garden that John Saxon kept close to the house for a few things that needed constant care to thrive. She shook the bright drops of water from the green leaves and laid them away in the porous earthen dish as Sam delivered his message. Then she looked up with such a radiant smile that Sam almost shielded his eyes from it, and said with a real lilt in her voice:

"Yes, tell him I'm coming right away, Sam!"

Mary Elizabeth came walking demurely around the house in her simple white dress with her sleeves rolled up above her elbows and her shining eyes looking down at the springy path of grass she trod.

She was trying to look casual and demure, as if she were coming out to take an order concerning something to be done in the house, but the smile on her lovely mouth belied her manner, and when she looked up and met John Saxon's gaze her face broke into radiance.

"Will you go somewhere with me for a few minutes, Mary Elizabeth? Somewhere where we can be alone? I've just read your letter. I hadn't been to the post office for days!"

Mary Elizabeth sprang into the car and settled down beside him, and the old flivver racketed joyously away down a sweep of sandy road that was seldom traveled, into a bit of scrub and hammock land, till they came out to a quiet shaded place with a glimpse of a little lake not far away, and there the flivver stopped.

Little creatures from the wildness scuttled about and sniffed, and cast curious bright-eyed glances from trees and ground, but John Saxon and Mary Elizabeth were not noticing them.

"Mary Elizabeth!" said John Saxon putting out his arms and gathering her close. "My darling!" He drew her head to his shoulder and her lips to his. And Mary Elizabeth lay close to his heart as if she had come home.

It was some time before they talked at all, and then the man, looking hungrily down into the girl's eyes as if he could not get enough of the sight of them, said:

"Mary Elizabeth! Why didn't you write sooner? I thought you didn't care! I thought you were scorning me and teaching me a lesson not to be so presumptuous!"

"I couldn't," said Mary Elizabeth, looking up into his dear face and softly smoothing the knot of the little old cotton tie he was wearing, as if it were costly silk and precious. "I didn't dare! John, I was afraid about your God! I was afraid He wouldn't think I was fit for you. I'd just found out I was a sinner. Sam made me see it. And I knew that something had to be done before I could ever be in the same class with you. I had to find out about that first before I wrote you."

He pressed his arms closer about her and touched her forehead and her eyes with reverent lips.

"Did you,—find out—?" he murmured gently as if the matter were too sacred to speak of aloud.

"I—think so. Sam said I had to accept Christ as my personal Saviour. I'm not sure that I know all that it means, but I did the best I could. I told Him I did! And the next day I wrote you my letter. I didn't feel that I was any more fit to be loved by one like you, but I had done the best I could, and so I wrote. But,—do you think your Christ will think it is all right for you to love me? I wouldn't want to come between Him and you in any way."

"Oh, my darling!" said John Saxon stooping to touch her lips once more with reverence, "My Christ *loves* you, don't you know that?"

"I don't see how He could," said Mary Elizabeth. "I've never paid the slightest attention to Him before! And I thought—well, I thought when you didn't look at me nor hardly speak to me that you thought I wasn't worthy, and you were sorry you had written me what you did when you didn't know my name."

"Oh, my blessed darling! I didn't know! I didn't understand!"

24

IT was on the way back that Mary Elizabeth told him her plan.

"Did you know we're going to take your mother up to my place at Seacrest?" she said.

He looked at her startled.

"Sometime," he said dreamily.

"Sometime *soon!*" said Mary Elizabeth. "The doctor says it may be in a very few days she will be able to travel."

John Saxon shook his head.

"You don't understand, dear," he said. "She would never consent to go anywhere and leave Father behind."

"Oh, your father is going too, of course! It wouldn't be any fun to leave him behind. He knows all about it. I told him last night and he was delighted. He said he had been praying for a way to get her out of this climate till the hot weather was over."

"So have I," said John Saxon sadly, "but I couldn't let you take all that burden on you. What will your family think?"

"My family think it's lovely. I wired Dad yesterday

morning when Sam went down to the village for bread and the answer came just now over the telephone while you were gone. He said 'The more the merrier. Give them my hearty welcome!'"

"Does he know who we are?" asked John Saxon grimly. His lips were set in a thin, firm line and Mary Elizabeth felt that this was going to be bad.

"You mean does he know that you are going to marry me?" asked Mary Elizabeth gaily. "Not officially yet, I'm leaving that for you to tell him. But I shouldn't be surprised if he suspects. He's a pretty canny man, my father is."

"Yes," said John Saxon still more grimly, "and you think I could have the face to go and ask the father of a Wainwright to give his daughter to a penniless man without a flicker of prospect for the future?"

"Why, yes," said Mary Elizabeth still gaily, "that is, if you still want to marry me!"

"I want to marry you, yes, God knows that, but I don't want you to be tied down to poverty, and I couldn't ask you, a Wainwright, to marry me a poor nothing, not until I was sure of a living."

"Forget that Wainwright business, will you?" said Mary Elizabeth crossly. "It's the first trace of snobbishness I've found in you and I wouldn't have suspected it. As if money made one person better than another."

"You'll find a father will think so."

"Not my father," said Mary Elizabeth. "If it did I'd disown him. However, of course," and Mary Elizabeth's chin went up a little proudly, "if you want to let your mother droop and die in this hot summer climate and want to send me off with a broken heart, and incidentally maybe knick a little crack out of your own heart, why keep your old pride!"

She turned her head away from him to hide the

tremble of her lip and the blinking of her eyes. Mary Elizabeth was not a crying girl, but she was tired and overwrought, and this man was going to be stubborn.

But John Saxon suddenly stopped his car and put his arms around her again.

"Mary Elizabeth," he said solemnly, "God knows I want to marry you, but I don't want to take any advantage of you."

"You already took advantage of me going down that church aisle," gurgled Mary Elizabeth from the shelter of his arms, "and now you've got to bear the consequences! Pride or no pride, money or no money, you're not going to stand aloof from me for months and years nor even weary weeks, until you've brought your bank account up to mine, for I won't stand it. You showed me what I wanted when you walked me down that church aisle, and now I can't be satisfied with any counterfeit. The men I used to know don't interest me any more. Please don't be difficult, John Saxon. I love you, you know. And you'll find that that will make all the difference with Dad, too. You see Dad loves *me,* and he's going to love *you!*"

They got back to the bungalow eventually, though they did not give very satisfactory accounts of where they had been. But everybody was too busy to notice much except Sam, and he kept his own counsel, and went around suppressing a perpetual whistle, grinning all to himself whenever he might not whistle for fear of disturbing the invalid. Twice he went off in the woods by himself just to whistle, he felt so glad.

There was another reason for whistling, too. Just that day the doctor had announced that if the patient's pulse and temperature stayed as they were for a couple more days he thought they could plan to take her away. That would mean that the horrible time of anxiety would be over. Sam drew a deep breath and said "Oh Boy!" out loud to the tall pines, palmettos and waving moss.

The doctor brought up the subject that very evening while he and the two Saxons and Cousin Richie Wainwright were eating a quiet family meal in the Saxon kitchen, with Sam acting as waiter and Mary Elizabeth doing a tasty bit of experimental cooking.

"By the way, John," he said genially, "I think it's imperative that we get that mother of yours away from this heat at once. How about starting day after to-morrow if she still continues to improve? Mary Elizabeth has invited us all to a wonderful place by the sea, and I think the quicker we get there the better. It will be a lot better for me, too. I need to run up to New York for a few hours and look after some matters, and of course after another week or so I'll only have to run down to the shore occasionally to look after her. You can do all that is necessary most of the time, and of course keep a watch on her. We mustn't stand any chances of relapse. It might go hard with her. What do you think?"

John Saxon looked at his beloved doctor with startled eyes, taking in the facts as the doctor put them, and realizing the good sense of his argument, but there was immediate trouble and anxiety in both voice and expression.

"I hadn't thought that far," he owned. "I didn't see how anything like that could be. It sounds wonderful of course, and Mary Elizabeth has been telling me, but I do not see how I could go. I didn't think I'd be needed. There is work here that I ought to be doing—"

"Certainly you'll be needed!" said the doctor brusquely. "I couldn't take the responsibility of the trip without you, nor of leaving your mother in her present condition, even for a few hours unless you were there. And your father is not able to take the responsibility yet.

You are the king pin of this expedition, young man, and you might as well make up your mind to let everything else go. Groves aren't in it when we're talking about life and death!"

"He's right, Son. Let the grove go. This does seem God-sent," said the father, turning his peaceful eyes earnestly on his son. Since God had given him back his beloved partner he felt that nothing else mattered.

"But Father, if we lose the grove——?" began John Saxon.

"I know, Son, but this comes first. And if—*when*—your mother gets well there'll be a way out of our difficulties somehow."

John Saxon looked troubled, and was silent through the rest of the meal, his eyes deeply thoughtful, and when they were finished he stepped out into the dark grove and wandered around among his trees, looking up to the dark blue above him studded with stars.

It was there Cousin Richie found him half an hour later,—just strolled around and stood beside him as if that was the most natural thing in the world to do.

"You've got a nice grove here," he said casually, as if groves were only incidental in the scheme of things.

"Yes," said John, "it will be if it can have the attention it needs. In a couple of years it will put Father and Mother in comfort."

"Well, of course, that's a thing to be considered, still I suppose it doesn't weigh against their health."

"No," said John with a sigh, "of course not. I don't just know what I ought to do."

Cousin Richie was still for a minute, then he said:

"Nice grove! I suppose the old folks are greatly attached to it, aren't they? They wouldn't want to leave it?"

"No," said John Saxon, "I don't think they are. But

it's all they have of course, and it would mean a big loss if it died out. They've often talked over the matter, and sometimes wished they had gone somewhere else when they were buying."

"They wouldn't think of selling, I suppose, would they?"

John Saxon smiled.

"You couldn't sell anything now," he said. "You could hardly give it away. People are not buying. We could never get our money out of it."

"*Some* people are buying. Some people think it is a good time to buy when things are cheap. What would you have to get for it to get your money out? Fertilizers, labor and all, I mean."

John Saxon thought for a minute and then named a sum that seemed so ridiculously low that Cousin Richie almost laughed aloud at how things were being thrown into his hand.

"I think I could get more than that for you," he said thoughtfully, "if you think your father would consider selling at all. I have a friend up in New York who is interested in real estate. You might speak to your father and find out if he would be interested. If you say so I'll call up my friend in the morning and see if I can get an offer. How many acres have you? How old are your trees?"

They stayed out in the starlight for some time, John giving information about the grove, details of expenses etc., telling the price of land in that section when they purchased several years ago. Then he went in and had a little talk with his father. Later he wandered over to the plane and sought out Richie Wainwright again.

"Father says he'd be glad to sell," said John Saxon. "He says Mother needs to get away, and he knows she's been longing to go north again. He'd be willing to sell at almost any figure that would cover what he's actually put out."

"All right. I'll see what I can do in the morning," said Cousin Richie, trying to appear most casual.

"Well, it would be great, of course," said John Saxon, "but I'm not entertaining any very high hopes. Florida has slumped, you know, and people are not running around paying anything for isolated orange groves in the wilderness."

"You're sure your mother won't mind? You don't have to ask her first?" said Cousin Richie.

"No, we'll tell her the good news if it ever happens," grinned John Saxon. "That will be better for her than hoping for something that never could be."

"Well, we'll try it out in the morning," said Cousin Richie dryly. "Now you run home and get some sleep, and don't fret about things."

John Saxon said good night and went to his bed. He was not taking the matter of a possible sale very seriously. He thought this rich man did not understand the present state of the market for Florida property, and he had even more serious problems to face than the possible loss of the grove. He couldn't rightly exult in the love of the girl he had chosen because the way ahead looked dark and blank. He couldn't possibly marry Mary Elizabeth in his present penniless state, and he had a struggle with himself to lay the whole matter before the Lord and go quietly to sleep, but he finally did, and the new day dawned with a joy over the whole little group that could not be daunted by poverty or pain or anxiety of any kind. John Saxon's mother was getting well and what more could be desired?

In the morning Cousin Richie borrowed John Saxon's old flivver and drove in to the village. In about an hour he returned and said that his friend in New York had offered a sum twice as large as the highest hopes of the Saxon family had ever dared go. Old Mr. Saxon sat with an incredulous look upon his face and laughed when they told him. It took a lot of talking to make him understand that the offer was genuine. When he was at last convinced he sat and beamed.

"How about this furniture?" asked Cousin Richie. "Old family heirlooms? Have to keep it or want to sell?"

"It's all very cheap furniture, bought down here, no heirlooms," said John, looking about him at the things that had made up his background of home for the last fifteen years. "It's not worth much, and not worth taking north. But you wouldn't get anything for it."

"Well, I told him I didn't know if you wanted to sell the furniture of course. I told him it was plain and comfortable, nothing fancy, but it would be worth a thousand more if it was left furnished. He said all right, that would be good. Then I could select a care-taker who could live here and get right to work on the grove. Know any such person?"

"Oh, yes," said John Saxon. "Eric Tanner over in the next county is an expert with orange trees, and he'd be glad to get the job. He lost a lot of money in the slump. But really, Mr. Wainwright, this furniture isn't worth a thousand dollars. It isn't worth half that, not even when it was new."

"That's all right. It's worth that much to the new owner, just to get the grove taken over right away. We'll fix up the papers this afternoon and take them with us to sign in New York. Now, how soon do you think you could get away? Are there any things Mrs. Saxon would want to keep? Better find that out right away, and after lunch I'll take a flivver or the plane and go hunt Eric Tanner."

"Gee!" said Sam, standing in the doorway listening.

"You certainly are a fast worker!" said John Saxon, looking dazed. "It seems as if this was too good to be true."

"It certainly does," said John Saxon's father. "I'm afraid the man will think he's been cheated when he gets down here and sees everything."

"Oh, he won't get down here," said Cousin Richie easily. "He's just buying this on speculation. He'll put money into it and make it a success. He'll sell it for a lot more by and by when things come up from the slump again. Don't you worry about him. He deals in large interests and buys widely. He's taken my word for it that this is worth buying, and I feel sure it is, if one has the money to develop it. There's land enough all around to buy up, too, and enlarge, if he wants to. He's glad to know about it!"

"Well, it's just a miracle," said the old man sweetly, "just another miracle our Heavenly Father has let you be the instrument of bringing to us. We can never be thankful enough to you for your part in it."

Cousin Richie hurried away from praise as from a plague, and he came out into the orange grove rubbing his eyes and clearing his throat. He had never met people quite like these before.

Sam watched him away and then he slipped out into the kitchen where Mary Elizabeth was doing some work.

"Say, Mary Beth, did Cousin Richie buy this grove himself?"

"Why, he *says* that a man named Westgate bought it," said Mary Elizabeth turning a radiant smile on Sam.

"Oh *yeah?*" said Sam speculatively.

25

IT was decided that Mother Saxon was well enough to be told one or two of the things that were about to happen. Father Saxon was to do the telling while he sat with her for a few minutes. He was warned that it must be done so that it couldn't possibly excite her.

"Well, Mother," said Mr. Saxon, settling down in his chair, "do you feel strong enough to hear some good news?"

"Good news?" said Mother Saxon slowly. "Why surely. Good news never hurts anybody, does it? I really think, dear, that I'll be well enough to sit up in a few days, don't you think so? What better news could there be for me than that?"

"Well, we'll have to ask the doctor about when you can sit up," said Father smiling, "we're not going to have any relapses, you know. But listen, Mother, the unexpected has happened. We've had an offer for the grove. How about it, shall we sell?"

"I suppose they haven't offered enough to pay half what you've put in," said the wife. "Are you sure it's a genuine offer? Or just another one of those fakes, people trying to get property for nothing?"

"No, it's genuine enough. A man in New York. Mr. Wainwright knows him. I'm pretty well convinced we should sell. I'd like to take you back north, at least for the summer."

"But Father, not at a great loss! I can't bear to have you lose everything you've put in. And all your hard work!"

But when he told her the price that was offered she gasped delightedly.

"Why, Father, it's just like the fairy tales I used to dream out when I was a child going to sleep! You're not 'kidding me' are you, as John says?"

"No, I'm not kidding you. It's a genuine offer. He wants to take it over right away. He wants to buy the furniture too. He'll pay a thousand more for everything just as it stands. Of course you're to take out anything you very much prize. Or, of course, if you want to keep the furniture you can."

"No, there's nothing but the old clock and grandmother's bureau and chair that is worth keeping," said the pleased old lady, "but I can't make it seem real. Why would he want furniture he'd never seen?"

"He's going to put a man in right away to work the grove. He said it would save time and trouble to have a place all ready for him to live."

"How soon does he want us to get out? We'd have to pack our personal things of course."

"Yes, but that wouldn't take long, I guess. The man would like to take over the place this week."

"But, dear, does the doctor think I'd be able to get up by then? And where could we go, with you not able to walk yet without a crutch?"

"Not to say exactly up," said the smiling old man.

"Yes, up, up in the air perhaps," he smiled again. "But he says you'll be able to be moved. And we're invited to a house party! Mary Elizabeth Wainwright has invited us to a house party at the seashore and the doctor says you can go!"

The old lady looked dazed.

"But I couldn't possibly go to a house party," she said, "I've nothing fit to wear. It's very lovely of her of course, but I couldn't possibly do it. Everything I have is quite worn and old. It was well enough for down here, but it wouldn't do for a seashore place nor a house party. And besides, I haven't even anything fit to wear traveling!"

"Well, you talk with Mary Elizabeth about it, Mother. She'll explain it all out to you. And John, he thinks it's all right!"

"He would!" said the woman who had come back to earth again from the borderland of heaven, and realized that her fig leaves were entirely out of date. "John is a dear lamb but he doesn't know about clothes!"

"Oh, but I do!" cried Mary Elizabeth entering at just the right minute from her station outside the door. "I'll tell you all about it. You see it isn't a fashionable summer resort where you are going. It's a dear old house where I used to go when I was a child, and I love it. There are no fashionable people around, and anyway our house party is just going to be us, and clothes don't matter."

"But I've really nothing to travel in, dear," said the old lady who had begun to love the lovely girl who seemed to be a sort of assistant to the nurse, and was yet a cousin of Jeffrey Wainwright of whom she was so fond.

"Oh, but don't you know, you're just going to travel in your nightie, so that needn't bother you at all," laughed Mary Elizabeth.

"In my *what?*" exclaimed Mother Saxon in horror.

Then appeared John Saxon on the scene.

"Mother, you see it's this way. You've got to go very quietly. You've been too sick for us to risk any excitement. So we're just going to carry you over across the road and put you in a nice bed, in an airplane. You know you've always wished you could ride in one, and now you've got your wish!"

"An airplane! Oh, John! And how much will that cost? Just because you are selling the orange grove for more than we expected, don't go and get extravagant. I can perfectly well go in the train. I couldn't think of letting you pay a lot for an airplane."

"But it isn't costing anything, Mother!" assured John with a lot of joy in his eyes and a more rested look than Mary Elizabeth had seen on his face since they came down. "Mary Elizabeth's cousin Richie is taking us all back in his plane that he brought the doctor and nurse and Sam and Mary Elizabeth down in. Isn't that nice? Now, will you tell us, please, just what you want to keep of the furniture in the house? Sam and I are going to pack whatever you want to keep this afternoon. We'll go away and leave you a while and let you think about it, but you mustn't get excited."

"Excited!" said Mother Saxon. "I guess I have a right to be excited over all that! But can't you wait till I'm up before you pack?"

"No, we can't! We've got to get out of the house! Is there much you want beside the pictures, and the chests and trunks in the attic? I'll send everybody else out and sit down beside you now with a pencil and write down all you think of, and then you must go to sleep. Those are the doctor's orders."

"There isn't much, dear. Our personal things. The curtains perhaps?"

"Leave the curtains," advised John. "You can get new

ones when you have a new home. It will make the house look more homelike to leave them."

"Why, of course!" said Mother, relaxing with a smile. "It's a little bit like going to live in heaven, isn't it? You won't need the things you leave behind because you'll have better ones."

John Saxon stooped and kissed his mother, with a breath of thanksgiving in his heart that she was not leaving them for heaven yet, and then went back to his list.

In ten minutes he came out and Mary Elizabeth went in, and wafted a big palm leaf fan till the sweet old invalid dropped off to sleep.

John Saxon went through the house picking out the things that had to be kept. He realized that now he had hopes of getting his family into the safety of a cooler world, nothing else seemed to matter. The actual packing was not arduous. John produced two big boxes from the little shanty that was dignified by the name of garage and he and Sam stowed away books and pictures, and the few little precious trifles that are found in every home.

Cousin Richie borrowed John's flivver and went to make arrangements with Eric Tanner, saying as he left that he would arrange to leave the Saxon belongings stored in the attic until fall till they would know where to have them sent. Things were assuming quickly the attitude of departure.

The doctor came and went with a light of satisfaction in his face. He had saved another life, and that was better to him than anything else in the world. He watched his patient carefully without seeming to do so. He stepped in several times during the afternoon, watched her breathing, listened to her heart, touched her pulse lightly, and slipped out again with almost a grin on his rugged face.

The nurse was washing out garments and hanging them to dry in the back yard. The doctor came out to her.

"I believe it's done her good to be told. Her pulse is as strong and steady as I've seen it." There was a ring of triumph in his voice.

"Perhaps!" said the nurse doubtfully.

"Perhaps, nothing of the kind," muttered the doctor. "The sooner she's out of this heat the better."

So the work went steadily, quietly on. In the sick room, Mary Elizabeth, cautiously opening drawers and folding garments, sorting them in neat piles, was selecting the things that would be needed by Mrs. Saxon on the way.

Night came on and found things well on the way to readiness for the journey.

Mary Elizabeth went over to the plane for the night and looked up at the velvet star-studded sky thinking how things had worked out even in the very small details so that there seemed to be nothing to worry about anywhere. She wondered if God would always do that with troublesome details, if she would trust them absolutely to Him?

But out on the highway, Boothby Farwell was speeding along in the blackness of night, turning over in his mind his well laid plans to ship that impertinent kid, Sam Wainwright, home to his mother on the first train, and kidnap Mary Elizabeth! He had hoped to make his destination by that afternoon, but in some unaccountable way he had got off the highway, and had to go miles to get back again. He must stop at the next possible resting place and wait till morning. He was almost out of gas, dog-weary and terribly thirsty. But in the morning he would start early and arrive in time to get the kid off on the night train. Then Mary Elizabeth would find out whether it was worth while to trifle with him or not!

But unfortunately for his plans someone had left a lot of broken glass in the way, and Farwell was not driving carefully through the night. The result was that he was laid up for several hours waiting for his car to be put in running order again, and thus it was the morning of the second day before he reached the village for which he was aiming. Still he felt reasonably sure that his prey would not escape. How could they get by him? This was the only highway, wasn't it?

26

A GREAT deal was accomplished the next morning at the bungalow before the invalid awoke, and during the day Mary Elizabeth and Nurse Noble did their best to keep her quietly interested in getting together such of her own garments as she wanted to take with her. Then when Mary Elizabeth felt she was getting a little weary she would tell her about the sea, and the whispering pines, and gently sing her to sleep.

It was planned that they should leave the next morning as early as possible, and Cousin Richie had spent time on his plane, getting it in perfect order for the start. John Saxon had errands here and there preparatory to leaving. Then toward night Eric Tanner arrived and had to be introduced to the needs of the grove. There really hadn't been any too much time anywhere since the decision had been made to start, and Mary Elizabeth had been busy too, for there were telegrams to send to Father, and Uncle, and the Bateman caretakers, to be sure that there were supplies in the house and a meal ready to serve almost any time.

It was with great eagerness that she got up the next

morning and dressed in her last clean white dress, ready to leave. They didn't even have to wash the breakfast dishes, Mr. Tanner had said, for he would do them. Though they did wash them. Nurse Noble wouldn't hear to anything else.

And indeed there was time enough, for at the last minute a man came to buy John Saxon's old flivver, and Eric Tanner offered to give a little more than the other man, and John Saxon had to do some dickering between them.

Then, just before they were to take Mrs. Saxon out to the plane the doctor discovered that his bottle of rubbing alcohol was empty, having been upset by somebody's carelessness when the cork was out. Also one or two other things needed replacing from the drug store. Sam eagerly offered to go for them on John's old bicycle, the flivver obviously being otherwise occupied at that moment, and so there was a short breathing space in which everybody went around being sure that nobody had left anything.

Sam was glad to have an outlet for his excitement. He bent low over the handle bars of the bicycle and rattled along over the resonant board walk, the little gay scared lizards whisking along before him and darting beneath the boards whenever they got too near. The sun beamed down hotly and the perspiration streamed down Sam's face, but he wore a broad grin of satisfaction, and he could scarcely restrain himself. Sometimes he whistled and sometimes he sang:

*"Everything's all right in my Father's house . . .
There'll be joy, joy, joy all the while!"*

But when he approached the sleepy little hamlet and drew near to the store he sobered down, and put on a grown-up air. He leaned his wheel against the building and sauntered in casually, in the regular boy way. No one would have dreamed he was in a terrible hurry, or that anything exciting was going on that morning.

He handed over the doctor's prescription and the bottles that were to be filled, and sauntered back to the end of the counter examining the dusty articles there on display.

The sound of an automobile horn drew his attention, and a great car flashed up, brilliant with chromium, a car with a familiar look about it. Sam turned and squinted at it carefully. He even came forward a step or two to make sure.

"Good night!" he said softly to himself. "If that poor fish hasn't butted in again!"

He stood there in consternation and watched the man get out of his car and come toward the drug store. Yes, it was Farwell, no mistake about it!

Sam stuffed his hands in his pockets and ducked casually behind the counter out of sight, keeping both eyes and ears open to developments.

"Is there a man named Saxon living around this neighborhood?" asked Farwell in his condescending tone.

"Yep!" snapped the clerk clipping off the string that tied Sam's alcohol bottle. "Lives about five and a half miles west of here, up the first road to the right, turn at the cross roads. You can't miss it!"

"Thanks! That sounds easy! Have you got anything to drink?"

The clerk named the various drinks as he sauntered back to Sam with his bundles.

Farwell gave his order curtly and then said:

"By the way, are there any people visiting these Saxons? A young woman and a red-haired kid?"

The clerk gave a quick startled look at Sam, met a deadly wink that only Sam's eye knew how to give, and sauntered back slowly, answering:

"Couldn't say. There might be and there might not be. You'd havta go and see." Slowly he went at the work of preparing the drink, and looked back where Sam had been standing. But Sam had made good his escape, informally, out of the back door.

"Good night!" thought Sam again. "I can't get out there ahead of him on this bike. I gotta do something! If he gets there before we get started he'll gum the works entirely! *Good night!*"

Sam gave a quick look at the big blue car with its silver trim, took in its direction from the window by the soda counter and ventured forth furtively.

Darting out into the road opposite the car, he stooped down, his bicycle leaning against his back as if he were doing something to its pedals, and reaching out a quick hand back of him he turned a tiny cap on the rear tire of the big blue car. A soft whistling sound ensued. Sam slid a length to the front wheel and did the same thing to that. Then with a furtive glance toward the drug store window, noting that the enemy was still standing with his back to the window, sipping his drink in a leisurely way, Sam slid his wheel around behind the car and doctored the other two tires, in spite of having to struggle with one cap that resisted.

He caught up his own wheel then and whirled out of sight, taking a short cut through the woods, which, though bad for bicycling, would at least hide him from immediate view.

Sometimes he had to jump down and run beside his wheel to make any time at all, until he came into the road again and could take to the rickety board walk. Then he raced along madly. How long would it take for that dumb fish to find a garage and get his tires pumped up again? Could he make it to the house and get the folks to start at once?

The alcohol bottle in its thin paper wrapping bumped around in the wire basket that was fastened to the front of the wheel. He must look out. If he broke that bottle there would be more delay.

The last half mile he was puffing like a porpoise, and he looked like anything but a neat boy prepared to go a journey.

Sam arrived just as they were carrying Mrs. Saxon across from the house on a mattress. John Saxon was carrying the head, Cousin Richie the foot, the nurse and Mary Elizabeth on either side.

Sam held his breath till they had lifted her up and carried her into the plane. Then he slid the old bicycle into its place in the garage and came on the run, just in time to help Mr. Saxon, who was trying to get along by himself to save trouble.

As he upheld Father Saxon he cast a furtive glance down the road looking for a flashy blue car with silver edges, but all was quiet and empty on the highroad so far.

"Is there anything else in the house to go?" he asked Cousin Richie when he had seated his passenger comfortably. "There's some poor fish down at the village on his way to find Mary Beth and I happen ta know she don't want him. Can't ya get started before he gets here?"

Cousin Richie cast a speculative eye at Sam, a keen glance at Mary Elizabeth, who was smiling down and giving some direction to John Saxon, and then said:

"Sure thing, son. Run after John and help him bring the rest of the things. There aren't many, and I'll get the engine ready."

Sam scuttled off, his eye down the road again.

Three minutes more and they were back with the last load, and nobody in sight yet. John Saxon was lingering to say a few last words to Eric Tanner. Would he never be done?

At last they were off. Sam felt the smooth vibration of the engine, the slow movement that seemed to be scarcely motion at all, for the ride was to be a quiet one not to excite the invalid. And now at last they were rising, a little, and a little, and now the ground was really quite far below them. Sam drew a deep breath.

Then, looking down the road from the height that gave him a better view he saw a great blue car flash into view, its shining trim casting sharp brightness in the sun. Sam looked down and grinned.

He cast one more look at the ground, measured the possibilities of turning around and going back again for callers and decided they were nil, then he slid over to Mary Elizabeth's side pointing down.

"There goes that poor fish of a Farwell, coming to call. Do you wantta go back and entertain him?" he said into her ear.

Mary Elizabeth gave a quick glance back and saw the bright car slowing down before the bungalow, saw Eric Tanner coming out to meet it, and a look of amazement grew upon her face. It couldn't be that Boothby had found out where she was and had dared to follow so far! It must be another car, like his, of course.

"What makes you think that is Mr. Farwell, Sam?" she asked.

"Because I saw him down at the village when I went after the alcohol. He was getting a drink, and asking the way out here! He wanted to know if the Saxons had company, a girl and a red-haired boy!"

Sam's face and voice expressed the scorn and disgust he did not put into words.

"But I don't understand," said Mary Elizabeth, "Why didn't he get here before you did? It's a long way into the village and you had only a bicycle?"

"Sure, I fixed him so he couldn't. I let the air out of his tires!"

"Sam! You didn't! Not *really?*"

"Sure I did! I wasn't going to have that poor dumb fish coming here gumming things all up just as we were getting off."

Suddenly Mary Elizabeth put her head down and laughed and laughed. Then she said:

"Sam, there are a great many things I have to thank you for, and this is not the least of them. Oh, Sam, Sam, for a person who knows as much about the Bible as you do, you certainly are the limit!"

Then Mary Elizabeth's eyes turned away and rested with great tenderness on John Saxon who was bending over his mother, smiling and holding her hand, helping her through the first startling idea of riding in the air.

The great bird lifted and soared aloft, smoothly, evenly, and suddenly the young man who had come out seeking a wild free thing, to bind and bend it to his will, found that his bird had flown away, and wildly he lifted a futile shout, and raised his hand in a gesture of command. Then he ran with all his might forward toward where the plane had been, dashing into the deep untrodden sand without looking where he stepped, and wallowed along screaming and shaking his fist up toward the vanishing plane. Suddenly his head and shoulders were going faster than his feet could get there, and the inevitable happened. Boothby Farwell went down ignominiously in the sand and literally bit the dust, sand in his eyes and sand in his ears and sand in his mouth, a sorry figure, stunned, and blinded, and so angry he was stupefied for the instant.

And the girl he was chasing did not even see him. She had eyes for only one man and he was up in the air with her.

Only Sam saw the downfall of his enemy and stood grinning with all his might and finally laughing aloud in a great boy roar, but the engine drowned the sound and nobody was the wiser.

27

THE great plane came to earth on the smooth, broad beach almost exactly in front of the Wainwright summer estate, taxi-ing over the hard, white sand as lightly as over a marble floor, and the invalid who had been greatly intrigued and unexpectedly invigorated by her flight, scarcely knew she had lit upon earth yet.

Almost at once, there appeared around the plane Mary Elizabeth's father, Sam's father, Frank Bateman wheeling an invalid chair-cot, and Susan Bateman, her hands wrapped in a neat white apron, standing respectfully in the background. It had the air of an occasion, almost of a celebration, and Mary Elizabeth's eyes shone with satisfaction as she looked upon the group. Not one of them was missing! Dad had been equal to the occasion as she knew he would be, as he always had been since she could remember, and Uncle Robert Wainwright was right behind him. They were great brothers, those two, of the House of Wainwright, and Mary Elizabeth was proud of them.

Then her glance went to John Saxon, who had suddenly straightened up from assuring his mother they had landed, and was taking in the situation. John Saxon's face was tense with a dawning comprehension of what all this might mean, suffused suddenly with a deep embarrassment, and then a quick misty realization of the kindness that had prompted it all.

Oh, he had met them both, those Brothers Wainwright, at the wedding; big, successful, kindly, blustering, but polished men of the world. Under the guise of a best man he had shaken their hands and let their hearty greetings at introduction roll off from his consciousness as something that didn't mean a thing to him personally, being only a part of the wedding ceremonies.

But now, suddenly brought face to face with them in a personal way, with the weight of a great debt of gratitude to them hung about his neck John Saxon was overwhelmed.

Mary Elizabeth saw and understood. It was like Mary Elizabeth to understand, even if he hadn't been John Saxon, and dearly beloved. Mary Elizabeth had an understanding mind. And quickly she moved over to stand beside John Saxon, and share the meeting, share the experience of whatever her man was passing through, and take the sting with him, protect his pride with her own hands and her own smiles, so that its gay plumage should not be permanently damaged.

"It's Dad and Uncle Bob!" she exclaimed, sliding her hand into John Saxon's! "Oh, aren't they the old darlings, John! They would leave their business and rush down to have fun with us when we arrive! They're just like kids! They couldn't wait to see you, and to help all they could!"

Somehow her words, and her shining eyes that she lifted to John Saxon's face, took the sting from the mortification, and suddenly put John Saxon and his honored father on a level with the whole Wainwright tribe. It made him forget that he was poor and struggling, and utterly presuming to dare to have aspired to the hand of Mary Elizabeth Wainwright, heir to millions, and choice of the whole universe of women.

Suddenly his hand folded the hand of Mary Elizabeth close in his own, and looking down into her shining happy eyes he felt for the first time utterly that he and she were one, and that it didn't matter if those two relatives out there on the sand had been a whole battalion of royal soldiers come out to battle with him for a princess, she would never leave him, nor would he have to let her go, for they belonged together, now and through eternity.

It was Sam who alighted first and did the honors of the ship as if he had been commander.

"Well, here we all are!" he announced importantly. "Howareya, Dad? Hello, Uncle Sam! All ready for us, aren't ya? Well, we're all okay!"

His father enveloped him quickly with a strong possessive arm and said with a relieved voice:

"Sure! I knew you would be! Great son you are, Kid! I'm proud of you. How's the invalid?"

"Oh, she's fine. The doctor says it did her good! She's a good sport, she is!" swaggered Sam as if she were a protégée of his.

Then all was quiet orderliness. Mary Elizabeth's father came forward and grasped John Saxon's hand as he alighted from the ship.

"Glad to see you! So good you could bring your mother right here. Nothing like sea air. Now, here's the outfit. Think this will be comfortable for her? Get her right up to the house in a jiffy and into her bed. How do you want this wheel-chair arrangement set? Head this way? Frank can wheel it and we'll steady it, or we could carry it if necessary. This the doctor? Glad to meet you,

Doctor. Great work you've been doing, I hear. Now, we're here to serve, just tell us how to move to cause the least excitement. And we've brought a wheeled chair for Mr. Saxon—"

Quiet, pleasant, business-like voices, steady, composed air as if they were all one family bent on doing the very best for the invalids. He was perfect, thought his daughter, listening with overflowing heart of joy. Dear Dad!

With the least noise and fuss possible the little procession formed, bearing the invalid gently, steadily up the beach, into the great grilled gateway, under the whispering pines, and into the hospitable old-fashioned mansion.

"I'm Mary Elizabeth's father," said Samuel Wainwright to the invalid just before they started, "and we're very glad to welcome you. Now we aren't going to bother you with any more introductions to-day till you're rested from your journey!"

Mother Saxon lifted her sweet eyes and smiled, and the brothers dropped behind to escort Father Saxon in his wheeled chair as if he were a king among his subjects.

So they came down from the sky, and went up from the sea, and the old Wainwright summer home came to life after many years of quietness.

Before she could possibly realize what was happening Mother Saxon was tenderly lifted and laid in the softest bed on which she had ever been and was swallowing a glass of orange juice in a fragrant darkened room, with flowers dimly lifting fairy faces in quiet corners. There was the dull gleam of old mahogany, the smooth feel of linen sheets and pillow cases, the soft murmur of whispering pines above, the deep undertone of the ocean not far away, all mingling softly into a delicious sleepy atmosphere, with the memory of Mary Elizabeth's soft lips, brushing her forehead, and her boy John's tender pat on her hand. Could mortal happy woman keep awake under those circumstances?

The doctor tiptoed in, touched her wrist, her brow, winked in satisfaction at the nurse, and nodded his approval, tiptoed out again and she never knew it.

Out around the side of the house Mother Saxon's old lover sat in a deep comfortable chair with his hurt foot on a cushion and enjoyed a real old-time talk with men of his own age and education, discovering mutual friends, similar experiences, and links of their younger days that made them friends at once. Till Mary Elizabeth and his son John suddenly descended upon him and swept him off to the little room adjoining the invalid's room, and made him take a nap.

Cousin Richie had taken the doctor up the beach fifty miles or so in his plane to visit a convalescent patient about whom he was a bit anxious, Mary Elizabeth and John Saxon had gone off down the beach hand in hand, and it was then that young Sam had his innings, sitting on the side steps with his father and his Uncle Sam who were lying back in two big old beach chairs listening to him proudly.

By the time the rest came back there was not an incident of the trip down and back that had not been recounted, and the two old men had laughed till they wept over the story of the deflated tires and Boothby Farwell wallowing in the sand, shaking his fist at the departing plane.

"Well, Samuel," said Robert Wainwright at last, wiping the tears from his pleased old face. "All I've got to say is, that girl of yours is smart as they make 'em. She knows her onions! And she certainly has picked a rare one! I like that John Saxon! Even if my Jeff hadn't picked him first as the best man he knew, I'd still have liked him!"

"Yes," said Mary Elizabeth's father with a faraway look in his eyes, "I consider that I've had a very narrow escape, to say nothing of Mary Elizabeth! Of course, we may be a little previous. They haven't said anything about it, but it sorta looks that way," and he nodded down toward the beach where a man and a maid could be seen walking very slowly along the bright sand.

"It certainly does!" agreed the uncle, "no mistake about that. Haven't I just been through one wedding? Can't I tell the look in the eye of a young lover? You certainly had a narrow escape if you ever considered that young ape of a Farwell in the light of a son-in-law."

"Well, I didn't know what to think, one time there. I didn't know but I was going to have to take Mary Elizabeth around the world again, or up to the moon or something. I guess I've got young Sam to thank for showing him up several times! Good work, Kid! Good work! I shan't forget it! Mary Elizabeth was telling me something about some empty bottles in a case of liquor. Sam ever tell you that tale, and the mystery of how they got empty? Get him to tell you that, Bob. It's a good one!"

And then they were off again listening to young Sam and laughing.

The days went by and the invalid improved in leaps and bounds. Dr. MacKelvie lingered a few days to be sure that all was well and then hurried away to his neglected vacation and patients, returning occasionally when Cousin Richie brought him down for a day or two to watch Mother Saxon.

The summer was slipping away fast now, and the invalid was able to walk on the piazza a few steps every day leaning on the arm of her strong son. Sometimes Mary Elizabeth walked on her other side encouraging her.

There came a day when John Saxon felt he might be spared to run up to New York for another interview with the great man who was to be his instructor during the winter.

While he was gone Mary Elizabeth and Sam took the honors of looking after the invalid upon themselves. Of course the nurse was there yet, but Mary Elizabeth knew that Mrs. Saxon felt a little formal with her in spite of the long weeks of her ministrations. So when the invalid was taken out on the piazza, either to walk or just to sit and enjoy the air and listen to the beating of the waves, or to watch a white sail flit, it was Mary Elizabeth who came out and occupied a chair near by with a nice book, often reading aloud to her; and it was Sam with his knife and a stick who sat on the top step not far away, whittling, sometimes softly whistling, ready to run for a glass of milk or orange juice, or a cup of broth or the medicine.

Sam was very happy in these days. It seemed to him that this last few weeks had been a special dispensation of Providence to show him exactly what like Heaven was going to be like some day.

He had been almost entirely free from being told what to do, or what not to do. In fact he didn't seem to want to do anything except what the people around him most desired. He had had long hours of close companionship with his beloved hero-doctor, walking on the beach, fishing, crabbing, swimming, and often getting a Bible lesson when he least expected it.

Mary Elizabeth, too, had often been with them, and that made it all the better. Sam believed that there were no two better in all the world than Mary Elizabeth and John Saxon. And he often marveled that they were willing to have him around when they were together. He had noticed that the way of the world with a man and a maid was that they had no time for small boys. So he adored them all the more, and was most humble and grateful, and as unobtrusive as possible.

In some of the long walks with John Saxon he had learned of a boys' school not far from home, where there were Christian teachers, and where many of the boys were Christians also. Listening to his friend's stories of the head master of that school Sam had acquired a deep desire to attend it.

He broached the matter to his father one weekend when he came down to the shore to see if his son were in the way and ought to be removed. His father had been interested, had read the catalogues carefully which Sam diligently acquired, and had written to the head master, finally giving his consent that Sam should go. Sam felt that a new world was opening before him. Of course there might be trouble when his mother arrived on the scene. This calamity was due to happen almost any day now, Sam realized, for it was getting toward the time for migrations back to the city, but his father had given him his word of honor that he would tell his mother that he felt it was time that Sam had a change of environment and that his father should choose the next school, because Sam was growing up. Jeff had written also his hearty approval of the plan, added his own knowledge of the head master to the argument, and promised to speak to his mother. There was due to be a battle, of course, but Sam had reasonable hopes of coming out victorious, and so he was very happy.

Mary Elizabeth had a quiet starry look in her eyes as she went about humming snatches of little tunes. Sam was sure she was happy.

One day her father talking to her over the telephone,

happened to mention a matter which the summer had entirely erased from his memory until then.

"Say, Mary Elizabeth, do you know, I promised Jeff that I would get you to run out sometime this summer and see if Camilla's mother is getting on all right, and it entirely slipped my mind. It won't be long now before Camilla and Jeff will be coming back from their trip, and I'd hate to say I hadn't even told you. I had it in mind that you might ask her and her companion down for a week-end sometime this summer but I guess that's out of the question now, isn't it, while the folks are there? Might be too many for the invalid. But can't you get away to run up to the city for a day and go out and call there?"

"Why, of course," promised Mary Elizabeth. "I've meant to do that all summer only there didn't seem to be any time. But I'm coming up to the city to-morrow, Dad, and I'll make it a point to call. I've got to get another nurse. The one we've had all along thinks she's got to get back to New York to look after her affairs, so I said I'd try and get another. Sam's driving up with me, wants to see his father about his new school, and why can't you come on back with us for over Sunday?"

"Well, perhaps," said her father. "I'm glad you can see Jeff's mother-in-law, that's weighed on my mind."

So Mary Elizabeth called on Camilla's mother. To her delight she discovered that the companion who was staying with her during Camilla's absence was a trained nurse, and before the call was concluded Mary Elizabeth arranged that the two should come down to the shore for the next week, Nurse York taking the place that Nurse Noble would leave vacant in a few days. It seemed an altogether happy arrangement. And so it proved to be.

John Saxon's mother was delighted to have the

mother of her son's dearest friend to visit with, and the two dear elderly ladies spent pleasant hours on the piazza together, drinking in health, and conversing like two girls of their life's experiences.

John Saxon came back from New York with a new light of hope in his eyes. He had not only made satisfactory arrangements about his winter's work with the great specialist, but he had spent an evening with Dr. MacKelvie in his city office, and had been offered an out and out partnership with that great man!

It would mean of course that his future was practically secured. A professional connection with Dr. MacKelvie was beyond compare. There was none better in the land.

"I'm getting old. I need help," said the doctor. "My son who had a bent toward medicine is dead. I've never seen a man before that I cared to work with till I knew you. Will you come and join forces?" He had sat back in his chair and studied the face of the younger man with a kind of wistful yearning.

"But I'm not through my studies yet," said John when he had recovered from his astonishment enough to speak. "I won't be worth anything to you for some time."

"That's all right," said the doctor wearily. "I want you to finish your course. But I believe you told me you were planning to work part time? Well, why not work for me in what leisure you have, and gradually work into things? No, this isn't a philanthropic proposition at all,—" he waved his hand impatiently as he saw that John was going to offer objections,—"I *want* you! I *need* you! There'll be times when I can leave matters with you that I wouldn't trust with an ordinary assistant. See? Because I know you as a man, and I know you've got something that will be dead sure to lean on. I need to lean on you sometimes when I'm hard pressed. Do you think you can stand it to hitch up for a time to an old crotchety man who is getting near the end of his career? I'll see that you don't lose anything by it."

The whole thing seemed too spectacular to be true, and on the way back to the shore John Saxon began strongly to suspect that Mary Elizabeth was somehow at the bottom of such a wonderful proposition. But when he told her about it he saw by her quick surprise and delight that it was as much a surprise to her as to him.

"It means," said John Saxon with a wonderful light in his face, "that now I can go to your father and put myself on something like a working basis with him. It's time he understood how things are between you and me, Mary Elizabeth."

"Yes?" said Mary Elizabeth, lifting her sparkling face with a twinkle in her eyes. "But you know, I sort of think he knows already."

"You haven't been telling him, Mary Elizabeth?" said John Saxon suddenly appalled. "You know I asked you not to till I could have some definite financial future in view."

"Oh, no!" grinned Mary Elizabeth. "I didn't need to tell him. My father has average intelligence. He doesn't need to be told what I like and what I don't like."

Mary Elizabeth's father came down to the shore that night for the week-end, just to look his family over and see how things were getting on. After dinner while it was yet sunset, and the waves were tossing rubies and diamonds and sapphires and amethysts and topazes and pearls about on their crest, John Saxon and Mary Elizabeth's father took a walk out along the many-colored sands together, while the younger man told of his love for Mary Elizabeth.

"Good news, Son!" said the old man in a hearty voice. "You couldn't tell me anything that I'd like better! I never saw a man before that I was willing to have marry Mary Elizabeth, and there's been a-plenty of 'em, I'm telling you! But I feel that you'll be a real son and I can welcome you heartily into the family. I'm going to feel comfortable about Mary Elizabeth with you for a husband. You see I was beginning to be afraid I'd been mistaken about you two after all, and maybe the way would still be open for that nincompoop Farwell yet. You never can tell what a woman will do you know, and that Farwell has ways past finding out. I didn't know but I might have to go out and shoot him or something to get rid of him, and I couldn't die happy leaving my girl open to such as he."

"I wanted to tell you at once, sir," said John eagerly, "but you see I hadn't so much as a shadow of prospect for the future until to-day."

"Stuff and nonsense!" said the father with happy eyes. "As if it wasn't prospect enough just for you and Mary Elizabeth to be together. My girl will have enough for both of you, and you're not to worry about prospects and money, do you understand, young man? You've got something worth far more than money. If we'd wanted more money that cur Farwell has gobs of it. But we didn't, Mary Beth and I, we wanted a real man, and I'm satisfied we've found him. You have my best wishes."

Wainwright put out a strong hand in a hearty grasp, and John Saxon had a sudden rush of warm liking for his girl's father come into his heart.

"There's another thing, too, John," said the older man, "better get married right away. You'll need your wife this winter in New York, and Mary Elizabeth needs you. It isn't as if you didn't know your own minds, and I don't see hanging around and being lonesome when a question like that is really settled."

John Saxon gave his future father-in-law a quick searching look, and then in a wistful voice:

"I wish that were possible, Mr. Wainwright, but I won't begin to have an adequate income for a little while yet, you know. I can give Dr. MacKelvie part time, and can't in honesty accept much for that. Of course, if I were to give up the idea of taking that special work with the other doctor—. But I should lose out in the end, for that special work is going to make me worth more money in the end."

"I understand all that of course," said the old man with a gesture as if he would brush the idea of such folly from the scene. "You must have all the advantages that are to be had. And as for income, that's all poppycock! There's no question of whose income it is between a husband and wife if they're both the right kind. Of course if you were some other style of man I might take your point of view, too,—a man who was out to get his hands on his wife's fortune,—but you're not. And Mary Elizabeth needs your care. I'm an old man. I can't look after her right. And besides, I may not last long. I wish you'd get married soon! I really do. It will be better for you both."

John Saxon's voice was husky with feeling.

"I certainly appreciate your confidence, sir," he said. "I'll never forget what you've said. But you don't realize, perhaps— You see, I couldn't possibly keep your daughter in the way she should be kept, not yet. I hope it won't be long before I can,—but—"

"Nonsense," said the old man testily. "Put your pride in your pocket and forget that idea. Mary Elizabeth has knocked around a lot and she would rather knock around with you than waste away in a mansion waiting for you. She's not so hard to please! And anyhow you wouldn't starve, I'd see to that. Oh, I know, your precious pride! But look here now, be reasonable! I want a chance to watch you two be happy a little while before I die, and if I get more pleasure out of using some of my money that way instead of hoarding it up for you to inherit when I'm gone, haven't I a right? Now, listen to me. I've got an apartment in New York, looking out on Gramercy Park. I've owned it for years, and the family used to live in it winters the years we summered down here, when Mary Elizabeth's mother was living. It's old-fashioned, and the neighborhood is not stylish any more, but I like to keep it because of old times. It's big and roomy and comfortable. There'd be plenty of room for your father and mother to be with you winters, at least till they want to go back to Florida, though privately I don't believe they should. I think they need to be with you and be looked after, especially not till your mother is thoroughly strong again. I know Mary Elizabeth thinks so too for she told me so. And there'll be room for me to drop in over night whenever I have business in New York, so I can keep in touch with you all now and then. Come, will you be reasonable and think it over? Here comes Mary Elizabeth now. Here, Mary Beth, come take your future husband and talk turkey to him. I've been offering him the New York apartment for you all to live in this winter. It's all repaired and done over, and if you want any more changes it's all right with me. Now you two run along down the beach and have it out. I'm going back to talk with Mr. and Mrs. Saxon a while. It's getting chilly out here for my rheumatic shoulders."

Mary Elizabeth came running up catching John's hand, the last glow of the sunset in her face, and together they walked slowly into the dying glow of the evening.

And so it came about quite quietly, that there was a

wedding in the old house at last, although there were almost no preparations.

Mary Elizabeth hunted out her mother's fine old wedding veil from a carved chest where it had lain wrapped in satin paper, for many years. And there was a sweet little white dress, very simple and plain and lovely, among her Parisian clothes, a dress which she had been keeping for some special time. There wasn't a thing that Mary Elizabeth needed to buy but a clean pair of white slippers, and those she could telephone for, and they would arrive the next day. In fact a half hour's telephoning completed all Mary Elizabeth's arrangements.

She called up her uncles and she called up her aunts, and a few favorite cousins, and invited them to come down for a house party. She called up Cousin Richie and asked him to meet Jeffrey and Camilla when their boat docked at New York, and fly them down also. He was to tell them that it was a celebration of their home coming and they *must* come! Then she called up the doctor, and the family caterer, giving a brief simple order, and Mary Elizabeth was ready. She didn't bother with any of the long lines of social acquaintances and friends. This was a family affair.

John Saxon's problems were not so easily solved. He had to get a suitable ring wherewith to wed a Wainwright, and he couldn't begin to afford the right kind.

He stayed awake half the night and came down to breakfast all perplexed, announcing that he must go up to town right away.

However, his mother called him to a conference and placed in his hand a little velvet box that he had often seen as a child, but had forgotten long ago.

"These were your Grandmother's, John. I was wondering if you wouldn't like to use them—at least for a little while till you could afford to get something more modern? They are tiny, but Mary Elizabeth has a very small hand. I think she could wear them. Do you think she would like them?"

John Saxon took the worn little velvet box reverently and pressed the tiny pearl button that sprang the lid open, and there were the dear old rings, the wonder of his childhood, in a setting of so long ago that it was almost modern. A plain gold band, and another with a great ruby like a drop of blood, and a pearl of rare luster.

"Oh, Mother!" breathed the son. "But they belonged to your mother! I couldn't let you give them up!"

"It's what I've been keeping them for, Son," said the mother with a pleased light in her eyes. "But you're not to make Mary Elizabeth wear them unless she really likes them."

"Mary Elizabeth will like them, I'm sure!" said John Saxon, stooping to place a reverent kiss on his mother's forehead. "Dear Mother!"

Mary Elizabeth did. They called her and she did. She said she would wear them always. She didn't want them changed for diamonds, ever! She loved them as they were, and when they went up to town John would put her name and his under the quaint old inscription that was still clearly to be read in the ring, announcing the former wearer and its giver.

Then John Saxon had only to telephone to a florist's shop in the city and get a bouquet.

It was Mary Elizabeth's father who supplied the minister. Mary Elizabeth was just back from a drive with John to get the license when he telephoned. She hadn't so much as remembered that a minister would be needed. She gave a little gasp when her father asked her who was going to perform the ceremony. The summer guests who might have a minister among them, had mostly gone back to the city now. Mary Elizabeth didn't number many ministers among her friends, and John Saxon had gone up the beach with Sam so she couldn't ask him what to do.

Mary Elizabeth hesitated so long that her father grew impatient. He waited another second or two and then said:

"Well, if you haven't anybody in mind, how would you like me to bring somebody down?"

"Who is he?" asked the bride-to-be in a perplexed tone.

"He's the young man who married your mother and me, only of course he isn't a *young* man any more. But he was young then and your mother and I thought there wasn't any minister like him, I remember. I just happened to run across him in the city to-day and it occurred to me you might like the idea. I could bring him down and park him at the hotel until the time for the ceremony so there wouldn't be any wondering about him, and then send the chauffeur after him when we're ready."

"Oh, Dad, that would be great!" said Mary Elizabeth delightedly. "I simply hadn't thought about a minister, and there isn't anybody I can think of I'd like. It would be lovely to have the same one you and Mother had!"

"All right!" said the father, "then I'll bring him down. I suppose there's still some place open where we can park him? Some hotel or boarding house open, either there or up the beach a way?"

"Oh, yes," said Mary Elizabeth. "I'll see to that. I'll send Sam up to engage a room somewhere as soon as he comes back. You'll be down early, won't you Dad?"

"Sure thing!" said the father happily. "I might come the night before. All right! Then that's settled."

The servants from the city house were to come down for the house party, but Susan Bateman had everything in such apple-pie order that they found little left to do until the guests arrived, so they made a regular holiday out of it.

Mary Elizabeth and John Saxon wandered off down the beach in the moonlight with no cares at all the night before the wedding.

Mary Elizabeth wore a simple little blue organdy the day of the house party. Of course it happened to be made in Paris and had very lovely lines, but for all that it had a simplicity about it that fitted seashore life, and its color matched her eyes. John Saxon told her so a dozen times an hour.

The guests came fairly early for they wanted to be on hand when Jeffrey and Camilla arrived. They thought it was merely a surprise party for them.

Uncle Warren Wainwright was there with Aunt Fannie, sleek and placid and beaming on everybody, enjoying the view and the pines and reminiscing delightfully about the house and grounds.

Father Wainwright came the night before as he had threatened, having parked his minister safely a mile up the shore, and went about doing the honors, introducing the elder Saxons delightedly as if they belonged to royalty, as in reality they did.

Sam's father and mother arrived a little late as usual, that is later than the rest, and it was plain to be seen that it hadn't been Uncle Robert who had been the cause of the delay.

"I really hadn't a rag left fit to wear," Aunt Clarice declared in apology, glancing down at the elaborate flowered chiffon she had finally elected to wear. "You know I'm only just back from the mountains, and everything is simply unspeakable after the entire summer away from home."

"Oh, but it's a very lovely dress," said Mary Elizabeth

cannily, pouring a few drops of her own sweet personality on the aunt who most frequently troubled the family waters.

"Well, it had to do," sighed the poor woman, dismissing the subject and lifting her lorgnette for a glimpse around at the place.

"Why dear me! The old house really looks quite livable again, doesn't it? I suppose you had to do a lot of replacing and repairing, and it was hardly worth it, was it? So utterly out of date, but it's nice to see it again, a quaint old setting of an age that is gone!" and Aunt Clarice heaved a sentimental sigh.

"And where is my infant son?" she next demanded, bringing down her lorgnette from a survey of fluted columns and giving a quick alert look about for Sam.

Now although Sam was fond of his mother, he had rather dreaded her coming, for she was apt to belittle him, and it embarrassed him exceedingly to be called her infant son, but he had prepared for the meeting by an elaborate toilet, the like of which he had not attempted since he last saw her, which explained the present immaculateness of his garments. They had lain in a bureau drawer all summer.

He came forward now dutifully with a gravity and grace that was astonishing considering his years, and gave his mother the kiss she expected. It quite took her off her balance, it was so unusual. Heretofore he had always had to be admonished about it before he reluctantly welcomed her.

She stood back and surveyed him through her lorgnette, as she had the fluted columns. Sam bore it very well. He had scrubbed unmercifully behind his ears, he had polished his shoes, cleaned his fingernails to a nicety, and put on a necktie he hated but knew she liked. What more could he do? Besides, he was going to a real school now and one had to concede something.

"Why Sam!" she exclaimed in pleased surprise, "you're quite grown up, aren't you? You did that very well. Betty dear, I believe you must have been good for him in spite of everything, though I do think you went a little beyond the limit when you took him up in an airplane."

"Oh, I didn't take him, he took me," laughed Mary Elizabeth.

"And what's this ridiculous idea I hear of, that you've been putting notions in his head about a new school?" said Aunt Clarice putting aside the matter of the airplane for a future time when she could hope to do justice to it. "I really can't think of countenancing his going away from home again when he's been away all summer—"

But just then to the distraction of everybody the buzz of an airplane was heard, and all heads were turned to the heavens. Presently Cousin Richie's big plane came sailing down neatly on the beach and taxied right up to the big iron gateway.

Aunt Clarice watched the performance with a shudder, and several gasps.

"I don't see how he dares!" she said in a terrified voice. "And to think he presumed to take my angel child and his bride up into the sky! I think it was criminal!"

But nobody heard her. They were all rushing down to greet Jeff and Camilla and Cousin Richie. All but John Saxon's mother who lay in her invalid chair, relaxed and happy, and amused at it all. For did she not know a secret that none of the other guests knew?

The dining room was ready in festive array with flowers that had been ordered from the city, a long family table, made up of several sections, a reminder of other days. There was no hint of the big bridal cake that had been hidden away. Not even Mary Elizabeth knew about it. For Mr. Wainwright had given the family servants carte blanche to order what was needed and nothing had been forgotten. But in it all there was nothing to suggest to a casual guest passing through that it was to be a wedding luncheon, and not just a plain house party. It was all quite simple and informal, and the various guests looked about upon each other smiling and relaxed, and thinking how nice it was for them all to be together once more like a big family.

They settled down to talk like a bunch of magpies, and Sam stood about grinning to himself at what was to come. It was going to be swell. Nothing to interfere with the fun, everybody here, nobody missing, no frumpy old cousins that were not wanted, just the ones who belonged. He smoothed a wrinkle out of his white linen coat, adjusted the unaccustomed, throttling tie, and smiled to himself. There were few duties ahead now, and those nice ones. Sam did a great deal of grinning to himself that morning, and in between he ran little pleasant errands, brought Mrs. Saxon's shawl, brought her a better footstool, adjusted the pillows for her, got Mr. Saxon's cane, hovered in the wake of his idol John Saxon, and admired his returned brother and the new unknown sister-in-law from afar.

No one saw the Wainwright car drive in from the back gate and the elderly stranger in a frock coat who got out and followed Sam up the back stairs to a room appointed for his use. No one even noticed that Mary Elizabeth had disappeared for a few minutes. It was getting near to lunch time and they were growing hungry. She had likely gone to give orders to the servants.

When Sam and Miss York helped Mrs. Saxon into the living room they merely thought she was chilly out on the piazza, and several of the guests drifted inside also. Then Sam appeared at the door and called the rest, supposedly to lunch.

"Will you all come in now?" he said pleasantly in quite a grown-up tone, and they responded to the call eagerly.

But inside they stood about uncertainly in the big living room, thinking how lovely it all looked with the airy muslin curtains blowing in the fresh sea breeze, and gorgeous fall roses in great bowls and vases everywhere, wondering why Mary Elizabeth didn't give the signal to come to the dining room.

They could see the long table through the archway now, and it looked so festive and inviting.

Then suddenly Mary Elizabeth appeared at the top of the stairs, with her father just behind her. She had changed her dress! She was wearing white! How strange! She must have soiled that pretty blue one! What a pity, it was so becoming! And what was that she was wearing over her hair? A veil? They gasped softly in amazement, those who stood in the hallway and saw her.

At that instant soft strains from the piano began to sound. They turned about and saw Camilla sitting at the old grand piano playing. Just soft chords, at first, blending in delightful harmony.

Then at the far end of the room, the place that strangely had no chairs in it, Jeff and John Saxon appeared, and a stranger with them, an elderly man! A stranger! In a frock coat! The family stiffened, and prepared to resent the stranger.

Then the music widened and grew stately and became unmistakably the wedding march!

Why, what was this? A wedding? Why, where was Mary Elizabeth, and had that really been a veil over her head?

But Mary Elizabeth was walking into their midst now, on her father's arm, smiling with happy eyes, looking toward John Saxon, and stepping to the well-known measures of the wedding march. That rare old lace that draped her head and flowed down over her lovely new white frock must be her mother's wedding veil. Aunt Clarice was studying it through her lorgnette as it passed her, and recognizing it as if she had memorized every flower on it long years ago.

A low, soft exclamation in chorus broke from all their throats and then they looked up to differentiate the group at the lower end of the room and single out the bridegroom.

John Saxon! Jeffrey Wainwright's best man!

And Mrs. Saxon was sitting in a deep comfortable chair just at the side where she could watch the faces of the two beloved children! She had come north to John's wedding even as she had dreamed! Ah! Was this what had been going on all this quiet summer? And Mary Elizabeth had done this, put this over on them!

"When she might have had that lovely rich Boothby Farwell," sighed Aunt Clarice into a costly handkerchief.

Then the quiet voice of the elderly stranger broke the silence of wonder:

"Dearly beloved, we are met together to join this man and this woman in the bonds of holy Matrimony—"

Sam standing in the doorway his hands gripped together behind his white linen back held his breath listening to every word, storing it away for the time when some great experience should perhaps come into his life, getting a sudden vision of what it might mean to join two souls in such a bond, remembering how John Saxon had taught him that marriage was meant to be a picture of Christ's relation to His true church. Sam's eyes grew misty with tenderness, big and faraway and serious, and his expression startled his mother as she suddenly turned and saw him standing there! Sam was growing up! She must get at him and teach him how to behave in society, she thought with a fleeting sense of her social duties, and then she turned back to take in the lovely scene again, to watch Camilla, playing so exquisitely! That was a revelation, too. She never knew that her new daughter-in-law was a musician. Perhaps she wasn't going to be so bad after all. And Camilla's mother over there in the corner really looked very smart in that lovely gray chiffon. She must ask her how she managed to keep so slim at her age.

Then it was over with a tender prayer. John Saxon had kissed his bride, and Mary Elizabeth was kissing her father, and everybody was stirring happily and milling around, trying to say how surprised they were, and rushing to congratulate the bride and groom.

There was so much gay laughter and talk going on that nobody heard the big showy car drive around the house and stop before the door. That is, nobody but Sam.

Sam caught a glimpse of the enemy approaching up the steps and grinned to himself.

"Good night!" he murmured under his breath. "Just too late, as usual! But let him come! He can't do any damage now."

And Boothby Farwell, frowning at the sight of the family gathering, walked into the hall without ceremony, and was in the midst of the living room staring grimly about him before he realized what was going on.

It was Mary Elizabeth who saved the situation.

"Why, Mr. Farwell!" she called cheerfully, "you've arrived just in time to congratulate me! How nice! Come over and meet my husband!"

Boothby Farwell with a baleful glare at the bridegroom, walked over and did the proper thing, but severely, disapprovingly, and then with an offended glance about him he turned and stalked out of the room.

Only Sam bothered to watch him as he strode down the steps, sprang into his car, and drove furiously away. Sam had to slip out on the porch after that, behind one of the fluted columns, and whistle. Then he heaved a sigh of utter satisfaction and whistled again. All was as it should be to his way of thinking, for the maid of honor had become the bride of John Saxon! What more was there to be desired?

About the Author

Grace Livingston Hill is well known as one of the most prolific writers of romantic fiction. Her personal life was fraught with joys and sorrows not unlike those experienced by many of her fictional heroines.

Born in Wellsville, New York, Grace nearly died during the first hours of life. But her loving parents and friends turned to God in prayer. She survived miraculously, thus her thankful father named her Grace.

Grace was always close to her father, a Presbyterian minister, and her mother, a published writer. It was from them that she learned the art of storytelling. When Grace was twelve, a close aunt surprised her with a hardbound, illustrated copy of one of Grace's stories. This was the beginning of Grace's journey into being a published author.

In 1892 Grace married Fred Hill, a young minister, and they soon had two lovely young daughters. Then came 1901, a difficult year for Grace—the year when, within months of each other, both her father and husband died. Suddenly Grace had to find a new place to live (her home was owned by the church where her husband had been pastor). It was a struggle for Grace to raise her young daughters alone, but through everything she kept writing. In 1902 she produced *The Angel of His Presence, The Story of a Whim,* and *An Unwilling Guest.* In 1903 her two books *According to the Pattern* and *Because of Stephen* were published.

It wasn't long before Grace was a well-known author, but she wanted to go beyond just entertaining her readers. She soon included the message of God's salvation through Jesus Christ in each of her books. For Grace, the most important thing she did was not write books but share the message of salvation, a message she felt God wanted her to share through the abilities he had given her.

In all, Grace Livingston Hill wrote more than one hundred books, all of which have sold thousands of copies and have touched the lives of readers around the world with their message of "enduring love" and the true way to lasting happiness: a relationship with God through his Son, Jesus Christ.

In an interview shortly before her death, Grace's devotion to her Lord still shone clear. She commented that whatever she had accomplished had been God's doing. She was only his servant, one who had tried to follow his teaching in all her thoughts and writing.

A VOICE IN THE WILDERNESS

LIVING BOOKS®
Tyndale House Publishers, Inc.
Wheaton, Illinois

This Tyndale House book
by Grace Livingston Hill
contains the complete text
of the original hardcover edition.
NOT ONE WORD
HAS BEEN OMITTED.

3-in-1 ISBN: 1-56865-181-3

Copyright © 1991 by Tyndale House Publishers, Inc.
All rights reserved
Cover illustration copyright © 1991 by Nathan Greene

Living Books is a registered trademark of Tyndale House
Publishers, Inc.

Library of Congress Catalog Card Number 90-70191
ISBN 0-8423-7908-8

Printed in the United States of America

WITH a lurch the train came to a dead stop and Margaret Earle, hastily gathering up her belongings, hurried down the aisle and got out into the night.

It occurred to her, as she swung her heavy suit-case down the rather long step to the ground, and then carefully swung herself after it, that it was strange that neither conductor, brakeman, nor porter had come to help her off the train, when all three had taken the trouble to tell her that hers was the next station; but she could hear voices up ahead. Perhaps something was the matter with the engine that detained them and they had forgotten her for the moment.

The ground was rough where she stood, and there seemed no sign of a platform. Did they not have platforms in this wild Western land, or was the train so long that her car had stopped before reaching it?

She strained her eyes into the darkness, and tried to make out things from the two or three specks of light that danced about like fireflies in the distance. She could dimly see moving figures away up near the engine, and each one evidently carried a lantern. The train was tremendously long. A sudden feeling of isolation took possession of her. Perhaps she

ought not to have got out until some one came to help her.
Perhaps the train had not pulled into the station yet and she
ought to get back on it and wait. Yet if the train started before she found the conductor she might be carried on somewhere and he justly blame her for a fool.

There did not seem to be any building on that side of the
track. It was probably on the other, but she was standing too
near the cars to see over. She tried to move back to look, but
the ground sloped and she slipped and fell in the cinders,
bruising her knee and cutting her wrist.

In sudden panic she arose. She would get back into the
train, no matter what the consequences. They had no right
to put her out here, away off from the station, at night, in
a strange country. If the train started before she could find
the conductor she would tell him that he must back it up
again and let her off. He certainly could not expect her to
get out like this.

She lifted the heavy suit-case up the high step that was even
farther from the ground than it had been when she came
down, because her fall had loosened some of the earth and
caused it to slide away from the track. Then, reaching to the
rail of the step, she tried to pull herself up, but as she did so
the engine gave a long snort and the whole train, as if it were
in league against her, lurched forward crazily, shaking off
her hold. She slipped to her knees again, the suit-case, top-
pled from the lower step, descending upon her, and together
they slid and rolled down the short bank, while the train, like
an irresponsible nurse who had slapped her charge and left
it to its fate, ran giddily off into the night.

The horror of being deserted helped the girl to rise in spite
of bruises and shock. She lifted imploring hands to the unresponsive cars as they hurried by her—one, two, three, with
bright windows, each showing a passenger, comfortable and
safe inside, unconscious of her need.

A moment of useless screaming, running, trying to attract
some one's attention, a sickening sense of terror and failure,

and the last car slatted itself past with a mocking clatter, as if it enjoyed her discomfort.

Margaret stood dazed, reaching out helpless hands, then dropped them at her sides and gazed after the fast-retreating train, the light on its last car swinging tauntingly, blinking now and then with a leer in its eye, rapidly vanishing from her sight into the depth of the night.

She gasped and looked about her for the station that but a short moment before had been so real to her mind; and, lo! on this side and on that there was none!

The night was wide like a great floor shut in by a low, vast dome of curving blue set with the largest, most wonderful stars she had ever seen. Heavy shadows of purple-green, smoke-like, hovered over earth darker and more intense than the unfathomable blue of the night sky. It seemed like the secret nesting-place of mysteries wherein no human foot might dare intrude. It was incredible that such could be but common sage-brush, sand, and greasewood wrapped about with the beauty of the lonely night.

No building broke the inky outlines of the plain, nor friendly light streamed out to cheer her heart. Not even a tree was in sight, except on the far horizon, where a heavy line of deeper darkness might mean a forest. Nothing, absolutely nothing, in the blue, deep, starry dome above and the bluer darkness of the earth below save one sharp shaft ahead like a black mast throwing out a dark arm across the track.

As soon as she sighted it she picked up her baggage and made her painful way toward it, for her knees and wrist were bruised and her baggage was heavy.

A soft drip, drip greeted her as she drew nearer; something splashing down among the cinders by the track. Then she saw the tall column with its arm outstretched, and looming darker among the sage-brush the outlines of a water-tank. It was so she recognized the engine's drinking-tank, and knew that she had mistaken a pause to water the engine for a regular stop at a station.

Her soul sank within her as she came up to the dripping water and laid her hand upon the dark upright, as if in some way it could help her. She dropped her baggage and stood, trembling, gazing around upon the beautiful, lonely scene in horror; and then, like a mirage against the distance, there melted on her frightened eyes a vision of her father and mother sitting around the library lamp at home, as they sat every evening. They were probably reading and talking at this very minute, and trying not to miss her on this her first venture away from the home into the great world to teach. What would they say if they could see their beloved daughter, whom they had sheltered all these years and let go forth so reluctantly now, in all her confidence of youth, bound by almost absurd promises to be careful and not run any risks.

Yet here she was, standing alone beside a water-tank in the midst of an Arizona plain, no knowing how many miles from anywhere, at somewhere between nine and ten o'clock at night! It seemed incredible that it had really happened! Perhaps she was dreaming! A few moments before in the bright car, surrounded by drowsy fellow-travelers, almost at her journey's end, as she supposed; and now, having merely done as she thought right, she was stranded here!

She rubbed her eyes and looked again up the track, half expecting to see the train come back for her. Surely, surely the conductor, or the porter who had been so kind, would discover that she was gone, and do something about it. They couldn't leave her here alone on the prairie! It would be too dreadful!

That vision of her father and mother off against the purple-green distance, how it shook her! The lamp looked bright and cheerful, and she could see her father's head with its heavy white hair. He turned to look at her mother to tell her of something he read in the paper. They were sitting there, feeling contented and almost happy about her, and she, their little girl—all her dignity as school-teacher dropped from her like a garment now—she was standing in this empty space alone, with only an engine's water-tank to keep her from dying, and only the barren, desolate track to connect her with the world of men and women. She dropped her head upon her breast and the tears came, sobbing, choking, raining down. Then off in the distance she heard a low, rising howl of some snarling, angry beast, and she lifted her head and stood in trembling terror, clinging to the tank.

That sound was coyotes or wolves howling. She had read about them, but had not expected to experience them in such a situation. How confidently had she accepted the position which offered her the opening she had sought for the splendid career that she hoped was to follow! How fearless had she been! Coyotes, nor Indians, nor wild cowboy students — nothing had daunted her courage. Besides, she told her mother it was very different going to a town from what it would be if she were a missionary going to the wilds. It was an important school she was to teach, where her Latin and German and mathematical achievements had won her the place above several other applicants, and where her well-known tact was expected to work wonders. But what were Latin and German and mathematics now? Could they show her how to climb a water-tank? Would tact avail with a hungry wolf?

The howl in the distance seemed to come nearer. She cast frightened eyes to the unresponsive water-tank looming high and dark above her. She must get up there somehow. It was not safe to stand here a minute. Besides, from that height she might be able to see farther, and perhaps there would be a light somewhere and she might cry for help.

Investigation showed a set of rude spikes by which the trainmen were wont to climb up, and Margaret prepared to ascend them. She set her suit-case dubiously down at the foot. Would it be safe to leave it there? She had read how coyotes carried off a hatchet from a camping-party, just to get the leather thong which was bound about the handle. She could not afford to lose her things. Yet how could she climb and carry that heavy burden with her? A sudden thought came.

Her simple traveling-gown was finished with a silken girdle, soft and long, wound twice about her waist and falling in tasseled ends. Swiftly she untied it and knotted one end firmly to the handle of her suit-case, tying the other end securely to her wrist. Then slowly, cautiously, with many a look upward, she began to climb.

It seemed miles, though in reality it was but a short distance. The howling beasts in the distance sounded nearer now and continually, making her heart beat wildly. She was stiff and bruised from her falls, and weak with fright. The spikes were far apart, and each step of progress was painful and difficult. It was good at last to rise high enough to see over the water-tank and feel a certain confidence in her defense.

But she had risen already beyond the short length of her silken tether, and the suit-case was dragging painfully on her arm. She was obliged to steady herself where she stood and pull it up before she could go on. Then she managed to get it swung up to the top of the tank in a comparatively safe place. One more long spike step and she was beside it.

The tank was partly roofed over, so that she had room enough to sit on the edge without danger of falling in and drowning. For a few minutes she could only sit still and be thankful and try to get her breath back again after the climb; but presently the beauty of the night began to cast its spell over her. That wonderful blue of the sky! It hadn't ever before impressed her that skies were blue at night. She would have said they were black or gray. As a matter of fact, she didn't remember to have ever seen so much sky at once before, nor to have noticed skies in general until now.

This sky was so deeply, wonderfully blue, the stars so real, alive and sparkling, that all other stars she had ever seen paled before them into mere imitations. The spot looked like one of Taylor's pictures of the Holy Land. She half expected to see a shepherd with his crook and sheep approaching her out of the dim shadows, or a turbaned, white-robed David with his lifted hands of prayer standing off among the depths of purple darkness. It would not have been out of keeping if a walled city with housetops should be hidden behind the clumps of sage-brush farther on. 'Twas such a night and such a scene as this, perhaps, when the wise men started to follow the star!

But one cannot sit on the edge of a water-tank in the desert night alone and muse long on art and history. It was cold up there, and the howling seemed nearer than before. There was no sign of a light or a house anywhere, and not even a freight-train sent its welcome clatter down the track. All was still and wide and lonely, save that terrifying sound of the beasts; such stillness as she had not ever thought could be — a fearful silence as a setting for the awful voices of the wilds.

The bruises and scratches she had acquired set up a fine stinging, and the cold seemed to sweep down and take possession of her on her high, narrow seat. She was growing stiff and cramped, yet dared not move much. Would there be no train, nor any help? Would she have to sit there all night? It looked so very near to the ground now. Could wild beasts climb, she wondered?

Then in the interval of silence that came between the calling of those wild creatures there stole a sound. She could not tell at first what it was. A slow, regular, plodding sound, and quite far away. She looked to find it, and thought she saw a shape move out of the sage-brush on the other side of the track, but she could not be sure. It might be but a figment of her brain, a foolish fancy from looking so long at the huddled bushes on the dark plain. Yet something prompted her to cry out, and when she heard her own voice she cried again and louder, wondering why she had not cried before.

"Help! Help!" she called; and again: "Help! Help!"

The dark shape paused and turned toward her. She was sure now. What if it were a beast instead of a human! Terrible fear took possession of her; then, to her infinite relief, a nasal voice sounded out:

"Who's thar?"

But when she opened her lips to answer, nothing but a sob would come to them for a minute, and then she could only cry, pitifully:

"Help! Help!"

"Whar be you?" twanged the voice; and now she could see a horse and rider like a shadow moving toward her down the track.

THE horse came to a standstill a little way from the track, and his rider let forth a stream of strange profanity. The girl shuddered and began to think a wild beast might be preferable to some men. However, these remarks seemed to be a mere formality. He paused and addressed her:

"Heow'd yeh git up thar? D'j'yeh drap er climb?"

He was a little, wiry man with a bristly, protruding chin. She could see that, even in the starlight. There was something about the point of that stubby chin that she shrank from inexpressibly. He was not a pleasant man to look upon, and even his voice was unprepossessing. She began to think that even the night with its loneliness and unknown perils was preferable to this man's company.

"I got off the train by mistake, thinking it was my station, and before I discovered it the train had gone and left me," Margaret explained, with dignity.

"Yeh didn't 'xpect it t' sit reound on th' plain while you was gallivantin' up water-tanks, did yeh?"

Cold horror froze Margaret's veins. She was dumb for a second. "I am on my way to Ashland station. Can you tell me how far it is from here and how I can get there?" Her tone was like icicles.

"It's a little matter o' twenty miles, more 'r less," said the man protruding his offensive chin. "The walkin's good. I don't know no other way from this p'int at this time o' night. Yeh might set still till th' mornin' freight goes by an' drap atop o' one of the kyars."

"Sir!" said Margaret, remembering her dignity as a teacher. The man wheeled his horse clear around and looked up at her impudently. She could smell bad whisky on his breath.

"Say, you must be some young highbrow, ain't yeh? Is thet all yeh want o' me? 'Cause ef 'tis I got t' git on t' camp. It's a good five mile yet, an' I 'ain't hed no grub sence noon."

The tears suddenly rushed to the girl's eyes as the horror of being alone in the night again took possession of her. This dreadful man frightened her, but the thought of the loneliness filled her with dismay.

"Oh!" she cried, forgetting her insulted dignity, "you're not going to leave me up here alone, are you? Isn't there some place near here where I could stay overnight?"

"Thur ain't no palace hotel round these diggin's, ef that's what you mean," the man leered at her. "You c'n come along t' camp 'ith me ef you ain't too stuck up."

"To camp!" faltered Margaret in dismay, wondering what her mother would say. "Are there any ladies there?"

A loud guffaw greeted her question. "Wal, my woman's thar, sech es she is; but she ain't no high-flier like you. We mostly don't hev ladies to camp. But I got t' git on. Ef you want to go too, you better light down pretty speedy, fer I can't wait."

In fear and trembling Margaret descended her rude ladder step by step, primitive man seated calmly on his horse, making no attempt whatever to assist her.

"This ain't no baggage-car," he grumbled, as he saw the suit-case in her hand. "Well, h'ist yerself up thar; I reckon we c'n pull through somehow. Gimme the luggage."

Margaret stood appalled beside the bony horse and his uncouth rider. Did he actually expect her to ride with him?

"Couldn't I walk?" she faltered, hoping he would offer to do so.

" 'T's up t' you," the man replied, indifferently. "Try 't an' see!"

He spoke to the horse, and it started forward eagerly, while the girl in horror struggled on behind. Over rough, uneven ground, between greasewood, sage-brush, and cactus, back into the trail. The man, oblivious of her presence, rode contentedly on, a silent shadow on a dark horse wending a silent way between the purple-green clumps of other shadows, until, bewildered, the girl almost lost sight of them. Her breath came short, her ankle turned, and she fell with both hands in a stinging bed of cactus. She cried out then and begged him to stop.

"L'arned yer lesson, hev yeh, sweety?" he jeered at her, foolishly. "Well, get in yer box, then."

He let her struggle up to a seat behind himself with very little assistance, but when she was seated and started on her way she began to wish she had stayed behind and taken any perils of the way rather than trust herself in proximity to this creature.

From time to time he took a bottle from his pocket and swallowed a portion of its contents, becoming fluent in his language as they proceeded on their way. Margaret remained silent, growing more and more frightened every time the bottle came out. At last he offered it to her. She declined it with cold politeness, which seemed to irritate the little man, for he turned suddenly fierce.

"Oh, yer too fine to take a drap fer good comp'ny, are yeh? Wal, I'll show yeh a thing er two, my pretty lady. You'll give me a kiss with yer two cherry lips before we go another step. D'yeh hear, my sweetie?" And he turned with a silly leer to enforce his command; but with a cry of horror Margaret slid to the ground and ran back down the trail as hard as she could go, till she stumbled and fell in the shelter of a great sage-brush, and lay sobbing on the sand.

The man turned bleared eyes toward her and watched until she disappeared. Then sticking his chin out wickedly, he slung her suit-case after her and called:

"All right, my pretty lady; go yer own gait an' l'arn yer own lesson." He started on again, singing a drunken song.

Under the blue, starry dome alone sat Margaret again, this time with no friendly water-tank for her defense, and took counsel with herself. The howling coyotes seemed to be silenced for the time; at least they had become a minor quantity in her equation of troubles. She felt now that man was her greatest menace, and to get away safely from him back to that friendly water-tank and the dear old railroad track she would have pledged her next year's salary. She stole softly to the place where she had heard the suit-case fall, and, picking it up, started on the weary road back to the tank. Could she ever find the way? The trail seemed so intangible a thing, her sense of direction so confused. Yet there was nothing else to do. She shuddered whenever she thought of the man who had been her companion on horseback.

When the man reached camp he set his horse loose and stumbled into the door of the log bunk-house, calling loudly for something to eat.

The men were sitting around the room on the rough benches and bunks, smoking their pipes or stolidly staring into the dying fire. Two smoky kerosene-lanterns that hung from spikes driven high in the logs cast a weird light over the company, eight men in all, rough and hardened with exposure to stormy life and weather. They were men with unkempt beards and uncombed hair, their coarse cotton shirts open at the neck, their brawny arms bare above the elbow, with crimes and sorrows and hard living written large across their faces.

There was one, a boy in looks, with smooth face and white skin healthily flushed in places like a baby's. His face, too, was hard and set in sternness like a mask, as if life had used him badly; but behind it was a fineness of feature and spirit that could not be utterly hidden. They called him the Kid, and thought it was his youth that made him different from them all, for he was only twenty-four, and not one of the rest was under forty. They were doing their best to help him get over that innate fineness that was his natural inheritance, but although he stopped at nothing, and played his part always with the ease of one old in the ways of the world, yet he kept a quiet reserve about him, a kind of charm beyond which they had not been able to go.

He was playing cards with three others at the table when the man came in, and did not look up at the entrance.

The woman, white and hopeless, appeared at the door of the shed-room when the man came, and obediently set about getting his supper; but her lifeless face never changed expression.

"Brung a gal 'long of me part way," boasted the man, as he flung himself into a seat by the table. "Thought you fellers might like t' see 'er, but she got too high an' mighty fer me, wouldn't take a pull at th' bottle 'ith me, 'n' shrieked like a catamount when I kissed 'er. Found 'er hangin' on th' water-tank. Got off 't th' wrong place. One o' yer highbrows out o' th' parlor car! Good lesson fer 'er!"

The Boy looked up from his cards sternly, his keen eyes boring through the man. "Where is she now?" he asked, quietly; and all the men in the room looked up uneasily. There was that tone and accent again that made the Boy alien from them. What was it?

The man felt it and snarled his answer angrily. "Dropped 'er on th' trail, an' threw her fine-lady b'longin's after 'er. 'Ain't got no use fer thet kind. Wonder what they was created fer? Ain't no good to nobody, not even 'emselves." And he laughed a harsh cackle that was not pleasant to hear.

The Boy threw down his cards and went out, shutting the door. In a few minutes the men heard two horses pass the end of the bunk-house toward the trail, but no one looked up nor spoke. You could not have told by the flicker of an eyelash that they knew where the Boy had gone.

She was sitting in the deep shadow of a sage-brush that lay on the edge of the trail like a great blot, her suit-case beside her, her breath coming short with exertion and excitement, when she heard a cheery whistle in the distance. Just an old love-song dating back some years and discarded now as hackneyed even by the street pianos at home; but oh, how good it sounded!

From the desert I come to thee!

The ground was cold, and struck a chill through her garments as she sat there alone in the night. On came the clear, musical whistle, and she peered out of the shadow with eager eyes and frightened heart. Dared she risk it again? Should she call, or should she hold her breath and keep still, hoping he would pass her by unnoticed? Before she could decide two horses stopped almost in front of her and a rider swung himself down. He stood before her as if it were day and he could see her quite plainly.

"You needn't be afraid," he explained, calmly. "I thought I had better look you up after the old man got home and gave his report. He was pretty well tanked up and not exactly a fit escort for ladies. What's the trouble?"

Like an angel of deliverance he looked to her as he stood in the starlight, outlined in silhouette against the wide, wonderful sky: broad shoulders, well-set head, close-cropped curls, handsome contour even in the darkness. There was about him an air of quiet strength which gave her confidence.

"Oh, thank you!" she gasped, with a quick little relieved sob in her voice. "I am so glad you have come. I was—just a little—frightened, I think." She attempted to rise, but her foot caught in her skirt and she sank wearily back to the sand again.

The Boy stooped over and lifted her to her feet. "You certainly are some plucky girl!" he commented, looking down at her slender height as she stood beside him. "A 'little frightened,' were you? Well, I should say you had a right to be."

"Well, not exactly frightened, you know," said Margaret, taking a deep breath and trying to steady her voice. "I think perhaps I was more mortified than frightened, to think I made such a blunder as to get off the train before I reached my station. You see, I'd made up my mind not to be frightened, but when I heard that awful howl of some beast— And then that terrible man!" She shuddered and put her hands suddenly over her eyes as if to shut out all memory of it.

"More than one kind of beasts!" commented the Boy, briefly. "Well, you needn't worry about him; he's having his supper and he'll be sound asleep by the time we get back."

"Oh, have we got to go where he is?" gasped Margaret. "Isn't there some other place? Is Ashland very far away? That is where I am going."

"No other place where you could go to-night. Ashland's a good twenty-five miles from here. But you'll be all right. Mom Wallis 'll look out for you. She isn't much of a looker, but she has a kind heart. She pulled me through once when I was just about flickering out. Come on. You'll be pretty tired. We better be getting back. Mom Wallis 'll make you comfortable, and then you can get off good and early in the morning."

Without an apology, and as if it were the common courtesy of the desert, he stooped and lifted her easily to the saddle of the second horse, placed the bridle in her hands, then swung the suit-case up on his own horse and sprang into the saddle.

3

HE turned the horses about and took charge of her just as if he were accustomed to managing stray ladies in the wilderness every day of his life and understood the situation perfectly; and Margaret settled wearily into her saddle and looked about her with content.

Suddenly, again, the wide wonder of the night possessed her. Involuntarily she breathed a soft little exclamation of awe and delight. Her companion turned to her questioningly:

"Does it always seem so big here — so — limitless?" she asked in explanation. "It is so far to everywhere it takes one's breath away, and yet the stars hang close, like a protection. It gives one the feeling of being alone in the great universe with God. Does it always seem so out here?"

He looked at her curiously, her pure profile turned up to the wide dome of luminous blue above. His voice was strangely low and wondering as he answered, after a moment's silence:

"No, it is not always so," he said. "I have seen it when it was more like being alone in the great universe with the devil."

There was a tremendous earnestness in his tone that the

girl felt meant more than was on the surface. She turned to look at the fine young face beside her. In the starlight she could not make out the bitter hardness of lines that were beginning to be carved about his sensitive mouth. But there was so much sadness in his voice that her heart went out to him in pity.

"Oh," she said, gently, "it would be awful that way. Yes, I can understand. I felt so, a little, while that terrible man was with me." And she shuddered again at the remembrance.

Again he gave her that curious look. "There are worse things than Pop Wallis out here," he said, gravely. "But I'll grant you there's some class to the skies. It's a case of 'Where every prospect pleases and only man is vile.' " And with the words his tone grew almost flippant. It hurt her sensitive nature, and without knowing it she half drew away a little farther from him and murmured, sadly:

"Oh!" as if he had classed himself with the "man" he had been describing. Instantly he felt her withdrawal and grew grave again, as if he would atone.

"Wait till you see this sky at the dawn," he said. "It will burn red fire off there in the east like a hearth in a palace, and all this dome will glow like a great pink jewel set in gold. If you want a classy sky, there you have it! Nothing like it in the East!"

There was a strange mingling of culture and roughness in his speech. The girl could not make him out; yet there had been a palpitating earnestness in his description that showed he had felt the dawn in his very soul.

"You are — a — poet, perhaps?" she asked, half shyly. "Or an artist?" she hazarded.

He laughed roughly and seemed embarrassed. "No, I'm just a — bum! A sort of roughneck out of a job."

She was silent, watching him against the starlight, a kind of embarrassment upon her after his last remark. "You — have been here long?" she asked, at last.

"Three years." He said it almost curtly and turned his head

away, as if there were something in his face he would hide.

She knew there was something unhappy in his life. Unconsciously her tone took on a sympathetic sound. "And do you get homesick and want to go back, ever?" she asked.

His tone was fairly savage now. "No!"

The silence which followed became almost oppressive before the Boy finally turned and in his kindly tone began to question her about the happenings which had stranded her in the desert alone at night.

So she came to tell him briefly and frankly about herself, as he questioned—how she came to be in Arizona all alone.

"My father is a minister in a small town in New York State. When I finished college I had to do something, and I had an offer of this Ashland school through a friend of ours who had a brother out here. Father and mother would rather have kept me nearer home, of course, but everybody says the best opportunities are in the West, and this was a good opening, so they finally consented. They would send post-haste for me to come back if they knew what a mess I have made of things right at the start—getting out of the train in the desert."

"But you're not discouraged?" said her companion, half wonderingly. "Some nerve you have with you. I guess you'll manage to hit it off in Ashland. It's the limit as far as discipline is concerned, I understand, but I guess you'll put one over on them. I'll bank on you after to-night, sure thing!"

She turned a laughing face toward him. "Thank you!" she said. "But I don't see how you know all that. I'm sure I didn't do anything particularly nervy. There wasn't anything else to do but what I did, if I'd tried."

"Most girls would have fainted and screamed, and fainted again when they were rescued," stated the Boy, out of a vast experience.

"I never fainted in my life," said Margaret Earle, with disdain. "I don't think I should care to faint out in the vast universe like this. It would be rather inopportune, I should think."

Then, because she suddenly realized that she was growing very chummy with this stranger in the dark, she asked the first question that came into her head.

"What was your college?"

That he had not been to college never entered her head. There was something in his speech and manner that made it a foregone conclusion.

It was as if she had struck him forcibly in his face, so sudden and sharp a silence ensued for a second. Then he answered, gruffly, "Yale," and plunged into an elaborate account of Arizona in its early ages, including a detailed description of the cliff-dwellers and their homes, which were still to be seen high in the rocks of the cañons not many miles to the west of where they were riding.

Margaret was keen to hear it all, and asked many questions, declaring her intention of visiting those cliff-caves at her earliest opportunity. It was so wonderful to her to be actually out here where were all sorts of queer things about which she had read and wondered. It did not occur to her, until the next day, to realize that her companion had of intention led her off the topic of himself and kept her from asking any more personal questions.

He told her of the petrified forest just over some low hills off to the left; acres and acres of agatized chips and trunks of great trees all turned to eternal stone, called by the Indians "Yeitso's bones," after the great giant of that name whom an ancient Indian hero killed. He described the coloring of the brilliant days in Arizona, where you stand on the edge of some flat-topped mesa and look off through the clear air to mountains that seem quite near by, but are in reality more than two hundred miles away. He pictured the strange colors and lights of the place; ledges of rock, yellow, white and green, drab and maroon, and tumbled piles of red boulders, shadowy buttes in the distance, serrated cliffs against the horizon, not blue, but rosy pink in the heated haze of the air, and perhaps a great, lonely eagle poised above the silent, brilliant waste.

He told it not in book language, with turn of phrase and smoothly flowing sentences, but in simple, frank words, as a boy might describe a picture to one he knew would appreciate it—for her sake, and not because he loved to put it into words; but in a new, stumbling way letting out the beauty that had somehow crept into his heart in spite of all the rough attempts to keep all gentle things out of his nature.

The girl, as she listened, marveled more and more what manner of youth this might be who had come to her out of the desert night.

She forgot her weariness as she listened, in the thrill of wonder over the new mysterious country to which she had come. She forgot that she was riding through the great darkness with an utter stranger, to a place she knew not, and to experiences most dubious. Her fears had fled and she was actually enjoying herself, and responding to the wonderful story of the place with soft-murmured exclamations of delight and wonder.

From time to time in the distance there sounded forth those awful blood-curdling howls of wild beasts that she had heard when she sat alone by the water-tank, and each time she heard a shudder passed through her and instinctively she swerved a trifle toward her companion, then straightened up again and tried to seem not to notice. The Boy saw and watched her brave attempts at self-control with deep appreciation. But suddenly, as they rode and talked, a dark form appeared across their way a little ahead, lithe and stealthy and furry, and two awful eyes like green lamps glared for an instant, then disappeared silently among the mesquite bushes.

She did not cry out nor start. Her very veins seemed frozen with horror, and she could not have spoken if she tried. It was all over in a second and the creature gone, so that she almost doubted her senses and wondered if she had seen aright. Then one hand went swiftly to her throat and she shrank toward her companion.

"There is nothing to fear," he said, reassuringly, and laid a strong hand comfortingly across the neck of her horse. "The pussy-cat was as unwilling for our company as we for hers. Besides, look here!"—and he raised his hand and shot into the air. "She'll not come near us now."

"I am not afraid!" said the girl, bravely. "At least, I don't think I am—very! But it's all so new and unexpected, you know. Do people around here always shoot in that—well—unpremeditated fashion?"

They laughed together.

"Excuse me," he said. "I didn't realize the shot might startle you even more than the wildcat. It seems I'm not fit to have charge of a lady. I told you I was a roughneck."

"You're taking care of me beautifully," said Margaret Earle, loyally, "and I'm glad to get used to shots if that's the thing to be expected often."

Just then they came to the top of the low, rolling hill, and ahead in the darkness there gleamed a tiny, wizened light set in a blotch of blackness. Under the great white stars it burned a sickly red and seemed out of harmony with the night.

"There we are!" said the Boy, pointing toward it. "That's the bunk-house. You needn't be afraid. Pop Wallis 'll be snoring by this time, and we'll come away before he's about in the morning. He always sleeps late after he's been off on a bout. He's been gone three days, selling some cattle, and he'll have a pretty good top on."

The girl caught her breath, gave one wistful look up at the wide, starry sky, a furtive glance at the strong face of her protector, and submitted to being lifted down to the ground.

Before her loomed the bunk-house, small and mean, built of logs, with only one window in which the flicker of the lanterns menaced, with unknown trials and possible perils for her to meet.

4

WHEN Margaret Earle dawned upon that bunk-room the men sat up with one accord, ran their rough, red hands through their rough, tousled hair, smoothed their beards, took down their feet from the benches where they were resting. That was as far as their etiquette led them. Most of them continued to smoke their pipes, and all of them stared at her unreservedly. Such a sight of exquisite feminine beauty had not come to their eyes in many a long day. Even in the dim light of the smoky lanterns, and with the dust and weariness of travel upon her, Margaret Earle was a beautiful girl.

"That's what's the matter, father," said her mother, when the subject of Margaret's going West to teach had first been mentioned. "She's too beautiful. Far too beautiful to go among savages! If she were homely and old, now, she might be safe. That would be a different matter."

Yet Margaret had prevailed, and was here in the wild country. Now, standing on the threshold of the log cabin, she read, in the unveiled admiration that startled from the eyes of the men, the meaning of her mother's fears.

Yet withal it was a kindly admiration not unmixed with awe. For there was about her beauty a touch of the spiritual which set her above the common run of women, making men feel her purity and sweetness, and inclining their hearts to worship rather than be bold.

The Boy had been right. Pop Wallis was asleep and out of the way. From a little shed room at one end his snoring marked time in the silence that the advent of the girl made in the place.

In the doorway of the kitchen offset Mom Wallis stood with her passionless face—a face from which all emotions had long ago been burned by cruel fires—and looked at the girl, whose expression was vivid with her opening life all haloed in a rosy glow.

A kind of wistful contortion passed over Mom Wallis's hopeless countenance, as if she saw before her in all its possibility of perfection the life that she herself had lost. Perhaps it was no longer possible for her features to show tenderness, but a glow of something like it burned in her eyes, though she only turned away with the same old apathetic air, and without a word went about preparing a meal for the stranger.

Margaret looked wildly, fearfully, around the rough assemblage when she first entered the long, low room, but instantly the Boy introduced her as "the new teacher for the Ridge School beyond the Junction," and these were Long Bill, Big Jim, the Fiddling Boss, Jasper Kemp, Fade-away Forbes, Stocky, Croaker, and Fudge. An inspiration fell upon the frightened girl, and she acknowledged the introduction by a radiant smile, followed by the offering of her small gloved hand. Each man in dumb bewilderment instantly became her slave, and accepted the offered hand with more or less pleasure and embarrassment. The girl proved her right to be called tactful, and, seeing her advantage, followed it up quickly by a few bright words. These men were of an utterly different type from any she had ever met before, but they had in their eyes a kind of homage which Pop Wallis had not shown and they were not repulsive to her. Besides, the Boy was in the background, and her nerve had returned. The Boy knew how a lady should be treated. She was quite ready to "play up" to his lead.

It was the Boy who brought the only chair the bunkhouse afforded, a rude, home-made affair, and helped her off with her coat and hat in his easy, friendly way, as if he had known her all his life; while the men, to whom such gallant ways were foreign, sat awkwardly by and watched in wonder and amaze.

Most of all they were astonished at "the Kid," that he could fall so naturally into intimate talk with this delicate, beautiful woman. She was another of his kind, a creature not made in the same mold as theirs. They saw it now, and watched the fairy play with almost childish interest. Just to hear her call him "Mr. Gardley"! — Lance Gardley, that was what he had told them was his name the day he came among them. They had not heard it since. The Kid! Mr. Gardley!

There it was, the difference between them! They looked at the girl half jealously, yet proudly at the Boy. He was theirs — yes, in a way he was theirs — had they not found him in the wilderness, sick and nigh to death, and nursed him back to life again? He was theirs; but he knew how to drop into her world, too, and not be ashamed. They were glad that he could, even while it struck them with a pang that some day he would go back to the world to which he belonged — and where they could never be at home.

It was a marvel to watch her eat the coarse cornbread and pork that Mom Wallis brought her. It might have been a banquet, the pleasant way she seemed to look at it. Just like a bird she tasted it daintily, and smiled, showing her white teeth. There was nothing of the idea of greediness that each man knew he himself felt after a fast. It was all beautiful, the way she handled the two-tined fork and the old steel knife. They watched and dropped their eyes abashed as at a lovely sacrament. They had not felt before that eating could be an art. They did not know what art meant.

Such strange talk, too! But the Kid seemed to understand. About the sky—their old, common sky, with stars that they saw every night—making such a fuss about that, with words like "wide," "infinite," "azure," and "gems." Each man went furtively out that night before he slept and took a new look at the sky to see if he could understand.

The Boy was planning so the night would be but brief. He knew the girl was afraid. He kept the talk going enthusiastically, drawing in one or two of the men now and again. Long Bill forgot himself and laughed out a hoarse guffaw, then stopped as if he had been choked. Stocky, red in the face, told a funny story when commanded by the Boy, and then dissolved in mortification over his blunders. The Fiddling Boss obediently got down his fiddle from the smoky corner beside the fireplace and played a weird old tune or two, and then they sang. First the men, with hoarse, quavering approach and final roar of wild sweetness; then Margaret and the Boy in duet, and finally Margaret alone, with a few bashful chords on the fiddle, feeling their way as accompaniment.

Mom Wallis had long ago stopped her work and was sitting huddled in the doorway on a nail-keg with weary, folded hands and a strange wistfulness on her apathetic face. A fine silence had settled over the group as the girl, recognizing her power, and the pleasure she was giving, sang on. Now and then the Boy, when he knew the song, would join in with his rich tenor.

It was a strange night, and when she finally lay down to rest on a hard cot with a questionable-looking blanket for covering and Mom Wallis as her room-mate, Margaret Earle could not help wondering what her mother and father would think now if they could see her. Would they not, perhaps, almost prefer the water-tank and the lonely desert for her to her present surroundings?

Nevertheless, she slept soundly after her terrible excitement, and woke with a start of wonder in the early morning, to hear the men outside splashing water and humming or whistling bits of the tunes she had sung to them the night before.

Mom Wallis was standing over her, looking down with a hunger in her eyes at the bright waves of Margaret's hair and the soft, sleep-flushed cheeks.

"You got dretful purty hair," said Mom Wallis, wistfully.

Margaret looked up and smiled in acknowledgment of the compliment.

"You wouldn't b'lieve it, but I was young an' purty oncet. Beats all how much it counts to be young—an' purty! But land! It don't last long. Make the most of it while you got it."

Browning's immortal words came to Margaret's lips—

> *Grow old along with me,*
> *The best is yet to be,*
> *The last of life for which the first was made—*

but she checked them just in time and could only smile mutely. How could she speak such thoughts amid these intolerable surroundings? Then with sudden impulse she reached up to the astonished woman and, drawing her down, kissed her sallow cheek.

"Oh!" said Mom Wallis, starting back and laying her bony hands upon the place where she had been kissed, as if it hurt her, while a dull red stole up from her neck over her cheeks and high forehead to the roots of her hay-colored hair. All at once she turned her back upon her visitor and the tears of the years streamed down her impassive face.

"Don't mind me," she choked, after a minute. "I liked it real good, only it kind of give me a turn." Then, after a second: "It's time t' eat. You c'n wash outside after the men is done."

That, thought Margaret, had been the scheme of this woman's whole life—"After the men is done!"

So, after all, the night was passed in safety, and a wonderful dawning had come. The blue of the morning, so different from the blue of the night sky, was, nevertheless, just as un-fathomable; the air seemed filled with straying star-beams, so sparkling was the clearness of the light.

But now a mountain rose in the distance with heliotrope-and-purple bounds to stand across the vision and dispel the illusion of the night that the sky came down to the earth all around like a close-fitting dome. There were mountains on all sides, and a slender, dark line of mesquite set off the more delicate colorings of the plain.

Into the morning they rode, Margaret and the Boy, be-fore Pop Wallis was yet awake, while all the other men stood round and watched, eager, jealous for the handshake and the parting smile. They told her they hoped she would come again and sing for them, and each one had an awkward word of parting. Whatever Margaret Earle might do with her school, she had won seven loyal friends in the camp, and she rode away amid their admiring glances, which lingered, too, on the broad shoulders and wide sombrero of her escort rid-ing by her side.

"Wal, that's the end o' him, I 'spose," drawled Long Bill, with a deep sigh, as the riders passed into the valley out of their sight.

"H'm!" said Jasper Kemp, hungrily. "I reck'n *he* thinks it's jes' th' beginnin'!"

"Maybe so! Maybe so!" said Big Jim, dreamily.

The morning was full of wonder for the girl who had come straight from an Eastern city. The view from the top of the mesa, or the cool, dim entrance of a cañon where great ferns fringed and feathered its walls, and strange caves hol-lowed out in the rocks far above, made real the stories she had read of the cave-dwellers. It was a new world.

The Boy was charming. She could not have picked out among her city acquaintances a man who would have done the honors of the desert more delightfully than he. She had thought him handsome in the starlight and in the lantern-light the night before, but now that the morning shone upon him she could not keep from looking at him. His fresh color, which no wind and weather could quite subdue, his gray-blue eyes with that mixture of thoughtfulness and reverence and daring, his crisp, brown curls glinting with gold in the sunlight—all made him good to look upon. There was something about the firm set of his lips and chin that made her feel a hidden strength about him.

When they camped a little while for lunch he showed the thoughtfulness and care for her comfort that many an older man might not have had. Even his talk was a mixture of boyishness and experience and he seemed to know her thoughts before she had them fully spoken.

"I do not understand it," she said, looking him frankly in the eyes at last. "How ever in the world did one like *you* get landed among all those dreadful men! Of course, in their way, some of them are not so bad; but they are not like you, not in the least, and never could be."

They were riding out upon the plain now in the full afternoon light, and a short time would bring them to her destination.

A sad, set look came quickly into the Boy's eyes and his face grew almost hard.

"It's an old story. I suppose you've heard it before," he said, and his voice tried to take on a careless note, but failed. "I didn't make good back there"—he waved his hand sharply toward the East—"so I came out here to begin again. But I guess I haven't made good here, either—not in the way I meant when I came."

"You can't, you know," said Margaret. "Not here."

"Why?" He looked at her earnestly, as if he felt the answer might help him.

"Because you have to go back where you didn't make good and pick up the lost opportunities. You can't really make good till you do that *right where you left off.*"

"But suppose it's too late?"

"It's never too late if we're in earnest and not too proud."

There was a long silence then, while the Boy looked thoughtfully off at the mountains, and when he spoke again it was to call attention to the beauty of a silver cloud that floated lazily on the horizon. But Margaret Earle had seen the look in his gray eyes and was not deceived.

A few minutes later they crossed another mesa and descended to the enterprising little town where the girl was to begin her winter's work. The very houses and streets seemed to rise briskly and hasten to meet them those last few minutes of their ride.

Now that the experience was almost over, the girl realized that she had enjoyed it intensely, and that she dreaded inexpressibly that she must bid good-by to this friend of a few hours and face an unknown world. It had been a wonderful day, and now it was almost done. The two looked at each other and realized that their meeting had been an epoch in their lives that neither would soon forget—that neither wanted to forget.

5

SLOWER the horses walked, and slower. The voices of the Boy and girl were low when they spoke about the common things by the wayside. Once their eyes met, and they smiled with something both sad and glad in them.

Margaret was watching the young man by her side and wondering at herself. He was different from any man whose life had come near to hers before. He was wild and worldly, she could see that, and unrestrained by many of the things that were vital principles with her, and yet she felt strangely drawn to him and wonderfully at home in his company. She could not understand herself nor him. It was as if his real soul had looked out of his eyes and spoken, untrammeled by the circumstances of birth or breeding or habit, and she knew him for a kindred spirit. And yet he was far from being one in whom she would have expected even to find a friend. Where was her confidence of yesterday? Why was it that she dreaded to have this strong young protector leave her to meet alone a world of strangers, whom yesterday at this time she would have gladly welcomed?

Now, when his face grew thoughtful and sad, she saw the

hard, bitter lines that were beginning to be graven about his lips, and her heart ached over what he had said about not making good. She wondered if there was anything else she could say to help him, but no words came to her, and the sad, set look about his lips warned her that perhaps she had said enough. He was not one who needed a long dissertation to bring a thought home to his consciousness.

Gravely they rode to the station to see about Margaret's trunks and make inquiries for the school and the house where she had arranged to board. Then Margaret sent a telegram to her mother to say that she had arrived safely, and so, when all was done and there was no longer an excuse for lingering, the Boy realized that he must leave her.

They stood alone for just a moment while the voluble landlady went to attend to something that was boiling over on the stove. It was an ugly little parlor that was to be her reception-room for the next year at least, with red-and-green ingrain carpet of ancient pattern, hideous chromos on the walls, and frantically common furniture setting up in its shining varnish to be pretentious; but the girl had not seen it yet. She was filled with a great homesickness that had not possessed her even when she said good-by to her dear ones at home. She suddenly realized that the people with whom she was to be thrown were of another world from hers, and this one friend whom she had found in the desert was leaving her.

She tried to shake hands formally and tell him how grateful she was to him for rescuing her from the perils of the night, but somehow words seemed so inadequate, and tears kept crowding their way into her throat and eyes. Absurd it was, and he a stranger twenty hours before, and a man of other ways than hers, besides. Yet he was her friend and rescuer.

She spoke her thanks as well as she could, and then looked up, a swift, timid glance, and found his eyes upon her earnestly and troubled.

"Don't thank me," he said, huskily. "I guess it was the best thing I ever did, finding you. I sha'n't forget, even if you never let me see you again — and — I hope you will." His eyes searched hers wistfully.

"Of course," she said. "Why not?"

"I thank you," he said in quaint, courtly fashion, bending low over her hand. "I shall try to be worthy of the honor."

And so saying, he left her and, mounting his horse, rode away into the lengthening shadows of the afternoon.

She stood in the forlorn little room staring out of the window after her late companion, a sense of utter desolation upon her. For the moment all her brave hopes of the future had fled, and if she could have slipped unobserved out of the front door, down to the station, and boarded some waiting express to her home, she would gladly have done it then and there.

Try as she would to summon her former reasons for coming to this wild, she could not think of one of them, and her eyes were very near to tears.

But Margaret Earle was not given to tears, and as she felt them smart beneath her lids she turned in a panic to prevent them. She could not afford to cry now. Mrs. Tanner would be returning, and she must not find the "new schoolma'am" weeping.

With a glance she swept the meager, pretentious room, and then, suddenly, became aware of other presences. In the doorway stood a man and a dog, both regarding her intently with open surprise, not unmixed with open appraisement and a marked degree of admiration.

The man was of medium height, slight, with a putty complexion; cold, pale-blue eyes; pale, straw-colored hair, and a look of self-indulgence around his rather weak mouth. He was dressed in a city business suit of the latest cut, however, and looked as much out of place in that crude little house as did Margaret Earle herself in her simple gown of dark-blue crêpe and her undeniable air of style and good taste.

His eyes, as they regarded her, had in them a smile that the girl instinctively resented. Was it a shade too possessive and complacently sure for a stranger?

The dog, a large collie, had great, liquid, brown eyes, menacing or loyal, as circumstances dictated, and regarded her with an air of brief indecision. She felt she was being weighed in the balance by both pairs of eyes. Of the two the girl preferred the dog.

Perhaps the dog understood, for he came a pace nearer and waved his plumy tail tentatively. For the dog she felt a glow of friendliness at once, but for the man she suddenly, and most unreasonably, of course, conceived one of her violent and unexpected dislikes.

Into this tableau bustled Mrs. Tanner. "Well, now, I didn't go to leave you by your lonesome all this time," she apologized, wiping her hands on her apron, "but them beans boiled clean over, and I hed to put 'em in a bigger kettle. You see, I put in more beans 'count o' you bein' here, an' I ain't uset to calca'latin' on two extry." She looked happily from the man to the girl and back again.

"Mr. West, I 'spose, o' course, you interjuced yerself? Bein' a preacher, you don't hev to stan' on ceremony like the rest of mankind. You 'ain't? Well, let me hev the pleasure of interjucin' our new school-teacher, Miss Margaret Earle. I 'spect you two 'll be awful chummy right at the start, both bein' from the East that way, an' both hevin' ben to college."

Margaret Earle acknowledged the bow with a cool little inclination of her head. She wondered why she didn't hate the garrulous woman who rattled on in this happy, take-it-for-granted way; but there was something so innocently pleased in her manner that she couldn't help putting all her wrath on the smiling man who came forward instantly with a low bow and a voice of fulsome flattery.

"Indeed, Miss Earle, I assure you I am happily surprised. I am sure Mrs. Tanner's prophecy will come true and we shall be the best of friends. When they told me the new teacher was to board here I really hesitated. I have seen something of these Western teachers in my time, and scarcely thought I should find you congenial; but I can see at a glance that you are the exception to the rule."

He presented a soft, unmanly white hand, and there was nothing to do but take it or seem rude to her hostess; but her manner was like icicles, and she was thankful she had not yet removed her gloves.

If the reverend gentleman thought he was to enjoy a lingering hand-clasp he was mistaken, for the gloved fingertips merely touched his hand and were withdrawn, and the girl turned to her hostess with a smile of finality as if he were dismissed. He did not seem disposed to take the hint and withdraw, however, until on a sudden the great dog came and stood between them with open-mouthed welcome and joyous greeting in the plumy, wagging tail. He pushed close to her and looked up into her face insistently, his hanging pink tongue and wide, smiling countenance proclaiming that he was satisfied with his investigation.

Margaret looked down at him, and then stooped and put her arms about his neck. Something in his kindly dog expression made her feel suddenly as if she had a real friend.

It seemed the man, however, did not like the situation. He kicked gingerly at the dog's hind legs, and said in a harsh voice:

"Get out of the way, sir. You're annoying the lady. Get out, I say!"

The dog, however, uttered a low growl and merely showed the whites of his menacing eyes at the man, turning his body slightly so that he stood across the lady's way protectingly, as if to keep the man from her.

Margaret smiled at the dog and laid her hand on his head, as if to signify her acceptance of the friendship he had offered her, and he waved his plume once more and attended her from the room, neither of them giving further attention to the man.

"Confound that dog!" said Rev. Frederick West, in a most unpreacher-like tone, as he walked to the window and looked out. Then to himself he mused: "A pretty girl. A *very pretty* girl. I really think it 'll be worth my while to stay a month at least."

Up in her room the "very pretty girl" was unpacking her suit-case and struggling with the tears. Not since she was a wee little girl and went to school all alone for the first time had she felt so very forlorn, and it was the little bare bedroom that had done it. At least that had been the final straw that had made too great the burden of keeping down those threatening tears.

It was only a bare, plain room with unfinished walls, rough woodwork, a cheap wooden bed, a bureau with a warped looking-glass, and on the floor was a braided rug of rags. A little wooden rocker, another small, straight wooden chair, a hanging wall-pocket decorated with purple roses, a hanging bookshelf composed of three thin boards strung together with maroon picture cord, a violently colored picture-card of "Moses in the Bulrushes" framed in straws and red worsted, and bright-blue paper shades at the windows. That was the room!

How different from her room at home, simply and sweetly finished anew for her home-coming from college! It rose before her homesick vision now. Soft gray walls, rose-colored ceiling, blended by a wreath of exquisite wild roses, whose pattern was repeated in the border of the simple curtains and chair cushions, white-enamel furniture, pretty brass bed soft as down in its luxurious mattress, spotless and inviting always. She glanced at the humpy bed with its fringed gray spread and lumpy-looking pillows in dismay. She had not thought of little discomforts like that, yet how they loomed upon her weary vision now!

The tiny wooden stand with its thick, white crockery seemed ill substitute for the dainty white bath-room at home. She had known she would not have her home luxuries, of course, but she had not realized until set down amid these barren surroundings what a difference they would make.

Going to the window and looking out, she saw for the first time the one luxury the little room possessed — a view! And such a view! Wide and wonderful and far it stretched, in colors unmatched by painter's brush, a purple mountain topped by rosy clouds in the distance. For the second time in Arizona her soul was lifted suddenly out of itself and its dismay by a vision of the things that God has made and the largeness of it all.

FOR some time she stood and gazed, marveling at the beauty and recalling some of the things her companion of the afternoon had said about his impressions of the place; then suddenly there loomed a dark speck in the near foreground of her meditation, and, looking down annoyed, she discovered the minister like a gnat between the eye and a grand spectacle, his face turned admiringly up to her window, his hand lifted in familiar greeting.

Vexed at his familiarity, she turned quickly and jerked down the shade; then throwing herself on the bed, she had a good cry. Her nerves were terribly wrought up. Things seemed twisted in her mind, and she felt that she had reached the limit of her endurance. Here was she, Margaret Earle, newly elected teacher to the Ashland Ridge School, lying on her bed in tears, when she ought to be getting settled and planning her new life; when the situation demanded her best attention she was wrought up over a foolish little personal dislike. Why did she have to dislike a minister, anyway, and then take to a wild young fellow whose life thus far had been anything but satisfactory even to himself? Was it her perverse nature that caused her to remember the look in the eyes of the Boy who had rescued her from a night in the wilderness, and to feel there was far more manliness in his face than in the face of the man whose profession surely would lead one to suppose he was more worthy of her respect and interest? Well, she was tired. Perhaps things would assume their normal relation to one another in the morning. And so, after a few minutes, she bathed her face in the little, heavy, ironstone wash-bowl, combed her hair, and freshened the collar and ruffles in her sleeves preparatory to going down for the evening meal. Then, with a swift thought, she searched through her suit-case for every available article wherewith to brighten that forlorn room.

The dainty dressing-case of Dresden silk with rosy ribbons that her girl friends at home had given as a parting gift covered a generous portion of the pine bureau, and when she had spread it out and bestowed its silver-mounted brushes, combs, handglass, and pretty sachet, things seemed to brighten up a bit. She hung up a cobweb of a lace boudoir cap with its rose-colored ribbons over the bleary mirror, threw her kimono of flowered challis over the back of the rocker, arranged her soap and toothbrush, her own washrag and a towel brought from home on the wash-stand, and somehow felt better and more as if she belonged. Last she ranged her precious photographs of father and mother and the dear vine-covered church and manse across in front of the mirror. When her trunks came there would be other things, and she could bear it, perhaps, when she had this room buried deep in the home belongings. But this would have to do for to-night, for the trunk might not come till morning, and, anyhow, she was too weary to unpack.

She ventured one more look out of her window, peering carefully at first to make sure her fellow-boarder was not still standing down below on the grass. A pang of compunction shot through her conscience. What would her dear father think of her feeling this way toward a minister, and before she knew the first thing about him, too? It was dreadful! She must shake it off. Of course he was a good man or he wouldn't be in the ministry, and she had doubtless mistaken mere friendliness for forwardness. She would forget it and try to go down and behave to him the way her father would want her to behave toward a fellow-minister.

Cautiously she raised the shade again and looked out. The mountain was bathed in a wonderful ruby light fading into amethyst, and all the path between was many-colored like a pavement of jewels set in filigree. While she looked the picture changed, glowed, softened, and changed again, making her think of the chapter about the Holy City in Revelation.

She started at last when some one knocked hesitatingly on the door, for the wonderful sunset light had made her forget for the moment where she was, and it seemed a desecration to have mere mortals step in and announce supper, although the odor of pork and cabbage had been proclaiming it dumbly for some time.

She went to the door, and, opening it, found a dark figure standing in the hall. For a minute she half feared it was the minister, until a shy, reluctant backwardness in the whole stocky figure and the stirring of a large furry creature just behind him made her sure it was not.

"Ma says you're to come to supper," said a gruff, untamed voice; and Margaret perceived that the person in the gathering gloom of the hall was a boy.

"Oh!" said Margaret, with relief in her voice. "Thank you for coming to tell me. I meant to come down and not give that trouble, but I got to looking at the wonderful sunset. Have you been watching it?" She pointed across the room to the window. "Look! Isn't that a great color there on the tip of the mountain? I never saw anything like that at home. I suppose you're used to it, though."

The boy came a step nearer the door and looked blankly, half wonderingly, across at the window, as if he expected to see some phenomenon. "Oh! *That!*" he exclaimed, carelessly. "Sure! We have them all the time."

"But that wonderful silver light pouring down just in that one tiny spot!" exclaimed Margaret. "It makes the mountain seem alive and smiling!"

The boy turned and looked at her curiously. "Gee!" said, he, "I c'n show you plenty like that!" But he turned and looked at it a long, lingering minute again.

"But we mustn't keep your mother waiting," said Margaret, remembering and turning reluctantly toward the door. "Is this your dog? Isn't he a beauty? He made me feel really as if he were glad to see me." She stooped and laid her hand on the dog's head and smiled brightly up at his master.

The boy's face lit with a smile, and he turned a keen, appreciative look at the new teacher, for the first time genuinely interested in her. "Cap's a good old scout," he admitted.

"So his name is Cap. Is that short for anything?"

"Cap'n."

"Captain. What a good name for him. He looks as if he were a captain, and he waves that tail grandly, almost as if it might be a badge of office. But who are you? You haven't told me your name yet. Are you Mrs. Tanner's son?"

The boy nodded. "I'm just Bud Tanner."

"Then you are one of my pupils, aren't you? We must shake hands on that." She put out her hand, but she was forced to go out after Bud's reluctant red fist, take it by force in a strange grasp, and do all the shaking; for Bud had never had that experience before in his life, and he emerged from it with a very red face and a feeling as if his right arm had been somehow lifted out of the same class with the rest of his body. It was rather awful, too, that it happened just in the open dining-room door, and that "preacher-boarder" watched the whole performance. Bud put on an extra-deep frown and shuffled away from the teacher, making a great show of putting Cap out of the dining-room, though he always sat behind his master's chair at meals, much to the discomfiture of the male boarder, who was slightly in awe of his dogship, not having been admitted into friendship as the lady had been.

Mr. West stood back of his chair, awaiting the arrival of the new boarder, an expectant smile on his face, and rubbing his hands together with much the same effect as a wolf licking his lips in anticipation of a victim. In spite of her resolves to like the man, Margaret was again struck with aversion as she saw him standing there, and was intensely relieved when she found that the seat assigned to her was on the opposite side of the table from him, and beside Bud. West, however, did not seem to be pleased with the arrangement, and, stepping around the table, said to his landlady:

"Did you mean me to sit over here?" and he placed a possessive hand on the back of the chair that was meant for Bud.

"No, Mister West, you jest set where you ben settin'," responded Mrs. Tanner. She had thought the matter all out and decided that the minister could converse with the teacher to the better advantage of the whole table if he sat across from her. Mrs. Tanner was a born match-maker. This she felt was an opportunity not to be despised, even if it sometime robbed the Ridge School of a desirable teacher.

But West did not immediately return to his place at the other side of the table. To Margaret's extreme annoyance he drew her chair and waited for her to sit down. The situation, however, was somewhat relieved of its intimacy by a sudden interference from Cap, who darted away from his frowning master and stepped up authoritatively to the minister's side with a low growl, as if to say:

"Hands off that chair! That doesn't belong to you!"

West suddenly released his hold on the chair without waiting to shove it up to the table, and precipitately retired to his own place. "That dog's a nuisance!" he said, testily, and was answered with a glare from Bud's dark eyes.

Bud came to his seat with his eyes still set savagely on the minister, and Cap settled down protectingly behind Margaret's chair.

Mrs. Tanner bustled in with the coffee-pot, and Mr. Tanner came last, having just finished his rather elaborate hair-comb at the kitchen glass with the kitchen comb, in full view of the assembled multitude. He was a little, thin, wiry, weather-beaten man, with skin like leather and sparse hair. Some of his teeth were missing, leaving deep hollows in his cheeks, and his kindly protruding chin was covered with scraggy gray whiskers, which stuck out ahead of him like a cow-catcher. He was in his shirt-sleeves and collarless, but looked neat and clean, and he greeted the new guest heartily before he sat down, and nodded to the minister:

"Naow, Brother West, I reckon we're ready fer your part o' the performance. You'll please to say grace."

Mr. West bowed his sleek, yellow head and muttered a formal blessing with an offhand manner, as if it were a mere ceremony. Bud stared contemptuously at him the while, and Cap uttered a low rumble as of a distant growl. Margaret felt a sudden desire to laugh, and tried to control herself, wondering what her father would feel about it all.

The genial clatter of knives and forks broke the stiffness after the blessing. Mrs. Tanner bustled back and forth from the stove to the table, talking clamorously the while. Mr. Tanner joined in with his flat, nasal twang, responding, and the minister, with an air of utter contempt for them both, endeavored to set up a separate and altogether private conversation with Margaret across the narrow table; but Margaret innocently had begun a conversation with Bud about the school, and had to be addressed by name each time before Mr. West could get her attention. Bud, with a boy's keenness, noticed her aversion, and put aside his own backwardness, entering into the contest with remarkably voluble replies. The minister, if he would be in the talk at all, was forced to join in with theirs, and found himself worsted and contradicted by the boy at every turn.

Strange to say, however, this state of things only served to make the man more eager to talk with the lady. She was not anxious for his attention. Ah! She was coy, and the acquaintance was to have the zest of being no lightly won friendship. All the better. He watched her as she talked, noted every charm of lash and lid and curving lip; stared so continually that she finally gave up looking his way at all, even when she was obliged to answer his questions.

Thus, at last, the first meal in the new home was concluded, and Margaret, pleading excessive weariness, went to her room. She felt as if she could not endure another half-hour of contact with her present world until she had had some rest. If the world had been just Bud and the dog she could have stayed below stairs and found out a little more about the new life; but with that oily-mouthed minister continually butting in her soul was in a tumult.

When she had prepared for rest she put out her light and drew up the shade. There before her spread the wide wonder of the heavens again, with the soft purple of the mountain under stars; and she was carried back to the experience of the night before with a vivid memory of her companion. Why, just *why* couldn't she be as interested in the minister down there as in the wild young man? Well, she was too tired to-night to analyze it all, and she knelt beside her window in the starlight to pray. As she prayed her thoughts were on Lance Gardley once more, and she felt her heart go out in longing for him, that he might find a way to "make good," whatever his trouble had been.

As she rose to retire she heard a step below, and, looking down, saw the minister stalking back and forth in the yard, his hands clasped behind, his head thrown back raptly. He could not see her in her dark room, but she pulled the shade down softly and fled to her hard little bed. Was that man going to obsess her vision everywhere, and must she try to like him just because he was a minister?

So at last she fell asleep.

THE next day was filled with unpacking and with writing letters home. By dint of being very busy Margaret managed to forget the minister, who seemed to·obtrude himself at every possible turn of the day, and would have monopolized her if she had given him half a chance.

The trunks, two delightful steamer ones, and a big packing-box with her books, arrived the next morning and caused great excitement in the household. Not since they moved into the new house had they seen so many things arrive. Bud helped carry them up-stairs, while Cap ran wildly back and forth, giving sharp barks, and the minister stood by the front door and gave ineffectual and unpractical advice to the man who had brought them. Margaret heard the man and Bud exchanging their opinion of West in low growls in the hall as they entered her door, and she couldn't help feeling that she agreed with them, though she might not have expressed her opinion in the same terms.

The minister tapped at her door a little later and offered his services in opening her box and unstrapping her trunks; but she told him Bud had already performed that service for her, and thanked him with a finality that forbade him to linger. She half hoped he heard the vicious little click with which she locked the door after him, and then wondered if she were wicked to feel that way. But all such compunctions were presently forgotten in the work of making over her room.

The trunks, after they were unpacked and repacked with the things she would not need at once, were disposed in front of the two windows with which the ugly little room was blessed. She covered them with two Bagdad rugs, relics of her college days, and piled several college pillows from the packing-box on each, which made the room instantly assume a homelike air. Then out of the box came other things. Framed pictures of home scenes, college friends and places, pennants, and flags from football, baseball, and basket-ball games she had attended; photographs; a few prints of rare paintings simply framed; a roll of rose-bordered white scrim like her curtains at home, wherewith she transformed the blue-shaded windows and the stiff little wooden rocker, and even made a valance and a bed-cover over pink cambric for her bed. The bureau and wash-stand were given pink and white covers, and the ugly walls literally disappeared beneath pictures, pennants, banners, and symbols.

When Bud came up to call her to dinner she flung the door open, and he paused in wide-eyed amazement over the transformation. His eyes kindled at a pair of golf-sticks, a hockey-stick, a tennis-racket, and a big basket-ball in the corner; and his whole look of surprise was so ridiculous that she had to laugh. He looked as if a miracle had been performed on the room, and actually stepped back into the hall to get his breath and be sure he was still in his father's house.

"I want you to come in and see all my pictures and get acquainted with my friends when you have time," she said. "I wonder if you could make some more shelves for my books and help me unpack and set them up?"

"Sure!" gasped Bud, heartily, albeit with awe. She hadn't asked the minister; she had asked *him* — *Bud!* Just a boy! He looked around the room with anticipation. What wonder and delight he would have looking at all those things!

Then Cap stepped into the middle of the room as if he belonged, mouth open, tongue lolling, smiling and panting a hearty approval, as he looked about at the strangenesss for all the world as a human being might have done. It was plain he was pleased with the change.

There was a proprietary air about Bud during dinner that was pleasant to Margaret and most annoying to West. It was plain that West looked on the boy as an upstart whom Miss Earle was using for the present to block his approach, and he was growing most impatient over the delay. He suggested that perhaps she would like his escort to see something of her surroundings that afternoon; but she smilingly told him that she would be very busy all the afternoon getting settled, and when he offered again to help her she cast a dazzling smile on Bud and said she didn't think she would need any more help, that Bud was going to do a few things for her, and that was all that was necessary.

Bud straightened up and became two inches taller. He passed the bread, suggested two pieces of pie, and filled her glass of water as if she were his partner. Mr. Tanner beamed to see his son in high favor, but Mrs. Tanner looked a little troubled for the minister. She thought things weren't just progressing as fast as they ought to between him and the teacher.

Bud, with Margaret's instructions, managed to make a very creditable bookcase out of the packing-box sawed in half, the pieces set side by side. She covered them deftly with green burlap left over from college days, like her other supplies, and then the two arranged the books. Bud was delighted over the prospect of reading some of the books, for they were not all school-books, by any means, and she had brought plenty of them to keep her from being lonesome on days when she longed to fly back to her home.

At last the work was done, and they stood back to survey

it. The books filled up every speck of space and overflowed to the three little hanging shelves over them; but they were all squeezed in at last except a pile of school-books that were saved out to take to the school-house. Margaret set a tiny vase on the top of one part of the packing-case and a small brass bowl on the top of the other, and Bud, after a knowing glance, scurried away for a few minutes and brought back a handful of gorgeous cactus blossoms to give the final touch.

"Gee!" he said, admiringly, looking around the room. "Gee! You wouldn't know it fer the same place!"

That evening after supper Margaret sat down to write a long letter home. She had written a brief letter, of course, the night before, but had been too weary to go into detail. The letter read:

> Dear Mother and Father, — I'm unpacked and settled at last in my room, and now I can't stand it another minute till I talk to you.
>
> Last night, of course, I was pretty homesick, things all looked so strange and new and different. I had known they would, but then I didn't realize at all how different they would be. But I'm not getting homesick already; don't think it. I'm not a bit sorry I came, or at least I sha'n't be when I get started in school. One of the scholars is Mrs. Tanner's son, and I like him. He's crude, of course, but he has a brain, and he's been helping me this afternoon. We made a bookcase for my books, and it looks fine. I wish you could see it. I covered it with the green burlap, and the books look real happy in smiling rows over on the other side of the room. Bud Tanner got me some wonderful cactus blossoms for my brass bowl. I wish I could send you some. They are gorgeous!
>
> But you will want me to tell about my arrival. Well, to begin with, I was late getting here *[Margaret had*

decided to leave out the incident of the desert altogether, for she knew by experience that her mother would suffer terrors all during her absence if she once heard of that wild adventure], which accounts for the lateness of the telegram I sent you. I hope its delay didn't make you worry any.

A very nice young man named Mr. Gardley piloted me to Mrs. Tanner's house and looked after my trunks for me. He is from the East. It was fortunate for me that he happened along, for he was most kind and gentlemanly and helpful. Tell Jane not to worry lest I'll fall in love with him; he doesn't live here. He belongs to a ranch or camp or something twenty-five miles away. She was so afraid I'd fall in love with an Arizona man and not come back home.

Mrs. Tanner is very kind and motherly according to her lights. She has given me the best room in the house, and she talks a blue streak. She has thin, brown hair turning gray, and she wears it in a funny little knob on the tip-top of her round head to correspond with the funny little tuft of hair on her husband's protruding chin. Her head is set on her neck like a clothes-pin, only she is squattier than a clothes-pin. She always wears her sleeves rolled up (at least so far she has) and she always bustles around noisily and apologizes for everything in the jolliest sort of way. I would like her, I guess, if it wasn't for the other boarder; but she has quite made up her mind that I shall like him, and I don't, of course, so she is a bit disappointed in me so far.

Mr. Tanner is very kind and funny, and looks something like a jack-knife with the blades half-open. He never disagrees with Mrs. Tanner, and I really believe he's in love with her yet, though they must have been married a good while. He calls her "Ma," and seems restless unless she's in the room. When she goes out to the kitchen to get some more soup or hash or bring in the pie, he shouts remarks at her all the time she's

gone, and she answers, utterly regardless of the conversation the rest of the family are carrying on. It's like
a phonograph wound up for the day.

Bud Tanner is about fourteen, and I like him. He's
well developed, strong, and almost handsome; at least
he would be if he were fixed up a little. He has fine,
dark eyes and a great shock of dark hair. He and I are
friends already. And so is the dog. The dog is a peach!
Excuse me, mother, but I just must use a little of the
dear old college slang somewhere, and your letters are
the only safety-valve, for I'm a schoolmarm now and
must talk "good and proper" all the time, you know.

The dog's name is Captain, and he looks the part.
He has constituted himself my bodyguard, and it's
going to be very nice having him. He's perfectly
devoted already. He's a great, big, fluffy fellow with
keen, intelligent eyes, sensitive ears, and a tail like a
spreading plume. You'd love him, I know. He has a
smile like the morning sunshine.

And now I come to the only other member of the
family, the boarder, and I hesitate to approach the topic,
because I have taken one of my violent and naughty
dislikes to him, and — awful thought — mother! father!
he's a minister! Yes, he's a *Presbyterian minister!* I know it
will make you feel dreadfully, and I thought some of
not telling you, but my conscience hurt me so I had
to. I just can't *bear* him, so there! Of course, I may get
over it, but I don't see how ever, for I can't think of anything that's more like him than *soft soap!* Oh yes, there
is one other word. Grandmother used to use it about
men she hadn't any use for, and that was "squash."
Mother, I can't help it, but he does seem something like
squash. One of that crook-necked, yellow kind with
warts all over it, and a great, big, splurgy vine behind
it to account for its being there at all. Insipid and
thready when it's cooked, you know, and has to have

a lot of salt and pepper and butter to make it go down at all. Now I've told you the worst, and I'll try to describe him and see what you think I'd better do about it. Oh, he isn't the regular minister here, or missionary—I guess they call *him*. *He's* located quite a distance off, and only comes once a month to preach here, and, anyhow, *he's* gone East now to take his wife to a hospital for an operation, and won't be back for a couple of months, perhaps, and this man isn't even taking his place. He's just here for his health or for fun or something, I guess. He says he had a large suburban church near New York, and had a nervous breakdown; but I've been wondering if he didn't make a mistake, and it wasn't the church had the nervous breakdown instead. He isn't very big nor very little; he's just insignificant. His hair is like wet straw, and his eyes like a fish's. His hand feels like a dead toad when you have to shake hands, which I'm thankful doesn't have to be done but once. He looks at you with a flat, sickening grin. He has an acquired double chin, acquired to make him look pompous, and he dresses stylishly and speaks of the inhabitants of this country with contempt. He wants to be very affable, and offers to take me to all sorts of places, but so far I've avoided him. I can't think how they ever came to let him be a minister—I really can't! And yet, I suppose it's all my horrid old prejudice, and father will be grieved and you will think I am perverse. But, really, I'm sure he's not one bit like father was when he was young. I never saw a minister like him. Perhaps I'll get over it. I do sometimes, you know, so don't begin to worry yet. I'll try real hard. I suppose he'll preach Sunday, and then, perhaps, his sermon will be grand and I'll forget how soft-soapy he looks and think only of his great thoughts.

But I know it will be a sort of comfort to you to know that there is a Presbyterian minister in the house with me, and I'll really try to like him if I can.

There's nothing to complain of in the board. It isn't luxurious, of course, but I didn't expect that. Everything is very plain, but Mrs. Tanner manages to make it taste good. She makes fine corn-bread, almost as good as yours — not quite.

My room is all lovely, now that I have covered its bareness with my own things, but it has one great thing that can't compare with anything at home, and that is its view. It is wonderful! I wish I could make you see it. There is a mountain at the end of it that has as many different garments as a queen. To-night, when sunset came, it grew filmy as if a gauze of many colors had dropped upon it and melted into it, and glowed and melted until it turned to slate blue under the wide, starred blue of the wonderful night sky, and all the dark about was velvet. Last night my mountain was all pink and silver, and I have seen it purple and rose. But you can't think the wideness of the sky, and I couldn't paint it for you with words. You must see it to understand. A great, wide, dark sapphire floor just simply ravished with stars like big jewels!

But I must stop and go to bed, for I find the air of this country makes me very sleepy, and my wicked little kerosene-lamp is smoking. I guess you would better send me my student-lamp, after all, for I'm surely going to need it.

Now I must turn out the light and say good night to my mountain, and then I will go to sleep thinking of you. Don't worry about the minister. I'm very polite to him, but I shall never — *no, never* — fall in love with *him* — tell Jane.

> Your loving little girl,
> Margaret

8

MARGARET had arranged with Bud to take her to the school-house the next morning, and he had promised to have a horse hitched up and ready at ten o'clock, as it seemed the school was a magnificent distance from her boarding-place. In fact, everything seemed to be located with a view to being as far from everywhere else as possible. Even the town was scattering and widespread and sparse.

When she came down to breakfast she was disappointed to find that Bud was not there, and she was obliged to suffer a breakfast tête-à-tête with West. By dint, however, of asking him questions instead of allowing him to take the initiative, she hurried through her breakfast quite successfully, acquiring a superficial knowledge of her fellow-boarder quite distant and satisfactory. She knew where he spent his college days and at what theological seminary he had prepared for the ministry. He had served three years in a prosperous church of a fat little suburb of New York, and was taking a winter off from his severe, strenuous pastoral labors to recuperate his strength, get a new stock of sermons ready, and possibly to write a book of some of his experiences. He flattened his weak, pink chin learnedly as he said this, and tried to look at her impressively. He said that he should probably take a large city church as his next pastorate when his health was fully recuperated. He had come out to study the West and enjoy its freedom, as he understood it was a good place to rest and do as you please unhampered by what people thought. He wanted to get as far away from churches and things clerical as possible. He felt it was due himself and his work that he should. He spoke of the people he had met in Arizona as a kind of tamed savages, and Mrs. Tanner, sitting behind her coffee-pot for a moment between bustles, heard his comments meekly and looked at him with awe. What a great man he must be, and how fortunate for the new teacher that he should be there when she came!

Margaret drew a breath of relief as she hurried away from the breakfast-table to her room. She was really anticipating the ride to the school with Bud. She liked boys, and Bud had taken her fancy. But when she came down-stairs with her hat and sweater on she found West standing out in front, holding the horse.

"Bud had to go in another direction, Miss Earle," he said, touching his hat gracefully, "and he has delegated to me the pleasant task of driving you to the school."

Dismay filled Margaret's soul, and rage with young Bud. He had deserted her and left her in the hands of the enemy! And she had thought he understood! Well, there was nothing for it but to go with this man, much as she disliked it. Her father's daughter could not be rude to a minister.

She climbed into the buckboard quickly to get the ceremony over, for her escort was inclined to be too officious about helping her in, and somehow she couldn't bear to have him touch her. Why was it that she felt so about him? Of course he must be a good man.

West made a serious mistake at the very outset of that ride. He took it for granted that all girls like flattery, and he proceeded to try it on Margaret. But Margaret did not enjoy being told how delighted he was to find that instead of the loud, bold "old maid" he had expected, she had turned out to be "so beautiful and young and altogether congenial"; and, coolly ignoring his compliments, she began a fire of questions again.

She asked about the country, because that was the most obvious topic of conversation. What plants were those that grew by the wayside? She found he knew greasewood from sage-brush, and that was about all. To some of her questions he hazarded answers that were absurd in the light of the explanations given her by Gardley two days before. However, she reflected that he had been in the country but a short time, and that he was by nature a man not interested in such topics. She tried religious matters, thinking that here at least they must have common interests. She asked him what he thought of Christianity in the West as compared with the East. Did he find these Western people more alive and awake to the things of the Kingdom?

West gave a startled look at the clear profile of the young woman beside him, thought he perceived that she was testing him on his clerical side, flattened his chin in his most learned, self-conscious manner, cleared his throat, and put on wisdom.

"Well, now, Miss Earle," he began, condescendingly, "I really don't know that I have thought much about the matter. Ah — you know I have been resting absolutely, and I really haven't had opportunity to study the situation out here in detail; but, on the whole, I should say that everything was decidedly primitive; yes — ah — I might say — ah — well, crude. Yes, *crude* in the extreme! Why, take it in this mission district. The missionary who is in charge seems to be teaching the most absurd of the old dogmas such as our forefathers used to teach. I haven't met him, of course. He is in the East with his wife for a time. I am told she had to go under some kind of an operation. I have never met him, and really don't care to do so; but to judge from all I hear, he is a most unfit man for a position of the kind. For example, he is teaching such exploded doctrines as the old view of the atonement, the infallibility of the Scriptures, the deity of Christ, belief in miracles, and the like. Of course, in one sense it really matters very little what the poor Indians believe, or what such people as the Tanners are taught. They have but little mind, and would scarcely know the difference; but you can readily see that with such a primitive, unenlightened man at the head of religious affairs, there could scarcely be much broadening and real religious growth. Ignorance, of course, holds sway out here. I fancy you will find that to be the case soon enough. What in the world ever led you to come to a field like this to labor? Surely there must have been many more congenial places open to such as you." He leaned forward and cast a sentimental glance at her, his eyes looking more "fishy" than ever.

"I came out here because I wanted to get acquainted with this great country, and because I thought there was an opportunity to do good," said Margaret, coldly. She did not care to discuss her own affairs with this man. "But, Mr. West, I don't know that I altogether understand you. Didn't you tell me that you were a Presbyterian minister?"

"I certainly did," he answered, complacently, as though he were honoring the whole great body of Presbyterians by making the statement.

"Well, then, what in the world did you mean? All Presbyterians, of course, believe in the infallibility of the Scriptures and the deity of Jesus — and the atonement!"

"Not necessarily," answered the young man, loftily. "You will find, my dear young lady, that there is a wide, growing feeling in our church in favor of a broader view. The younger men, and the great student body of our church, have thrown to the winds all their former beliefs and are ready to accept new light with open minds. The findings of science have opened up a vast store of knowledge, and all thinking men must acknowledge that the old dogmas are rapidly vanishing away. Your father doubtless still holds to the old faith, perhaps, and we must be lenient with the older men who have done the best they could with the light they had; but all younger, broad-minded men are coming to the new way of looking at things. We have had enough of the days of preaching hell-fire and damnation. We need a religion of love to man, and good works. You should read some of the books that have been written on this subject if you care to understand. I really think it would be worth your while. You look to me like a young woman with a mind. I have a few of the latest with me. I shall be glad to read and discuss them with you if you are interested."

"Thank you, Mr. West," said Margaret, coolly, though her eyes burned with battle. "I think I have probably read most of those books and discussed them with my father. He may be old, but he is not without 'light,' as you call it, and he always believed in knowing all that the other side was saying. He brought me up to look into these things for myself. And, anyhow, I should not care to read and discuss any of these subjects with a man who denies the deity of my Saviour and does not believe in the infallibility of the Bible. It seems to me you have nothing left—"

"Ah! Well—now—my dear young lady—you mustn't misjudge me! I should be sorry indeed to shake your faith, for an innocent faith is, of course, a most beautiful thing, even though it may be unfounded."

"Indeed, Mr. West, that would not be possible. You could not shake my faith in my Christ, because *I know Him.* If I had not ever felt His presence, nor been guided by His leading, such words might possibly trouble me, but having seen 'Him that is invisible,' *I know.*" Margaret's voice was steady and gentle. It was impossible for even that man not to be impressed by her words.

"Well, let us not quarrel about it," he said, indulgently, as to a little child. "I'm sure you have a very charming way of stating it, and I'm not sure that it is not a relief to find a woman of the old-fashioned type now and then. It really is man's place to look into these deeper questions, anyway. It is woman's sphere to live and love and make a happy home — "

His voice took on a sentimental purr, and Margaret was fairly boiling with rage at him; but she would not let her temper give way, especially when she was talking on the sacred theme of the Christ. She felt as if she must scream or jump out over the wheel and run away from this obnoxious man, but she knew she would do neither. She knew she would sit calmly through the expedition and somehow control that conversation. There was one relief, anyway. Her father would no longer expect respect and honor and liking toward a minister who denied the very life and foundation of his faith.

"It can't be possible that the school-house is so far from the town," she said, suddenly looking around at the widening desert in front of them. "Haven't you made some mistake?"

"Why, I thought we should have the pleasure of a little drive first," said West, with a cunning smile. "I was sure you would enjoy seeing the country before you get down to work, and I was not averse myself to a drive in such delightful company."

"I would like to go back to the school-house at once, please," said Margaret, decidedly, and there was that in her voice that caused the man to turn the horse around and head it toward the village.

"Why, yes, of course, if you prefer to see the school-house first, we can go back and look it over, and then, perhaps, you will like to ride a little farther," he said. "We have plenty of time. In fact, Mrs. Tanner told me she would not expect us home to dinner, and she put a very promising-looking basket of lunch under the seat for us in case we got hungry before we came back."

"Thank you," said Margaret, quite freezingly now. "I really do not care to drive this morning. I would like to see the

school-house, and then I must return to the house at once.
I have a great many things to do this morning."

Her manner at last penetrated even the thick skin of the
self-centered man, and he realized that he had gone a step
too far in his attentions. He set himself to undo the mischief,
hoping perhaps to melt her yet to take the all-day drive with
him. But she sat silent during the return to the village, answering his volubility only by yes or no when absolutely
necessary. She let him babble away about college life and tell
incidents of his late pastorate, at some of which he laughed
immoderately; but he could not even bring a smile to her dignified lips.

He hoped she would change her mind when they got to
the school building, and he even stooped to praise it in a kind
of contemptuous way as they drew up in front of the large
adobe building.

"I suppose you will want to go through the building," he
said, affably, producing the key from his pocket and putting
on a pleasant anticipatory smile, but Margaret shook her
head. She simply would not go into the building with that
man.

"It is not necessary," she said again, coldly. "I think I will
go home now, please." And he was forced to turn the horse
toward the Tanner house, crestfallen, and wonder why this
beautiful girl was so extremely hard to win. He flattered himself that he had always been able to interest any girl he chose.
It was really quite a bewildering type. But he would win her
yet.

He set her down silently at the Tanner door and drove off,
lunch-basket and all, into the wilderness, vexed that she was
so stubbornly unfriendly, and pondering how he might
break down the dignity wherewith she had surrounded herself. There would be a way and he would find it. There was
a stubbornness about that weak chin of his, when one observed it, and an ugliness in his pale-blue eye; or perhaps you
would call it a hardness.

9

SHE watched him furtively from her bedroom window, whither she had fled from Mrs. Tanner's exclamations. He wore his stylish derby tilted down over his left eye and slightly to one side in a most unministerial manner, showing too much of his straw-colored back hair, which rose in a cowlick at the point of contact with the hat, and he looked a small, mean creature as he drove off into the vast beauty of the plain. Margaret, in her indignation, could not help comparing him with the young man who had ridden away from the house two days before.

"And he to set up to be a minister of Christ's gospel and talk like that about the Bible and Christ!" Oh, what was the church of Christ coming to, to have ministers like that? How ever did he get into the ministry, anyway? Of course, she knew there were young men with honest doubts who sometimes slid through nowadays, but a mean little silly man like that? How ever did he get in? What a lot of ridiculous things he had said! He was one of those described in the Bible who "darken counsel with words." He was not worth noticing. And yet, what a lot of harm he could do in an unlearned community. Just see how Mrs. Tanner hung upon his words, as though they were law and gospel! How *could* she?

Margaret found herself trembling yet over the words he had spoken about Christ, the atonement, and the faith. They meant so much to her and to her mother and father. They were not mere empty words of tradition that she believed because she had been taught. She had lived her faith and proved it; and she could not help feeling it like a personal insult to have him speak so of her Saviour. She turned away and took her Bible to try and get a bit of calmness.

She fluttered the leaves for something — she could not just tell what — and her eye caught some of the verses that her father had marked for her before she left home for college, in the days when he was troubled for her going forth into the world of unbelief.

> As ye have therefore received Christ Jesus the Lord, so walk ye in him: Rooted and built up in him, and established in the faith, as ye have been taught, abounding therein with thanksgiving. Beware lest any man spoil you through philosophy and vain deceit, after the tradition of men, after the rudiments of the world, and not after Christ. For in him dwelleth all the fullness of the Godhead bodily. . . .

How the verses crowded upon one another, standing out clearly from the pages as she turned them, marked with her father's own hand in clear ink underlinings. It almost seemed as if God had looked ahead to these times and set these words down just for the encouragement of his troubled servants who couldn't understand why faith was growing dim. God knew about it, had known it would be, all this doubt, and had put words here just for troubled hearts to be comforted thereby.

> For I know whom I have believed *[How her heart echoed to that statement!]*, and am persuaded that he is able to

keep that which I have committed unto him against that day.

And on a little further:

> Nevertheless the foundation of God standeth sure, having this seal, The Lord knoweth them that are his.

There was a triumphant look to the words as she read them.

Then over in Ephesians her eye caught a verse that just seemed to fit that poor blind minister:

> Having the understanding darkened, being alienated from the life of God through the ignorance that is in them, because of the blindness of their heart.

And yet he was set to guide the feet of the blind into the way of life! And he had looked on her as one of the ignorant. Poor fellow! He couldn't know the Christ who was her Saviour or he never would have spoken in that way about Him. What could such a man preach? What was there left to preach, but empty words, when one rejected all these doctrines? Would she have to listen to a man like that Sunday after Sunday? Did the scholars in her school, and their parents, and the young man out at the camp, and his rough, simple-hearted companions have to listen to preaching from that man, when they listened to any? Her heart grew sick within her, and she knelt beside her bed for a strengthening word with the Christ who since her little childhood had been a very real presence in her life.

When she arose from her knees she heard the kitchen door slam down-stairs and the voice of Bud calling his mother. She went to her door and opened it, listening a moment, and then called the boy.

There was a dead silence for an instant after her voice was

heard, and then Bud appeared at the foot of the stairs, very frowning as to brow, and very surly as to tone:

"What d'ye want?"

It was plain that Bud was "sore."

"Bud" — Margaret's voice was sweet and a bit cool as she leaned over the railing and surveyed the boy; she hadn't yet got over her compulsory ride with that minister — "I wanted to ask you, please, next time you can't keep an appointment with me don't ask anybody else to take your place. I prefer to pick out my own companions. It was all right, of course, if you had to go somewhere else, but I could easily have gone alone or waited until another time. I'd rather not have you ask Mr. West to go anywhere with me again."

Bud's face was a study. It cleared suddenly and his jaw dropped in surprise; his eyes fairly danced with dawning comprehension and pleasure, and then his brow drew down ominously.

"I never ast him," he declared, vehemently. "He told me you wanted him to go, and fer me to get out of the way 'cause you didn't want to hurt my feelings. Didn't you say nothing to him about it at all this morning?"

"No, indeed!" said Margaret, with flashing eyes.

"Well, I just thought he was that kind of a guy. I told ma he was lying, but she said I didn't understand young ladies, and, of course, you didn't want me when there was a man, and especially a preacher, round. Some preacher he is! This 's the second time I've caught him lying. I think he's the limit. I just wish you'd see our missionary. If he was here he'd beat the dust out o' that poor stew. *He's* some man, he is. He's a regular man, *our missionary!* Just you wait till *he* gets back."

Margaret drew a breath of relief. Then the missionary was a real man, after all. Oh, for his return!

"Well, I'm certainly very glad it wasn't your fault, Bud. I didn't feel very happy to be turned off that way," said the teacher, smiling down upon the rough head of the boy.

"You bet it wasn't my fault!" said the boy, vigorously. "I

was sore's a pup at you, after you'd made a date and all, to
do like that; but I thought if you wanted to go with that guy
it was up to you."

"Well, I didn't and I don't. You'll please understand hereafter that I'd always rather have your company than his. How
about going down to the school-house some time to-day?
Have you time?"

"Didn't you go yet?" The boy's face looked as if he had
received a kingdom, and his voice had a ring of triumph.

"We drove down there, but I didn't care to go in without
you, so we came back."

"Wanta go now?" The boy's face fairly shone.

"I'd love to. I'll be ready in three minutes. Could we carry
some books down?"

"Sure! Oh—gee! That guy's got the buckboard. We'll have
to walk. Doggone him!"

"I shall enjoy a walk. I want to find out just how far it is,
for I shall have to walk every day, you know."

"No, you won't, neither, 'nless you wanta. I c'n always hitch
up."

"That 'll be very nice sometimes, but I'm afraid I'd get
spoiled if you babied me all the time that way. I'll be right
down."

They went out together into the sunshine and wideness
of the morning, and it seemed a new day had been created
since she got back from her ride with the minister. She looked
at the sturdy, honest-eyed boy beside her, and was glad to
have him for a companion.

Just in front of the school-house Margaret paused. "Oh,
I forgot! The key! Mr. West has the key in his pocket! We can't
get in, can we?"

"Aw, we don't need a key," said her escort. "Just you wait!"
And he whisked around to the back of the building, and in
about three minutes his shock head appeared at the window.
He threw the sash open and dropped out a wooden box.
"There!" he said, triumphantly, "you c'n climb up on that,

cantcha? Here, I'll holdya steady. Take holta my hand."

And so it was through the front window that the new teacher of the Ridge School first appeared on her future scene of action and surveyed her little kingdom.

Bud threw open the shutters, letting the view of the plains and the sunshine into the big, dusty room, and showed her the new blackboard with great pride.

"There's a whole box o' chalk up on the desk, too; 'ain't never been opened yet. Dad said that was your property. Want I should open it?"

"Why, yes, you might, and then we'll try the blackboard, won't we?"

Bud went to work gravely opening the chalk-box as if it were a small treasure-chest, and finally produced a long, smooth stick of chalk and handed it to her with shining eyes.

"You try it first, Bud," said the teacher, seeing his eagerness; and the boy went forward awesomely, as if it were a sacred precinct and he unworthy to intrude.

Shyly, awkwardly, with infinite painstaking, he wrote in a cramped hand, "William Budlong Tanner," and then, growing bolder, "Ashland, Arizona," with a big flourish underneath.

"Some class!" he said, standing back and regarding his handiwork with pride. "Say, I like the sound the chalk makes on it, don't you?"

"Yes, I do," said Margaret, heartily, "so smooth and business-like, isn't it? You'll enjoy doing examples in algebra on it, won't you?"

"Good night! Algebra! Me? No chance. I can't never get through the arithmetic. The last teacher said if he'd come back twenty years from now he'd still find me working compound interest."

"Well, we'll prove to that man that he wasn't much of a judge of boys," said Margaret, with a tilt of her chin and a glint of her teacher-mettle showing in her eyes. "If you're not in algebra before two months are over I'll miss my guess.

We'll get at it right away and show him."

Bud watched her, charmed. He was beginning to believe that almost anything she tried would come true.

"Now, Bud, suppose we get to work. I'd like to get acquainted with my class a little before Monday. Isn't it Monday school opens? I thought so. Well, suppose you give me the names of the scholars and I'll write them down, and that will help me to remember them. Where will you begin? Here, suppose you sit down in the front seat and tell me who sits there and a little bit about him, and I'll write the name down; and then you move to the next seat and tell me about the next one, and so on. Will you?"

"Sure!" said Bud, entering into the new game. "But it ain't a 'he' sits there. It's Susie Johnson. She's Bill Johnson's smallest girl. She has to sit front 'cause she giggles so much. She has yellow curls and she ducks her head down and snickers right out this way when anything funny happens in school." And Bud proceeded to duck and wriggle in perfect imitation of the small Susie.

Margaret saw the boy's power of imitation was remarkable, and laughed heartily at his burlesque. Then she turned and wrote "Susie Johnson" on the board in beautiful script.

Bud watched with admiration, saying softly under his breath; "Gee! that's great, that blackboard, ain't it?"

Amelia Schwartz came next. She was long and lank, with the buttons off the back of her dress, and hands and feet too large for her garments. Margaret could not help but see her in the clever pantomime the boy carried on. Next was Rosa Rogers, daughter of a wealthy cattleman, the pink-cheeked, blue-eyed beauty of the school, with all the boys at her feet and a perfect knowledge of her power over them. Bud didn't, of course, state it that way, but Margaret gathered as much from his simpering smile and the coy way he looked out of the corner of his eyes as he described her.

Down the long list of scholars he went, row after row, and when he came to the seats where the boys sat his tone changed. She could tell by the shading of his voice which boys were the ones to look out for.

Jed Brower, it appeared, was a name to conjure with. He could ride any horse that ever stood on four legs, he could outshoot most of the boys in the neighborhood, and he never allowed any teacher to tell him what to do. He was Texas Brower's only boy, and always had his own way. His father was on the school board. Jed Brower was held in awe, even while his methods were despised, by some of the younger boys. He was big and powerful, and nobody dared fool with him. Bud did not exactly warn Margaret that she must keep on the right side of Jed Brower, but he conveyed that impression without words. Margaret understood. She knew also that Tad Brooks, Larry Parker, Jim Long, and Dake Foster were merely henchmen of the worthy Jed, and not negligible quantities when taken by themselves. But over the name of Timothy Forbes — "Delicate Forbes," Bud explained was his nickname — the boy lingered with that loving inflection of admiration that a younger boy will sometimes have for a husky, courageous older lad. The second time Bud spoke of him he called him "Forbeszy," and Margaret perceived that here was Bud's model of manhood. Delicate Forbes could outshoot and outride even Jed Brower when he chose, and his courage with cattle was that of a man. Moreover, he was good to the younger boys and wasn't above pitching baseball with them when he had nothing better afoot. It became evident from the general description that Delicate Forbes was not called so from any lack of inches to his stature. He had a record of having licked every man teacher in the school, and beaten by guile every woman teacher they had had in six years. Bud was loyal to his admiration, yet it could be plainly seen that he felt Margaret's greatest hindrance in the school would be Delicate Forbes.

Margaret mentally underlined the names in her memory that belonged to the back seats in the first and second rows of desks, and went home praying that she might have wisdom and patience to deal with Jed Brower and Timothy Forbes, and through them to manage the rest of her school.

She surprised Bud at the dinner-table by handing him a neat diagram of the school-room desks with the correct names of all but three or four of the scholars written on them. Such a feat of memory raised her several notches in his estimation.

"Say, that's going some! Guess you won't forget nothing, no matter how much they try to make you."

10

THE minister did not appear until late in the evening, after Margaret had gone to her room, for which she was sincerely thankful. She could hear his voice, fretful and complaining, as he called loudly for Bud to take the horse. It appeared he had lost his way and wandered many miles out of the trail. He blamed the country for having no better trails, and the horse for not being able to find his way better. Mr. Tanner had gone to bed, but Mrs. Tanner bustled about and tried to comfort him.

"Now that's too bad! Dearie me! Bud oughta hev gone with you, so he ought. Bud! *Oh,* Bud, you 'ain't gonta sleep yet, hev you? Wake up and come down and take this horse to the barn."

But Bud declined to descend. He shouted some sleepy directions from his loft where he slept, and said the minister could look after his own horse, he "wasn't a gonta!" There was "plentya corn in the bin."

The minister grumbled his way to the barn, highly incensed at Bud, and disturbed the calm of the evening view of Margaret's mountain by his complaints when he returned.

He wasn't accustomed to handling horses, and he thought Bud might have stayed up and attended to it himself. Bud chuckled in his loft and stole down the back kitchen roof while the minister ate his late supper. Bud would never leave the old horse to that amateur's tender mercies, but he didn't intend to make it easy for the amateur. Margaret, from her window-seat watching the night in the darkness, saw Bud slip off the kitchen roof and run to the barn, and she smiled to herself. She liked that boy. He was going to be a good comrade.

The Sabbath morning dawned brilliantly, and to the homesick girl there suddenly came a sense of desolation on waking. A strange land was this, without church-bells or sense of Sabbath fitness. The mountain, it is true, greeted her with a holy light of gladness, but mountains are not dependent upon humankind for being in the spirit on the Lord's day. They are "continually praising Him." Margaret wondered how she was to get through this day, this dreary first Sabbath away from her home and her Sabbath-school class, and her dear old church with father preaching. She had been away, of course, a great many times before, but never to a churchless community. It was beginning to dawn upon her that that was what Ashland was — a churchless community. As she recalled the walk to the school and the ride through the village she had seen nothing that looked like a church, and all the talk had been of the missionary. They must have services of some sort, of course, and probably that flabby, fish-eyed man, her fellow-boarder, was to preach; but her heart turned sick at thought of listening to a man who had confessed to the unbeliefs that he had. Of course, he would likely know enough to keep such doubts to himself; but he had told her, and nothing he could say now would help or uplift her in the least.

She drew a deep sigh and looked at her watch. It was late. At home the early Sabbath-school bells would be ringing, and little girls in white, with bunches of late fall flowers for their teachers, and holding hands with their little brothers, would be hurrying down the street. Father was in his study, going over his morning sermon, and mother putting her little pearl pin in her collar, getting ready to go to her Bible class. Margaret decided it was time to get up and stop thinking of it all.

She put on a little white dress that she wore to church at home and hurried down to discover what the family plans were for the day, but found, to her dismay, that the atmosphere below-stairs was just like that of other days. Mr. Tanner sat tilted back in a dining-room chair, reading the weekly paper, Mrs. Tanner was bustling in with hot cornbread, Bud was on the front-door steps teasing the dog, and the minister came in with an air of weariness upon him, as if he quite intended taking it out on his companions that he had experienced a trying time on Saturday. He did not look in the least like a man who expected to preach in a few minutes. He declined to eat his egg because it was cooked too hard, and poor Mrs. Tanner had to try it twice before she succeeded in producing a soft-boiled egg to suit him. Only the radiant outline of the great mountain, which Margaret could see over the minister's head, looked peaceful and Sabbath-like.

"What time do you have service?" Margaret asked, as she rose from the table.

"Service?" It was Mr. Tanner who echoed her question as if he did not quite know what she meant.

Mrs. Tanner raised her eyes from her belated breakfast with a worried look, like a hen stretching her neck about to see what she ought to do next for the comfort of the chickens under her care. It was apparent that she had no comprehension of what the question meant. It was the minister who answered, condescendingly:

"Um! Ah! There is no church edifice here, you know, Miss Earle. The mission station is located some miles distant."

"I know," said Margaret, "but they surely have some religious service?"

"I really don't know," said the minister, loftily, as if it were something wholly beneath his notice.

"Then you are not going to preach this morning?" In spite of herself there was relief in her tone.

"Most certainly not," he replied, stiffly. "I came out here to rest, and I selected this place largely because it was so far from a church. I wanted to be where I should not be annoyed by requests to preach. Of course, ministers from the East would be a curiosity in these Western towns, and I should really get no rest at all if I had gone where my services would have been in constant demand. When I came out here I was in much the condition of our friend the minister of whom you have doubtless heard. He was starting on his vacation, and he said to a brother minister, with a smile of joy and relief, 'No preaching, no praying, no reading of the Bible for six whole weeks'!"

"Indeed!" said Margaret, freezingly. "No, I am not familiar with ministers of that sort." She turned with dismissal in her manner and appealed to Mrs. Tanner. "Then you really have no Sabbath service of any sort whatever in town?" There was something almost tragic in her face. She stood aghast at the prospect before her.

Mrs. Tanner's neck stretched up a little longer, and her lips dropped apart in her attempt to understand the situation. One would scarcely have been surprised to hear her say, "Cut-cut-cut-ca-daw-cut?" so fluttered did she seem.

Then up spoke Bud. "We gotta Sunday-school, ma!" There was pride of possession in Bud's tone, and a kind of triumph over the minister, albeit Bud had adjured Sunday-school since his early infancy. He was ready now, however, to be offered on the altar of Sunday-school, even, if that would please the new teacher — and spite the minister. "I'll take you ef you wanta go." He looked defiantly at the minister as he said it.

But at last Mrs. Tanner seemed to grasp what was the matter. "Why!—why!—why! You mean preaching service!" she clucked out. "Why, yes, Mr. West, wouldn't that be fine? You could preach for us. We could have it posted up at the saloon, and the crossings, and out a ways on both trails, and you'd have quite a crowd. They'd come from over to the camp, and up the cañon way, and round-abouts. They'd do you credit, they surely would, Mr. West. And you could have the school-house for a meeting-house. Pa, there, is one of the school board. There wouldn't be a bit of trouble—"

"Um! Ah! Mrs. Tanner, I assure you it's quite out of the question. I told you I was here for absolute rest. I couldn't think of preaching. Besides, it's against my principles to preach without remuneration. It's a wrong idea. The workman is worthy of his hire, you know, Mrs. Tanner, the Good Book says." Mr. West's tone took on a self-righteous inflection.

"Oh! Ef that's all, that 'u'd be all right!" she said, with relief. "You could take up a collection. The boys would be real generous. They always are when any show comes along. They'd appreciate it, you know, and I'd like fer Miss Earle here to hear you preach. It 'u'd be a real treat to her, her being a preacher's daughter and all." She turned to Margaret for support, but that young woman was talking to Bud. She had promptly closed with his offer to take her to Sunday-school, and now she hurried away to get ready, leaving Mrs. Tanner to make her clerical arrangements without aid.

The minister, meantime, looked after her doubtfully. Perhaps, after all, it would have been a good move to have preached. He might have impressed that difficult young woman better that way than any other, seeing she posed as being so interested in religious matters. He turned to Mrs. Tanner and began to ask questions about the feasibility of a church service. The word "collection" sounded good to him. He was not averse to replenishing his somewhat depleted treasury if it could be done so easily as that.

Meantime Margaret, up in her room, was wondering again how such a man as Mr. West ever got into the Christian ministry.

West was still endeavoring to impress the Tanners with the importance of his late charge in the East as Margaret came down-stairs. His pompous tones, raised to favor the deafness that he took for granted in Mr. Tanner, easily reached her ears.

"I couldn't, of course, think of doing it every Sunday, you understand. It wouldn't be fair to myself nor my work which I have just left; but, of course, if there were sufficient inducement I might consent to preach some Sunday before I leave."

Mrs. Tanner's little satisfied cluck was quite audible as the girl closed the front door and went out to the waiting Bud.

The Sunday-school was a desolate affair, presided over by an elderly and very illiterate man, who nursed his elbows and rubbed his chin meditatively between the slow questions which he read out of the lesson-leaf. The woman who usually taught the children was called away to nurse a sick neighbor, and the children were huddled together in a restless group. The singing was poor, and the whole of the exercises dreary, including the prayer. The few women present sat and stared in a kind of awe at the visitor, half belligerently, as if she were an intruder. Bud lingered outside the door and finally disappeared altogether, reappearing when the last hymn was sung. Altogether the new teacher felt exceedingly homesick as she wended her way back to the Tanners' beside Bud.

"What do you do with yourself on Sunday afternoons, Bud?" she asked, as soon as they were out of hearing of the rest of the group.

The boy turned wondering eyes toward her. "Do?" he repeated, puzzled. "Why, we pass the time away, like 'most any day. There ain't much difference."

A great desolation possessed her. No church! Worse than no minister! No Sabbath! What kind of a land was this to which she had come?

The boy beside her smelled of tobacco smoke. He had been off somewhere smoking while she was in the dreary little Sunday-school. She looked at his careless boy-face furtively as they walked along. He smoked, of course, like most boys of his age, probably, and he did a lot of other things he ought not to do. He had no interest in God or righteousness, and he did not take it for granted that the Sabbath was different from any other day. A sudden heart-sinking came upon her. What was the use of trying to do anything for such as he? Why not give it up now and go back where there was more promising material to work upon and where she would be welcome indeed? Of course, she had known things would be discouraging, but somehow it had seemed different from a distance. It all looked utterly hopeless now, and herself crazy to have thought she could do any good in a place like this.

And yet the place needed somebody! That pitiful little Sunday-school! How forlorn it all was! She was almost sorry she had gone. It gave her an unhappy feeling for the morrow, which was to be her first day of school.

Then, all suddenly, just as they were nearing the Tanner house, there came one riding down the street with all the glory of the radiant morning in his face, and a light in his eyes at seeing her that lifted away her desolation, for here at last was a friend!

She wondered at herself. An unknown stranger, and a self-confessed failure so far in his young life, and yet he seemed so good a sight to her amid these uncongenial surroundings!

THIS stranger of royal bearing, riding a rough Western pony as if it were decked with golden trappings, with his bright hair gleaming like Roman gold in the sun, and his blue-gray eyes looking into hers with the gladness of his youth; this one who had come to her out of the night-shadows of the wilderness and led her into safety! Yes, she was glad to see him.

He dismounted and greeted her, his wide hat in his hand, his eyes upon her face, and Bud stepped back, watching them in pleased surprise. This was the man who had shot all the lights out the night of the big riot in the saloon. He had also risked his life in a number of foolish ways at recent festal carouses. Bud would not have been a boy had he not admired the young man beyond measure; and his boy worship of the teacher yielded her to a fitting rival. He stepped behind and walked beside the pony, who was following his master meekly, as though he, too, were under the young man's charm.

"Oh, and this is my friend, William Tanner," spoke Margaret, turning toward the boy loyally. (Whatever good angel made her call him William? Bud's soul swelled with new dignity as he blushed and acknowledged the introduction by a grin.)

"Glad to know you, Will," said the new-comer, extending his hand in a hearty shake that warmed the boy's heart in a trice. "I'm glad Miss Earle has so good a protector. You'll have to look out for her. She's pretty plucky and is apt to stray around the wilderness by herself. It isn't safe, you know, boy, for such as her. Look after her, will you?"

"Right I will," said Bud, accepting the commission as if it were Heaven-sent, and thereafter walked behind the two with his head in the clouds. He felt that he understood this great hero of the plains and was one with him at heart. There could be no higher honor than to be the servitor of this man's lady. Bud did not stop to question how the new teacher became acquainted with the young rider of the plains. It was enough that both were young and handsome and seemed to belong together. He felt they were fitting friends.

The little procession walked down the road slowly, glad to prolong the way. The young man had brought her handkerchief, a filmy trifle of an excuse that she had dropped behind her chair at the bunk-house, where it had lain unnoticed till she was gone. He produced it from his inner pocket, as though it had been too precious to carry anywhere but over his heart, yet there was in his manner nothing presuming, not a hint of any intimacy other than their chance acquaintance of the wilderness would warrant. He did not look at her with any such look as West had given every time he spoke to her. She felt no desire to resent his glance when it rested upon her almost worshipfully, for there was respect and utmost humility in his look.

The men had sent gifts: some arrow-heads and a curiously fashioned vessel from the cañon of the cave-dwellers; some chips from the petrified forest; a fern with wonderful fronds, root and all; and a sheaf of strange, beautiful blossoms carefully wrapped in wet paper, and all fastened to the saddle. Margaret's face kindled with interest as he showed them to her one by one, and told her the history of each and a little message from the man who had sent it. Mom Wallis, too, had baked a queer little cake and sent it. The young man's face was tender as he spoke of it. The girl saw that he knew what her coming had meant to Mom Wallis. Her memory went quickly back to those few words the morning she had wakened in the bunk-house and found the withered old woman watching her with tears in her eyes. Poor Mom Wallis, with her pretty girlhood all behind her and such a blank, dull future ahead! Poor, tired, ill-used, worn-out Mom Wallis! Margaret's heart went out to her.

"They want to know," said the young man, half hesitatingly, "if some time, when you get settled and have time, you would come to them again and sing? I tried to make them understand, of course, that you would be busy, your time taken with other friends and your work, and you would not want to come; but they wanted me to tell you they never enjoyed anything so much in years as your singing. Why, I heard Long Jim singing 'Old Folks at Home' this morning when he was saddling his horse. And it's made a difference. The men sort of want to straighten up the bunk-house. Jasper made a new chair yesterday. He said it would do when you came again." Gardley laughed diffidently, as if he knew their hopes were all in vain.

But Margaret looked up with sympathy in her face. "I'll come! Of course I'll come some time," she said, eagerly. "I'll come as soon as I can arrange it. You tell them we'll have more than one concert yet."

The young man's face lit up with a quick appreciation, and the flash of his eyes as he looked at her would have told any onlooker that he felt here was a girl in a thousand, a girl with an angel spirit, if ever such a one walked the earth.

Now it happened that Rev. Frederick West was walking impatiently up and down in front of the Tanner residence, looking down the road about that time. He had spent the morning in looking over the small bundle of "show sermons" he had brought with him in case of emergency, and had about decided to accede to Mrs. Tanner's request and preach in Ashland before he left. This decision had put him in so self-satisfied a mood that he was eager to announce it before his fellow-boarder. Moreover, he was hungry, and he could not understand why that impudent boy and that coquettish young woman should remain away at Sunday-school such an interminable time.

Mrs. Tanner was frying chicken. He could smell it every time he took a turn toward the house. It really was ridiculous that they should keep dinner waiting this way. He took one more turn and began to think over the sermon he had decided to preach. He was just recalling a particularly eloquent passage when he happened to look down the road once more, and there they were, almost upon him! But Bud was no longer walking with the maiden. She had acquired a new escort, a man of broad shoulders and fine height. Where had he seen that fellow before? He watched them as they came up, his small, pale eyes narrowing under their yellow lashes with a glint of slyness, like some mean little animal that meant to take advantage of its prey. It was wonderful how many different things that man could look like for a person as insignificant as he really was!

Well, he saw the look between the man and maiden; the look of sympathy and admiration and a fine trust that is not founded on mere outward show, but has found some hidden fineness of the soul. Not that the reverend gentleman understood that, however. He had no fineness of soul himself. His mind had been too thoroughly taken up with himself all his life for him to have cultivated any.

Simultaneous with the look came his recognition of the man or, at least, of where he had last seen him, and his little soul rejoiced at the advantage he instantly recognized.

He drew himself up importantly, flattened his chin upward until his lower lip protruded in a pink roll across his mouth, drew down his yellow brows in a frown of displeasure, and came forward mentor-like to meet the little party as it neared the house. He had the air of coming to investigate and possibly oust the stranger, and he looked at him keenly, critically, offensively, as if he had the right to protect the lady. They might have been a pair of naughty children come back from a forbidden frolic, from the way he surveyed them. But the beauty of it was that neither of them saw him, being occupied with each other, until they were fairly upon him. Then, there he stood offensively, as if he were a great power to be reckoned with.

"Well, well, well, Miss Margaret, you have got home at last!" he said, pompously and condescendingly, and then he looked into the eyes of her companion as if demanding an explanation of *his* presence there.

Margaret drew herself up haughtily. His use of her Christian name in that familiar tone annoyed her exceedingly. Her eyes flashed indignantly, but the whole of it was lost unless Bud saw it, for Gardley had faced his would-be adversary with a keen, surprised scrutiny, and was looking him over coolly. There was that in the young man's eye that made the eye of Frederick West quail before him. It was only an instant the two stood challenging each other, but in that short time each knew and marked the other for an enemy. Only a brief instant and then Gardley turned to Margaret, and before she had time to think what to say, he asked:

"Is this man a friend of yours, Miss *Earle?*" with marked emphasis on the last word.

"No," said Margaret, coolly, "not a friend—a boarder in the house." Then most formally, "Mr. West, my *friend* Mr. Gardley."

If the minister had not been possessed of the skin of a rhinoceros he would have understood himself to be dismissed at that; but he was not a man accustomed to accepting dismissal, as his recent church in New York State might have testified. He stood his ground, his chin flatter than ever, his little eyes mere slits of condemnation. He did not acknowledge the introduction by so much as the inclination of his head. His hands were clasped behind his back, and his whole attitude was one of righteous belligerence.

Gardley gazed steadily at him for a moment, a look of mingled contempt and amusement gradually growing upon his face. Then he turned away as if the man were too small to notice.

"You will come in and take dinner with me?" asked Margaret, eagerly. "I want to send a small package to Mrs. Wallis if you will be so good as to take it with you."

"I'm sorry I can't stay to dinner, but I have an errand in another direction and at some distance. I am returning this way, however, and, if I may, will call and get the package toward evening."

Margaret's eyes spoke her welcome, and with a few formal words the young man sprang on his horse, said, "So long, Will!" to Bud, and, ignoring the minister, rode away.

They watched him for an instant, for, indeed, he was a goodly sight upon a horse, riding as if he and the horse were utterly one in spirit; then Margaret turned quickly to go into the house.

"Um! Ah! Miss Margaret!" began the minister, with a commandatory gesture for her to stop.

Margaret was the picture of haughtiness as she turned and said, "Miss *Earle,* if you please!"

"Um! Ah! Why, certainly, Miss — ah — *Earle,* if you wish it. Will you kindly remain here for a moment? I wish to speak with you. Bud, you may go on."

"I'll go when I like, and it's none of your business!" muttered Bud, ominously, under his breath. He looked at Margaret to see if she wished him to go. He had an idea that this might be one of the times when he was to look after her.

She smiled at him understandingly. "William may remain, Mr. West," she said, sweetly. "Anything you have to say to me can surely be said in his presence," and she laid her hand lightly on Bud's sleeve.

Bud looked down at the hand proudly and grew inches taller enjoying the minister's frown.

"Um! Ah!" said West, unabashed. "Well, I merely wished to warn you concerning the character of that person who has just left us. He is really not a proper companion for you. Indeed, I may say he is quite the contrary, and that to my personal knowledge—"

"He's as good as you are and better!" growled Bud, ominously.

"Be quiet, boy! I wasn't speaking to you!" said West, as if he were addressing a slave. "If I hear another word from your lips I shall report it to your father!"

"Go 's far 's you like and see how much I care!" taunted Bud, but was stopped by Margaret's gentle pressure on his arm.

"Mr. West, I thought I made you understand that Mr. Gardley is my friend."

"Um! Ah! Miss Earle, then all I have to say is that you have formed a most unwise friendship, and should let it proceed no further. Why, my dear young lady, if you knew all there is to know about him you would not think of speaking to that young man."

"Indeed! Mr. West, I suppose that might be true of a good many people, might it not, *if we knew all there is to know about them?* Nobody but God could very well get along with some of us."

"But, my dear young lady, you don't understand. This young person is nothing but a common ruffian, a gambler, in fact, and an habitué at the saloons. I have seen him myself sitting in a saloon at a very late hour playing with a vile, dirty pack of cards, and in the company of a lot of low-down creatures—"

"May I ask how you came to be in a saloon at that hour, Mr. West?" There was a gleam of mischief in the girl's eyes, and her mouth looked as if she were going to laugh, but she controlled it.

The minister turned very red indeed. "Well, I — ah — I had been called from my bed by shouts and the report of a pistol. There was a fight going on in the room adjoining the bar, and I didn't know but my assistance might be needed!" (At this juncture Bud uttered a sort of snort and, placing his hands over his heart, ducked down as if a sudden pain had seized him.) "But imagine my pain and astonishment when I was informed that the drunken brawl I was witnessing was but a nightly and common occurrence. I may say I remained for a few minutes, partly out of curiosity, as I wished to see all kinds of life in this new world for the sake of a book I am thinking of writing. I therefore took careful note of the persons present, and was thus able to identify the person who has just ridden away as one of the chief factors in that evening's entertainment. He was, in fact, the man who, when he had pocketed all the money on the gaming-table, arose and, taking out his pistol, shot out the lights in the room, a most dangerous and irregular proceeding — "

"Yes, and you came within an ace of being shot, pa says. The Kid's a dead shot, he is, and you were right in the way. Served you right for going where you had no business!"

"I did not remain longer in that place, as you may imagine," went on West, ignoring Bud, "for I found it was no place for a — for — a — ah — minister of the gospel; but I remained long enough to hear from the lips of this person with whom you have just been walking some of the most terrible language my ears have ever been permitted to — ah — witness!"

But Margaret had heard all that she intended to listen to on that subject. With decided tone she interrupted the voluble speaker, who was evidently enjoying his own eloquence.

"Mr. West, I think you have said all that it is necessary to say. There are still some things about Mr. Gardley that you evidently do not know, but I think you are in a fair way to learn them if you stay in this part of the country long. William, isn't that your mother calling us to dinner? Let us go in; I'm hungry."

Bud followed her up the walk with a triumphant wink at the discomfited minister, and they disappeared into the house; but when Margaret went up to her room and took off her hat in front of the little warped looking-glass there were angry tears in her eyes. She never felt like crying in her life. Chagrin and anger and disappointment were all struggling in her soul, yet she must not cry, for dinner would be ready and she must go down. Never should that mean little meddling man see that his words had pierced her soul.

For, angry as she was at the minister, much as she loathed his petty, jealous nature and saw through his tale-bearing, something yet told her that his picture of young Gardley's wildness was probably true, and her soul sank within her at the thought. It was just what had come in shadowy, instinctive fear to her heart when he had hinted at his being a "roughneck," yet to have it put baldly into words by an enemy hurt her deeply, and she looked at herself in the glass half frightened. "Margaret Earle, have you come out to the wilderness to lose your heart to the first handsome sower of wild oats that you meet?" her true eyes asked her face in the glass, and Margaret Earle's heart turned sad at the question and shrank back. Then she dropped upon her knees beside her gay little rocking-chair and buried her face in its flowered cushions and cried to her Father in heaven:

"Oh, my Father, let me not be weak, but with all my heart I cry to Thee to save this young, strong, courageous life and not let it be a failure. Help him to find Thee and serve Thee, and if his life has been all wrong—and I suppose it has—oh, make it right for Jesus' sake! If there is anything that I can do to help, show me how, and don't let me make mistakes. Oh, Jesus, Thy power is great. Let this young man feel it and yield himself to it."

She remained silently praying for a moment more, putting her whole soul into the prayer and knowing that she had been called thus to pray for him until her prayer was answered.

She came down to dinner a few minutes later with a calm, serene face, on which was no hint of her recent emotion, and she managed to keep the table conversation wholly in her own hands, telling Mr. Tanner about her home town and her father and mother. When the meal was finished the minister had no excuse to think that the new teacher was careless about her friends and associates, and he was well informed about the high principles of her family.

But West had retired into a sulky mood and uttered not a word except to ask for more chicken and coffee and a second helping of pie. It was, perhaps, during that dinner that he decided it would be best for him to preach in Ashland on the following Sunday. The young lady could be properly impressed with his dignity in no other way.

12

WHEN Lance Gardley came back to the Tanners' the sun was preparing the glory of its evening setting, and the mountain was robed in all its rosiest veils.

Margaret was waiting for him, with the dog Captain beside her, wandering back and forth in the unfenced dooryard and watching her mountain. It was a relief to her to find that the minister occupied a room on the first floor in a kind of ell on the opposite side of the house from her own room and her mountain. He had not been visible that afternoon, and with Captain by her side and Bud on the front-door step reading *The Sky Pilot* she felt comparatively safe. She had read to Bud for an hour and a half, and he was thoroughly interested in the story; but she was sure he would keep the minister away at all costs. As for Captain, he and the minister were sworn enemies by this time. He growled every time West came near or spoke to her.

She made a picture standing with her hand on Captain's shaggy, noble head, the lace of her sleeve falling back from the white arm, her other hand raised to shade her face as she looked away to the glorified mountain, a slim, white figure looking wistfully off at the sunset. The young man took off his hat and rode his horse more softly, as if in the presence of the holy.

The dog lifted one ear, and a tremor passed through his frame as the rider drew near; otherwise he did not stir from his position; but it was enough. The girl turned, on the alert at once, and met him with a smile, and the young man looked at her as if an angel had deigned to smile upon him. There was a humility in his fine face that sat well with the courage written there, and smoothed away all hardness for the time, so that the girl, looking at him in the light of the revelations of the morning, could hardly believe it had been true, yet an inner fineness of perception taught her that it was.

The young man dismounted and left his horse standing quietly by the roadside. He would not stay, he said, yet lingered by her side, talking for a few minutes, watching the sunset and pointing out its changes.

She gave him the little package for Mom Wallis. There was a simple lace collar in a little white box, and a tiny leather-bound book done in russet suède with gold lettering.

"Tell her to wear the collar and think of me whenever she dresses up."

"I'm afraid that 'll never be, then," said the young man, with a pitying smile. "Mom Wallis never dresses up."

"Tell her I said she must dress up evenings for supper, and I'll make her another one to change with that and bring it when I come."

He smiled upon her again, that wondering, almost worshipful smile, as if he wondered if she were real, after all, so different did she seem from his idea of girls.

"And the little book," she went on, apologetically; "I suppose it was foolish to send it, but something she said made me think of some of the lines in the poem. I've marked them for her. She reads, doesn't she?"

"A little, I think. I see her now and then read the papers that Pop brings home with him. I don't fancy her literary range is very wide, however."

"Of course, I suppose it is ridiculous! And maybe she'll not understand any of it; but tell her I sent her a message. She must see if she can find it in the poem. Perhaps you can explain it to her. It's Browning's 'Rabbi Ben Ezra.' You know it, don't you?"

"I'm afraid not. I was intent on other things about the time when I was supposed to be giving my attention to Browning, or I wouldn't be what I am to-day, I suppose. But I'll do my best with what wits I have. What's it about? Couldn't you give me a pointer or two?"

"It's the one beginning:

> *Grow old along with me!*
> *The best is yet to be,*
> *The last of life, for which the first was made:*
> *Our times are in His hand*
> *Who saith, 'A whole I planned,*
> *Youth shows but half; trust God: see all, nor*
> *be afraid!' "*

He looked down at her still with that wondering smile. "Grow old along with you!" he said, gravely, and then sighed. "You don't look as if you ever would grow old."

"That's it," she said, eagerly. "That's the whole idea. We don't ever grow old and get done with it all, we just go on to bigger things, wiser and better and more beautiful, till we come to understand and be a part of the whole great plan of God!"

He did not attempt an answer, nor did he smile now, but just looked at her with that deeply quizzical, grave look as if his soul were turning over the matter seriously. She held her peace and waited, unable to find the right word to speak. Then he turned and looked off, an infinite regret growing in his face.

"That makes living a different thing from the way most

people take it," he said, at last, and his tone showed that he was considering it deeply.

"Does it?" she said, softly, and looked with him toward the sunset, still half seeing his quiet profile against the light. At last it came to her that she must speak. Half fearfully she began: "I've been thinking about what you said on the ride. You said you didn't make good. I—wish you would. I—I'm sure you could—"

She looked up wistfully and saw the gentleness come into his face as if the fountain of his soul, long sealed, had broken up, and as if he saw a possibility before him for the first time through the words she had spoken.

At last he turned to her with that wondering smile again. "Why should you care?" he asked. The words would have sounded harsh if his tone had not been so gentle.

Margaret hesitated for an answer. "I don't know how to tell it," she said, slowly. "There's another verse, a few lines more in that poem, perhaps you know them?—

> 'All I never could be, All, men ignored in me,
> This I was worth to God, whose wheel the pitcher shaped.'

I want it because—well, perhaps because I feel you are worth all that to God. I would like to see you be that."

He looked down at her again, and was still so long that she felt she had failed miserably.

"I hope you will excuse my speaking," she added. "I— It seems there are so many grand possibilities in life, and for you—I couldn't bear to have you say you hadn't made good, as if it were all over."

"I'm glad you spoke," he said, quickly. "I guess perhaps I have been all kinds of a fool. You have made me feel how many kinds I have been."

"Oh no!" she protested.

"You don't know what I have been," he said, sadly, and

then with sudden conviction, as if he read her thoughts: "You *do* know! That prig of a parson has told you! Well, it's just as well you should know. It's right!"

A wave of misery passed over his face and erased all its brightness and hope. Even the gentleness was gone. He looked haggard and drawn with hopelessness all in a moment.

"Do you think it would matter to me — *anything* that man would say?" she protested, all her woman's heart going out in pity.

"But it was true, all he said, probably, and more — "

"It doesn't matter," she said, eagerly. "The other is true, too. Just as the poem says, 'All that man ignores in you, just that you are worth to God!' And you *can* be what He meant you to be. I have been praying all the afternoon that He would help you to be."

"Have you?" he said, and his eyes lit up again as if the altar-fires of hope were burning once more. "Have you? I thank you."

"You came to me when I was lost in the wilderness," she said, shyly. "I wanted to help *you* back — if — I might."

"You will help — you have!" he said, earnestly. "And I was far enough off the trail, too, but if there's any way to get back I'll get there." He grasped her hand and held it for a second. "Keep up that praying," he said. "I'll see what can be done."

Margaret looked up. "Oh, I'm so glad, so glad!"

He looked reverently into her eyes, all the manhood in him stirred to higher, better things. Then, suddenly, as they stood together, a sound smote their ears as from another world.

"Um! Ah! — "

The minister stood within the doorway, barred by Bud in scowling defiance, and guarded by Cap, who gave an answering growl.

Gardley and Margaret looked at each other and smiled, then turned and walked slowly down to where the pony stood. They did not wish to talk here in that alien presence. Indeed, it seemed that more words were not needed — they would be a desecration.

So he rode away into the sunset once more with just another look and a handclasp, and she turned, strangely happy at heart, to go back to her dull surroundings and her uncongenial company.

"Come, William, let's have a praise service," she said, brightly, pausing at the doorway, but ignoring the scowling minister.

"A praise service! What's a praise service?" asked the wondering Bud, shoving over to let her sit down beside him.

She sat with her back to West, and Cap came and lay at her feet with the white of one eye on the minister and a growl ready to gleam between his teeth any minute. There was just no way for the minister to get out unless he jumped over them or went out the back door; but the people in the doorway had the advantage of not having to look at him, and he couldn't very well dominate the conversation standing so behind them.

"Why, a praise service is a service of song and gladness, of course. You sing, don't you? Of course. Well, what shall we sing? Do you know this?" And she broke softly into song:

> *"When peace like a river attendeth my way;*
> *When sorrows like sea-billows roll;*
> *Whatever my lot Thou hast taught me to say,*
> *It is well, it is well with my soul."*

Bud did not know the song, but he did not intend to be balked with the minister standing right behind him, ready, no doubt, to jump in and take the precedence; so he growled away at a note in the bass, turning it over and over and trying to make it fit, like a dog gnawing at a bare bone; but he managed to keep time and make it sound a little like singing.

The dusk was falling fast as they finished the last verse, Margaret singing the words clear and distinct, Bud growling unintelligibly and snatching at words he had never heard before. Once more Margaret sang:

> *"Abide with me; fast falls the eventide;*
> *The darkness deepens; Lord, with me abide!*
> *When other refuge fails and comforts flee,*
> *Help of the helpless, oh, abide with me!"*

Out on the lonely trail wending his way toward the purple mountain—the silent way to the bunk-house at the camp—in that clear air where sound travels a long distance the traveler heard the song, and something thrilled his soul. A chord that never had been touched in him before was vibrating, and its echoes would be heard through all his life.

On and on sang Margaret, just because she could not bear to stop and hear the commonplace talk which would be about her. Song after song thrilled through the night's wideness. The stars came out in thick clusters. Father Tanner had long ago dropped his weekly paper and tilted his chair back against the wall, with his eyes half closed to listen, and his wife had settled down comfortably on the carpet sofa, with her hands nicely folded in her lap, as if she were at church. The minister, after silently surveying the situation for a song or two, attempted to join his voice to the chorus. He had a voice like a cross-cut saw, but he didn't do much harm in the background that way, though Cap did growl now and then, as if it put his nerves on edge. And by and by Mr. Tanner quavered in with a note or two.

Finally Margaret sang:

> *"Sun of my soul, Thou Saviour dear,*
> *It is not night if Thou art near,*
> *Oh, may no earth-born cloud arise*
> *To hide Thee from Thy servant's eyes."*

During this hymn the minister had slipped out the back door and gone around to the front of the house. He could not stand being in the background any longer; but as the last note died away Margaret arose and, bidding Bud good night, slipped up to her room.

There, presently, beside her darkened window, with her face toward the mountain, she knelt to pray for the wanderer who was trying to find his way out of the wilderness.

MONDAY morning found Margaret at the school-house nerved for her new task.

One by one the scholars trooped in, shyly or half defiantly, hung their hats on the hooks, put their dinner-pails on the shelf, looked furtively at her, and sank into their accustomed seats; that is, the seats they had occupied during the last term of school. The big boys remained outside until Bud, acting under instructions from Margaret — after she had been carefully taught the ways of the school by Bud himself — rang the big bell. Even then they entered reluctantly and as if it were a great condescension that they came at all, Jed and "Delicate" coming in last, with scarcely a casual glance toward the teacher's desk, as if she were a mere fraction in the scheme of the school. She did not need to be told which was Timothy and which was Jed. Bud's description had been perfect. Her heart, by the way, instantly went out to Timothy. Jed was another proposition. He had thick, overhanging eyebrows, and a mouth that loved to make trouble and laugh over it. He was going to be hard to conquer. She wasn't sure the conquering would be interesting, either.

Margaret stood by the desk, watching them all with a

pleasant smile. She did not frown at the unnecessary shuffling of feet nor the loud remarks of the boys as they settled into their seats. She just stood and watched them interestedly, as though her time had not yet come.

Jed and Timothy were carrying on a rumbling conversation. Even after they took their seats they kept it up. It was no part of their plan to let the teacher suppose they saw her or minded her in the least. They were the dominating influences in that school, and they wanted her to know it, right at the start; then a lot of trouble would be saved. If they didn't like her and couldn't manage her they didn't intend she should stay, and she might as well understand that at once.

Margaret understood it fully. Yet she stood quietly and watched them with a look of deep interest on her face and a light almost of mischief in her eyes, while Bud grew redder and redder over the way his two idols were treating the new teacher. One by one the school became aware of the twinkle in the teacher's eyes, and grew silent to watch, and one by one they began to smile over the coming scene when Jed and Timothy should discover it, and, worst of all, find out that it was actually directed against them. They would expect severity, or fear, or a desire to placate; but a twinkle—it was more than the school could decide what would happen under such circumstances. No one in that room would ever dare to laugh at either of those two boys. But the teacher was almost laughing now, and the twinkle had taken the rest of the room into the secret, while she waited amusedly until the two should finish the conversation.

The room grew suddenly deathly still, except for the whispered growls of Jed and Timothy, and still the silence deepened, until the two young giants themselves perceived that it was time to look up and take account of stock.

The perspiration by this time was rolling down the back of Bud's neck. He was about the only one in the room who was not on a broad grin, and he was wretched. What a fearful mistake the new teacher was making right at the start!

She was antagonizing the two boys who held the whole school in their hands. There was no telling what they wouldn't do to her now. And he would have to stand up for her. Yes, no matter what they did, he would stand up for her! Even though he lost his best friends, he must be loyal to her; but the strain was terrible! He did not dare to look at them, but fastened his eyes upon Margaret, as if keeping them glued there was his only hope. Then suddenly he saw her face break into one of the sweetest, merriest'smiles he ever witnessed, with not one single hint of reproach or offended dignity in it, just a smile of comradeship, understanding, and pleasure in the meeting; and it was directed to the two seats where Jed and Timothy sat.

With wonder he turned toward the two big boys, and saw, to his amazement, an answering smile upon their faces; reluctant, 'tis true, half sheepish at first, but a smile with lifted eyebrows of astonishment and real enjoyment of the joke.

A little ripple of approval went round in half-breathed syllables, but Margaret gave no time for any restlessness to start. She spoke at once, in her pleasantest partnership tone, such as she had used to Bud when she asked him to help her build her book-case. So she spoke now to that school, and each one felt she was speaking just to him especially, and felt a leaping response in his soul. Here, at least, was something new and interesting, a new kind of teacher. They kept silence to listen.

"Oh, I'm not going to make a speech now," she said, and her voice sounded glad to them all. "I'll wait till we know one another before I do that. I just want to say how do you do to you, and tell you how glad I am to be here. I hope we shall like one another immensely and have a great many good times together. But we've got to get acquainted first, of course, and perhaps we'd better give most of the time to that to-day. First, suppose we sing something. What shall it be? What do you sing?"

Little Susan Johnson, by virtue of having seen the teacher

at Sunday-school, made bold to raise her hand and suggest, "Thar-thpangle Banner, pleath!" And so they tried it; but when Margaret found that only a few seemed to know the words, she said, "Wait!" Lifting her arm with a pretty, imperative gesture, and taking a piece of chalk from the box on her desk, she went to the new blackboard that stretched its shining black length around the room.

The school was breathlessly watching the graceful movement of the beautiful hand and arm over the smooth surface, leaving behind it the clear, perfect script. Such wonderful writing they had never seen; such perfect, easy curves and twirls. Every eye in the room was fastened on her, every breath was held as they watched and spelled out the words one by one.

"Gee!" said Bud, softly, under his breath, nor knew that he had spoken, but no one else moved.

"Now," she said, "let us sing," and when they started off again Margaret's strong, clear soprano leading, every voice in the room growled out the words and tried to get in step with the tune.

They had gone thus through two verses when Jed seemed to think it was about time to start something. Things were going altogether too smoothly for an untried teacher, if she *was* handsome and unabashed. If they went on like this the scholars would lose all respect for him. So, being quite able to sing a clear tenor, he nevertheless puckered his lips impertinently, drew his brows in an ominous frown, and began to whistle a somewhat erratic accompaniment to the song. He watched the teacher closely, expecting to see the color flame in her cheeks, the anger flash in her eyes; he had tried this trick on other teachers and it always worked. He gave the wink to Timothy, and he too left off his glorious bass and began to whistle.

But instead of the anger and annoyance they expected, Margaret turned appreciative eyes toward the two back seats, nodding her head a trifle and smiling with her eyes as she sang; and when the verse was done she held up her hand for silence and said:

"Why, boys, that's beautiful! Let's try that verse once more, and you two whistle the accompaniment a little stronger in the chorus; or how would it do if you just came in on the chorus? I believe that would be more effective. Let's try the first verse that way; you boys sing during the verse and then whistle the chorus just as you did now. We really need your voices in the verse part, they are so strong and splendid. Let's try it now." And she started off again, the two big astonished fellows meekly doing as they were told, and really the effect was beautiful. What was their surprise when the whole song was finished to have her say, "Now everybody whistle the chorus softly," and then pucker up her own soft lips to join in. That completely finished the whistling stunt. Jed realized that it would never work again, not while she was here, for she had turned the joke into beauty and made them all enjoy it. It hadn't annoyed her in the least.

Somehow by that time they were all ready for anything she had to suggest, and they watched again breathlessly as she wrote another song on the blackboard, taking the other side of the room for it, and this time a hymn — "I Need Thee Every Hour."

When they began to sing it, however, Margaret found the tune went slowly, uncertainly.

"Oh, how we need a piano!" she exclaimed. "I wonder if we can't get up an entertainment and raise money to buy one. How many will help?"

Every hand in the place went up, Jed's and Timothy's last and only a little way, but she noted with triumph that they went up.

"All right; we'll do it! Now let's sing that verse correctly." And she began to sing again, while they all joined anxiously in, really trying to do their best.

The instant the last verse died away, Margaret's voice took their attention.

"Two years ago in Boston two young men, who belonged to a little group of Christian workers who were going around from place to place holding meetings, sat talking together in their room in the hotel one evening."

There was instant quiet, a kind of a breathless quiet. This was not like the beginning of any lesson any other teacher had ever given them. Every eye was fixed on her.

"They had been talking over the work of the day, and finally one of them suggested that they choose a Bible verse for the whole year —"

There was a movement of impatience from one back seat, as if Jed had scented an incipient sermon, but the teacher's voice went steadily on:

"They talked it over, and at last they settled on 2 Timothy 2:15. They made up their minds to use it on every possible occasion. It was time to go to bed, so the man whose room adjoined got up and, instead of saying good night, he said, 'Well, 2 Timothy 2:15,' and went to his room. Pretty soon, when he put out his light, he knocked on the wall and shouted '2 Timothy 2:15,' and the other man responded, heartily, 'All right, 2 Timothy 2:15.' The next morning when they wrote their letters each of them wrote '2 Timothy 2:15' on the lower left-hand corner of the envelope, and sent out a great handful of letters to all parts of the world. Those letters passed through the Boston post-office, and some of the clerks who sorted them saw that queer legend written down in the lower left-hand corner of the envelope, and they wondered at it, and one or two wrote it down, to look it up afterward. The letters reached other cities and were put into the hands of mail-carriers to distribute, and they saw the queer little sentence '2 Timothy 2:15,' and they wondered, and some of them looked it up."

By this time the entire attention of the school was upon the story, for they perceived that it was a story.

"The men left Boston and went across the ocean to hold meetings in other cities, and one day at a little railway station in Europe a group of people were gathered, waiting for a train, and those two men were among them. Pretty soon the train came, and one of the men got on the back end of the last car, while the other stayed on the platform, and as the train moved off the man on the last car took off his hat and said, in a good, loud, clear tone, 'Well, take care of yourself, 2 Timothy 2:15,' and the other one smiled and waved his hat and answered, 'Yes, 2 Timothy 2:15.' The man on the train, which was moving fast now, shouted back, '2 Timothy 2:15,' and the man on the platform responded still louder, waving his hat, '2 Timothy 2:15,' and back and forth the queer sentence was flung until the train was too far away for them to hear each other's voices. In the mean time all the people on the platform had been standing there listening and wondering what in the world such a strange salutation could mean. Some of them recognized what it was, but many did not know, and yet the sentence was said over so many times that they could not help remembering it; and some went away to recall it and ask their friends what it meant. A young man from America was on that platform and heard it, and he knew it stood for a passage in the Bible, and his curiosity was so great that he went back to his boarding-house and hunted up the Bible his mother had packed in his trunk when he came away from home, and he hunted through the Bible until he found the place, '2 Timothy 2:15,' and read it; and it made him think about his life and decide that he wasn't doing as he ought to do. I can't tell you all the story about that queer Bible verse, how it went here and there and what a great work it did in people's hearts; but one day those Christian workers went to Australia to hold some meetings, and one night, when the great auditorium was crowded, a man who was leading the meeting got up and told the story of this verse, how it had been chosen, and how it had gone over the world in strange ways, even told about the morning at the little railway station when the two men said good-by. Just as he got to that place in his story a man in the audience stood up and said: 'Brother, just let me say a word, please. I never knew anything about all this before, but I was at that railway station, and I heard those two men shout that strange good-by, and I went home and read that verse, and it's made a great difference in my life.'

"There was a great deal more to the story, how some Chicago policemen got to be good men through reading that verse, and how the story of the Australia meetings was printed in an Australian paper and sent to a lady in America who sent it to a friend in England to read about the meetings. And this friend in England had a son in the army in India, to whom she was sending a package, and she wrapped it around something in that package, and the young man read all about it, and it helped to change his life. Well, I thought of that story this morning when I was trying to decide what to read for our opening chapter, and it occurred to me that perhaps you would be interested to take that verse for our school verse this term, and so if you would like it I will put it on the blackboard. Would you like it, I wonder?"

She paused wistfully, as if she expected an answer, and there was a low, almost inaudible growl of assent; a keen listener might almost have said it had an impatient quality in it, as if they were in a hurry to find out what the verse was that had made such a stir in the world.

"Very well," said Margaret, turning to the board; "then I'll put it where we all can see it, and while I write it will you please say over where it is, so that you will remember it and hunt it up for yourselves in your Bibles at home?"

There was a sort of snicker at that, for there were probably not half a dozen Bibles, if there were so many, represented in that school; but they took her hint as she wrote, and chanted, "2 Timothy 2:15, 2 Timothy 2:15," and then spelled out after her rapid crayon, "Study to show thyself approved unto God, a workman that needeth not to be ashamed."

They read it together at her bidding, with a wondering,

half-serious look in their faces, and then she said, "Now, shall we pray?"

The former teacher had not opened her school with prayer. It had never been even suggested in that school. It might have been a dangerous experiment if Margaret had attempted it sooner in her program. As it was, there was a shuffling of feet in the back seats at her first word; but the room grew quiet again, perhaps out of curiosity to hear a woman's voice in prayer:

"Our Heavenly Father, we want to ask Thee to bless us in our work together, and to help us to be such workmen that we shall not need to be ashamed to show our work to Thee at the close of the day. For Christ's sake we ask it. Amen."

They did not have time to resent that prayer before she had them interested in something else. In fact, she had planned her whole first day out so that there should not be a minute for misbehavior. She had argued that if she could just get time to become acquainted with them she might prevent a lot of trouble before it ever started. Her first business was to win her scholars. After that she could teach them easily if they were once willing to learn.

She had a set of mental arithmetic problems ready which she propounded to them next, some of them difficult and some easy enough for the youngest child who could think, and she timed their answers and wrote on the board the names of those who raised their hands first and had the correct answers. The questions were put in a fascinating way, many of them having curious little catches in them for the scholars who were not on the alert, and Timothy presently discovered this and set himself to get every one, coming off victorious at the end. Even Jed roused himself and was interested, and some of the girls quite distinguished themselves.

When a half-hour of this was over she put the word "TRANSFIGURATION" on the blackboard, and set them to playing a regular game out of it. If some of the school-board had come in just then they might have lifted up hands of horror at the idea of the new teacher setting the whole school to playing a game. But they certainly would have been delightfully surprised to see a quiet and orderly room with bent heads and knit brows, all intent upon papers and pencils. Never before in the annals of that school had the first day held a full period of quiet or orderliness. It was expected to be a day of battle; a day of trying out the soul of the teacher and proving whether he or she were worthy to cope with the active minds and bodies of the young bullies of Ashland. But the expected battle had been forgotten. Every mind was busy with the matter in hand.

Margaret had given them three minutes to write as many words as they could think of, of three letters or more, beginning with T, and using only the letters in the word she had put on the board. When time was called there was a breathless rush to write a last word, and then each scholar had to tell how many words he had, and each was called upon to read his list. Some had only two or three, some had ten or eleven. They were allowed to mark their words, counting one for each person present who did not have that word and doubling if it were two syllables, and so on. Excitement ran high when it was discovered that some had actually made a count of thirty or forty, and when they started writing words beginning with R every head was bent intently from the minute time was started.

Never had three minutes seemed so short to those unused brains, and Jed yelled out: "Aw, gee! I only got three!" when time was called next.

It was recess-time when they finally finished every letter in that word, and, adding all up, found that Timothy had won the game. Was that school? Why, a barbecue couldn't be named beside it for fun! They rushed out to the school-yard with a shout, and the boys played leap-frog loudly for the first few minutes. Margaret, leaning her tired head in her hands, elbows on the window-seat, closing her eyes and gathering strength for the after-recess session, heard one boy say: "Wal, how d'ye like 'er?" And the answer came: "Gee! I didn't think she'd be that kind of a guy! I thought she'd be some stiff old Ike! Ain't she a peach, though?" She lifted up her head and laughed triumphantly to herself, her eyes alight, herself now strengthened for the fray. She wasn't wholly failing, then?

After recess there was a spelling-match, choosing sides, of course, "Because this is only the first day, and we must get acquainted before we can do real work, you know," she explained.

The spelling-match proved an exciting affair also, with new features that Ashland had never seen before. Here the girls began to shine into prominence, but there were very few good spellers, and they were presently reduced to two girls — Rosa Rogers, the beauty of the school, and Amanda Bounds, a stolid, homely girl with deep eyes and a broad brow.

"I'm going to give this as a prize to the one who stands up the longest," said Margaret, with sudden inspiration as she saw the boys in their seats getting restless; and she unpinned a tiny blue-silk bow that fastened her white collar.

The girls all said "Oh-h-h!" and immediately every one in the room straightened up. The next few minutes those two girls spelled for dear life, each with her eye fixed upon the tiny blue bow in the teacher's white hands. To own that bow, that wonderful, strange bow of the heavenly blue, with the graceful twist to the tie! What delight! The girl who won that would be the admired of all the school. Even the boys sat up and took notice, each secretly thinking that Rosa, the beauty, would get it, of course.

But she didn't; she slipped up on the word "receive," after all, putting the i before the e; and her stolid companion, catching her breath awesomely, slowly spelled it right and received the blue prize, pinned gracefully at the throat of her old brown gingham by the teacher's own soft, white fingers, while the school looked on admiringly and the blood rolled hotly up the back of her neck and spread over her face and forehead. Rosa, the beauty, went crestfallen to her seat.

It was at noon, while they ate their lunch, that Margaret tried to get acquainted with the girls, calling most of them by name, to their great surprise, and hinting of delightful possibilities in the winter's work. Then she slipped out among the boys and watched their sports, laughing and applauding when some one made a particularly fine play, as if she thoroughly understood and appreciated.

She managed to stand near Jed and Timothy just before Bud rang the bell. "I've heard you are great sportsmen," she said to them, confidingly. "And I've been wondering if you'll teach me some things I want to learn? I want to know how to ride and shoot. Do you suppose I could learn?"

"Sure!" they chorused, eagerly, their embarrassment forgotten. "Sure, you could learn fine! Sure, *we'll learn* you!"

And then the bell rang and they all went in.

The afternoon was a rather informal arrangement of classes and schedule for the next day, Margaret giving out slips of paper with questions for each to answer, that she might find out just where to place them; and while they wrote she went from one to another, getting acquainted, advising, and suggesting about what they wanted to study. It was all so new and wonderful to them! They had not been used to caring what they were to study. Now it almost seemed interesting.

But when the day was done, the school-house locked, and Bud and Margaret started for home, she realized that she was weary. Yet it was a weariness of success and not of failure, and she felt happy in looking forward to the morrow.

14

THE minister had decided to preach in Ashland, and on the following Sabbath. It became apparent that if he wished to have any notice at all from the haughty new teacher he must do something at once to establish his superiority in her eyes. He had carefully gone over his store of sermons that he always carried with him, and decided to preach on "The Dynamics of Altruism."

Notices had been posted up in saloons and stores and post-office. He had made them himself after completely tabooing Mr. Tanner's kindly and blundering attempt, and they gave full information concerning "the Rev. Frederick West, Ph.D., of the vicinity of New York City, who had kindly consented to preach in the school-house on 'The Dynamics of Altruism.' "

Several of these elaborately printed announcements had been posted up on big trees along the trails, and in other conspicuous places, and there was no doubt but that the coming Sabbath services were more talked of than anything else in that neighborhood for miles around, except the new teacher and her extraordinary way of making all the scholars fall in love with her. It is quite possible that the Reverend Frederick might not have been so flattered at the size of his audience when the day came if he could have known how many of them came principally because they thought it would be a good opportunity to see the new teacher.

However, the announcements were read, and the preacher became an object of deep interest to the community when he went abroad. Under this attention he swelled, grew pleased, bland, and condescending, wearing an oily smile and bowing most conceitedly whenever anybody noticed him. He even began to drop his severity and silence at the table, toward the end of the week, and expanded into dignified conversation, mainly addressed to Mr. Tanner about the political situation in the State of Arizona. He was trying to impress the teacher with the fact that he looked upon her as a most insignificant mortal who had forfeited her right to his smiles by her headstrong and unseemly conduct when he had warned her about "that young ruffian."

Out on the trail Long Bill and Jasper Kemp paused before a tree that bore the Reverend Frederick's church notice, and read in silence while the wide wonder of the desert spread about them.

"What d'ye make out o' them cuss words, Jap?" asked Long Bill, at length. "D'ye figger the parson's goin' to preach on swearin' ur gunpowder?"

"Blowed ef I know," answered Jasper, eying the sign ungraciously; "but by the looks of him he can't say much to suit me on neither one. He resembles a yaller cactus bloom out in a rain-storm as to head, an' his smile is like some of them prickles on the plant. He can't be no 'sky-pilot' to me, not just yet."

"You don't allow he b'longs in any way to *her?*" asked Long Bill, anxiously, after they had been on their way for a half-hour.

"B'long to *her?* Meanin' the schoolmarm?"

"Yes; he ain't sweet on her nor nothin'?"

"Wal, I guess not," said Jasper, contentedly. "She's got eyes sharp's a needle. You don't size her up so small she's goin' to take to a sickly parson with yaller hair an' sleek ways when she's seen the Kid, do you?"

"Wal, no, it don't seem noways reasonable, but you never can tell. Women gets notions."

"She ain't that kind! You mark my words, *she ain't that kind.* I'd lay she'd punch the breeze like a coyote ef he'd make up to her. Just you wait till you see him. He's the most no-'count, measleyest little thing that ever called himself a man. My word! I'd like to see him try to ride that colt o' mine. I really would. It would be some sight for sore eyes, it sure would."

"Mebbe he's got a intellec'," suggested Long Bill, after another mile. "That goes a long ways with women-folks with a education."

"No chance!" said Jasper, confidently. " 'Ain't got room fer one under his yaller thatch. You wait till you set your lamps on him once before you go to gettin' excited. Why, he ain't one-two-three with our missionary! Gosh! I wish *he'd* come back an' see to such goin's-on — I certainly do."

"Was you figgerin' to go to that gatherin' Sunday?"

"I sure was," said Jasper. "I want to see the show, an', besides, we might be needed ef things got too high-soundin'. It ain't good to have a creature at large that thinks he knows all there is to know. I heard him talk down to the post-office the day after that little party we had when the Kid shot out the lights to save Bunchy from killin' Crapster, an' it's my opinion he needs a good spankin'; but I'm agoin' to give him a fair show. I ain't much on religion myself, but I do like to see a square deal, especially in a parson. I've sized it up he needs a lesson."

"I'm with ye, Jap," said Long Bill, and the two rode on their way in silence.

Margaret was so busy and so happy with her school all

the week that she quite forgot her annoyance at the minister. She really saw very little of him, for he was always late to breakfast, and she took hers early. She went to her room immediately after supper, and he had little opportunity for pursuing her acquaintance. Perhaps he judged that it would be wise to let her alone until after he had made his grand impression on Sunday, and let her "make up" to him.

It was not until Sunday morning that she suddenly recalled that he was to preach that day. She had indeed seen the notices, for a very large and elaborate one was posted in front of the school-house, and some anonymous artist had produced a fine caricature of the preacher in red clay underneath his name. Margaret had been obliged to remain after school Friday and remove as much of this portrait as she was able, not having been willing to make it a matter of discipline to discover the artist. In fact, it was so true to the model that the young teacher felt a growing sympathy for the one who had perpetrated it.

Margaret started to the school-house early Sunday morning, attended by the faithful Bud. Not that he had any more intention of going to Sunday-school than he had the week before, but it was pleasant to be the chosen escort of so popular a teacher. Even Jed and Timothy had walked home with her twice during the week. He did not intend to lose his place as nearest to her. There was only one to whom he would surrender that, and he was too far away to claim it often.

Margaret had promised to help in the Sunday-school that morning, for the woman who taught the little ones was still away with her sick neighbor, and on the way she persuaded Bud to help her.

"You'll be secretary for me, won't you, William?" she asked, brightly. "I'm going to take the left-front corner of the room for the children, and seat them on the recitation-benches, and that will leave all the back part of the room for the older people. Then I can use the blackboard and not disturb the rest."

"Secretary?" asked the astonished Bud. He was, so to speak, growing accustomed to surprises. "Secretary" did not sound like being "a nice little Sunday-school boy."

"Why, yes! take up the collection, and see who is absent, and so on. I don't know all the names, perhaps, and, anyhow, I don't like to do that when I have to teach!"

Artful Margaret! She had no mind to leave Bud floating around outside the school-house, and though she had ostensibly prepared her lesson and her blackboard illustration for the little children, she had hidden in it a truth for Bud—poor, neglected, devoted Bud!

The inefficient old man who taught the older people that day gathered his forces together and, seated with his back to the platform, his spectacles extended upon his long nose, he proceeded with the questions on the lesson-leaf, as usual, being more than ordinarily unfamiliar with them; but before he was half through he perceived by the long pauses between the questions and answers that he did not have the attention of his class. He turned slowly around to see what they were all looking at, and became so engaged in listening to the lesson the new teacher was drawing on the blackboard that he completely forgot to go on, until Bud, very important in his new position, rang the tiny desk-bell for the close of school, and Margaret, looking up, saw in dismay that she had been teaching the whole school.

While they were singing a closing hymn the room began to fill up, and presently came the minister, walking importantly beside Mr. Tanner, his chin flattened upward as usual, but bent in till it made a double roll over his collar, his eyes rolling importantly, showing much of their whites, his sermon, in an elaborate leather cover, carried conspicuously under his arm, and the severest of clerical coats and collars setting out his insignificant face.

Walking behind him in single file, measured step, just so far apart, came the eight men from the bunk-house—Long Bill, Big Jim, Fiddling Boss, Jasper Kemp, Fade-away Forbes,

Stocky, Croaker, and Fudge; and behind them, looking like a scared rabbit, Mom Wallis scuttled into the back seat and sank out of sight. The eight men, however, ranged themselves across the front of the room on the recitation-bench, directly in front of the platform, removing a few small children for that purpose.

They had been lined up in a scowling row along the path as the minister entered, looking at them askance under his aristocratic yellow eyebrows, and as he neared the door the last man followed in his wake, then the next, and so on.

Margaret, in her seat half-way back at the side of the school-house near a window, saw through the trees a wide sombrero over a pair of broad shoulders; but, though she kept close watch, she did not see her friend of the wilderness enter the school-house. If he had really come to meeting, he was staying outside.

The minister was rather nonplussed at first that there were no hymn-books. It almost seemed that he did not know how to go on with divine service without hymn-books, but at last he compromised on the long-meter Doxology, pronounced with deliberate unction. Then, looking about for a possible pipe-organ and choir, he finally started it himself; but it is doubtful whether any one would have recognized the tune enough to help it on if Margaret had not for very shame's sake taken it up and carried it along, and so they came to the prayer and Bible-reading.

These were performed with a formal, perfunctory style calculated to impress the audience with the importance of the preacher rather than the words he was speaking. The audience was very quiet, having the air of reserving judgment for the sermon.

Margaret could not just remember afterward how it was she missed the text. She had turned her eyes away from the minister, because it somehow made her feel homesick to compare him with her dear, dignified father. Her mind had

wandered, perhaps, to the sombrero she had glimpsed outside, and she was wondering how its owner was coming on
with his resolves, and just what change they would mean in
his life, anyway. Then suddenly she awoke to the fact that
the sermon had begun.

15

"CONSIDERED in the world of physics," began the lordly tones of the Reverend Frederick, "dynamics is that branch of mechanics that treats of the effects of forces in producing motion, and of the laws of motion thus produced; sometimes called kinetics, opposed to statics. It is the science that treats of the laws of force, whether producing equilibrium or motion; in this sense including both statics and kinetics. It is also applied to the forces producing or governing activity or movement of any kind; also the methods of such activity."

The big words rolled out magnificently over the awed gathering, and the minister flattened his chin and rolled his eyes up at the people in his most impressive way.

Margaret's gaze hastily sought the row of rough men on the front seat, sitting with folded arms in an attitude of attention, each man with a pair of intelligent eyes under his shaggy brows regarding the preacher as they might have regarded an animal in a zoo. Did they understand what had been said? It was impossible to tell from their serious faces.

"Philanthropy has been called the dynamics of Christianity; that is to say, it is Christianity in action," went on the preacher. "It is my purpose this morning to speak upon the dynamics of altruism. Now altruism is the theory that inculcates benevolence to others in subordination to self-interest; interested benevolence as opposed to disinterested; also, the practice of this theory."

He lifted his eyes to the audience once more and nodded his head slightly, as if to emphasize the deep truth he had just given them, and the battery of keen eyes before him never flinched from his face. They were searching him through and through. Margaret wondered if he had no sense of the ridiculous, that he could, to such an audience, pour forth such a string of technical definitions. They sounded strangely like dictionary language. She wondered if anybody present besides herself knew what the man meant or got any inkling of what his subject was. Surely he would drop to simpler language, now that he had laid out his plan.

It never occurred to her that the man was trying to impress *her* with his wonderful fluency of language and his marvelous store of wisdom. On and on he went in much the same trend he had begun, with now and then a flowery sentence or whole paragraph of meaningless eloquence about the "brotherhood of man"—with a roll to the r's in brotherhood.

Fifteen minutes of this profitless oratory those men of the wilderness endured, stolidly and with fixed attention; then, suddenly, a sentence of unusual simplicity struck them and an almost visible thrill went down the front seat.

"For years the church has preached a dead faith, without works, my friends, and the time has come to stop preaching faith! I repeat it—fellow-men. I repeat it. The time has come *to stop preaching faith* and begin to do good works!" He thumped the desk vehemently. "Men don't need a superstitious belief in a Saviour to save them from their sins; they need to go to work and save themselves! As if a man dying two thousand years ago on a cross could do any good to you and me to-day!"

It was then that the thrill passed down that front line, and Long Bill, sitting at their head, leaned slightly forward and looked full and frowning into the face of Jasper Kemp; and the latter, frowning back, solemnly winked one eye. Margaret sat where she could see the whole thing.

Immediately, still with studied gravity, Long Bill cleared his throat impressively, arose, and, giving the minister a full look in the eye, of the nature almost of a challenge, he turned and walked slowly, noisily down the aisle and out the front door.

The minister was visibly annoyed, and for the moment a trifle flustered; but, concluding his remarks had been too deep for the rough creature, he gathered up the thread of his argument and proceeded:

"We need to get to work at our duty toward our fellow-men. We need to down trusts and give the laboring-man a chance. We need to stop insisting that men shall believe in the inspiration of the entire Bible and get to work at something practical!"

The impressive pause after this sentence was interrupted by a sharp, rasping sound of Big Jim clearing his throat and shuffling to his feet. He, too, looked the minister full in the face with a searching gaze, shook his head sadly, and walked leisurely down the aisle and out of the door. The minister paused again and frowned. This was becoming annoying.

Margaret sat in startled wonder. Could it be possible that these rough men were objecting to the sermon from a theological point of view, or was it just a happening that they had gone out at such pointed moments. She sat back after a minute, telling herself that of course the men must just have been weary of the long sentences, which no doubt they could not understand. She began to hope that Gardley was not within hearing. It was not probable that many others understood enough to get harm from the sermon, but her soul boiled with indignation that a man could go forth and call himself a minister of an evangelical church and yet talk such terrible heresy.

Big Jim's steps died slowly away on the clay path outside, and the preacher resumed his discourse.

"We have preached long enough of hell and torment. It is time for a gospel of love to our brothers. Hell is a superstition of the Dark Ages. *There is no hell!*"

Fiddling Boss turned sharply toward Jasper Kemp, as if waiting for a signal, and Jasper gave a slight, almost imperceptible nod. Whereupon Fiddling Boss cleared his throat loudly and arose, faced the minister, and marched down the aisle, while Jasper Kemp remained quietly seated as if nothing had happened, a vacancy each side of him.

By this time the color began to rise in the minister's cheeks. He looked at the retreating back of Fiddling Boss, and then suspiciously down at the row of men, but every one of them sat with folded arms and eyes intent upon the sermon, as if their comrades had not left them. The minister thought he must have been mistaken and took up the broken thread once more, or tried to, but he had hopelessly lost the place in his manuscript, and the only clue that offered was a quotation of a poem about the devil; to be sure, the connection was somewhat abrupt, but he clutched it with his eye gratefully and began reading it dramatically:

> " '*Men don't believe in the devil now*
> *As their fathers used to do—*' "

But he had got no further when a whole clearing-house of throats sounded, and Fade-away Forbes stumbled to his feet frantically, bolting down the aisle as if he had been sent for. He had not quite reached the door when Stocky clumped after him, followed at intervals by Croaker and Fudge, and each just as the minister had begun:

"Um! Ah! To resume—"

And now only Jasper Kemp remained of the front-seaters, his fine gray eyes boring through and through the minister as he floundered through the remaining portion of his manuscript up to the point where it began, "And finally—" which opened with another poem:

" 'I need no Christ to die for me.' "

The sturdy, gray-haired Scotchman suddenly lowered his folded arms, slapping a hand resoundingly on each knee, bent his shoulders the better to pull himself to his feet, pressing his weight on his hands till his elbows were akimbo, uttered a deep sigh and a, "Yes—well—ah!"

With that he got to his feet and dragged them slowly out of the school-house.

By this time the minister was ready to burst with indignation. Never before in all the bombastic days of his egotism had he been so grossly insulted, and by such rude creatures! And yet there was really nothing that could be said or done. These men appeared to be simple creatures who had wandered in idly, perhaps for a few moments' amusement, and, finding the discourse above their caliber, had innocently wandered out again. That was the way it had been made to appear. But his plans had been cruelly upset by such actions, and he was mortified in the extreme. His face was purple with his emotions, and he struggled and spluttered for a way out of his trying dilemma. At last he spoke, and his voice was absurdly dignified:

"Is there—ah—any other—ah—auditor—ah—who is desirous of withdrawing before the close of service? If so he may do so now, or—ah—" He paused for a suitable ending, and familiar words rushed to his lips without consciousness for the moment of their meaning—"or forever after hold their peace—ah!"

There was a deathly silence in the school-house. No one offered to go out, and Margaret suddenly turned her head and looked out of the window. Her emotions were almost beyond her control.

Thus the closing eloquence proceeded to its finish, and at last the service was over. Margaret looked about for Mom Wallis, but she had disappeared. She signed to Bud, and together they hastened out; but a quiet Sabbath peace reigned about the door of the school-house, and not a man from the camp was in sight; no, nor even the horses upon which they had come.

And yet, when the minister had finished shaking hands with the worshipful women and a few men and children, and came with Mr. Tanner to the door of the school-house, those eight men stood in a solemn row, four on each side of the walk, each holding his chin in his right hand, his right elbow in his left hand, and all eyes on Jasper Kemp, who kept his eyes thoughtfully up in the sky.

"H'w aire yeh, Tanner? Pleasant 'casion. Mind steppin' on a bit? We men wanta have a word with the parson."

Mr. Tanner stepped on hurriedly, and the minister was left standing nonplussed and alone in the doorway of the school-house.

16

"UM! Ah!" began the minister, trying to summon his best clerical manner to meet—what? He did not know. It was best to assume they were a penitent band of inquirers for the truth. But the memory of their recent exodus from the service was rather too clearly in his mind for his pleasantest expression to be uppermost toward these rough creatures. Insolent fellows! He ought to give them a good lesson in behavior!

"Um! Ah!" he began again, but found to his surprise that his remarks thus far had had no effect whatever on the eight stolid countenances before him. In fact, they seemed to have grown grim and menacing even in their quiet attitude, and their eyes were fulfilling the promise of the look they had given him when they left the service.

"What does all this mean, anyway?" he burst forth, suddenly.

"Calm yourself, elder! Calm yourself," spoke up Long Bill. "There ain't any occasion to get excited."

"I'm not an elder; I'm a minister of the gospel," exploded West, in his most pompous tones. "I should like to know who you are and what all this means?"

"Yes, parson, we understand who you are. We understand quite well, an' we're agoin' to tell you who we are. We're a band of al-tru-ists! That's what we are. We're *altruists!*" It was Jasper Kemp of the keen eyes and sturdy countenance who spoke. "And we've come here in brotherly love to exercise a little of that dynamic force of altruism you was talkin' about. We just thought we'd begin on you so's you could see that we got some works to go 'long with our faith."

"What do you mean, sir?" said West, looking from one grim countenance to another. "I — I don't quite understand." The minister was beginning to be frightened, he couldn't exactly tell why. He wished he had kept Brother Tanner with him. It was the first time he had ever thought of Mr. Tanner as "brother."

"We mean just this, parson; you been talkin' a lot of lies in there about there bein' no Saviour an' no hell, ner no devil, an' while we ain't much credit to God ourselves, bein' just common men, we know all that stuff you said ain't true about the Bible an' the devil bein' superstitions, an' we thought we better exercise a little of that there altruism you was talkin' about an' teach you better. You see, it's real brotherly kindness, parson. An' now we're goin' to give you a sample of that dynamics you spoke about. Are you ready, boys?"

"All ready," they cried as one man.

There seemed to be no concerted motion, nor was there warning. Swifter than the weaver's shuttle, sudden as the lightning's flash, the minister was caught from where he stood pompously in that doorway, hat in hand, all grandly as he was attired, and hurled from man to man. Across the walk and back; across and back; across and back; until it seemed to him it was a thousand miles all in a minute of time. He had no opportunity to prepare for the onslaught. He jammed his high silk hat, wherewith he had thought to over-awe the community, upon his sleek head, and grasped his precious sermon-case to his breast; the sermon, as it well deserved, was flung to the four winds of heaven and fortunately was no more — that is, existing as a whole. The time came when each of those eight men recovered and retained a portion of that learned oration, and Mom Wallis, not quite understanding, pinned up and used as a sort of shrine the portion about doubting the devil; but as a sermon the parts were never assembled on this earth, nor could be, for some of it was ground to powder under eight pairs of ponderous heels. But the minister at that trying moment was too much otherwise engaged to notice that the child of his brain lay scattered on the ground.

Seven times he made the round up and down, up and down that merciless group, tossed like a thistle-down from man to man. And at last, when his breath was gone, when the world had grown black before him, and he felt smaller and more inadequate than he had ever felt in his whole conceited life before, he found himself bound, helplessly bound, and cast ignominiously into a wagon. And it was a strange thing that, though seemingly but five short minutes before the place had been swarming with worshipful admirers thanking him for his sermon, now there did not seem to be a creature within hearing, for he called and cried aloud and roared with his raucous voice until it would seem that all the surrounding States might have heard that cry from Arizona, yet none came to his relief.

They carried him away somewhere, he did not know where; it was a lonely spot and near a water-hole. When he protested and loudly blamed them, threatening all the law in the land upon them, they regarded him as one might a naughty child who needed chastisement, leniently and with sorrow, but also with determination.

They took him down by the water's side and stood him up among them. He began to tremble with fear as he looked from one to another, for he was not a man of courage, and he had heard strange tales of this wild, free land, where every man was a law unto himself. Were they going to drown him then and there? Then up spoke Jasper Kemp:

"Mr. Parson," he said, and his voice was kind but firm; one might almost say there was a hint of humor in it, and there surely was a twinkle in his eye; but the sternness of his lips belied it, and the minister was in no state to appreciate humor—"Mr. Parson, we've brought you here to do you good, an' you oughtn't to complain. This is altruism, an' we're but actin' out what you been preachin'. You're our brother an' we're tryin' to do you good; an' now we're about to show you what a dynamic force we are. You see, Mr. Parson, I was brought up by a good Scotch grandmother, an' I know a lie when I hear it, an' when I hear a man preach error I know it's time to set him straight; so now we're agoin' to set you straight. I don't know where you come from, nor who brang you up, nor what church set you afloat, but I know enough by all my grandmother taught me—even if I hadn't been a-listenin' off and on for two years back to Mr. Brownleigh, our missionary—to know you're a dangerous man to have at large. I'd as soon have a mad dog let loose. Why, what you preach ain't the gospel, an' it ain't the truth, and the time has come for you to know it, an' own it and recant. Recant! That's what they call it. That's what we're here to see 't you do, or we'll know the reason why. That's the *dynamics* of it. See?"

The minister saw. He saw the deep, muddy water-hole. He saw nothing more.

"Folks are all too ready to believe them there things you was gettin' off without havin' 'em *preached* to justify 'em in their evil ways. We gotta think of those poor ignorant brothers of ours that might listen to you. See? That's the *altruism* of it!"

"What do you want me to do?" The wretched man's tone was not merely humble—it was abject. His grand Prince Albert coat was torn in three places; one tail hung down dejectedly over his hip; one sleeve was ripped half-way out. His collar was unbuttoned and the ends rode up hilariously over his cheeks. His necktie was gone. His sleek hair stuck out in damp wisps about his frightened eyes, and his hat had been "stove in" and jammed down as far as it would go until his ample ears stuck out like sails at half-mast. His feet were imbedded in the heavy mud on the margin of the water-hole, and his fine silk socks, which had showed at one time above the erstwhile neat tyings, were torn and covered with mud.

"Well, in the first place," said Jasper Kemp, with a slow wink around at the company, "that little matter about hell needs adjustin'. Hell ain't no superstition. I ain't dictatin' what kind of a hell there is; you can make it fire or water or anything else you like, but *there is a hell,* an' *you believe in it.* D'ye understand? We'd just like to have you make that statement publicly right here an' now."

"But how can I say what I don't believe?" whined West, almost ready to cry. He had come proudly through a trial by Presbytery on these very same points, and had posed as being a man who had the courage of his convictions. He could not thus easily surrender his pride of original thought and broad-mindedness. He had received congratulations from a number of noble martyrs who had left their chosen church for just such reasons, congratulating him on his brave stand. It had been the first notice from big men he had ever been able to attract to himself, and it had gone to his head like wine. Give that up for a few miserable cowboys! It might get into the papers and go back East. He must think of his reputation.

"That's just where the dynamics of the thing comes in, brother," said Jasper Kemp, patronizingly. "We're here to *make* you believe in a hell. We're the force that will bring you back into the right way of thinkin' again. Are you ready, boys?"

The quiet utterance brought goose-flesh up to West's very ears, and his eyes bulged with horror.

"Oh, that isn't necessary! I believe—yes, I believe in hell!" he shouted, as they seized him.

But it was too late. The Rev. Frederick West was plunged into the water-hole, from whose sheep-muddied waters he came up spluttering, "Yes, I believe in *hell!*" and for the first time in his life, perhaps, he really did believe in it, and thought that he was in it.

The men were standing knee-deep in the water and holding their captive lightly by his arms and legs, their eyes upon their leader, waiting now.

Jasper Kemp stood in the water, also, looking down benevolently upon his victim, his chin in his hand, his elbow in his other hand, an attitude which carried a feeling of hopelessness to the frightened minister.

"An' now there's that little matter of the devil," said Jasper Kemp, reflectively. "We'll just fix that up next while we're near his place of residence. You believe in the devil, Mr. Parson, from now on? If you'd ever tried resistin' him I figger you'd have b'lieved in him long ago. But *you believe in him* from *now on,* an' you *don't preach against him any more!* We're not goin' to have our Arizona men gettin' off their guard an' thinkin' their enemy is dead. There *is* a devil, parson, and you believe in him! Duck him, boys!"

Down went the minister into the water again, and came up sputtering, "Yes, I—I—I—believe—in—the—devil." Even in this strait he was loath to surrender his pet theme—no devil.

"Very well, so far as it goes," said Jasper Kemp, thoughtfully. "But now, boys, we're comin' to the most important of all, and you better put him under about three times, for there mustn't be no mistake about this matter. You believe in the Bible, parson—*the whole Bible?*"

"Yes!" gasped West, as he went down the first time and got a mouthful of the bitter water, "I believe—" The voice was fairly anguished. Down he went again. Another mouthful of water. *"I believe in the whole Bible!"* he screamed, and went down the third time. His voice was growing weaker, but he came up and reiterated it without request, and was lifted out upon the mud for a brief respite. The men of the bunk-house were succeeding better than the Presbytery back in the East had been able to do. The conceit was no longer visible in the face of the Reverend Frederick. His teeth were chattering, and he was beginning to see one really needed to believe in something when one came as near to his end as this.

"There's just one more thing to reckon with," said Jasper Kemp, thoughtfully. "That line of talk you was handin' out about a man dyin' on a cross two thousand years ago bein' nothin' to you. You said you *an' me,* but you can speak for *yourself.* We may not be much to look at, but we ain't goin' to stand for no such slander as that. Our missionary preaches all about that Man on the Cross, an' if you don't need Him before you get through this little campaign of life I'll miss my guess. Mebbe we haven't been all we might have been, but we ain't agoin' to let you ner no one else go back on that there Cross!"

Jasper Kemp's tone was tender and solemn. As the minister lay panting upon his back in the mud he was forced to acknowledge that at only two other times in his life had a tone of voice so arrested his attention and filled him with awe; once when as a boy he had been caught copying off another's paper at examination-time, and he had been sent to the principal's office; and again on the occasion of his mother's funeral, as he sat in the dim church a few years ago and listened to the old minister. For a moment now he was impressed with the wonder of the Cross, and it suddenly seemed as if he were being arraigned before the eyes of Him with Whom we all have to do. A kind of shame stole into his pale, flabby face, all the smugness and complacence gone, and he a poor wretch in the hands of his accusers. Jasper Kemp, standing over him on the bank, looking down grimly upon him, seemed like the emissary of God sent to condemn him, and his little, self-centered soul quailed within him.

"Along near the end of that *dis*course of yours you mentioned that sin was only misplaced energy. Well, if that's so there's a heap of your energy gone astray this mornin', an' the time has come for you to pay up. Speak up now an' say

what you believe or whether you want another duckin' —
an' it 'll be seven times this time!"

The man on the ground shut his eyes and gasped. The silence was very solemn. There seemed no hint of the ridiculous in the situation. It was serious business now to all those men. Their eyes were on their leader.

"Do you solemnly declare before God — I s'pose you still believe in a God, as you didn't say nothin' to the contrary — that from now on you'll stand for that there Cross and for Him that hung on it?"

The minister opened his eyes and looked up into the wide brightness of the sky, as if he half expected to see horses and chariots of fire standing about to do battle with him then and there, and his voice was awed, and frightened as he said:
"I do!"

There was silence, and the men stood with half-bowed heads, as if some solemn service were being performed that they did not quite understand, but in which they fully sympathized. Then Jasper Kemp said, softly:

"Amen!" And after a pause: "I ain't any sort of a Christian myself, but I just can't stand it to see a parson floatin' round that don't even know the name of the firm he's workin' for. Now, parson, there's just one more requirement, an' then you can go home."

The minister opened his eyes and looked around with a frightened appeal, but no one moved, and Jasper Kemp went on:

"You say you had a church in New York. What was the name and *ad*dress of your workin'-boss up there?"

"What do you mean? I hadn't any boss."

"Why, him that hired you an' paid you. The chief elder or whatever you called him."

"Oh!" The minister's tone expressed lack of interest in the subject, but he answered, languidly, "Ezekiel Newbold, Hazelton."

"Very good. Now, parson, you'll just kindly write two copies of a letter to Mr. Ezekiel Newbold statin' what you've just said to us concernin' your change of faith, sign your name, address one to Mr. Newbold, an' give the duplicate to me. We just want this little matter put on record so you can't change your mind any in future. Do you get my idea?"

"Yes," said the minister, dispiritedly.

"Will you do it?"

"Yes," apathetically.

"Well, now I got a piece of advice for you. It would be just as well for your health for you to leave Arizona about as quick as you can find it convenient to pack, but you won't be allowed to leave this town, day or night, cars or afoot, until them there letters are all O. K. Do you get me?"

"Yes," pathetically.

"I might add, by way of explainin', that if you had come to Arizona an' minded your own business you wouldn't have been interfered with. You mighta preached whatever bosh you darned pleased so far as we was concerned, only you wouldn't have had no sorta audience after the first try of that stuff you give to-day. But when you come to Arizona an' put your fingers in other folks' pie, when you tried to 'squeal' on the young gentleman who was keen enough to shoot out the lights to save a man's life, why, we 'ain't no further use for you. In the first place, you was all wrong. You thought the Kid shot out the lights to steal the gamin'-money; but he didn't. He put it all in the hands of the sheriff some hours before your 'private information' reached him through the mail. You thought you were awful sharp, you little sneak! But I wasn't the only man present who saw you put your foot out an' cover a gold piece that rolled on the floor just when the fight began. You thought nobody was a-lookin', but you'll favor us, please, with that identical gold piece along with the letter before you leave. Well, boys, that 'll be about all, then. Untie him!"

In silence and with a kind of contemptuous pity in their

faces the strong men stooped and unbound him; then, without another word, they left him, tramping solemnly away single file to their horses, standing at a little distance.

Jasper Kemp lingered for a moment, looking down at the wretched man. "Would you care to have us carry you back to the house?" he asked, reflectively.

"No!" said the minister, bitterly. "No!" And without another word Jasper Kemp left him.

Into the mesquite-bushes crept the minister, his glory all departed, and hid his misery from the light, groaning in bitterness of spirit. He who had made the hearts of a score of old ministers to sorrow for Zion, who had split in two a pleasantly united congregation, disrupted a session, and brought about a scandalous trial in Presbytery was at last conquered. The Rev. Frederick West had recanted!

WHEN Margaret left the school-house with Bud she had walked but a few steps when she remembered Mom Wallis and turned back to search for her; but nowhere could she find a trace of her, and the front of the school-house was as empty of any people from the camp as if they had not been there that morning. The curtain had not yet risen for the scene of the undoing of West.

"I suppose she must have gone home with them," said the girl, wistfully. "I'm sorry not to have spoken with her. She was good to me."

"You mean Mom Wallis?" said the boy. "No, she ain't gone home. She's hiking 'long to our house to see you. The Kid went along of her. See, there — down by those cottonwood-trees? That's them."

Margaret turned with eagerness and hurried along with Bud now. She knew who it was they called the Kid in that tone of voice. It was the way the men had spoken of and to him, a mingling of respect and gentling that showed how much beloved he was. Her cheeks wore a heightened color, and her heart gave a pleasant flutter of interest.

They walked rapidly and caught up with their guests before they had reached the Tanner house, and Margaret had the pleasure of seeing Mom Wallis's face flush with shy delight when she caught her softly round the waist, stealing quietly up behind, and greeted her with a kiss. There had not been many kisses for Mom Wallis in the later years, and the two that were to Margaret Earle's account seemed very sweet to her. Mom Wallis's eyes shone as if she had been a young girl as she turned with a smothered "Oh!" She was a woman not given to expressing herself; indeed, it might be said that the last twenty years of her life had been mainly of self-repression. She gave that one little gasp of recognition and pleasure, and then she relapsed into embarrassed silence beside the two young people who found pleasure in their own greetings. Bud, boylike, was after a cottontail, along with Cap, who had appeared from no one knew where and was attending the party joyously.

Mom Wallis, in her big, rough shoes, on the heels of which her scant brown calico gown was lifted as she walked, trudged shyly along between the two young people, as carefully watched and helped over the humps and bumps of the way as if she had been a princess. Margaret noticed with a happy approval how Gardley's hand was ready under the old woman's elbow to assist her as politely as he might have done for her own mother had she been walking by his side.

Presently Bud and Cap returned, and Bud, with observant eye, soon timed his step to Margaret's on her other side and touched her elbow lightly to help her over the next rut. This was his second lesson in manners from Gardley. He had his first the Sunday before, watching the two while he and Cap walked behind. Bud was learning. He had keen eyes and an alert brain. Margaret smiled understandingly at him, and his face grew deep red with pleasure.

"He was bringin' me to see where you was livin'," explained Mom Wallis, suddenly, nodding toward Gardley as if he had been a king. "We wasn't hopin' to see you, except mebbe just as you come by goin' in."

"Oh, then I'm so glad I caught up with you in time. I wouldn't have missed you for anything. I went back to look for you. Now you're coming in to dinner with me, both of you," declared Margaret, joyfully. "William, your mother will have enough dinner for us all, won't she?"

"Sure!" said Bud, with that assurance born of his life acquaintance with his mother, who had never failed him in a trying situation so far as things to eat were concerned.

Margaret looked happily from one of her invited guests to the other, and Gardley forgot to answer for himself in watching the brightness of her face, and wondering why it was so different from the faces of all other girls he knew anywhere.

But Mom Wallis was overwhelmed. A wave of red rolled dully up from her withered neck in its gala collar over her leathery face to the roots of her thin, gray hair.

"Me! Stay to dinner! Oh, I couldn't do that nohow! Not in these here clo'es. 'Course I got that pretty collar you give me, but I couldn't never go out to dinner in this old dress an' these shoes. I know what folks ought to look like an' I ain't goin' to shame you."

"Shame me? Nonsense! Your dress is all right, and who is going to see your shoes? Besides, I've just set my heart on it. I want to take you up to my room and show you the pictures of my father and mother and home and the church where I was christened, and everything."

Mom Wallis looked at her with wistful eyes, but still shook her head. "Oh, I'd like to mighty well. It's good of you to ast me. But I couldn't. I just couldn't. 'Sides, I gotta go home an' git the men's grub ready."

"Oh, can't she stay this time, Mr. Gardley?" appealed Margaret. "The men won't mind for once, will they?"

Gardley looked into her true eyes and saw she really meant the invitation. He turned to the withered old woman by his side. "Mom, we're going to stay," he declared, joyously. "She wants us, and we have to do whatever she says. The men will rub along. They all know how to cook. Mom, *we're going to stay.*"

"That's beautiful!" declared Margaret. "It's so nice to have some company of my own." Then her face suddenly sobered. "Mr. Wallis won't mind, will he?" And she looked with troubled eyes from one of her guests to the other. She did not want to prepare trouble for poor Mom Wallis when she went back.

Mom Wallis turned startled eyes toward her. There was contempt in her face and outraged womanhood. "Pop's gone off," she said, significantly. "He went yist'day. But he 'ain't got no call t' mind. I ben waitin' on Pop nigh on to twenty year, an' I guess I'm goin' to a dinner-party, now't I'm invited. Pop 'd better *not* mind, I guess!"

And Margaret suddenly saw how much, how very much, her invitation had been to the starved old soul. Margaret took her guests into the stiff little parlor and slipped out to interview her landlady. She found Mrs. Tanner, as she had expected, a large-minded woman who was quite pleased to have more guests to sit down to her generous dinner, particularly as her delightful boarder had hinted of ample recompense in the way of board money; and she fluttered about, sending Tanner after another jar of pickles, some more apple-butter, and added another pie to the menu.

Well pleased, Margaret left Mrs. Tanner and slipped back to her guests. She found Gardley making arrangements with Bud to run back to the church and tell the men to leave the buckboard for them, as they would not be home for dinner. While this was going on she took Mom Wallis up to her room to remove her bonnet and smooth her hair.

It is doubtful whether Mom Wallis ever did see such a room in her life; for when Margaret swung open the door the poor little woman stopped short on the threshold, abashed, and caught her breath, looking around with wondering eyes and putting out a trembling hand to steady herself against the door-frame. She wasn't quite sure whether things in that room were real, or whether she might not by chance have caught a glimpse into heaven, so beautiful did it seem to her. It was not till her eyes, in the roving, suddenly rested on the great mountain framed in the open window that she felt anchored and sure that this was a tangible place. Then she ventured to step her heavy shoe inside the door. Even then she drew her ugly calico back apologetically, as if it were a desecration to the lovely.

But Margaret seized her and drew her into the room, placing her gently in the rose-ruffled rockingchair as if it were a throne and she a queen, and the poor little woman sat entranced, with tears springing to her eyes and trickling down her cheeks.

Perhaps it was an impossibility for Margaret to conceive what the vision of that room meant to Mom Wallis. The realization of all the dreams of a starved soul concentrated into a small space; the actual, tangible proof that there might be a heaven some day—who knew?—since beauties and comforts like these could be real in Arizona.

Margaret brought the pictures of her father and mother, of her dear home and the dear old church. She took her about the room and showed her the various pictures and reminders of her college days, and when she saw that the poor creature was overwhelmed and speechless she turned her about and showed her the great mountain again, like an anchorage for her soul.

Mom Wallis looked at everything speechlessly, gasping as her attention was turned from one object to another, as if she were unable to rise beyond her excitement; but when she saw the mountain again her tongue was loosed, and she turned and looked back at the girl wonderingly.

"Now, ain't it strange! Even that old mounting looks diffrunt—it do look diffrunt from a room like this. Why, it looks like it got its hair combed an' its best collar on!" And Mom Wallis looked down with pride and patted the simple net ruffle about her withered throat. "Why, it looks like a picter painted an' hung up on this yere wall, that's what that mounting looks like! It kinda ain't no mounting any more; it's jest a picter in your room!"

Margaret smiled. "It is a picture, isn't it? Just look at that silver light over the purple place. Isn't it wonderful? I like to think it's mine — my mountain. And yet the beautiful thing about it is that it's just as much yours, too. It will make a picture of itself framed in your bunk-house window if you let it. Try it. You just need to let it."

Mom Wallis looked at her wonderingly. "Do you mean," she said, studying the girl's lovely face, "that ef I should wash them there bunk-house winders, an' string up some posy caliker, an' stuff a chair, an' have a pin-cushion, I could make that there mounting come in an' set fer me like a picter the way it does here fer you?"

"Yes, that's what I mean," said Margaret, softly, marveling how the uncouth woman had caught the thought. "That's exactly what I mean. God's gifts will be as much to us as we will let them, always. Try it and see."

Mom Wallis stood for some minutes looking out reflectively at the mountain. "Wal, mebbe I'll try it!" she said, and turned back to survey the room again.

And now the mirror caught her eye, and she saw herself, a strange self in a soft white collar, and went up to get a nearer view, laying a toil-worn finger on the lace and looking half embarrassed at sight of her own face.

"It's a real purty collar," she said, softly, with a choke in her voice. "It's too purty fer me. I told him so, but he said as how you wanted I should dress up every night fer supper in it. It's 'most as strange as havin' a mounting come an' live with you, to wear a collar like that — me!"

Margaret's eyes were suddenly bright with tears. Who would have suspected Mom Wallis of having poetry in her nature? Then, as if her thoughts anticipated the question in Margaret's mind, Mom Wallis went on:

"He brang me your little book," she said. "I ain't goin' to

say thank yeh, it ain't a big-'nuf word. An' he read me the poetry words it says. I got it wropped in a hankercher on the top o' the beam over my bed. I'm goin' to have it buried with me when I die. Oh, I *read* it. I couldn't make much out of it, but I read the words *thor*ough. An' then *he* read 'em — the Kid did. He reads just beautiful. He's got education, he has. He read it, and he talked a lot about it. Was this what you mean? Was it that we ain't really growin' old at all, we're jest goin' on, *gettin'* there, if we go right? Did you mean you think Him as planned it all wanted some old woman right thar in the bunk-house, an' it's *me*? Did you mean there was agoin' to be a chanct fer me to be young an' beautiful somewheres in creation yit, 'fore I git through?"

The old woman had turned around from looking into the mirror and was facing her hostess. Her eyes were very bright; her cheeks had taken on an excited flush, and her knotted hands were clutching the bureau. She looked into Margaret's eyes earnestly, as though her very life depended upon the answer; and Margaret, with a great leap of her heart, smiled and answered:

"Yes, Mrs. Wallis, yes, that is just what I meant. Listen, these are God's own words about it: 'For I reckon that the sufferings of this present time are not worthy to be compared with the glory that shall be revealed in us.' "

A kind of glory shone in the withered old face now. "Did you say them was God's words?" she asked in an awed voice.

"Yes," said Margaret; "they are in the Bible."

"But you couldn't be sure it meant *me?*" she asked, eagerly. "They wouldn't go to put *me* in the Bible, o' course."

"Oh yes, you could be quite sure, Mrs. Wallis," said Margaret, gently. "Because if God was making you and had a plan for you, as the poem says, He would be sure to put down something in His book about it, don't you think? He would want you to know."

"It does sound reasonable-like now, don't it?" said the woman, wistfully. "Say them glory words again, won't you?"

Margaret repeated the text slowly and distinctly.

"Glory!" repeated Mom Wallis, wonderingly. "Glory! Me!" and turned incredulously toward the glass. She looked a long time wistfully at herself, as if she could not believe it, and pulled reproachfully at the tight hair drawn away from her weather-beaten face. "I useta have purty hair onct," she said, sadly.

"Why, you have pretty hair now!" said Margaret, eagerly. "It just wants a chance to show its beauty. Here, let me fix it for dinner, will you?"

She whisked the bewildered old woman into a chair and began unwinding the hard, tight knot of hair at the back of her head and shaking it out. The hair was thin and gray now, but it showed signs of having been fine and thick once.

"It's easy to keep your hair looking pretty," said the girl, as she worked. "I'm going to give you a little box of my nice sweet-smelling soap-powder that I use to shampoo my hair. You take it home and wash your hair with it every two or three weeks and you'll see it will make a difference in a little while. You just haven't taken time to take care of it, that's all. Do you mind if I wave the front here a little? I'd like to fix your hair the way my mother wears hers."

Now nothing could have been further apart than this little weather-beaten old woman and Margaret's gentle, dove-like mother, with her abundant soft gray hair, her cameo features, and her pretty, gray dresses; but Margaret had a vision of what glory might bring to Mom Wallis, and she wanted to help it along. She believed that heavenly glory can be hastened a good deal on earth if one only tries, and so she set to work. Glancing out the window, she saw with relief that Gardley was talking interestedly with Mr. Tanner and seemed entirely content with their absence.

Mom Wallis hadn't any idea what "waving" her hair meant, but she readily consented to anything this wonderful girl proposed, and she sat entranced, looking at her mountain and thrilling with every touch of Margaret's satin fingers against her leathery old temples. And so, Sunday though it was, Margaret lighted her little alcohol-lamp and heated a tiny curling-iron which she kept for emergencies. In a few minutes' time Mom Wallis's astonished old gray locks lay soft and fluffy about her face, and pinned in a smooth coil behind, instead of the tight knot, making the most wonderful difference in the world in her old, tired face.

"Now look!" said Margaret, and turned her about to the mirror. "If there's anything at all you don't like about it I can change it, you know. You don't have to wear it so if you don't like it."

The old woman looked, and then looked back at Margaret with frightened eyes, and back to the vision in the mirror again.

"My soul!" she exclaimed in an awed voice. "My soul! It's come a'ready! Glory! I didn't think I could look like that! I wonder what Pop 'd say! My land! Would you mind ef I kep' it on a while an' wore it back to camp this way? Pop might uv come home an' I'd like to see ef he'd take notice to it. I used to be purty onct, but I never expected no sech thing like this again on earth. Glory! Glory! Mebbe I *could* get some glory, *too.*"

" 'The glory that shall be revealed' is a great deal more wonderful than this," said Margaret, gently. "This was here all the time, only you didn't let it come out. Wear it home that way, of course, and wear it so all the time. It's very little trouble, and you'll find your family will like it. Men always like to see a woman looking her best, even when she's working. It helps to make them good. Before you go home I'll show you how to fix it. It's quite simple. Come, now, shall we go down-stairs? We don't want to leave Mr. Gardley alone too long, and, besides, I smell the dinner. I think they'll be waiting for us pretty soon. I'm going to take a few of these pictures down to show Mr. Gardley."

She hastily gathered a few photographs together and led the bewildered little woman down-stairs again, and out in the yard, where Gardley was walking up and down now, looking off at the mountain. It came to Margaret, suddenly, that the minister would be returning to the house soon, and she wished he wouldn't come. He would be a false note in the pleasant harmony of the little company. He would be disagreeable to manage, and perhaps hurt poor Mom Wallis's feelings. Perhaps he had already come. She looked furtively around as she came out the door, but no minister was in sight, and then she forgot him utterly in the look of bewildered astonishment with which Gardley was regarding Mom Wallis.

He had stopped short in his walk across the little yard, and was staring at Mom Wallis, recognition gradually growing in his gaze. When he was fully convinced he turned his eyes to Margaret, as if to ask: "How did you do it? Wonderful woman!" and a look of deep reverence for her came over his face.

Then suddenly he noticed the shy embarrassment on the old woman's face, and swiftly came toward her, his hands outstretched, and, taking her bony hands in his, bowed low over them as a courtier might do.

"Mom Wallis, you are beautiful. Did you know it?" he said, gently, and led her to a little stumpy rocking-chair with a gay red-and-blue rag cushion that Mrs. Tanner always kept sitting by the front door in pleasant weather. Then he stood off and surveyed her, while the red stole into her cheeks becomingly. "What has Miss Earle been doing to glorify you?" he asked, again looking at her earnestly.

The old woman looked at him in awed silence. There was that word again—glory! He had said the girl had glorified her. There was then some glory in her, and it had been brought out by so simple a thing as the arrangement of her hair. It frightened her, and tears came and stood in her tired old eyes.

It was well for Mom Wallis's equilibrium that Mr. Tanner came out just then with the paper he had gone after, for the stolidity of her lifetime was about breaking up. But, as he turned, Gardley gave her one of the rarest smiles of sympathy and understanding that a young man can give to an old woman; and Margaret, watching, loved him for it. It seemed to her one of the most beautiful things a young man had ever done.

They had discussed the article in the paper thoroughly, and had looked at the photographs that Margaret had brought down; and Mrs. Tanner had come to the door numberless times, looking out in a troubled way down the road, only to trot back again, look in the oven, peep in the kettle, sigh, and trot out to the door again. At last she came and stood, arms akimbo, and looked down the road once more.

"Pa, I don't just see how I can keep the dinner waitin' a minute longer. The potatoes 'll be sp'iled. I don't see what's keepin' that preacher-man. He musta been invited out, though I don't see why he didn't send me word."

"That's it, likely, Ma," said Tanner. He was growing hungry. "I saw Mis' Bacon talkin' to him. She's likely invited him there. She's always tryin' to get ahead o' you, Ma, you know, 'cause you got the prize fer your marble cake."

Mrs. Tanner blushed and looked down apologetically at her guests. "Well, then, ef you'll just come in and set down, I'll dish up. My land! Ain't that Bud comin' down the road, Pa? He's likely sent word by Bud. I'll hurry in an' dish up."

Bud slid into his seat hurriedly after a brief ablution in the kitchen, and his mother questioned him sharply.

"Bud, wher you be'n? Did the minister get invited out?"

The boy grinned and slowly winked one eye at Gardley. "Yes, he's invited out, all right," he said, meaningly. "You don't need to wait fer him. He won't be home fer some time, I don't reckon."

Gardley looked keenly, steadily, at the boy's dancing eyes, and resolved to have a fuller understanding later, and his own eyes met the boy's in a gleam of mischief and sympathy.

It was the first time in twenty years that Mom Wallis had

eaten anything which she had not prepared herself, and now, with fried chicken and company preserves before her, she could scarcely swallow a mouthful. To be seated beside Gardley and waited on like a queen! To be smiled at by the beautiful young girl across the table, and deferred to by Mr. and Mrs. Tanner as "Mrs. Wallis," and asked to have more pickles and another helping of jelly, and did she take cream and sugar in her coffee! It was too much, and Mom Wallis was struggling with the tears. Even Bud's round, blue eyes regarded her with approval and interest. She couldn't help thinking, if her own baby boy had lived, would he ever have been like Bud? And once she smiled at him, and Bud smiled back, a real boy-like, frank, hearty grin. It was all like taking dinner in the Kingdom of Heaven to Mom Wallis, and getting glory aforetime.

It was a wonderful afternoon, and seemed to go on swift wings. Gardley went back to the school-house, where the horses had been left, and Bud went with him to give further particulars about that wink at the dinner-table. Mom Wallis went up to the rose-garlanded room and learned how to wash her hair, and received a roll of flowered scrim wherewith to make curtains for the bunk-house. Margaret had originally intended it for the school-house windows in case it proved necessary to make that place habitable, but the school-room could wait.

And there in the rose-room, with the new curtains in her trembling hands, and the great old mountain in full view, Mom Wallis knelt beside the little gay rocking-chair, while Margaret knelt beside her and prayed that the Heavenly Father would show Mom Wallis how to let the glory be revealed in her now on the earth.

Then Mom Wallis wiped the furtive tears away with her calico sleeve, tied on her funny old bonnet, and rode away with her handsome young escort into the silence of the desert, with the glory beginning to be revealed already in her countenance.

Quite late that evening the minister returned.

He came in slowly and wearily, as if every step were a pain to him, and he avoided the light. His coat was torn and his garments were mud-covered. He murmured of a "slight accident" to Mrs. Tanner, who met him solicitously in a flowered dressing-gown with a candle in her hand. He accepted greedily the half a pie, with cheese and cold chicken and other articles, she proffered on a plate at his door, and in the reply to her query as to where he had been for dinner, and if he had a pleasant time, he said:

"Very pleasant, indeed, thank you! The name? Um-ah—I disremember! I really didn't ask, That is—"

The minister did not get up to breakfast. In fact, he remained in bed for several days, professing to be suffering with an attack of rheumatism. He was solicitously watched over and fed by the anxious Mrs. Tanner, who was much disconcerted at the state of affairs, and couldn't understand why she could not get the school-teacher more interested in the invalid.

On the fourth day, however, the Reverend Frederick crept forth, white and shaken, with his sleek hair elaborately combed to cover a long scratch on his forehead, and announced his intention of departing from the State of Arizona that evening.

He crept forth cautiously to the station as the shades of evening drew on, but found Long Bill awaiting him, and Jasper Kemp not far away. He had the two letters ready in his pocket, with the gold piece, though he had entertained hopes of escaping without forfeiting them, but he was obliged to wait patiently until Jasper Kemp had read both letters through twice, with the train in momentary danger of departing without him, before he was finally allowed to get on board. Jasper Kemp's parting word to him was:

"Watch your steps spry, parson. I'm agoin' to see that you're shadowed wherever you go. You needn't think you can get shy on the Bible again. It won't pay."

There was menace in the dry remark, and the Reverend Frederick's professional egotism withered before it. He bowed his head, climbed on board the train, and vanished from the scene of his recent discomfiture. But the bitterest thing about it all was that he had gone without capturing the heart or even the attention of that haughty little school-teacher. "And she was such a pretty girl," he said, regretfully, to himself. "Such a *very* pretty girl!" He sighed deeply to himself as he watched Arizona speed by the window. "Still," he reflected, comfortably, after a moment, "there are always plenty more! What was that remarkably witty saying I heard just before I left home? 'Never run after a street-car or a woman. There'll be another one along in a minute.' Um—ah—yes—very true—there'll be another one along in a minute."

18

SCHOOL had settled down to real work by the opening of the new week. Margaret knew her scholars and had gained a personal hold on most of them already. There was enough novelty in her teaching to keep the entire school in a pleasant state of excitement and wonder as to what she would do next, and the word had gone out through all the country round about that the new teacher had taken the school by storm. It was not infrequent for men to turn out of their way on the trail to get a glimpse of the school as they were pasing, just to make sure the reports were true. Rumor stated that the teacher was exceedingly pretty; that she would take no nonsense, not even from the big boys; that she never threatened nor punished, but that every one of the boys was her devoted slave. There had been no uprising, and it almost seemed as if that popular excitement was to be omitted this season, and school was to sail along in an orderly and proper manner. In fact, the entire school as well as the surrounding population were eagerly talking about the new piano, which seemed really to be a coming fact. Not that there had been anything done toward it yet, but the teacher had promised that just as soon as every one was really studying hard and doing his best, she was going to begin to get them ready for an entertainment to raise money for that piano. They couldn't begin until everybody was in good working order, because they didn't want to take the interest away from the real business of school; but it was going to be a Shakespeare play, whatever that was, and therefore of grave import. Some people talked learnedly about Shakespeare and hinted of poetry; but the main part of the community spoke the name joyously and familiarly and without awe, as if it were milk and honey in their mouths. Why should they reverence Shakespeare more than any one else?

Margaret had grown used to seeing a head appear suddenly at one of the school-room windows and look long and frowningly first at her, then at the school, and then back to her again, as if it were a nine days' wonder. Whoever the visitor was, he would stand quietly, watching the process of the hour as if he were at a play, and Margaret would turn and smile pleasantly, then go right on with her work. The visitor would generally take off a wide hat and wave it cordially, smile back a curious, softened smile, and by and by he would mount his horse and pass on reflectively down the trail, wishing he could be a boy and go back again to school — such a school!

Oh, it was not all smooth, the way that Margaret walked. There were hitches, and unpleasant days when nothing went right, and when some of the girls got silly and rebellious, and the boys followed in their lead. She had her trials like any teacher, skilful as she was, and not the least of them because Rosa Rogers, the petted beauty, who presently manifested a childish jealousy of her in her influence over the boys. Noting this, Margaret went out of her way to win Rosa, but found it a difficult matter.

Rosa was proud, selfish, and unprincipled. She never forgave any one who frustrated her plans. She resented being made to study like the rest. She had always compelled the teacher to let her do as she pleased and still give her a good report. This she found she could not do with Margaret, and for the first time in her career she was compelled to work or fall behind. It presently became not a question of how the new teacher was to manage the big boys and the bad boys of the Ashland Ridge School, but how she was to prevent Rosa Rogers and a few girls who followed her from upsetting all her plans. The trouble was, Rosa was pretty and knew her power over the boys. If she chose she could put them all in a state of insubordination, and this she chose very often during those first few weeks.

But there was one visitor who did not confine himself to looking in at the window.

One morning a fine black horse came galloping up to the school-house at recess-time, and a well-set-up young man in wide sombrero and jaunty leather trappings sprang off and came into the building. His shining spurs caught the sunlight and flashed as he moved. He walked with the air of one who regards himself of far more importance than all who may be watching him. The boys in the yard stopped their ball-game, and the girls huddled close in whispering groups and drew near to the door. He was a young man from a ranch near the fort some thirty miles away, and he had brought an invitation for the new school-teacher to come over to dinner on Friday evening and stay until the following Monday morning. The invitation was from his sister, the wife of a wealthy cattleman whose home and hospitality were noted for miles around. She had heard of the coming of the beautiful young teacher, and wanted to attach her to her social circle.

The young man was deference itself to Margaret, openly admiring her as he talked, and said the most gracious things to her; and then, while she was answering the note, he smiled over at Rosa Rogers, who had slipped into her seat and was studiously preparing her algebra with the book upside down.

Margaret, looking up, caught Rosa's smiling glance and

the tail end of a look from the young man's eyes, and felt a passing wonder whether he had ever met the girl before. Something in the boldness of his look made her feel that he had not. Yet he was all smiles and deference to herself, and his open admiration and pleasure that she was to come to help brighten this lonely country, and that she was going to accept the invitation, was really pleasant to the girl, for it was desolate being tied down to only the Tanner household and the school, and she welcomed any bit of social life.

The young man had light hair, combed very smooth, and light-blue eyes. They were bolder and handsomer than the minister's, but the girl had a feeling that they were the very same cold color. She wondered at her comparison, for she liked the handsome young man, and in spite of herself was a little flattered at the nice things he had said to her. Nevertheless, when she remembered him afterward it was always with that uncomfortable feeling that if he hadn't been so handsome and polished in his appearance he would have seemed just a little bit like that minister, and she couldn't for the life of her tell why.

After he was gone she looked back at Rosa, and there was a narrowing of the girl's eyes and a frown of hate on her brows. Margaret turned with a sigh back to her school problem—what to do with Rosa Rogers?

But Rosa did not stay in the school-house. She slipped out and walked arm in arm with Amanda Bounds down the road.

Margaret went to the door and watched. Presently she saw the rider wheel and come galloping back to the door. He had forgotten to tell her that an escort would be sent to bring her as early on Friday afternoon as she would be ready to leave the school, and he intimated that he hoped he might be detailed for that pleasant duty.

Margaret looked into his face and warmed to his pleasant smile. How could she have thought him like West? He touched his hat and rode away, and a moment later she saw him draw rein beside Rosa and Amanda, and presently dismount.

Bud rang the bell just then, and Margaret went back to her desk with a lingering look at the three figures in the distance. It was full half an hour before Rosa came in, with Amanda looking scared behind her; and troubled Margaret watched the sly look in the girl's eyes and wondered what she ought to do about it. As Rosa was passing out of the door after school she called her to the desk.

"You were late in coming in after recess, Rosa," said Margaret, gently. "Have you any excuse?"

"I was talking to a friend," said Rosa, with a toss of her head which said, as plainly as words could have done, "I don't intend to give an excuse."

"Were you talking to the gentleman who was here?"

"Well, if I was, what is that to you, Miss Earle?" said Rosa, haughtily. "Did you think you could have all the men and boys to yourself?"

"Rosa," said Margaret, trying to speak calmly, but her voice trembling with suppressed indignation, "don't talk that way to me. Child, did you ever meet Mr. Forsythe before?"

"I'm not a child, and it's none of your business!" flouted Rosa, angrily, and she twitched away and flung herself out of the school-house.

Margaret, trembling from the disagreeable encounter, stood at the window and watched the girl going down the road, and felt for the moment that she would rather give up her school and go back home than face the situation. She knew in her heart that this girl, once an enemy, would be a bitter one, and this her last move had been a most unfortunate one, coming out, as it did, with Rosa in the lead. She could, of course, complain to Rosa's family, or to the school-board, but such was not the policy she had chosen. She wanted to be able to settle her own difficulties. It seemed strange that she could not reach this one girl — who was in a way the key to the situation. Perhaps the play would be able to help her.

She spent a long time that evening going over the different plays in her library, and finally, with a look of apology toward a little photographed head of Shakespeare, she decided on "Midsummer-Night's Dream." What if it was away above the heads of them all, wouldn't a few get something from it? And wasn't it better to take a great thing and try to make her scholars and a few of the community understand it, rather than to take a silly little play that would not amount to anything in the end? Of course, they couldn't do it well; that went without saying. Of course it would be away beyond them all, but at least it would be a study of something great for her pupils, and she could meantime teach them a little about Shakespeare and perhaps help some of them to learn to love his plays and study them.

The play she had selected was one in which she herself had acted the part of Puck, and she knew it by heart. She felt reasonably sure that she could help some of the more adaptable scholars to interpret their parts, and, at least, it would be good for them just as a study in literature. As for the audience, they would not be critics. Perhaps they would not even be able to comprehend the meaning of the play, but they would come and they would listen, and the experiment was one worth trying.

Carefully she went over the parts, trying to find the one which she thought would best fit Rosa Rogers, and please her as well, because it gave her opportunity to display her beauty and charm. She really was a pretty girl, and would do well. Margaret wondered whether she were altogether right in attempting to win the girl through her vanity, and yet what other weak place was there in which to storm the silly little citadel of her soul?

And so the work of assigning parts and learning them began that very week, though no one was allowed a part until his work for the day had all been handed in.

At noon Margaret made one more attempt with Rosa Rogers. She drew her to a seat beside her and put aside as much as possible her own remembrance of the girl's disagreeable actions and impudent words.

"Rosa," she said, and her voice was very gentle, "I want to have a little talk with you. You seem to feel that you and I are enemies, and I don't want you to have that attitude. I hoped we'd be the best of friends. You see, there isn't any other way for us to work well together. And I want to explain why I spoke to you as I did yesterday. It was not, as you hinted, that I want to keep all my acquaintances to myself. I have no desire to do that. It was because I feel responsible for the girls and boys in my care, and I was troubled lest perhaps you had been foolish—"

Margaret paused. She could see by the bright hardness of the girl's eyes that she was accomplishing nothing. Rosa evidently did not believe her.

"Well, Rosa," she said, suddenly, putting an impulsive kindly hand on the girl's arm, "suppose we forget it this time, put it all away, and be friends. Let's learn to understand each other if we can, but in the mean time I want to talk to you about the play."

And then, indeed, Rosa's hard manner broke, and she looked up with interest, albeit there was some suspicion in the glance. She wanted to be in that play with all her heart; she wanted the very showiest part in it, too; and she meant to have it, although she had a strong suspicion that the teacher would want to keep that part for herself, whatever it was.

But Margaret had been wise. She had decided to take time and explain the play to her, and then let her choose her own part. She wisely judged that Rosa would do better in the part in which her interest centered, and perhaps the choice would help her to understand her pupil better.

And so for an hour she patiently stayed after school and went over the play, explaining it carefully, and it seemed at one time as though Rosa was about to choose to be Puck, because with quick perception she caught the importance of that character; but when she learned that the costume must be a quiet hood and skirt of green and brown she scorned it, and chose, at last, to be Titania, queen of the fairies. So, with a sigh of relief, and a keen insight into the shallow nature, Margaret began to teach the girl some of the fairy steps, and found her quick and eager to learn. In the first lesson Rosa forgot for a little while her animosity and became almost as one of the other pupils. The play was going to prove a great means of bringing them all together.

Before Friday afternoon came the parts had all been assigned and the plans for the entertainment were well under way.

Jed and Timothy had been as good as their word about giving the teacher riding-lessons, each vying with the other to bring a horse and make her ride at noon hour, and she had already had several good lessons and a long ride or two in company with both her teachers.

The thirty-mile ride for Friday, then, was not such an undertaking as it might otherwise have been, and Margaret looked forward to it with eagerness.

19

THE little party of escort arrived before school was closed on Friday afternoon, and came down to the school-house in full force to take her away with them. The young man Forsythe, with his sister, the hostess herself, and a young army officer from the fort, comprised the party. Margaret dismissed school ten minutes early and went back with them to the Tanners' to make a hurried change in her dress and pick up her suit-case, which was already packed. As they rode away from the school-house Margaret looked back and saw Rosa Rogers posing in one of her sprite dances in the school-yard, saw her kiss her hand laughingly toward their party, and saw the flutter of a handkerchief in young Forsythe's hand. It was all very general and elusive, a passing bit of fun, but it left an uncomfortable impression on the teacher's mind. She looked keenly at the young man as he rode up smiling beside her, and once more experienced that strange, sudden change of feeling about him.

She took opportunity during that long ride to find out if the young man had known Rosa Rogers before; but he frankly told her that he had just come West to visit his sister, was bored to death because he didn't know a soul in the whole State, and until he had seen her had not laid eyes on one whom he cared to know. Yet while she could not help enjoying the gay badinage, she carried a sense of uneasiness whenever she thought of the young girl Rosa in her pretty fairy pose, with her fluttering pink fingers and her saucy, smiling eyes. There was something untrustworthy, too, in the handsome face of the man beside her.

There was just one shadow over this bit of a holiday. Margaret had a little feeling that possibly some one from the camp might come down on Saturday or Sunday, and she would miss him. Yet nothing had been said about it, and she had no way of sending word that she would be away. She had meant to send Mom Wallis a letter by the next messenger that came that way. It was all written and lying on her bureau, but no one had been down all the week. She was, therefore, greatly pleased when an approaching rider in the distance proved to be Gardley, and with a joyful little greeting she drew rein and hailed him, giving him a message for Mom Wallis.

Only Gardley's eyes told what this meeting was to him. His demeanor was grave and dignified. He acknowledged the introductions to the rest of the party gracefully, touched his hat with the ease of one to the manner born, and rode away, flashing her one gleam of a smile that told her he was glad of the meeting; but throughout the brief interview there had been an air of question and hostility between the two men, Forsythe and Gardley. Forsythe surveyed Gardley rudely, almost insolently, as if his position beside the lady gave him rights beyond the other, and he resented the coming of the stranger. Gardley's gaze was cold, too, as he met the look, and his eyes searched Forsythe's face keenly, as though they would find out what manner of man was riding with his friend.

When he was gone Margaret had the feeling that he was somehow disappointed, and once she turned in the saddle and looked wistfully after him; but he was riding furiously into the distance, sitting his horse as straight as an arrow and already far away upon the desert.

"Your friend is a reckless rider," said Forsythe, with a sneer in his voice that Margaret did not like, as they watched the speck in the distance clear a steep descent from the mesa at a bound and disappear from sight in the mesquite beyond.

"Isn't he fine-looking? Where did you find him, Miss Earle?" asked Mrs. Temple, eagerly. "I wish I'd asked him to join us. He left so suddenly I didn't realize he was going."

Margaret felt a wondering and pleasant sense of possession and pride in Gardley as she watched, but she quietly explained that the young stranger was from the East, and that he was engaged in some kind of cattle business at a distance from Ashland. Her manner was reserved, and the matter dropped. She naturally felt a reluctance to tell how her acquaintance with Gardley began. It seemed something between themselves. She could fancy the gushing Mrs. Temple saying, "How romantic!" She was that kind of a woman. It was evident that she was romantically inclined herself, for she used her fine eyes with effect on the young officer who rode with her, and Margaret found herself wondering what kind of a husband she had and what her mother would think of a woman like this.

There was no denying that the luxury of the ranch was a happy relief from the simplicity of life at the Tanners'. Iced drinks and cushions and easy-chairs, feasting and music and laughter! There were books, too, and magazines, and all the little things that go to make up a cultured life; and yet they were not people of Margaret's world, and when Saturday evening was over she sat alone in the room they had given her and, facing herself in the glass, confessed to herself that she looked back with more pleasure to the Sabbath spent with Mom Wallis than she could look forward to a Sabbath here. The morning proved her forebodings well founded.

Breakfast was a late, informal affair, filled with hilarious gaiety. There was no mention of any church service, and

Margaret found it was quite too late to suggest such a thing when breakfast was over, even if she had been sure there was any service.

After breakfast was over there were various forms of amusement proposed for her pleasure, and she really felt very much embarrassed for a few moments to know how to avoid what to her was pure Sabbath-breaking. Yet she did not wish to be rude to these people who were really trying to be kind to her. She managed at last to get them interested in music, and, grouping them around the piano after a few preliminary performances by herself at their earnest solicitation, coaxed them into singing hymns.

After all, they really seemed to enjoy it, though they had to get along with one hymn-book for the whole company; but Margaret knew how to make hymn-singing interesting, and her exquisite voice was never more at its best than when she led off with "My Jesus, as Thou Wilt," or "Jesus, Saviour, Pilot Me."

"You would be the delight of Mr. Brownleigh's heart," said the hostess, gushingly, at last, after Margaret had finished singing "Abide With Me" with wonderful feeling.

"And who is Mr. Brownleigh?" asked Margaret. "Why should I delight his heart?"

"Why, he is our missionary—that is, the missionary for this region—and you would delight his heart because you are so religious and sing so well," said the superficial little woman. "Mr. Brownleigh is really a very cultured man. Of course, he's narrow. All clergymen are narrow, don't you think? They have to be to a certain extent. He's really *quite* narrow. Why, he believes in the Bible *literally,* the whale and Jonah, and the Flood, and making bread out of stones, and all that sort of thing, you know. Imagine it! But he does. He's sincere! Perfectly sincere. I suppose he has to be. It's his business. But sometimes one feels it a pity that he can't relax a little, just among us here, you know. We'd never tell. Why, he won't even play a little game of poker! And he doesn't smoke!

Imagine it — *not even when he's by himself,* and *no one would know!* Isn't that odd? But he can preach. He's really very interesting; only a little too Utopian in his ideas. He thinks everybody ought to be good, you know, and all that sort of thing. He really thinks it's possible, and he lives that way himself. He really does. But he is a wonderful person; only I feel sorry for his wife sometimes. She's quite a cultured person. Has been wealthy, you know. She was a New York society girl. Just imagine it; out in these wilds taking gruel to the dirty little Indians! How she ever came to do it! Of course she adores him, but I can't really believe she is happy. No woman could be quite blind enough to give up everything in the world for one man, no matter how good he was. Do you think she could? It wasn't as if she didn't have plenty of other chances. She gave them all up to come out and marry him. She's a pretty good sport, too; she never lets you know she isn't perfectly happy."

"She *is* happy; mother, she's happier than *anybody* I ever saw," declared the fourteen-year-old daughter of the house, who was home from boarding-school for a brief visit during an epidemic of measles in the school.

"Oh yes, she manages to make people think she's happy," said her mother, indulgently; "but you can't make me believe she's satisfied to give up her house on Fifth Avenue and live in a two-roomed log cabin in the desert, with no society."

"Mother, you don't know! Why, *any* woman would be satisfied if her husband adored her the way Mr. Brownleigh does her."

"Well, Ada, you're a romantic girl, and Mr. Brownleigh is a handsome man. You've got a few things to learn yet. Mark my words, I don't believe you'll see Mrs. Brownleigh coming back next month with her husband. This operation was all well enough to talk about, but I'll not be surprised to hear that he has come back alone or else that he has accepted a call to some big city church. And he's equal to the city church, too; that's the wonder of it. He comes of a fine family himself, I've heard. Oh, people can't keep up the pose of saints forever, even though they do adore each other. But Mr. Brownleigh *certainly* is a good man!"

The vapid little woman sat looking reflectively out of the window for a whole minute after this deliverance. Yes, certainly Mr. Brownleigh was a good man. He was the one man of culture, education, refinement, who had come her way in many a year who had patiently and persistently and gloriously refused her advances at a mild flirtation, and refused to understand them, yet remained her friend and reverenced hero. He was a good man, and she knew it, for she was a very pretty woman and understood her art well.

Before the day was over Margaret had reason to feel that a Sabbath in Arizona was a very hard thing to find. The singing could not last all day, and her friends seemed to find more amusements on Sunday that did not come into Margaret's code of Sabbath-keeping than one knew how to say no to. Neither could they understand her feeling, and she found it hard not to be rude in gently declining one plan after another.

She drew the children into a wide, cozy corner after dinner and began a Bible story in the guise of a fairy-tale, while the hostess slipped away to take a nap. However, several other guests lingered about, and Mr. Temple strayed in. They sat with newspapers before their faces and got into the story, too, seeming to be deeply interested, so that, after all, Margaret did not have an unprofitable Sabbath.

But altogether, though she had a gay and somewhat frivolous time, a good deal of admiration and many invitations to return as often as possible, Margaret was not sorry when she said good night to know that she was to return in the early morning to her work.

Mr. Temple himself was going part way with them, accompanied by his niece, Forsythe, and the young officer who came over with them. Margaret rode beside Mr. Temple until his way parted from theirs, and had a delightful talk about Arizona. He was a kindly old fellow who adored his frivolous little wife and let her go her own gait, seeming not to mind how much she flirted.

The morning was pink and silver, gold and azure, a wonderful specimen of an Arizona sunrise for Margaret's benefit, and a glorious beginning for her day's work in spite of the extremely early hour. The company was gay and blithe, and the Eastern girl felt as if she were passing through a wonderful experience.

They loitered a little on the way to show Margaret the wonders of a fern-plumed cañon, and it was almost schooltime when they came up the street, so that Margaret rode straight to the school-house instead of stopping at Tanners'. On the way to the school they passed a group of girls, of whom Rosa Rogers was the center. A certain something in Rosa's narrowed eyelids as she said good morning caused Margaret to look back uneasily, and she distinctly saw the girl give a signal to young Forsythe, who, for answer, only tipped his hat and gave her a peculiar smile.

In a moment more they had said good-by, and Margaret was left at the school-house door with a cluster of eager children about her, and several shy boys in the background, ready to welcome her back as if she had been gone a month.

In the flutter of opening school Margaret failed to notice that Rosa Rogers did not appear. It was not until the roll was called that she noticed her absence, and she looked uneasily toward the door many times during the morning, but Rosa did not come until after recess, when she stole smilingly in, as if it were quite the thing to come to school late. When questioned about her tardiness she said she had torn her dress and had to go home and change it. Margaret knew by the look in her eyes that the girl was not telling the truth, but what was she to do? It troubled her all the morning and went with her to a sleepless pillow that night. She was beginning to see that life as a school-teacher in the far West was not all she had imagined it to be. Her father had been right. There would likely be more thorns than roses on her way.

THE first time Lance Gardley met Rosa Rogers riding with Archie Forsythe he thought little of it. He knew the girl by sight, because he knew her father in a business way. That she was very young and one of Margaret's pupils was all he knew about her. For the young man he had conceived a strong dislike, but as there was no reason whatever for it he put it out of his mind as quickly as possible.

The second time he met them it was toward evening and they were so wholly absorbed in each other's society that they did not see him until he was close upon them. Forsythe looked up with a frown and a quick hand to his hip, where gleamed a weapon.

He scarcely returned the slight salute given by Gardley, and the two young people touched up their horses and were soon out of sight in the mesquite. But something in the frightened look of the girl's eyes caused Gardley to turn and look after the two.

Where could they be going at that hour of the evening? It was not a trail usually chosen for rides. It was lonely and unfrequented, and led out of the way of travelers. Gardley himself had been a far errand for Jasper Kemp, and had taken this short trail back because it cut off several miles and he was weary. Also, he was anxious to stop in Ashland and leave Mom Wallis's request that Margaret would spend the next Sabbath at the camp and see the new curtains. He was thinking what he should say to her when he saw her in a little while now, and this interruption to his thoughts was unwelcome. Nevertheless, he could not get away from that frightened look in the girl's eyes. Where could they have been going? That fellow was a new-comer in the region; perhaps he had lost his way. Perhaps he did not know that the road he was taking the girl led into a region of outlaws, and that the only habitation along the way was a cabin belonging to an old woman of weird reputation, where wild orgies were sometimes celebrated, and where men went who loved darkness rather than light, because their deeds were evil.

Twice Gardley turned in his saddle and scanned the desert. The sky was darkening, and one or two pale stars were impatiently shadowing forth their presence. And now he could see the two riders again. They had come up out of the mesquite to the top of the mesa, and were outlined against the sky sharply. They were still on the trail to old Ouida's cabin!

With a quick jerk Gardley reined in his horse and wheeled about, watching the riders for a moment; and then, setting spurs to his beast, he was off down the trail after them on one of his wild, reckless rides. Down through the mesquite he plunged, through the darkening grove, out, and up to the top of the mesa. He had lost sight of his quarry for the time, but now he could see them again riding more slowly in the valley below, their horses close together, and even as he watched the sky took on its wide night look and the stars blazed forth.

Suddenly Gardley turned sharply from the trail and made a detour through a grove of trees, riding with reckless speed, his head down to escape low branches; and in a minute or two he came with unerring instinct back to the trail some distance ahead of Forsythe and Rosa. Then he wheeled his horse and stopped stock-still, awaiting their coming.

By this time the great full moon was risen and, strangely enough, was at Gardley's back, making a silhouette of man and horse as the two riders came on toward him.

They rode out from the cover of the grove, and there he was across their path. Rosa gave a scream, drawing nearer her companion, and her horse swerved and reared; but Gardley's black stood like an image carved in ebony against the silver of the moon, and Gardley's quiet voice was in strong contrast to the quick, unguarded exclamation of Forsythe, as he sharply drew rein and put his hand hastily to his hip for his weapon.

"I beg your pardon, Mr. Forsythe" — Gardley had an excellent memory for names — "but I thought you might not be aware, being a new-comer in these parts, that the trail you are taking leads to a place where ladies do not like to go."

"Really! You don't say so!" answered the young man, insolently. "It's very kind of you, I'm sure, but you might have saved yourself the trouble. I know perfectly where I am going, and so does the lady, and we choose to go this way. Move out of the way, please. You are detaining us."

But Gardley did not move out of the way. "I am sure the lady does not know where she is going," he said, firmly. "I am sure that she does not know that it is a place of bad reputation, even in this unconventional land. At least, if she knows, I am sure that *her father* does not know, and I am well acquainted with her father."

"Get out of the way, sir," said Forsythe, hotly. "It certainly is none of your business, anyway, whoever knows what. Get out of the way or I shall shoot. This lady and I intend to ride where we please."

"Then I shall have to say you *cannot*," said Gardley; and his voice still had that calm that made his opponent think him easy to conquer.

"Just how do you propose to stop us?" sneered Forsythe, pulling out his pistol.

"This way," said Gardley, lifting a tiny silver whistle to his lips and sending forth a peculiar, shrilling blast. "And this way," went on Gardley, calmly lifting both hands and showing a weapon in each, wherewith he covered the two.

Rosa screamed and covered her face with her hands, cowering in her saddle.

Forsythe lifted his weapon, but looked around nervously. "Dead men tell no tales," he said, angrily.

"It depends upon the man," said Gardley, meaningly, "especially if he were found on this road. I fancy a few tales could be told if you happened to be the man. Turn your horses around at once and take this lady back to her home. My men are not far off, and if you do not wish the whole story to be known among your friends and hers you would better make haste."

Forsythe dropped his weapon and obeyed. He decidedly did not wish his escapade to be known among his friends. There were financial reasons why he did not care to have it come to the ears of his brother-in-law just now.

Silently in the moonlight the little procession took its way down the trail, the girl and the man side by side, their captor close behind, and when the girl summoned courage to glance fearsomely behind her she saw three more men riding like three grim shadows yet behind. They had fallen into the trail so quietly that she had not heard them when they came. They were Jasper Kemp, Long Bill, and Big Jim. They had been out for other purposes, but without question followed the call of the signal.

It was a long ride back to Rogers's ranch, and Forsythe glanced nervously behind now and then. It seemed to him that the company was growing larger each time he turned. He tried hurrying his horse, but when he did so the followers were just as close without any seeming effort. He tried to laugh it all off.

Once he turned and tried to placate Gardley with a few shakily jovial words:

"Look here, old fellow, aren't you the man I met on the trail the day Miss Earle went over to the fort? I guess you've made a mistake in your calculations. I was merely out on a pleasure ride with Miss Rogers. We weren't going anywhere in particular, you know. Miss Rogers chose this way, and I wanted to please her. No man likes to have his pleasure interfered with, you know. I guess you didn't recognize me?"

"I recognized you," said Gardley. "It would be well of you to be careful where you ride with ladies, especially at night. The matter, however, is one that you would better settle with Mr. Rogers. My duty will be done when I have put it into his hands."

"Now, my good fellow," said Forsythe, patronizingly, "you surely don't intend to make a great fuss about this and go telling tales to Mr. Rogers about a trifling matter — "

"I intend to do my duty, Mr. Forsythe," said Gardley; and Forsythe noticed that the young man still held his weapons. "I was set this night to guard Mr. Rogers's property. That I did not expect his daughter would be a part of the evening's guarding has nothing to do with the matter. I shall certainly put the matter into Mr. Rogers's hands."

Rosa began to cry softly.

"Well, if you want to be a fool, of course," laughed Forsythe, disagreeably; "but you will soon see Mr. Rogers will accept my explanation."

"That is for Mr. Rogers to decide," answered Gardley, and said no more.

The reflections of Forsythe during the rest of that silent ride were not pleasant, and Rosa's intermittent crying did not tend to make him more comfortable.

The silent procession at last turned in at the great ranch gate and rode up to the house. Just as they stopped and the door of the house swung open, letting out a flood of light, Rosa leaned toward Gardley and whispered:

"Please, Mr. Gardley, don't tell papa. I'll do *anything* in the world for you if you won't tell papa."

He looked at the pretty, pitiful child in the moonlight. "I'm sorry, Miss Rosa," he said, firmly. "But you don't understand. I must do my duty."

"Then I shall hate you!" she hissed. "Do you hear? I shall *hate* you forever, and you don't know what that means. It means I'll take my *revenge* on you and on *everybody you like.*"

He looked at her half pityingly as he swung off his horse and went up the steps to meet Mr. Rogers, who had come out and was standing on the top step of the ranch-house in the square of light that flickered from a great fire on the hearth of the wide fireplace. He was looking from one to another of the silent group, and as his eyes rested on his daughter he said, sternly:

"Why, Rosa, what does this mean? You told me you were going to bed with a headache!"

Gardley drew his employer aside and told what had happened in a few low-toned sentences; and then stepped down and back into the shadow, his horse by his side, the three men from the camp grouped behind him. He had the delicacy to withdraw after his duty was done.

Mr. Rogers, his face stern with sudden anger and alarm, stepped down and stood beside his daughter. "Rosa, you may get down and go into the house to your own room. I will talk with you later," he said. And then to the young man, "You, sir, will step into my office. I wish to have a plain talk with you."

A half-hour later Forsythe came out of the Rogers house and mounted his horse, while Mr. Rogers stood silently and watched him.

"I will bid you good evening, sir," he said, formally, as the young man mounted his horse and silently rode away. His back had a defiant look in the moonlight as he passed the group of men in the shadow; but they did not turn to watch him.

"That will be all to-night, Gardley, and I thank you very much," called the clear voice of Mr. Rogers from his front steps.

The four men mounted their horses silently and rode down a little distance behind the young man, who wondered in his heart just how much or how little Gardley had told Rosa's father.

The interview to which young Forsythe had just been subjected had been chastening in character, of a kind to baffle curiosity concerning the father's knowledge of details, and to discourage any further romantic rides with Miss Rosa. It had been left in abeyance whether or not the Temples should be made acquainted with the episode, dependent upon the future conduct of both young people. It had not been satisfactory from Forsythe's point of view; that is, he had not been so easily able to disabuse the father's mind of suspicion, nor to establish his own guileless character as he had hoped; and some of the remarks Rogers made led Forsythe to think that the father understood just how unpleasant it might become for him if his brother-in-law found out about the escapade.

This is why Archie Forsythe feared Lance Gardley, although there was nothing in the least triumphant about the set of that young man's shoulders as he rode away in the moonlight on the trail toward Ashland. And this is how it came about that Rosa Rogers hated Lance Gardley, handsome and daring though he was; and because of him hated her teacher, Margaret Earle.

An hour later Lance Gardley stood in the little dim Tanner parlor, talking to Margaret.

"You look tired," said the girl, compassionately, as she saw the haggard shadows on the young face, showing in spite of the light of pleasure in his eyes. "You look *very* tired. What in the world have you been doing?"

"I went out to catch cattle-thieves," he said, with a sigh, "but I found there were other kinds of thieves abroad. It's all in the day's work. I'm not tired now." And he smiled at her with beautiful reverence.

Margaret, as she watched him, could not help thinking that the lines in his face had softened and strengthened since she had first seen him, and her eyes let him know that she was glad he had come.

"And so you will really come to us, and it isn't going to be asking too much?" he said, wistfully. "You can't think what it's going to be to the men — to *us!* And Mom Wallis is so excited she can hardly get her work done. If you had said no I would be almost afraid to go back." He laughed, but she could see there was deep earnestness under his tone.

"Indeed I will come," said Margaret. "I'm just looking forward to it. I'm going to bring Mom Wallis a new bonnet like one I made for mother; and I'm going to teach her how to make corn gems and steamed apple dumplings. I'm bringing some songs and some music for the violin; and I've got something for you to help me do, too, if you will?"

He smiled tenderly down on her. What a wonderful girl she was, to be willing to come out to the old shack among a lot of rough men and one uncultured old woman and make them happy, when she was fit for the finest in the land!

"You're *wonderful!*" he said, taking her hand with a quick pressure for good-by. "You make every one want to do his best."

He hurried out to his horse and rode away in the moonlight. Margaret went up to her "mountain window" and watched him far out on the trail, her heart swelling with an unnamed gladness over his last words.

"Oh, God, keep him, and help him to make good!" she prayed.

21

THE visit to the camp was a time to be remembered long by all the inhabitants of the bunk-house, and even by Margaret herself. Margaret wondered Thursday evening, as she sat up late, working away braiding a lovely gray bonnet out of folds of malines, and fashioning it into form for Mom Wallis, why she was looking forward to the visit with so much more real pleasure than she had done to the one the week before at the Temples'. And so subtle is the heart of a maid that she never fathomed the real reason.

The Temples', of course, was interesting and delightful as being something utterly new in her experience. It was comparatively luxurious, and there were pleasant, cultured people there, more from her own social class in life. But it was going to be such fun to surprise Mom Wallis with that bonnet and see her old face light up when she saw herself in the little folding three-leaved mirror she was taking along with her and meant to leave for Mom Wallis's log boudoir. She was quite excited over selecting some little thing for each one of the men—books, pictures, a piece of music, a bright cushion, and a pile of picture magazines. It made a big bundle when she had them together, and she was dubious if she ought to try to carry them all; but Bud, whom she consulted on the subject, said, loftily, it "wasn't a flea-bite for the Kid; he could carry *any*thing on a horse."

Bud was just a little jealous to have his beloved teacher away from home so much, and rejoiced greatly when Gardley, Friday afternoon, suggested that he come along, too. He made quick time to his home, and secured a hasty permission and wardrobe, appearing like a footman on his father's old horse when they were half a mile down the trail.

Mom Wallis was out at the door to greet her guest when she arrived, for Margaret had chosen to make her visit last from Friday afternoon after school, until Monday morning. It was the generosity of her nature that she gave to her utmost when she gave.

The one fear she had entertained about coming had been set at rest on the way when Gardley told her that Pop Wallis was off on one of his long trips, selling cattle, and would probably not return for a week. Margaret, much as she trusted Gardley and the men, could not help dreading to meet Pop Wallis again.

There was a new trimness about the old bunk-house. The clearing had been cleaned up and made neat, the grass cut, some vines set out and trained up limply about the door, and the windows shone with Mom Wallis's washing.

Mom Wallis herself was wearing her best white apron, stiff with starch, her lace collar, and her hair in her best imitation of the way Margaret had fixed it, although it must be confessed she hadn't quite caught the knack of arrangement yet. But the one great difference Margaret noticed in the old woman was the illuminating smile on her face. Mom Wallis had learned how to let the glory gleam through all the hard sordidness of her life, and make earth brighter for those about her.

The curtains certainly made a great difference in the looks of the bunk-house, together with a few other changes. The men had made some chairs — three of them, one out of a barrel; and together they had upholstered them roughly. The cots around the walls were blazing with their red blankets folded smoothly and neatly over them, and on the floor in front of the hearth, which had been scrubbed, Gardley had spread a Navajo blanket he had bought of an Indian.

The fireplace was piled with logs ready for the lighting at night, and from somewhere a lamp had been rigged up and polished till it shone in the setting sun that slanted long rays in at the shining windows.

The men were washed and combed, and had been huddled at the back of the bunk-house for an hour, watching the road, and now they came forward awkwardly to greet their guest, their horny hands scrubbed to an unbelievable whiteness. They did not say much, but they looked their pleasure, and Margaret greeted every one as if he were an old friend, the charming part about it all to the men being that she remembered every one's name and used it.

Bud hovered in the background and watched with starry eyes. Bud was having the time of his life. He preferred the teacher's visiting the camp rather than the fort. The "Howdy, sonny!" which he had received from the men, and the "Make yourself at home, Bill" from Gardley, had given him great joy; and the whole thing seemed somehow to link him to the teacher in a most distinguishing manner.

Supper was ready almost immediately, and Mom Wallis had done her best to make it appetizing. There was a lamb stew with potatoes, and fresh corn bread with coffee. The men ate with relish, and watched their guest of honor as if she had been an angel come down to abide with them for a season. There was a tablecloth on the old table, too — a *white* tablecloth. It looked remarkably like an old sheet, to be sure, with a seam through the middle where it had been worn and turned and sewed together; but it was a tablecloth now, and a marvel to the men. And the wonder about Margaret was that she could eat at such a table and make it seem as though that tablecloth were the finest damask, and the two-tined forks the heaviest of silver.

After the supper was cleared away and the lamp lighted, the gifts were brought out. A book of Scotch poetry for Jasper Kemp, bound in tartan covers of the Campbell clan; a small illustrated pamphlet of Niagara Falls for Big Jim, because he had said he wanted to see the place and never could manage it; a little picture folder of Washington City for Big Jim; a book of old ballad music for Fiddling Boss; a book of jokes for Fade-away Forbes; a framed picture of a beautiful shepherd dog for Stocky; a big, red, ruffled denim pillow for Croaker, because when she was there before he was always complaining about the seats being hard; a great blazing crimson pennant bearing the name HARVARD in big letters for Fudge, because she had remembered he was from Boston; and for Mom Wallis a framed text beautifully painted in water-colors, done in rustic letters twined with stray forget-me-nots, the words, "Come unto Me, all ye that labor and are heavy laden, and I will give you rest." Margaret had made that during the week and framed it in a simple raffia braid of brown and green.

It was marvelous how these men liked their presents; and while they were examining them and laughing about them and putting their pictures and Mom Wallis's text on the walls, and the pillow on a bunk, and the pennant over the fireplace, Margaret shyly held out a tiny box to Gardley.

"I thought perhaps you would let me give you this," she said. "It isn't much; it isn't even new, and it has some marks in it; but I thought it might help with your new undertaking."

Gardley took it with a lighting of his face and opened the box. In it was a little, soft, leather-bound Testament, showing the marks of usage, yet not worn. It was a tiny thing, very thin, easily fitting in a vest-pocket, and not a burden to carry. He took the little book in his hand, removed the silken rubber band that bound it, and turned the leaves reverently in his fingers, noting that there were pencil-marks here and there. His face was all emotion as he looked up at the giver.

"I thank you," he said, in a low tone, glancing about to see that no one was noticing them. "I shall prize it greatly. It surely will help. I will read it every day. Was that what you wanted? And I will carry it with me always."

His voice was very earnest, and he looked at her as though she had given him a fortune. With another glance about at the preoccupied room—even Bud was busy studying Jasper Kemp's oldest gun—he snapped the band on the book again and put it carefully in his inner breast-pocket. The book would henceforth travel next his heart and be his guide. She thought he meant her to understand that, as he put out his hand unobtrusively and pressed her fingers gently with a quick, low "Thank you!"

Then Mom Wallis's bonnet was brought out and tied on her, and the poor old woman blushed like a girl when she stood with meek hands folded at her waist and looked primly about on the family for their approval at Margaret's request. But that was nothing to the way she stared when Margaret got out the threefold mirror and showed her herself in the new headgear. She trotted away at last, the wonderful bonnet in one hand, the box in the other, a look of awe on her face, and Margaret heard her murmur as she put it away: "Glory! *Me!* Glory!"

Then Margaret had to read one or two of the poems for Jasper Kemp, while they all sat and listened to her Scotch and marveled at her. A woman like that condescending to come to visit them!

She gave a lesson in note-reading to the Fiddling Boss, pointing one by one with her white fingers to the notes until he was able to creep along and pick out "Suwanee River" and "Old Folks at Home" to the intense delight of the audience.

Margaret never knew just how it was that she came to be telling the men a story, one she had read not long before in a magazine, a story with a thrilling national interest and a keen personal touch that searched the hearts of men; but they listened as they had never listened to anything in their lives before.

And then there was singing, more singing, until it bade fair to be morning before they slept, and the little teacher was weary indeed when she lay down on the cot in Mom Wallis's room, after having knelt beside the old woman and prayed.

The next day there was a wonderful ride with Gardley and Bud to the cañon of the cave-dwellers, and a coming home to the apple dumplings she had taught Mom Wallis to make before she went away. All day Gardley and she, with Bud for delighted audience, had talked over the play she was getting up at the school, Gardley suggesting about costumes and tree boughs for scenery, and promising to help in any way she wanted. Then after supper there were jokes and songs around the big fire, and some popcorn one of the men had gone a long ride that day to get. They called for another story, too, and it was forthcoming.

It was Sunday morning after breakfast, however, that Margaret suddenly wondered how she was going to make the day helpful and different from the other days.

She stood for a moment looking out of the clear little window thoughtfully, with just the shadow of a sigh on her lips, and as she turned back to the room she met Gardley's questioning glance.

"Are you homesick?" he asked, with a sorry smile. "This must all be very different from what you are accustomed to."

"Oh no, it isn't that." She smiled, brightly. "I'm not a baby for home, but I do get a bit homesick about church-time. Sunday is such a strange day to me without a service."

"Why not have one, then?" he suggested, eagerly. "We can sing and—you could—do the rest!"

Her eyes lighted at the suggestion, and she cast a quick

glance at the men. Would they stand for that sort of thing?

Gardley followed her glance and caught her meaning. "Let them answer for themselves," he said quickly in a low tone, and then, raising his voice: "Speak up, men. Do you want to have church? Miss Earle here is homesick for a service, and I suggest that we have one, and she conduct it."

"Sure!" said Jasper Kemp, his face lighting. "I'll miss my guess if she can't do better than the parson we had last Sunday. Get into your seats, boys; we're goin' to church."

Margaret's face was a study of embarrassment and delight as she saw the alacrity with which the men moved to get ready for "church." Her quick brain turned over the possibility of what she could read or say to help this strange congregation thus suddenly thrust upon her.

It was a testimony to her upbringing by a father whose great business of life was to preach the gospel that she never thought once of hesitating or declining the opportunity, but welcomed it as an opportunity, and only deprecated her unreadiness for the work.

The men stirred about, donned their coats, furtively brushing their hair, and Long Bill insisted that Mom Wallis put on her new bonnet; which she obligingly did, and sat down carefully in the barrel-chair, her hands neatly crossed in her lap, supremely happy. It really was wonderful what a difference that bonnet made in Mom Wallis.

Gardley arranged a comfortable seat for Margaret at the table and put in front of her one of the hymn-books she had brought. Then, after she was seated, he took the chair beside her and brought out the little Testament from his breast-pocket, gravely laying it on the hymn-book.

Margaret met his eyes with a look of quick appreciation. It was wonderful the way these two were growing to understand each other. It gave the girl a thrill of wonder and delight to have him do this simple little thing for her, and the smile that passed between them was beautiful to see.

Long Bill turned away his head and looked out of the window with an improvised sneeze to excuse the sudden mist that came into his eyes.

Margaret chose "My Faith Looks Up to Thee" for the first hymn, because Fiddling Boss could play it, and while he was tuning up his fiddle she hastily wrote out two more copies of the words. And so the queer service started with a quaver of the old fiddle and the clear, sweet voices of Margaret and Gardley leading off, while the men growled on their way behind, and Mom Wallis, in her new gray bonnet, with her hair all fluffed softly gray under it, sat with eyes shining like a girl's.

So absorbed in the song were they all that they failed to hear the sound of a horse coming into the clearing. But just as the last words of the final verse died away the door of the bunk-house swung open, and there in the doorway stood Pop Wallis!

The men sprang to their feet with one accord, ominous frowns on their brows, and poor old Mom Wallis sat petrified where she was, the smile of relaxation frozen on her face, a look of fear growing in her tired old eyes.

Now Pop Wallis, through an unusual combination of circumstances, had been for some hours without liquor and was comparatively sober. He stood for a moment staring amazedly at the group around his fireside. Perhaps because he had been so long without his usual stimulant his mind was weakened and things appeared as a strange vision to him. At any rate, he stood and stared, and as he looked from one to another of the men, at the beautiful stranger, and across to the strangely unfamiliar face of his wife in her new bonnet, his eyes took on a frightened look. He slowly took his hand from the doorframe and passed it over his eyes, then looked again, from one to another, and back to his glorified wife.

Margaret had half risen at her end of the table, and Gardley stood beside her as if to reassure her; but Pop Wallis was not looking at any of them any more. His eyes were on his wife.

He passed his hand once more over his eyes and took one step gropingly into the room, a hand reached out in front of him, as if he were not sure but he might run into something on the way, the other hand on his forehead, a dazed look in his face.

"Why, Mom—that ain't really—*you*, now, *is* it?" he said, in a gentle, insinuating voice like one long unaccustomed making a hasty prayer.

The tone made a swift change in the old woman. She gripped her bony hands tight and a look of beatific joy came into her wrinkled face.

"Yes, it's really *me*, Pop!" she said, with a kind of triumphant ring to her voice.

"But—but—you're right *here*, ain't you? You ain't *dead*, an'—an'—gone to—gl-oo-ry, be you? You're right *here?*"

"Yes, I'm right *here*, Pop. I ain't dead! Pop—glory's *come to me!*"

"Glory?" repeated the man, dazedly. "Glory?" And he gazed around the room and took in the new curtains, the pictures on the wall, the cushions and chairs, and the bright, shining windows. "You don't mean it's *heav'n*, do you, Mom? 'Cause I better go back—*I* don't belong in heav'n. Why, Mom, it can't be glory, *'cause* it's the same old bunk-house outside, anyhow."

"Yes, it's the same old bunk-house, and it ain't heaven, but it's *goin'* to be. The glory's come all right. You sit down, Pop; we're goin' to have church, and this is my new bonnet. *She* brang it. This is the new school-teacher, Miss Earle, and she's goin' to have church. She done it *all!* You sit down and listen."

Pop Wallis took a few hesitating steps into the room and dropped into the nearest chair. He looked at Margaret as if she might be an angel holding open the portal to a kingdom in the sky. He looked and wondered and admired, and then he looked back to his glorified old wife again in wonder.

Jasper Kemp shut the door, and the company dropped back into their places. Margaret, because of her deep embarrassment, and a kind of inward trembling that had taken possession of her, announced another hymn.

It was a solemn little service, quite unique, with a brief, simple prayer and an expository reading of the story of the blind man from the sixth chapter of John. The men sat attentively, their eyes upon her face as she read; but Pop Wallis sat staring at his wife, an awed light upon his scared old face, the wickedness and cunning all faded out, and only fear and wonder written there.

In the early dawning of the pink-and-silver morning Margaret went back to her work, Gardley riding by her side, and Bud riding at a discreet distance behind, now and then going off at a tangent after a stray cottontail. It was wonderful what good sense Bud seemed to have on occasion.

The horse that Margaret rode, a sturdy little Western pony, with nerve and grit and a gentle common sense for humans, was to remain with her in Ashland, a gift from the men of the bunk-house. During the week that followed Archie Forsythe came riding over with a beautiful shining saddle-horse for her use during her stay in the West; but when he went riding back to the ranch the shining saddle-horse was still in his train, riderless, for Margaret told him that she already had a horse of her own. Neither had Margaret accepted the invitation to the Temples' for the next week-end. She had other plans for the Sabbath, and that week there appeared on all the trees and posts about the town, and on the trails, a little notice of a Bible class and vesper service to be held in the school-house on the following Sabbath afternoon; and so Margaret, true daughter of her minister-father, took up her mission in Ashland for the Sabbaths that were to follow; for the school-board had agreed with alacrity to such use of the school-house.

NOW when it became noised abroad that the new teacher wanted above all things to purchase a piano, and that to that end she was getting up a wonderful Shakespeare play in which the scholars were to act upon a stage set with tree boughs after the manner of some new kind of players, the whole community round about began to be excited.

Mrs. Tanner talked much about it. Was not Bud to be a prominent character? Mr. Tanner talked about it everywhere he went. The mothers and fathers and sisters talked about it, and the work of preparing the play went on.

Margaret had discovered that one of the men at the bunk-house played a flute, and she was working hard to teach him and Fiddling Boss and Croaker to play a portion of the elfin dance to accompany the players. The work of making costumes and training the actors became more and more strenuous, and in this Gardley proved a fine assistant. He undertook to train some of the older boys for their parts, and did it so well that he was presently in the forefront of the battle of preparation and working almost as hard as Margaret herself.

The beauty of the whole thing was that every boy in the

school adored him, even Jed and Timothy, and life took on a different aspect to them in company with this high-born college-bred, Eastern young man who yet could ride and shoot with the daringest among the Westerners.

Far and wide went forth the fame of the play that was to be. The news of it reached to the fort and the ranches, and brought offers of assistance and costumes and orders for tickets. Margaret purchased a small duplicator and set her school to printing tickets and selling them, and before the play was half ready to be acted tickets enough were sold for two performances, and people were planning to come from fifty miles around. The young teacher began to quake at the thought of her big audience and her poor little amateur players; and yet for children they were doing wonderfully well, and were growing quite Shakespearian in their manner of conversation.

"What say you, sweet Amanda?" would be a form of frequent address to that stolid maiden Amanda Bounds; and Jed, instead of shouting for "Delicate" at recess, as in former times, would say, "My good Timothy, I swear to thee by Cupid's strongest bow; by his best arrow with the golden head"—until all the school yard rang with classic phrases; and the whole country round was being addressed in phrases of another century by the younger members of their households.

Then Rosa Rogers's father one day stopped at the Tanners' and left a contribution with the teacher of fifty dollars toward the new piano; and after that it was rumored that the teacher said the piano could be sent for in time to be used at the play. Then other contributions of smaller amounts came in, and before the date of the play had been set there was money enough to make a first payment on the piano. That day the English exercise for the whole school was to compose the letter to the Eastern piano firm where the piano was to be purchased, ordering it to be sent on at once. Weeks before this Margaret had sent for a number of piano catalogues beautifully illustrated, showing by cuts how the whole instruments were made, with full illustrations of the factories where they were manufactured, and she had discussed the selection with the scholars, showing them what points were to be considered in selecting a good piano. At last the order was sent out, the actual selection itself to be made by a musical friend of Margaret's in New York, and the school waited in anxious suspense to hear that it had started on its way.

The piano arrived at last, three weeks before the time set for the play, which was coming on finely now and seemed to the eager scholars quite ready for public performance. Not so to Margaret and Gardley, as daily they pruned, trained, and patiently went over and over again each part, drawing all the while nearer to the ideal they had set. It could not be done perfectly, of course, and when they had done all they could there would yet be many crudities; but Margaret's hope was to bring out the meaning of the play and give both audience and performers the true idea of what Shakespeare meant when he wrote it.

The arrival of the piano was naturally a great event in the school. For three days in succession the entire school marched in procession down to the incoming Eastern train to see if their expected treasure had arrived, and when at last it was lifted from the freight-car and set upon the station platform the school stood awe-struck and silent, with half-bowed heads and bated breath, as though at the arrival of some great and honorable guest.

They attended it on the roadside as it was carted by the biggest wagon in town to the school-house door; they stood in silent rows while the great box was peeled off and the instrument taken out and carried into the school-room; then they filed in soulfully and took their accustomed seats without being told, touching shyly the shining case as they passed. By common consent they waited to hear its voice for the first time. Margaret took the little key from the envelope tied to the frame, unlocked the cover, and, sitting down, began to play. The rough men who had brought it stood in awesome adoration around the platform; the silence that spread over that room would have done honor to Paderewski or Josef Hoffman.

Margaret played and played, and they could not hear enough. They would have stayed all night listening, perhaps, so wonderful was it to them. And then the teacher called each one and let him or her touch a few chords, just to say they had played on it. After which she locked the instrument and sent them all home. That was the only afternoon during that term that the play was forgotten for a while.

After the arrival of the piano the play went forward with great strides, for now Margaret accompanied some of the parts with the music; and the flute and violin were also practised in their elfin dance with much better effect. It was about this time that Archie Forsythe discovered the rehearsals and offered his assistance, and, although it was declined, he frequently managed to ride over about rehearsal time, finding ways to make himself useful in spite of Margaret's polite refusals. Margaret always felt annoyed when he came, because Rosa Rogers instantly became another creature on his arrival, and because Gardley simply froze into a polite statue, never speaking except when spoken to. As for Forsythe, his attitude toward Gardley was that of a contemptuous master toward a slave, and yet he took care to cover it always with a form of courtesy, so that Margaret could say or do nothing to show her displeasure, except to be grave and dignified. At such times Rosa Rogers's eyes would be upon her with a gleam of hatred, and the teacher felt that the scholar was taking advantage of the situation. Altogether it was a trying time for Margaret when Forsythe came to the schoolhouse. Also, he discovered to them that he played the violin, and offered to assist in the orchestral parts. Margaret really could think of no reason to decline this offer, but she was sadly upset by the whole thing. His manner to her was too pronounced, and she felt continually uncomfortable under it, what with Rosa Rogers's jealous eyes upon her and Gardley's eyes turned haughtily away.

She planned a number of special rehearsals in the evenings, when it was difficult for Forsythe to get there, and managed in this way to avoid his presence; but the whole matter became a source of much vexation, and Margaret even shed a few tears wearily into her pillow one night when things had gone particularly hard and Forsythe had hurt the feelings of Fiddling Boss with his insolent directions about playing. She could not say or do anything much in the matter, because the Temples had been very kind in helping to get the piano, and Mr. Temple seemed to think he was doing the greatest possible kindness to her in letting Forsythe off duty so much to help with the play. The matter became more and more of a distress to Margaret, and the Sabbath was the only day of real delight.

The first Sunday after the arrival of the piano was a great day. Everybody in the neighborhood turned out to the Sunday-afternoon class and vesper service, which had been growing more and more in popularity, until now the school-room was crowded. Every man from the bunk-house came regularly, often including Pop Wallis, who had not yet recovered fully from the effect of his wife's new bonnet and fluffy arrangement of hair, but treated her like a lady visitor and deferred to her absolutely when he was at home. He wasn't quite sure even yet but he had strayed by mistake into the outermost courts of heaven and ought to get shooed out. He always looked at the rose-wreathed curtains with a mingling of pride and awe.

Margaret had put several hymns on the black-board in clear, bold printing, and the singing that day was wonderful. Not the least part of the service was her own playing over of the hymns before the singing began, which was listened to with reverence as if it had been the music of an angel playing on a heavenly harp.

Gardley always came to the Sunday services, and helped her with the singing, and often they two sang duets together.

The service was not always of set form. Usually Margaret taught a short Bible lesson, beginning with the general outline of the Bible, its books, their form, substance, authors, etc. — all very brief and exceedingly simple, putting a wide space of music between this and the vesper service, into which she wove songs, bits of poems, passages from the Bible, and often a story which she told dramatically, illustrating the Scripture read.

But the very Sunday before the play, just the time Margaret had looked forward to as being her rest from all the perplexities of the week, a company from the fort, including the Temples, arrived at the school-house right in the midst of the Bible lesson.

The ladies were daintily dressed, and settled their frills and ribbons amusedly as they watched the embarrassed young teacher trying to forget that there was company present. They were in a distinct sense "company," for they had the air, as they entered, of having come to look on and be amused, not to partake in the worship with the rest.

Margaret found herself trembling inwardly as she saw the supercilious smile on the lips of Mrs. Temple and the amused stares of the other ladies of the party. They did not take any notice of the other people present any more than if they had been so many puppets set up to show off the teacher; their air of superiority was offensive. Not until Rosa Rogers entered with her father, a little later, did they condescend to bow in recognition, and then with that pretty little atmosphere as if they would say, "Oh, you've come, too, to be amused."

Gardley was sitting up in front, listening to her talk, and she thought he had not noticed the strangers. Suddenly it came to her to try to keep her nerve and let him see that they were nothing to her; and with a strong effort and a swift prayer for help she called for a hymn. She sat coolly down at the piano, touching the keys with a tender chord or two and beginning to sing almost at once. She had sent home for some old hymn-books from the Christian Endeavor Society in her father's church, so the congregation were supplied with the notes and words now; and everybody took part eagerly, even the people from the fort condescendingly joining in.

But Gardley was too much alive to every expression on that vivid face of Margaret's to miss knowing that she was annoyed and upset. He did not need to turn and look back to immediately discover the cause. He was a young person of keen intuition. It suddenly gave him great satisfaction to see that look of consternation on Margaret's face. It settled for him a question he had been in great and anxious doubt about, and his soul was lifted up with peace within him. When, presently, according to arrangement, he rose to sing a duet with Margaret, no one could have possibly told by so much as the lifting of an eyelash that he knew there was an enemy of his in the back of the room. He sang, as did Margaret, to the immediate audience in front of him, those admiring children and adoring men in the forefront who felt the school-house had become for them the gate of heaven for the time being; and he sang with marvelous feeling and sympathy, letting out his voice at its best.

"Really," said Mrs. Temple, in a loud whisper to the wife of one of the officers, "that young man has a fine voice, and he isn't bad-looking, either. I think he'd be worth cultivating. We must have him up and try him out."

But when she repeated this remark in another stage whisper to Forsythe he frowned haughtily.

The one glimpse Margaret caught of Forsythe during that afternoon's service was when he was smiling meaningly at Rosa Rogers; and she had to resolutely put the memory of their look from her mind or the story which she was about to tell would have fled.

It was the hunger in Jasper Kemp's eyes that finally anchored Margaret's thoughts and helped her to forget the company at the back of the room. She told her story, and she told it wonderfully and with power, interpreting it now and then for the row of men who sat in the center of the room drinking in her every word; and when the simple service was concluded with another song, in which Gardley's voice rang forth with peculiar tenderness and strength, the men filed forth silently, solemnly, with bowed heads and thoughtful eyes. But the company from the fort flowed up around Margaret like flood-tide let loose and gushed upon her.

"Oh, my dear!" said Mrs. Temple. "How beautifully you do it! And such attention as they give you! No wonder you are willing to forego all other amusements to stay here and preach! But it was perfectly sweet the way you made them listen and the way you told that story. I don't see how you do it. I'd be scared to death!"

They babbled about her awhile, much to her annoyance, for there were several people to whom she had wanted to speak, who drew away and disappeared when the newcomers took possession of her. At last, however, they mounted and rode away, to her great relief. Forsythe, it is true, tried to make her go home with them; tried to escort her to the Tanners'; tried to remain in the school-house with her awhile when she told him she had something to do there; but she would not let him, and he rode away half sulky at the last, a look of injured pride upon his face.

Margaret went to the door finally, and looked down the road. He was gone, and she was alone. A shade of sadness came over her face. She was sorry that Gardley had not waited. She had wanted to tell him how much she liked his singing, what a pleasure it was to sing with him, and how glad she was that he came up to her need so well with the strangers there and helped to make it easy. But Gardley had melted away as soon as the service was over, and had probably gone home with the rest of the men. It was disappointing, for she had come to consider their little time together on Sunday as a very pleasant hour, this few minutes after the service when they would talk about real living and the vital things of existence. But he was gone!

She turned, and there he was, quite near the door, coming toward her. Her face lighted up with a joy that was unmistakable, and his own smile in answer was a revelation of his deeper self.

"Oh, I'm so glad you are not gone!" she said, eagerly. "I wanted to tell you—" And then she stopped, and the color flooded her face rosily, for she saw in his eyes how glad he was and forgot to finish her sentence.

He came up gravely, after all, and, standing just a minute so beside the door, took both her hands in both his. It was only for a second that he stood so, looking down into her eyes. I doubt if either of them knew till afterward that they had been holding hands. It seemed the right and natural thing to do, and meant so much to each of them. Both were glad beyond their own understanding over that moment and its tenderness.

It was all very decorous, and over in a second, but it meant much to remember afterward, that look and hand-clasp.

"I wanted to tell you," he said, tenderly, "how much that story did for me. It was wonderful, and it helped me to decide something I have been perplexed over—"

"Oh, I am glad!" she said, half breathlessly.

So, talking in low, broken sentences, they went back to the piano and tried over several songs for the next Sunday, lingering together, just happy to be there with each other, and not half knowing the significance of it all. As the purple lights on the school-room wall grew long and rose-edged, they walked slowly to the Tanner house and said good night.

There was a beauty about the young man as he stood for a moment looking down upon the girl in parting, the kind of beauty there is in any strong, wild thing made tame and tender for a great love by a great uplift. Gardley had that look of self-surrender, and power made subservient to right, that crowns a man with strength and more than physical beauty. In his fine face there glowed high purpose, and deep devotion to the one who had taught it to him. Margaret, looking up at him, felt her heart go out with that great love, half maiden, half divine, that comes to some favored women even here on earth, and she watched him down the road toward the mountain in the evening light and marveled how her trust had grown since first she met him; marveled and reflected that she had not told her mother and father much about him yet. It was growing time to do so; yes — *it was growing time!* Her cheeks grew pink in the darkness and she turned and fled to her room.

That was the last time she saw him before the play.

23

THE play was set for Tuesday. Monday afternoon and evening were to be the final rehearsals, but Gardley did not come
to them. Fiddling Boss came late and said the men had been
off all day and had not yet returned. He himself found it hard
to come at all. They had important work on. But there was
no word from Gardley.

Margaret was disappointed. She couldn't get away from
it. Of course they could go on with the rehearsal without
him. He had done his work well, and there was no real reason why he had to be there. He knew every part by heart,
and could take any boy's place if any one failed in any way.
There was nothing further really for him to do until the performance, as far as that was concerned, except be there and
encourage her. But she missed him, and an uneasiness grew
in her mind. She had so looked forward to seeing him, and
now to have no word! He might at least have sent her a note
when he found he could not come.

Still she knew this was unreasonable. His work, whatever
it was—he had never explained it very thoroughly to her,
perhaps because she had never asked—must, of course, have

kept him. She must excuse him without question and go on with the business of the hour.

Her hands were full enough, for Forsythe came presently and was more trying than usual. She had to be very decided and put her foot down about one or two things, or some of here actors would have gone home in the sulks, and Fiddling Boss, whose part in the program meant much to him, would have given it up entirely.

She hurried everything through as soon as possible, knowing she was weary, and longing to get to her room and rest. Gardley would come and explain to-morrow, likely in the morning on his way somewhere.

But the morning came and no word. Afternoon came and he had not sent a sign yet. Some of the little things that he had promised to do about the setting of the stage would have to remain undone, for it was too late now to do it herself, and there was no one else to call upon.

Into the midst of her perplexity and anxiety came the news that Jed on his way home had been thrown from his horse, which was a young and vicious one, and had broken his leg. Jed was to act the part of Nick Bottom that evening, and he did it well! Now what in the world was she to do? If only Gardley would come!

Just at this moment Forsythe arrived.

"Oh, it is you, Mr. Forsythe!" And her tone showed plainly her disappointment. "Haven't you seen Mr. Gardley to-day? I don't know what I shall do without him."

"I certainly have seen Gardley," said Forsythe, a spice of vindictiveness and satisfaction in his tone. "I saw him not two hours ago, drunk as a fish, out at a place called Old Ouida's Cabin, as I was passing. He's in for a regular spree. You'll not see him for several days, I fancy. He's utterly helpless for the present, and out of the question. What is there I can do for you? Present your request. It's yours—to the half of my kingdom."

Margaret's heart grew cold as ice and then like fire. Her

blood seemed to stop utterly and then to go pounding through her veins in leaps and torrents. Her eyes grew dark, and things swam before her. She reached out to a desk and caught at it for support, and her white face looked at him a moment as if she had not heard. But when in a second she spoke, she said, quite steadily:

"I thank you, Mr. Forsythe; there is nothing just at present—or, yes, there is, if you wouldn't mind helping Timothy put up those curtains. Now, I think I'll go home and rest a few minutes; I am very tired."

It wasn't exactly the job Forsythe coveted, to stay in the school-house and fuss over those curtains; but she made him do it, then disappeared, and he didn't like the memory of her white face. He hadn't thought she would take it that way. He had expected to have her exclaim with horror and disgust. He watched her out of the door, and then turned impatiently to the waiting Timothy.

Margaret went outside the school-house to call Bud, who had been sent to gather sage-brush for filling in the background, but Bud was already out of sight far on the trail toward the camp on Forsythe's horse, riding for dear life. Bud had come near to the school-house door with his armful of sage-brush just in time to hear Forsythe's flippant speech about Gardley and see Margaret's white face. Bud had gone for help!

But Margaret did not go home to rest. She did not even get half-way home. When she had gone a very short distance outside the school-house she saw some one coming toward her, and in her distress of mind she could not tell who it was. Her eyes were blinded with tears, her breath was constricted, and it seemed to her that a demon unseen was gripping her heart. She had not yet taken her bearings to know what she thought. She had only just come dazed from the shock of Forsythe's words, and had not the power to think. Over and over to herself, as she walked along, she kept repeating the words: "I *do not* believe it! It is *not* true!" but her inner consciousness had not had time to analyze her soul and be sure that she believed the words wherewith she was comforting herself.

So now, when she saw some one coming, she felt the necessity of bringing her telltale face to order and getting ready to answer whoever she was to meet. As she drew nearer she became suddenly aware that it was Rosa Rogers coming with her arms full of bundles and more piled up in front of her on her pony. Margaret knew at once that Rosa must have seen Forsythe go by her house, and had returned promptly to the school-house on some pretext or other. It would not do to let her go there alone with the young man; she must go back and stay with them. She could not be sure that if she sent Rosa home with orders to rest she would be obeyed. Doubtless the girl would take another way around and return to the school again. There was nothing for it but to go back and stay as long as Rosa did.

Margaret stooped and, hastily plucking a great armful of sage-brush, turned around and retraced her steps, her heart like lead, her feet suddenly grown heavy. How could she go back and hear them laugh and chatter, answer their many silly, unnecessary questions, and stand it all? How could she, with that great weight at her heart?

She went back with a wonderful self-control. Forsythe's face lighted, and his reluctant hand grew suddenly eager as he worked. Rosa came presently, and others, and the laughing chatter went on quite as Margaret had known it would. And she—so great is the power of human will under pressure—went calmly about and directed here and there; planned and executed; put little, dainty, wholly unnecessary touches to the stage; and never let any one know that her heart was being crushed with the weight of a great, awful fear, and yet steadily upborne by the rising of a great, deep trust. As she worked and smiled and ordered, she was praying: "Oh, God, don't let it be true! Keep him! Save him! Bring him! Make him true! I *know* he is true! Oh, God, bring him safely *soon!*"

Meantime there was nothing she could do. She could not send Forsythe after him. She could not speak of the matter to one of those present, and Bud—where was Bud? It was the first time since she came to Arizona that Bud had failed her. She might not leave the school-house, with Forsythe and Rosa there, to go and find him, and she might not do anything else. There was nothing to do but work on feverishly and pray as she had never prayed before.

By and by one of the smaller boys came, and she sent him back to the Tanners' to find Bud, but he returned with the message that Bud had not been home since morning; and so the last hours before the evening, that would otherwise have been so brief for all there was to be done, dragged their weary length away and Margaret worked on.

She did not even go back for supper at the last, but sent one of the girls to her room for a few things she needed, and declined even the nice little chicken sandwich that thoughtful Mrs. Tanner sent back along with the things. And then, at last, the audience began to gather.

By this time her anxiety was so great for Gardley that all thought of how she was to supply the place of the absent Jed had gone from her mind, which was in a whirl. Gardley! Gardley! If only Gardley would come! That was her one thought. What should she do if he didn't come at all? How should she explain things to herself afterward? What if it had been true? What if he were the kind of man Forsythe had suggested? How terrible life would look to her! But it was not true. No, it *was not* true! She trusted him! With her soul she trusted him! He would come back some time and he would explain all. She could not remember his last look at her on Sunday and not trust him. He was true! He would come!

Somehow she managed to get through the terrible interval, to slip into the dressing-room and make herself sweet and comely in the little white gown she had sent for, with its delicate blue ribbons and soft lace ruffles. Somehow she managed the expected smiles as one and another of the audience came around to the platform to speak to her. There were dark hollows under her eyes, and her mouth was drawn and weary, but they laid that to the excitement. Two bright-red spots glowed on her cheeks; but she smiled and talked with her usual gaiety. People looked at her and said how beautiful she was, and how bright and untiring; and how wonderful it was that Ashland School had drawn such a prize of a teacher. The seats filled, the noise and the clatter went on. Still no sign of Gardley or any one from the camp, and still Bud had not returned! What could it mean?

But the minutes were rushing rapidly now. It was more than time to begin. The girls were in a flutter in one cloak-room at the right of the stage, asking more questions in a minute than one could answer in an hour; the boys in the other cloak-room wanted all sorts of help; and three or four of the actors were attacked with stage-fright as they peered through a hole in the curtain and saw some friend or relative arrive and sit down in the audience. It was all a mad whirl of seemingly useless noise and excitement, and she could not, no, she *could not,* go on and do the necessary things to start that awful play. Why, oh, *why* had she ever been left to think of getting up a play?

Forsythe, up behind the piano, whispered to her that it was time to begin. The house was full. There was not room for another soul. Margaret explained that Fiddling Boss had not yet arrived, and caught a glimpse of the cunning designs of Forsythe in the shifty turning away of his eyes as he answered that they could not wait all night for him; that if he wanted to get into it he ought to have come early. But even as she turned away she saw the little, bobbing, eager faces of Pop and Mom Wallis away back by the door, and the grim, towering figure of the Boss, his fiddle held high, making his way to the front amid the crowd.

She sat down and touched the keys, her eyes watching eagerly for a chance to speak to the Boss and see if he knew anything of Gardley; but Forsythe was close beside her all the time, and there was no opportunity. She struck the opening chords of the overture they were to attempt to play, and somehow got through it. Of course, the audience was not a critical one, and there were few real judges of music present; but it may be that the truly wonderful effect she produced upon the listeners was due to the fact that she was playing a prayer with her heart as her fingers touched the keys, and that instead of a preliminary to a fairy revel the music told the story of a great soul struggle, and reached hearts as it tinkled and rolled and swelled on to the end. It may be, too, that Fiddling Boss was more in sympathy that night with his accompanist than was the other violinist, and that was why his old fiddle brought forth such weird and tender tones.

Almost to the end, with her heart sobbing its trouble to the keys, Margaret looked up sadly, and there, straight before her through a hole in the curtain made by some rash youth to glimpse the audience, or perhaps even put there by the owner of the nose itself, she saw the little, freckled, turned-up member belonging to Bud's face. A second more and a big, bright eye appeared and solemnly winked at her twice, as if to say, "Don't you worry; it's all right!"

She almost started from the stool, but kept her head enough to finish the chords, and as they died away she heard a hoarse whisper in Bud's familiar voice:

"Whoop her up, Miss Earle. We're all ready. Raise the curtain there, you guy. Let her rip. Everything's O.K."

With a leap of light into her eyes Margaret turned the leaves of the music and went on playing as she should have done if nothing had been the matter. Bud was there, anyway, and that somehow cheered her heart. Perhaps Gardley had come or Bud had heard of him—and yet, Bud didn't know he had been missing, for Bud had been away himself.

Nevertheless, she summoned courage to go on playing. Nick Bottom wasn't in this first scene, anyway, and this would have to be gone through with somehow. By this time she was in a state of daze that only thought from moment to moment. The end of the evening seemed now to her as far off as the end of a hale old age seems at the beginning of a lifetime. Somehow she must walk through it; but she could only see a step at a time.

Once she turned half sideways to the audience and gave a hurried glance about, catching sight of Fudge's round, near-sighted face, and that gave her encouragement. Perhaps the others were somewhere present. If only she could get a chance to whisper to some one from the camp and ask when they had seen Gardley last! But there was no chance, of course!

The curtain was rapidly raised and the opening scene of the play began, the actors going through their parts with marvelous ease and dexterity, and the audience silent and charmed, watching those strangers in queer costumes that were their own children, marching around there at their ease and talking weird language that was not used in any class of society they had ever come across on sea or land before.

But Margaret, watching her music as best she could, and playing mechanically rather than with her mind, could not tell if they were doing well or ill, so loudly did her heart pound out her fears—so stoutly did her heart proclaim her trust.

And thus, without a flaw or mistake in the execution of the work she had struggled so hard to teach them, the first scene of the first act drew to its close, and Margaret struck the final chords of the music and felt that in another minute she must reel and fall from that piano-stool. And yet she sat and watched the curtain fall with a face as controlled as if nothing at all were the matter.

A second later she suddenly knew that to sit in that place calmly another second was a physical impossibility. She must get somewhere to the air at once or her senses would desert her.

With a movement so quick that no one could have anticipated it, she slipped from her piano-stool, under the curtain to the stage, and was gone before the rest of the orchestra had noticed her intention.

24

SINCE the day that he had given Margaret his promise to make good, Gardley had been regularly employed by Mr. Rogers, looking after important matters of his ranch. Before that he had lived a free and easy life, working a little now and then when it seemed desirable to him, having no set interest in life, and only endeavoring from day to day to put as far as possible from his mind the life he had left behind him. Now, however, all things became different. He brought to his service the keen mind and ready ability that had made him easily a winner at any game, a brave rider, and a never-failing shot. Within a few days Rogers saw what material was in him, and as the weeks went by grew to depend more and more upon his advice in matters.

There had been much trouble with cattle thieves, and so far no method of stopping the loss or catching the thieves had been successful. Rogers finally put the matter into Gardley's hands to carry out his own ideas, with the men of the camp at his command to help him, the camp itself being only a part of Rogers's outlying possessions, one of several such centers from which he worked his growing interests.

Gardley had formulated a scheme by which he hoped

eventually to get hold of the thieves and put a stop to the trouble, and he was pretty sure he was on the right track; but his plan required slow and cautious work, that the enemy might not suspect and take to cover. He had for several weeks suspected that the thieves made their headquarters in the region of Old Ouida's Cabin, and made their raids from that direction. It was for this reason that of late the woods and trails in the vicinity of Ouida's had been secretly patrolled day and night, and every passer-by taken note of, until Gardley knew just who were the frequenters of that way and mostly what was their business. This work was done alternately by the men of the Wallis camp and two other camps, Gardley being the head of all and carrying all responsibility; and not the least of that young man's offenses in the eyes of Rosa Rogers was that he was so constantly at her father's house and yet never lifted an eye in admiration of her pretty face. She longed to humiliate him, and through him to humiliate Margaret, who presumed to interfere with her flirtations, for it was a bitter thing to Rosa that Forsythe had no eyes for her when Margaret was about.

When the party from the fort rode homeward that Sunday after the service at the school-house, Forsythe lingered behind to talk to Margaret, and then rode around by the Rogers place, where Rosa and he had long ago established a trysting-place.

Rosa was watching for his passing, and he stopped a half-hour or so to talk to her. During this time she casually disclosed to Forsythe some of the plans she had overheard Gardley laying before her father. Rosa had very little idea of the importance of Gardley's work to her father, or perhaps she would not have so readily prattled of his affairs. Her main idea was to pay back Gardley for his part in her humiliation with Forsythe. She suggested that it would be a great thing if Gardley could be prevented from being at the play Tuesday evening, and told what she had overheard him saying to her father merely to show Forsythe how easy it would be to have Gardley detained on Tuesday. Forsythe questioned Rosa keenly. Did she know whom they suspected? Did she know what they were planning to do to catch them, and when?

Rosa innocently enough disclosed all she knew, little thinking how dishonorable to her father it was, and perhaps caring as little, for Rosa had ever been a spoiled child, accustomed to subordinating everything within reach to her own uses. As for Forsythe, he was nothing loath to get rid of Gardley, and he saw more possibilities in Rosa's suggestion than she had seen herself. When at last he bade Rosa good night and rode unobtrusively back to the trail he was already formulating a plan.

It was, therefore, quite in keeping with his wishes that he should meet a dark-browed rider a few miles farther up the trail whose identity he had happened to learn a few days before.

Now Forsythe would, perhaps, not have dared to enter into any compact against Gardley with men of such illrepute had it been a matter of money and bribery, but, armed as he was with information valuable to the criminals, he could so word his suggestion about Gardley's detention as to make the hunted men think it to their advantage to catch Gardley some time the next day when he passed their way and imprison him for a while. This would appear to be but a friendly bit of advice from a disinterested party deserving a good turn some time in the future and not get Forsythe into any trouble. As such it was received by the wretch, who clutched at the information with ill-concealed delight and rode away into the twilight like a serpent threading his secret, gliding way among the darkest places, scarcely rippling the air, so stealthily did he pass.

As for Forsythe, he rode blithely to the Temple ranch, with no thought of the forces he had set going, his life as yet one round of trying to please himself at others' expense, if need be, but please himself, *anyway,* with whatever amusement the hour afforded.

At home in the East, where his early life had been spent, a splendid girl awaited his dilatory letters and set herself patiently to endure the months of separation until he should have attained a home and a living and be ready for her to come to him.

In the South, where he had idled six months before he went West, another lovely girl cherished mementoes of his tarrying and wrote him loving letters in reply to his occasional erratic epistles.

Out on the Californian shore a girl with whom he had traveled West in her uncle's luxurious private car, with a gay party of friends and relatives, cherished fond hopes of a visit he had promised to make her during the winter.

Innumerable maidens of this world, wise in the wisdom that crushes hearts, remembered him with a sigh now and then, but held no illusions concerning his kind.

Pretty little Rosa Rogers cried her eyes out every time he cast a languishing look at her teacher, and several of the ladies of the fort sighed that the glance of his eye and the gentle pressure of his hand could only be a passing joy. But the gay Lothario passed on his way as yet without a scratch on the hard enamel of his heart, till one wondered if it were a heart, indeed, or perhaps only a metal imitation. But girls like Margaret Earle, though they sometimes were attracted by him, invariably distrusted him. He was like a beautiful spotted snake that was often caught menacing something precious, but you could put down anywhere after punishment or imprisonment and he would slide on his same slippery way and still be a spotted, deadly snake.

When Gardley left the camp that Monday morning following the walk home with Margaret from the Sabbath service, he fully intended to be back at the school-house Monday by the time the afternoon rehearsal began. His plans were so laid that he thought relays from other camps were to guard the suspected ground for the next three days and he could be free. It had been a part of the information that Forsythe had given the stranger that Gardley would likely pass a certain lonely crossing of the trail at about three o'clock that afternoon, and, had that arrangement been carried out, the men who lay in wait for him would doubtless have been pleased to have their plans mature so easily; but they would not have been pleased long, for Gardley's men were so near at hand at that time, watching that very spot with eyes and ears and long-distance glasses, that their chief would soon have been rescued and the captors be themselves the captured.

But the men from the farther camp, called "Lone Fox" men, did not arrive on time, perhaps through some misunderstanding, and Gardley and Kemp and their men had to do double time. At last, later in the afternoon, Gardley volunteered to go to Lone Fox and bring back the men.

As he rode his thoughts were of Margaret, and he was seeing again the look of gladness in her eyes when she found he had not gone yesterday; feeling again the thrill of her hands in his, the trust of her smile! It was incredible, wonderful, that God had sent a veritable angel into the wilderness to bring him to himself; and now he was wondering, could it be that there was really hope that he could ever make good enough to dare to ask her to marry him. The sky and the air were rare, but his thoughts were rarer still, and his soul was lifted up with joy. He was earning good wages now. In two more weeks he would have enough to pay back the paltry sum for the lack of which he had fled from his old home and come to the wilderness. He would go back, of course, and straighten out the old score. Then what? Should he stay in the East and go back to the old business wherewith he had hoped to make his name honored and gain wealth, or should he return to this wild, free land again and start anew?

His mother was dead. Perhaps if she had lived and cared

he would have made good in the first place. His sisters were both married to wealthy men and not deeply interested in him. He had disappointed and mortified them; their lives were filled with social duties; they had never missed him. His father had been dead many years. As for his uncle, his mother's brother, whose heir he was to have been before he got himself into disgrace, he decided not to go near him. He would stay as long as he must to undo the wrong he had done. He would call on his sisters and then come back; come back and let Margaret decide what she wanted him to do — that is, if she would consent to link her life with one who had been once a failure. Margaret! How wonderful she was! If Margaret said he ought to go back and be a lawyer, he would go — yes, even if he had to enter his uncle's office as an underling to do it. His soul loathed the idea, but he would do it for Margaret, if she thought it best. And so he mused as he rode!

When the Lone Fox camp was reached and the men sent out on their belated task, Gardley decided not to go with them back to meet Kemp and the other men, but sent word to Kemp that he had gone the short cut to Ashland, hoping to get to a part of the evening rehearsal yet.

Now that short cut led him to the lonely crossing of the trail much sooner than Kemp and the others could reach it from the rendezvous; and there in cramped positions, and with much unnecessary cursing and impatience, four strong masked men had been concealed for four long hours.

Through the stillness of the twilight rode Gardley, thinking of Margaret, and for once utterly off his guard. His long day's work was done, and though he had not been able to get back when he planned, he was free now, free until the day after to-morrow. He would go at once to her and see if there was anything she wanted him to do.

Then, as if to help along his enemies, he began to hum a song, his clear, high voice reaching keenly to the ears of the men in ambush:

" 'Oh, the time is long, mavourneen,
Till I come again, O mavourneen —' "

"And the toime'll be longer thun iver, oim thinkin', ma purty little voorneen!" said an unmistakable voice of Erin through the gathering dusk.

Gardley's horse stopped and Gardley's hand went to his revolver, while his other hand lifted the silver whistle to his lips; but four guns bristled at him in the twilight, the whistle was knocked from his lips before his breath had even reached it, some one caught his arms from behind, and his own weapon was wrenched from his hand as it went off. The cry which he at once sent forth was stifled in its first whisper in a great muffling garment flung over his head and drawn tightly about his neck. He was in a fair way to strangle, and his vigorous efforts at escape were useless in the hands of so many. He might have been plunged at once into a great abyss of limitless, soundless depths, so futile did any resistance seem. And so, as it was useless to struggle, he lay like one dead and put all his powers into listening. But neither could he hear much, muffled as he was, and bound hand and foot now, with a gag in his mouth and little care taken whether he could even breathe.

They were leading him off the trail and up over rough ground; so much he knew, for the horse stumbled and jolted and strained to carry him. To keep his whirling senses alive and alert he tried to think where they might be leading him; but the darkness and the suffocation dulled his powers. He wondered idly if his men would miss him and come back when they got home to search for him, and then remembered with a pang that they would think him safely in Ashland, helping Margaret. They would not be alarmed if he did not return that night, for they would suppose he had stopped at Rogers's on the way and perhaps stayed all night, as he had done once or twice before. *Margaret!* When should he see Margaret now? What would she think?

And then he swooned away.

When he came somewhat to himself he was in a close, stifling room where candle-light from a distance threw weird shadows over the adobe walls. The witch-like voices of a woman and a girl in harsh, cackling laughter, half suppressed, were not far away, and some one, whose face was covered, was holding a glass to his lips. The smell was sickening, and he remembered that he hated the thought of liquor. It did not fit with those who companied with Margaret. He had never cared for it, and had resolved never to taste it again. But whether he chose or not, the liquor was poured down his throat. Huge hands held him and forced it, and he was still bound and too weak to resist, even if he had realized the necessity.

The liquid burned its way down his throat and seethed into his brain, and a great darkness, mingled with men's wrangling voices and much cursing, swirled about him like some furious torrent of angry waters that finally submerged his consciousness. Then came deeper darkness and a blank relief from pain.

-Hours passed. He heard sounds sometimes, and dreamed dreams which he could not tell from reality. He saw his friends with terror written on their faces, while he lay apathetically and could not stir. He saw tears on Margaret's face; and once he was sure he heard Forsythe's voice in contempt: "Well, he seems to be well occupied for the present! No danger of his waking up for a while!" and then the voices all grew dim and far away again, and only an old crone and the harsh girl's whisper over him; and then Margaret's tears — tears that fell on his heart from far above, and seemed to melt out all his early sins and flood him with their horror. Tears and the consciousness that he ought to be doing something for Margaret now and could not. Tears — and more darkness!

25

WHEN Margaret arrived behind the curtain she was aware of many cries and questions hurled at her like an avalanche, but, ignoring them all, she sprang past the noisy, excited group of young people, darted through the dressing-room to the right and out into the night and coolness. Her head was swimming, and things went black before her eyes. She felt that her breath was going, going, and she must get to the air.

But when she passed the hot wave of the schoolroom, and the sharp air of the night struck her face, consciousness seemed to turn and come back into her again; for there over her head was the wideness of the vast, starry Arizona night, and there, before her, in Nick Bottom's somber costume, eating one of the chicken sandwiches that Mrs. Tanner had sent down to her, stood Gardley! He was pale and shaken from his recent experience; but he was undaunted, and when he saw Margaret coming toward him through the doorway with her soul in her eyes and her spirit all aflame with joy and relief, he came to meet her under the stars, and, forgetting everything else, just folded her gently in his arms!

It was a most astonishing thing to do, of course, right there outside the dressing-room door, with the curtain just about to rise on the scene and Gardley's wig was not on yet. He had not even asked nor obtained permission. But the soul sometimes grows impatient waiting for the lips to speak, and Margaret felt her trust had been justified and her heart had found its home. Right there behind the school-house, out in the great wide night, while the crowded, clamoring audience waited for them, and the young actors grew frantic, they plighted their troth, his lips upon hers, and with not a word spoken.

Voices from the dressing-room roused them. "Come in quick, Mr. Gardley; it's time for the curtain to rise, and everybody is ready. Where on earth has Miss Earle vanished? Miss Earle! Oh, Miss Earle!"

There was a rush to the dressing-room to find the missing ones; but Bud, as ever, present where was the most need, stood with his back to the outside world in the door of the dressing-room and called loudly:

"They're comin', all right. Go on! Get to your places. Miss Earle says to get to your places."

The two in the darkness groped for each other's hands as they stood suddenly apart, and with one quick pressure and a glance hurried in. There was not any need for words. They understood, these two, and trusted.

With her cheeks glowing now, and her eyes like two stars, Margaret fled across the stage and took her place at the piano again, just as the curtain began to be drawn; and Forsythe, who had been slightly uneasy at the look on her face as she left them, wondered now and leaned forward to tell her how well she was looking.

He kept his honeyed phrase to himself, however, for she was not heeding him. Her eyes were on the rising·curtain, and Forsythe suddenly remembered that this was the scene in which Jed was to have appeared—and Jed had a broken leg! What had Margaret done about it? It was scarcely a part that could be left out. Why hadn't he thought of it sooner and offered to take it? He could have bluffed it out somehow—he had heard it so much—made up words where he couldn't remember them all, and it would have been a splendid opportunity to do some real love-making with Rosa. Why hadn't he thought of it? Why hadn't Rosa? Perhaps she hadn't heard about Jed soon enough to suggest it.

The curtain was fully open now, and Bud's voice as Peter Quince, a trifle high and cracked with excitement, broke the stillness, while the awed audience gazed upon this new, strange world presented to them.

"Is all our company here?" lilted out Bud, excitedly, and Nick Bottom replied with Gardley's voice:

"You were best to call them generally, man by man, according to the scrip."

Forsythe turned deadly white. Jasper Kemp, whose keen eye was upon him, saw it through the tan, saw his lips go pale and purple points of fear start in his eyes, as he looked and looked again, and could not believe his senses.

Furtively he darted a glance around, like one about to steal away; then, seeing Jasper Kemp's eyes upon him, settled back with a strained look upon his face. Once he stole a look at Margaret and caught her face all transfigured with great joy; looked again and felt rebuked somehow by the pureness of her maiden joy and trust.

Not once had she turned her eyes to his. He was forgotten, and somehow he knew the look he would get if she should see him. It would be contempt and scorn that would burn his very soul. It is only a maid now and then to whom it is given thus to pierce and bruise the soul of a man who plays with love and trust and womanhood for selfishness. Such a woman never knows her power. She punishes all unconscious to herself. It was so that Margaret Earle, without being herself aware, and by her very indifference and contempt, showed the little soul of this puppet man to himself.

He stole away at last when he thought no one was looking, and reached the back of the school-house at the open door of the girls' dressing-room, where he knew Titania would be posing in between the acts. He beckoned her to his side and began to question her in quick, eager, almost angry tones, as if the failure of their plans were her fault. Had her father been at home all day? Had anything happened — any one been there? Did Gardley come? Had there been any report from the men? Had that short, thick-set Scotchman with the ugly grin been there? She must remember that she was the one to suggest the scheme in the first place, and it was her business to keep a watch. There was no telling now what might happen. He turned, and there stood Jasper Kemp close to his elbow, his short stature drawn to its full, his thick-set shoulders squaring themselves, his ugly grin standing out in bold relief, menacingly, in the night.

The young man let forth some words not in a gentleman's code, and turned to leave the frightened girl, who by this time was almost crying; but Jasper Kemp kept pace with Forsythe as he walked.

"Was you addressing me?" he asked, politely; "because I could tell you a few things a sight more appropriate for you than what you just handed to me."

Forsythe hurried around to the front of the school-house, making no reply.

"Nice, pleasant evening to be *free,*" went on Jasper Kemp, looking up at the stars. "Rather unpleasant for some folks that have to be shut up in jail."

Forsythe wheeled upon him. "What do you mean?" he demanded, angrily, albeit he was white with fear.

"Oh, nothing much," drawled Jasper, affably. "I was just thinking how much pleasanter it was to be a free man than shut up in prison on a night like this. It's so much healthier, you know."

Forsythe looked at him a moment, a kind of panic of intelligence growing in his face; then he turned and went toward the back of the school-house, where he had left his horse some hours before.

"Where are you going?" demanded Jasper. "It's 'most time you went back to your fiddling, ain't it?"

But Forsythe answered him not a word. He was mounting his horse hurriedly—his horse, which, all unknown to him, had been many miles since he last rode him.

"You think you have to go, then?" said Jasper, deprecatingly. "Well, now, that's a pity, seeing you was fiddling so nice an' all. Shall I tell them you've gone for your health?"

Thus recalled, Forsythe stared at his tormentor wildly for a second. "Tell her—tell her"—he muttered, hoarsely—"tell her I've been taken suddenly ill." And he was off on a wild gallop toward the fort.

"I'll tell her you've gone for your health!" called Jasper Kemp, with his hands to his mouth like a megaphone. "I reckon he won't return again very soon, either," he chuckled. "This country's better off without such pests as him an' that measley parson." Then, turning, he beheld Titania, the queen of the fairies, white and frightened, staring wildly into the starry darkness after the departed rider. "Poor little fool!" he muttered under his breath as he looked at the girl and turned away. "Poor, pretty little fool!" Suddenly he stepped up to her side and touched her white-clad shoulder gently. "Don't you go for to care, lassie," he said in a tender tone. "He ain't worth a tear from your pretty eye. He ain't fit to wipe your feet on—your pretty wee feet!"

But Rosa turned angrily and stamped her foot.

"Go away! You bad old man!" she shrieked. "Go away! I shall tell my father!" And she flouted herself into the school-house.

Jasper stood looking ruefully after her, shaking his head. "The little de'il!" he said aloud; "the poor, pretty little de'il. She'll get her dues aplenty afore she's done." And Jasper went back to the play.

Meantime, inside the school-house, the play went gloriously on to the finish, and Gardley as Nick Bottom took the house by storm. Poor absent Jed's father, sent by the sufferer to report it all, stood at the back of the house while tears of pride and disappointment rolled down his cheeks—pride that Jed had been so well represented, disappointment that it couldn't have been his own son up there play-acting like that.

The hour was late when the play was over, and Margaret stood at last in front of the stage to receive the congratulations of the entire countryside, while the young actors posed and laughed and chattered excitedly, then went away by two and threes, their tired, happy voices sounding back along the road. The people from the fort had been the first to surge around Margaret with their eager congratulations and gushing sentiments: "So sweet, my dear! So perfectly wonderful! You really have got some dandy actors!" And, "Why don't you try something lighter—something simpler, don't you know. Something really popular that these poor people could understand and appreciate? A little farce! I could help you pick one out!"

And all the while they gushed Jasper Kemp and his men, grim and forbidding, stood like a cordon drawn about her to protect her, with Gardley in the center, just behind her, as though he had a right there and meant to stay; till at last the fort people hurried away and the school-house grew suddenly empty with just those two and the eight men behind; and by the door Bud, talking to Pop and Mom Wallis in the buckboard outside.

Amid this admiring body-guard at last Gardley took Margaret home. Perhaps she wondered a little that they all went along, but she laid it to their pride in the play and their desire to talk it over.

They had sent Mom and Pop Wallis home horse-back, after all, and put Margaret and Gardley in the buckboard, Margaret never dreaming that it was because Gardley was not fit to walk. Indeed, he did not realize himself why they all stuck so closely to him. He had lived through so much since Jasper and his men had burst into his prison and freed him, bringing him in hot haste to the school-house, with Bud wildly riding ahead. But it was enough for him to sit beside Margaret in the sweet night and remember how she had come out to him under the stars. Her hand lay beside him on the seat, and without intending it his own brushed it. Then he laid his gently, reverently, down upon hers with a quiet pressure, and her smaller fingers thrilled and nestled in his grasp.

In the shadow of a big tree beside the house he bade her good-by, the men busying themselves with turning about the buckboard noisily, and Bud discreetly taking himself to the back door to get one of the men a drink of water.

"You have been suffering in some way," said Margaret, with sudden intuition, as she looked up into Gardley's face. "You have been in peril, somehow—"

"A little," he answered, lightly. "I'll tell you about it to-morrow. I mustn't keep the men waiting now. I shall have a great deal to tell you to-morrow—if you will let me. Good night, *Margaret!*" Their hands lingered in a clasp, and then he rode away with his body-guard.

But Margaret did not have to wait until the morrow to hear the story, for Bud was just fairly bursting.

Mrs. Tanner had prepared a nice little supper—more cold chicken, pie, doughnuts, coffee, some of her famous marble cake, and preserves—and she insisted on Margaret's coming into the dining-room and eating it, though the girl would much rather have gone with her happy heart up to her own room by herself.

Bud did not wait on ceremony. He began at once when Margaret was seated, even before his mother could get her properly waited on.

"Well, we had *some ride,* we sure did! The Kid's a great old scout."

Margaret perceived that this was a leader. "Why, that's so, what became of you, William? I hunted everywhere for you.

Things were pretty strenuous there for a while, and I needed you dreadfully."

"Well, I know," Bud apologized. "I'd oughta let you know before I went, but there wasn't time. You see, I had to pinch that guy's horse to go, and I knew it was just a chance if we could get back, anyway; but I had to take it. You see, if I could 'a gone right to the cabin it would have been a dead cinch, but I had to ride to camp for the men, and then, taking the short trail across, it was some ride to Ouida's Cabin!"

Mrs. Tanner stopped aghast as she was cutting a piece of dried-apple pie for Margaret. "Now, Buddie—mother's boy—you don't mean to tell me *you* went to *Ouida's Cabin?* Why, sonnie, that's an *awful place!* Don't you know your pa told you he'd whip you if you ever went on that trail?"

"I should worry, Ma! I *had* to go. They had Mr. Gardley tied up there, and we had to go and get him rescued."

"*You* had to go, Buddie—now what could *you* do in that awful place?" Mrs. Tanner was almost reduced to tears. She saw her offspring at the edge of perdition at once.

But Bud ignored his mother and went on with his tale. "You jest oughta seen Jap Kemp's face when I told him what that guy said to you! Some face, b'lieve me! He saw right through the whole thing, too, I could see that! He ner the men hadn't had a bite o' supper yet; they'd just got back from somewheres. They thought the Kid was over here all day helping you. He said yesterday when he left 'em here's where he's a-comin' " —Bud's mouth was so full he could hardly articulate—"an' when I told 'em, he jest blew his little whistle—like what they all carry—three times, and those men every one jest stopped right where they was, whatever they was doin'. Long Bill had the comb in the air gettin' ready to comb his hair, an' he left it there and come away, and Big Jim never stopped to wipe his face on the roller-towel, he just let the wind dry it; and they all hustled on their horses fast as ever they could and beat it after Jap Kemp. Jap, he rode alongside o' me and asked me questions. He made me tell all what the guy from the fort said over again, three or four times, and then he ast what time he got to the school-house, and whether the Kid had been there at all yest'iday ur t'day; anda lot of other questions, and then he rode alongside each man and told him in just a few words where we was goin' and what the guy from the for had said. Gee! but you'd oughta heard what the men said when he told 'em! Gee! but they was some mad! Bimeby we came to the woods round the cabin, and Jap Kemp made me stick alongside Long Bill, and he sent the men off in different directions all in a big cir- cle, and waited till each man was in his place, and then we all rode hard as we could and came softly up round that cabin just as the sun was goin' down. Gee! but you'd oughta seen the scairt look on them women's faces; there was two of 'em — an old un an' a skinny-looking long-drink-o'-pump- water. I guess she was a girl. I don't know. Her eyes looked real old. There was only three men in the cabin; the rest was off somewheres. They wasn't looking for anybody to come that time o' day, I guess. One of the men was sick on a bunk in the corner. He had his head tied up, and his arm, like he'd been shot, and the other two men cam jumping up to the door with their guns, but when they saw how many men *we* had they looked awful scairt. *We* all had *our* guns out, too! — Jap Kemp gave me one to carry — " Bud tried not to swagger as he told this, but it was almost too much for him. "Two of our men held the horses, and all the rest of us got down and went into the cabin. Jap Kemp, sounded his whis- tle and all our men done the same just as they went in the door — some kind of signals they have for the Lone Fox Camp! The two men in the doorway aimed straight at Jap Kemp and fired, but Jap was onto 'em and jumped one side, and our men fired, too, and we soon had 'em tied up and went in — that is, Jap and me and Long Bill went in, the rest stayed by the door — and it wasn't long 'fore their other men came riding back hot hast; they'd heard the shots, you know —

and some more of *our* men—why, most twenty or thirty there was, I guess, altogether; some from Lone Fox Camp that was watching off in the woods came, and when we got outside again there they all were, like a big army. Most of the men belonging to the cabin was tied and harmless by that time, for our men took 'em one at a time as they came riding in. Two of 'em got away, but Jap Kemp said they couldn't go far without being caught, 'cause there was a watch out for 'em—they'd been stealing cattle long back something terrible. Well, so Jap Kemp and Long Bill and I went into the cabin after the two men that shot was tied with ropes we'd brung along, and handcuffs, and we went hunting for the Kid. At first we couldn't find him at all. Gee! It was something fierce! And the old woman kep' a-crying and saying we'd kill her sick son, and she didn't know nothing about the man we was hunting for. But pretty soon I spied the Kid's foot stickin' out from under the cot where the sick man was, and when I told Jap Kemp that sick man pulled out a gun he had under the blanket and aimed it right at me!"

"Oh, mother's little Buddie!" whimpered Mrs. Tanner, with her apron to her eyes.

"*Aw, Ma,* cut it out! *he* didn't *hurt* me! The gun just went off crooked, and grazed Jap Kemp's hand a little, not much. Jap knocked it out of the sick man's hand just as he was pullin' the trigger. Say, Ma, ain't you got any more of those cucumber pickles? It makes a man mighty hungry to do all that riding and shooting. Well, it certainly was something fierce—Say, Miss Earle, you take that last piece o' pie. Oh, g'wan! *Take* it! *You* worked hard. No, I don't want it, really! Well, if you won't take it *anyway,* I might eat it just to save it. Got any more coffee, Ma?"

But Margaret was not eating. Her face was pale and her eyes were starry with unshed tears, and she waited in patient but breathless suspense for the vagaries of the story to work out to the finish.

"Yes, it certainly was something fierce, that cabin," went

on the narrator. "Why, Ma, it looked as if it had never been swept under that cot when we hauled the Kid out. He was tied all up in knots, and great heavy ropes wound tight from his shoulders down to his ankles. Why, they were bound so tight they made great heavy welts in his wrists and shoulders and round his ankles when we took 'em off; and they had a great big rag stuffed into his mouth so he couldn't yell. Gee! It was something fierce! He was 'most dippy, too; but Jap Kemp brought him round pretty quick and got him outside in the air. That was the worst place I ever was in myself. You couldn't breathe, and the dirt was something fierce. It was like a pigpen. I sure was glad to get outdoors again. And then—well, the Kid came around all right and they got him on a horse and gave him something out of a bottle Jap Kemp had, and pretty soon he could ride again. Why, you'd oughta seen his nerve. He just sat up there as straight, his lips all white yet and his eyes looked some queer; but he straightened up and he looked those rascals right in the eye, and told 'em a few things, and he gave orders to the other men from Lone Fox Camp what to do with 'em; and he had the two women disarmed—they had guns, too—and carried away, and the cabin nailed up, and a notice put on the door, and every one of those men were handcuffed—the sick one and all—and he told 'em to bring a wagon and put the sick one's cot in and take 'em over to Ashland to the jail, and he sent word to Mr. Rogers. Then we rode home and got to the school-house just when you was playing the last chords of the ov'rtcher. Gee! It was some fierce ride and some *close shave!* The Kid he hadn't had a thing to eat since Monday noon, and he was some hungry! I found a sandwich on the window of the dressing-room, and he ate it while he got togged up—'course I told him 'bout Jed soon's we left the cabin, and Jap Kemp said he'd oughta go right home to camp after all he had been through; but he wouldn't; he said he was goin' to *act.* So 'course he had his way! But, gee! You could see it wasn't any cinch game for him! He 'most fell over every time after the curtain fell.

You see, they gave him some kind of drugged whisky up there at the cabin that made his head feel queer. Say, he thinks that guy from the fort came in and looked at him once while he was asleep. He says it was only a dream, but I bet he did. Say, Ma, ain't you gonta give me another doughnut?"

In the quiet of her chamber at last, Margaret knelt before her window toward the purple, shadowy mountain under the starry dome, and gave thanks for the deliverance of Gardley; while Bud, in his comfortable loft, lay down to his well-earned rest and dreamed of pirates and angels and a hero who looked like the Kid.

26

THE Sunday before Lance Gardley started East on his journey of reparation two strangers slipped quietly into the back of the school-house during the singing of the first hymn and sat down in the shadow by the door.

Margaret was playing the piano when they came in, and did not see them, and when she turned back to her Scripture lesson she had time for but the briefest of glances. She supposed they must be some visitors from the fort, as they were speaking to the captain's wife—who came over occasionally to the Sunday service, perhaps because it afforded an opportunity for a ride with one of the young officers. These occasional visitors who came for amusement and curiosity had ceased to trouble Margaret. Her real work was with the men and women and children who loved the services for their own sake, and she tried as much as possible to forget outsiders. So, that day everything went on just as usual, Margaret putting her heart into the prayer, the simple, storylike reading of the Scripture, and the other story-sermon which followed it. Gardley sang unusually well at the close, a wonderful bit from an oratorio that he and Margaret had been practising.

But when toward the close of the little vesper service Margaret gave opportunity, as she often did, for others to take part in sentence prayers, one of the strangers from the back of the room stood up and began to pray. And such a prayer! Heaven seemed to bend low, and earth to kneel and beseech as the stranger-man, with a face like an archangel, and a body of an athlete clothed in a brown-flannel shirt and khakis, besought the Lord of heaven for a blessing on this gathering and on the leader of this little company who had so wonderfully led them to see the Christ and their need of salvation through the lesson of the day. And it did not need Bud's low-breathed whisper, "The missionary!" to tell Margaret who he was. His face told her. His prayer thrilled her, and his strong, young, true voice made her sure that here was a man of God in truth.

When the prayer was over and Margaret stood once more shyly facing her audience, she could scarcely keep the tremble out of her voice:

"Oh," said she, casting aside ceremony, "if I had known the missionary was here I should not have dared to try and lead this meeting to-day. Won't you please come up here and talk to us for a little while now, Mr. Brownleigh?"

At once he came forward eagerly, as if each opportunity were a pleasure. "Why, surely, I want to speak a word to you, just to say how glad I am to see you all, and to experience what a wonderful teacher you have found since I went away; but I wouldn't have missed this meeting to-day for all the sermons I ever wrote or preached. You don't need any more sermon than the remarkable story you've just been listening to, and I've only one word to add; and that is, that I've found since I went away that Jesus Christ, the only-begotten Son of God, is just the same Jesus to me to-day that He was the last time I spoke to you. He is just as ready to forgive your sin, to comfort you in sorrow, to help you in temptation, to raise your body in the resurrection, and to take you home to a mansion in His Father's house as He was the day He hung upon the cross to save your soul from death. I've found I can rest just as securely upon the Bible as the word of God as when I first tested its promises. Heaven and earth may pass away, but His word shall *never* pass away."

"*Go to it!*" said Jasper Kemp under his breath in the tone some men say "Amen!" and his brows were drawn as if he were watching a battle. Margaret couldn't help wondering if he were thinking of the Rev. Frederick West just then.

When the service was over the missionary brought his wife forward to Margaret, and they loved each other at once. Just another sweet girl like Margaret. She was lovely, with a delicacy of feature that betokened the high-born and high-bred, but dressed in a dainty khaki riding costume, if that uncompromising fabric could ever be called dainty. Margaret, remembering it afterward, wondered what it had been that gave it that unique individuality, and decided it was perhaps a combination of cut and finish and little dainty accessories. A bit of creamy lace at the throat of the rolling collar, a touch of golden-brown velvet in a golden clasp, the flash of a wonderful jewel on her finger, the modeling of the small, brown cap with its two eagle quills — all set the little woman apart and made her fit to enter any well-dressed company of riders in some great city park or fashionable drive. Yet here in the wilderness she was not overdressed.

The eight men from the camp stood in solemn row, waiting to be recognized, and behind them, abashed and grinning with embarrassment, stood Pop and Mom Wallis, Mom with her new gray bonnet glorifying her old face till the missionary's wife had to look twice to be sure who she was.

"And now, surely, Hazel, we must have these dear people come over and help us with the singing sometimes. Can't we try something right now?" said the missionary, looking first at his wife and then at Margaret and Gardley. "This man is a newcomer since I went away, but I'm mighty sure he is the right kind, and I'm glad to welcome him — or perhaps I would better ask if he will welcome me?" And with his rare smile the missionary put out his hand to Gardley, who took it with an eager grasp. The two men stood looking at each other for a moment, as rare men, rarely met, sometimes do even on a sinful earth; and after that clasp and that look they turned away, brothers for life.

That was a most interesting song rehearsal that followed. It would be rare to find four voices like those even in a cultivated musical center, and they blended as if they had been made for one another. The men from the bunk-house and a lot of other people silently dropped again into their seats to listen as the four sang on. The missionary took the bass, and his wife the alto, and the four made music worth listening to. The rare and lovely thing about it was that they sang to souls, not alone for ears, and so their music, classical though it was and of the highest order, appealed keenly to the hearts of these rough men, and made them feel that heaven had opened for them, as once before for untaught shepherds, and let down a ladder of angelic voices.

"I shall feel better about leaving you out here while I am gone, since they have come," said Gardley that night when he was bidding Margaret good night. "I couldn't bear to think there were none of your own kind about you. The others are devoted and would do for you with their lives if need be, as far as they know; but I like you to have *real friends* — real *Christian* friends. This man is what I call a Christian. I'm not sure but he is the first minister that I have ever come close to who has impressed me as believing what he preaches, and living it. I suppose there are others. I haven't known many. That man West that was here when you came was a mistake!"

"He didn't even preach much," smiled Margaret, "so how could he live it? This man is real. And there are others. Oh, I have known a lot of them that are living lives of sacrifice and loving service and are yet just as strong and happy and delightful as if they were millionaires. But they are the men who have not thrown away their Bibles and their Christ.

They believe every promise in God's word, and rest on them day by day, testing them and proving them over and over. I wish you knew my father!"

"I am going to," said Gardley, proudly. "I am going to him just as soon as I have finished my business and straightened out my affairs; and I am going to tell him *everything*—with your permission, Margaret!"

"Oh, how beautiful!" cried Margaret, with happy tears in her eyes. "To think you are going to see father and mother. I have wanted them to know the real you. I couldn't half *tell* you, the real you, in a letter!"

"Perhaps they won't look on me with your sweet blindness, dear," he said, smiling tenderly down on her. "Perhaps they will see only my dark, past life—for I mean to tell your father everything. I'm not going to have any skeletons in the closet to cause pain hereafter. Perhaps your father and mother will not feel like giving their daughter to me after they know. Remember, I realize just what a rare prize she is."

"No, father is not like that, Lance," said Margaret, with her rare smile lighting up her happy eyes. "Father and mother will understand."

"But if they should not?" There was the shadow of sadness in Gardley's eyes as he asked the question.

"I belong to you, dear, anyway," she said, with sweet surrender. "I trust you though the whole world were against you!"

For answer Gardley took her in his arms, a look of awe upon his face, and, stooping, laid his lips upon hers in tender reverence.

"Margaret—you wonderful Margaret!" he said. "God has blessed me more than other men in sending you to me! With His help I will be worthy of you!"

Three days more and Margaret was alone with her school work, her two missionary friends thirty miles away, her eager watching for the mail to come, her faithful attendant

Bud, and for comfort the purple mountain with its changing glory in the distance.

A few days before Gardley left for the East he had been offered a position by Rogers as general manager of his estate at a fine salary, and after consultation with Margaret he decided to accept it, but the question of their marriage they had left by common consent unsettled until Gardley should return and be able to offer his future wife a record made as fair and clean as human effort could make it after human mistakes had unmade it. As Margaret worked and waited, wrote her charming letters to father and mother and lover, and thought her happy thoughts with only the mountain for confidant, she did not plan for the future except in a dim and dreamy way. She would make those plans with Gardley when he returned. Probably they must wait some time before they could be married. Gardley would have to earn some money, and she must earn, too. She must keep the Ashland School for another year. It had been rather understood, when she came out, that if at all possible she would remain two years at least. It was hard to think of not going home for the summer vacation; but the trip cost a great deal and was not to be thought of. There was already a plan suggested to have a summer session of the school, and if that went through, of course she must stay right in Ashland. It was hard to think of not seeing her father and mother for another long year, but perhaps Gardley would be returning before the summer was over, and then it would not be so hard. However, she tried to put these thoughts out of her mind and do her work happily. It was incredible that Arizona should have become suddenly so blank and uninteresting since the departure of a man whom she had not known a few short months before.

Margaret had long since written to her father and mother about Gardley's first finding her in the desert. The thing had become history and was not likely to alarm them. She had been in Arizona long enough to be acquainted with things, and they would not be always thinking of her as sitting on stray water-tanks in the desert; so she told them about it, for she wanted them to know Gardley as he had been to her. The letters that had traveled back and forth between New York and Arizona had been full of Gardley; and still Margaret had not told her parents how it was between them. Gardley had asked that he might do that. Yet it had been a blind father and mother who had not long ago read between the lines of those letters and understood. Margaret fancied she detected a certain sense of relief in her mother's letters after she knew that Gardley had gone East. Were they worrying about him, she wondered, or was it just the natural dread of a mother to lose her child?

So Margaret settled down to school routine, and more and more made a confidant of Bud concerning little matters of the school. If it had not been for Bud at that time Margaret would have been lonely indeed.

Two or three times since Gardley left, the Brownleighs had ridden over to Sunday service, and once had stopped for a few minutes during the week on their way to visit some distant need. These occasions were a delight to Margaret, for Hazel Brownleigh was a kindred spirit. She was looking forward with pleasure to the visit she was to make them at the mission station as soon as school closed. She had been there once with Gardley before he left, but the ride was too long to go often, and the only escort available was Bud. Besides, she could not get away from school and the Sunday service at present; but it was pleasant to have something to look forward to.

Meantime the spring Commencement was coming on and Margaret had her hands full. She had undertaken to inaugurate a real Commencement with class day and as much form and ceremony as she could introduce in order to create a good school spirit; but such things are not done with the turn of a hand, and the young teacher sadly missed Gardley in all these preparations.

At this time Rosa Rogers was Margaret's particular thorn in the flesh.

Since the night that Forsythe had quit the play and ridden forth into the darkness Rosa had regarded her teacher with baleful eyes. Gardley, too, she hated, and was only waiting with smoldering wrath until her wild, ungoverned soul could take its revenge. She felt that but for those two Forsythe would still have been with her.

Margaret, realizing the passionate, untaught nature of the motherless girl and her great need of a friend to guide her, made attempt after attempt to reach and befriend her; but every attempt was met with repulse and the sharp word of scorn. Rosa had been too long the petted darling of a father who was utterly blind to her faults to be other than spoiled. Her own way was the one thing that ruled her. By her will she had ruled every nurse and servant about the place, and wheedled her father into letting her do anything the whim prompted. Twice her father, through the advice of friends, had tried the experiment of sending her away to school, once to an Eastern finishing school, and once to a convent on the Pacific coast, only to have her return shortly by request of the school, more wilful than when she had gone away. And now she ruled supreme in her father's home, disliked by most of the servants save these whom she chose to favor because they could be made to serve her purposes. Her father, engrossed in his business and away much of the time, was bound up in her and saw few of her faults. It is true that when a fault of hers did come to his notice, however, he dealt with it most severely, and grieved over it in secret, for the girl was much like the mother whose loss had emptied the world of its joy for him. But Rosa knew well how to manage her father and wheedle him, and also how to hide her own doings from his knowledge.

Rosa's eyes, dimples, pink cheeks, and coquettish little mouth were not idle in these days. She knew how to have every pupil at her feet and ready to obey her slightest wish.

She wielded her power to its fullest extent as the summer drew near, and day after day saw a slow torture for Margaret. Some days the menacing air of insurrection fairly bristled in the room, and Margaret could not understand how some of her most devoted followers seemed to be in the forefront of battle, until one day she looked up quickly and caught the lynx-eyed glance of Rosa as she turned from smiling at the boys in the back seat. Then she understood. Rosa had cast her spell upon the boys, and they were acting under it and not of their own clear judgment. It was the world-old battle of sex, of woman against woman for the winning of the man to do her will. Margaret, using all the charm of her lovely personality to uphold standards of right, truth, purity, high living, and earnest thinking; Rosa striving with her impish beauty to lure them into *any* mischief so it foiled the other's purposes. And one day Margaret faced the girl alone, looking steadily into her eyes with sad, searching gaze, and almost a yearning to try to lead the pretty child to finer things.

"Rosa, why do you always act as if I were your enemy?" she said, sadly.

"Because you are!" said Rosa, with a toss of her independent head.

"Indeed I'm not, dear child," she said, putting out her hand to lay it on the girl's shoulder kindly. "I want to be your friend."

"I'm not a child!" snapped Rosa, jerking her shoulder angrily away; "and you can *never* be my friend, because I *hate* you!"

"Rosa, look here!" said Margaret, following the girl toward the door, the color rising in her cheeks and a desire growing in her heart to conquer this poor, passionate creature and win her for better things. "Rosa, I cannot have you say such things. Tell me why you hate me? What have I done that you should feel that way? I'm sure if we should talk it over we might come to some better understanding."

Rosa stood defiant in the doorway. "We could never come to any better understanding, Miss Earle," she declared in a cold, hard tone, "because I understand you now and I hate you. You tried your best to get my friend away from me, but you couldn't do it; and you would like to keep me from having any boy friends at all, but you can't do that, either. You think you are very popular, but you'll find out I always do what I like, and you needn't try to stop me. I don't have to come to school unless I choose, and as long as I don't break your rules you have no complaint coming; but you needn't think you can pull the wool over my eyes the way you do the others by pretending to be friends. I won't be friends! I hate you!" And Rosa turned grandly and marched out of the school-house.

Margaret stood gazing sadly after her and wondering if her failure here were her fault—if there was anything else she ought to have done—if she had let her personal dislike of the girl influence her conduct. She sat for some time at her desk, her chin in her hands, her eyes fixed on vacancy with a hopeless, discouraged expression in them, before she became aware of another presence in the room. Looking around quickly, she saw that Bud was sitting motionless at his desk, his forehead wrinkled in a fierce frown, his jaw set belligerently, and a look of such unutterable pity and devotion in his eyes that her heart warmed to him at once and a smile of comradeship broke over her face.

"Oh, William! Were you here? Did you hear all that? What do you suppose is the matter? Where have I failed?"

"You 'ain't failed anywhere! You should worry 'bout her! She's a nut! If she was a boy I'd punch her head for her! But seeing she's only a girl, *you should worry!* She always was the limit!"

Bud's tone was forcible. He was the only one of all the boys who never yielded to Rosa's charms, but sat in glowering silence when she exercised her powers on the school and created pandemonium for the teacher. Bud's attitude was comforting. It had a touch of manliness and gentleness about it quite unwonted for him. It suggested beautiful possibilities for the future of his character, and Margaret smiled tenderly.

"Thank you, dear boy!" she said, gently. "You certainly are a comfort. If every one was as splendid as you are we should have a model school. But I do wish I could help Rosa. I can't see why she should hate me so! I must have made some big mistake with her in the first place to antagonize her."

"Naw!" said Bud, roughly. "No chance! She's just a *nut,* that's all. She's got a case on that Forsythe guy, the worst kind, and she's afraid somebody 'll get him away from her, the poor stew, as if anybody would get a case on a tough guy like that! Gee! You should worry! Come on, let's take a ride over t' camp!"

With a sign and a smile Margaret accepted Bud's consolations and went on her way, trying to find some manner of showing Rosa what a real friend she was willing to be. But Rosa continued obdurate and hateful, regarding her teacher with haughty indifference except when she was called upon to recite, which she did sometimes with scornful condescension, sometimes with pert perfection, and sometimes with saucy humor which convulsed the whole room. Margaret's patience was almost ceasing to be a virtue, and she meditated often whether she ought not to request that the girl be withdrawn from the school. Yet she reflected that it was a very short time now until Commencement, and that Rosa had not openly defied any rules. It was merely a personal antagonism. Then, too, if Rosa were taken from the school there was really no other good influence in the girl's life at present. Day by day Margaret prayed about the matter and hoped that something would develop to make plain her way.

After much thought in the matter she decided to go on with her plans, letting Rosa have her place in the Commencement program and her part in the class-day doings as if nothing were the matter. Certainly there was nothing laid down in the rules of a public school that proscribed a scholar who did not love her teacher. Why should the fact that one had incurred the hate of a pupil unfit that pupil for her place in her class so long as she did her duties? And Rosa did hers promptly and deftly, with a certain piquant originality that Margaret could not help but admire.

Sometimes, as the teacher cast a furtive look at the pretty girl working away at her desk, she wondered what was going on behind the lovely mask. But the look in Rosa's eyes when she raised them, was both deep and sly.

Rosa's hatred was indeed deep rooted. Whatever heart she had not frivoled away in wilfulness had been caught and won by Forsythe, the first grown man who had ever dared to make real love to her. Her jealousy of Margaret was the most intense thing that had ever come into her life. To think of him looking at Margaret, talking to Margaret, smiling at Margaret, walking or riding with Margaret, was enough to send her writhing upon her bed in the darkness of a wakeful night. She would clench her pretty hands until the nails dug into the flesh and brought the blood. She would bite the pillow or the blankets with an almost fiendish clenching of her teeth upon them and mutter, as she did so: "I hate her! I *hate* her! I could *kill* her!"

The day her first letter came from Forsythe, Rosa held her head high and went about the school as if she were a princess royal and Margaret were the dust under her feet. Triumph sat upon her like a crown and looked forth regally from her eyes. She laid her hand upon her heart and felt the crackle of his letter inside her blouse. She dreamed with her eyes upon the distant mountain and thought of the tender names he had called her: "Little wild Rose of his heart," "No rose in all the world until you came," and a lot of other meaningful sentences. A real love-letter all her own! No sharing him with any hateful teachers! He had implied in her letter that she was the only one of all the people in that region to whom he cared to write. He had said he was coming back some day to get her. Her young, wild heart throbbed exultantly, and her eyes looked forth their triumph malignantly. When he did come she would take care that he stayed close by her. No conceited teacher from the East should lure him from her side. She would prepare her guiles and smile her sweetest. She would wear fine garments from abroad, and show him she could far outshine that quiet, common Miss Earle, with all her airs. Yet to this end she studied hard. It was no part of her plan to be left behind at graduating-time. She would please her father by taking a prominent part in things and outdoing all the others. Then he would give her what she liked—jewels and silk dresses, and all the things a girl should have who had won a lover like hers.

The last busy days before Commencement were especially trying for Margaret. It seemed as if the children were possessed with the very spirit of mischief, and she could not help but see that it was Rosa who, sitting demurely in her desk, was the center of it all. Only Bud's steady, frowning countenance of all that rollicking, roistering crowd kept loyalty with the really beloved teacher. For, indeed, they loved her, every one but Rosa, and would have stood by her to a man and girl when it really came to the pinch, but in a matter like a little bit of fun in these last few days of school, and when challenged to it by the school beauty who did not usually condescend to any but a few of the older boys, where was the harm? They were so flattered by Rosa's smiles that they failed to see Margaret's worn, weary wistfulness.

Bud, coming into the school-house late one afternoon in search of her after the other scholars had gone, found Margaret with her head down upon the desk and her shoulders shaken with soundless sobs. He stood for a second silent in the doorway, gazing helplessly at her grief, then with the delicacy of one boy for another he slipped back outside the door and stood in the shadow, grinding his teeth.

"Gee!" he said, under his breath. "Oh, gee! I'd like to punch her fool head. I don't care if she is a girl! She needs it. Gee!

if she was a boy wouldn't I settle her, the little darned mean sneak!"

His remarks, it is needless to say, did not have reference to his beloved teacher.

It was in the atmosphere everywhere that something was bound to happen if this strain kept up. Margaret knew it and felt utterly inadequate to meet it. Rosa knew it and was awaiting her opportunity. Bud knew it and could only stand and watch where the blow was to strike first and be ready to ward it off. In these days he wished fervently for Gardley's return. He did not know just what Gardley could do about "that little fool," as he called Rosa, but it would be a relief to be able to tell some one all about it. If he only dared leave he would go over and tell Jasper Kemp about it, just to share his burden with somebody. But as it was he must stick to the job for the present and bear his great responsibility, and so the days hastened by to the last Sunday before Commencement, which was to be on Monday.

MARGARET had spent Saturday in rehearsals, so that there had been no rest for her. Sunday morning she slept late, and awoke from a troubled dream, unrested. She almost meditated whether she would not ask some one to read a sermon at the afternoon service and let her go on sleeping. Then a memory of the lonely old woman at the camp, and the men, who came so regularly to the service, roused her to effort once more, and she arose and tried to prepare a little something for them.

She came into the school-house at the hour, looking fagged, with dark circles under her eyes; and the loving eyes of Mom Wallis already in her front seat watched her keenly.

"It's time for *him* to come back," she said, in her heart. "She's gettin' peeked! I wisht he'd come!"

Margaret had hoped that Rosa would not come. The girl was not always there, but of late she had been quite regular, coming in late with her father just a little after the story had begun, and attracting attention by her smiles and bows and giggling whispers, which sometimes were so audible as to create quite a diversion from the speaker.

But Rosa came in early to-day and took a seat directly in

front of Margaret, in about the middle of the house, fixing her eyes on her teacher with a kind of settled intention that made Margaret shrink as if from a danger she was not able to meet. There was something bright and hard and daring in Rosa's eyes as she stared unwinkingly, as if she had come to search out a weak spot for her evil purposes, and Margaret was so tired she wanted to lay her head down on her desk and cry. She drew some comfort from the reflection that if she should do so childish a thing she would be at once surrounded by a strong battalion of friends from the camp, who would shield her with their lives if necessary.

It was silly, of course, and she must control this choking in her throat, only how was she ever going to talk, with Rosa looking at her that way? It was like a nightmare pursuing her. She turned to the piano and kept them all singing for a while, so that she might pray in her heart and grow calm; and when, after her brief, earnest prayer, she lifted her eyes to the audience, she saw with intense relief that the Brownleighs were in the audience.

She started a hymn that they all knew, and when they were well in the midst of the first verse she slipped from the pianostool and walked swiftly down the aisle to Brownleigh's side.

"Would you please talk to them a little while?" she pleaded, wistfully. "I am so tired I feel as if I just couldn't, to-day."

Instantly Brownleigh followed her back to the desk and took her place, pulling out his little, worn Bible and opening it with familiar fingers to a beloved passage:

" 'Come unto me, all ye that labor and are heavy laden, and I will give you rest.' "

The words fell on Margaret's tired heart like balm, and she rested her head back against the wall and closed her eyes to listen. Sitting so away from Rosa's stare, she could forget for a while the absurd burdens that had got on her nerves, and could rest down hard upon her Saviour. Every word that the man of God spoke seemed meant just for her, and brought strength, courage, and new trust to her heart. She forgot the little crowd of other listeners and took the message to herself, drinking it in eagerly as one who has been a long time ministering accepts a much-needed ministry. When she moved to the piano again for the closing hymn she felt new strength within her to bear the trials of the week that were before her. She turned, smiling and brave, to speak to those who always crowded around to shake hands and have a word before leaving.

Hazel, putting a loving arm around her as soon as she could get up to the front, began to speak soothingly: "You poor, tired child!" she said; "you are almost worn to a frazzle. You need a big change, and I'm going to plan it for you just as soon as I possibly can. How would you like to go with us on our trip among the Indians? Wouldn't it be great? It'll be several days, depending on how far we go, but John wants to visit the Hopi reservation, if possible, and it 'll be so interesting. They are a most strange people. We'll have a delightful trip, sleeping out under the stars, you know. Don't you just love it? I do. I wouldn't miss it for the world. I can't be sure, for a few days yet, when we can go, for John has to make a journey in the other direction first, and he isn't sure when he can return; but it might be this week. How soon can you come to us? How I wish we could take you right home with us to-night. You need to get away and rest. But your Commencement is to-morrow, isn't it? I'm so sorry we can't be here, but this other matter is important, and John has to go early in the morning. Some one very sick who wants to see him before he dies — an old Indian who didn't know a thing about Jesus till John found him one day. I suppose you haven't anybody who could bring you over to us after your work is done here to-morrow night or Tuesday, have you? Well, we'll see if we can't find some one to send for you soon. There's an old Indian who often comes this way, but he's away buying cattle. Maybe John can think of a way we could send for you early in the week. Then you would be ready to go with us on the trip. You would like to go, wouldn't you?"

"Oh, so much!" said Margaret, with a sigh of wistfulness. "I can't think of anything pleasanter!"

Margaret turned suddenly, and there, just behind her, almost touching her, stood Rosa, that strange, baleful gleam in her eyes like a serpent who was biding her time, drawing nearer and nearer, knowing she had her victim where she could not move before she struck.

It was a strange fancy, of course, and one that was caused by sick nerves, but Margaret drew back and almost cried out, as if for some one to protect her. Then her strong common sense came to the rescue and she rallied and smiled at Rosa a faint little sorry smile. It was hard to smile at the bright, baleful face with the menace in the eyes.

Hazel was watching her. "You poor child! You're quite worn out! I'm afraid you're going to be sick."

"Oh, no," said Margaret, trying to speak cheerfully; "things have just got on my nerves, that's all. It's been a particularly trying time. I shall be all right when to-morrow night is over."

"Well, we're going to send for you very soon, so be ready!" and Hazel followed her husband, waving her hand in gay parting.

Rosa was still standing just behind her when Margaret turned back to her desk, and the younger girl gave her one last dagger look, a glitter in her eyes so sinister and vindictive that Margaret felt a shudder run through her whole body, and was glad that just then Rosa's father called to her that they must be starting home. Only one more day now of Rosa, and she would be done with her, perhaps forever. The girl was through the school course and was graduating. It was not likely she would return another year. Her opportunity was over to help her. She had failed. Why, she couldn't tell, but she had strangely failed, and all she asked now was not to have to endure the hard, cold, young presence any longer.

"Sick nerves, Margaret!" she said to herself. "Go home and go to bed. You'll be all right to-morrow!" And she locked the school-house door and walked quietly home with the faithful Bud.

The past month had been a trying time also for Rosa. Young, wild, and motherless, passionate, wilful and impetuous, she was finding life tremendously exciting just now. With no one to restrain her or warn her she was playing with forces that she did not understand.

She had subjugated easily all the boys in school, keeping them exactly where she wanted them for her purpose, and using methods that would have done credit to a woman of the world. But by far the greatest force in her life was her infatuation for Forsythe.

The letters had traveled back and forth many times between them since Forsythe wrote that first love-letter. He found a whimsical pleasure in her deep devotion and naïve readiness to follow as far as he cared to lead her. He realized that, young as she was, she was no innocent, which made the acquaintance all the more interesting. He, meantime, idled away a few months on the Pacific coast, making mild love to a rich California girl and considering whether or not he was ready yet to settle down.

In the mean time his correspondence with Rosa took on such a nature that his volatile, impulsive nature was stirred with a desire to see her again. It was not often that once out of sight he looked back to a victim, but Rosa had shown a daring and a spirit in her letters that sent a challenge to his sated senses. Moreover, the California heiress was going on a journey; besides, an old enemy of his who knew altogether too much of his past had appeared on the scene; and as Gardley had been removed from the Ashland vicinity for a time, Forsythe felt it might be safe to venture back again. There was always that pretty, spirited little teacher if Rosa failed to charm. But why should Rosa not charm? And why should he not yield? Rosa's father was a good sort and had all kinds of property. Rosa was her father's only heir. On the whole, Forsythe decided that the best move he could make next would be to return to Arizona. If things turned out well he might even think of marrying Rosa.

This was somewhat the train of thought that led Forsythe at last to write to Rosa that he was coming, throwing Rosa into a panic of joy and alarm. For Rosa's father had been most explicit about her ever going out with Forsythe again. It had been the most relentless command he had ever laid upon her, spoken in a tone she hardly ever disobeyed. Moreover, Rosa was fearfully jealous of Margaret. If Forsythe should come and begin to hang around the teacher Rosa felt she would go wild, or do something terrible, perhaps even kill somebody. She shut her sharp little white teeth fiercely down into her red under lip and vowed with flashing eyes that he should never see Margaret again if power of hers could prevent it.

The letter from Forsythe had reached her on Saturday evening, and she had come to the Sunday service with the distinct idea of trying to plan how she might get rid of Margaret. It would be hard enough to evade her father's vigilance if he once found out the young man had returned; but to have him begin to go and see Margaret again was a thing she could not and would not stand.

The idea obsessed her to the exclusion of all others, and made her watch her teacher as if by her very concentration of thought upon her some way out of the difficulty might be evolved; as if Margaret herself might give forth a hint of weakness somewhere that would show her how to plan.

To that intent she had come close in the group with the others around the teacher at the close of meeting, and, so standing, had overheard all that the Brownleighs had said. The lightning flash of triumph that she cast at Margaret as she left the school-house was her own signal that she had found a way at last. Her opportunity had come, and just in time. Forsythe was to arrive in Arizona some time on Tuesday, and wanted Rosa to meet him at one of their old trysting-places, out some distance from her father's house. He knew that school would just be over, for she had written him about Commencement, and so he understood that she would be free. But he did not know that the place he had selected to meet her was on one of Margaret's favorite trails where she and Bud often rode in the late afternoons, and that above all things Rosa wished to avoid any danger of meeting her teacher; for she not only feared that Forsythe's attention would be drawn away from her, but also that Margaret might feel it her duty to report to her father about her clandestine meeting.

Rosa's heart beat high as she rode demurely home with her father, answering his pleasantries with smiles and dimples and a coaxing word, just as he loved to have her. But she was not thinking of her father, though she kept well her mask of interest in what he had to say. She was trying to plan how she might use what she had heard to get rid of Margaret Earle. If only Mrs. Brownleigh would do as she had hinted and send some one Tuesday morning to escort Miss Earle over to her home, all would be clear sailing for Rosa; but she dared not trust to such a possibility. There were not many escorts coming their way from Ganado, and Rosa happened to know that the old Indian who frequently escorted parties was off in another direction. She could not rest on any such hope. When she reached home she went at once to her room and sat beside her window, gazing off at the purple mountains in deep thought. Then she lighted a candle and went in search of a certain little Testament, long since neglected and covered with dust. She found it at last on top of a pile of books in a dark closet, and dragged it forth, eagerly turning the pages. Yes, there is was, and in it a small envelope directed to "Miss Rosa Rogers" in a fine angular handwriting. The letter was from the missionary's wife to the little girl who had recited her texts so beautifully as to earn the Testament.

Rosa carried it to her desk, secured a good light, and sat down to read it over carefully.

No thought of her innocent childish exultation over that letter came to her now. She was intent on one thing—the handwriting. Could she seize the secret of it and reproduce it? She had before often done so with great success. She could imitate Miss Earle's writing so perfectly that she often took an impish pleasure in changing words in the questions on the blackboard and making them read absurdly for the benefit of the school. It was such good sport to see the amazement on Margaret's face when her attention would be called to it by a hilarious class, and to watch her troubled brow when she read what she supposed she had written.

When Rosa was but a little child she used to boast that she could write her father's name in perfect imitation of his signature; and often signed some trifling receipt for him just for amusement. A dangerous gift in the hands of a conscienceless girl! Yes this was the first time that Rosa had really planned to use her art in any serious way. Perhaps it never occurred to her that she was doing wrong. At present her heart was too full of hate and fear and jealous love to care for right or wrong or anything else. It is doubtful if she would have hesitated a second even if the thing she was planning had suddenly appeared to her in the light of a great crime. She seemed sometimes almost like a creature without moral sense, so swayed was she by her own desires and feelings. She was blind now to everything but her great desire to get Margaret out of the way and have Forsythe to herself.

Long after her father and the servants were asleep Rosa's light burned while she bent over her desk, writing. Page after page she covered with careful copies of Mrs. Brownleigh's letter written to herself almost three years before. Finally she wrote out the alphabet, bit by bit as she picked it from the words, learning just how each letter was habitually formed, the small letters and the capitals, with the peculiarities of connection and ending. At last, when she lay down to rest, she felt herself capable of writing a pretty fair letter in Mrs. Brownleigh's handwriting. The next thing was to make her plan and compose her letter. She lay staring into the darkness and trying to think just what she could do.

In the first place, she settled it that Margaret must be gotten to Walpi at least. It would not do to send her to Ganado, where the mission station was, for that was a comparatively short journey, and she could easily go in a day. When the fraud was discovered, as of course it would be when Mrs. Brownleigh heard of it, Margaret would perhaps return to find out who had done it. No, she must be sent all the way to Walpi if possible. That would take at least two nights and the most of two days to get there. Forsythe had said his stay was to be short. By the time Margaret got back from Walpi Forsythe would be gone.

But how manage to get her to Walpi without her suspicions being aroused? She might word the note so that Margaret would be told to come half-way, expecting to meet the missionaries, say at Keams. There was a trail straight up from Ashland to Keams, cutting off quite a distance and leaving Ganado off at the right. Keams was nearly forty miles west of Ganado. That would do nicely. Then if she could manage to have another note left at Keams, saying they could not wait and had gone on, Margaret would suspect nothing and go all the way to Walpi. That would be fine and would give the school-teacher an interesting experience which wouldn't hurt her in the least. Rosa thought it might be rather interesting than otherwise. She had no compunctions whatever about how Margaret might feel when she arrived in that strange Indian town and found no friends awaiting her. Her only worry was where she was to find a suitable escort, for she felt assured that Margaret would not start out alone with one man servant on an expedition that would keep her out overnight. And where in all that region could she find a woman whom she could trust to send on the errand? It almost looked as though the thing were an impossibility. She lay tossing and puzzling over it till gray dawn stole into the room. She mentally reviewed every servant on the place on whom she could rely to do her bidding and keep her secret, but there was some reason why each one would not do. She scanned the country, even considering old Ouida, who had been living in a shack over beyond the fort ever since her cabin had been raided; but old Ouida was too notorious. Mrs. Tanner would keep Margaret from going with her, even if Margaret herself did not know the old woman's reputation. Rosa considered if there were any way of wheedling Mom Wallis into the affair, and gave that up, remembering the suspicious little twinkling eyes of Jasper Kemp. At last she fell asleep, with her plan still unformed but her determination to carry it through just as strong as ever. If worst came to worst she would send the half-breed cook from the ranch kitchen and put something in the note about his expecting to meet his sister an hour's ride out on the trail. The half-breed would do anything in the world for money, and Rosa had no trouble in getting all she wanted of that commodity. But the half-breed was an evil-looking fellow, and she feared lest Margaret would not like to go with him. However, he should be a last resort. She would not be balked in her purpose.

28

ROSA awoke very early, for her sleep had been light and troubled. She dressed hastily and sat down to compose a note which could be altered slightly in case she found some one better than the half-breed; but before she was half through the phrasing she heard a slight disturbance below her window and a muttering in guttural tones from a strange voice. Glancing hastily out, she saw some Indians below, talking with one of the men, who was shaking his head and motioning to them that they must go on, that this was no place for them to stop. The Indian motioned to his squaw, sitting on a dilapidated little moth-eaten burro with a small papoose in her arms and looking both dirty and miserable. He muttered as though he were pleading for something.

We believe that God's angels follow the feet of little children and needy ones to protect them; does the devil also send his angels to lead unwary ones astray, and to protect the plans of the erring ones? If so then he must have sent these Indians that morning to further Rosa's plans, and instantly she recognized her opportunity. She leaned out of her window and spoke in a clear, reproving voice:

"James, what does he want? Breakfast? You know father

wouldn't want any hungry person to be turned away. Let them sit down on the bench there and tell Dorset I said to give them a good hot breakfast, and get some milk for the baby. Be quick about it, too!"

James started and frowned at the clear, commanding voice. The squaw turned grateful animal eyes up to the little beauty in the window, muttering some inarticulate thanks, while the stolid Indian's eyes glittered hopefully, though the muscles of his masklike countenance changed not an atom.

Rosa smiled radiantly and ran down to see that her orders were obeyed. She tried to talk a little with the squaw, but found she understood very little English. The Indian spoke better and gave her their brief story. They were on their way to the Navajo reservation to the far north. They had been unfortunate enough to lose their last scanty provisions by prowling coyotes during the night, and were in need of food. Rosa gave them a place to sit down and a plentiful breakfast, and ordered that a small store of provisions should be prepared for their journey after they had rested. Then she hurried up to her room to finish her letter. She had her plan well fixed now. These strangers should be her willing messengers. Now and then, as she wrote she lifted her head and gazed out of the window, where she could see the squaw busy with her little one, and her eyes fairly glittered with satisfaction. Nothing could have been better planned than this.

She wrote her note carefully:

> Dear Margaret *[she had heard Hazel call Margaret by her first name, and rightly judged that their new friendship was already strong enough to justify this intimacy]*, — I have found just the opportunity I wanted for you to come to us. These Indians are thoroughly trustworthy and are coming in just the direction to bring you to a point where we will meet you. We have decided to go on to Walpi at once, and will probably meet you near Keams,

or a little farther on. The Indian knows the way, and you need not be afraid. I trust him perfectly. Start at once, please, so that you will meet us in time. John has to go on as fast as possible. I know you will enjoy the trip, and am so glad you are coming.

Lovingly,
Hazel Radcliffe Brownleigh

Rosa read it over, comparing it carefully with the little yellow note from her Testament, and decided that it was a very good imitation. She could almost hear Mrs. Brownleigh saying what she had written. Rosa really was quite clever. She had done it well.

She hastily sealed and addressed her letter, and then hurried down to talk with the Indians again.

The place she had ordered for them to rest was at some distance from the kitchen door, a sort of outshed for the shelter of certain implements used about the ranch. A long bench ran in front of it, and a big tree made a goodly shade. The Indians had found their temporary camp quite inviting.

Rosa made a detour of the shed, satisfied herself that no one was within hearing, and then sat down on the bench, ostensibly playing with the papoose, dangling a red ball on a ribbon before his dazzled, bead-like eyes and bringing forth a gurgle of delight from the dusky little mummy. While she played she talked idly with the Indians. Had they money enough for their journey? Would they like to earn some? Would they act as guide to a lady who wanted to go to Walpi? At least she wanted to go as far as Keams, where she might meet friends, missionaries, who were going on with her to Walpi to visit the Indians. If they didn't meet her she wanted to be guided all the way to Walpi. Would they undertake it? It would pay them well. They would get money enough for their journey and have some left when they got to the reservation. And Rosa displayed two gold pieces temptingly in her small palms.

The Indian uttered a guttural sort of gasp at sight of so much money, and sat upright. He gasped again, indicating by a solemn nod that he was agreeable to the task before him, and the girl went gaily on with her instructions:

"You will have to take some things along to make the lady comfortable. I will see that those are got ready. Then you can have the things for your own when you leave the lady at Walpi. You will have to take a letter to the lady and tell her you are going this afternoon, and she must be ready to start at once or she will not meet the missionary. Tell her you can only wait until three o'clock to start. You will find the lady at the school-house at noon. You must not come till noon—" Rosa pointed to the sun and then straight overhead. The Indian watched her keenly and nodded.

"You must ask for Miss Earle and give her this letter. She is the school-teacher."

The Indian grunted and looked at the white missive in Rosa's hand, noting once more the gleam of the gold pieces.

"You must wait till the teacher goes to her boarding-house and packs her things and eats her dinner. If anybody asks where you came from you must say the missionary's wife from Ganado sent you. Don't tell anybody anything else. Do you understand? More money if you don't say anything?" Rosa clinked the gold pieces softly.

The strange, sphinx-like gaze of the Indian narrowed comprehensively. He understood. His native cunning was being bought for this girl's own purposes. He looked greedily at the money. Rosa had put her hand in her pocket and brought out yet another gold piece.

"See! I give you this one now"—she laid one gold piece in the Indian's hand—"and these two I put in an envelope and pack with some provisions and blankets on another horse. I will leave the horse tied to a tree up where the big trail crosses this big trail out that way. You know?"

Rosa pointed in the direction she meant, and the Indian looked and grunted, his eyes returning to the two gold pieces in her hand. It was a great deal of money for the little lady to give. Was she trying to cheat him? He looked down at the gold he already held. It was good money. He was sure of that. He looked at her keenly.

"I shall be watching and I shall know whether you have the lady or not," went on the girl, sharply. "If you do not bring the lady with you there will be no money and no provisions waiting for you. But if you bring the lady you can untie the horse and take him with you. You will need the horse to carry the things. When you get to Walpi you can set him free. He is branded and he will likely come back. We shall find him. See, I will put the gold pieces in this tin can."

She picked up a sardine-tin that lay at her feet, slipped the gold pieces in an envelope from her pocket, stuffed it in the tin, bent down the cover, and held it up.

"This can will be packed on the top of the other provisions, and you can open it and take the money out when you untie the horse. Then hurry on as fast as you can and get as far along the trail as possible to-night before you camp. Do you understand?"

The Indian nodded once more, and Rosa felt that she had a confederate worthy of her need.

She stayed a few minutes more, going carefully over her directions, telling the Indian to be sure his squaw was kind to the lady, and that on no account he should let the lady get uneasy or have cause to complain of her treatment, or trouble would surely come to him. At last she felt sure she had made him understand, and she hurried away to slip into her pretty white dress and rose-colored ribbons and ride to school. Before she left her room she glanced out of the window at the Indians, and saw them sitting motionless, like a group of bronze. Once the Indian stirred and, putting his hand in his bosom, drew forth the white letter she had given him, gazed at it a moment, and hid it in his breast again. She nodded her satisfaction as she turned from the window. The next thing was to get to school and play her own part in the Commencement exercises.

The morning was bright, and the school-house was already filled to overflowing when Rosa arrived. Her coming, as always, made a little stir among admiring groups, for even those who feared her admired her from afar. She fluttered into the school-house and up the aisle with the air of a princess who knew she had been waited for and was condescending to come at all.

Rosa was in everything — the drills, the march, the choruses, and the crowning oration. She went through it all with the perfection of a bright mind and an adaptable nature. One would never have dreamed, to look at her pretty dimpling face and her sparking eyes, what diabolical things were moving in her mind, nor how those eyes, lynx-soft with lurking sweetness and treachery, were watching all the time furtively for the appearance of the old Indian.

At last she saw him, standing in a group just outside the window near the platform, his tall form and stern countenance marking him among the crowd of familiar faces. She was receiving her diploma from the hand of Margaret when she caught his eye, and her hand trembled just a quiver as she took the dainty roll tied with blue and white ribbons. That he recognized her she was sure; that he knew she did not wish him to make known his connection with her she felt equally convinced he understood. His eye had that comprehending look of withdrawal. She did not look up directly at him again. Her eyes were daintily downward. Nevertheless, she missed not a turn of his head, not a glance from that stern eye, and she knew the moment when he stood at the front door of the school-house with the letter in his hand, stolid and indifferent, yet a great force to be reckoned with.

Some one looked at the letter, pointed to Margaret, called her, and she came. Rosa was not far away all the time, talking with Jed; her eyes downcast, her cheeks dimpling, missing nothing that could be heard or seen.

Margaret read the letter. Rosa watched her, knew every curve of every letter and syllable as she read, held her breath, and watched Margaret's expression. Did she suspect? No. A look of intense relief and pleasure had come into her eyes. She was glad to have found a way to go. She turned to Mrs. Tanner.

"What do you think of this, Mrs. Tanner? I'm to go with Mrs. Brownleigh on a trip to Walpi. Isn't that delicious? I'm to start at once. Do you suppose I could have a bite to eat? I won't need much. I'm too tired to eat and too anxious to be off. If you give me a cup of tea and a sandwich I'll be all right. I've got things about ready to go, for Mrs. Brownleigh told me she would send some one for me."

"H'm!" said Mrs. Tanner, disapprovingly. "Who you goin' with? Just *him?* I don't much like *his* looks!"

She spoke in a low tone so the Indian would not hear, and it was almost in Rosa's very ear, who stood just behind. Rosa's heart stopped a beat and she frowned at the toe of her slipper. Was this common little Tanner woman going to be the one to balk her plans?

Margaret raised her head now for her first good look at the Indian, and it must be admitted a chill came into her heart. Then, as if he comprehended what was at stake, the Indian turned slightly and pointed down the path toward the road. By common consent the few who were standing about the door stepped back and made a vista for Margaret to see the squaw sitting statue-like on her scraggy little pony, gazing off at the mountain in the distance, as if she were sitting for her picture, her solemn little papoose strapped to her back.

Margaret's troubled eyes cleared. The family aspect made things all right again. "You see, he has his wife and child," she said. "It's all right. Mrs. Brownleigh says she trusts him perfectly, and I'm to meet them on the way. Read the letter."

She thrust the letter into Mrs. Tanner's hand, and Rosa trembled for her scheme once more. Surely, surely Mrs.

Tanner would not be able to detect the forgery!

"H'm! Well, I s'pose it's all right if she says so, but I'm sure I don't relish them pesky Injuns, and I don't think that squaw wife of his looks any great shakes, either. They look to me like they needed a good scrub with Bristol brick. But then, if you're set on going, you'll go, 'course. I jest wish Bud hadn't 'a' gone home with that Jasper Kemp. He might 'a' gone along, an' then you'd 'a' had somebody to speak English to."

"Yes, it would have been nice to have William along," said Margaret; "but I think I'll be all right. Mrs. Brownleigh wouldn't send anybody that wasn't nice."

"H'm! I dun'no'! She's an awful crank. She just loves them Injuns, they say. But I, fer one, draw the line at holdin' 'em in my lap. I don't b'lieve in mixin' folks up that way. Preach to 'em if you like, but let 'em keep their distance, I say."

Margaret laughed and went off to pick up her things. Rosa stood smiling and talking to Jed until she saw Margaret and Mrs. Tanner go off together, the Indians riding slowly along behind.

Rosa waited until the Indians had turned off the road down toward the Tanners', and then she mounted her own pony and rode swiftly home.

She rushed up to her room and took off her fine apparel, arraying herself quickly in a plain little gown, and went down to prepare the provisions. There was none too much time, and she must work rapidly. It was well for her plans that she was all-powerful with the servants and could send them about at will to get them out of her way. She invented a duty for each now that would take them for a few minutes well out of sight and sound; then she hurried together the provisions in a basket, making two trips to get them to the shelter where she had told the Indian he would find the horse tied. She had to make a third trip to bring the blankets and a few other things she knew would be indispensable, but the whole outfit was really but carelessly gotten together, and it was just by chance that some things got in at all.

It was not difficult to find the old cayuse she intended using for a pack-horse. He was browsing around in the corral, and she soon had a halter over his head, for she had been quite used to horses from her babyhood.

She packed the canned things, tinned meats, vegetables, and fruit into a couple of large sacks, adding some fodder for the horses, a box of matches, some corn bread, of which there was always plenty on hand in the house, some salt pork, and a few tin dishes. These she slung pack fashion over the old horse, fastened the sardine-tin containing the gold pieces where it would be easily found, tied the horse to a tree, and retired behind a shelter of sage-brush to watch.

It was not long before the little caravan came, the Indians riding ahead single file, like two graven images, moving not a muscle of their faces, and Margaret a little way behind on her own pony, her face as happy and relieved as if she were a child let out from a hard task to play.

The Indian stopped beside the horse, a glitter of satisfaction in his eyes as he saw that the little lady had fulfilled her part of the bargain. He indicated to the squaw and the lady that they might move on down the trail, and he would catch up with them; and then dismounted, pouncing warily upon the sardine-tin at once. He looked furtively about, then took out the money and tested it with his teeth to make sure it was genuine.

He grunted his further satisfaction, looked over the pack-horse, made more secure the fastenings of the load, and, taking the halter, mounted and rode stolidly away toward the north.

Rosa waited in her covert until they were far out of sight, then made her way hurriedly back to the house and climbed to a window where she could watch the trail for several miles. There, with a field-glass, she kept watch until the procession had filed across the plains, down into a valley, up over a hill, and dropped to a farther valley out of sight. She looked at the sun and drew a breath of satisfaction. She had done it at last! She had got Margaret away before Forsythe came! There was no likelihood that the fraud would be discovered until her rival was far enough away to be safe. A kind of reaction came upon Rosa's overwrought nerves. She laughed out harshly, and her voice had a cruel ring to it. Then she threw herself upon the bed and burst into a passionate fit of weeping, and so, by and by, fell asleep. She dreamed that Margaret had returned like a shining, fiery angel, a two-edged sword in her hand and all the Wallis camp at her heels, with vengeance in their wake. That hateful little boy, Bud Tanner, danced around and made faces at her, while Forsythe had forgotten her to gaze at Margaret's face.

29

TO Margaret the day was very fair, and the omens all auspicious. She carried with her close to her heart two precious letters received that morning and scarcely glanced at as yet, one from Gardley and one from her mother. She had had only time to open them and be sure that all was well with her dear ones, and had left the rest to read on the way.

She was dressed in the khaki riding-habit she always wore when she went on horseback; and in the bag strapped on behind she carried a couple of fresh white blouses, a thin, white dress, a little soft dark silk gown that folded away almost into a cobweb, and a few other necessities. She had also slipped in a new book her mother had sent her, into which she had had as yet no time to look, and her chessmen and board, besides writing materials. She prided herself on having got so many necessaries into so small a compass. She would need the extra clothing if she stayed at Ganado with the missionaries for a week on her return from the trip, and the book and chessmen would amuse them all by the way. She had heard Brownleigh say he loved to play chess.

Margaret rode on the familiar trail, and for the first hour just let herself be glad that school was over and she could rest and have no responsibility. The sun shimmered down brilliantly on the white, hot sand and gray-green of the greasewood and sage-brush. Tall spikes of cactus like lonely spires shot up now and again to vary the scene. It was all familiar ground to Margaret around here, for she had taken many rides with Gardley and Bud, and for the first part of the way every turn and bit of view was fraught with pleasant memories that brought a smile to her eyes as she recalled some quotation of Gardley's or some prank of Bud's. Here was where they first sighted the little cottontail the day she took her initial ride on her own pony. Off there was the mountain where they saw the sun drawing silver water above a frowning storm. Yonder was the group of cedars where they had stopped to eat their lunch once, and this water-hole they were approaching was the one where Gardley had given her a drink from his hat.

She was almost glad that Bud was not along, for she was too tired to talk and liked to be alone with her thoughts for this few minutes. Poor Bud! He would be disappointed when he got back to find her gone, but then he had expected she was going in a few days, anyway, and she had promised to take long rides with him when she returned. She had left a little note for him, asking him to read a certain book in her bookcase while she was gone, and be ready to discuss it with her when she got back, and Bud would be fascinated with it, she knew. Bud had been dear and faithful, and she would miss him, but just for this little while she was glad to have the great out-of-doors to herself.

She was practically alone. The two sphinx-like figures riding ahead of her made no sign, but stolidly rode on hour after hour, nor turned their heads even to see if she were coming. She knew that Indians were this way; still, as the time went by she began to feel an uneasy sense of being alone in the universe with a couple of bronze statues. Even the papoose had erased itself in sleep, and when it awoke partook so fully of its racial peculiarities as to hold its little peace and make no fuss. Margaret began to feel the baby was hardly human, more like a little brown doll set up in a missionary meeting to teach white children what a papoose was like.

By and by she got out her letters and read them over carefully, dreaming and smiling over them, and getting precious bits by heart. Gardley hinted that he might be able very soon to visit her parents, as it looked as though he might have to make a trip on business in their direction before he could go further with what he was doing in his old home. He gave no hint of soon returning to the West. He said he was awaiting the return of one man who might soon be coming from abroad. Margaret sighed and wondered how many weary months it would be before she would see him. Perhaps, after all, she ought to have gone home and stayed them out with her mother and father. If the school-board could be made to see that it would be better to have no summer session, perhaps she would even yet go when she returned from the Brownleighs'. She would see. She would decide nothing until she was rested.

Suddenly she felt herself overwhelmingly weary, and wished that the Indians would stop and rest for a while; but when she stirred up her sleepy pony and spurred ahead to broach the matter to her guide he shook his solemn head and pointed to the sun:

"No get Keams good time. No meet Aneshodi."

"Aneshodi," she knew, was the Indians' name for the missionary, and she smiled her acquiescence. Of course they must meet the Brownleighs and not detain them. What was it Hazel had said about having to hurry? She searched her pocket for the letter, and then remembered she had left it with Mrs. Tanner. What a pity she had not brought it! Perhaps there was some caution or advice in it that she had not taken note of. But then the Indian likely knew all about it, and she could trust him. She glanced at his stolid face and wished she could make him smile. She cast a sunny smile at him and said something pleasant about the beautiful day, but he only looked her through as if she were not there, and after one or two more attempts she fell back and tried to talk to the squaw; but the squaw only looked stolid, too, and shook her head. She did not seem friendly. Margaret drew back into her old position and feasted her eyes upon the distant hills.

The road was growing unfamiliar now. They were crossing rough ridges with cliffs of red sandstone, and every step of the way was interesting. Yet Margaret felt more and more how much she wanted to lie down and sleep, and when at last in the dusk the Indians halted not far from a little pool of rainwater and indicated that here they would camp for the night, Margaret was too weary to question the decision. It had not occurred to her that she would be on the way overnight before she met her friends. Her knowledge of the way, and of distances, was but vague. It is doubtful if she would have ventured had she known that she must pass the night thus in the company of two strange savage creatures. Yet, now that she was here and it was inevitable, she would not shrink, but make the best of it. She tried to be friendly once more, and offered to look out for the baby while the squaw gathered wood and made a fire. The Indian was off looking after the horses, evidently expecting his wife to do all the work.

Margaret watched a few minutes, while pretending to play with the baby, who was both sleepy and hungry, yet held his emotions as stolidly as if he were a grown person. Then she decided to take a hand in the supper. She was hungry and could not bear that those dusky, dirty hands should set forth her food, so she went to work cheerfully, giving directions as if the Indian woman understood her, though she very soon discovered that all her talk was as mere babbling to the other, and she might as well hold her peace. The woman set a kettle of water over the fire, and Margaret forestalled her next movement by cutting some pork and putting it to cook in a little skillet she found among the provisions. The woman watched her solemnly, not seeming to care; and so, silently, each went about her own preparations.

The supper was a silent affair, and when it was over the squaw handed Margaret a blanket. Suddenly she understood that this, and this alone, was to be her bed for the night. The earth was there for a mattress, and the sage-brush lent a partial shelter, the canopy of stars was overhead.

A kind of panic took possession of her. She stared at the squaw and found herself longing to cry out for help. It seemed as if she could not bear this awful silence of the mortals who were her only company. Yet her common sense came to her aid, and she realized that there was nothing for it but to make the best of things. So she took the blanket and, spreading it out, sat down upon it and wrapped it about her shoulders and feet. She would not lie down until she saw what the rest did. Somehow she shrank from asking the bronze man how to fold a blanket for a bed on the ground. She tried to remember what Gardley had told her about folding the blanket bed so as best to keep out snakes and ants. She shuddered at the thought of snakes. Would she dare call for help from those stolid companions of hers if a snake should attempt to molest her in the night? And would she ever dare to go to sleep?

She remembered her first night in Arizona out among the stars, alone on the water-tank, and her first frenzy of loneliness. Was this as bad? No, for these Indians were trustworthy and well known by her dear friends. It might be unpleasant, but this, too, would pass and the morrow would soon be here.

The dusk dropped down and the stars loomed out. All the world grew wonderful, like a blue jeweled dome of a palace with the lights turned low. The fire burned brightly as the man threw sticks upon it, and the two Indians moved stealthily about in the darkness, passing silhouetted before the fire this way and that, and then at last lying down wrapped in their blankets to sleep.

It was very quiet about her. The air was so still she could hear the hobbled horses munching away in the distance, and moving now and then with the halting gait a hobble gives a horse. Off in the farther distance the blood-curdling howl of the coyotes rose, but Margaret was used to them, and knew they would not come near a fire.

She was growing very weary, and at last wrapped her blanket closer and lay down, her head pillowed on one corner of it. Committing herself to her Heavenly Father, and breathing a prayer for father, mother, and lover, she fell asleep.

It was still almost dark when she awoke. For a moment she thought it was still night and the sunset was not gone yet, the clouds were so rosy tinted.

The squaw was standing by her, touching her shoulder roughly and grunting something. She perceived, as she rubbed her eyes and tried to summon back her senses, that she was expected to get up and eat breakfast. There was a smell of pork and coffee in the air, and there was scorched corn bread beside the fire on a pan.

Margaret got up quickly and ran down to the water-hole to get some water, dashing it in her face and over her arms and hands, the squaw meanwhile standing at a little distance, watching her curiously, as if she thought this some kind of an oblation paid to the white woman's god before she ate. Margaret pulled the hair-pins out of her hair, letting it down and combing it with one of her side combs; twisted it up again in its soft, fluffy waves; straightened her collar, set on her hat, and was ready for the day. The squaw looked at her with both awe and contempt for a moment, then turned and stalked back to her papoose and began preparing it for the journey.

Margaret made a hurried meal and was scarcely done before she found her guides were waiting like two pillars of the desert, but watching keenly, impatiently, her every mouthful, and anxious to be off.

The sky was still pink-tinted with the semblance of a sunset, and Margaret felt, as she mounted her pony and followed her companions, as if the day was all turned upside down. She almost wondered whether she hadn't slept through a whole twenty-four hours, and it were not, after all, evening again, till by and by the sun rose clear and the wonder of the cloud-tinting melted into day.

The road lay through sage-brush and old barren cedar-trees, with rabbits darting now and then between the rocks. Suddenly from the top of a little hill they came out to a spot where they could see far over the desert. Forty miles away three square, flat hills, or mesas, looked like a gigantic train of cars, and the clear air gave everything a strange vastness. Farther on beyond the mesas dimly dawned the Black Mountains. One could even see the shadowed head of "Round Rock," almost a hundred miles away. Before them and around was a great plain of sage-brush, and here and there was a small bush that the Indians call "the weed that was not scared." Margaret had learned all these things during her winter in Arizona, and keenly enjoyed the vast, splendid view spread before her.

They passed several little mud-plastered hogans that Margaret knew for Indian dwellings. A fine band of ponies off in the distance made an interesting spot on the landscape, and twice they passed bands of sheep. She had a feeling of great isolation from everything she had ever known, and seemed going farther and farther from life and all she loved. Once she ventured to ask the Indian what time he expected to meet her friends, the missionaries, but he only shook his head and murmured something unintelligible about "Keams" and pointed to the sun. She dropped behind again, vaguely uneasy, she could not tell why. There seemed something so altogether sly and wary and unfriendly in the faces of the two that she almost wished she had not come. Yet the way was beautiful enough and nothing very unpleasant was happening to her. Once she dropped the envelope of her mother's letter and was about to dismount and recover it. Then some strange impulse made her leave it on the sand of the desert. What if they should be lost and that paper should guide them back? The notion stayed by her, and once in a while she dropped other bits of paper by the way.

About noon the trail dropped off into a cañon, with high, yellow-rock walls on either side, and stifling heat, so that she felt as if she could scarcely stand it. She was glad when they emerged once more and climbed to higher ground. The noon camp was a hasty affair, for the Indian seemed in a hurry. He scanned the horizon far and wide and seemed searching keenly for some one or something. Once they met a lonely Indian, and he held a muttered conversation with him, pointing off ahead and gesticulating angrily. But the words were unintelligible to Margaret. Her feeling of uneasiness was growing, and yet she could not for the life of her tell why, and laid it down to her tired nerves. She was beginning to think she had been very foolish to start on such a long trip before she had had a chance to get rested from her last days of school. She longed to lie down under a tree and sleep for days.

Toward night they sighted a great blue mesa about fifty miles south, and at sunset they could just see the San Francisco peaks more than a hundred and twenty-five miles away. Margaret, as she stopped her horse and gazed, felt a choking in her heart and throat and a great desire to cry. The glory and awe of the mountains, mingled with her own weariness and nervous fear, were almost too much for her. She was glad to get down and eat a little supper and go to sleep again. As she fell asleep she comforted herself with repeating over a few precious words from her Bible:

"The angel of the Lord encampeth round about them that fear Him and delivereth them. Thou wilt keep him in perfect peace whose mind is stayed on Thee because he trusteth in Thee. I will both lay me down in peace and sleep, for Thou Lord only makest me to dwell in safety. . . ."

The voice of the coyotes, now far, now near, boomed out on the night; great stars shot dartling pathways across the heavens; the fire snapped and crackled, died down and flickered feebly; but Margaret slept, tired out, and dreamed the angels kept close vigil around her lowly couch.

She did not know what time the stars disappeared and the rain began to fall. She was too tired to notice the drops that fell upon her face. Too tired to hear the coyotes coming nearer, nearer, yet in the morning there lay one dead, stretched not thirty feet from where she lay. The Indian had shot him through the heart.

Somehow things looked very dismal that morning, in spite of the brightness of the sun after the rain. She was stiff and sore with lying in the dampness. Her hair was wet, her blanket was wet, and she woke without feeling rested. Almost the trip seemed more than she could bear. If she could have wished herself back that morning and have stayed at Tanners' all summer she certainly would have done it rather than to be where and how she was.

The Indians seemed excited — the man grim and forbidding, the woman appealing, frightened, anxious. They were near to Keams Cañon. "Aneshodi" would be somewhere about. The Indian hoped to be rid of his burden then and travel on his interrupted journey. He was growing impatient. He felt he had earned his money.

But when they tried to go down Keams Cañon they found the road all washed away by flood, and must needs go a long way around. This made the Indian surly. His countenance was more forbidding than ever. Margaret, as she watched him with sinking heart, altered her ideas of the Indian as a whole to suit the situation. She had always felt pity for the poor Indians, whose land had been seized and whose kindred had been slaughtered. But this Indian was not an object of pity. He was the most disagreeable, cruel-looking Indian Margaret had ever laid eyes on. She had felt it innately the first time she saw him, but now, as the situation began to bring him out, she knew that she was dreadfully afraid of him. She had a feeling that he might scalp her if he got tired of her. She began to alter her opinion of Hazel Brownleigh's judgment as regarded Indians. She did not feel that she would ever send this Indian to any one for a guide and say he was perfectly trustworthy. He hadn't done anything very dreadful yet, but she felt he was going to.

He had a number of angry confabs with his wife that morning. At least, he did the confabbing and the squaw protested. Margaret gathered after a while that it was something about herself. The furtive, frightened glances that the squaw cast in her direction sometimes, when the man was not looking, made her think so. She tried to say it was all imagination, and that her nerves were getting the upper hand of her, but in spite of her she shuddered sometimes, just as she had done when Rosa looked at her. She decided that she must be going to have a fit of sickness, and that just as soon as she got in the neighborhood of Mrs. Tanner's again she would pack her trunk and go home to her mother. If she was going to be sick she wanted her mother.

About noon things came to a climax. They halted on the top of the mesa, and the Indians had another altercation, which ended in the man descending the trail a fearfully steep way, down four hundred feet to the trading-post in the cañon. Margaret looked down and gasped and thanked a kind Providence that had not made it necessary for her to make that descent; but the squaw stood at the top with her baby and looked down in silent sorrow—agony perhaps would be a better name. Her face was terrible to look upon.

Margaret could not understand it, and she went to the woman and put her hand out sympathetically, asking, gently:

"What is the matter, you poor little thing? Oh, what is it?"

Perhaps the woman understood the tenderness in the tone, for she suddenly turned and rested her forehead against Margaret's shoulder, giving one great, gasping sob, then lifted her dry, miserable eyes to the girl's face as if to thank her for her kindness.

Margaret's heart was touched. She threw her arms around the poor woman and drew her, papoose and all, comfortingly toward her, patting her shoulder and saying gentle, soothing words as she would to a little child. And by and by the woman lifted her head again, the tears coursing down her face, and tried to explain, muttering her queer gutturals and making eloquent gestures until Margaret felt she understood. She gathered that the man had gone down to the trading-post to find the "Aneshodi," and that the squaw feared that he would somehow procure firewater either from the trader or from some Indian he might meet, and would come back angrier than he had gone, and without his money.

If Margaret also suspected that the Indian had desired to get rid of her by leaving her at that desolate little trading-station down in the cañon until such time as her friends should call for her, she resolutely put the thought out of her mind and set herself to cheer the poor Indian woman.

She took a bright, soft, rosy silk tie from her own neck and knotted it about the astonished woman's dusky throat, and then she put a silver dollar in her hand, and was thrilled with wonder to see what a change came over the poor, dark face. It reminded her of Mom Wallis when she got on her new bonnet, and once again she felt the thrill of knowing the whole world kin.

The squaw cheered up after a little, got sticks and made a fire, and together they had quite a pleasant meal. Margaret exerted herself to make the poor woman laugh, and finally succeeded by dangling a bright-red knight from her chessmen in front of the delighted baby's eyes till he gurgled out a real baby crow of joy.

It was the middle of the afternoon before the Indian returned, sitting crazily his struggling beast as he climbed the trail once more. Margaret, watching, caught her breath and prayed. Was this the trustworthy man, this drunken, reeling creature, clubbing his horse and pouring forth a torrent of indistinguishable gutturals? It was evident that his wife's worst fears were verified. He had found the firewater.

The frightened squaw set to work putting things together as fast as she could. She well knew what to expect, and when the man reached the top of the mesa he found his party packed and mounted, waiting fearsomely to take the trail.

Silently, timorously, they rode behind him, west across the great wide plain.

In the distance gradually there appeared dim mesas like great fingers stretching out against the sky; miles away they seemed, and nothing intervening but a stretch of varying color where sage-brush melted into sand, and sage-brush and greasewood grew again, with tall cactus startling here and there like bayonets at rest but bristling with menace.

The Indian had grown silent and sullen. His eyes were like deep fires of burning volcanoes. One shrank from looking at them. His massive, cruel profile stood out like bronze against the evening sky. It was growing night again, and still they had not come to anywhere or anything, and still her friends seemed just as far away.

Since they had left the top of Keams Cañon Margaret had been sure all was not right. Aside from the fact that the guide was drunk at present, she was convinced that there had been something wrong with him all along. He did not act like the Indians around Ashland. He did not act like a trusted guide that her friends would send for her. She wished once more that she had kept Hazel Brownleigh's letter. She wondered how her friends would find her if they came after her. It was then she began in earnest to systematically plan to leave a trail behind her all the rest of the way. If she had only done it thoroughly when she first began to be uneasy. But now she was so far away, so many miles from anywhere! Oh, if she had not come at all!

And first she dropped her handkerchief, because she happened to have it in her hand—a dainty thing with lace on the edge and her name written in tiny script by her mother's careful hand on the narrow hem. And then after a little, as soon as she could scrawl it without being noticed, she wrote a note which she twisted around the neck of a red chessman, and left behind her. After that scraps of paper, as she could reach them out of the bag tied on behind her saddle; then a stocking, a bedroom slipper, more chessmen, and so, when they halted at dusk and prepared to strike camp, she had quite a good little trail blazed behind her over that wide, empty plain. She shuddered as she looked into the gathering darkness ahead, where those long, dark lines of mesas looked like barriers in the way. Then, suddenly, the Indian pointed ahead to the first mesa and uttered one word—"Walpi!" So that was the Indian village to which she was bound? What was before her on the morrow? After eating a pretense of supper she lay down. The Indian had more firewater with him. He drank, he uttered cruel gutturals at his squaw, and even kicked the feet of the sleeping papoose as he passed by till it awoke and cried sharply, which made him more angry, so he struck the squaw.

It seemed hours before all was quiet. Margaret's nerves were strained to such a pitch she scarcely dared to breathe, but at last, when the fire had almost died down, the man lay quiet, and she could relax and close her eyes.

Not to sleep. She must not go to sleep. The fire was almost gone and the coyotes would be around. She must wake and watch!

That was the last thought she remembered—that and a prayer that the angels would keep watch once again.

When she awoke it was broad daylight and far into the morning, for the sun was high overhead and the mesas in the distance were clear and distinct against the sky.

She sat up and looked about her, bewildered, not knowing at first where she was. It was so still and wide and lonely.

She turned to find the Indians, but there was no trace of them anywhere. The fire lay smoldering in its place, a thin trickle of smoke curling away from a dying stick, but that was all. A tin cup half full of coffee was beside the stick, and a piece of blackened corn bread. She turned frightened eyes to east, to west, to north, to south, but there was no one in sight, and out over the distant mesa there poised a great eagle alone in the vast sky keeping watch over the brilliant, silent waste.

30

WHEN Margaret was a very little girl her father and mother had left her alone for an hour with a stranger while they went out to make a call in a strange city through which they were passing on a summer trip. The stranger was kind, and gave to the child a large green box of bits of old black lace and purple ribbons to play with, but she turned sorrowfully from the somber array of finery, which was the only thing in the way of a plaything the woman had at hand, and stood looking drearily out of the window on the strange, new town, a feeling of utter loneliness upon her. Her little heart was almost choked with the awfulness of the thought that she was a human atom drifted apart from every other atom she had ever known, that she had a personality and a responsibility of her own, and that she must face this thought of herself and her aloneness for evermore. It was the child's first realization that she was a separate being apart from her father and mother, and she was almost consumed with the terror of it.

As she rose now from her bed on the ground and looked out across that vast waste, in which the only other living creature was that sinister, watching eagle, the same feeling returned to her and made her tremble like the little child who had turned from her box of ancient finery to realize her own little self and its terrible aloneness.

For an instant even her realization of God, which had from early childhood been present with her, seemed to have departed. She could not grasp anything save the vast empty silence that loomed about her so awfully. She was alone, and about as far from anywhere or anything as she could possibly be in the State of Arizona. Would she ever get back to human habitations? Would her friends ever be able to find her?

Then her heart flew back to its habitual refuge, and she spoke aloud and said, "God is here!" and the thought seemed to comfort her. She looked about once more on the bright waste, and now it did not seem so dreary.

"God is here!" she repeated, and tried to realize that this was a part of His habitation. She could not be lost where God was. He knew the way out. She had only to trust. So she dropped upon her knees in the sand and prayed for trust and courage.

When she rose again she walked steadily to a height a little above the camp-fire, and, shading her eyes, looked carefully in every direction. No, there was not a sign of her recent companions. They must have stolen away in the night quite soon after she fell asleep, and have gone fast and far, so that they were now beyond the reach of her eyes, and not anywhere was there sign of living thing, save that eagle still sweeping in great curves and poising again above the distant mesa.

Where was her horse? Had the Indians taken that, too? She searched the valley, but saw no horse at first. With sinking heart she went back to where her things were and sat down by the dying fire to think, putting a few loose twigs and sticks together to keep the embers bright while she could. She reflected that she had no matches, and this was probably the last fire she would have until somebody came to her rescue or she got somewhere by herself. What was she to do? Stay right where she was or start out on foot? And should she go backward or forward? Surely, surely the Brownleighs would miss her pretty soon and send out a search-party for her. How could it be that they trusted an Indian who had done such a cruel thing as to leave a woman unprotected in the desert? And yet, perhaps, they did not know his temptation to drink. Perhaps they had thought he could not get any firewater. Perhaps he would return when he came to himself and realized what he had done.

And now she noticed what she had not seen at first — a small bottle of water on a stone beside the blackened bread. Realizing that she was very hungry and that this was the only food at hand, she sat down beside the fire to eat the dry bread and drink the miserable coffee. She must have strength to do whatever was before her. She tried not to think how her mother would feel if she never came back, how anxious they would be as they waited day by day for her letters that did not come. She reflected with a sinking heart that she had, just before leaving, written a hasty note to her mother telling her not to expect anything for several days, perhaps even as much as two weeks, as she was going out of civilization for a little while. How had she unwittingly sealed her fate by that! For now not even by way of her alarmed home could help come to her.

She put the last bit of hard corn bread in her pocket for a further time of need, and began to look about her again. Then she spied with delight a moving object far below her in the valley, and decided it was a horse, perhaps her own. He was a mile away, at least, but he was there, and she cried out with sudden joy and relief.

She went over to her blanket and bags, which had been beside her during the night, and stood a moment trying to think what to do. Should she carry the things to the horse or risk leaving them here while she went after the horse and brought him to the things? No, that would not be safe. Some one might come along and take them, or she might not be able to find her way back again in this strange, wild waste. Besides, she might not get the horse, after all, and would lose everything. She must carry her things to the horse. She stooped to gather them up, and something bright beside her bag attracted her. It was the sun shining on the silver dollar she had given to the Indian woman. A sudden rush of tears came to her eyes. The poor creature had tried to make all the reparation she could for thus hastily leaving the white woman in the desert. She had given back the money—all she had that was valuable! Beside the dollar rippled a little chain of beads curiously wrought, an inanimate appeal for forgiveness and a grateful return for the kindness shown her. Margaret smiled as she stooped again to pick up her things. There had been a heart, after all, behind that stolid countenance, and some sense of righteousness and justice. Margaret decided that Indians were not all treacherous. Poor woman! What a life was hers—to follow her grim lord whither he would lead, even as her white sister must sometimes, sorrowing, rebelling, crying out, but following! She wondered if into the heart of this dark sister there ever crept any of the rebellion which led some of her white sisters to cry aloud for "rights" and "emancipation."

But it was all a passing thought to be remembered and turned over at a more propitious time. Margaret's whole thoughts now were bent on her present predicament.

The packing was short work. She stuffed everything into the two bags that were usually hung across the horse, and settled them carefully across her shoulders. Then she rolled the blanket, took it in her arms, and started. It was a heavy burden to carry, but she could not make up her mind to part with any of her things until she had at least made an effort to save them. If she should be left alone in the desert for the night the blanket was indispensable, and her clothes would at least do to drop as a trail by which her friends might find her. She must carry them as far as possible. So she started.

It was already high day, and the sun was intolerably hot.

Her heavy burden was not only cumbersome, but very warm, and she felt her strength going from her as she went; but her nerve was up and her courage was strong. Moreover, she prayed as she walked, and she felt now the presence of her Guide and was not afraid. As she walked she faced a number of possibilities in the immediate future which were startling, and to say the least, undesirable. There were wild animals in this land, not so much in the daylight, but what of the night? She had heard that a woman was always safe in that wild Western land; but what of the prowling Indians? What of a possible exception to the Western rule of chivalry toward a decent woman? One small piece of corn bread and less than a pint of water were small provision on which to withstand a siege. How far was it to anywhere?

It was then she remembered for the first time that one word — "Walpi!" uttered by the Indian as he came to a halt the night before and pointed far to the mesa — "Walpi." She lifted her eyes now and scanned the dark mesa. It loomed like a great battlement of rock against the sky. Could it be possible there were people dwelling there? She had heard, of course, about the curious Hopi villages, each village a gigantic house of many rooms, called pueblos, built upon the lofty crags, sometimes five or six hundred feet above the desert.

Could it be that that great castle-looking outline against the sky before her, standing out on the end of the mesa like a promontory above the sea, was Walpi? And if it was, how was she to get up there? The rock rose sheer and steep from the desert floor. The narrow neck of land behind it looked like a slender thread. Her heart sank at thought of trying to storm and enter, single-handed, such an impregnable fortress. And yet, if her friends were there, perhaps they would see her when she drew near and come to show her the way. Strange that they should have gone on and left her with those treacherous Indians! Strange that they should have trusted them so, in the first place! Her own instincts had been against trusting the man from the beginning. It must be confessed that during her reflections at this point her opinion of the wisdom and judgment of the Brownleighs was lowered several notches. Then she began to berate herself for having so easily been satisfied about her escort. She should have read the letter more carefully. She should have asked the Indians more questions. She should, perhaps, have asked Jasper Kemp's advice, or got him to talk to the Indian. She wished with all her heart for Bud, now. If Bud were along he would be saying some comical boy-thing, and be finding a way out of the difficulty. Dear, faithful Bud!

The sun rose higher and the morning grew hotter. As she descended to the valley her burdens grew intolerable, and several times she almost cast them aside. Once she lost sight of her pony among the sage-brush, and it was two hours before she came to him and was able to capture him and strap on her burdens. She was almost too exhausted to climb into the saddle when all was ready; but she managed to mount at last and started out toward the rugged crag ahead of her.

The pony had a long, hot climb out of the valley to a hill where she could see very far again, but still that vast emptiness reigned. Even the eagle had disappeared, and she fancied he must be resting like a great emblem of freedom on one of the points of the castle-like battlement against the sky. It seemed as if the end of the world had come, and she was the only one left in the universe, forgotten, riding on her weary horse across an endless desert in search of a home she would never see again.

Below the hill there stretched a wide, white strip of sand, perhaps two miles in extent, but shimmering in the sun and seeming to recede ahead of her as she advanced. Beyond was soft greenness — something growing — not near enough to be discerned as cornfields. The girl drooped her tired head upon her horse's mane and wept, her courage going from her with her tears. In all that wide universe there seemed no way to go, and she was so very tired, hungry, hot, and discouraged! There was always that bit of bread in her pocket and that muddy-looking, warm water for a last resort; but she must save them as long as possible, for there was no telling how long it would be before she had more.

There was no trail now to follow. She had started from the spot where she had found the horse, and her inexperienced eyes could not have searched out a trail if she had tried. She was going toward that distant castle on the crag as to a goal, but when she reached it, if she ever did, would she find anything there but crags and lonesomeness and the eagle?

Drying her tears at last, she started the horse on down the hill, and perhaps her tears blinded her, or because she was dizzy with hunger and the long stretch of anxiety and fatigue she was not looking closely. There was a steep place, a sharp falling away of the ground unexpectedly as they emerged from a thicket of sage-brush, and the horse plunged several feet down, striking sharply on some loose rocks, and slipping to his knees; snorting, scrambling, making brave effort, but slipping, half rolling, at last he was brought down with his frightened rider, and lay upon his side with her foot under him and a sensation like a red-hot knife running through her ankle.

Margaret caught her breath in quick gasps as they fell, lifting a prayer in her heart for help. Then came the crash and the sharp pain, and with a quick conviction that all was over she dropped back unconscious on the sand, a blessed oblivion of darkness rushing over her.

When she came to herself once more the hot sun was pouring down upon her unprotected face, and she was conscious of intense pain and suffering in every part of her body. She opened her eyes wildly and looked around. There was sage-brush up above, waving over the crag down which they had fallen, its gray-greenness shimmering hotly in the sun; the sky was mercilessly blue without a cloud. The great beast, heavy and quivering, lay solidly against her, half pinning her to earth, and the helplessness of her position was

like an awful nightmare from which she felt she might waken
if she could only cry out. But when at last she raised her voice
its empty echo frightened her, and there, above her, with
wide-spread wings, circling for an instant, then poised in
motionless survey of her, with cruel eyes upon her, loomed
that eagle — so large, so fearful, so suggestive in its curious
stare, the monarch of the desert come to see who had invaded
his precincts and fallen into one of his snares.

With sudden frenzy burning in her veins Margaret struggled and tried to get free, but she could only move the slightest bit each time, and every motion was an agony to the hurt
ankle.

It seemed hours before she writhed herself free from that
great, motionless horse, whose labored breath only showed
that he was still alive. Something terrible must have happened
to the horse or he would have tried to rise, for she had coaxed,
patted, cajoled, tried in every way to rouse him. When at last
she crawled free from the hot, horrible body and crept with
pained progress around in front of him, she saw that both
his forelegs lay limp and helpless. He must have broken them
in falling. Poor fellow! He, too, was suffering and she had
nothing to give him! There was nothing she could do for
him!

Then she thought of the bottle of water, but, searching
for it, found that her good intention of dividing it with him
was useless, for the bottle was broken and the water already
soaked into the sand. Only a damp spot on the saddle-bag
showed where it had departed.

Then indeed did Margaret sink down in the sand in despair
and begin to pray as she had never prayed before.

31

THE morning after Margaret's departure Rosa awoke with no feelings of self-reproach, but rather a great exultation at the way in which she had been able to get rid of her rival.

She lay for a few minutes thinking of Forsythe, and trying to decide what she would wear when she went forth to meet him, for she wanted to charm him as she had never charmed any one before.

She spent some time arraying herself in different costumes, but at last decided on her Commencement gown of fine white organdie, hand-embroidered and frilled with filmy lace, the product of a famous house of gowns in the Eastern city where she had attended school for a while and acquired expensive tastes.

Daintily slippered, beribboned with coral-silk girdle, and with a rose from the vine over her window in her hair, she sallied forth at last to the trysting-place.

Forsythe was a whole hour late, as became a languid gentleman who had traveled the day before and idled at his sister's house over a late breakfast until nearly noon. Already his fluttering fancy was apathetic about Rosa, and he wondered, as he rode along, what had become of the interesting young teacher who had charmed him for more than a passing moment. Would he dare to call upon her, now that Gardley was out of the way? Was she still in Ashland or had she gone home for vacation? He must ask Rosa about her.

Then he came in sight of Rosa sitting picturesquely in the shade of an old cedar, reading poetry, a little lady in the wilderness, and he forgot everything else in his delight over the change in her. For Rosa had changed. There was no mistake about it. She had bloomed out into maturity in those few short months of his absence. Her soft figure had rounded and developed, her bewitching curls were put up on her head, with only a stray tendril here and there to emphasize a dainty ear or call attention to a smooth, round neck; and when she raised her lovely head and lifted limpid eyes to his there was about her a demureness, a coolness and charm that he had fancied only ladies of the city could attain. Oh, Rosa knew her charms, and had practised many a day before her mirror till she had appraised the value of every curving eyelash, every hidden dimple, every cupid's curve of lip. Rosa had watched well and learned from all with whom she had come in contact. No woman's guile was left untried by her.

And Rosa was very sweet and charming. She knew just when to lift up innocent eyes of wonder; when to not understand suggestions; when to exclaim softly with delight or shrink with shyness that nevertheless did not repulse.

Forsythe studied her with wonder and delight. No maiden of the city had ever charmed him more, and withal she seemed so innocent and young, so altogether pliable in his hands. His pulses beat high, his heart was inflamed, and passion came and sat within his handsome eyes.

It was easy to persuade her, after her first seemingly shy reserve was overcome, and before an hour was passed she had promised to go away with him. He had very little money, but what of that? When he spoke of that feature Rosa declared she could easily get some. Her father gave her free access to his safe, and kept her plentifully supplied for the household use. It was nothing to her—a passing incident. What should it matter whose money took them on their way?

When she went demurely back to the ranch a little before sunset she thought she was very happy, poor little silly sinner! She met her father with her most alluring but most furtive smile. She was charming at supper, and blushed as her mother used to do when he praised her new gown and told her how well she looked in it. But she professed to be weary yet from the last days of school—to have a headache—and so she went early to her room and asked that the servants keep the house quiet in the morning, that she might sleep late and get really rested. Her father kissed her tenderly and thought what a dear child she was and what a comfort to his ripening years; and the house settled down into quiet.

Rosa packed a bag with some of her most elaborate garments, arrayed herself in a charming little outfit of silk for the journey, dropped her baggage out of the window; and when the moon rose and the household were quietly sleeping she paid a visit to her father's safe, and then stole forth, taking her shadowy way to the trail by a winding route known well to herself and secure from the watch of vigilant servants who were ever on the lookout for cattle thieves.

Thus she left her father's house and went forth to put her trust in a man whose promises were as ropes of sand and whose fancy was like a wave of the sea, tossed to and fro by every breath that blew. Long ere the sun rose the next morning the guarded, beloved child was as far from her safe home and her father's sheltering love as if alone she had started for the mouth of the bottomless pit. Two days later, while Margaret lay unconscious beneath the sage-brush, with a hovering eagle for watch, Rosa in the streets of a great city suddenly realized that she was more alone in the universe than ever she could have been in a wide desert, and her plight was far worse than the girl's with whose fate she had so lightly played.

Quite early on the morning after Rosa left, while the household was still keeping quiet for the supposed sleeper, Gardley rode into the inclosure about the house and asked for Rogers.

Gardley had been traveling night and day to get back. Matters had suddenly arranged themselves so that he could finish up his business at his old home and go on to see Margaret's father and mother, and he had made his visit there and hurried back to Arizona, hoping to reach Ashland in time for Commencement. A delay on account of a washout on the road had brought him back two days late for Commencement. He had ridden to camp from a junction forty miles away to get there the sooner, and this morning had ridden straight to the Tanners' to surprise Margaret. It was, therefore, a deep disappointment to find her gone and only Mrs. Tanner's voluble explanations for comfort. Mrs. Tanner exhausted her vocabulary in trying to describe the "Injuns," her own feeling of protest against them, and Mrs. Brownleigh's foolishness in making so much of them; and then she bustled in to the old pine desk in the dining-room and produced the letter that had started Margaret off as soon as Commencement was over.

Gardley took the letter eagerly, as though it were something to connect him with Margaret, and read it through carefully to make sure just how matters stood. He had looked troubled when Mrs. Tanner told how tired Margaret was, and how worried she seemed about her school and glad to get away from it all; and he agreed that the trip was probably a good thing.

"I wish Bud could have gone along, though," he said, thoughtfully, as he turned away from the door. "I don't like her to go with just Indians, though I suppose it is all right. You say he had his wife and child along? Of course Mrs.

Brownleigh wouldn't send anybody that wasn't perfectly all right. Well, I suppose the trip will be a rest for her. I'm sorry I didn't get home a few days sooner. I might have looked out for her myself."

He rode away from the Tanners', promising to return later with a gift he had brought for Bud that he wanted to present himself, and Mrs. Tanner bustled back to her work again.

"Well, I'm glad he's got home, anyway," she remarked, aloud, to herself as she hung her dish-cloth tidily over the upturned dish-pan and took up her broom. "I 'ain't felt noways easy 'bout her sence she left, though I do suppose there ain't any sense to it. But I'm *glad he's back!*"

Meantime Gardley was riding toward Rogers's ranch, meditating whether he should venture to follow the expedition and enjoy at least the return trip with Margaret, or whether he ought to remain patiently until she came back and go to work at once. There was nothing really important demanding his attention immediately, for Rogers had arranged to keep the present overseer of affairs until he was ready to undertake the work. He was on his way now to report on a small business matter which he had been attending to in New York for Rogers. When that was over he would be free to do as he pleased for a few days more if he liked, and the temptation was great to go at once to Margaret.

As he stood waiting beside his horse in front of the house while the servant went to call Rogers, he looked about with delight on the beauty of the day. How glad he was to be back in Arizona again! Was it the charm of the place or because Margaret was there, he wondered, that he felt so happy? By all means he must follow her. Why should he not?

He looked at the clambering rose-vine that covered one end of the house, and noticed how it crept close to the window casement and caressed the white curtain as it blew. Margaret must have such a vine at her window in the house he would build for her. It might be but a modest house that he could give her now, but it should have a rose-vine just like that; and he would train it round her window where she could smell the fragrance from it every morning when she awoke, and where it would breathe upon her as she slept.

Margaret! How impatient he was to see her again! To look upon her dear face and know that she was his! That her father and mother had been satisfied about him and sent their blessing, and he might tell her so. It was wonderful! His heart thrilled with the thought of it. Of course he would go to her at once. He would start as soon as Rogers was through with him. He would go to Ganado. No, Keams. Which was it? He drew the letter out of his pocket and read it again, then replaced it.

The fluttering curtain up at the window blew out and in, and when it blew out again it brought with it a flurry of papers like white leaves. The curtain had knocked over a paper-weight or vase or something that held them and set the papers free. The breeze caught them and flung them about erratically, tossing one almost at his feet. He stooped to pick it up, thinking it might be of value to some one, and caught the name "Margaret" and "Dear Margaret" written several times on the sheet, with "Walpi, Walpi, Walpi," filling the lower half of the page, as if some one had been practising it.

And because these words were just now keenly in his mind he reached for the second paper just a foot or two away and found more sentences and words. A third paper contained an exact reproduction of the letter which Mrs. Tanner had given him purporting to come from Mrs. Brownleigh to Margaret. What could it possibly mean?

In great astonishment he pulled out the other letter and compared them. They were almost identical save for a word here and there crossed out and rewritten. He stood looking mutely at the papers and then up at the window, as though an explanation might somehow be wafted down to him, not knowing what to think, his mind filled with vague alarm.

Just at that moment the servant appeared.

"Mr. Rogers says would you mind coming down to the corral. Miss Rosa has a headache, and we're keeping the house still for her to sleep. That's her window up there — " And he indicated the rose-bowered window with the fluttering curtain.

Dazed and half suspicious of something, Gardley folded the two letters together and crushed them into his pocket, wondering what he ought to do about it. The thought of it troubled him so that he only half gave attention to the business in hand; but he gave his report and handed over certain documents. He was thinking that perhaps he ought to see Miss Rosa and find out what she knew of Margaret's going and ask how she came in possession of this other letter.

"Now," said Rogers, as the matter was concluded, "I owe you some money. If you'll just step up to the house with me I'll give it to you. I'd like to settle matters up at once."

"Oh, let it go till I come again," said Gardley, impatient to be off. He wanted to get by himself and think out a solution of the two letters. He was more than uneasy about Margaret without being able to give any suitable explanation of why he should be. His main desire now was to ride to Ganado and find out if the missionaries had left home, which way they had gone, and whether they had met Margaret as planned.

"No, step right up to the house with me," insisted Rogers. "It won't take long, and I have the money in my safe."

Gardley saw that the quickest way was to please Rogers, and he did not wish to arouse any questions, because he supposed, of course, his alarm was mere foolishness. So they went together into Rogers's private office, where his desk and safe were the principal furniture, and where no servants ventured to come without orders.

Rogers shoved a chair for Gardley and went over to his

safe, turning the little nickel knob this way and that with the skill of one long accustomed, and in a moment the thick door swung open and Rogers drew out a japanned cash-box and unlocked it. But when he threw the cover back he uttered an exclamation of angry surprise. The box was empty!

32

MR. Rogers strode to the door, forgetful of his sleeping daughter overhead, and thundered out his call for James. The servant appeared at once, but he knew nothing about the safe, and had not been in the office that morning. Other servants were summoned and put through a rigid examination. Then Rogers turned to the woman who had answered the door for Gardley and sent her up to call Rosa.

But the woman returned presently with word that Miss Rosa was not in her room, and there was no sign that her bed had been slept in during the night. The woman's face was sullen. She did not like Rosa, but was afraid of her. This to her was only another of Miss Rosa's pranks, and very likely her doting father would manage to blame the servants with the affair.

Mr. Rogers's face grew stern. His eyes flashed angrily as he turned and strode up the stairs to his daughter's room, but when he came down again he was holding a note in his trembling hand and his face was ashen white.

"Read that, Gardley," he said, thrusting the note into Gardley's hands and motioning at the same time for the servants to go away.

Gardley took the note, yet even as he read he noticed that the paper was the same as those he carried in his pocket. There was a peculiar watermark that made it noticeable.

The note was a flippant little affair from Rosa, telling her father she had gone away to be married and that she would let him know where she was as soon as they were located. She added that he had forced her to this step by being so severe with her and not allowing her lover to come to see her. If he had been reasonable she would have stayed at home and let him give her a grand wedding; but as it was she had only this way of seeking her happiness. She added that she knew he would forgive her, and she hoped he would come to see that her way had been best, and Forsythe was all that he could desire as a son-in-law.

Gardley uttered an exclamation of dismay as he read, and, looking up, found the miserable eyes of the stricken father upon him. For the moment his own alarm concerning Margaret and his perplexity about the letters was forgotten in the grief of the man who had been his friend.

"When did she go?" asked Gardley, quickly looking up.

"She took supper with me and then went to her room, complaining of a headache," said the father, his voice showing his utter hopelessness. "She may have gone early in the evening, perhaps, for we all turned in about nine o'clock to keep the house quiet on her account."

"Have you any idea which way they went, east or west?" Gardley was the keen adviser in a crisis now, his every sense on the alert.

The old man shook his head. "It is too late now," he said, still in that colorless voice. "They will have reached the railroad somewhere. They will have been married by this time. See, it is after ten o'clock!"

"Yes, if he marries her," said Gardley, fiercely. He had no faith in Forsythe.

"You think—you don't think he would *dare!*" The old man straightened up and fairly blazed in his righteous wrath.

"I think he would dare anything if he thought he would not be caught. He is a coward, of course."

"What can we do?"

"Telegraph to detectives at all points where they would be likely to arrive and have them shadowed. Come, we will ride to the station at once; but, first, could I go up in her room and look around? There might be some clue."

"Certainly," said Rogers, pointing hopelessly up the stairs; "the first door to the left. But you'll find nothing. I looked everywhere. She wouldn't have left a clue. While you're up there I'll interview the servants. Then we'll go."

As he went up-stairs Gardley was wondering whether he ought to tell Rogers of the circumstance of the two letters. What possible connection could there be between Margaret Earle's trip to Walpi with the Brownleighs and Rosa Rogers's elopement? When you come to think of it, what possible explanation was there for a copy of Mrs. Brownleigh's letter to blow out of Rosa Rogers's bedroom window? How could it have got there?

Rosa's room was in beautiful order, the roses nodding in at the window, the curtain blowing back and forth in the breeze and rippling open the leaves of a tiny Testament lying on her desk, as if it had been recently read. There was nothing to show that the owner of the room had taken a hasty flight. On the desk lay several sheets of note-paper with the peculiar water-mark. These caught his attention, and he took them up and compared them with the papers in his pocket. It was a strange thing that that letter which had sent Margaret off into the wilderness with an unknown Indian should be written on the same kind of paper as this; and yet, perhaps, it was not so strange, after all. It probably was the only note-paper to be had in that region, and must all have been purchased at the same place.

The rippling leaves of the Testament fluttered open at the fly-leaf and revealed Rosa's name and a date with Mrs. Brownleigh's name written below, and Gardley took it up, startled again to find Hazel Brownleigh mixed up with the Rogers. He had not known that they had anything to do with each other. And yet, of course, they would, being the missionaries of the region.

The almost empty waste-basket next caught his eye, and here again were several sheets of paper written over with words and phrases, words which at once he recognized as part of the letter Mrs. Tanner had given him. He emptied the waste-basket out on the desk, thinking perhaps there might be something there that would give a clue to where the elopers had gone; but there was not much else in it except a little yellowed note with the signature "Hazel Brownleigh" at the bottom. He glanced through the brief note, gathered its purport, and then spread it out deliberately on the desk and compared the writing with the others, a wild fear clutching at his heart. Yet he could not in any way explain why he was so uneasy. What possible reason could Rosa Rogers have for forging a letter to Margaret from Hazel Brownleigh?

Suddenly Rogers stood behind him looking over his shoulder. "What is it, Gardley? What have you found? Any clue?"

"No clue," said Gardley, uneasily, "but something strange I cannot understand. I don't suppose it can possibly have anything to do with your daughter, and yet it seems almost uncanny. This morning I stopped at the Tanners' to let Miss Earle know I had returned, and was told she had gone yesterday with a couple of Indians as guide to meet the Brownleighs at Keams or somewhere near there, and take a trip with them to Walpi to see the Hopi Indians. Mrs. Tanner gave me this letter from Mrs. Brownleigh, which Miss Earle had left behind. But when I reached here and was waiting for you some papers blew out of your daughter's window. When I picked them up I was startled to find that one of them was an exact copy of the letter I had in my pocket. See! Here they are! I don't suppose there is anything to it, but in spite of me

I am a trifle uneasy about Miss Earle. I just can't understand how that copy of the letter came to be here."

Rogers was leaning over, looking at the papers. "What's this?" he asked, picking up the note that came with the Testament. He read each paper carefully, took in the little Testament with its fluttering fly-leaf and inscription, studied the pages of words and alphabet, then suddenly turned away and groaned, hiding his face in his hands.

"What is it?" asked Gardley, awed with the awful sorrow in the strong man's attitude.

"My poor baby!" groaned the father. "My poor little baby girl! I've always been afraid of that fatal gift of hers. Gardley, she could copy any handwriting in the world perfectly. She could write my name so it could not be told from my own signature. She's evidently written that letter. Why, I don't know, unless she wanted to get Miss Earle out of the way so it would be easier for her to carry out her plans."

"It can't be!" said Gardley, shaking his head. "I can't see what her object would be. Besides, where would she find the Indians? Mrs. Tanner saw the Indians. They came to the school after her with the letter, and waited for her. Mrs. Tanner saw them ride off together."

"There were a couple of strange Indians here yesterday, begging something to eat," said Rogers, settling down on a chair and resting his head against the desk as if he had suddenly lost the strength to stand.

"This won't do!" said Gardley. "We've got to get down to the telegraph-office, you and I. Now try to brace up. Are the horses ready? Then we'll go right away."

"You better question the servants about those Indians first," said Rogers; and Gardley, as he hurried down the stairs, heard groan after groan from Rosa's room, where her father lingered in agony.

Gardley got all the information he could about the Indians, and then the two men started away on a gallop to the station. As they passed the Tanner house Gardley drew rein to call to Bud, who hurried out joyfully to greet his friend, his face lighting with pleasure.

"Bill, get on your horse in double-quick time and beat it out to camp for me, will you?" said Gardley, as he reached down and gripped Bud's rough young paw. "Tell Jasper Kemp to come back with you and meet me at the station as quick as he can. Tell him to have the men where he can signal them. We may have to hustle out on a long hunt; and, Bill, keep your head steady and get back yourself right away. Perhaps I'll want you to help me. I'm a little anxious about Miss Earle, but you needn't tell anybody that but old Jasper. Tell him to hurry for all he's worth."

Bud, with his eyes large with loyalty and trouble, nodded understandingly, returned the grip of the young man's hand with a clumsy squeeze, and sprang away to get his horse and do Gardley's bidding. Gardley knew he would ride as for his life, now that he knew Margaret's safety was at stake.

Then Gardley rode on to the station and was indefatigable for two hours hunting out addresses, writing telegrams, and calling up long-distance telephones.

When all had been done that was possible Rogers turned a haggard face to the young man. "I've been thinking, Gardley, that rash little girl of mine may have got Miss Earle into some kind of a dangerous position. You ought to look after her. What can we do?"

"I'm going to, sir," said Gardley, "just as soon as I've done everything I can for you. I've already sent for Jasper Kemp, and we'll make a plan between us and find out if Miss Earle is all right. Can you spare Jasper or will you need him?"

"By all means! Take all the men you need. I sha'n't rest easy till I know Miss Earle is safe."

He sank down on a truck that stood on the station platform, his shoulders slumping, his whole attitude as of one who was fatally stricken. It came over Gardley how suddenly old he looked, and haggard and gray! What a thing for the selfish child to have done to her father! Poor, silly child, whose fate with Forsythe would in all probability be anything but enviable!

But there was no time for sorrowful reflections. Jasper Kemp, stern, alert, anxious, came riding furiously down the street, Bud keeping even pace with him.

33

WHILE Gardley briefly told his tale to Jasper Kemp, and the Scotchman was hastily scanning the papers with his keen, bright eyes, Bud stood frowning and listening intently.

"Gee!" he burst forth. "That girl's a mess! 'Course she did it! You oughta seen what all she didn't do the last six weeks of school. Miss Mar'get got so she shivered every time that girl came near her or looked at her. She sure had her goat! Some nights after school, when she thought she's all alone, she just cried, she did. Why, Rosa had every one of those guys in the back seat acting like the devil, and nobody knew what was the matter. She wrote things on the blackboard right in the questions, so's it looked like Miss Mar'get's writing; fierce things, sometimes; and Miss Mar'get didn't know who did it. And she was jealous as a cat of Miss Mar'get. You all know what a case she had on that guy from over by the fort; and she didn't like to have him even look at Miss Mar'get. Well, she didn't forget how he went away that night of the play. I caught her looking at her like she would like to murder her. *Good night!* Some look! The guy had a case on Miss Mar'get, all right, too, only she was onto him and wouldn't look at him nor let him spoon nor nothing. But Rosa saw it all, and she just hated Miss Mar'get. Then once Miss Mar'get stopped her from going out to meet that guy, too. Oh, she hated her, all right! And you can bet she wrote the letter! Sure she did! She wanted to get her away when that guy came back. He was back yesterday. I saw him over by the run on that trail that crosses the trail to the old cabin. He didn't see me. I got my eye on him first, and I chucked behind some sage-brush, but he was here, all right, and he didn't mean any good. I follahed him awhile till he stopped and fixed up a place to camp. I guess he must 'a' stayed out last night — "

A heavy hand was suddenly laid from behind on Bud's shoulder, and Rogers stood over him, his dark eyes on fire, his lips trembling.

"Boy, can you show me where that was?" he asked, and there was an intensity in his voice that showed Bud that something serious was the matter. Boylike he dropped his eyes indifferently before this great emotion.

"Sure!"

"Best take Long Bill with you, Mr. Rogers," advised Jasper Kemp, keenly alive to the whole situation. "I reckon we'll all have to work together. My men ain't far off," and he lifted his whistle to his lips and blew the signal blasts. "The Kid here 'll want to ride to Keams to see if the lady is all safe and has met her friends. I reckon mebbe I better go straight to Ganado and find out if them mission folks really got started, and put 'em wise to what's been going on. They'll mebbe know who them Injuns was. I have my suspicions they weren't any friendlies. I didn't like that Injun the minute I set eyes on him hanging round the school-house, but I wouldn't have stirred a step toward camp if I'd 'a' suspected he was come fur the lady. 'Spose you take Bud and Long Bill and go find that camping-place and see if you find any trail showing which way they took. If you do, you fire three shots, and the men 'll be with you. If you want the Kid, fire four shots. He can't be so fur away by that time that he can't hear. He's got to get provisioned 'fore he starts. Lead him out, Bud. We 'ain't got no time to lose."

Bud gave one despairing look at Gardley and turned to obey.

"That's all right, Bud," said Gardley, with an understanding glance. "You tell Mr. Rogers all you know and show him the place, and then when Long Bill comes you can take the cross-cut to the Long Trail and go with me. I'll just stop at the house as I go by and tell your mother I need you."

Bud gave one radiant, grateful look and sprang upon his horse, and Rogers had hard work to keep up with him at first, till Bud got interested in giving him a detailed account of Forsythe's looks and acts.

In less than an hour the relief expedition had started. Before night had fallen Jasper Kemp, riding hard, arrived at the mission, told his story, procured a fresh horse, and after a couple of hours' rest started with Brownleigh and his wife for Keams Cañon.

Gardley and Bud, riding for all they were worth, said little by the way. Now and then the boy stole glances at the man's face, and the dead weight of sorrow settled like lead, the heavier, upon his heart. Too well he knew the dangers of the desert. He could almost read Gardley's fears in the white, drawn look about his lips, the ashen circles under his eyes, the tense, strained pose of his whole figure. Gardley's mind was urging ahead of his steed, and his body could not relax. He was anxious to go a little faster, yet his judgment knew it would not do, for his horse would play out before he could get another. They ate their corn bread in the saddle, and only turned aside from the trail once to drink at a water-hole and fill their cans. They rode late into the night, with only the stars and their wits to guide them. When they stopped to rest they did not wait to make a fire, but hobbled the horses where they might feed, and, rolling quickly in their blankets, lay down upon the ground.

Bud, with the fatigue of healthy youth, would have slept till morning in spite of his fears, but Gardley woke him in a couple of hours, made him drink some water and eat a bite of food, and they went on their way again. When morning broke they were almost to the entrance of Keams Cañon and both looked haggard and worn. Bud seemed to have aged in the night, and Gardley looked at him almost tenderly.

"Are you all in, kid?" he asked.

"Naw!" answered Bud, promptly, with an assumed cheerfulness. "Feeling like a four-year-old. Get on to that sky? Guess we're going to have some day! Pretty as a red wagon!"

Gardley smiled sadly. What would that day bring forth for the two who went in search of her they loved? His great anxiety was to get to Keams Cañon and inquire. They would surely know at the trading-post whether the missionary and his party had gone that way.

The road was still almost impassable from the flood; the two dauntless riders picked their way slowly down the trail to the post.

But the trader could tell them nothing comforting. The missionary had not been that way in two months, and there had been no party and no lady there that week. A single strange Indian had come down the trail above the day before, stayed awhile, picked a quarrel with some men who were there, and then ridden back up the steep trail again. He might have had a party with him up on the mesa, waiting. He had said something about his squaw. The trader admitted that he might have been drunk, but he frowned as he spoke of him. He called him a "bad Indian." Something unpleasant had evidently happened.

The trader gave them a good, hot dinner, of which they stood sorely in need, and because they realized that they must keep up their strength they took the time to eat it. Then, procuring fresh horses, they climbed the steep trail in the direction the trader said the Indian had taken. It was a slender clue, but it was all they had, and they must follow it. And now the travelers were very silent, as if they felt they were drawing near to some knowledge that would settle the question for them one way or the other. As they reached the top at last, where they could see out across the plain, each drew a long breath like a gasp and looked about, half fearing what he might see.

Yes, there was the sign of a recent camp-fire, and a few tin cans and bits of refuse, nothing more. Gardley got down and searched carefully. Bud even crept about upon his hands and knees, but a single tiny blue bead like a grain of sand was all that rewarded his efforts. Some Indian had doubtless camped here. That was all the evidence. Standing thus in hopeless uncertainty what to do next, they suddenly heard voices. Something familiar once or twice made Gardley lift his whistle and blow a blast. Instantly a silvery answer came ringing from the mesa a mile or so away and woke the echoes in the cañon. Jasper Kemp and his party had taken the longer way around instead of going down the cañon, and were just arriving at the spot where Margaret and the squaw had waited two days before for their drunken guide. But Jasper Kemp's whistle rang out again, and he shot three times into the air, their signal to wait for some important news.

Breathlessly and in silence the two waited till the coming of the rest of the party, and cast themselves down on the ground, feeling the sudden need of support. Now that there was a possibility of some news, they felt hardly able to bear it, and the waiting for it was intolerable, to such a point of anxious tension were they strained.

But when the party from Ganado came in sight their faces wore no brightness of good news. Their greetings were quiet, sad, anxious, and Jasper Kemp held out to Gardley an envelope. It was the one from Margaret's mother's letter that she had dropped upon the trail.

"We found it on the way from Ganado, just as we entered Steamboat Cañon," explained Jasper.

"And didn't you search for a trail off in any other direction?" asked Gardley, almost sharply. "They have not been here. At least only one Indian has been down to the trader's."

"There was no other trail. We looked," said Jasper, sadly.

"There was a camp-fire twice, and signs of a camp. We felt sure they had come this way."

Gardley shook his head and a look of abject despair came over his face. "There is no sign here," he said. "They must have gone some other way. Perhaps the Indian has carried her off. Are the other men following?"

"No, Rogers sent them in the other direction after his girl. They found the camp all right. Bud tell you? We made sure we had found our trail and would not need them."

Gardley dropped his head and almost groaned.

Meanwhile the missionary had been riding around in radiating circles from the dead camp-fire, searching every step of the way; and Bud, taking his cue from him, looked off toward the mesa a minute, then struck out in a straight line for it and rode off like mad. Suddenly there was heard a shout loud and long, and Bud came riding back, waving something small and white above his head.

They gathered in a little knot, waiting for the boy, not speaking; and when he halted in their midst he fluttered down the handkerchief to Gardley.

"It's hers, all right. Gotter name all written out on the edge!" he declared, radiantly.

The sky grew brighter to them all now. Eagerly Gardley sprang into his saddle, no longer weary, but alert and eager for the trail.

"You folks better go down to the trader's and get some dinner. You'll need it! Bud and I'll go on. Mrs. Brownleigh looks all in."

"No," declared Hazel, decidedly. "We'll just snatch a bite here and follow you at once. I couldn't enjoy a dinner till I know she is safe." And so, though both Jasper Kemp and her husband urged her otherwise, she would take a hasty meal by the way and hurry on.

But Bud and Gardley waited not for others. They plunged wildly ahead.

It seemed a long way to the eager hunters, from the place where Bud had found the handkerchief to the little note twisted around the red chessman. It was perhaps nearly a mile, and both the riders had searched in all directions for some time before Gardley spied it. Eagerly he seized upon the note, recognizing the little red manikin with which he had whiled away an hour with Margaret during one of her visits at the camp.

The note was written large and clear upon a sheet of writing-paper:

"I am Margaret Earle, school-teacher at Ashland. I am supposed to be traveling to Walpi, by way of Keams, to meet Mr. and Mrs. Brownleigh of Ganado. I am with an Indian, his squaw and papoose. The Indian said he was sent to guide me, but he is drunk now and I am frightened. He has acted strangely all the way. I do not know where I am. Please come and help me."

Bud, sitting anxious like a statue upon his horse, read Gardley's face as Gardley read the note. Then Gardley read it aloud to Bud, and before the last word was fairly out of his mouth both man and boy started as if they had heard Margaret's beloved voice calling them. It was not long before Bud found another scrap of paper a half-mile farther on, and then another and another, scattered at great distances along the way. The only way they had of being sure she had dropped them was that they seemed to be the same kind of paper as that upon which the note was written.

How that note with its brave, frightened appeal wrung the heart of Gardley as he thought of Margaret, unprotected, in terror and perhaps in peril, riding on she knew not where. What trials and fears had she not already passed through! What might she not be experiencing even now while he searched for her?

It was perhaps two hours before he found the little white stocking dropped where the trail divided, showing which way she had taken. Gardley folded it reverently and put it in his pocket. An hour later Bud pounced upon the bedroom slipper and carried it gleefully to Gardley; and so by slow degrees, finding here and there a chessman or more paper, they came at last to the camp where the Indians had abandoned their trust and fled, leaving Margaret alone in the wilderness.

It was then that Gardley searched in vain for any further clue, and, riding wide in every direction, stopped and called her name again and again, while the sun grew lower and lower and shadows crept in lurking-places waiting for the swift-coming night. It was then that Bud, flying frantically from one spot to another, got down upon his knees behind a sage-bush when Gardley was not looking and mumbled a rough, hasty prayer for help. He felt like the old woman who, on being told that nothing but God could save the ship, exclaimed, "And has it come to that?" Bud had felt all his life that there was a remote time in every life when one might need to believe in prayer. The time had come for Bud.

Margaret, on her knees in the sand of the desert praying for help, remembered the promise, "Before they call I will answer, and while they are yet speaking I will hear," and knew not that her deliverers were on the way.

The sun had been hot as it beat down upon the whiteness of the sand, and the girl had crept under a sage-brush for shelter from it. The pain in her ankle was sickening. She had removed her shoe and bound the ankle about with a handkerchief soaked with half of her bottle of witch-hazel, and so, lying quiet, had fallen asleep, too exhausted with pain and anxiety to stay awake any longer.

When she awoke again the softness of evening was hovering over everything, and she started up and listened. Surely,

surely, she had heard a voice calling her! She sat up sharply and listened. Ah! There is was again, a faint echo in the distance. Was it a voice, or was it only her dreams mingling with her fancies?

Travelers in deserts, she had read, took all sorts of fancies, saw mirages, heard sounds that were not. But she had not been out long enough to have caught such a desert fever. Perhaps she was going to be sick. Still that faint echo made her heart beat wildly. She dragged herself to her knees, then to her feet, standing painfully with the weight on her well foot.

The suffering horse turned his anguished eyes and whinnied. Her heart ached for him, yet there was no way she could assuage his pain or put him out of his misery. But she must make sure if she had heard a voice. Could she possibly scale that rock down which she and her horse had fallen? For then she might look out farther and see if there were any one in sight.

Painfully she crawled and crept, up and up, inch by inch, until at last she gained the little height and could look afar.

There was no living thing in sight. The air was very clear. The eagle had found his evening rest somewhere in the quiet crag. The long corn waved on the distant plain, and all was deathly still once more. There was a hint of coming sunset in the sky. Her heart sank, and she was about to give up hope entirely, when, rich and clear, there it came again! A voice in the wilderness calling her name: "Margaret! Margaret!"

The tears rushed to her eyes and crowded in her throat. She could not answer, she was so overwhelmed; and though she tried twice to call out, she could make no sound. But the call kept coming again and again: "Margaret! Margaret!" and it was Gardley's voice. Impossible! For Gardley was far away and could not know her need. Yet it was his voice. Had she died, or was she in delirium that she seemed to hear him calling her name?

But the call came clearer now: "Margaret! Margaret! I am

coming!" and like a flash her mind went back to the first night in Arizona when she heard him singing, "From the Desert I Come to Thee!"

Now she struggled to her feet again and shouted, inarticulately and gladly through her tears. She could see him. It was Gardley. He was riding fast toward her, and he shot three shots into the air above him as he rode, and three shrill blasts of his whistle rang out on the still evening air.

She tore the scarf from her neck that she had tied about it to keep the sun from blistering her, and waved it wildly in the air now, shouting in happy, choking sobs.

And so he came to her across the desert!

He sprang down before the horse had fairly reached her side, and, rushing to her, took her in his arms.

"Margaret! My darling! I have found you at last!"

She swayed and would have fallen but for his arms, and then he saw her white face and knew she must be suffering.

"You are hurt!" he cried. "Oh, what have they done to you?" And he laid her gently down upon the sand and dropped on his knees beside her.

"Oh, no," she gasped, joyously, with white lips. "I'm all right now. Only my ankle hurts a little. We had a fall, the horse and I. Oh, go to him at once and put him out of his pain. I'm sure his legs are broken."

For answer Gardley put the whistle to his lips and blew a blast. He would not leave her for an instant. He was not sure yet that she was not more hurt than she had said. He set about discovering at once, for he had brought with him supplies for all emergencies.

It was Bud who came riding madly across the mesa in answer to the call, reaching Gardley before any one else. Bud with his eyes shining, his cheeks blazing with excitement, his hair wildly flying in the breeze, his young, boyish face suddenly grown old with lines of anxiety. But you wouldn't have known from his greeting that it was anything more than a pleasure excursion he had been on the past two days.

"Good work, Kid! Whatcha want me t' do?"

It was Bud who arranged the camp and went back to tell the other detachments that Margaret was found; Bud who led the pack-horse up, unpacked the provisions, and gathered wood to start a fire. Bud was everywhere, with a smudged face, a weary, gray look around his eyes, and his hair sticking "seven ways for Sunday." Yet once, when his labors led him near to where Margaret lay weak and happy on a couch of blankets, he gave her an unwonted pat on her shoulder and said in a low tone: "Hello, Gang! See you kept your nerve with you!" and then he gave her a grin all across his dirty, tired face, and moved away as if he were half ashamed of his emotion. But it was Bud again who came and talked with her to divert her so that she wouldn't notice when they shot her horse. He talked loudly about a coyote they shot the night before, and a cottontail they saw at Keams, and when he saw that she understood what the shot meant, and there were tears in her eyes, he gave her hand a rough, bear squeeze and said, gruffly: "You should worry! He's better off now!" And when Gardley came back he took himself thoughtfully to a distance and busied himself opening tins of meat and soup.

In another hour the Brownleighs arrived, having heard the signals, and they had a supper around the camp-fire, everybody so rejoiced that there were still quivers in their voices; and when any one laughed it sounded like the echo of a sob, so great had been the strain of their anxiety.

Gardley, sitting beside Margaret in the starlight afterward, her hand in his, listened to the story of her journey, the strong, tender pressure of his fingers telling her how deeply it affected him to know the peril through which she had passed. Later, when the others were telling gay stories about the fire, and Bud lying full length in their midst had fallen fast asleep, these two, a little apart from the rest, were murmuring their innermost thoughts in low tones to each other, and rejoicing that they were together once more.

34

THEY talked it over the next morning at breakfast as they sat around the fire. Jasper Kemp thought he ought to get right back to attend to things. Mr. Rogers was all broken up, and might even need him to search for Rosa if they had not found out her whereabouts yet. He and Fiddling Boss, who had come along, would start back at once. They had had a good night's rest and had found their dear lady. What more did they need? Besides, there were not provisions for an indefinite stay for such a large party, and there were none too many sources of supply in this region.

The missionary thought that, now he was here, he ought to go on to Walpi. It was not more than two hours' ride there, and Hazel could stay with the camp while Margaret's ankle had a chance to rest and let the swelling subside under treatment.

Margaret, however, rebelled. She did not wish to be an invalid, and was very sure she could ride without injury to her ankle. She wanted to see Walpi and the queer Hopi Indians, now she was so near. So a compromise was agreed upon. They would all wait in camp a couple of days, and then if

Margaret felt well enough they would go on, visit the Hopis, and so go home together.

Bud pleaded to be allowed to stay with them, and Jasper Kemp promised to make it all right with his parents.

So for two whole, long, lovely days the little party of five camped on the mesa and enjoyed sweet converse. It is safe to say that never in all Bud's life will he forget or get away from the influences of that day in such company.

Gardley and the missionary proved to be the best of physicians, and Margaret's ankle improved hourly under their united treatment of compresses, lotions, and rest. About noon on Saturday they broke camp, mounted their horses, and rode away across the stretch of white sand, through tall cornfields growing right up out of the sand, closer and closer to the great mesa with the castle-like pueblos five hundred feet above them on the top. It seemed to Margaret like suddenly being dropped into Egypt or the Holy Land, or some of the Babylonian excavations, so curious and primitive and altogether different from anything else she had ever seen did it all appear. She listened, fascinated, while Brownleigh told about this strange Hopi land, the strangest spot in America. Spanish explorers found them away back years before the Pilgrims landed, and called the country Tuscayan. They built their homes up high for protection from their enemies. They lived on the corn, pumpkins, peaches, and melons which they raised in the valley, planting the seeds with their hands. It is supposed they got their seeds first from the Spaniards years ago. They make pottery, cloth, and baskets, and are a busy people.

There are seven villages built on three mesas in the northern desert. One of the largest, Orabi, has a thousand inhabitants. Walpi numbers about two hundred and thirty people, all living in this one great building of many rooms. They are divided into brotherhoods, or phratries, and each brotherhood has several large families. They are ruled by a speaker chief and a war chief elected by a council of clan elders.

Margaret learned with wonder that all the water these people used had to be carried by the women in jars on their backs five hundred feet up the steep trail.

Presently, as they drew nearer, a curious man with his hair "banged" like a child's, and garments much like those usually worn by scarecrows—a shapeless kind of shirt and trousers—appeared along the steep and showed them the way up. Margaret and the missionary's wife exclaimed in horror over the little children playing along the very edge of the cliffs above as carelessly as birds in trees.

High up on the mesa at last, how strange and weird it seemed! Far below the yellow sand of the valley; fifteen miles away a second mesa stretching dark; to the southwest, a hundred miles distant, the dim outlines of the San Francisco peaks. Some little children on burros crossing the sand below looked as if they were part of a curious moving-picture, not as if they were little living beings taking life as seriously as other children do. The great, wide desert stretching far! The bare, solid rocks beneath their feet! The curious houses behind them! It all seemed unreal to Margaret, like a great picture-book spread out for her to see. She turned from gazing and found Gardley's eyes upon her adoringly, a tender understanding of her mood in his glance. She thrilled with pleasure to be here with him; a soft flush spread over her cheeks and a light came into her eyes.

They found the Indians preparing for one of their most famous ceremonies, the snake dance, which was to take place in a few days. For almost a week the snake priests had been busy hunting rattlesnakes, building altars, drawing figures in the sand, and singing weird songs. On the ninth day the snakes are washed in a pool and driven near a pile of sand. The priests, arrayed in paint, feathers, and charms, come out in line and, taking the live snakes in their mouths, parade up and down the rocks, while the people crowd the roofs and terraces of the pueblos to watch. There are helpers to whip the snakes and keep them from biting, and catchers to see that none get away. In a little while the priests take the snakes down on the desert and set them free, sending them north, south, east, and west, where it is supposed they will take the people's prayers for rain to the water serpent in the under-world, who is in some way connected with the god of the rain-clouds.

It was a strange experience, that night in Walpi: the primitive accommodations; the picturesque, uncivilized people; the shy glances from dark, eager eyes. To watch two girls grinding corn between two stones, and a little farther off their mother rolling out her dough with an ear of corn, and cooking over an open fire, her pot slung from a crude crane over the blaze — it was all too unreal to be true.

But the most interesting thing about it was to watch the "Aneshodi" going about among them, his face alight with warm, human love; his hearty laugh ringing out in a joke that the Hopis seemed to understand, making himself one with them. It came to Margaret suddenly to remember the pompous little figure of the Rev. Frederick West, and to fancy him going about among these people and trying to do them good. Before she knew what she was doing she laughed aloud at the thought. Then, of course, she had to explain to Bud and Gardley, who looked at her inquiringly.

"Aw! Gee! *Him? He* wasn't a minister! He was a *mistake!* Fergit him, the poor simp!" growled Bud, sympathetically. Then his eyes softened as he watched Brownleigh playing with three little Indian maids, having a fine romp. "Gee! he certainly is a peach, isn't he?" he murmured, his whole face kindling appreciatively. "Gee! I bet that kid never forgets that!"

The Sunday was a wonderful day, when the missionary gathered the people together and spoke to them in simple words of God — their god who made the sky, the stars, the mountains, and the sun, whom they call by different names, but whom He called God. He spoke of the Book of Heaven that told about God and His great love for men, so great that

He sent His son to save them from their sin. It was not a long sermon, but a very beautiful one; and, listening to the simple, wonderful words of life that fell from the missionary's earnest lips and were translated by his faithful Indian interpreter, who always went with him on his expeditions, watching the faces of the dark, strange people as they took in the marvelous meaning, the little company of visitors was strangely moved. Even Bud, awed beyond his wont, said, shyly, to Margaret:

"Gee! It's something fierce not to be born a Christian and know all that, ain't it?"

Margaret and Gardley walked a little way down the narrow path that led out over the neck of rock less than a rod wide that connects the great promontory with the mesa. The sun was setting in majesty over the desert, and the scene was one of breathless beauty. One might fancy it might look so to stand on the hills of God and look out over creation when all things have been made new.

They stood for a while in silence. Then Margaret looked down at the narrow path worn more than a foot deep in the solid rock by the ten generations of feet that had been passing over it.

"Just think," she said, "of all the feet, little and big, that have walked here in all the years, and of all the souls that have stood and looked out over this wonderful sight! It must be that somehow in spite of their darkness they have reached out to the God who made this, and have found a way to His heart. They couldn't look at this and not feel Him, could they? It seems to me that perhaps some of those poor creatures who have stood here and reached up blindly after the Creator of their souls have, perhaps, been as pleasing to Him as those who have known about Him from childhood."

Gardley was used to her talking this way. He had not been in her Sunday meetings for nothing. He understood and sympathized, and now his hand reached softly for hers and held it tenderly. After a moment of silence he said:

"I surely think if God could reach and find me in the desert of my life, He must have found them. I sometimes think I was a greater heathen than all these, because I knew and would not see."

Margaret nestled her hand in his and looked up joyfully into his face. "I'm so glad you know Him now!" she murmured, happily.

They stood for some time looking out over the changing scene, till the crimson faded into rose, the silver into gray; till the stars bloomed out one by one, and down in the valley across the desert a light twinkled faintly here and there from the camps of the Hopi shepherds.

They started home at daybreak the next morning, the whole company of Indians standing on the rocks to send them royally on their way, pressing simple, homely gifts upon them and begging them to return soon again and tell the blessed story.

A wonderful ride they had back to Ganado, where Gardley left Margaret for a short visit, promising to return for her in a few days when she was rested, and hastened back to Ashland to his work; for his soul was happy now and at ease, and he felt he must get to work at once. Rogers would need him. Poor Rogers! Had he found his daughter yet? Poor, silly child-prodigal!

But when Gardley reached Ashland he found among his mail awaiting him a telegram. His uncle was dead, and the fortune which he had been brought up to believe was his, and which he had idly tossed away in a moment of recklessness, had been restored to him by the uncle's last will, made since Gardley's recent visit home. The fortune was his again!

Gardley sat in his office on the Rogers ranch and stared hard at the adobe wall opposite his desk. That fortune would be great! He could do such wonderful things for Margaret now. They could work out their dreams together for the people they loved. He could see the shadows of those dreams—a beautiful home for Margaret out on the trail she loved, where wildness and beauty and the mountain she called hers were not far away; horses in plenty and a luxurious car when they wanted to take a trip; journeys East as often as they wished; some of the ideal appliances for the school that Margaret loved; a church for the missionary and convenient halls where he could speak at his outlying districts; a trip to the city for Mom Wallis, where she might see a real picture-gallery, her one expressed desire this side of heaven, now that she had taken to reading Browning and had some of it explained to her. Oh, and a lot of wonderful things! These all hung in the dream-picture before Gardley's eyes as he sat at his desk with that bit of yellow paper in his hand.

He thought of what that money had represented to him in the past. Reckless days and nights of folly as a boy and young man at college; ruthless waste of time, money, youth; shriveling of soul, till Margaret came and found and rescued him! How wonderful that he had been rescued! That he had come to his senses at last, and was here in a man's position, doing a man's work in the world! Now, with all that money, there was no need for him to work and earn more. He could live idly all his days and just have a good time — make others happy, too. But still he would not have this exhilarating feeling that he was supplying his own and Margaret's necessities by the labor of hand and brain. The little telegram in his hand seemed somehow to be trying to snatch from him all this material prosperity that was the symbol of that spiritual regeneration which had become so dear to him.

He put his head down on his clasped hands upon the desk then and prayed. Perhaps it was the first great prayer of his life.

"O God, let me be strong enough to stand this that has come upon me. Help me to be a man in spite of money! Don't let me lose my manhood and my right to work. Help me to use the money in the right way and not to dwarf myself, nor spoil our lives with it." It was a great prayer for a man such as Gardley had been, and the answer came swiftly in his conviction.

He lifted up his head with purpose in his expression, and, folding the telegram, put it safely back into his pocket. He would not tell Margaret of it—not just yet. He would think it out—just the right way—and he did not believe he meant to give up his position with Rogers. He had accepted it for a year in good faith, and it was his business to fulfil the contract. Meantime, this money would perhaps make possible his marriage with Margaret sooner than he had hoped.

Five minutes later Rogers telephoned to the office.

"I've decided to take that shipment of cattle and try that new stock, provided you will go out and look at them and see that everything is all O.K. I couldn't go myself now. Don't feel like going anywhere, you know. You wouldn't need to go for a couple of weeks. I've just had a letter from the man, and he says he won't be ready sooner. Say, why don't you and Miss Earle get married and make this a wedding-trip? She could go to the Pacific coast with you. It would be a nice trip. Then I could spare you for a month or six weeks when you got back if you wanted to take her East for a little visit."

Why not? Gardley stumbled out his thanks and hung up the receiver, his face full of the light of a great joy. How were the blessings pouring down upon his head these days? Was it a sign that God was pleased with his action in making good what he could where he had failed? And Rogers! How kind he was! Poor Rogers, with his broken heart and his stricken home! For Rosa had come home again a sadder, wiser child; and her father seemed crushed with the disgrace of it all.

Gardley went to Margaret that very afternoon. He told her only that he had had some money left him by his uncle, which would make it possible for him to marry at once and keep her comfortably now. He was to be sent to California on a business trip. Would she be married and go with him?

Margaret studied the telegram in wonder. She had never asked Gardley much about his circumstances. The telegram merely stated that his uncle's estate was left to him. To her simple mind an estate might be a few hundred dollars, enough to furnish a plain little home; and her face lighted with joy over it. She asked no questions, and Gardley said no more about the money. He had forgotten that question, comparatively, in the greater possibility of joy.

Would she be married in ten days and go with him?

Her eyes met his with an answering joy, and yet he could see that there was a trouble hiding somewhere. He presently saw what it was without needing to be told. Her father and mother! Of course, they would be disappointed! They would want her to be married at home!

"But Rogers said we could go and visit them for several weeks on our return," he said; and Margaret's face lighted up.

"Oh, that would be beautiful," she said, wistfully; "and perhaps they won't mind so much—though I always expected father would marry me if I was ever married; still, if we can go home so soon and for so long—and Mr. Brownleigh would be next best, of course."

"But, of course, your father must marry you," said Gardley, determinedly. "Perhaps we could persuade him to come, and your mother, too."

"Oh no, they couldn't possibly," said Margaret, quickly, a shade of sadness in her eyes. "You know it costs a lot to come out here, and ministers are never rich."

It was then that Gardley's eyes lighted with joy. His money could take this bugbear away, at least. However, he said nothing about the money.

"Suppose we write to your father and mother and put the matter before them. See what they say. We'll send the letters to-night. You write your mother and I'll write your father."

Margaret agreed and sat down at once to write her letter, while Gardley, on the other side of the room, wrote his, scratching away contentedly with his fountain-pen and looking furtively now and then toward the bowed head over at the desk.

Gardley did not read his letter to Margaret. She wondered a little at this, but did not ask, and the letters were mailed, with special-delivery stamps on them. Gardley awaited their replies with great impatience.

He filled in the days of waiting with business. There were letters to write connected with his fortune, and there were arrangements to be made for his trip. But the thing that occupied the most of his time and thought was the purchase and refitting of a roomy old ranch-house in a charming location, not more than three miles from Ashland, on the road to the camp.

It had been vacant for a couple of years past, the owner having gone abroad permanently and the place having been offered for sale. Margaret had often admired it in her trips to and from the camp, and Gardley thought of it at once when it became possible for him to think of purchasing a home in the West.

There was a great stone fireplace, and the beams of the ceilings and pillars of the porch and wide, hospitable rooms were of tree-trunks with the bark on them. With a little work it could be made roughly but artistically habitable. Gardley had it cleaned up, not disturbing the tangle of vines and shrubbery that had had their way since the last owner had left them and which had made a perfect screen from the road for the house.

Behind this screen the men worked—most of them the men from the bunk-house, whom Gardley took into his confidence.

The floors were carefully scrubbed under the direction of Mom Wallis, and the windows made shining. Then the men spent a day bringing great loads of tree-boughs and filling the place with green fragrance, until the big living-room looked like a woodland bower. Gardley made a raid upon some Indian friends of his and came back with several fine Navajo rugs and blankets, which he spread about the room luxuriously on the floor and over the rude benches which the men had constructed. They piled the fireplace with big logs, and Gardley took over some of his own personal possessions that he had brought back from the East with him to give the place a livable look. Then he stood back satisfied. The place was fit to bring his bride and her friends to. Not that it was as it should be. That would be for Margaret to do, but it would serve as a temporary stopping-place if there came need. If no need came, why, the place was there, anyway, hers and his. A tender light grew in his eyes as he looked it over in the dying light of the afternoon. Then he went out and rode swiftly to the telegraph-office and found these two telegrams, according to the request in his own letter to Mr. Earle.

Gardley's telegram read:

> Congratulations. Will come as you desire. We await your advice. Have written.—Father.

He saddled his horse and hurried to Margaret with hers, and together they read:

> Dear child! So glad for you. Of course you will go. I am sending you some things. Don't take a thought for us. We shall look forward to your visit. Our love to you both.—Mother.

Margaret, folded in her lover's arms, cried out her sorrow and her joy, and lifted up her face with happiness. Then Gardley, with great joy, thought of the surprise he had in store for her and laid his face against hers to hide the telltale smile in his eyes.

For Gardley, in his letter to his future father-in-law, had written of his newly inherited fortune, and had not only enclosed a check for a good sum to cover all extra expense of the journey, but had said that a private car would be at their disposal, not only for themselves, but for any of Margaret's friends and relatives whom they might choose to invite. As he had written this letter he was filled with deep thanksgiving that it was in his power to do this thing for his dear girl-bride.

The morning after the telegrams arrived Gardley spent several hours writing telegrams and receiving them from a big department store in the nearest great city, and before noon a big shipment of goods was on its way to Ashland. Beds, bureaus, washstands, chairs, tables, dishes, kitchen utensils, and all kinds of bedding, even to sheets and pillow-cases, he ordered with lavish hand. After all, he must furnish the house himself, and let Margaret weed it out or give it away afterward, if she did not like it. He was going to have a house party and he must be ready. When all was done and he was just about to mount his horse again he turned back and sent another message, ordering a piano.

"Why, it's *great!*" he said to himself, as he rode back to his office. "It's simply great to be able to do things just when I need them! I never knew what fun money was before. But then I never had Margaret to spend it for, and she's worth the whole of it at once!"

The next thing he ordered was a great easy carriage with plenty of room to convey Mother Earle and her friends from the train to the house.

The days went by rapidly enough, and Margaret was so busy that she had little time to wonder and worry why her mother did not write her the long, loving, motherly good-by letter to her little girlhood that she had expected to get. Not until three days before the wedding did it come over her that she had had but three brief, scrappy letters from her mother, and they not a whole page apiece. What could be the matter with mother? She was almost on the point of panic when Gardley came and bundled her on to her horse for a ride.

Strangely enough, he directed their way through Ashland and down to the station, and it was just about the time of the arrival of the evening train.

Gardley excused himself for a moment, saying something about an errand, and went into the station. Margaret sat on her horse, watching the oncoming train, the great connecting link between East and West, and wondered if it would bring a letter from mother.

The train rushed to a halt, and behold some passengers were getting off from a private car! Margaret watched them idly, thinking more about an expected letter than about the people. Then suddenly she awoke to the fact that Gardley was greeting them. Who could they be?

There were five of them, and one of them looked like Jane! Dear Jane! She had forgotten to write her about this hurried wedding. How different it all was going to be from what she and Jane had planned for each other in their dear old school-day dreams! And that young man that Gardley was shaking hands with now looked like Cousin Dick! She hadn't seen him for three years, but he must look like that now; and the younger girl beside him might be Cousin Emily! But, oh, who were the others? *Father!* And MOTHER!

Margaret sprang from her horse with a bound and rushed into her mother's arms. The interested passengers craned their necks and looked their fill with smiles of appreciation as the train took up its way again, having dropped the private car on the side track.

Dick and Emily rode the ponies to the house, while Margaret nestled in the back seat of the carriage between her father and mother, and Jane got acquainted with Gardley in the front seat of the carriage. Margaret never even noticed where they were going until the carriage turned in and stopped before the door of the new house, and Mrs. Tanner, furtively casting behind her the checked apron she had worn, came out to shake hands with the company and tell them supper was all ready, before she went back to her deserted boarding-house. Even Bud was going to stay at the new house that night, in some cooked-up capacity or other, and all the men from the bunk-house were hiding out among the trees to see Margaret's father and mother and shake hands if the opportunity offered.

The wonder and delight of Margaret when she saw the house inside and knew that it was hers, the tears she shed and smiles that grew almost into hysterics when she saw some of the incongruous furnishings, are all past describing. Margaret was too happy to think. She rushed from one room to another. She hugged her mother and linked her arm in her father's for a walk across the long piazza; she talked to Emily and Dick and Jane; and then rushed out to find Gardley and thank him again. And all this time she could not understand how Gardley had done it, for she had not yet comprehended his fortune.

Gardley had asked his sisters to come to the wedding, not much expecting they would accept, but they had telegraphed at the last minute they would be there. They arrived an hour or so before the ceremony; gushed over Margaret; told Gardley she was a "sweet thing"; said the house was "dandy for a house party if one had plenty of servants, but they should think it would be dull in winter"; gave Margaret a diamond sunburst pin, a string of pearls, and an emerald bracelet set in diamond chips; and departed immediately after the ceremony. They had thought they were the chief guests, but the relief that overspread the faces of those guests who were best beloved by both bride and groom was at once visible on their departure. Jasper Kemp drew a long breath and declared to Long Bill that he was glad the air was growing pure again. Then all those old friends from the bunk-house filed in to the great tables heavily loaded with good things, the abundant gift of the neighborhood, and sat down to the wedding supper, heartily glad that the "city lady and her gals"—as Mom Wallis called them in a suppressed whisper—had chosen not to stay over a train.

The wedding had been in the school-house, embowered in foliage and all the flowers the land afforded, decorated by the loving hands of Margaret's pupils, old and young. She was attended by the entire school marching double file before her, strewing flowers in her way. The missionary's wife played the wedding-march, and the missionary assisted the bride's father with the ceremony. Margaret's dress was a simple white muslin, with a little real lace and embroidery handed down from former generations, the whole called into being by Margaret's mother. Even Gardley's sisters had said it was "perfectly dear." The whole neighborhood was at the wedding.

And when the bountiful wedding-supper was eaten the entire company of favored guests stood about the new piano and sang "Blest Be the Tie that Binds"—with Margaret playing for them.

Then there was a little hurry at the last, Margaret getting into the pretty traveling dress and hat her mother had brought, and kissing her mother good-by—though happily not for long this time.

Mother and father and the rest of the home party were to wait until morning, and the missionary and his wife were to stay with them that night and see them to their car the next day.

So, waving and throwing kisses back to the others, they rode away to the station, Bud pridefully driving the team from the front seat.

Gardley had arranged for a private apartment on the train, and nothing could have been more luxurious in traveling than the place where he led his bride. Bud, scuttling behind with a suit-case, looked around him with all his eyes before he said a hurried good-by, and murmured under his breath: "Gee! Wisht I was goin' all the way!"

Bud hustled off as the train got under way, and Margaret and Gardley went out to the observation platform to wave a last farewell.

The few little blurring lights of Ashland died soon in the distance, and the desert took on its vast wideness beneath a starry dome; but off in the East a purple shadow loomed, mighty and majestic, and rising slowly over its crest a great silver disk appeared, brightening as it came and pouring a silver mist over the purple peak.

"My mountain!" said Margaret, softly.

And Gardley, drawing her close to him, stooped to lay his lips upon hers.

"My darling!" he answered.

THE END

About the Author

Grace Livingston Hill is well known as one of the most prolific writers of romantic fiction. Her personal life was fraught with joys and sorrows not unlike those experienced by many of her fictional heroines.

Born in Wellsville, New York, Grace nearly died during the first hours of life. But her loving parents and friends turned to God in prayer. She survived miraculously, thus her thankful father named her Grace.

Grace was always close to her father, a Presbyterian minister, and her mother, a published writer. It was from them that she learned the art of storytelling. When Grace was twelve, a close aunt surprised her with a hardbound, illustrated copy of one of Grace's stories. This was the beginning of Grace's journey into being a published author.

In 1892 Grace married Fred Hill, a young minister, and they soon had two lovely young daughters. Then came 1901, a difficult year for Grace—the year when, within months of each other, both her father and husband died. Suddenly Grace had to find a new place to live (her home was owned by the church where her husband had been pastor). It was a struggle for Grace to raise her young daughters alone, but through everything she kept writing. In 1902 she produced *The Angel of His Presence, The Story of a Whim,* and *An Unwilling Guest.* In 1903 her two books *According to the Pattern* and *Because of Stephen* were published.

It wasn't long before Grace was a well-known author, but she wanted to go beyond just entertaining her readers. She soon included the message of God's salvation through Jesus Christ in each of her books. For Grace, the most important thing she did was not write books but share the message of salvation, a message she felt God wanted her to share through the abilities he had given her.

In all, Grace Livingston Hill wrote more than one hundred books, all of which have sold thousands of copies and have touched the lives of readers around the world with their message of "enduring love" and the true way to lasting happiness: a relationship with God through his Son, Jesus Christ.

In an interview shortly before her death, Grace's devotion to her Lord still shone clear. She commented that whatever she had accomplished had been God's doing. She was only his servant, one who had tried to follow his teaching in all her thoughts and writing.

MARY ARDEN

Living Books ®
Tyndale House Publishers, Inc.
Wheaton, Illinois

This Tyndale House book
by Grace Livingston Hill
contains the complete text
of the original hardcover edition..
NOT ONE WORD
HAS BEEN OMITTED.

3-in-1 ISBN: 1-56865-181-3

Living Books is a registered trademark of Tyndale House
Publishers, Inc.

Library of Congress Catalog Card Number 94-60545
ISBN 0-8423-3883-7

Printed in the United States of America

FOR three generations there had been a Mary Arden at the old home on the edge of the village of Ardenville and now the fourth Mary Arden had come back there to live.

She was just out of college and had inherited the old Arden homestead, a simple plain colonial house, with four white pillars across the front and a big round window over the front door.

Her father had been sent to China suddenly by the government on some urgent business and her mother was planning to go to a fashionable coastal resort where they often spent much time in the summers. But Mary Arden had not chosen to go with her. She was not fond of the life there and told her mother she would rather run down to Ardenville and look over her new inheritance.

Mrs. Arden had argued the matter at length. She felt that Mary, now that she was out of college, should begin to take a more active part in her own social world, and that there was no place as suitable for Mary to begin as Castanza, the resort where they had spent their summers for years, and where many of their friends, the best people, always went.

"But I don't want to go there, mother," Mary had insisted. "I want to go back to the house where I used to visit grandmother and have such good times. The house that is mine now. I want to go and get acquainted with it all over again. The house that belongs to my name."

"What nonsense!" said her mother contemptuously. "If your father were at home he would soon make you understand."

"If dad were home he would make *you* understand, mother, why I feel as I do. Dad is an Arden, and that house in Ardenville is where he was born and brought up. It was where his mother lived and his grandmother, and it was dad who wanted me named Mary Arden, you told me so yourself. Why shouldn't I want to go and get acquainted all over again with my namesake house that I'm so proud of, now that I own it?"

Her mother signed annoyedly:

"Oh, Mary, child, you don't understand. You don't realize that you would be bored to death if you went down there in the country. Not a friend of your own age who is worth cultivating, just a lot of country bumpkins!"

"I don't care, mother, I want to go and remember all the beautiful times I had as a child."

"But you're not a child, now, my dear! You are just coming into young womanhood and this is the time when you can lay the foundation for a successful life. Listen, my dear, I have private information that three young officers of very high rank have engaged apartments at Castanza for the summer. There will be all sorts of gaieties planned to include them. I am very anxious to have you in on this. In fact Mrs. Worthington Warden has given me this information ahead of time because she is anxious that you should be there and help in all these festivities. She told me that she was counting on you to help her, and she personally would see that you had a good time."

Mary's face grew very grave.

"Well, that's very kind of her, of course, but I've never felt the need of Mrs. Worthington Warden before to give me a good time. And that doesn't change my plans. I simply must go down to Ardenville this summer. I really have my heart set on it. I mentioned it once to dad before he knew he had to go away, and he seemed pleased that I wanted to go there."

"He would, of course!" said Mrs. Arden with a deprecating sigh. "He has always been utterly childish about that place. Even wanted me to go there and live when we were married. Imagine it! I went through two weeks of it and that was all I could stand. Oh, I've been back occasionally, to your Aunt Cathie's wedding, to the golden wedding of the old Ardens, and a few occasions like that. I did manage to escape the funerals. Ardenville and funerals was a combination I could not stand, and it was very fortunate for me that I usually had a severe cold, or a sprained ankle or something of the sort to prevent my going. I was always glad to be relieved from the trip to Ardenville. And, my dear, you are very like your mother in your emotional make-up. I'm sure you will feel the same way I do about the place, when you once see it."

"But I have seen it, mother dear, and I don't feel that way at all. I have a lovely photograph of the house that dad got for me, and I always cherished it. You don't know how I love it and have longed to see it again."

"But you were a mere child when you were there the last time."

"I was sixteen years old, mother, and I remember everything about it."

"Nonsense! You were just barely sixteen, and besides sixteen-year-old memories are soon dispelled. Why, my dear, you'll have no companions, and no servants."

"Oh, mother, grandmother's old servants are still there. Dear old Nannie, and Orrin, her husband, and their daughter Randa. They've kept the house for years. Goodness knows I have to pay them little enough, and the inheritance takes care of that little. I shall keep them on, for there couldn't be better servants."

"My dear! You don't realize what you're saying. They are simply antiquated, like the house itself. They wouldn't know how to do anything in the modern way. I grant you they can make buckwheat cakes and queer old-fashioned hash, and cook baked beans, and brown bread—that's about all. But you just go down there and try it. Invite some of your friends from college, or from New York, to visit you there, and you'll sink through the floor with shame when you take them out to your table. Just try it for a week and find out for yourself! That will cure you of this absurd obsession."

"All right, mother, I will. Only I won't promise to come back in a week. I'm going to stay the whole summer long."

"But, Mary, I've accepted several invitations for you already. You'll simply have to come up to attend them, you know. They are counting on you for them all."

"Sorry, mother, but I can't make it."

"Such an absurd notion!" sighed her mother distressfully, settling in her mind that this should never be.

Yet Mary Arden went to Ardenville, on the strength of a cablegram received from her father, giving hearty permission and commendation to the idea:

"Delighted that you are going. Wish I could be with you.

Lovingly, Dad."

But as she drove away her mother's words of warning sounded clearly in her ears.

"Now remember, Mary dear, that your room in the hotel at Castanza is engaged for the season, and any time when you get fed up with that silly old country place you can come right up to Castanza and find a gay welcome and plenty of good times. And you don't need to worry about clothes. I've had all your evening dresses and a few new sports things sent up, so they'll be there waiting for you, and you needn't pack a thing except your overnight bag when you get ready to come back to your own natural world."

A shadow flitted across the girl's eyes as she listened, and she feared that there might still be some plot afoot to try to stop her. So she drove away into the lovely summer morning and tried for the thousandth time to see if she might possibly be in the wrong.

Each time she had approached the subject it had come to her with a shock that she was deliberately planning to stay away from her own mother for the whole summer, perhaps for even longer, the mother from whom she had been so long separated by her college days. And yet behind it all there had been reasons which she had not ventured to bring forward in her arguing with her mother that had made her feel entirely justified in her decision. They were reasons which she had not openly owned even to herself as she thought it over. She had not been willing even to think about it much because she shrank from the subject, did not want to acknowledge that there was anything in it. But now speeding far away with no one beside her to watch the thoughts in her eyes, she realized that she must face the matter and have it out with herself once and for all.

And so as she drove along the smooth highway, and now and again into lovely fragrant country roads, gay with spring flowers, she deliberately brought out the main immediate question and braced herself to settle it.

For there was a certain Brooke Haven, tall, handsome, cultured, well-thought-of, and almost fabulously wealthy, who had been hovering about her vicinity this year every time she came home from college, with a possessiveness that was becoming annoying to her. His mother, too, was taking the attitude that Mary *belonged* exclusively to her son. He and his family were to be at Castanza this summer, and were fairly gloating over the fact that the two young people were to be together. And it made it all the worse for Mary that Mrs. Haven was an intimate friend of Mrs. Arden, and the two mothers evidently shared their hopes and aspirations regarding their children.

Mary shrank from acknowledging that her own mother had a part in this conspiracy. But she was sure of it in spite of the fact that Mrs. Arden had of late taken pains to stress, albeit halfheartedly, other young men also, such as the young officers who were going to be at Castanza, who were Mrs. Worthington Warden's contribution to the list of attractions offered Mary recently.

Of these attractions Jinnie Randall's birthday party was the first definite engagement. How little attraction it offered! The thought of it left Mary simply cold and blank. She wondered why she had used to thrill so at the thought of parties. Of course, she had been ill this winter and was still feeling rather dragged out. And there had been that tragedy at college that had upset her more than she was willing to admit. The thought of it still brought a sinking feeling in the pit of her stomach. So far she had found no one to answer her desperate questions about it. That was one thing she planned to do at Arden, the other main reason why she had wanted to go. She would be quiet, and she would go over that whole terrible experience and find an answer to it. But she must not think of it again now. Wait until she could get settled.

Well, perhaps she could avoid all these parties until she felt more like herself. If she sent a rather good birthday present and a nice letter of excuse to Jinnie Randall she *could* get out of that. Then there was Earle Warren's coming-of-age party. But why should she care about that? She was definitely not his girl, and even though her mother was a good friend of his mother, another stunning present would make that all right. That is, with everybody but her own mother who would certainly reproach her with rudeness. But there would be some way to get out of it.

Then her heart suddenly froze with the remembrance of another engagement that she had entirely forgotten. Floss Fairlee's wedding! And she had tentatively promised to be maid of honor. But perhaps it wouldn't take place until fall! If she could only get out of all these dates how wonderful it would be! If she went back for that wedding it would mean that Brooke Haven would take possession of her, and arrange to walk up the aisle with her. No, she simply would not be caught in that trap! Somehow she must have a real summer to herself, without any strings to it.

With a sigh of relief that at least she was out of tangible reach for the present, she found a pleasant little tea room and stopped for lunch. She had made up her mind to cancel *all* those engagements the first thing when she got to her new home. Then she could really enjoy her summer.

But after lunch she started worrying about presents!

What presents could she think up that would adequately make up for what her mother would consider extreme rudeness? The problem stung her like a gigantic thorn, and stayed with her as she rode along the pleasant way spoiling her anticipation of the new, exciting joy that she hoped was before her. She simply must think up some wonderful presents and have them ordered and sent in plenty of time to evade the invitations that would follow one another all too quickly if she wasn't ready for them. The wedding, of all other engagements, she simply would not attend, for she knew it would mean the constant attendance of Brooke Haven, who was Floss Fairlee's cousin, and the inevitable conclusion in the minds of all present that he and she were pledged to one another. This of all the other anxieties was most repellent to her. Yet she knew she must say nothing about it to her mother until the time was at hand, or somehow her mother would plan it so that she *had* to be in the party.

She felt a little guilty as she thought these things over. It seemed rather wicked to be so definitely planning to disappoint the mother who had planned for her youthful joy all her life. But she saw plainly that if she did not take a stand now, and make it quite plain, that she would be trapped for life in ways that she would never choose for herself. Oh, if daddy would only hurry back and be her ally it would not be so hard. He always understood, and sided with her!

Then the town appeared in the distance and she began to watch for familiar landmarks. Yes, there was the old Harmon farm where she once went with her grandfather to see a horse he was thinking of buying. There had been a little pony there and the owner had put her on its back and let her ride around the lot while her grandfather was talking with the man about the horse.

And next was the little white cottage where Granny McVicker used to live. It did not look so immaculately white as she remembered it. Probably Granny was gone now, and somebody else lived there. There seemed to be several little children playing around the yard. And then the row of brown houses facing on the railroad street, and off in the distance the old red brick school house where she had gone sometimes to visit school with Angie Perkins and had had such fun at recess time playing blind man's buff. Then the spire of the big old Presbyterian church came into view; a little farther on, the Methodist church, and to the left the Baptist church. She had gone to each of them once or twice with the little girls she played with, and once to a Sunday School picnic in the woods up over the hillside. How it all came back to her like a moving picture now, as one after another the scenes of beloved summers long cherished in memory, swept into view. And now the old freight station flashed by, and then a broad new platform paved with cement, and a name posted in bright letters, AR-DEN. Not Arden*ville* as it used to be, but ARDEN. It came with almost a shock and made it seem like a new place at which she was arriving. Yet they had retained the family name, Arden, after her great grandfather! That was nice.

Mary had a passing sense of pride in the name. It was a pretty name. Prettier than Ardenville.

She felt like one about to arrive in a long-hoped-for heaven where she could look around with shining eyes on the idols of her childhood.

With happy eyes she swept her glance over the scene before her. Just the same little old brick station, with gray stone trimmings, but it had always seemed to her the most beautiful little station in the world. Of course it was dirty now, and old-looking, but that seemed to make it all the more precious to her.

There was the old drug store across the street, and the grocery next door. She remembered how she used to go down with her dimes or her nickels to get peanuts, and pink-and-white-striped mint candy.

And there was the little real estate building, now enlarged, with a neat little second story, advertising a beauty parlor, presided over by one Sylva Grannis. Mary read it over twice. Why, Sylva Grannis used to be a senior in the high school when she was there last. She used to be a very popular girl with a wonderful hair-do and very red lips. So that was what she was doing now! Running a beauty parlor! And she was the girl that so many of the high-school boys had been crazy about!

Some men along the road had ceased their work and were gazing after the new arrival, speculating as to who she was and where she was going, no doubt.

As she bumped along the rough cobblestones of the poor old road that hadn't had time or men or material to get itself mended during the war, Mary cast an amused glance at the old houses by the way. She half smiled at the expression that she felt sure would be on her mother's face if she could see her treasured daughter now, and see how humbly she was riding to her own ancestral home. It was almost as if that mother were sitting beside her. She could fairly hear the scorn in her voice as she would say in her polite taunting voice:

"There, now, I hope you see what kind of a place you have come to. Imagine an *Arden* riding on little bumpy streets like this, and living in a shabby town! It is unthinkable, Mary. I hope you understand. If I were you I would turn right around and start home at once. I wouldn't go a step farther. Nobody knows you are coming. You won't have to explain a thing to anybody!

You told me yourself you didn't even send a telegram to the servants, so even they cannot be disappointed about having to get up a dinner for somebody who won't be there!"

Mary drew a long breath and set her pretty lips. She had no idea of turning around or going back. She had come thus far in good faith to find her beloved inheritance, and if it was *all* shabby, why then she would simply set about bringing back its charm. She hadn't expected perfection when she came back here. It would be old-fashioned of course, but she loved old-fashioned things. At least she believed she did, and she meant to find out for herself whether or not it was true that she did.

She knew that the station was almost a mile from the old Arden home, and she watched anxiously as she drove along the way to see some of the old places she remembered. There were some new stores, one quite large one, like a department store, and next a very large up-to-date market. Then a barbershop, a shoe shop, and another grocery. These were built where the Whites used to live, next the yellow boardinghouse where the men from the factory used to board, and where the laundry used to be. Well, they were no loss. They had only been an eyesore in her memory. The blacksmith shop was gone, and in its place was a grand new fire house with a bright red chrome-trimmed fire engine standing grandly within its open doors.

And now she turned into the wider avenue, and swept up past the better houses. There was a big new hotel, towering up several stories. And then she came to the fine old houses she remembered, with now and then a new one sandwiched in. The new ones were fairly good-looking and did not seem out of place between the handsome Tracy mansion, and the Rathbone house where she used to go and play with Celia Rathbone, and love it so. She glanced up to the upper porch where the door of Celia's playroom opened out. Where was Celia now, she wondered?

Up the pleasant hill she went, and now she could catch a glimpse of her own stone house at the top, a little back from the street, so sweetly pleasant and cosy, yet spacious in the lovely setting of trees and lawn. Thanks be, it didn't look run-down as her mother had said that it would. It looked well groomed, as if every blade of grass had been newly brushed and combed that morning, and every flower set right for blooming to welcome her home. It looked just as it had looked in her grandmother's day, just as she had known Nannie and Orrin and Randa would keep it, even if it were only in memory of the adored mistress who had lived there for years. Even though they had no possible way of knowing that the present new owner was arriving that night. Her heart thrilled as she thought of this. This was something she could be proud to tell her mother, something mother would appreciate: that the servants had kept up their traditions, the ways in which they had been trained, even with no one to watch over them.

Then she was at the house, turning up the well-remembered drive. Mary stood still on the step, slowly looking around the old familiar scene, down the smooth-sloping lawns, over to the summer pergola, drawing a deep breath of delight that at last she was here and was seeing it all again, and that it wasn't changed in the least. At least the outside wasn't changed. And now she almost dreaded to go in lest something would have been moved before she saw it again. She wanted so much to see it as it had been in her girlhood when she had learned to love it so much.

Suddenly she turned and went to the door touching

the bell and thrilling to hear it bring to life the old house. Almost at once she heard footsteps. Nannie's, shuffling along in felt slippers, to meet, as she supposed, some book agent or a man selling a new kind of cleaner.

A moment more and Mary was in the old woman's arms. Mary gave a glance around. There was the wide cool living room where the white curtains were floating gently in the breeze, just as they always had. A big brass jardiniere of black-eyed Susans stood on the hearth, just as grandmother always fixed them. One might have thought that Nannie had expected her Arden chick this very morning.

A glimpse toward the far wing, through the dining room with its spacious bay window, showed the same beautiful willow furniture in the wide sunroom, with the gray-flowered chintz covers as crisp as ever. Flowers in there, too. How homey it all looked.

The wonderful old grandfather clock, in its accustomed place beneath the gallery of the stairway, struck the half-hour with its welcoming voice, and Mary felt as if it were one of the family, too. Over Nannie's shoulder her eyes swept downward and she saw the big wide random-width floor boards. Yes, they were just as smooth and well kept as ever. What wonderful people Nannie and Orrin were.

"Oh, Nannie, Nannie!" she cried softly. "You're just the same. You haven't changed at all."

"Oh, my darlin'!" said Nannie as she emerged from the smothering young arms that enveloped her. And then she stood her off and looked at her.

"Oh, my little darlin'! How you've growed up. I'd scarce know you. And yet, you've the same big eyes. Yes, it's you yerself, darlin'!"

And then appeared Randa on the scene, solid, shy, but with eyes full of joy. Randa, grown to be a woman, capable and strong and ready to take all burdens from her mother's frail arms, fully aware of her responsibilities now that her mother was growing old.

"Dad! Come here! See who's come! Our Miss Mary, all lovely and golden and grown up," she called.

Then came old Orrin, eagerly, to greet her.

"Oh, my little lady! You have come at last to claim your own. We have been hankerin' after you, my dear! All's right now with an Arden in the old house again!"

They drew her into the living room at last and seated her in the best chair, and flocked around her, as if to show her that now at last they had their own again.

Then, although it seemed early to Mary, it was time to get supper. She remembered that she was in the country now.

"There's some fried mush ready for the griddle," said Nannie.

"Fried mush!" reproved the embarrassed Randa, red showing in her solid square face. "A city lady wouldn't eat the like of that!"

"Oh, but I *would*. I'd *love* it," cried Mary. "I always remembered it as the best thing I ever ate. I've begged our cook to make it for me but she always says she doesn't know how. And once the maid said she knew how, but it didn't taste like yours. Let me have some. It makes me hungry just to think about it. And may I have a glass of milk with it? Do you still have Taffy the cow?"

"We have Taffy's calf—we call her M'lasses," laughed Nannie, "and she gives wonderful milk. Come out in the kitchen an' see!"

"Oh, but mom, don't you want I should set a place in the dining room?" protested Randa, her precise brows and straight hair fairly bristling with disapproval of her mother's informality.

"No," put in Mary. "I want to eat in the kitchen the

way we used to do when we had fried mush and wanted it hot off the griddle."

So they went joyously to the kitchen.

The two old people sat there beaming. Their little girl was back unchanged and happy to be with them. This was what they had been wanting but had scarcely dared to hope for, and now that she was here they felt as if they were in a dream.

She insisted that they sit down with her. "I hate to eat alone!" she cried.

So even Randa delightedly succumbed though she was firm about being the one to hop up and tend to the griddle.

They were consuming an enormous amount of the delicious fried mush. The big bowl was almost empty now. Only a few more slices left, and the bowl had been full. Usually it lasted for two or sometimes three days. But oh how good it tasted to them all, enjoying it together, with plenty of Orrin's fresh garden peas and a big dish of fluffy scrambled eggs from their own hens.

And then suddenly the back door opened and a tall young man stepped in with a cheery good evening and set a brimming pail of milk down.

"Got your pans ready, Randa?" he called laughingly, and then suddenly he realized there was a stranger there. A stranger? Or was she a stranger? His merry face fairly shone.

"Mary Arden!" he cried. "As I live! Is it really you, Merry Arden, or am I dreaming?" He came over toward her with a joyful welcome, that matched her own glad look, both his hands extended.

"And you look just like yourself when I went away, the day you and your father came down to see me off and you gave me that farewell kiss! Do you remember?"

Mary's face flamed scarlet and her eyes were dancing.

"It's Laurie Judson!" she exclaimed joyously. "The very same Jud, come home again."

"Yes, and don't I rate a welcome kiss? For bringing myself home alive?"

Mary hesitated an instant, then suddenly lifted her laughing face with lips delicately offered, as she gaily answered, "Why of course," and received in return a courteous, grateful, almost reverent salute. Even the fun was subdued as he lifted his head and gave a quick glance around among the old servants to make sure they had understood, and that there was nothing impertinent in what he had done.

But Nannie and her family had not lived all these years with such people as the Ardens without having developed a discernment beyond most people, and they understood and sanctioned the action with tender smiles.

But suddenly Mary's cheeks grew rosier, and her eyes filled with a gentle wonder. Oh, Mary had been kissed before, even since she grew up, but seldom according to her liking. Brooke Haven had been the last offender in that line, and the memory of his fervent lips upon hers was one of the strong reasons why she had run away to Arden for the summer. And now, what was this that she had done?

Yet study her old friend searchingly as she could she saw nothing offensive in his attitude. There was, instead, a look upon him as if he had received a sudden benediction.

Ah! After all, he was her old childhood friend, older by four years or more than herself. Doubtless he still felt her to be but a child. She had often gone out and helped rake the yard with him when he was earning money toward his college expenses. No doubt she had only hindered him but they had had lots of fun at it.

He had lived next door to her grandfather, in a rambling, cosy farmhouse that made no pretense at being a mansion; that fact in her mother's eyes would be a terrible drawback to her having anything to do with him. She recalled that her father had spoken of him as coming from a fine family and that his father was a former classmate of her father in college. But of course mother would know nothing of all this. Mother never paid attention to details like this if she chose to put someone out of her "class" as she called it. And somehow Mary felt condemned before her mother, as if by kissing Laurie she had transgressed some law of good breeding, which was about the only law her mother reckoned to be of any great value. She suddenly felt as if her mother had just walked into the room and were looking at her, and it made her self-conscious and silent. Then she became aware that the young man was looking at her earnestly. There was something questioning, almost troubled in his glance and she gave him a lovely smile, as if she had understood his question and were reassuring him.

He turned then to Randa.

"Where are your pans, Randa? Shall I pour this milk into them for you?" he asked pleasantly as if she too were a young woman worthy of attention. Randa appreciated this attitude of his, and gave him back frank friendliness, but only that.

So he carried the pail into the wide cool buttery where the pans stood, and poured the milk for her, and then came back to the kitchen.

"Well, I'm terribly glad you've come back, Mary," he said, just as if it were only the other day when she'd been fifteen or so and he about to go away to war. "I hope we'll be seeing something of each other now and then. I'm still looking after the cows when I can get down this way for a few minutes. Can I take your bags up before I go? I have classes all this evening."

He gathered up the bags as if they had no weight at all, and Mary took in the broadness of his shoulders, and his fine upstanding figure as she passed him to lead the way up to her room.

Upstairs he put the bags down and stood a minute by the door before Nannie came puffing up the stairs.

"Mary," he said in a low tone, "you aren't angry, are you? You didn't mind that I kissed you, did you? I really meant no disrespect. I forgot you are grown up now and it was just so wonderful to see you again."

"Of course not, Laurie!" She smiled straight back into his eyes.

"I'll be seeing you soon," he said relieved, and went whistling cheerily down the stairs.

Mary, upstairs, stepped softly over to the window and looked out, watching the young man as he walked thoughtfully down to the gate and swung out into the highway.

She was getting a new view of her old-time friend and remembering that merry kiss he had given her which so electrically had turned into a grave tender kiss. Did he realize that? Had he sensed it too, and was that why he had seemed to think he must apologize?

Then as she heard Nannie coming briskly from the linen closet with her arms full of towels, she turned sharply from the window and from her strange unexpected thoughts. This was ridiculous of course. He was just an old friend, and she would always think of him that way, no matter what, and she must not harbor silly thoughts any more. She must be getting morbid with all she had been through. No, she would just be glad and not think such foolishness any more.

2

BUT Nannie had caught a glimpse of her dear Mary looking out of the window at the moonlit lawn, and her quick mind figured out what Mary was thinking.

"That's a mighty fine young man," she remarked casually, as if they had just been talking about him. "Do you know he's that thoughtful for his old friends that when he found out Orrin's knees were hurting him, he just walks all this way down here every night to save him milking. And mornings too, so Randa won't have to do it. That's a lot to do for old friends who are just working folks, and he what he is! There's not many would even remember just old servants. It's a long walk to take twice a day, and him in his good clothes mostly."

"Long walk?" said Mary looking puzzled. "But doesn't he live just next door where he used to?"

"No. Not any more after his father died." Mary had a feeling that Nannie was about to say more in explanation, then thought better of it. "I miss them a lot," went on Nannie after a troubled pause. "Mrs. Judson is a sweet body and was always doing kind things, just like her boy. They live over the other side of the highway in that new development. Orrin took me over the day they moved in. I wanted to take her a loaf of bread and a fresh apple pie I baked. Their house is very small but it's clean and new. I'd think Mrs. Judson would feel terrible cramped after the big rooms at the farm but she don't make no complaint." Nannie's brow puckered again in a little troubled frown but she offered no more information.

"But what's Laurie doing, Nannie? Isn't he working somewhere?"

"Why yes, they say he has a fine job. It's something about a thing they call radar. Ever hear about it?"

"Oh, yes! I've heard about radar. It's pretty important I guess. A job like that ought to pay well. But Nannie, he said he had to go to a class. Did he mean he's teaching something?"

"No, he's not teaching. He's studying, hisself."

"Studying! But Nannie, I thought he graduated from college! He'd had two years already when I was here last."

"Oh yes, he went to college, but he didn't get all through at first 'count o' the war. You know he was called and he hadta go and so he hadta finish when he got back. He graduated all right, but he's still at the studyin'."

"Oh, is he trying for a higher degree?" asked Mary with respect in her tone.

"Well, you'll just havta ask him," said Nannie with a satisfied smile. "He mebbe can make you understand. But I'll tell you what I think he has in mind. I think he wants ta get ta be a preacher, and that's what he's studying for."

"A preacher! You mean he wants to be a minister?" asked Mary in astonishment. "Why, I never knew he was religious."

"Oh yes, he was. Even when he was a boy. Don't you mind how he used to be so conscientious? Nobody ever doubted his word, and you could always trust him. And he didn't swear like the other boys."

"Yes, he was good," said Mary thoughtfully, "but that's not exactly being religious."

"Well, I s'pose not, but then it's a part of it. A person can't be religious and go around swearing and lying and stealing and killing."

"No, of course not," said Mary, "but then Laurie always was so full of fun and laughter. It would seem strange to think of him preaching."

"I don't know's there's anything in the Bible that says a Christian minister can't laugh and be happy," said Nannie, a bit belligerently.

"Well, perhaps not," said Mary. "I never thought about it, but all the ministers I've met seemed rather old and grim. That's the reason I never cared to go to service in college, because the old chaplain was always so severe and lofty. He used to look at us girls as if he saw sins written all over our faces, and I used to go around a whole block to escape having to meet him. I can't think of Laurie ever getting to be old and grim like that."

"He won't!" said Nannie with assurance. "And I can tell you the folks in his chapel where he preaches don't feel that way about him. They're just crazy about him, and are always rushing right to him whenever they have any trouble knowing he always can find a way out for them."

"Chapel!" said Mary in astonishment. "Do you mean to say he preaches now?"

"Oh yes. He's been preaching ever since he came back from war. He ain't through studyin' yet, but he's got him a little chapel where the minister moved away and it's full every Sunday. Orrin and I go there all the time now, and what he says is good! You'd be surprised. Orrin and I decided we'd rather hear him preach than any minister we ever heard."

"Why, that's wonderful!" said Mary with amazement in her voice. "I'd like to hear him."

"Well, you certainly shall if you want to," said the old servant, happy that there was something pleasant she could give her child to entertain her. "But you wouldn't want to go to church with us!"

"I certainly would, Nannie. Don't you know I'm not like that? I'd love to go with you, you know that! If it's such a grand church that they have to judge me by who I'm with I certainly wouldn't want to go."

"Oh, it's not a grand church, lambkin, it's just a very plain little chapel, and they're all plain people. But I thought you might not like to go with us."

"Now Nannie! You know better than that. Why do you think I came here at all if I didn't want to see you again and be with you?"

"There, my lambkin, I knew you wouldn't be like that. And besides you've got your own pretty car. We could go in that, and Orrin could be your driver if you want a chauffeur."

"Why, of course, we can go in any car, sometimes one, sometimes the other. I'm not a snob, Nannie, and we won't talk like that any more. I came down to visit you and to look my house over. I may stay all summer if it seems best. Will you mind that?"

"Mind! Dear child, I'd be only too happy! I hadn't dared hope that you would come again, and to have a whole summer with you will be wonderful."

"Well, I'm not sure about how long I can stay. My mother wants very much that I should come up to Castanza where she will be, but I've been there a great many summers, and I did so want to try another summer here."

"Blessed child!" said the old woman, throwing her loving arms around the young shoulders, and patting her gently until Mary looked up and smiled.

"And now, child, you must get to your bed. You're tired as you can be, and this is no way to take care of you to let you stay up till all hours."

So Mary went to her rest, and lay at last in the big four-poster bed that used to be her great admiration. She was here again, and it was good to lie down and stretch out, and relax.

Then her thoughts drifted over the happenings of the last few hours since she had arrived, and she remembered again the young man Laurie, her old admiration, now grown into a man with a fine dependable face and a merry look. And soon he would be a regular full-fledged minister, perhaps! Laurie! It seemed incredible. And then she remembered the laughing kiss she had given him, a minister! Just the way the fresh girls she despised would have done. What had she been thinking of to do it! Well, forget it. He doubtless took it just as a joke, too. Although he had seemed troubled lest she was angry. Well, she probably wouldn't see him much anyway, and if she did she would be most discreet. She didn't want him to think she had grown into a silly modern girl who went around flirting. But she wouldn't see him much of course, since they had moved away. She would like to hear him preach once though. Perhaps she and Nannie could manage it unobtrusively, and slip out during a closing hymn.

So she dropped off to sleep, planning to waken early in the morning and enjoy the new day.

But the sun stole a march on her and had climbed high before she awoke. Nannie had kept everything very quiet about the house so that she might have a good sleep after her long drive.

The house was full of a delicious fragrance of fresh-baked bread and something spicy and sweet. She had visions of loaves of brown and white bread, delicious looking pies, maybe a pudding, brown and delectable, and a big round cake with icing, the way it used to be when grandmother was alive. How she had loved the fragrance of the wide old kitchen. She used to feast her eyes on the table where stood the finished product of Nannie's morning baking. She hurried down to see it before it was put away in bread box and cake closet.

Nannie greeted her with a happy smile, and a bright good morning, and motioned her toward the table where was set a plate with new baked brown bread and butter, a glass of rich creamy milk, and a bunch of ripe red cherries.

"Just a little snack to keep you till lunch time," she said with a motherly smile. "It won't be so long now. Orrin generally comes in a little before twelve. You see, we don't keep fashionable hours here, but if you want any change you've just to say what you like and we'll change."

"Oh, no," said Mary. "I like the old ways, the way grandmother had them. That's why I came this summer. I wanted to get back to that dear time."

The old servant gave her a quick appreciative look. Mary was still a sweet unspoiled girl, loving and kind as her father used to be when he was a boy, liking simple joys. Well, that was going to be a comfort. But how long would that high and mighty mother of hers let her stay on here? Not long likely, but at least she would enjoy her while she had her, and if she was anything at all like the rest of the Arden family, the chances were she would remain fine and good even when she grew as old as her fussy mother.

So Nannie contented herself and set about getting ready for a good time while it lasted.

As soon as Mary had finished her delicious breakfast she went out the kitchen door and stood on the old flagstone platform that formed the lower step, and revisioned the old days again. She took a quick trip around the yard, just to take it all in, and then she came into the house.

"What time does the postman come, Nannie?" she asked.

"Oh, he's been here already while you were sleeping. He'll not be here again till between one and two o'clock. Would you be expecting some letters?"

"Oh, no, I was just thinking I ought to write some. You see I came away in rather a hurry, and there are a few things I ought to attend to. I think I'll send a telegram to mother. She might get uneasy about me you know, driving all alone. Though she isn't very scary."

"No?" said Nannie in a tone that was aware of the type of mother Mary had, and was merely assenting.

So Mary sent off her telegram to her mother, and then spent a little while writing notes to the various people who had invited her to officiate at their important festivities. Floss Fairlee was obviously the first one, because that wedding was probably just in the offing and someone would have to take her place. She must let Floss know at once.

Dear Floss:—

As you can see by my address, I am at Arden. I came away a little sooner than I had anticipated, and that is why I did not get in touch with you before I left. I haven't picked up my strength yet from that illness this spring and when I went to the doctor for a check-up he said I should get away as soon as possible. I am planning to stay here at the old home in Arden all summer and try to get my pep back.

Now I don't know whether you are planning for your wedding any time soon or not, or whether you still have me down for maid of honor. I think it was perfectly sweet of you to ask me to do that and I only wish I could. But I won't be able to do it if you are married this summer, and so I am writing you at the earliest possible moment to give you a chance to get someone else. I know I shall miss a lot of fun, and it's an honor I hate to hand over to someone else, but it just can't be me, this time. I'm sorry.

Let me know, though, when the date is, and write me all the plans! I shall be thinking of you and wishing you all the happiness possible.

Lovingly,
As ever, Mary.

Mary read the letter over when it was finished and a great burden rolled from her shoulders. With the writing of that letter she felt that the worst was over. Now Jinnie Randall's birthday dinner came next, for that was soon. And then Earle Warren's party. All these important dates could be gotten out of the way before her mother was likely to object to her cancelling them. More and more as her pen flew over the paper wiping her calendar free from engagements that would make it imperative for her to get to Castanza at a certain date, her heart grew lighter.

Yet it did trouble her when she had finished them all and put them down in the post box at the gate for the postman to take on his next round, to realize how disappointed her mother would be about all this. Mother did want her to be popular, and sought after. But it was getting to be such a burden, especially with Brooke Haven in such constant attendance. She simply must stay away this summer and get her bearings and feel free to plan her own life. When her father came home he would surely be able to make her mother understand.

She was surprised to hear the little silver bell ringing for lunch. She hadn't realized how late it was.

But she did justice to the delicious lunch. Just old-fashioned rice pancakes and honey, tiny little sausages such as she used to remember, more cherries to finish off with. How good everything tasted!

"And now what can I do to help?" she asked when at last she finished the last mouthful of delicate pancake and took a good drink of the delicious milk. "Let me wash the dishes, won't you? You know I'm not very well versed in much housework, but surely I couldn't do any harm washing a few dishes."

Randa smiled and her honest blue eyes twinkled as if it were a joke.

"How do you think I'd feel letting you get your pretty hands all red and rough, when I've been used to it all my life? No, Miss Mary, you are the lady here and I am the servant."

"But I don't feel that way, Randa!"

"But *I* do!" said Randa very decidedly. "If you should insist on doing my work I'd simply have to go away and get another job somewhere."

"Randa! How silly! You don't mean that!"

"I certainly do!" said Randa with a setting of her chin that meant insurmountable determination.

"Oh, Randa! I'm sorry. I didn't mean to hurt you. But I do want to be doing something helpful. You know I can't just sit around and do nothing. I've got to have some part in the house while I'm here. What are you going to do next after you get the dishes washed?"

"Why, I'm going down to the store to do the shopping for the day."

"Well, then, couldn't I take you down in my car? That would be fun, and it would certainly be better than having you carry a lot of big bundles up. Then your father wouldn't have to go out while his knee is still lame."

And so it was finally arranged and Mary and Randa started off amicably. Randa settled down to enjoy herself, amazed to find that she was wrong, and Mary really wanted to be friendly. So Mary learned a little about how to pick out vegetables and meat and fruit. Shopping for food was something she had never experienced before, and she certainly enjoyed it. Then when the shopping was over Mary suggested that they take a little ride if Randa had time.

"Just to show me any changes that have come in the town since I was here. Have you time?"

Randa's tense expression softened.

"Why, yes," she said hesitantly, "I guess so, if we don't stay more than a half hour. I've got to get back to get those chickens on to cook or they won't be tender."

So they took a ride, and Randa showed her all the new houses and told her a lot of the family history of the people who were living in them.

"And now," said Randa, "before we head home perhaps you'd like to see Laurie Judson's church."

"Why yes," said Mary, "I would. And the house the Judsons bought. Your mother told me about it."

"Oh, that. Yes, it's right up that street on the top of the hill. Real cosy house, I think. But it seems lonesome on our street without them, and I think they miss their old friends too."

"Yes," said Mary. "It does seem too bad. I always hate changes in a nice neighborhood."

"I don't like changes either. It was awful hard when your grandmother passed away. It just seemed as if life couldn't go on. My mother and father were all beat out."

"Yes," said Mary sadly, "I felt that way too, though of course I hadn't seen her in a long time. But she made my visit here so wonderful that I felt I had to come back this summer, and live it all over again, and do you know, just in the short time I've been here I feel as if grandmother were still here. Her spirit seems to sort of hover over things."

"Say, do you feel that way too?" asked Randa.

"Yes, I felt that way this morning when I came down the stairs. I can't get myself to forget any of the little things she taught me to do about the house. Of course when I was a little girl I used to think some things she insisted on were unnecessary, but afterwards I found why she made some of these rules. And now I can't seem to get away from them. I've tried to tell myself that was superstition, but still I don't know as it is."

Randa looked at the other girl admiringly.

"That sounds awful nice, and I guess that's true, but I couldn't have said it as handsomely as you did. I suppose that's because you've gone to college. I wish I could have had a good education. But then, what difference would it have made? I was born a cook and houseworker, I guess."

"But that's important, too. What would become of us all if somebody didn't like cooking? But there's no reason why you can't have more education too, Randa. Do you like to read?"

"Not so much," said the older girl with a sigh. "I might if I knew what books to pick out. But I never bothered with books much. There was always so much to be done that there wasn't time."

"Well, we'll have to find some books you like," said Mary. "I've brought some delightful books with me. I'm quite sure we can find something you will like. And now where is that chapel you talked about?"

"Just down this next street," said Randa. "It isn't a grand church you know, but it's very pleasant inside and I think it looks mighty cosy."

Mary studied the little plain church with interest. It was not large nor ostentatious, just built of the native stone and without adornment. But the lines of the building were good, and there was an honest simplicity about it that somehow reminded Mary of Laurie Judson although of course he couldn't have had anything to do with building it.

And then as if her thoughts had reached Randa's mind the older girl said:

"Mr. Bowers built it, you know, in memory of his little girl who used to go to Sunday School there. She died when she was a little thing and her father was terribly upset. He and his wife are regular attendants there, and very much interested in the work. He is always doing something nice for the Sunday School. Gave a whole library once."

Somehow the sight of that little simple church gave Mary a new view of the boy who used to be her friend, and she was silent almost all the rest of the way home. It was Randa who rambled on, giving little side lights of the services that she had attended in that chapel. Telling more than she dreamed of the young man who was its earnest young pastor, more than she had any conception she was revealing.

"He goes to a town twenty miles away, twice a week," she announced, as they turned into the home street, "to some kind of a Bible School. That's why he won't come to milk tonight. He offered to send somebody else, but Pa told him his knee was better now and it wasn't necessary any more. He's awful kind that way. He doesn't need ta come. He knew I could milk whenever Pa wasn't well enough. But he just comes, that's all. It seems somehow as if he was fond of us all, just for old times' sake. Why, when Ma was sick the month he got home from overseas, he usta bring her white grapes and things like that that he knew she never would likely get anywhere. He knew we didn't get down to shop very often, and anyway, it wasn't our way to buy white grapes and things out of season. But you'd be surprised to know how much Ma enjoyed 'em. Now here we are, and I've got ta get those chickens in ta cook or they'll be tough and Ma never would forgive me for feeding you tough chickens."

Two days later Laurie came back. He dropped in around suppertime with the full pail of milk, his face on a broad grin.

"Stole a march on you, didn't I?" he said giving a genial wink toward Orrin. "But I guess it won't hurt you to have another night's rest, will it? And M'lasses seemed real glad to see me."

"Well then, you've just got to stay to supper," said Nannie, ostentatiously setting a place for him at the table.

It was a cheery supper table, and Mary enjoyed every minute of the time he stayed.

"I saw your church," she said, "and I'm coming pretty soon to hear you preach!"

The young man gave her a quick keen look, as if he wondered about it.

"I'm not much of a preacher," he said simply. "I'm just trying to do a little witnessing."

Mary looked at him questioningly as if she didn't quite understand.

"It's what we're told to do, you know, be witnesses."

But just then the doorbell rang announcing the arrival of some neighbors who had come to call on Mary because they had known her family for years, and Mary had to go without waiting to find out what he meant by witnessing.

Laurie declined to come into the living room to meet the callers.

"Sorry," he said, "I've a great deal of studying to do. I'll have to skip home very soon. You'll excuse me, I know. I shall be looking for you at church. Good night."

There was a disappointed feeling in her, but she went to the living room to meet her callers, and they filled her mind with other thoughts. There were some young people among them, and the home of her heritage seemed to be taking on new form, and filling in the empty places that memory did not supply. She saw that she was not going to be lonely here in Arden. It was a normal pleasant town. She must write to her mother in the morning and tell her about it all. Of course her mother did not want her to like it, she knew that, but she must be true to her plans and make an honest pleasant picture of it all. Perhaps some day when her father returned they would all come back there to live. Wouldn't mother like it then? There would likely be bridge clubs here as there were everywhere. And best of all there would be no Brooke Haven, for he was the burden she desired most of all to be rid of.

But would her mother like Laurie Judson? Of course Laurie was not in the position of an ardent suitor, but would her mother tolerate even a casual occasional friendship? Or would she remember that he had once cut the grass for Mary's grandfather, and because of that count him a "working man"? She must remember to say nothing about her having known him before. At least not now.

3

THE CALLERS stayed late. When they were gone Mary found that Laurie had also been sometime gone. She was disappointed; she had wanted to ask him some questions about the thing he called "witnessing." He had seemed to expect that she would understand what he meant by it. She puzzled over it quite a bit, while she was preparing for rest, but did not seem to find any explanation of the word. Some sort of a religious word it must be, that had a special meaning. She wished she knew what it meant. But there was no one she felt like asking. It did not seem as if it would be something that Randa would understand, even if she were willing to show her own ignorance by asking. So she went to sleep trying to puzzle it out, and thinking with satisfaction that tomorrow was Sunday and perhaps there would be something said in the church service that would make her understand.

It was a pleasant sunny day to which she awoke the next morning, with a clear golden light in the air and a clear sharp sparkle in the sunshine. A day of loveliness with joy in the air, and a breathless waiting note for something good or better to come as the day went on.

Mary felt a great happiness in her heart as she awoke. She did not stop to question why it was, she just knew it was there, and was satisfied at that. She hoped the day would fulfill it and make it really a happy time. But when she came to think it over and examine herself she couldn't believe that just the thought of going to church was making her happy. It had never made her happy before just to go to church. But of course, someone she knew, an old friend, was going to preach, and that seemed really funny. She couldn't somehow think of the merry boy she used to rake leaves with, and climb trees and play ball with, preaching, unless he was doing it as some kind of joke. And somehow her soul rejected such a thought in connection with Laurie.

There was a cheery atmosphere in the house, for the old servants were very happy at the thought of taking their beloved little lady to their church. Even the breakfast seemed to be a gala affair. Strawberries, the finest of the season, fresh from the garden, tiny sausages, nice little brown potato balls, and waffles for a fine finish. There never was such a breakfast, Mary thought as she enjoyed every mouthful.

There had been no letters for her since she arrived except a cold little note from her mother, still utterly disapproving her daughter's action.

"I'm sure I hope you're enjoying your crazy action in going off to the country when your duty and certainly your pleasure, all lie in another direction. However you did it yourself, and you'll have to bear the consequences. I hope you won't rue the day you made this stubborn decision."

It was not a loving letter, and Mary's lips closed firmly to keep them from trembling. She couldn't bear to have a difference between herself and her dear mother.

But then she told herself things were no different from

what they had been when she left home. Her mother was only hoping that the separation might have made a difference in her feeling and that she would soon change her mind and return. She knew her mother's methods very well, and though during her short life she had seldom gone directly contrary to her mother's expressed wishes, she knew the time had come to stick to her decision. If Brooke Haven had not been so much concerned in the matter she might have given in, but Brooke was there and she felt she must do something definite about it.

So although her mother's letter had troubled her from time to time, she had managed to keep it in the back of her mind, especially this bright Sunday morning. She flew around after breakfast, tidying her room, making her bed, and getting ready for church. Now and again trilling a bit of a song half under her breath. She didn't know the songs Randa sang very well, hymn tunes. She had not been drilled in that kind of music, and she was extremely desirous of not doing anything that would break the holy quiet of that day in the dear old house. She almost felt as if her grandmother were alive again and sitting in her comfortable rocking chair across the hall.

The ride to church seemed a pleasant thing to the girl who had been brought up to very little churchgoing, and that attended by a formal mother who went occasionally because it was the thing to do among many of her associates. Going in a costly limousine with a liveried uniform on the front seat was somehow more of a form than going in her own car with the honored servants as attendants. Somehow the day seemed brighter and the sunshine warmer, the birds more tuneful, than any Sunday she remembered, and she felt in her heart that she was glad she had carried out her plan and come here to this dear place.

There was none of the stately formality of her mother's church in the little white chapel where they presently arrived, and she drew a breath of relief as they parked the car and got out.

And straightway they walked into a friendly atmosphere. The people did not look at the house servants as if they were servants. They treated them as if they were Christian brothers and sisters. There were several as well dressed as her own mother would have been if she had been there; and some whom she had heard mentioned as being friends of her grandmother. They welcomed her most heartily, and she could see that Nannie and Orrin had a respected standing among them all, old retainers of a much beloved family. She felt from the first that she was in a happy friendly atmosphere. Everything simple and plain but comfortable. A sweet-faced girl was at the cabinet organ playing the hymns and the singing was from the heart. Mary was surprised that such plain unsophisticated people could yet make a melody that seemed like real worship. Although Mary had very little idea of what real worship was, yet her heart was convinced that this was.

For the first few minutes Mary did not see Laurie, though she was looking around with a vague idea of seeing him in a gown and gravity, and she couldn't help wondering how that could be.

Then she saw him coming toward the plain little desk that served as a pulpit, dressed in a plain blue suit. No pretense of superiority, no posing as a divine. Just Laurie, and she looked at him in wonder, as he sat down behind the desk and bowed his head for a moment's prayer. As he lifted it there was a sweet look of light on his face, as if he had just exchanged a word with his Lord whom he was about to serve.

It was a beautiful look, and Mary instantly lost that half fear she had had that Laurie would be just playing a part, an irreverence that she had half dreaded, although when one has nothing but form in place of religion it is difficult to understand why there would be any sense of shock at the lack of it.

Then he rose and instantly every head was bowed for the beautiful humble prayer that followed, a prayer that gave Mary the feeling that God was there, as she had never felt in any of the more formal churches she had attended. Laurie was speaking as if he knew God well, as if the whole congregation were well beloved of the Father, and suddenly Mary felt that she too might be a part of this petition if she would. And involuntarily she recognized the invisible Presence that for the first time in her life she felt was real.

And then Mary Arden began to take out some of those painful thoughts she had hitherto avoided, and look at them honestly. For they were her other reason, besides escape from Brooke Haven, for wanting to take refuge in Arden this summer. During this last winter in college a classmate of hers had died very suddenly. She was not an especially close friend of Mary's, but she knew her fairly well as a girl who was rather wild in her social life and who delighted in risque situations. It had happened to be Mary who was alone with the girl just before she died. The girl's terror at the thought of death facing her was indescribably horrible to Mary. She had tried to soothe her with quiet words and tell her to take courage, but Mary found during that desperate hour that that was not enough to give a soul about to go out into the dark.

Mary had sent for the chaplain of the college, but he

was out playing golf and the girl was gone before he reached her. She had gone with a moan and a curse on her lips. For a time Mary could not get the scene out of her mind.

And so now, although the desire was still vague in her mind, she had hoped that at Arden she might somehow recover for herself whatever it was that had sustained her grandmother and grandfather and made them the fine characters they were. They had lived such brave lives full of troubles, including the loss of a little son. But their lives had also had a full measure of peace.

So she found herself listening intently, almost desperately, for a note of reality and sincerity that would give her assurance to go on in her search for—whatever it was she felt she needed.

Nannie stole a shy sweet adoring look at Mary now and again, and was satisfied. She had so hoped that Mary would like this service. Of course everything was simple, and plain, and not at all what Mary would be supposed to be used to at home, but was she enough unspoiled to see the beauty in their beloved service?

Laurie was at the door at the close of service with his own wide beautiful smile, and his warm handclasp, making every member feel that the smile and the greeting were personal.

Quietly they went home; scarcely a word was spoken by any of them until they got out of the car. There was an almost holy look on each of their faces. Even old Orrin looked as if he had been blest.

The silence except for necessary questions, lasted until they sat down to dinner, and Orrin had bowed his gray head in a slow hesitant blessing, during which a new truth entered Mary's mind. This something with which she had today come in touch down at the little church was something they all had, themselves. Therefore it was doubly real.

That afternoon after the dinner was cleared away, the household settled down to quiet, and Mary in her room wrote a few more letters, making it plain to a number of her friends at home that she would be away all summer. She had a feeling that this would save complications if her mother tried to change her plans. For now Mary was sure she wanted to stay here all summer. She wanted very much to look into this matter of a God and find out if it was true that just anyone could get to know Him. Now she had an overwhelming desire to settle this matter right away, while her mind was on it and her interest stirred. If she waited and had to go back to some of those tiresome parties, perhaps she might not be able to get back to the same point of view and give this thing a real try out.

This matter being settled, she went to the little book-case in her room to find a book to read, and there right on the top shelf was a soft old Bible, undoubtedly her grandmother's.

She took it down with reverent hands and turned its worn pages softly. It seemed a great thing to be handling grandmother's Bible. She had never owned one of her own, except a little Testament acquired in a briefly attended Sunday School. It had been amusedly stuck away high in the closet, with a casual remark about how silly it was to give a thing like that to a mere baby. But she had always grieved over that, and once long years after, she found it among some dusty books in the attic and retrieved it, hiding it safely away among her private treasures. It was not that she had at that time entertained any great reverence for the Bible, but it was something that was connected with her little-girl life, a recognition that she had been a bona fide member of a certain

Sunday School. So she had put it safely away, but she had never read it. In fact it was almost too fine print to read. It was just a thing with a bright red cover, now stained with age and lack of care, that stood for something in her past. She recognized that her mother would say it was silly sentimentality, superstition, but she had treasured it. So now as she took out her grandmother's old Bible and handled it reverently, it seemed somehow connected with her own little old discarded Testament.

As she turned the thin pages worn by the dear fingers, her eyes caught the words "And this is life eternal, that they might know Thee, the only true God, and Jesus Christ whom Thou hast sent."

She paused and read the words over again. Why, that was what the sermon had been about. That very verse had been read!

She read it over again and tried to remember some of the things her preacher-friend had said.

Then she heard the others stirring about downstairs, putting dishes on the table. Was it possible that it was near to tea time? She put the Bible away carefully, slipping a bit of paper in the place where she had been reading. Strange, she had never known before how interesting a book the Bible was. She wondered if it was as interesting everywhere as the place where she had been reading. It seemed a pretty big book. Perhaps she would start some time pretty soon and try to read it through.

Then she ran a comb through her curls and hurried down to see if she could be of any use.

She was delighted to find that the whole family were planning to go to church again that night, for the taste she had had that morning made her eager to hear more. Perhaps she had an intuition that her pleasant interlude into freedom and a world that was all so new to her might possibly be interrupted, and she was anxious to get into the real heart of this life if there was any fear she might be snatched away and put back into the world that her mother had chosen for her. She just wanted to make sure that this new life which she had barely glimpsed was really worth while.

The night service was even more interesting than the morning one had been, perhaps because she had been reading and thinking about it, and she found that she understood much better this time, and that it was just as intriguing as before. It was incredible that this should have been in the world and she so far have seen nothing of it. How was it that nothing of this sort had been taught in college? What a difference it might have made to that girl who had died. They had had a course in Bible there, though it hadn't interested Mary and she had chosen psychology instead, which seemed far more popular with the students.

Monday morning things began to happen.

First there came a special delivery letter from Floss.

Mary dear, you saved my life! Not that I didn't want you for my maid of honor just as we planned, for I still do. But something has occurred that put me in a hole and I just didn't know what to do about it until your letter came saying that you wouldn't be able to be back here all summer.

You see, my cousin Sue has arrived most unexpectedly from California and she says that she promised long ago to come on for my wedding and be my maid of honor. Of course I don't remember that for I must have been quite young when that happened, and I don't really know her so very well, but when she started to unpack and get out this perfect duck of a dress she says she had made especially for my wedding, I just didn't know what to do, for Dad was standing there looking awfully pleased. She is the only one of his close relatives who has ever been here much. I knew he would feel hurt if I told her someone else already had that place, so I just smiled and passed it off, but I knew the reckoning would come the next day when mother found out, although really she cares more for what your mother thinks than for anything else. I had my mind all made up to tell Sue about you this morning when nobody was around. And then your letter came!

Of course I feel terribly bad you are not going to be here, but certainly your letter helped me out a lot. You understand, I'm sure, and won't mind that we aren't having the wedding fun together after all. Of course I know it was hard to plan things exactly when I wasn't sure when Jim would get here. But now it looks as if it might be pretty soon, so I'm hurrying everything to be ready if—

Mary laid down the letter with a sigh of satisfaction. Now everything was fixed and mother wouldn't feel bad when she found out that she had written to Floss and cancelled that maid of honor business. Of course it was an important wedding; Flossie's family were an important family, and her own mother had been proud that Mary had been selected for the honorable position, and had talked a good deal about it, advising about the color and style of the garment she was to wear. But so far nothing definite had been done, because the bridegroom was so uncertain in his coming. Well, at least she had her reprieve.

But just after lunch there arrived a special delivery letter from her mother which threw everything into a dither.

Dear Mary:

You are to get the first plane you can for home. Floss has just had word that her fiancé will be home in a few days now, and perhaps be ordered away again almost immediately. Her mother phoned me that she was getting everything ready for a swift wedding if necessary. So Mary, come home quickly! I have just phoned our dressmaker to be ready to make alterations in that aqua dress we looked at last week, and I called the store and had them send it up. Of course if you and Floss prefer another color you can likely find something. But don't wait. Get the first reservation you can. This is important. Don't fail me! I mean what I say.

Mother.

Mary read the letter with a puzzled expression. Surely Floss must by this time have told her mother that she wasn't coming to the wedding!

Well, anyway, this thing had to be settled at once!

So she went to the telephone and called long distance, but after some delay was told that her mother was not at home. She had gone to Chicago to take someone's place making a speech at an important convention. And no, Hetty didn't know the address, nor just when she would be home. She had spoken as if it might be a couple of days before she could get back.

"But she said you would likely be home tonight, and I was to show you just what changes she thought ought to be made in the dress. And Miss Renaud wants to get the measurements at once so she can get an early start."

"But Hetty," urged Mary, "I am not coming to that wedding."

"But your mother said I was to insist upon your

coming. She said you did not realize what you were doing to everybody."

"Listen, Hetty," explained Mary. "I wrote to Floss the very day after I got here that I could not possibly get back, and she is entirely satisfied. She has asked her cousin from California to take my place, and she understands the situation perfectly."

"But Miss Mary, your mother made me promise that I would make you understand this was something you simply had to do. She said there were several reasons why you couldn't afford to stay away from this wedding, reasons that would affect other people——"

"Yes, I know, Hetty, but I'm not coming! Please tell mother not to worry, I'll make it all right with everybody. And Hetty, you telephone Miss Renaud and call off her appointment, and also telephone the store and tell them not to send the dress."

"But Miss Mary, if I do all that your mamma will be very angry with me. She will think I have failed her."

"Oh, no, she won't, Hetty. I'll tell her it was all my fault."

"Oh, but Miss Mary, you never was like this before, not when your mamma wanted something important."

"I'm sorry, Hetty," said Mary firmly, "but I know what I'm doing. And please don't let the chauffeur come down after my car, for I need it here, and he'll just have an extra trip on the train if he comes."

Mary hung up at last with a sigh. It was not easy to argue with her mother's trained servants, whom she had all her life been expected to obey. But this was the time she had to be firm. And perhaps it was easier that her mother was away and she need not immediately explain the situation to her.

However the trouble stayed with her, and lingered into the night. Morning found her tired and still troubled. She was not accustomed to going against her mother's advice, and she readily saw that her mother's letter had been in the nature of an order, practically a command, as if she were still a little girl subject to command. Well, that was all right of course. Not for anything would she choose to disappoint or distress her mother. Yet this was something that mother didn't quite understand. Floss had agreed to this and seemed glad of it. She simply must make her mother understand that, that was all! But how could she do it until her mother got home from Chicago?

She went down to a late breakfast with the little worry pucker in her forehead. And she had scarcely finished her breakfast before there came another telegram, this time a day letter from her mother, for of course Hetty must have telephoned her or communicated with her somehow and told her the whole thing.

With trembling fingers she tore open the envelope and read:

> *Am sending a friend down after you this morning. I want you to be ready to start as soon as he gets there. This is imperative, and most important. I expect to be back by the time you get there and will explain it all.*

> *Your mother.*

There was something dictatorial about that signature, which wasn't a real signature. That little word "Your" seemed to have a defiant note in it. Mary knew she must do something about it at once.

She knew in her heart that the friend her mother would send would be without doubt the young man from whom she had run away down here, and she simply would not be caught and carried back home by him like a naughty child. A journey in his company was the last thing she wanted to endure. She looked up with a frightened something in her eyes, and Randa recognized a need for help in that glance.

"Something the matter?" she asked as casually as she thought befitted the inquiry of a mere servant.

Mary gave her an answering nod.

"Yes, there is something mother seems to think is important and she has sent for me. I guess if you'll excuse me I'll go right up and get ready. I ought to start at once I suppose. But I'll be back later, and I'll only be taking one suitcase. I'll certainly be back as soon as I can get away. No, nobody is sick. It's just a complication about somebody's wedding. I thought I had got out of it, but it seems I haven't."

She rushed upstairs and flung a few things into her suitcase meanwhile trying to think her way through. She mustn't try to drive home for it would take too long, and if the person who was being sent down for her was Brooke Haven, as she strongly suspected, she knew that he would somehow trace her and catch up with her. It was no part of her plan to travel with him anywhere if she could avoid it. Yet she must not leave her car here, for somehow it would be sent home, and she wanted it down here. It needed a check-up and a few minor repairs. She would just take it to the garage and leave it in their care to repair till her return.

That is, she would do that provided she could get a reservation on the plane, or the train.

She had studied those timetables so much since her mother had first demanded to have her come home that she did not have to look at them, though she had the time cards in her purse. She gave a quick glance at the clock. There was at least twenty minutes before that plane left, and then, if there wasn't any room left on it, there would be time, if she hurried, to get to the train before it left.

Rapidly she explained to the garage keeper what she wanted done to her car while she was gone, told him about when she expected to return, and wheedled him into taking her to the airport which was not far away. Now, if only she could get a reservation!

Out of breath she hurried to the ticket window and asked a wistful question, and strange to say the agent smiled.

"Yes, young lady," he said, "you're in luck. A cancellation just came in, and you get the seat."

Almost startled at her good fortune Mary paid her money and accepted the ticket, and then, suddenly remembering that it would be kind to stop Brooke Haven before he left home, she stepped over to the telegraph desk, and wrote hastily:

Am starting home at once! Don't send anybody after me,

Mary.

She addressed it to her mother, or in case of her absence, to Hetty. Then she heard them calling for the plane passengers, and hurried breathlessly to embark.

Seated quietly at last, her few belongings about her, she began to review her activities of the last hour. Had she forgotten anything? Maybe she should have told Randa what she was doing with her car. But no, if Brooke did fail to hear she was on her way, and arrive sometime that day, he would ask how she had gone, and he did not need to know that she had not driven in her car. The less he knew the better.

Also there was the possibility that someone would call up from home, and demand to know how she was coming, and then heaven and earth would be turned to have someone meet her at station or airport or somewhere. And she didn't want to be met by anyone, especially Brooke Haven.

She settled back in her seat and closed her eyes for a moment as she carefully went over all her precautions. Of course there was another matter to be considered. They would probably try their best to get her into that wedding procession. But unless that visiting cousin from California had *died* in the meantime, she positively would not do it! She spent some little time coining pleasant phrases of refusal and excuse to meet this possibility. Her mother and Brooke would of course be the hardest ones to deal with. She was thankful that she had had the presence of mind to bring Floss's letter along, for surely her mother would understand that situation and know that she simply could not be a part of the wedding group now. However she would just laugh it off pleasantly with Floss and tell her she found it possible to get away just for a day or so, but had to hurry right back. Oh, there were pleasant ways of making excuses that would not involve anyone with embarrassment.

These matters settled comfortably, she let her mind drift back to Arden and the pleasant days she had spent there getting acquainted with the dear old times. And especially the wonderful services in the little white chapel. Then there struck a warning note in her mind. She must not talk at home about this plain little church. Nobody would understand. She was not just sure that she fully understood herself, but she had to learn to understand now that she had gone this far. She had to get this matter cleared up before she settled down to a life of comfort and ease.

4

AS the plane flew on toward the north and Mary began to recognize the region into which they were coming, her thoughts went ahead to what was before her, and suddenly it came to her that she must get Floss a wedding present. Why, it just might be that the bridegroom had already arrived, and had but a short time. The wedding might even be set for tomorrow, or the next day, and she certainly wanted that present to be delivered before she had an opportunity to see Floss. Also, she wanted the gift to be a definite finished fact. Yes, even before she saw her mother and had an opportunity to talk with her. She wanted her mother to know that she had not acted wildly in trying to evade that wedding. She wanted her to understand that her plans had been kind and courteous and that she and Floss understood each other.

There had been no opportunity for her to select the gift she wanted Floss to have, for she wanted it to be something very special, and she didn't know the stores down near Arden well enough to find what she wanted there. But now, pretty soon, she would be landing in her own home city, and instead of taking a taxi right to the house, she could just take one to the store where she was used to purchasing extra special fine things. She could have a gift sent right out to Floss. It would perhaps reach her that night if she made a special arrangement for its delivery. At least it would be there in the morning.

So Mary spent the rest of the time before she landed in thinking out just what she wanted to give. Something that Floss would like immensely, and that nobody else would duplicate. Something in crystal and silver perhaps, and she thought back over their various shopping trips, in the days when she and Floss used to be a great deal together, and tried to remember what Floss had admired. Such things would be frightfully expensive now with a federal tax besides; but Floss loved expensive things.

So, when they landed Mary took a taxi and went at once to her favorite store where she was sure she would find something very lovely.

There were still two hours before the stores would close, so she had plenty of time. And the people at home did not yet know how or when she was arriving, so she could take her time.

Then just as she was about to leave, feeling she had done everything necessary, she came upon some charming little salt and pepper shakers that just matched some her mother cherished very much. Several of her mother's had been broken and were greatly regretted. She paused and invested in a half dozen and had them wrapped. These she would carry with her and present to her mother when she arrived. If there were just a little more time she would try to buy presents for all the other friends who were giving parties she didn't wish to attend, but it was getting late and she could buy them another time. So at last she took her familiar way home, comfortable in the thought that no one knew exactly when she was coming, and so there would be no fuss about her arriving.

The telephone was ringing as she fitted her key into the lock. She wondered if that could be her mother somewhere, not yet back from Chicago. There was no telling. Those committee meetings were sometimes long-drawn-out affairs. Then she could hear Hetty's voice answering upstairs:

"Yes, Mrs. Arden. I got your instructions, and Mr. Haven started down after Miss Mary this morning. . . . Yes, he went on the plane. But before his plane could have left I received a day letter from Miss Mary, addressed to us both, saying she was on her way home. Ma'am? . . . No, I couldn't get hold of Mr. Haven and stop his trip. I did my best but his mother said some friend of his had already taken him to the airport. I had him paged, but couldn't reach him no matter how hard I tried. . . . No, Miss Mary hasn't come yet, but she'll likely be here soon. . . . No, she didn't say how she was coming. But I'm sure you needn't worry. Miss Mary is pretty levelheaded, and since she took the trouble to say she was on her way I suppose we can expect her sometime soon. . . . Ma'am? . . . The bridegroom? Why yes, Mrs. Arden, he's expected tomorrow night, and Miss Floss is all for having the wedding the next day. You'll be coming home tonight? . . . Well, that's good. They'll want your help in planning, I'm sure. And yes, Mr. Haven said he'd be returning at once as soon as he got in touch with Miss Mary. . . . No, I can't say. But he said he'd been makin' a big fuss to have Miss Mary maid of honor. He says he positively won't serve as best man unless she is."

Mary listened with foreboding in her heart, and because she did not feel just ready to discuss these matters with her mother then, she stood quietly by the door and made no move for several minutes, waiting until Hetty had hung up, thinking over what she had heard. Well, at least there was time for her to make her plans carefully. Then slowly she picked up her suitcase and went silently upstairs, meeting Hetty in the hall as she came from the telephone.

"Miss Mary!" said Hetty with a relieved note in her voice. "Did you just come in? Oh, I'm glad. Your mother was on the phone. She was troubled that you wired you were on the way. Did Mr. Haven get there before you started? And did you come with him? You'd best be asking him in for dinner. Is he downstairs?"

"Mr. Haven?" said Mary pleasantly. "No, I haven't seen Mr. Haven. Has he been here?"

"Here!" said Hetty indignantly. "Didn't I wire you he was coming after you? He started on the eleven o'clock plane and was to bring you back tonight."

"But I had no telegram about Brooke Haven. My mother said she would send someone after me if I didn't come at once, so I started on the quickest plane I could get. But anyway I would not have come with Brooke Haven!" she said determinedly. "He would have no right to come after me, and I would certainly not have come home with him. When is my mother getting here?"

"Why, she'll be here in the morning, Miss Mary," said Hetty with the troubled look of a trusted servant, "but there'll be all kinds of fuss about Mr. Haven. Your mother won't like it a bit you didn't wait and come with him."

"I'm sorry, Hetty, but I don't care to have Brooke Haven or any other young man sent after me. I'm not a child and I can take care of myself and make my own plans."

"But that's not like you, Miss Mary. You always was considerate of other people's feelings."

"Yes?" said Mary quietly. "Well, this is different. Now, Hetty, I wonder if I can have a tray in my room tonight? I'm a bit tired, and I've some plans to make, some letters to write and a few phone calls to make."

Hetty with a half-frightened look toward this new Mary Arden, scuttled down to the lower hall phone and called up Mary's mother but found to her dismay that she had gone out to dinner and would not return until midnight, so with a troubled sigh she went down to get Mary's dinner tray.

"Do ya mean she didn't come back with that Haven fella?" questioned the cook as Hetty prepared the dainty tray.

"No, she didn't!" snapped Hetty. "I can't think what's taken her. She never was like this before. Why, they've gone together for years."

"He must've done something she didn't like," said the cook.

"But we'd have been sure to hear about it if he had. He's lived around here all his life. Of course he's gone with a few other nice girls, but he always showed his preference for Mary."

"Well, if you ask me," said Anna the cook, "I'll bet he's been goin' with somebody else on the sly, or she'd never have missed marchin' up the aisle beside that good-looker, and if you ask me I think she's takin' a big chance, gettin' him sore at her."

"Oh, she's taking no chance. He's crazy about her, and if she sees he needs a good lesson it's up to her to give it to him. Besides, he's not sore at her. You should have seen his face when I told him Mrs. Arden wanted him to go after her."

"Well, that's not saying how his face'll look when he

gets away down there and finds her gone. Did she come in her car?"

"Why, I don't just know. I didn't ask her. She just walked in. Anyhow, I'm glad she's here! That's a great load off my mind, with her mother gone and all."

"Yes, it's good to have her home, an' I hope she don't go away again. The house isn't the same with her away."

"That's right," said Hetty as she took the tray and started upstairs, wondering just what her next move should be. Should she try to get her mistress again, or just wait? Well, at least she could try.

So she took Mary's tray to her room, had a nice little pleasant talk with her, asking her how she found the old house, and wasn't it terribly lonesome down there with nobody around she knew? Mary blossomed out surprisingly and told her how sweet and dear it was, and how much she had enjoyed herself down there, and then began to dilate about Nannie and Randa, until Hetty grew quite jealous and troubled.

"But you're glad to get home, aren't you, Miss Mary?" she asked anxiously.

"Why yes," said Mary, "home is always good. But I wasn't ready to come just yet. There are things I have to do down there. You know it is my house now, Hetty."

"Oh, you mean you are getting it ready to sell?"

"Oh no, Hetty. I wouldn't sell it for anything. It is mine, you know, and I love it."

"Oh, but Miss Mary! This is your home!"

"Why yes," said Mary hesitantly, "but remember that is where I went when I was a little girl, and I remember my dear grandmother there, and all the things we used to do. I don't think I shall ever want to sell it. It was my father's home, too, and he loves it. He was a little boy there, and he wanted me to go down and take over."

Hetty gave her a despairing look.

"Well, yes," she grudgingly agreed. "I suppose that would make a difference. But I hope you'll not be going back again soon. We miss you something terrible. Would you like another cup of coffee with your pie? Cook made that pie just with you in mind, you know."

"Oh, that was sweet of her," said Mary appreciatively. "Thank her for it, please. Tell her it's delicious."

So they drifted into talk of other things and Hetty presently went down to the kitchen phone and tried to call Mrs. Arden again, but was told she was still out.

Mrs. Arden arrived the next morning and met her daughter with a quick questioning look, as if she didn't quite trust what she saw.

"I don't understand," she said as she examined the letters and telegrams that had arrived during her absence. "What time did you get here?"

Mary smiled quietly.

"Why, I got here last night just in time for dinner."

"But Mary, how could Brooke get down there in time to get you back here for dinner?"

"Brooke?" said Mary with a lifting of her pretty brows. "Did Brooke go down after me?"

"Why certainly. Didn't I telegraph you I was sending someone?"

"Why, yes, mother, but you didn't say who, and I telegraphed back that I was starting at once. I thought it would reach you in time to stop him. I was very much annoyed that you were sending someone after me."

"Well, it seemed the only way to get you here in time for the wedding."

"But mother, I wrote you that I was not coming to the wedding. You haven't read all your letters yet and don't understand. You see, I had written Floss that I was not coming back in time, and I found she was greatly relieved. She had a cousin arrive from California, expecting to be maid of honor. Wait! I'll show you her letter."

"Does her mother know this?"

"I'm sure I don't know, mother, but you can see that my plans have not upset her in the least."

"Well, I can tell you they have upset someone else's plans. You'll find Brooke Haven will make a terrible disturbance about it.".

"Brooke Haven? What on earth has he got to do with it? It's Floss's wedding, isn't it? He's nothing but the best man."

"Yes," said Mrs. Arden, "and as such was to march down the aisle with you, and he certainly won't like this change. He dislikes that California cousin of Floss's very much, and he said he simply wouldn't be in the procession if he had to walk with her. We'll have to do something about this before Brooke gets back. He never will stand for this."

Mary looked at her mother steadily, realizing that her mother must have talked the matter over, cousin and all, with Brooke Haven. Then she spoke very quietly:

"Mother, if you must know the truth of this, I went away *because* I didn't want to be in that wedding procession with Brooke Haven! I simply won't be coupled with him any longer. I've tried various ways to get rid of his exclusive escort, and when they all failed I simply ran away. And if you try to do anything about this now and change things I'll take the next plane back to Arden and stay, for I will not be in this affair."

"But Mary! You and Brooke have been friends a long time. How can you feel this way? What has he done to offend you?"

"Nothing, mother, except to park on my footsteps and take possession of me wherever I dare to go. I'm just getting fed up with it, mother, and I thought it was time to put a stop to it. I won't be tagged and labelled as his exclusive property!"

"Mary! Why that's very indelicate of you! And he is such a nice boy; we all love him so much, and there is nothing objectionable about him."

"I can't help it, I just don't want him no matter how unobjectionable he is. You may love him if you like, but I don't, and I am done running around with him."

"But my dear! You can't do a thing like this!"

"Yes, I can, mother. I must. I can't go on any longer this way, and if you try to make an issue of this wedding I'll simply clear out before any of them have any opportunity to see me. I mean it, mother!"

"Oh, Mary, how can you be so rude and unkind? What will my friend Mrs. Haven think?"

"Oh, mother, I don't mean to be rude and unkind. Not to you anyway, and of course not to your friends, but this is a case where I will have to take a stand!"

"But Mary, why should you suddenly turn everything upside down, right in the midst of an important wedding, and break up a friendship that has existed pleasantly for years? You've never made any such fuss as this about going places with Brooke. Have you and he had an argument and are you trying to pay him back for something he has said or done? Because I'm quite sure if he were spoken to in the right way he would be entirely willing to apologize. For I happen to know that it is quite important to him that you march with him in this procession. What has he done? I insist upon knowing why you have suddenly grown so stubborn."

"Mother, it's nothing he has said or done recently any more than many other times. It's just that I have come to the place where I won't take his constant attendance any longer. I'm of age now, and I have a right to make my own decisions, and after thinking it all over I decided it would be easier on everybody concerned and less noticeable to everybody if I slipped off to Arden suddenly, unobtrusively. There would be no need of any explanation to anybody. Just that I found it necessary to go down and 'attend to some business matters connected with my recent inheritance.'"

"Mary! You know that that is absurd! There are no imperative business matters of that sort. It would make no difference to your inheritance if you never went down, and I sincerely hope you never will."

"Mother, you are mistaken. There are papers I have to sign, and there is the possible sale of some land that may be important. I can't tell you all the items now because I have been waiting for the lawyer to return from a trip, and I must go right back."

"I think this is the most absurd nonsense I ever heard of. I've owned property all my life, but your father's lawyer has looked after these matters for me, and told me when to sign papers."

"But I'm not going to own property that way, mother. I'm looking after my own, and learning how to run it in the best way. And anyway, mother, this really has nothing to do with the present state of things. I wanted to get away from these various social functions for a special reason, and I thought this was a good chance without hurting anybody. Now, would you rather I went right back before I've been seen, or stay long enough to attend the wedding in the church and then leave? I would rather go now if you don't mind, for then I wouldn't have to have any arguments with Brooke Haven, but I'll stay if you think that will be any the less embarrassing for you."

"But Mary!" went on Mrs. Arden still avoiding an answer, "how long do you expect this thing to go on?

Do you look on this as a permanent break with Brooke?"

"I certainly do. I thought I could stay out of his vicinity until he begins to get interested in somebody else, or gets over being silly about me. For I simply won't put up with him any longer!"

"Has Brooke ever proposed to you, Mary? Don't you think you are taking a good deal for granted?"

"No, mother, I don't. No, he hasn't ever proposed in regular words. But he's often remarked with one of his hazy grins, 'When we're married I'll see that you don't do that any more'."

"Mary! I think you're just being silly!"

"No, mother, I'm not. I'm just getting out of the picture. Now, there's a plane in an hour and a half and I can take a taxi to the airport and keep out of sight. Would you rather I'd do that?"

Mrs. Arden put on her most disturbed air.

"And what am I to say to Brooke when he comes back?"

"Well, you sent him down, you know, not I. I suppose you can say there was a mix-up in dates or telegrams or something like that, if you feel you must. I certainly telegraphed before I left."

"What will they have told him down there?" asked her mother anxiously. "Did they know you had come home?"

"Oh yes, I told them you sent for me."

"Did they know how you came?"

"No, I went away in a hurry in my car and left it at a garage for some repairs. But they wouldn't know that."

The worry deepened on the mother's face.

"I don't know what to tell you to do. I don't even know positively whether Brooke went in his own car or took a plane. I had to hurry away to make my Chicago train. But I made it plain to him that I wanted you here as soon as possible to get your dresses ready. Oh dear! Why do you have to be so very difficult, my child?"

Mary's eyes were troubled.

"I'm truly sorry, mother, but 1 just couldn't have things go on as they were any longer, and I thought this was the best way to do it."

"Well, it certainly isn't very good from my point of view," said her mother with a sigh. "I'm sure I don't see how I'm going to explain myself. I shall be mortified to death! Brooke's mother is one of my best friends."

"Now look, mother! If you want me to I'll take over and explain it all."

"But how could you explain?"

"Why, I'd simply say you sent for me, and I came on the first plane I could get. Sorry if it inconvenienced Brooke. You simply said you were sending someone for me. There was no name mentioned, and I came at once, telegraphing that I was on my way. Of course since you were not here you didn't get it in time."

Then she heard the front door open, quite accustomedly, as if the one who entered had come often, and instantly Mary knew who it was.

5

WHEN Mary Arden had made her sudden departure from the dear cheery home that seemed to have come alive since her presence there, Nannie and Randa paused in their work with broom and with dishcloth to stare disconsolately at each other.

Randa was the first to speak, in an almost hard, resentful tone.

"I knew it wouldn't last!" She bit off her words in her disappointment. "I knew she couldn't take it, here. Not after the life she's had with parties and beaux and servants to wait on her hand and foot."

But old Nannie shook her head slowly, tiredly. "Don't blame Miss Mary, Randa. No, 'tain't her that's done it. It's that mother of hers. Didn't ya take notice to the worry in her face this mornin'? She didn't want to leave here. That's why I feel so sorry. She'd like to stay. I really believe she likes our quiet ways, an' this old place, an' all. No, I'm real sorry fer her, cause it don't look as if she'll ever get what she wants. That's the way it often is, you know, with rich people an' princesses an' the like. Everything that money can buy, but not what they really want."

Nannie sighed, a heavy sympathetic sigh after she had delivered this bit of sound philosophy. Then she went back to her dishes.

Randa wielded her broom again, gustily, still bitterly. "Hunh! It may be so," she grumbled. "I dunno."

"You talk about beaux," went on her mother, "what finer man would any girl want than our Laurie Judson, I'd like to know?" Nannie used the personal pronoun advisedly. She knew that her daughter shared her own almost adoration for the young man who cared to be friendly to three servants. Into her talks with Randa about him through the years, she had woven many strands of sound common sense gleaned from anxious hours spent on her old bony knees. She and Orrin had been quite aware of the effect Laurie's friendliness might have upon the heart of their plain hard-working daughter. They had taken pains to see to it that he was kept upon the pedestal they chose to place him on, and that she was supplied with plenty of good times with young friends of her own station in life so that no foolishness should creep into her heart about him. They were even aware that at one time in her teens in spite of all they could do, she had had a struggle with just such thoughts, but they had redoubled their agonized prayers that God would shield their girl and lead her aright. And soon after that a new young chauffeur had appeared at the big adjoining estate, who now bid fair to take sole place in Randa's life. They could breathe easily again, and speak without inward trembling when Laurie Judson's name was mentioned. But Randa still held for him the greatest respect.

"He hasn't got enough money for her, likely," she sniffed.

"Oh, Randa," gently reproved her mother, "surely you can see that our Miss Mary isn't like that. And didn't ya hear the happy lilt in her voice when she spoke his name? No, Miss Mary's all right, an' always will be whether she comes back here or not, if only her mother doesn't interfere and spoil her life—"

Just then the doorbell rang. A long insistent peal. And before either could reach the front of the house, it rang again.

Randa, indignant, flung it open, all her resentfulness over Miss Mary's departure still upon her like a dark cloud.

There stood a tall arrogantly handsome young man. His impeccable pearl-grey felt hat was in his hand, disclosing a head of shining sleek black hair. His eyes were black, too, and his brows, which slanted slightly upward where they nearly met above his nose. The straightness of his nose was accentuated by a straight little black mustache below it.

"I want to see Miss Arden!" he demanded as if this plain-faced person who opened the door had been keeping her hidden. Randa glared.

"Miss Arden is out." She stated it with finality and seemed about to close the door.

But the young man was determined. "Then I'll come in and wait for her." He was in the hall and aimed for the big easy chair in the quaint low-ceilinged living room before Randa knew what to do. She had not had a great deal of experience in edging out unwelcome callers in this friendly little town. Her impulse would have been to present solid resistance to this stranger, if only because she was in a resentful mood at the moment. But probably he was one of Miss Mary's city friends, and much as she herself intended to dislike him for that reason, still Miss Mary would not be pleased if she were rude to him. And he was handsome, strikingly so. Randa had to admit that to herself grudgingly as she stood in the hallway, uncertain what to say to him.

Nannie arrived then and in her kindly courteous way informed the gentleman that "Miss Arden will not be in soon, sir. She has had to leave town unexpectedly."

The young man paused in the act of seating himself and whirled on the old servant.

"Leave *town!*" he repeated with rising indignation. "You must be mistaken, whoever you are. Miss Arden was to go with me, under my escort. Her mother requested me to see her safely to her home." He accented the word home as if this quiet cosy spot could not by any chance deserve the name of home. "Who are you two, anyway, and what are you doing in this place?"

Randa gave a furious gasp. But Nannie silenced her with a look and answered in her calm way, ignoring the rudeness, "We have been caretakers of the Arden home here for twenty-five years, sir. If you care to call again—"

"Call again!" the young man blazed. "Where do you think I live? Certainly not in this God-forsaken dump. Where did she go? I'll go and get her."

"May I first ask who you are, and what right you have to know Miss Arden's affairs?" Nannie's voice had taken on a cool edge now.

Impatiently the young man reached into his pocket and drew forth an engraved card. Very deliberately Nannie pulled down her glasses from her front hair and adjusted them, while Randa, unable to curb her curiosity, sidled closer and looked over her shoulder.

R. Brooke Haven was the name on the card. It also bore a fashionable address. Neither meant anything at all to Nannie or Randa. Slowly Nannie looked up from her careful reading, trying to think how to handle this unknown imperious youth.

Just then firm steps bounded joyously in at the back

door and an eager bass voice called through the house familiarly, "Anybody home? Oh-h Ma-ry! Merry Arden!"

Laurie Judson came into view from the hallway and stopped short. There was a sudden silence.

The two men faced each other, the black piercing eyes staring insolently, hatefully into the cool brown ones that were busy sizing up the other man.

The air was so tense that poor old Nannie began to tremble, hardly knowing why. Randa stood her ground and glared. But old Orrin, coming in right after Laurie, in his patched overalls with his battered straw hat still on his head, took in at a glance the strained situation and startled them all with a hoarse old cackle of a laugh.

"What-all goin's on have we got here?" he asked not unkindly. "Who are ye, young feller? State yer business."

"I want Mary Arden!" roared Brooke Haven furiously. "I don't know what kind of dive this is, nor why we have to have such a mystery about it. Mrs. Arden asked me to come down here and bring her daughter home, and I intend to do it. Now where is she?"

Orrin raised his brows and nodded reasonably enough.

"Well, now, I reckon if ye can calm down a little the wimmin here can tell ye whar she is. I ain't seen her meself yet today. Ben out in the south field since sunup. Nannie," he turned placidly to his wife, "help the gentleman to find Miss Mary, and," he added remembering courtesies, "did ye interduce him to Laurie?"

"I have no interest in meeting your son, old man, nor in anything but in getting Mary Arden out of here. I demand to know where she is."

Nannie would have struggled out of her daze then and told him, but Laurie spoke.

"Just a minute—dad!" he grinned and winked at Orrin who chuckled with glee. "As this person seems so concerned over Miss Arden's safety, perhaps we would do well ourselves to examine his credentials before we turn her over to him." He looked Haven squarely in the eye and waited.

Flustered and sputtering, Brooke Haven gave in under that steady gaze and reached in his pocket for another card. But his rage broke out afresh as he handed it over to Laurie.

"It's high time Mrs. Arden got her out of here, when a decent man has to answer to a lot of yokels for the right to see the girl he expects to marry. There is my name and address, bud, though I don't suppose that could possibly mean anything to you. You can have the police check on me if you like," he added sarcastically. "Now where is Mary Arden?"

They all turned to Nannie then, who had by this time recovered her poise.

"She has gone back to her mother's house in the city."

"Back to the city! Why, I was to take her back! Didn't she get the message?"

"She got a message, I don't know who from. She up and left a half-hour ago."

"Did she drive? Or take the train?" Brooke Haven stammered.

"She left here in her car. I don't know if she was goin' to park it and take the train, or the plane, or drive all the way. I couldn't say."

Brooke Haven was wild. "What time does the train leave?" he burst out. "Quick! You've kept me here talking all this time and I might have caught her."

"I don't rightly know," Nannie started to answer.

"Oh!"—and he flung a mouthful of oaths at them all impartially and tore down the driveway.

In a sort of stunned silence the little group watched him go, then Orrin let out his amused cackle and turned to Laurie:

"Well, son, ya didn't get a chanct to shake his hand after all, did ya?"

The tension was broken and they all laughed.

"I'd far rather shake him all over till his bones rattled!" responded Laurie heatedly.

Nannie's eyes twinkled and Randa looked her approval and then all started back to their work.

But Laurie's day was spoiled. He had intended asking Mary Arden to take a walk with him out to the woods near the old paper mill where they had picnicked once years ago. There were canoes there, and lovely nooks for quiet talks. He knew Nannie would fix them something for supper. His heart had been pounding with eagerness ever since he thought of it on the way home from church last night. He had scarcely been able to sleep for thinking of her sweet eyes turned so earnestly up to him as he gave the simple message of the gospel in the chapel. She had seemed really interested in what he was saying.

The day looked as if it might be a blessed bright interval between his hours of hard work, for he was trying to do two years' work in one, at the Bible School, besides holding down his job. Today he had an unexpected half holiday. But with Mary Arden gone it seemed suddenly that there was no reason to take a holiday. Why did people take holidays, anyway? Just a waste of time. He might as well get back to work on that thesis that had to be finished before next week.

But even his absorbing interest in the theme he had chosen had vanished. Everything was dull and meaningless. He felt as if there were a heavy weight dragging his feet down. And some unoutlined subtle danger was hovering in the offing. He took a deep breath and tried to shake off the ridiculous unreasonable dread that had taken hold of him. What was the root of this sudden unhappiness? Was it just that Mary Arden was away? He took himself to task.

Surely he could manage to exist in a reasonably cheerful manner even though he had been disappointed about a picnic. Was he a child, that he must sulk over disappointments? No, this thing that was bothering him was more than a disappointment. Ah! Now he knew. It was that insolent fellow at Mary Arden's house, who acted as if he possessed every right to her. Who was he? One of her friends from the city, no doubt. But if he was a chosen friend of Mary Arden, then definitely Laurie Judson was not. The two men had measured each other in that instant of meeting and each had sensed the immeasurable distance between their thoughts and ways and standards, between their very spheres of being.

Brooke Haven was the source of this uneasiness in Laurie's mind. Could it be that Mary Arden was actually pledged to him in any way? She *must* be saved from what Laurie knew in his soul that this man must be. But what right had he to step in and try to save her? None at all. A childhood companion for a brief summer. That's all he was to her. A gay memory. And now a country preacher! She was probably laughing now with this debonair socialite from her own sphere about her country preacher friend. The thought ground pain through Laurie's soul as his pride writhed in torture.

Then suddenly, through his self-made agony words came winging as sweet as the song of spring birds on a rainy day: "For we preach not ourselves, but Christ Jesus the Lord . . . we are fools for Christ's sake . . . that we may be glorified with him."

Laurie straightened up and raised his head with a look that was beautiful to see. "Thank you, Lord, for reminding me," he said humbly, as he walked through the quiet wooded lane on his way home. The burden of the morning's dark disappointment was gone. In its stead there was a great earnestness of desire that the beautiful girl who had flashed twice into his life and out again might be guarded from all harm.

And back at the lovely low rambling house that was Mary Arden's the three loving servants who were devoted to her went about their work forlornly, till at last, seated together at the lunch table old Orrin broke out:

"Fer goodness sake stop snifflin', you two. Miss Mary's still Miss Mary. She ain't a bit diffrunt from what she was two hours ago. You don't think fer a minit that she's goin' ta take up with that little upstart prig, do ya?" He laughed his jolly old cackle. "What do ya s'pose she ran off *fer?* I never did see two sech dumb wimmin! Talk about a man not bein' able to understand a woman, it's you two that can't tell a-b-c about her. Ner that fella Laurie Judson neither. He walked outa here as if an atom bomb was goin' to fall today. Perk up, Nannie! You got more sense'n that!"

So with his grumbling gaiety he jollied his own two women into their usual steady pace again.

But Brooke Haven had no help on his stormy homeward way.

IF Mary Arden hadn't been quite sure who it was that came in the front door, her mother's little gasp of dismay would have told her.

With a quick glance toward her distressed mother she arose and went without hesitation to the top of the stairway and spoke in a clear voice of assurance.

"Oh, it's you, Brooke? We were troubled that we had not heard from you. I am so sorry that there was a misunderstanding and you had that long trip for nothing. I do hope you'll pardon me. I didn't know who was being sent after me, of course, but I hoped that my telegram would reach here in time to stop whoever it was. Of course mother's not being here when it was received made the mix-up, but you mustn't blame mother. We all thought we were doing the right thing."

"Oh, of course," said the young man half mollified by Mary's apology, unusually abject for her. "Don't think a thing about it." He came on up the stairs in his old friendly way but his voice was still rather cold and sarcastic. "I was glad to help out in any way I could. I had a delightful trip! But nobody seemed to know at that address your mother gave me just how you were travelling, or I might have caught up with you. I suppose servants are hard to get now and you take what you can, but such a pack of nitwits as you have there I never did see. There was a moment when I didn't know but that old fellow's presumptuous son was going to have me locked up in the town jail till he could look up my references." Brooke ended his tirade with a sneer yet withal a bit of laughter. He was home at last and had got the wrath out of his system, now he was ready to forgive and forget it all, if he could put Mary where he wanted her.

Mary's indignation rose as she heard him malign her beloved servants, but she quickly decided to control it and let the whole unfortunate incident be smoothed over as lightly as possible. So she too gave a deprecatory little laugh, saying gaily, "Oh, you mustn't be upset by old Orrin and Nannie. They are really wonderful servants, and after all, weren't they trying to take the best of care of me?"

But afterward Mary puzzled over the "son" Brooke had mentioned. Who on earth could he mean? Had prim Randa borne down upon him in slacks and had he mistaken her plain face for a man's? She laughed to herself at the thought. Well, the least said about the whole thing, and especially about matters at Arden, the better, as long as her mother felt the way she did.

And Brooke was ready now to put the whole thing aside and get down to present events.

"Well, have it your way," he carelessly dismissed it. "But now there are some things we'll have to talk over that we might have settled on the trip home. Floss wants—"

"Oh," interrupted Mary with lifted brows, "but you

know I'm not to be in Floss's wedding. Hadn't you heard?"

The dark storm bore down again upon Mary from Brooke's black brows.

"What!" he roared. "You certainly are to be in the wedding. You'll be the whole show as far as I'm concerned."

"Oh, but you don't know the latest," answered Mary sweetly. "As soon as I saw that I might not get back in time I wrote to Floss about it and I found she was really quite relieved. It seems that in an impulsive moment she had asked a cousin of hers to be maid of honor, long ago, and then she forgot about it. Well, this cousin turned up a few days ago and took it all for granted. It was making all kinds of a family feud, so Floss was glad to let me off. See? Now," Mary hastened on all too conscious of dark looks, before her mother or Brooke could say a word, "if you will excuse me, I'll run down and do a couple of errands that have to be done before noon or they will be too late. See you later."

Mary flitted down the stairs, or rather she started to but she was suddenly confronted by a long strong arm. Determined to ease out of the scene without causing an actual explosion of wills, she quickly ducked under the arm with a gay laugh and flew down the rest of the way and out the back hall toward the garage. But anticipating her scheme Brooke as swiftly turned and fairly slid down the back stairs, catching her at the kitchen door in both arms this time.

"No, you don't, my girl!" he cried, half laughing, half angry. "You'll not pull that again with me. You ran away from that ghastly dump called Arden thinking you'd fool me! Come now, you know you did!" He gave her a little shake. "And I won't have any more of it. Fun is fun but enough's enough."

He pinned her arms behind her and held her to him kissing her fiercely on the mouth. Then he held her off and laughed delightedly, gleefully to see her eyes blazing angry blue sparks.

"You look lovely that way, beauty!" he smiled into her face. "I hope we will have a little tiff now and then all our lives if you can always be so beautiful."

Struggling desperately, perfectly furious, Mary freed one hand and struck him as hard as she could across his face. He dropped her hands but she did not try to run. She walked in quiet fury back into the lower hall where her mother had followed. She was angry, but still calm enough to realize that she must not be tricked into acting like a childish runaway.

Brooke followed her, ready to laugh off the whole thing. He pretended to pout.

"Why didn't you bring up your daughter better?" he demanded half jokingly of Mrs. Arden. "Do you think it's nice of her to go around slapping people in the face?" He put his hand up to the bright pink place, rubbing it tenderly.

"Why, daughter! How terribly unladylike! Even in fun there is no excuse for such rudeness." She smiled a gentle apologetic smile.

Mary did not smile.

"It was not in fun, mother. Now I really must go. I shall be late."

She walked calmly out the front door and down the street, while her unwanted lover and her mother stood and looked at each other waiting each for the other to make a move.

"I can't think what has come over Mary," excused Mrs. Arden. "I'm sure I hope she will come to her senses before long. Do try to be patient with her, you poor dear boy. You have had a trying two days and I fear it was partly my fault. I'm so sorry things got mixed up."

Gruffly Brooke Haven muttered an "Oh, it's nothing," took his hat and hurried out, saying, "I'll catch her in the car and we'll make up. Don't you worry."

Even as he said the words he pushed from him any anxiety he might have had that all would not be as he wished it to be. It was the way he had pushed aside unpleasant things all his life. It was an easy way, and generally worked. He had not taken Mary's resistance too seriously. Plenty of girls had pretended to be outraged at his demonstrations of affection. True, Mary had seemed to mean it, and probably did. That made her all the more interesting. She'd get over her little rage.

He looked up and down the street but no Mary was in sight. Silly girl, to waste all that energy in running when it would be so easy for him to find her with his car. He got in and started toward the shopping center a few blocks away, looking up and down every cross street. Finally he shrugged his shoulders and betook himself to Floss Fairlee's to see what new developments promised interest.

But Mary's rage was no small matter. It was not that Brooke Haven had kissed her against her will for the first time. There had been other kisses; once when she first knew him and she was almost pleased that he wanted to kiss her, or at least she had not learned to dislike his attentions. Later a time or two when to gain some other freedom from him she had submitted to a good-night kiss. But never had he kissed her with this fierce passion—or had he? It was not really very different from some of those other kisses which he had almost forced upon her. Well, what was it then that had made her very soul shrink from him in disgust? Why did she feel so degraded now? Just because she had come to despise him so? Or was it—stay! There came a memory now of other lips, another kiss, treasured as something most precious. A kiss that had begun in gay friendliness and ended in a tender benediction. That was it. She had a sudden feeling that Brooke Haven's fierce caress had somehow sullied that other that she had meant to keep sacred in her heart. And then she wondered how she ever could have allowed any of those other kisses from this man she so disliked. Now that she knew what the meeting of lips could mean, the tenderness, the sweetness and almost holiness of such a caress, it seemed a terrible soil upon her soul, all those other ugly kisses that meant nothing; they were like a child's idle snatching after a goody.

And now she wanted to get away, somewhere where she could get her balance again and find her lost self respect.

Just as she reached the corner of the street she heard the faint sound of the Arden front door closing. She knew instantly that it would be Brooke, come to overtake her. She turned the corner, though she had not meant to go that way, and slipped into a yard behind a huge oak tree. She felt like a small boy hiding from his teacher, and she feared to peer out from behind her shelter until the sound of Brooke's car was dim in the distance. Then, wondering what on earth the people who owned the oak tree were thinking if they had seen her, she guiltily hastened down the wrong street and walked on far away from the downtown section, into a part of town where Brooke would never think to search.

Her anger was beginning to subside and the whole scene seemed to her now so childish, so ridiculously melodramatic that she was filled with contempt for herself. When she finally began to get desperate and felt as if she couldn't stand to go back and face her family and friends again, she suddenly remembered what her father had told her so many times: "If you can learn to laugh at yourself, child, you'll never entirely lose your balance." A quick rush of longing for her father came over her as she recalled the depth of understanding and comfort she always found in him, and the tears almost came in a flood, threatening to humiliate her still further, right out there on the street. Then because she had to laugh or cry, she did laugh, heartily, all to herself.

"If I'm not a silly!" she thought. "First I put on the third act of a melodrama, then I get sorry for myself. Wouldn't daddy tease me!"

Thus, gradually, the whole affair shrank to normal size again and she briskly started home, making up her mind on the way that she would take the first train back to Arden tomorrow morning, before the household was stirring and could stop her.

But when she reached home and opened the front door, there was the telephone ringing again. Her mother appeared from somewhere and answered it, motioning to Mary as she did so to wait till she had finished.

Mary thought she knew what was coming, a sound scolding from her mother for being so rude, and she tried to grasp at her sense of humor to keep it from slipping away from her as it so often seemed to do in these sessions with her mother, leaving her exposed, as it were, to the deadly emotional currents that always ran riot.

Her mother was smiling into the phone, however, and answering "Oh, isn't that too bad!" in a pleased voice.

Then, motioning again to Mary to come, she went on, "Yes, fortunately she returned last night and we hope she will not be having to leave again, at least for the present. Yes, here she is now."

Deftly Mrs. Arden placed the receiver in Mary's hand

and slid away, leaving Mary rooted to the spot, whether she wished it or not.

Without the slightest idea of who was holding up the other end of this disturbing conversation, Mary managed a hesitating, "Yes?"

It was Floss's voice, eager, troubled, that came to her over the wire. Mary's heart sank.

"Oh, darling! I'm *so* relieved to find you there. The most awful thing has happened, and I'm in a terrible fix again. Jim is actually coming tonight! Oh, I don't mean that's the terrible thing. I'm thrilled to a peanut. Imagine. And the wedding will be Thursday, because he has only five days, but that will give us a little honeymoon. Oh, I'm so excited I don't know which end I'm standing on!"

Mary waited, murmuring appropriate "Ohs!" at the right time, but with an awful foreboding in her heart.

"But, darling," rattled on the bride, "you don't *know* what has happened to Cousin Sue—the one, you know who was to have taken your place as maid of honor—I never *did* want to make that change, as you very well know, for Cousin Sue never meant anything really special to me and you do—"

"Oh, will she never come out with it?" thought Mary hopelessly, certain now of what Floss was going to ask.

"Well, Sue has come down with *chicken pox!* Can you imagine? Yes, at her age! She says there was a child on the train with some spots on her, when she left California. That's likely where she picked it up. But—oh, Mary I'm glad you are back. Now we can go ahead and have the wedding party the way I really planned it. You will, won't you, now you're home? And we are going to have the rehearsal tonight. Of course Jim may not get here until late tonight, but he'll find out quickly enough what to do. Brooke can nudge him when to march and all that. Oh, I'm so happy I could hug you right now. Well, I'll be seeing you tonight—and oh, about your dress!" And then came a long discussion of colors and styles.

Mary turned away from the phone feeling as if she had been tricked. Although she could not actually blame her mother. Her mother certainly hadn't inoculated Cousin Sue with chicken pox. It seemed as if there were no way for her to step out of the current that carried her straight back into the arms of Brooke Haven. For of course, with Brooke Haven as best man, and Mary as maid of honor, they would be thrown together constantly during the next few days.

Well, there was nothing for it but to go through with it now. Mary sighed heavily. Her head was aching, and she felt tired all over. Strange, she had felt so rested from just those few days at Arden. Arden! What a refuge it seemed. She could almost see those thin white curtains moving with the gentle breeze in her cool living room. And perhaps even now there was a firm step on the back porch and a cheery whistle announcing the arrival of a tall young man with clear brown eyes and a merry smile, a man who treated her tenderly and knew how to speak of heavenly things with joy. The surge of longing to be back at her own dear house made Mary fly up the stairs and into her own room to shut the door against anyone who should pry into her soul and see the sweet images there.

It came to her as she lay upon her bed to wonder whether Laurie Judson had always worn that look of joy, and perhaps she had only just now noticed it. Just to be with him was to expect something perfectly delightful to happen any minute. Did he know joy like that when he was overseas in the mud and heat and danger, she wondered. His joy seemed an inward thing, independent of outward circumstances. Were some people just naturally made that way? Could she perhaps learn to be that way, in this ordeal that she had to endure these next few days, for instance. It pleased her to think she might try, if only because it would be like sharing something with her friend Laurie. It was not that she was getting foolish about Laurie, certainly not. He was her old friend, older than herself by—well, four years. He was like a haven in a storm. Haven! What a travesty for Brooke to be named that. How was she ever to keep him at arm's length till she could escape again? Perhaps just keep everything on a gay laughing level, making constant fun of herself and of him, never allowing a serious moment to settle upon them. At any rate that seemed the best way she knew.

And then Hetty called her to lunch.

It was a delicious lunch of delicate pink ham slices, with tiny sandwiches of some delectable new cheese spread, and a cool salad, for the day was warm for the middle of June.

Yet Mary, seated at the massive walnut table in the great shadowed dining room could not seem to enjoy it or even the dainty dessert the cook had fixed "specially for Miss Mary." Every little while would come a vision of the cosy kitchen where even now Nannie and Randa were probably sitting at their little lunch, mourning the bird that had flown and wondering whether she would ever come back to them. It was not that Mary was so much more fond of those servants than these whom her mother had trained and who had waited upon her all her life. But there was an air of loving friendliness and a lack of tension about the old place at Arden that was infinitely restful. Here there seemed to be a constant fever to be sure to do everything just as the rest of society dictated. It irked Mary.

She would not admit to herself that the possibility of a visit from that merry-eyed tall young man down at Arden had anything special to do with the attraction of the place for her.

After several long silent minutes during which Mary's mother watched her sharply Mrs. Arden said, "Well, anyone would think you were to take part in a funeral, not a wedding."

Mary looked up with a guilty start. "Oh! Why—" she had actually been staring out the windows of her room at Arden, letting her eyes follow the winding of the little brook that flowed at the bottom of the hill back of the house. "Why, I wasn't even thinking about the wedding." She gave a little laugh.

"It's about time you did think about it, I should say," responded her mother irritably. "It's the greatest piece of fortune that you happened back just in time for it. Now let's get everything planned so that there will be no hitch in your part, at least. You know how Mrs. Fairlee is, she must have everything just right."

Mrs. Arden set out under full sail into a discussion of what each member of the wedding party would wear, where each would stand, and then told of the long argument Mrs. Fairlee had had with the caterer.

Mary would try to listen, fade off to Arden, and jerk back just in time to say "Oh, really?" or, "Yes, I guess so," until she realized all of a sudden that her mother was talking about Brooke Haven.

Gradually her subconscious mind warned her that there was something she should be aware of. With an effort she slowly recalled her mother's last sentence to which she had murmured a wordless assent.

Yes, it had been about Brooke Haven.

"—you know, he was planning that you and he would announce your engagement at the wedding rehearsal—"

Horrified, Mary tried to cancel her vague assent with: "Oh, no! *No, mother!*" But her mother was already halfway out of the room responding to another telephone call, and she didn't answer Mary.

7

MRS. Judson looked up from her needlework alertly as she caught the sound of unexpected footsteps on the front walk.

Laurie's mother was an attractive woman in her early fifties. She had Laurie's soft brown eyes with the dancing twinkles in them, and her brown hair waved from her forehead just as his did. But he had inherited his father's strong height, for she was a fragile little body, with dainty feet and hands. Her mouth showed sweetness at first glance, then determination which gave the sweetness a firm dependable quality. Both of these virtues had been learned the hard way, through her having plenty of trying circumstances in which to practice them. The climax had come two years ago when her beloved husband had suddenly been called from this earth, leaving a heavy burden of debt.

That had happened while Laurie was overseas. Mr. Judson had had to arrange a personal loan from a friend to stall off a mortgage foreclosure on the farm they owned up near the Arden house where they had lived ever since they were married. But soon after the borrowed money was paid out, he suffered a heart attack and died in a few minutes.

Of course the mortgage was foreclosed, as the loan had covered only a part of the sum. Laurie, sent home on furlough fortunately, shared with his mother the great grief that seemed to them both the end of all happy living, then he bravely shouldered the responsibility as head of the house. He went out and hunted up this little cottage for his mother to live in, moved what goods he felt she must have, and sold the rest. Then before he went back to his outfit he paid a visit to the bank president, who was his father's best friend and who had loaned him the few thousand dollars which he had thought would see him through the hard times.

Laurie had his figures down in black and white. He showed what he was making in the service now, quite a goodly sum on account of promotions for his splendid work. He subtracted his mother's expenses, which he had pared down as far as he dared without actually making her suffer, and then he proposed to pay back monthly from what was left, the loan that his father had made.

"You see," he finished earnestly, his young face set in grim lines, "if all goes well, I shall be able to finish the payments in even less time than father had calculated. Now sir, is this agreeable to you? Of course, I shall pay the same rate of interest that my father would have paid."

The older man looked into the worried, brave young face and shook his head gently.

"No, my boy," he said kindly, "I'm afraid it is not. I shall have to make some changes in your plan, excellent as it seems. After all, you know, your father was like a brother to me. I loved him. And knowing him as I did, I am well aware of some of the plans he cherished. I propose to see that those plans are carried out as far as possible. One of them was that his son should have a full college education, and more, if he desired. Now wait just a minute," he held up his hand as the boy started to shake his head proudly, "let me explain *my* plan, since you have told me yours. You realize, I suppose, that as a GI you will have your education provided for without charge. Now, I shall not accept this plan of yours at all, unless you first finish your last two years of schooling. Then if you care to repay me you may put your plan into effect. It will take you, I should think, only a little longer to finish that way, since your earning power will be so much more after you have your degree. Now I want you to understand that if anything happens to make it impossible or difficult for you to pay this money, at any time, you will let me know. I would gladly forgive the whole amount and cross it off my books. You know that, son. If I had known that your father was in such a tight place I would gladly have offered him the few thousand as a gift. Another thing, I never intended to accept a cent of interest from him and I shall not ask it of you."

Then Laurie's mouth took on the determined look his mother's often wore.

"Mr. Winters, you knew my father and you know he would rather have lost his right hand than leave a debt unpaid. He would have considered the interest on the money part of the debt. I feel I owe it to him as well as to you and to my mother and myself to pay in full with interest. I *really want* to do it. I appreciate your letting me wait to finish college, and I know father wanted that. So I will concede that point gladly. All this will take a long time, I know, but I *must* pay that debt."

The two men stood up and shook hands, then Laurie went out. But Mr. Winters stood for several minutes seeing the straight brave figure still facing him. It was as if the shining of Laurie's clean young manhood left a bright glow there in the office.

But Laurie never said a word of all this to his mother. He was afraid if she knew he was trying to pay off that debt, that she would bend her own frail strength beyond its limits and force herself to economies unnecessary, to try to ease the burden from him.

So when he chose for her the smallest, cheapest house he could find that was at all fit, he thought, "She'll take it for granted that I am trying to save to finish college."

But he should have known his mother better than that. She was the old-fashioned kind of mother who wondered, but said nothing. Her brows were often drawn in a little puzzled frown when she took note of his small economies. She sought at first for a girl in the picture, but there seemed to be none; that is, no special one. Then she began to realize the extra pride in his carriage, the straight-up way he wore his young manhood when he walked abroad. And that was what gave away his secret. She suddenly sensed it one day when they had passed Mr. Winters on the street. She knew that her Laurie could never bear himself with that straightforward look of self-respect if there remained any hidden question of honor unsettled.

It was then that she redoubled her own efforts to use her spare moments to turn into pennies every scrap of skill and strength she had, besides practising her own private ways of "going without." She longed to help shoulder what to her boy must seem an endless burden stretching out ahead for years. And the joy in her heart over the man he had become overwhelmed the tiredness of her frail body and helped her to fight on when her poor eyesight seemed too great an obstacle.

Even when Laurie came home to stay, finished up his college course in record time, and was chosen for the finest position a young graduate could have in the new radar laboratory, he never made any explanation to his mother of why he did not give her more comforts. In fact he never had mentioned the exact sum of his salary, only announced casually, "The boss gave me a good break. Dad would be pleased!" And because they were like that with one another, his mother never asked him more, but her brown eyes shone through tender tears in her quiet rejoicing with him.

Oh, it was not that he made his mother suffer hardships, or that he left her without any of the little attentions that can make such extraordinarily sweet spots in the long monotonous workdays that most widowed mothers put through. Laurie would always go out of his way in the springtime to run down to the woods and find the first arbutus, he knew she loved it so. Often in summer he would gather a capful of those incredibly sweet wild strawberries that grew in the meadow beyond their old south pasture. Then stealing up behind her chair he would slip the luscious fragrant offering into her lap. Then he would laugh with the simple joy of his surprise. It reminded her of his first year at school when he made some astonishing picture, or paper basket, and brought it to her with a triumphant "For you, mommie!"

His mother would still be surprised and delighted in the old way and she would pull his brown head down from his tall height behind her and give him a hug and a kiss. Together they would go to the kitchen, give a quick sparkling rinse to the berries, get out the cream and perhaps some cookies she had made as her surprise for him and they would enjoy the little feast together because it savored of love.

Yes, Mrs. Judson was quite satisfied with Laurie's care of her. As time went on she sensed with more keen certainty the longing he had now and again to buy little luxuries for her. And so she dried the tears that gradually flowed less often, and happily struggled with the old worn-out washing machine that creaked and groaned in all its joints, and threatened nearly every week to quit its job entirely. She always took care, however, to do the wash when Laurie was out lest he discover how wobbly the old washer was and find out that the drain was not set low enough in this house, so that she had either to scoop all the water out with a dipper or else let it run into a bucket and run the risk of flooding the whole floor.

She had managed through the long months and years to help out quite a little by doing beautiful needlepoint and petit point, though it was terribly hard on her eyes. She never handed over to Laurie the money she received. She knew that would hurt him. She simply used the money for supplies, explaining casually at dinner time, "The price of peas was down this week, and bacon's not so high either." She always watched the prices carefully so that she could truthfully say it even though the drop was only half a cent. "I do believe the prices are actually going down. I didn't need all you gave me last week. Don't give me so much this time."

Oh, she couldn't say that too often, or her son's keen eyes would look at her suspiciously and he would demand "Are you eating enough, mother, when I'm not here? We don't want you getting sick, you know. Why, who would take care of you when I'm at work!" as if the problem of a nurse were far more important than her health and comfort. Then they would share their laugh together and rest in the love that was in all their unspoken words.

This bright June day Mrs. Judson had taken her place in the worn old rocker by the window where she always sat to sew because the light was best there. Just as soon as Laurie went out she hurried to get started. For she knew that he had planned to be gone the rest of the day on a picnic with Mary Arden, and that would give her a chance to finish the chair seat for Mrs. Sewell who was so anxious to get it.

"I'll pay you a dollar extra," that condescending lady had stated, "if you can finish it for me in time so that I can have it put on before Lady Somerset arrives. She is used to everything beautiful about her, you know, and I am just *so* anxious to have things just as nice as can be. You know she is to stay with me when she comes to speak at our Club."

Mrs. Judson's soft brown eyes could throw sparks on occasion and how they would have enjoyed doing so then, as accompaniment to a curt refusal of the little bonus. But Laurie's mother remembered in time and quietly answered, "I'll do my best to have it for you, Mrs. Sewell." Oh, if Laurie had known! But he didn't know, not yet, anyway. Some day when the whole debt was settled perhaps she would tell him some of the little things that had happened, the funny ones, or the ones that showed how marvelously their God was guiding and caring for them.

So she sat and sewed, taking her careful stitches efficiently, swiftly. And she thought with almost a pang of pleasure of the outing that Laurie was to have. It was not that she did not want him to go. He deserved all the good times there were, and she exulted in every bit of pleasure that came his way, so long as it was the right kind of pleasure, and Laurie had proved to her anxious mother heart now that he did not have a taste for any other than good clean fun.

No, it was that lovely girl! Mrs. Judson had not seen her, it is true, since she was sixteen years old. But she had been like an exquisite bud then. It was not hard to imagine how beautifully she had blossomed. In the few days since she had been back at Arden, Laurie had talked constantly of her.

"Yes," muttered his mother to herself pleating her soft brown brows as she turned her work to start across the other way, "he's spent more words on her in three days than he ever wasted on all other girls put together. This is *it!* I knew it would have to come, and it ought to. But oh, I wish she weren't so rich, and if she only didn't have that mother!"

For Mrs. Judson, having been "next farm neighbor" in the days when Mr. Arden had inveigled his young bride to visit his old home, had had many a social slap from that fine lady. She had good reason to know what her standards of life must be. And what a girl would turn out to be who had been exposed to such ideals all her life.

And so Mrs. Judson as she worked breathed a cry for help for her son. "Let him see, Lord, right away before it's too late, if she is not the one for him. And help me to keep my hands off!"

Then she heard the footsteps.

The Fuller brush man, likely. He generally came about this time of day. Or the scissors grinder. No, the steps were too crisp for his. Then she looked out the window.

It was Laurie!

Quick as a flash she whisked her needlepoint into her capacious knitting bag and grabbed out a sock. It turned out to be one she had already darned two days ago and had forgot to put away, but Laurie need not know that. She pretended to be rethreading her needle.

But why was he back? Had the girl turned him down? And now her silly heart was ready to take offense at this girl who could not see the worth of her splendid Laurie-boy. Yet stay—wasn't that perhaps the answer to her prayer?

She looked up casually as Laurie came in.

"What, no picnic? Or is it to be later?" she said it still casually, as if of course everything must be all right. But she could not help noting the little disappointed droop to those broad shoulders.

"No picnic." He answered trying to smile indifferently. "She's gone."

Mrs. Judson's heart gave a leap. Was this over so soon then? Before any harm had been done? Or *was* it "before?" Had her laddie's heart indeed gone out from him already? She waited. When he said nothing she asked,

"You mean gone, for good? This was just a little visit?"

"I don't know," sighed Laurie. "Her mother sent for her, it seems. At least some drip with a soiled upper lip was there to get her. She had left already." He slumped down on the edge of the couch with his head in his hands. "I might have known it was too nice to last. She probably couldn't take it after all the dance and song of the city. Yokels have no appeal." He tried to smile grimly. "Guess I'll get to work on that thesis and get it off my mind."

Just as he was going out the door his mother's voice stopped him.

"Laurie." He turned. She spoke gently but with the clear incisive wisdom of a man. "If she's like that, you know, it's just as well—isn't it?"

He sighed again. "Oh, I know it, mums. And I probably needed this to get sane again, but still," he flashed a real smile now, "God never said that His disappointments wouldn't hurt while they were going on, did He?"

Mrs. Judson nodded understandingly, smiling too as Laurie started up the stairs.

"'Okay,' son. You'll do!"

8

FLOSS Fairlee's wedding rehearsal was a gay affair. Floss and her mother had every detail of the ceremony planned so accurately that little time was wasted on such questions as who should walk on which side of whom, and all those other fine points that usually snag every wedding party and have to be discussed for hours on end until everyone almost wishes the bride and groom had been married quietly and had it over with.

Floss's mother was like a commanding general ordering everyone about, yet with a smiling graciousness that somewhat concealed the inflexibility of her commands. Floss had few ideas of her own. She had always been quite content to accept her mother's excellent readymade ones. Floss had pale gold fuzzy hair brushed out in a becoming halo around her face. Her mother had decided that this coiffure best shortened and widened her daughter's rather long face. Also it enhanced the ethereal quality of her pale fair skin and pale blue eyes. Therefore there was no argument about it, that was the way she wore her hair.

And Floss's upper teeth were a trifle over normal

length; so her mother had trained her not to raise her lips too high when she smiled. The effect was something like a sweet well groomed sheep.

But Floss was a sweet girl, and Mary Arden liked her, in a way. Still, it was Floss who was especially fond of Mary and sought her out to cling to, though Floss's family and financial standing were even more enviable from a worldly standpoint than Mary Arden's. Mrs. Arden was most flattered at Floss's interest in her daughter.

Brooke Haven was a nephew of Mrs. Fairlee's, and a pet of the whole family. So it was no wonder that he had no trouble in getting acquiescence in his plans for the night of the rehearsal, and, if other factors proved favorable, even for the aftermath of the wedding itself, which was to be in the living room of the enormous Fairlee home.

There were two bridesmaids besides Mary Arden, who was to be maid of honor. It was well known that the two men who were ushers were practically engaged to the two girls with whom they were to march and stand in the receiving line. So it was not difficult to draw them into Brooke Haven's clever plans.

Lovely Mary Arden appeared at her friend's house promptly for the rehearsal, wearing her best smile and dressed in all the gaiety she could muster after her unsettling tiff with Brooke Haven that morning.

She had intercepted her mother when she came from the telephone call and demanded to know what Brooke meant by planning to announce their engagement when she who was expected to be the bride had not given consent. But her mother, quick to sense that she had spoken too soon, responded, "Oh, that was a silly plan he mentioned once. If he has said nothing to you about it, I suppose of course he has given it up."

So Mary had had to be content with that hope. Still she felt most uneasy and dreaded the evening and the next day. Again and again she told herself that it was absurd to be nervous about this situation, for after all, she was sane and of age, she could do as she pleased. Surely no one could *force* her to marry Brooke Haven. But she was perfectly aware that Brooke Haven was clever and that he could put her into a most unwelcome situation if he chose.

Her natural desire was to freeze up and never speak to him again after what had happened already. But she finally decided once more that she would gain nothing by that attitude, and she would only make the whole affair most unpleasant for everyone concerned. It would be rude in the extreme to vent her own indignation on Floss by spoiling her party. No, her only defense would be gaiety. Just laugh off anything he tried to do or say. That would keep the bright atmosphere of the party intact, and make it impossible for Brooke to take seriously anything either of them said.

So the evening struck a note of something like hilarity in tune with Mary Arden's keen repartee.

Brooke noted her gay laughter and her playfulness with them all, even with himself, and smiled with satisfaction. She had got over her little pique, as he had expected, and was herself again, even more fascinating than usual. Her manner showed not the slightest trace of annoyance at him; just cheerful banter met everything he said.

After the brief rehearsal was over and Brooke had been instructed as to how and when to nudge the bridegroom, who had not yet arrived, they all sat down to a delectable repast in the Fairlees' handsome dining room.

Of course Mary was seated next to Brooke, with an

empty chair on her other side, next to Floss, waiting for the groom who might turn up at any moment.

But Mary had no difficulty in keeping their conversation on a general level, for Brooke seemed quite willing for the present at least, to be his most charming self, gracious and courteous. Mary almost relaxed her excited vigilance.

Then after a goodly amount of the dainty ice cream molds had disappeared, and many little cakes and confections, besides drinks of various kinds, a bit of a break came in the gay crosscurrents of joking and repartee.

The couple across the round table from Floss caught her quick nod and smile, and suddenly the young man arose. With an elaborate bow and flowery language he proceeded to address the girl beside him, beseeching her hand in marriage. With much ado she tried to keep her face perfectly straight and serious, but found it impossible as chuckle followed giggle around the intimate circle of her friends, and finally she broke down with smiles and blushes and made a most satisfactory response to her lover which sent them all off into peals of laughter. Since this engagement was one which had been taken for granted by them all for some time, it was not especially surprising to anyone there, just a clever unusual way of announcing the fact that these two were planning to marry. They were showered with congratulations and good wishes with Mary's brightly topping them all. Though a little shiver of dread shook her again as she recalled what her mother had said that afternoon.

Then when the excitement and teasing had subsided and another moment of calm arrived, what did the next couple do but put on their little act. In a slightly different way, of course, just to make it entertaining, but most obviously planned and possibly rehearsed. Then did Mary Arden's heart begin to gallop in panic. So this was what her mother had meant. Brooke Haven had planned this. It was like him. And just as surely as she knew that she sat there, she was certain that he intended to climax the little play with his own proposal, unrehearsed it is true, but nevertheless an obvious finish to a very unusual situation. There was nothing unexpected in the other two engagements, nor would anyone be surprised if she and Brooke would follow suit, for they had been seen together so very much during the past weeks.

Had Brooke told them she was willing for this? Was he actually counting on the presence of others to force her consent to save herself embarrassment? What could she do? What *could* she say to them all? Could she blaze up in anger and deny it? In the mood they were in that would probably accomplish just nothing at all. More than likely they would whoop with laughter and think she was pretending, for they all knew that she and Brooke had been together a great deal. This whole thing would be in the papers, undoubtedly, by tomorrow morning. Very likely Brooke had already given the news to the social column reporters and it was being printed right now for morning papers! Oh! What could she do to stop it! For she had no illusions any longer about Brooke. He would stop at nothing.

Then like a sudden frightening calm before a clap of thunder came a third silence. Mary's heart froze within her. It was coming. Now! Oh, was there no one to take her part? If only her father were home. At least she could go to him after it was over—if this horrible evening would ever be over—and ask him what to do, beg him to call the papers and cancel the news. But no, he was still far away across the water, too distant to help even tomorrow. She must face this thing herself and carry it through somehow! But how?

Then her mind suddenly flashed to Laurie. He seemed

like a strong refuge. But he could do nothing, of course, even if he were here and she could get in touch with him. Laurie had a God, though. Couldn't a God help at a time like this? But she didn't know Laurie's God. Why had she never realized that life could hold times of dread and stress when she would be absolutely on her own—and helpless!

Of course all this went through her racing mind in a second, while her lips smiled and she laughed with glee over something someone had said about the second couple whose engagement had been so cleverly announced. In this way the silence was broken, that silence that she knew had been a preparation for Brooke's speech, whatever it should be. She must not allow another silence. He must have no chance to get on his feet and start this farce. Yet even as she rattled on, gasping after silly gay remarks like straws floating by her, saying any ridiculous thing just to keep going, she was conscious that they were all watching her, with knowing smiles on their faces, waiting, willing to wait, another few moments, for the sake of the fun that was coming.

Then all at once there were no more straws floating by, no more words came to her. In sudden blank, stunned silence she felt Brooke beside her rise to his feet. Her face was ghastly white behind her forced gay smile.

"Well, boys and girls," he smiled his easy confident smile, "since you are all planning to walk down the aisle together I suppose it won't be any surprise to you if we do the same thing. How about it, Mary?" He leaned down and raised Mary to her feet, putting his arm familiarly around her, his face close to hers waiting for her kiss to seal her assent. But she pulled away, still with that merry hard bright smile upon her face, to say in her most joking tones, "Oh, part way down, if that's what we are to do, but not *all* the way, Brooke!" But most of her words were drowned in a shout of welcome, for there stood the bridegroom in the doorway!

Floss rushed to him and received her own embrace and then they all crowded round to greet him, squealing with excitement.

Mary Arden, aghast to think that perhaps she had not succeeded in making even one of them realize that she had *not* accepted Brooke Haven's casual proposal, slid into the other room to the telephone booth under the stairs to call the newspapers, any one, all of them, to find out whether Brooke had put in the notice, for that was what she was certain he had done this for, so that it would be practically irrevocable. But Mary had not realized the lateness of the hour. It was already past midnight. The morning papers were even now on sale at newsstands all over the city. And yes, the notice was in.

"I made sure to get it right," the man at the other end of the wire assured her confidently. "It's all O.K."

"But it isn't so!" choked out Mary.

But the satisfied social editor had clicked off.

With dull horror beating on her heart Mary went back into the other room. It made little difference now whether she was gay or sad, or even mad. They were all so excited over the return of their hero that even Mary Arden's engagement announcement had become just another incident in the whole delightful affair.

Short of blazing at them all with anger until she got their attention, Mary knew there was nothing she could do. And it seemed hardly fair to Floss to make such a scene when her bridegroom had just arrived and her wedding was tomorrow. After all, it was her trouble, not theirs. And nobody, not even Brooke Haven, could *make* her marry him. The announcement was humiliating, infuriating beyond words. It would make her no end of explanation. But there was nothing to be done

about it now. Absolutely nothing, until she could perhaps insert a notice in the column herself that the
announcement had been a mistake. It would be embarrassing, but—well, it would have to be so. Just one of
those things she had to take whether she liked it or not.
It seemed that a good many of such things were coming
her way all at once. Her life heretofore had been so
comparatively easy.

She thought of her father's warning to remember to
laugh at herself. But this time it just seemed impossible.

She wanted to run away but she made herself stay, to
see if things wouldn't quiet down a bit and perhaps she
would have a chance to explain that she hadn't given
Brooke a green light at all, quite the contrary.

She went upstairs when the girls went up, but the wild
hilarity continued.

Finally she thought her chance had come. Just before
they all started downstairs to say good night and take
their several departures, Mary found Floss next to her
and Floss was hugging her ecstatically and saying how
glad she was for her. "And you'll be my very own cousin
now in a little while, won't you?" she almost screamed
with glee.

Mary shook her head as hard as she could and tried to
speak above the din, "No, Floss, no! I didn't tell him I
would marry him at all. You didn't understand." But her
words were scarcely heard. The second bridesmaid
caught a little of what she was saying and laughed loudly.

"Oh, listen girls," she said, "revolt in the Haven
family already! Mary is trying to go back on it! Can you
tie that? He! He!" But her words were as the voice of
one blackbird in a flock. Nobody listened. Everybody
laughed because they were laughing at everything, but
nobody knew what had been said.

Mary tried again downstairs, but again she was drowned by uproarious joking. So she gave it up.

Brooke was of course to be her escort home. She had no other way home. She climbed into his car and sat in the farthest corner of the seat. She spoke not one word all the way home. She had decided that the time had come to cease the cheery gay attitude and let Brooke Haven understand that she meant no friendliness to him by her brave attempts to keep these two days cheerful for her friend Floss.

Brooke had sat silently also, gloomily aware that Mary was angry. He had hoped against hope that her gay manner tonight had meant that she would be cheerful and reasonable about this. But if she meant to carry on the feud, well, she'd get over it again, as she had before. Anyway, he meant to marry her. Then he'd make her behave herself.

As they drew up at the Arden house Mary said coldly, "You need not come to the door with me, now or ever again. You will see, please, that the notice in the papers is denied immediately. If you do not, my father will!"

Without so much as a good night she marched up into the house.

In the darkness she left behind her, Brooke raised his black eyebrows in amused admiration of her cleverness at guessing that he would have put that notice in the papers. She was so altogether desirable! If he could only get her over this infernal idea of holding him off. He frowned. It had never yet occurred to him that Mary Arden would not yield in the end, for it was inconceivable that he was not altogether desirable himself. If she were married to him she would *have* to submit, at least in public, and as for their private life, well, she was so attractive when she was angry that he wouldn't in the least mind a little quarrel now and then.

So he smiled grimly to himself as he drove off into the dark beginning of a new day that might mean a great deal to both him and Mary Arden.

But Mary stumbled desperately into the house that all unawares had become to her an unfriendly place. She climbed the stairs lugging her burden with her, torn between discouragement and fierce anger. At the top of the stairs her mother was waiting with a fond light in her eyes to greet her. But Mary forestalled all her questions by a weary: "Good night, mother. I'd like to get right to bed. I'm so tired, and tomorrow will be a big day."

So her mother wisely but reluctantly drew her soft silk robe about her and retired again to her own room to wonder and weep. Her daughter certainly did not seem as elated as a newly engaged girl should look but Mary was queer about some things, and no doubt she was tired. She sighed but she set her lips more grimly, awaiting tomorrow's enlightenment.

Mary Arden slid out of her dress and her shoes and turned out her light so that her mother would suppose she had gone to bed. But her mind was in too much turmoil to lie down yet. She went over to the open window and sat on the arm of a chair there, staring bitterly out into the urban darkness. Somewhere out among those dots of light and those buzzing engines was the man she had come to loathe. For a few minutes she simply let herself seethe with hatred for him. To think that he would *dare* to put her into a position like this! And then pretend he cared enough for her to marry her. Although it was true he had never made much pretense at loving her. He had admired her, yes. She sniffed indignantly. As if she were a costly painting, or a fine work of art! She shrank now from the very thought of his eyes upon her. The horrid memory of that kiss he had given her yesterday made her writhe. Did other girls

feel this way about the man they were going to marry?—
Oh! Horrors! What was she thinking? Had even she
come to the place where she felt a marriage to this man
was inevitable? Everyone in the world seemed to be
forcing it upon her. *Was* it inevitable? Was there no way
of escape? She shook the thought from her. What
nonsense. She had the right to marry whom she pleased
or not marry at all! She had tried her best to be courteous
and thoughtful for others in this situation but if worst
came to worst she would just have to make a big scene
and bring it to a head, news scandal or no.

She thought of trying to get in touch with her father
by long distance telephone, but she knew she would
have to ask her mother's help, for she did not know his
itinerary nor where to reach him just now. And she did
not want her mother's help in this, for she was sure it
would not be help.

Then she tried to think what her father would tell her
if she asked him. But her tired shocked mind was not
able to imagine what her father's gentle wise counsel
would be.

Then once more the thought of Laurie came to her.
Strange what a refuge he seemed, little as she really knew
him. Her cheeks burned with shame to think that he
could ever know of this awful situation she had got
herself into. Or had she? Was it her own fault, or just
that everybody seemed bent on planning her life for her?
That question made her stop and really think seriously.
Ye-es, she slowly admitted to herself, perhaps she had
been a little silly with Brooke Haven, right at the start of
their acquaintance. She had been flattered that such a
wealthy, good-looking young man whom any one of
her friends would have considered a marvelous "catch"
had showered such exclusive attention upon her. And,
yes, she had willingly let him kiss her once or twice,

even responded a little, gaily, carelessly. All the girls in her crowd did it, she knew, though she had never liked the idea. She was not ordinarily one to collect kisses from any and all. But she had toyed with the idea of caring enough some day to want his kisses. She had tried to make herself attractive with him in mind. Well, there was nothing basically wrong in that, surely. What then had made her feel so differently?

When was it that she began to notice this change in her own feelings toward Brooke? She had been home from college scarcely a month now, and had gone constantly with him at first. After seeing him at Christmas and holidays, and hearing from him often all winter, she had actually looked forward to being with him again. For two weeks they had been together almost constantly. He had taken her here and taken her there, had showered flowers and candy and presents of all kinds upon her. The rush had taken her off her balance. Then what happened? She had never stopped before to find out. She simply realized one day that she had had enough. She knew that she did not care to marry this man, and yet he evidently was bearing strongly toward that goal. That was when she made up her mind to go to Arden.

Arden! What made her think of going there, anyway? She searched her subconscious memories, clipping off day after day, until at last she came upon the very day and time when she felt she had begun to wake up to what was going on. It was when Aunt Cora was there visiting. Not that poor old Aunt Cora had the slightest power to influence Mary in her romances. No, but Mary had been left to entertain her one afternoon until her mother should return from her bridge club. Desperately after a half-hour of desultory cropping about on the bare prairie of common interests, Mary had seized upon her old photograph album. Aunt Cora had settled her spectacles upon her thin Roman nose and looked down through the bifocal part at the small snapshots that Mary tried to make interesting to her. Aunt Cora had not discovered much to interest her, except as she gave a sniff or two when she came on the pictures of some modern bathing suits.

But the snapshots had done something for Mary Arden that nothing else could have done. Those pages that showed snaps she had taken that summer at Arden were the ones that Mary had lingered over. They brought back all the sweet simple joys of that time that seemed so long ago now. The dear old house, the swing that carried one out over the brow of the hill, the little canoe down on the creek. And then there was one that had brought a sweet tingling thrill. Strange that it should! It was a picture of Laurie Judson. He was on one knee beside his canoe, smiling up at Mary as she had snapped the picture, with that joyous light in his eyes that she remembered with a sudden lift of the heart. It was the end of the summer. They had been about to take one of those delightful rides up the stream and down, through the lanes of yellow leaves that lay like a priceless rug on the polished still water; they would glide under soft sweeping pine branches that smelled oh so sweet as they snatched at a needle or two in passing and let the perfume steal out; then they would climb nimbly out, tie their craft, and, near a little fire Laurie would build, they would eat their picnic supper. Mary remembered her happy anticipation of that ride. And she recalled with another little thrill how gently and courteously Laurie had helped her out of the boat that day when they returned, and how deeply he had looked into her eyes as he stood there on the little landing slip, with a tender wistful farewell without words because he was going away to war. Of course she had been young, scarcely sixteen then, and not supposed to know her own mind. Laurie had been older, by nearly four years. But the memories of him were sweet clean memories. Laurie had never taken advantage of her as this man Brooke Haven had done. Yet Laurie had had more chance, and more right, if he had cared to be that kind of man. For she had known him summers, for years. And he was of a beloved next-door-neighbor family. That counted in Arden.

Yes, thought Mary as she still stood there at her window looking out into the hot night, it was that day, when she saw Laurie's picture again that she realized afresh what a man can be, and ought to be. It must have been then that she came to her senses. She was not conscious of having compared the two men that day, but the manliness, and the clean brave strength of Laurie Judson had swept through her being like a breath of fresh air that cleared her mind and heart.

Oh, to be back in Arden right now. Why had she ever come up here to the city again? What a mess had been stirred up. Yet she had thought she was doing her duty to come in answer to her mother's insistence. She wondered whether it really was right to try to obey someone's else whims continually, even a mother's. That problem was one she must ask Laurie about some day. He was a preacher, he ought to know. Probably he'd *have* to say obey.

At any rate, she made up her mind that now she had responded to her mother's call, and also pleased her friend, she would get right back to Arden as fast as any vehicle could carry her. But how was she to manage that?

How she wished now that she had brought her car so that she could just slide right out of the house after the wedding, and start off alone unnoticed. But she did not have the car.

There would have to be a valid reason she could give to Mrs. Fairlee for running off soon. For she had no intention of staying even one minute more than was absolutely dictated by the minimum of courtesy. She was quite sure that Brooke Haven would make some further attempt to enmesh her. The fact that he said nothing on the way home last night was no indication that he was accepting her verdict. He had not accepted it in the afternoon, had he? And he would not now. He simply did not consider others, only himself.

Having decided that she would get back to Arden, Mary felt a little easier in her mind and undressed quickly, even managing a little wan laugh at herself to think that here she was, apparently engaged to a millionaire, and planning to run away from him like a silly romantic kid.

She lay a long time planning her course of action for the next day. When at last she fell asleep it was nearly dawn.

And just a few hours later as Laurie strode downtown to get his bus out to the plant, he stopped at the corner newsstand and bought a paper. Propped in the rack near the paper of his nearby city were papers from other cities and his eye caught the name of the city where Mary Arden lived. With a little quickening of interest he threw down another nickel and picked one up. He had visited her city, though not her house, more than once, and would be not too unintelligent about its local news.

He found himself scanning only hastily the front page political news, and without realizing that he was looking for a certain name, turned over the pages until he came to the notes of society doings.

There at the top of a column was Mary Arden's lovely

face! Laurie's heart beat a little faster as he pulled the paper closer to read every word that was printed about her. Then almost a groan escaped him there in the crowded bus. He was too late! She belonged already to that unspeakable *cad*. That insolent fellow who had come and tried to claim her yesterday. The chump had been right then, in saying she was the girl he was going to marry! Laurie crushed the paper in his big hands and turned his hot despairing gaze out the window lest someone should see the suffering in his soul.

9

MARY detoured the storm that would have made havoc of the breakfast table, by sleeping too late to have anything but a cup of coffee in her room. The wedding was to be at noon, so she had to dress quickly.

She knew exactly how trying her mother could be after she had seen the announcement in the papers, and she had no heart to try to reason with her. She had made her plans and hoped to be able to carry them out without any horrible scenes.

When she woke it was nearly eleven o'clock. She rang for Hetty and asked her for coffee and the morning paper.

"Oh, yes! Miss Mary," simpered Hetty in a meaningful tone of voice. "Of *course* you'll be wanting to see it this morning!"

Then Hetty knew! She had seen the announcement, or else her mother had told the servants, with how much elation Mary could very well surmise. Or stay! Did Hetty simply mean that the news of Floss's wedding would be printed this morning, with all the items concerning the wedding party and its garments. Perhaps, oh, perhaps that was why she had spoken in that silly tone of voice. Was there just the least possibility that the awful thing had not happened and last night had been a dream?

Then Hetty returned with the steaming coffee daintily served, and an unctuous smile on her face as she nodded to the newspaper neatly folded on the tray, with the cut of Mary's lovely face at the very top of a column.

"We're all very happy for you, Miss Mary," beamed the servant. "And we hope you will have many happy years with your handsome bridegroom." Hetty was obviously proud of her little speech, which she had carefully prepared down in the kitchen, with the critical aid of the cook and chauffeur.

But Mary froze.

"Hetty!" she said sternly, "this is a terrible mistake. The papers had no right to print this for it is not true. Mr. Haven and I are *not* engaged, and I don't ever intend to be engaged to him! I shall appreciate it if you will correct the rumor wherever you have opportunity."

Crestfallen and shocked, Hetty started to withdraw.

"And Hetty," added Mary, "I shall dress alone this morning. Please see that no one at all disturbs me. Ask Henry to have the car ready in half an hour, please."

"Yes, Miss Mary." Hetty's deflated voice was barely audible and she closed the door noiselessly and hastened below stairs to give out the latest news note in the servants' quarters.

The first thing Mary did was to repack the little bag she had brought with her from Arden. She clicked it shut and placed it far back in her closet behind some long dresses.

Then she went to her desk and wrote a note to her mother. She would not have time later.

Dear mother: I am sorry not to say good by to you
properly, but I am very much upset by the trick that was
played on me last night and I am anxious to get away.
Please do not try to call me back. I shall no doubt get my
balance again one of these days but it has been horrible.

Mary.

She was conscious that it bore no loving message, but
just now she was not feeling very loving toward anyone.
Perhaps later she would be able to forgive and forget.
She did not know of course just what part her mother
had taken in the whole scheme, or whether she had
helped it on, but she had certainly known of it from
what she said yesterday. Mary would not blame her
mother in so many words but it was not easy to think
kindly this morning of anyone who had had anything to
do with Brooke Haven's plan.

For Floss's sake she would go through with the wedding, although it meant bearing looks and glances from
everyone there, pleased glances, to be sure, for all of
Floss's crowd seemed to think there was no one like
Brooke Haven.

"Well, I agree with them!" she muttered angrily to
her powder puff. "There is nobody like him, and it's a
mighty good thing there isn't."

But oh, how those glances would change to indignant
scorn when they heard her denial of the engagement.
For deny it she would. Every chance she got. If she
stayed to the reception, as she practically was forced to
do as maid of honor, she would have to meet every one
of those people in that awful line and tell them, with
Brooke Haven standing there beside her. Oh, how *could*
she get through this unspeakable day!

She had already looked up the trains last night. There

was one at one thirty, the only one that would get her to Arden before midnight. The only plane left before noon and that would not do. Could she possibly get away in time for the train?

She glanced at the little electric clock on her bedside table. Eleven twenty-five! Henry had been waiting ten minutes. Well, he was good natured, and he had nothing else to do. But she was supposed to be at the bride's house at half past.

She slid into the filmy blue dress, pulled up its tiny zipper, and hastily tied the big taffeta bow sash. Adjusting could come later. The girls would all fuss over each other anyway, and fix her up. She was not conscious that she was utterly lovely, no matter whether she was properly adjusted or not, and that her carefree naturalness was a part of her charm.

Giving a little fluff to her hair she snatched up her little bag that contained all the necessities for last minute touches, and fairly tore down the stairs.

But she knew all the time that her mother would be waiting down there; that Hetty and Henry had been questioned carefully as to her schedule.

It was just as well. Better let her mother know how she felt now, before she got to the Fairlees' house.

Mary drew her mother hastily into the library.

"Mother," she spoke in a tense, firm voice, although so quietly that Hetty, listening outside, could not make out more than a word or two, "that notice in the paper must be corrected. It is not true! Brooke Haven and I are *not* engaged and never will be. I would like you to correct it every chance there is, today. Good by, I'm late. Henry will be right back for you."

Without waiting for her mother's astonishment and chagrin to find words, she flew out the door and into the big family car.

As she sped along the familiar streets they suddenly seemed alien to her. She found herself imagining how she would tell the people who lived in each of these big houses they passed, and how each one would react. She made haste to tell even Henry, in tones that tried to be matter-of-fact, as though this thing were merely a mistaken rumor about a war or a strike being over when it really was not. Poor Henry stiffened in the chauffeur's seat and took it properly, with only a "Yes, Miss Mary." But he would have done that even though he hadn't heard it already mouthed in the servants' quarters.

Then came the problem of telling the excited wedding party. Oh, what a long task this was that was set before her! How could anyone be so cruel as to put another person in such a position as this. The thought of how she would treat Brooke Haven she pushed away from her. She simply would not waste a thought, even of anger on him now. Her main aim was to get through the next two hours and get away home, home to Arden. There she felt she would like to bury her head like a child in her pillow and cry herself to calmness.

Somehow Mary got the truth into the confused and bewildered minds of Floss and her friends. She tackled the first one she met and made her step aside to a comparatively quiet corner. Her serious face startled the girl into listening.

"Betty," said Mary, "you've just got to listen to me! You were all too addled last night to hear what I said. Brooke Haven has pulled a trick on me. We *are not* engaged, and don't expect to be! Is that plain? Because I shall have to depend on my friends to straighten this out. Please, Betty, tell everyone you know. It will be a scandal, I know, but I'm sure I did nothing to bring it on, and I'm perfectly furious."

The astounded girl gasped and stammered, thinking

only of the immediate crisis. "But Mary, won't you even be in the wedding? What'll we all do-o-o?" she wailed.

Mary gave her a little shake. "Of course, Betty, don't be so stupid. I'll go through with the wedding for Floss's sake. But I want this *lie* corrected. Do you understand?" Mary was so solemn and so insistent that the little bridesmaid was fairly frightened. She nodded in an awed way and fluttered off to try to get the ear of some other merrymaker to tell her astonishing news.

When it finally got around Mary was conscious of the whispers and looks in her direction as she stood at the mirror and fussed with her hair and her bouquet.

Then at last her father's daughter rose up in her and she turned to them all, maids and bridesmaids, and laughed. "You don't all need to stand and talk *about* me, girls. I'm not an object of fear, or even pity. Just please accept the fact that Brooke and I are not going to be married, and correct the thought in anybody else's mind. Now, let's see if Floss is ready."

Cheered to find their old Mary as ready as ever to join their fun, they flocked around her, but Mary in spite of her forced smile felt tired, tired down to her very heart. Would this never end so that she could get away?

The wedding march seemed endless, and the service, which Mary had always before enjoyed hearing, seemed a cruel chain, slowly binding, binding till the last prayer was said and the padlock was snapped shut. How, she wondered, could any girl ever be willing to promise all those things? How could she be sure enough of any man to trust him like that? For *all* her life? Oh, of course, there was divorce, it was common enough among the circle in which Mary moved. But she always had despised people who couldn't stick to their vows, or who hadn't known their own minds well enough not to get into something they couldn't finish. Now she was not sure. If by any chance a girl had married a man such as she now believed Brooke Haven to be, a man who would pull a dastardly, dishonorable trick on a girl he pretended to love as himself, what would be right? Should she still try to stick it out? Mary's very soul shrank with horror at the thought, but her honesty made her admit that, yes, she would feel that having promised, a girl ought to stick it out, that is—with practically no exceptions. But oh! how careful Mary meant to be before she ever made any promises like that to any man.

Then she found herself in the receiving line, receiving almost as many good wishes as the bride. To each gushing congratulator she turned her most cordial smile, frosted albeit with dignity, and shook her pretty head, explaining that there had been a mistake in the papers, there was no cause for best wishes. And Brooke Haven stood stonily by her side. When the guests turned to him for confirmation or denial of what his problematical financée had told them he raised his black eyebrows and ironically answered, "That's what Mary says," and shrugged. Most people went away still mystified. And Mary grew more and more indignant. She did not converse with Brooke, and he made no attempt to speak to her.

The heat of the day and the long standing in line began to make her head swim. At last she felt she could take it no longer. The line of guests were only the stragglers now, and a few close friends who were making the tour twice over. She glanced at her little jeweled watch. Oh! Five minutes after one. Could she try for that one-thirty train?

Without a word of apology or warning to Brooke Haven she turned to the usher on her other side, whispering, "I feel faint, Bill. I want to lie down. No, don't send anyone with me, I'll be all right in a minute or two.

They'll soon be going out to the dining room now and I'll feel better when I get a cup of coffee or something. Close up the line, will you, please? And don't say anything."

She slid out behind some palms. But instead of going upstairs she made her swift way out to the kitchen where she surprised the staid Henry with his arm around the Fairlees' second maid. He turned crimson but came to attention at once.

Mary smiled. Perhaps she would have to use pressure, for Henry was most loyal to Mrs. Arden, but she would surely have Henry on her side now!

"Will you take me home right away, please? I don't feel well and I want to lie down."

"Oh, yes, miss. Shall I call your mother?"

"No, Henry, don't disturb her now. It's nothing serious. I guess I'm just too tired. Come on, quickly."

Back at the big house she sent Henry speedily back to the Fairlees'.

"Here's a note for mother," she said as she gave him the one she had prepared. "If anyone asks about me just say I felt faint and wanted to lie down. Otherwise don't say anything at all. Thank you, Henry."

As soon as she heard the car start down the street she called a taxi. She was going to take no chances with Henry taking her to that train.

In ten minutes more she was at the station and had her ticket. She had not even waited to hang up her blue maid of honor dress. Hetty would do that later. She had moved as silently about her room as possible and got out of the house, she devoutly hoped, before any of the servants knew she was there. She had taken her own front-door key with that in mind.

But now that she was ready ahead of time for the train she began to get panicky for fear her absence would be discovered and a search made for her. If only the train would come and take her before they could discover where she was. They might make a hue and cry for her after that; her disappearance might even get into the papers, but she felt that that would not matter so much now. After all that had been in the papers about her, a little more could be no worse. But her mother might suspect where she had gone and follow her here to the station and make a terrible scene if she refused to come back! Her tired confused brain finally wound itself into such a turmoil of fretting in the few minutes left that she noticed a little girl looking at her strangely. She must present a woebegone picture, the child had such troubled pity in her glance. Then all at once she laughed. It *was* funny, after finding that her plans had worked out so well up to this point, for her to get herself into a perfect stew because they might fail now. She smiled brightly back at the little girl who slowly returned the smile with a sigh of relief although it was tinged with bewilderment. The child was plainly wondering how a grown-up who had obviously been in such desperate straits a minute ago could laugh it off and look gay without anything happening to change the situation. She stared at Mary a while then looked away and gave up the riddle.

But Mary had been jolted out of her depression, and for the first time in two days she took a deep breath. The train pulled in just then and she got in and found her seat. Now she was almost happy. She was going back to Arden. Going back home! Strange, that it should seem like home to her more than the place where she had been brought up and lived most of her life. Was it just that she was selfish and liked it because it was her own? No, she thought not. Perhaps it was that the life there was the kind she had always subconsciously yearned for.

Simplicity. Sincerity. Friendliness. The clean clear sun-shine and breezes. The wholesome smell of the fresh hay from her own fields. No ugly emulations rearing up their lustful heads to make bitter the sweetness of boys' and girls' good times. Oh, she supposed the striving and coveting and the jealousies must be there in Arden as well as anywhere else, but at least she did not have them to battle with, not yet, anyway.

There were Nannie and Randa, and good old Orrin. They plodded faithfully on, apparently satisfied with their life of service, doing their simple work as well as they could, interested in their little church.

Their church. Ah! That seemed a good, sweet safe place to go to. How glad she would be to get back to it. Would there be any answer there to all her problems? Any solution to why she was here on this earth that had suddenly become unfriendly?

Would the tall strong gentle young pastor of that little chapel be able to tell her anything that would help her particular situation? Or was his preaching just theories that would not stand practice like those of the cleric at college?

At any rate, she experienced the keenest longing to get back to that tall young pastor, to sense his great strength as she walked a country road beside him, to watch his merry smile and rest in the carefree joy of him. Would he be there when she returned? Or would he be away perhaps, at some business or religious conference, as he had been for a day or two when she was there before. Her heart sank and she realized how much she counted on seeing him. Yet what a mystery he was! How little she really knew about his private life. When she had been a young girl she had not thought to inquire further than that he was coming over the next day for a picnic, or that they were to go canoeing Saturday. Now she began to realize what a stranger to her he actually was. If her mother, for instance, should discover his existence, and ask about him, what could she tell her, beyond the fact that he lived next door and that he had been in the service? Only that he was tall and very muscular, and extremely good-looking, according to her point of view, and that he was a preacher! A preacher! What would her mother have said to that! Oh, a distinguished scholar in a great city church, well, perhaps her mother would not have objected to a friendship with such a one. But a country preacher, who cared enough to do that on the side, and hold down a regular job besides, apparently a very humble one. Well, her mother did not know of him, and she would take good care that she did not until Mary had had time to learn more of him herself and decide whether she cared to go on with the friendship. Although there was something in her heart now that told her that there had never been a friendship in her life that she did care about as much as this one. It seemed the one fine jewel of her social contacts thus far.

The train jogged on and on, now and then stopping for a minute in a small city. Each time it left a city behind and travelled again through fields and farms and forests Mary felt relieved.

"I'm just a little old country girl, I guess," she laughed at herself. "Why am I so different from mother?"

Then she fell to thinking of her mother and what she would say when she discovered that her daughter bird had flown. Poor mother! Why would she try so hard to force those around her into her own molds? This much Mary was determined on: she would not leave Arden again until she wanted to, for any reason whatever! Her mother would leave for Castanza now in a few days and the gay life there would occupy her. Perhaps she would let her alone for a time. But Mary had yet to discover that the very thing she vowed she would not do was the one generally laid out by her Heavenly Tutor for her to do.

At last the darkness came and with it the old depression settled down once more. Would Arden be as she had thought? Or would even that turn unfriendly if she knew it better? On and on went Mary's tired discouraged thoughts until she heard with great relief the raucous voice of the conductor shouting "Arden, Arden!"

Mary had sent a couple of telegrams ahead while she waited at the station for the train. One was to Alvin Burgett, Arden Garage.

> *Arriving 10:20 tonight. Please leave my car outside. I have duplicate keys. Thank you.*

And now there was her car waiting for her, drawn up to the platform, and there was Alvin Burgett himself, a lean soiled young man with kind eyes and a two or three days' growth of dark beard. Mary found herself wondering how he kept it always just that length. If he ever did shave, why wouldn't it *sometimes* look clean? And if he didn't why didn't it get longer? Or perhaps he knew how to shave it to just the length to give that two-day effect!

But she was glad to see him. It seemed as if somebody cared that she had come home.

"Thought ya might uv fergot yer other keys, mebbe, an' I was down taown here anyhow. Ya okay? Okay, then. G' night." And he loped away to his own jalopy.

Oh, it was good to get home, even to see Alvin Burgett, mechanic.

10

THERE was a bright welcoming light on the wide front porch as Mary drove up the long drive to her house.

Nannie and Randa had rejoiced when they received her telegram that she was returning that evening. Randa hustled up and made up Mary's bed freshly with sheets just off their lavender scented shelves. She flung open the windows and let the June breezes fluff out the white ruffled curtains. Then she sped downstairs and picked a large handful of flowers. Their stems were all the same length, almost mathematically accurate, and there was precious little foliage to frame their bright pinks; they were bunched tightly together and thrust into a thick-necked shiny blue vase—but they were fairly bursting with affection and Mary noted them when she came with a queer twist of warmth in her heart.

Nannie baked brown bread and cherry pies and made feathery doughnuts enough for an army, so that Orrin when he trudged in from his work at suppertime asked if they were expecting the church meetin' there.

"If our Miss Mary really stays awhile," prophesied

Nannie gleefully, "we'll be havin' plenty o' meetin's o' some kind, I reckon."

"Oh. Humph. She comin' back? Didn't I tell ye?" Orrin carefully scraped his boots on the backdoor mat. "I said she was jes a-runnin' away from that feller that come here after her, and—" Orrin chuckled as he wiped his hot wet forehead with his dusty cotton handkerchief—"it's my guess she's a-runnin' back here away from him again. Don't you say so, son?" He turned to greet the tall figure that suddenly filled the doorway.

"Say what?" questioned Laurie in a tired voice. He was not wearing his usual joyous smile and his face looked white and drawn into deep lines.

Orrin looked puzzled at him as he repeated his surmise. He had never seen Laurie look so depressed, even when his father died.

For answer Laurie took a clipping of newspaper out of his pocket and handed it to the old man. Laurie opened his mouth but no words came at first. Then he managed in a dull voice, "Looks like you're wrong this time, friend."

Nannie and Randa seeing the expression on the two faces came over to look too. A heavy silence settled on them all.

Finally Orrin took out his cotton handkerchief and blew his nose hard. Slow tears rolled down Nannie's wrinkled cheeks, and Randa's face was red with indignation.

Then Orrin spoke gruffly and he tossed the bit of paper back to Laurie as if it did not matter.

"Somethin' wrong there. Miss Mary ain't two people. The Miss Mary that was here couldn't love that feller that come after her. She may be fooled for a spell, I'll admit that, but it won't last. When's supper, Nannie?"

The tension broken, Nannie and Randa scurried

around getting a spic-and-span cloth on the big kitchen table.

It seemed a ray of hope, the confident way that Orrin had said it. Even Laurie almost allowed himself to wonder if maybe, maybe, there was some mistake. But his reason told him better instantly, and his step was slow and heavy as he took the milk pails out for Orrin.

He wouldn't admit to himself why he had stopped in here on his way home from work. He took for granted that it was what he often did, and it being a hot day, old Orrin would appreciate a little help. Had he looked farther into his heart he might have found a hidden yearning for just such comfort as Orrin had given, groundless though it might be.

The day had been a long dreary plod for him, with his heart like lead in him. He kept trying to tell himself that it was just because that fellow was so worthless; it was a shame for any nice girl to be tied to a man who was obviously a selfish boor. But every time he would even contemplate the picture of Mary Arden in that man's arms his heart would give an awful lunge and sink away down till he felt he couldn't carry the burden any longer.

He had sought out these plain people who loved Mary Arden in the hope that they might have further news of her. Well, they did. She was coming back. Tonight. Small comfort in that, though, he thought as he squirted the sweet warm milk into Orrin's shining pails. He had better keep a good distance or he might let Mary see how he felt about her accepted lover. No need in hurting Mary, if she really cared enough about him to marry him.

He said a preoccupied sad good night to the three waiting in the Arden house for their beloved mistress and went home with his heart still heavy.

During supper Nannie and Randa had a lengthy

discussion over what they should say to Miss Mary about her engagement, or whether they would let her tell them and pretend not to know of it.

"I declare," announced Randa hotly, "I've a mind just to keep Miss Mary home here next time she tries to go off, and I'll not let that city slicker see her at all."

"I'll be gormed!" ejaculated Orrin after two platefuls of his hash had been peppered with their worries. "Why can't you two let things be? You're still fond o' Miss Mary, ain't you? An' you're nothin' but her servants anyhow, are you? You don't need to try to run her life for her. Keep out of this thing fer land's sakes and let the Lord have a little say in what he'll do with her."

So the two distraught women obediently quieted down, but the welcome they had planned for their Miss Mary was somewhat dampened. However, they were there, all three of them, when her car swept up the drive, though it was long past their usual bedtime, Mary knew.

"Oh, it's *so* good to be back!" she called eagerly to them. Orrin took her car around to the garage while Randa grabbed her light suitcase.

"You wait on me hand and foot, you three. It isn't good for me, but oh, I'm glad to be back here with you all."

Nannie took her in her motherly arms and gave her a good warm hug. She had forgotten all about her worries as to how she should meet Miss Mary and what should be said to her.

They ushered Mary up to her peaceful airy room and left her, glad that at least tonight she was theirs, and safe.

With thankful heart Mary rested at last between the sweet smelling sheets that Randa had smoothed with such loving care and as she drifted off to sleep she felt as if some of the horror of the past two or three days had dropped away.

But Laurie was still on his knees beside his bed in the hot little room that he had insisted on taking, because the other bedroom in the tiny house had two windows, cross ventilation, and his mother must have that.

Over and over he poured out the hurt of his soul to God, but still the grief was there, eating and burning him, for he at last admitted to himself that he loved Mary Arden, loved her with all the strength of his heart. Gladly, he told his Heavenly Father, he would have died for her, but to see her loveliness soiled by the touch of that man seemed more than he could bear.

At last when he was so exhausted with his sorrow that his mind did not seem to function any more, he folded his hands like a child and looked upward. "Father," he said simply, "if this thing is according to Thy will, show me the rightness of it, and help me bear it, but if it is not Thy plan, then for the sake of Thine own Son stop it!" And then he crawled into bed.

It was Sunday morning before Mary saw him.

The two days after she got home were filled with resting and enjoying Nannie's delicious cooking, between intervals of going about her beloved house and grounds, planning what she would do. She made Orrin hunt up the old swing and finding that the rope was old and worn she went down town and bought new rope. But she insisted on having the same old wooden seat that she had used when she had had such good times years ago. It had Laurie's initials cut on one end of it and hers on the other. She cherished it. But she did not mention those initials to Orrin.

Then she decided that the pretty vine-covered summerhouse near where the swing hung from the old oak tree, needed paint. She went down again and bought some white paint—Orrin told her what kind to get—and she painted it herself. Orrin carefully pulled back the thorny rose ramblers from the bars they clung to, so that he could put them back after the paint was dry. The little place had a lovely flagstone floor and after the second coat of paint was finished, Randa came out and scrubbed the stones till the soft pastel colors shone out like an oriental rug. But Mary looked at the two old white wooden benches and decided there should be something more comfortable there. So she called a big store in the nearby city and ordered a delightful rolling chaise longue and three chairs all with gleaming chrome frames and bright varicolored cushions.

Although Nannie and Orrin had always kept the place immaculate, the little brightening changes that Mary made here and there gave evidence that someone was living there now who had a right to dress it up. The townspeople noticed, and nodded toward the place, as much as to say that the old Arden home had come alive again.

And Mary made up her mind to get acquainted with the people of Arden. She wanted to be counted as one of them. She hoped that many of them would soon feel free to drop in, and she meant to interest herself in the town doings.

It was on the way to church Sunday that she asked Randa to introduce her to some of the young people.

"Oh, my lands!" exclaimed Randa. "Why, I'd hardly know how, Miss Mary! I never know which name to say first an' I'd get all flustered, trying to interduce *you*. Besides, the folks I'd know wouldn't be the kind you'd want for friends."

"Now, Randa, I thought we had had that all out," remonstrated Mary. "I want you to understand that I live here in Arden now. I want to belong! I really do! I have chosen this place as my home and I intend to consider it so. I don't suppose my mother will come here often, but

I'm sure my father will, if he ever gets done with his government work and gets home from abroad."

"Well, I think that's very nice that you are going to stay, Miss Mary, and I'm sure all the people of the town will be glad to hear it but, you see, I don't know any but the plain common people, and they aren't the ones you'll want to invite to your home."

"I want them all, Randa, I want to be friends with everybody."

"Oh, you are so nice, Miss Mary! But much as you feel that way yourself there are all your city friends to think of. When you're married you'll—"

A loud harrumph came from the front seat where Orrin was driving silently along beside Nannie whose ears were well tuned to the conversation on the back seat.

Randa well knew what that sound meant from her father and she stopped short.

But Mary just laughed, a merry, but decided laugh. "I'm not thinking of getting married any time soon, Randa," she said, then had to hold tight to her side of the car for Orrin had nearly thrown them off their seats by swerving just in time to avoid a telephone pole he had evidently forgotten about.

When they were seated in the church Mary had a glimpse again of Laurie. His dark brown head was bowed reverently in prayer. A thrill shot through her to think she was here at home, where this splendid young man lived and worked and she could listen to him again. Would he seem as interesting now as he had before? Would he make the Bible seem real again? Oh, if only she might find some of the answers to her own problems. It suddenly occurred to her that that would be a valid sensible reason for going to church. In her experience, church going had been a fine respectable thing to do but only that. It was done because nice people did it. If one wanted to be correct in every department of life, that was one thing that must be attended to, like keeping oneself well groomed and repaying social obligations. It had never entered her mind before that some people found help and strength in fellowship with God's people.

The little organ ceased its murmur and Laurie stood up and gave a fleeting smile of good morning to the people. How delightfully informal and genuine this place seemed to be, thought Mary. Yet she noted a background of—was it sadness?—in Laurie's face that she had never seen before. She did not know that the very sight of her there had set Laurie's heart to thumping and he cried out silently again for strength.

"Oh, God, hide *me* today. May that little girl down there find Jesus Christ as her Saviour, but let me forget her, Lord, and be only Thy messenger."

To Mary his face seemed as the face of an angel as he sang in his rich baritone the wonderful words of the opening hymn.

> *"The soul that on Jesus hath leaned for repose*
> *I'll never, no never, desert to his foes."*

The tide of song swelled out and Mary glanced around the little building. It was full, but even at that there were comparatively few people, less than two hundred, probably. Yet they sang with their hearts and the place rang with their praises. A face here and there shone with a glad light as if the singer was delighted to have this chance to reaffirm his trust in the Saviour he sang about. The faces were lined and worn, and had evidently seen sorrow and trouble, yet there was peace in most of them, and real joy, Mary decided. How did they get that way?

She herself had had a very easy happy life thus far, barring the trying events of the past few days, and yet she felt she had never known such depth of joy as shone out in some of those worshippers.

They all paused after the song while Laurie spoke to the Lord simply, without any intoning or hypocritical piety in his voice, just, as it were, saying a glad good morning to Him for them all, rejoicing in the brightness of another new day untouched as yet by sin or wayward-ness, and then he ended with an earnest petition that they all might behold His glory as they delved into His Book and waited humbly before Him.

It was refreshing to Mary. She had never heard any-thing like it, only that other time she was here at the little chapel. She was glad that it all bore the test of a second visit. These people had a reason for coming here; it was a vital part of their everyday lives.

Laurie read a fascinating story from the Old Testament that Mary vaguely recalled having heard but it never had seemed real before. It was about a great multitude of people who were on a journey through the wilderness and had no water to drink. The story told of how God commanded Moses to strike a certain rock with his rod and water gushed forth, enough for all the people and all their animals.

"Now we know," explained Laurie, "according to the word in First Corinthians, that all these things hap-pened—" he interrupted himself, smiling his merry smile—"oh, yes, they really happened! But they hap-pened for a reason! We are told that these things hap-pened as types, or pictures, of spiritual things, and are written for our learning. What then, does this story mean? Why did God take this strange spectacular way of providing life-giving water for His people? Does the Bible itself give us any clue to understanding it? For of course we dare not make up our own explanation. We read the Psalms and find that David many times refers to God as a rock: 'a rock in a weary land,' 'my rock and my fortress,' he calls Him. Then we come back to our New Testament and the letters to the churches, and what do we find? Why, here in First Corinthians again, in so many words, referring to this very story of Moses and the rock, Paul says 'and that Rock was Christ'! Could any teaching be plainer?" Laurie smiled again as if in delight as he said intimately, "That is the way the Spirit of God teaches us, you know, for we are only little children, all of us."

Mary thought, This man is a master teacher! He has these people completely won. His words are clear as crystal and his pulpit manner is charming. Why, he should be in a great city church! Why doesn't someone discover him? Then she forgot the man in her interest at what he was saying. But Nannie glanced now and again out of the corner of her loving old eye to see and rejoice that her young lamb was listening with eagerness and taking in the words of life.

"Now let us see how Christ was struck as Moses struck the rock. Hear the words of Isaiah foretelling His sufferings. 'It pleased Jehovah to bruise Him.' It was God the Father who struck His Son on the Cross in punishment for your sins and mine! And what was the result? 'Whosoever will, let him take the water of life freely.' His death meant life for us.

"Of course, there might have been some foolish persons among that crowd on the mountain who refused to drink of the water! Just as there are some poor foolish ones today who refuse salvation. But there was enough for all and it was offered to all. Do you see it? Is it any wonder that the Lord Jesus when He talked with the Samaritan woman at the well, offered her water that would satisfy her so that she would never need to thirst again?"

Mary was listening now in amazement. Never before had she seen any reason satisfactory to her own mind why Jesus Christ let Himself die on the cross, if He had the power He seemed to have. Now she saw, and felt she had a starting point for answers to other problems.

As they all filed out of the little building, Laurie stood again at the front door, shaking hands and smiling, listening to a word of praise from one, a whispered cry of sorrow from another; comforting, encouraging, or perhaps rebuking as each one of his flock touched their lives to his for that brief moment.

Mary found herself almost embarrassed to greet him, she was so eager. She felt ashamed of herself and tried to explain it by telling herself that she had heard some helpful things this morning and would like to thank him and hear more some time. But that did not explain the tremble of her hand in his big warm one, nor the flutter of her heart as she said a simple "Good morning, sir," in mock formality. She did not know that his own heart was racing with just the nearness of her, nor that the rather solemn greeting he gave her with a mere "Glad to see you back" was a reproof to his own soul for caring so much about a girl who was pledged to another man.

Mary wanted to stop and ask him to come over soon, that she would like to ask more about his talk that morning but the people behind her were pressing and she was ashamed to stand longer and keep them waiting. In fact, when she looked up into his face, she found herself suddenly shy with this old friend. After this service he seemed more than just a boy she used to know, perhaps like one of God's servants of old, or one of the disciples, as if he were in another sphere from her. So she passed on down the steps, wordless, but longing to go on from this new starting point. Her soul felt somehow clean and refreshed by this morning's experience; she had a feeling that Brooke Haven and all her troubles were just a bad dream.

Mary hoped that Laurie would drop around that afternoon, or after church that evening, but she did not see him again for several days, except during the evening church service. Even then she had no further word with him for Nannie and the others slipped out by a side door to catch some friend whom they wished to see and she had no course but to follow.

Monday came and went. The new summerhouse furniture arrived and Mary unwrapped it and set it out enjoying the brightness of its fresh coloring. She took a new book she had bought down town and lay in the new chaise longue where the sweet smell of clover and roses was wafted to her. But she was not interested in the book. She kept glancing down the little path to see if a tall figure was striding that way to hunt her up. And instead of delighting in the thrushes' lovely songs she kept her ear tuned for footsteps on the flagstones.

Finally she threw her book down in impatience at her own restlessness.

"Well, what *do* I want?" she asked herself. "I come down here to Arden because it's peaceful and I'm not satisfied yet!" Then she laughed at herself. "Oh, yes, I really am. I love it. But I guess I am kind of lonely for young people. That's all." She did not specify just which young people she wanted.

So she got up and went into the house to hunt up Randa and ask her whether Celia Rathbone still lived in the old house.

"No, they moved away two years ago. A family from

California lives there now. Betty Tracy? Yes, she's still here. Going to be married I hear. Yes, next week. To a fella she met in Germany when she was over there in war work. Oh, yes, he's an American himself, right good-looking too, so they say."

But Mary shuddered. The very thought of a wedding was unpleasant to her just now. She had no desire to become involved with the festivities at the Tracys'. They would be only a reminder of what she had gone through the last few days. And no doubt the Tracys might have seen her picture and the write-up in the paper. There would be sure to be questions, and long explanations. No, she would not go there now.

"Does Mr. Harmon still live out near Windham?" she wondered. "I've a notion to go out and see his horses."

Yes, he was still there, and still had fine horses. Sold them for fancy prices sometimes to high class New Yorkers who came all the way down just for that.

So Mary spent a pleasant afternoon at the Harmons' discussing the fine points of horses with Mr. Harmon who said afterward, "That girl knows a thing or two about horses. I'll bet she can handle 'em!" And then she went into the house where Mrs. Harmon with whom she had always been a favorite, taught her how to bake cookies.

Mary went home feeling that at last she had made a start toward putting in roots in this delightful country.

Mary had seen a horse or two that she was sure would take her some enjoyable rides around the country lanes. Why shouldn't she get a couple of horses? Orrin could easily stable them in the big barn, and they wouldn't be so very much extra care. She would think about that. But why she thought of buying *two* horses she did not explain to herself.

The rest of the week passed in the same way for Mary.

She took some definite steps toward making friends in the village. And Saturday morning she made up her mind to go out to Harmons' and look at those horses again. She drove downtown first to get the groceries Nannie had said she needed. On the way she found herself wondering once more as she had every day, why Laurie Judson had not been around. Orrin had reported one evening that he had stopped in at the barn during milking time and helped him, but that he said he had some extra work and would not be able to come up to the house. It was at the supper table Orrin told them. As he happened to be looking Mary's way anyway when he spoke, he did not need to glance at her over his funny steel spectacles to see that little start of interest, and the tiny pucker of a puzzled frown that came into Mary's smooth forehead. But he said nothing more, and no Laurie appeared the next night or even the next. Whether he came to the barn again or not Mary did not know.

Mary had allowed herself to drive twice past the little house that Randa had pointed out that first day they rode together. She tried not to stare as she went past, but she noted the tiny paned windows and the almost flat roof that meant stifling heat this summer weather, and she wondered. Laurie likely had a very humble position in the radar plant if that was the best he could manage. Not that Mary thought the less of him for that. She knew he was a hard worker, and that was what really mattered after all. If he did the best he could, she was not one to despise poverty.

But she looked in vain for a glimpse of him anywhere around the house. She thought once that she saw a little figure bent over some sewing at the front window but she wasn't sure. She had met Mrs. Judson, of course, many times, when she was in Arden before, and she had loved the little brown-eyed energetic woman. She would like to go and call on her, but she had a feeling that it would look as if she were chasing Laurie and she scorned that sort of thing, although she knew plenty of girls who did it.

She was thinking about it that Saturday morning, whether she perhaps ought to go and call on Mrs. Judson, whether it wasn't rude of her not to, trying to persuade herself with all kinds of reasoning that it really was the thing to do, never once admitting to herself that it was Laurie she wanted to see, when all at once she turned a corner and there he was, just coming out of the post office.

Her heart gave a glad leap and she drew her car in quickly to the curb, thankful that for once there was parking space in front of the post office.

"Hi!" she called, tooting her horn ever so softly. He turned and saw her, and smiled. But did she imagine it or not? Was there a withdrawing in his glance? He came over to her car, and stood outside the open window.

"It sure is fine to have you care to come back to our little burg," he said cordially. But there was still that aloofness. What did it mean? He had never been so with her. They had always been on terms of the greatest frankness and informality.

"Well, I can tell you it surely is good to be back. I didn't want to leave anyway, and I had a horrid time and I am just gloating in the peace and quiet here."

He smiled again and wondered what she meant. It was not usual for a girl to call her engagement announcement a horrid time. His heart tried to grasp at hope but he sternly reasoned it away.

"Of course," she gave a wry little smile, "the peace and quiet here does amount almost to loneliness at times, especially, when I don't see any of my friends from one week's end to another!" She twinkled her eyes at him to let him know what friends she meant that she hadn't seen and he grinned with pleasure.

"If that's the way it is, I'd be glad to do anything I could for you. How did I know you wanted company?"

"I always did, didn't I?" she countered. "I'm just the same as I ever was."

"Are you?" he looked steadily at her.

"I thought so. Aren't I?" she giggled at her choice of grammar.

He looked long at her again and then away. Then he said "I—don't know. Of course you were just a little girl when I knew you."

"Well, heaven forbid I should ever grow up. Please take me in hand and knock it out of me if I do!" She laughed gaily, lightheartedly. She had not felt so happy since before she left Arden last week. It was a bright, precious thing, just to talk to Laurie. And she felt there was so much of treasure in him that she had not begun to discover.

But his brown eyes gave back only a sad serious smile at her and he said nothing.

Then she sobered. "Seriously, Laurie, you may think I'm screwy, but I would love to have you come and tell me more about what you've been telling those people in church. I guess I'm pretty much of a heathen, but I never heard anybody talk like you do before in my life. I think you've got something. Something I don't have. Would you come?"

And then a deep shining light came into his eyes. He said uncertainly, "Are you sure you want me to come?"

"Sure. You're my new pastor, aren't you?" she laughed half embarrassedly.

"Well, if you put it that way, I'll come. Gladly. Tonight?"

"Why not this afternoon, if you're not busy? Couldn't we talk in a canoe as well as on the front porch or the living room?"

He caught his breath. Dared he come into that much intimacy with her? Could he trust himself not to look or say more than he should? Nonsense. If he couldn't trust himself he could trust his Lord. Here was a soul who needed help. If that was the way she wanted it, all right.

"I'll come!" he said, as if he were repeating a vow.

"About half-past three? All right?"

He nodded and strode off, taking a deep breath and feeling as he did once when he took a tremendously high dive to pull a child who was drowning out of the water.

II

THERE was quiet relief in Mary Arden's house that afternoon and a feeling that all was again as it should be. Though Mary would have been amazed could she have known how troubled her three servants had been about her.

As the two young people strolled down the orchard path to the wooded creek behind the house Nannie happened to be scraping up the last little flakes of tart pastry from her board where she had been fixing a most delectable picnic lunch. And the board was directly under the back kitchen window. So she watched the two young people with utmost satisfaction.

And Randa just happened to be working upstairs in the back bedroom taking down the curtains to wash them, although it wasn't a month since they had been freshly laundered. So she saw the two stroll down the path to the canoe landing and she gave a little grunt of satisfaction. True, she had hoped to see them holding hands the way she and Horace would have done, but perhaps Miss Mary considered that not quite nice to do in the daytime, and with the pastor, at that!

And old Orrin also happened to be pulling weeds just then in the strawberry patch near the path that led down to the creek, although anyone else would surely have had to use a magnifying glass to discover any weeds in that garden. Orrin watching the young couple spat out of the corner of his mouth with satisfaction.

"Can't tell me that girl's not fond o' young Judson. Look at the skip in her walk! An' the way she looks up at him! An' the set o' her shoulders!" He cackled happily to the strawberries. "Drat that other fella comin' here and makin' trouble. I'd like to blast the dinged daylights outa him."

But the two who were unbeknownst under such loving surveillance sauntered happily on.

Laurie was almost like his old self again, for he had spent much time in prayer about this outing and he had decided to accept it as a God-given opportunity to help the one he loved. Further than that he would not think. Let God work out what His plan might be. And so Laurie had forgotten himself in his longing to introduce Mary Arden to his Heavenly Companion.

Mary skipped gaily along, eagerly looking forward to a good time such as she remembered from long ago. The nightmare of last week had faded at least for the time being. She had said not a word to anyone in Arden about what happened while she was away and it never entered her head that any of the people here might have seen her local newspaper's announcement. After Orrin's caution Nannie and Randa had never referred to it.

It was a perfect afternoon such as June sometimes can produce even when her store of rare days is almost exhausted. Mary drank in the quiet beauty of the trees and mirroring water. After they had paddled a little distance in contented silence, Laurie remembered to curve the little craft shoreward a bit to sail underneath a certain long lacy branch of hemlock that hung far over the brink of the stream. This had been a favorite spot of Mary's and she always used to beg him to go under the branch every time they passed that way. She loved the mysterious cosy intimacy of the cool green nook. When he steered toward it without her asking she gently tossed a smile straight into his eyes. Laurie's old smile blazed forth in answer to hers, and Mary almost felt that all was right again with the world. But in another instant that strange sadness seemed to veil once more the rich joyousness that had always been a part of Laurie's charm. What could it mean? Had some sorrow come into his life that she did not know? Some hardship? Had he got into trouble during his time in service? Surely not through his own wrongdoing. She could never believe that of Laurie. Yet he had not been sad like this before she went away this last time. It was a mystery to her.

Mary began slowly, hesitantly with her questions, for now she felt as if they were silly and stupid, though that night when her girl friend died they had been vividly challenging. But when she found that Laurie did not laugh at her, and that he had real satisfying answers, straight out of the Bible, she went on with eagerness. Their talk was long and earnest, interrupted now and then as they would stop to notice a blue jay scolding a squirrel high up in a pine tree, or a cardinal showing off his red feathers against the dark green of hemlocks. Their talk was not all serious, either, for every little way down the stream they had to recall with delight some little incident that had taken place here or there: the spot where Mary upset the canoe once with all the lunch aboard; the hole under the rock where they had found a whole family of opossums; countless little happenings that seemed precious to them now because they had been shared. Once as Mary lay back in the bottom of the

canoe against the back rest, looking up at the green
tracery against the sky, she suddenly glanced down at
Laurie to say something and caught him looking at her
with his soul in his eyes, so that she quickly shot her own
glance away and tried to hide the uncontrollable catching of her breath by some inane remark concerning the
beauty of the day. But they both were conscious that
their souls had met in that brief glance, and both treasured the moment.

They idled up the stream until they came to the dear
old flat-topped rock where they had sat so many times
and had their lunch. Laurie tied the canoe to the very
same old branch, and helped Mary out. The touch of
their hands brought once more the consciousness of that
thrill that had come to them a few moments before, and
Mary instinctively knew that Laurie's hand was mightily
aware of hers. But he held it not an instant longer than
any gentleman would have held it while helping a girl
out of a canoe, and a sort of disappointment stirred in
Mary.

They opened their delicate sandwiches and pickles
and cherry tarts, exclaiming with glee over each, and
remarking on Nannie's faithful care as they ate.

It was almost dusk as they finally pulled the little boat
ashore again at its own slip and started the climb up the
hill. Their talk turned again to things of the Spirit.

They were nearly to the summerhouse when Mary
said, "Well, I don't see anything in this life on earth
without God. I don't see how anyone can expect to be
glad at the end of it without Him. So I'm quite sure that
His way is the way I want to go. If it's really as simple as
you say to be born again, I will take Jesus Christ right
now as my Saviour."

Mary could not see the glow of radiant joy on Laurie's
face, and she had spoken in a low tone. But a man sitting

in the summerhouse saw them, and caught a word here and there as they passed. An angry look flashed from his black eyes.

"So that's what's changed my lady so suddenly, is it?" he muttered under his breath. "She's got a crush on this country preacher and she's hipped on religion! Well, we'll soon settle that. We won't have much trouble in showing up his blasted religion, and if I know my Mary she'll soon be disgusted with him and ready to come back."

He swore silently and after the others had passed into the house he took his way down the hill and back to his car.

Brooke Haven had not been waiting in the summerhouse by invitation. He had called at the house that afternoon and got the information about where Mary Arden was and what she was doing in the confident determined voice of Randa who, in her inexperience, felt that all was safe and settled now that Mary Arden and Laurie Judson had gone out canoeing together at last. It was beyond her imagination to conceive how either could withstand the charms of the other, and she was taking for granted that their future was by now assured, since they must be nearly up to the narrows at this hour. So she unfortunately took great delight in rolling out the fact of the canoe trip and she fairly smacked her lips over the taste of triumph. She gave Brooke Haven to understand thoroughly that Miss Mary Arden would not be at home to callers the rest of the day at least.

Randa saw him turn his car and start down the drive as if he were accepting defeat, whereat she strode back to the kitchen and told her mother what she had done. But when her mother had finished with her she was in tears wailing bitterly over the trouble she might have made for Miss Mary. "An' I never meant to at all!" she sobbed.

But Orrin chuckled when he heard what had happened. "Do 'em all good, mebbe. Might bring things to a head! We'll see. Dry up, Randa, and let's eat."

Meanwhile Brooke Haven drove all the way down the drive, hesitated, and then turned and went up again as far as a bend in the drive. There he stopped, parked his car behind a big clump of bushes and got out. The car was hidden from the house here. He had no desire for another argument with those stubborn servants. His intention was to skirt the grounds and slide into that little summerhouse he had seen which was evidently near the path from the creek, and to wait there till the absentees returned. Then he would waylay Mary and take possession of her.

But when he had put through two or three hours of doing nothing, and had smoked all the cigarettes he had with him his anger and his hunger grew more and more insistent. Then he heard that impossible conversation! He changed his plan and, waiting until the two had passed into the house, he retraced his way down the front lawn and got into his car and drove off.

But he had not yet finished the work he meant to do in the little town of Arden.

Mary Arden waved good by to Laurie as he left by the back door after helping Orrin with his night chores. She drew a deep happy breath as if she had at last reached a place where she could begin afresh, and find the answers to all her problems. She did not actually *feel* any different since she had taken this strange new step, but then Laurie had assured her that most people didn't have any sense of exaltation or any special feeling any more than a baby has a feeling of gladness at being born.

"The joy," he said, "is in Heaven, in the heart of your

new Heavenly Father," and then he smiled that warm smile again.

Oh, how good it was to be with Laurie again. How sane and right life seemed as he saw it.

Mary gave Nannie a brilliant happy smile and thanked her heartily for the wonderful lunch.

"You are so good to me, Nannie! I don't deserve it all."

But Nannie's eyes filled with tears as she smiled at the girl she loved almost as her own. And she said:

"That young fella was here again while you was gone, Miss Mary."

"Young fellow? Who?" Mary's brows knit as she wondered what young man knew her well enough in Arden to call.

"Why, that city fella. I don't know as I told you he was here before, just after you left for your mother's. I kinda fergot, I—g-g-guess," added Nannie trying to fit her words to her conscience, "you was so long comin' back. But he went away again when Randa told him you was down on the creek taking a boat ride."

Gradually it dawned on Mary who it was Nannie meant.

"Oh! You mean Mr. Haven? Well, that's all right. I'm glad he didn't wait."

But Nannie could not tell from her tone whether she was glad or sorry that she didn't see him.

Impatience and indignation that Brooke would be brazen enough to turn up again were all that Mary felt as she took her way upstairs. And it was not long before she forgot all about him as she went over the afternoon's pleasure in her mind. Again and again she recalled that look she had caught in Laurie's eyes as he watched her in the canoe. But if he cared as much as that look said he did, why did the sadness come? Well she was probably just imagining a lot about him, that was all. He had helped her wonderfully and she was grateful. After all that she had been through two weeks ago she had no desire even to think of love or marriage. It almost frightened her. Then she realized that she was never frightened in company with Laurie. It was always the greatest joy and delight to be with him. But she must not get any foolish ideas about him. He might be promised to some other girl for all she knew. Then why that loving adoring look she had seen? Oh well, that was probably her imagination. And so she argued herself around and around. Till finally she remembered Laurie had given her a little slip of paper with a few Bible references jotted on it for her to look up so that she would have the answers to some of her questions down in black and white.

She took the paper out of her pocket and went in search of her grandmother's Bible, suddenly ashamed that she had not one of her own at hand. What would Laurie think if he knew she had scarcely looked into a Bible for years except for reading her required chapters for lit. class in college.

She was embarrassed, too, to ask Nannie for the Bible. Nannie would have expected her to have her own with her. How she knew this she could not have told. But Nannie had high standards.

Finally she found it. Randa had evidently found it lying where she had left it Sunday and put it on a little table at the far end of the living room. Clasping it under her arm she flew up again to her room.

For an hour she read, coming on more and more verses, beyond the ones that Laurie had given her, amazed at how simple and clear and reasonable some of the verses were to her now. Laurie had said it would be so, as soon as she was born again. Well, even if she hadn't felt any funny way when she took that step, this was proof enough that something had happened, for never before had she made sense of anything she read in the Bible.

She did not know that Laurie was over across the town in his hot little room again, down on his knees, pouring out his heart for her, pleading God's promises that this newly born one might grow in grace through the knowledge of His Word.

But Brooke Haven was downtown, too, and not on his knees. He first hunted up the one little hotel in Arden and stalking up to the desk ostentatiously pulled out his solid gold cigarette case and lit a cigarette between words as he asked:

"Do you have such a thing as a room and bath in this dump?"

Joe Webb, the plain little room clerk with sandy hair and eyebrows shrank with awe as he gazed on that mustache of Brooke Haven's. For months he had nursed his few little bristles but still no sign of a mustache could be seen more than four feet away from his mirror. He had measured the distance. He opened his mouth to speak but he simply stared.

"Well?" burst out the would-be guest, "do you or don't you have a room and bath? Or perhaps you never heard of such a thing? Is there any other shack around here that could be called a hotel?"

"Oh! Why, ah—yes, of course," responded Joe at last.

"Of course what? Of course there's another hotel? I should hope there might be. What a dive!"

"Oh, I mean, that is, we have one, sir. A room and bath. Very nice, sir." Joe had finally got himself into his normal clerkly state of mind. "Would you like to see it, sir? Just sign here, please."

Brooke Haven snorted, made a few scratches with the

pen, swore at the pen and got out his own handsome one and signed his name with a flourish.

A little boy with a thin wizened face like a monkey darted in and seized his bag. Brooke half expected to see a tail whisk out from beneath the bell boy's uniform.

The room and bath were only fair but he tossed the little monkey boy a half dollar for carrying his one small bag up the one flight, not out of generosity but from a desire to show this scamp that he was somebody to be treated with respect. He was annoyed that the child was so young. He had hoped to have a word or two possibly with some older man who might give him a little data on the feminine population of the town of Arden.

Instead he sauntered downstairs and discovered a taproom into which he entered. He ordered a drink and sat looking around at the patrons. It being Saturday evening, all who so desired came from the surrounding countryside from farms and even smaller towns into Arden which was considered by them quite a center of news and high life. The place was full of farm hands mostly, Brooke guessed. There was a scattering of women. He scanned them all looking for just the type he had in mind.

At last he thought he had found her. She had been seated in a booth behind where he was sitting alone, and she was now out on the floor dancing in such a way as to attract the attention of every man in the place.

Brooke watched her for some time. She had reddish blonde hair done in an amazing coiffure that fairly outreached the latest style. Her dress was black, made in an off the white, white shoulder design; and it showed her rather full curves to what she evidently considered her advantage. Her make-up was startling, carefully planned to harmonize with her hair.

Brooke noticed that she talked a great deal, gaily, and

was apparently quite a wit, since the man with whom she was dancing laughed heartily every time she said anything.

Brooke noticed all the yokels in the place guffawing with maudlin pleasure as they watched her. When her partner seated her again in the booth and left her for a moment he quickly forestalled any other visits and slid in beside her.

"Well, beautiful, how does a town like this happen to produce a you?" He lowered his handsome head until his sparkling black eyes could look up into hers with a flattering smile.

"You're here yourself, I see!" she retorted coquettishly, raising her brows and flashing her own black eyes at him.

"Quick on the trigger, eh?" Her reply pleased him. She would do. She was smart. He smiled showing his perfect white teeth. All girls everywhere fell for that smile. He realized that his time was short; her companion might return at any moment. He lit a cigarette for her.

"Surely there's something better than this place for you and me, isn't there?" The diamonds set in that gold cigarette case glittered fascinatingly.

"In a town like this?" she mocked.

"Well, there are other towns, or even a city nearby, n'est-ce pas?" He knew she would be flattered that he thought she understood French.

"Weston, yes. If you call it a city," she said haughtily.

"It might do for a start," he said. "How about a getaway? Right now?"

The girl glanced around startled. A daring look came into her black eyes. She looked full at Brooke again, and then asked,

"Well, what are we waiting for?"

Brooke laughed. "You'll do," he said admiringly.

They arose and walked to the door but the young man who had been with her before turned his head just at that instant from where he had been standing talking at another table in the far corner of the room. A dark anger came into his face and he started toward them.

"Make it snappy!" commanded the girl under her breath to Brooke, and she slid like a shadow out the swinging doors.

Brooke wasted no time, for a public brawl was not in his plans. They fairly flew to his car and pulled away just as they heard a shout in the darkness. The girl flung a mocking laugh out of the car for her frustrated escort to pick up if he chose.

"Will this make trouble for you later?" questioned Brooke, more because he wanted to keep out of trouble himself than because he cared what happened to her.

"Trouble? With that chinless wonder? I can settle him. I'll just tell him he ran off and left me and he'll be down on his knees before I'm through with him. We didn't really have to hurry away from him, for you could've licked him easy. He's no he-man."

Brooke responded to her compliment by putting one arm around her and giving her plump shoulder a little squeeze. This was as he had planned it, but perhaps a shade more interesting than he had thought it would be, for the girl was nobody's dumb bunny.

They grew more intimate as the car proceeded toward Weston. Brooke cleverly drew from her various details of her background, telling only what he chose about himself. His home he decided to set in the far west. That would be safer.

The place of gaiety to which the girl was directing Brooke was one which she considered the most high-class resort within range of Arden. She had longed to go there ever since its swank had been noised abroad. But none of her various escorts up to now had warmed up to the idea, as they were all somewhat strapped for funds. This man, she felt, would be equal to anything. And so they arrived at its imposing portal, and Brooke's largesse was evidently sufficient to provide the fullest entree. The attention and respect of the men-in-waiting were enough to satisfy the most exacting demands of any lady. Gloriously happy for once, the girl lapped up the glamour. She was so obviously revelling in it that Brooke was more than half embarrassed. Yet for the sake of his own private scheme he stuck it out and entertained her to her heart's content.

It was not until the wee small hours had grown into fairly large ones that they took their way back to Arden. By that time he had accomplished the first step in his plan. He had made sure that his charge did not take aboard more liquor than she could carry, for he wanted her keenest attention while he unfolded to her his plan. But he found to his relief that she was too clever herself to drink too much. She realized that if she did she would not be in a state to enjoy this event to the fullest. So she was quite alert to his proposition and even managed to suggest a few fine points of operation herself. She entered into the plan with interest, especially as the successful carrying out of her end of it insured her, according to Brooke, another visit to such a place as this only in another city still more glamorous.

Brooke retired at last in his third-class hotel room, feeling that he deserved a good rest. The evening had been not too bad, although the girl was not up to his usual choice for such entertainment. But it was worth it, for he felt that now he was on the right track to break up this ridiculous fanatical streak that had come over his future bride, as he still considered Mary Arden.

He gave himself a smile in the wavy little mirror as he prepared for bed. How easy it had been to enchant that girl! They were all alike, except Mary Arden.

He need not take this girl out again if he did not care to. He would just disappear, perhaps, when she had accomplished what he wanted. Though he did get rather a kick out of seeing her eyes bulge at his extravagance. A little whisper of annoyance disturbed him as he realized afresh that Mary Arden never gave him that kick. She simply did not care about money or show. Well, there would always be girls who did, even after he had won Mary. And so he climbed into the hard bed.

12

MARY Arden woke the next morning with peace in her heart. It was Sunday and the birds were telling everybody what a glorious morning it was. Mary lay a few moments listening. It seemed to her that they never had sounded so sweet. The perfume of the regal lilies that Orrin tended so carefully came from the garden below her front window. Oh, what a blessed place this was! If she could only have known that this was ahead for her those awful days up in the city. Was that the way all of this earth's trials would seem, when she reached Heaven? As half-forgotten dreams?

And there was more than a delight in the quiet beauty of the day for Mary this morning. For the first time in her life she knew that her feet were planted in a definite path with a definite goal—the right path, the right goal! What a relief it was. To know where one was going, and that there would be joy, even though the going might be rough. For Laurie had done his work well, in teaching this precious newborn soul, and she had an assurance of her acceptance with God; she understood that that came from the work of His beloved Son, and not from her own attempts to please Him. She smiled in utter joy as she caught a glimpse of the blue, blue sky. Its light reminded her of the light in Laurie's face as he had looked at her yesterday that one time in the canoe. Oh, here! She must not begin thinking foolish thoughts about Laurie again. What if she should find that he really was engaged to some other girl! How ashamed she would feel.

She jumped out of bed and ran happily in to take her morning shower. She was singing as she dressed. Nothing could down the joy that surged up in her today, she felt.

Now wasn't that the fragrance of bacon she caught? Nannie must be getting breakfast.

As Nannie heard her lighthearted song and her tripping feet down the stairs her own heart felt easier of its burden about Mary Arden. For knowing Mary's mother as she did, old Nannie had taken on almost the responsibility of a mother for this sweet girl who seemed actually to love her grandmother's old home, and its servants as well.

There was joy in the simple companionship of the four around the kitchen table that morning. Mary found time to wonder at it herself. She felt one with these people even more than ever. She wondered if it was because of the new step she had taken last night. She wanted to tell these kind friends all about it, but a sudden shyness came over her and she could not bring herself to speak of it. Perhaps sometime when she was alone with Nannie she would tell her. Nannie would understand, she knew.

Mary insisted on helping again with the dishes, and then she hovered over Nannie while she put in the roast for dinner and whipped up a light fluffy Spanish cream dessert.

"I really want to learn to cook," she explained. "I think every girl ought to know how. I'll be stupid about it, I suppose," she sighed wistfully, "and I know you'll have plenty of chances to laugh at me, but I want you to let me make things sometimes. Why! just suppose," she went on with an impish grin, "that sometime I should marry and have four or five children! Little boys, for instance! What kind of a mother would I be if I couldn't even make cookies for them?"

Nannie laughed at her, and gave her one or two simple tasks about the preparing of dinner, but her casual reference to possible marriage worried Nannie. It all depended, of course, on whom she married!

Mary was as eager over going to church as any of them this morning.

Once she laughed quietly all to herself. Imagine being *eager* to go to any kind of church service! She could remember the many and various excuses the girls at college used to get up to avoid chapel exercises. How dull they had seemed. But the service here was not dull. And she was sure that that was so, it was not simply because a very good-looking young man was the preacher. Mary was actually looking forward to hearing what he would say. She thought she would be able to understand better now that she was born again. Once more that strange thought thrilled her that she *belonged,* belonged to the family of God in a very special way.

When she had taken her seat beside Randa she glanced up casually. She met a blinding smile from Laurie that sent her heart a-racing off again in wild ecstasy.

But Laurie seemed master of himself this morning. He wore the calm elation as of one who has won a secret victory.

His talk was about the Cross and some of the many

things Christ accomplished by it. Mary Arden sat and drank in the wonderful truths, rejoicing that at last they seemed clear to her.

She drove home in the same happy mood that had wakened with her. Her joyousness bubbled up easily and naturally over even small happenings. It seemed as if life would always be bright like this.

It was after Nannie's good dinner, in which Mary could take some pride because she had done little things to help, and after a good time of reading and a nap in the new summerhouse, that Mary suddenly became aware of footsteps on the flagstones. She knew before she opened her eyes that they were a man's footsteps. Was it Laurie? Had he come to see if she understood what he said this morning, and to give her more help? She smiled in her half sleep. The footsteps paused, then came on. She listened again. No, they were not Laurie's. Even in her doze she knew it was not Laurie. Something firm and dependable was lacking in these steps. Or was it that she missed Laurie's whistle? He nearly always whistled when he walked, especially when he came in search of her.

Then she roused enough to realize that it would be well to discover who it was. She opened her eyes.

There stood Brooke Haven.

He wore a humble look that Mary had never seen on him before. It was ill-fitting, unlike the immaculate sport suit he had on; but it was there.

He moved toward where Mary where she lay, her book fallen open in her lap.

Her eyes opened wide almost in terror.

"Mary," he said, more gently than she had ever heard him speak, "I've come to apologize."

Apologize! Whoever heard of Brooke Haven apologizing? Never had he been known to do that in all of his eventful life, although there had been many times when he should have.

Mary continued to stare unbelievingly, rubbing her eyes.

He smiled, deprecatingly. A smile reeking with humility.

"You don't trust me, Mary? You won't forgive me? I know now that that was an unfair thing to do, letting them all think we were engaged when we weren't—yet. I—well, somehow I didn't realize until afterwards how mean it was. I didn't intend any rudeness to you. I thought it would be fun for all of us to be—in the same boat, as it were." He attempted an embarrassed little laugh.

Mary still looked at him, with a puzzled stare, and said nothing.

He came closer and knelt down on one perfectly creased beige knee on the flagstone, to try to reach her across the chasm that was still between them. There was almost a sob in his voice as he begged again,

"Won't you ever forgive me, Mary, and let us be friends again?"

As he drew nearer Mary sat up with a jerk and straightened herself, pulling away as far as she could. But she listened to his apology with sober thoughtfulness. Could it be sincere? She wondered.

She looked off at a distant hillside, while he waited for her answer, his handsome head sorrowfully bowed. He did not attempt to touch her.

At last she turned back and gazed at him again.

"Why—yes," she said slowly, "I suppose I'll have to *forgive* you."

He raised his head, a great relief showing in his black eyes. He looked at her soulfully and murmured, "Thank you, Mary."

Then he drew a chair near her couch and sat down. He still spoke in that sorrowful humble voice.

"I wanted to tell you, Mary, first of anybody, that I have begun to realize that I have not always been what I should have been. I want you to help me."

Mary was appalled. If Brooke had come to her with joking, or even with a report that the story he started had all been denied and forgotten, she would have coldly sent him off again. But whoever would have expected this? Her first impulse in spite of his apology had been to send him away and refuse to see him again. Yet he seemed sincere enough, and had asked her help. What should she do? As a child of God who had been helped could she refuse help to someone else? She was very young in the faith yet and knew so little herself. Would he even listen if she told him of her new Saviour? Was his repentance that deep? Oh, if she only had someone to advise her. If only Laurie were here. Then suddenly a daring thought came to her, but still she hesitated.

"What kind of help do you want?" she parried.

"I want you to help me be the kind of man I ought to be." Again his shiny black head bowed and he gave a deep sigh.

Mary thought again a long moment. Then she looked at her watch and made her decision. It was almost suppertime now, and there would not need to be any lengthy discussions with him. Yes, she could manage that much.

"Well," she threw her challenge, "will you go to church tonight with me?"

His head was still bowed, and she did not see the angry sneer flash across his face. He raised his solemn eyes and said, "I will go anywhere you want me to go."

She arose, picking up her book, and said, albeit rather

uncordially, "Well, come in to the house and Nannie will soon have supper ready."

She walked ahead of him, saying no more on the walk to the house.

But Nannie saw them coming and her heart sank.

"Now how long has that good-fer-nothin' fella been out there with our Miss Mary, Randa? Did you tell him she was there?"

Randa came swiftly, starchily, to look out the window.

" 'Deed I did not, ma!" she protested hotly. "He never came to the door at all. He must've gone right on out there. Oh, ma! What'll Mr. Laurie say?"

"Mr. Laurie!" blurted her heavy-hearted mother. "I only wish he *would* say somep'n. Now I s'pose Miss Mary won't be goin' to church tonight, with comp'ny an' all. Oh me!"

But Mary, after pointing her unwelcome guest up the stairs to "the first door on the left," stepped out to the kitchen with a worried look on her face.

"Nannie!" she called peremptorily. Nannie told Orrin after they were in bed that night: "She didn't speak like herself. It ain't like her to give orders. She's always acted like we was all her family. Not that I mind. It's her right. But she just wasn't natural!"

"Nannie, set the table for two in the dining room tonight. I have company. Don't get anything extra. Just whatever you had planned will be all right." Then in a preoccupied manner she closed the kitchen door again and went upstairs to her own room.

Nannie and Randa just stood and looked at each other in despair. Great tears rolled down Randa's solid face. Glumly they set about doing what their beloved, mysterious mistress had ordered. But when Orrin came in, saw only three places set at the kitchen table and his womenfolk going about in a funereal dither, he stood watching a minute and then opened the kitchen door again and spat far out into the yard.

"Well, I'll be gormed! What's it all about now? Miss Mary gone again?"

Nannie sadly shook her head. Then glancing up at the guest window above them, she told him in a hoarse whisper: "It's that creek fella come again! Ta supper! He snuk out to the summerhouse an' found her 'thout comin' to the house at all."

"Creek fella?" Orrin was puzzled. "You mean Laurie Judson she went down on the creek with yesterday? That's swell."

Nannie gave him a scornful look.

"No, not Laurie Judson! Wouldn't I and Randa be singin' and dancin' if 'twas? No, that other one. Name of Creek or River, or some such."

"Oh!" snorted Orrin. "I know. *Him,* huh!" Then he grinned wickedly. "Goin' to put pisen in his supper, are ya?"

Nannie stamped her foot at him but had to laugh in spite of herself. "I wouldn't mind makin' him the least mite sick, that I wouldn't!" Then she pushed Orrin firmly out of her way, indignant with him for not offering more practical help. "Go on now, I've got to get comp'ny supper."

And such a supper as she got! She was determined that Miss Mary should not have need to be ashamed before this fine gentleman, despise him though she did. Her best puffy biscuits were not too much trouble, though she muttered and fretted all the time she was making them. Slices of cold chicken, tender as air. A tossed up salad from Orrin's garden with a sauce that only Nannie knew how to make. A jar of their own honey to go with the biscuits; and sunshine-sweet strawberries with rich cream for dessert, accompanied by some delectable little cookies that Randa had baked the day before.

No, Mary Arden had no need to hide her head in shame the way her mother had prophesied she would if any of her friends came to visit. Even Randa's service was impeccable. Not for nothing had old Grandmother Arden noted every detail of the kitchen and dining room in the old days, and required perfection of every servant.

But the atmosphere in the dining room was almost as stiff as the starched uniform and apron that Randa wore.

Mary politely asked after the young people at home, and Brooke gravely told her all she asked, but took no advantage in the conversation. He had taken this role seriously and he meant to play it through to the bitter end. He had won the first round of his fight, and if the next went well, and then Sylva did her part he thought the prize would be his at the payoff; but he was taking no chances. He was quite satisfied at his progress. Even a bit elated at the turn of events for the evening. A well-planned word, possibly only one, would plant a doubt of that young preacher that would grow.

Mary had determined that she would not subject herself to the sole company of Brooke during the interval between supper and going to church. So she asked Orrin to show the visitor around the gardens and the farm. She trailed along for a few minutes and then excused herself, feeling that she had carried out the most that convention would require of her, especially in view of Brooke's recent treatment of her. Of course, she was supposed to have forgiven that, but she still did not trust him in spite of his meek consent to go to church with her. She had little faith in his announced desire to reform.

If Mary Arden had had the slightest inkling of how hard she was making that evening service for Laurie she might never have gone so far as to invite Brooke to church. She had no notion that the two had ever met, of course, so she did not surmise the struggle that Laurie had within himself when he looked up from his place in the pulpit and saw who was sitting with Mary Arden.

He felt suddenly as if someone had thrown a ton of lead at his heart. All the joyous elation he had known as a result of Saturday's canoe trip with Mary vanished. The man was her guest evidently, no doubt a welcome guest, and she must of course be pledged to him. How could he ever have hoped otherwise? Mary's obvious pleasure in their time together yesterday had meant nothing except the friendliness that she had always shown for the neighbor boy who was older than herself. Naturally, she would choose a life companion from among her own kind. He knew it all along. Why had he allowed himself to hope? He had not even realized that he was hoping that the newspaper notice was a mistake. Of course, she wore no ring yet, but how could that notice possibly be a mistake? Over and over these thoughts whirled through his distraught mind. He kept his head bowed lest anyone should see the turmoil in him. How could he *ever* get up and preach before this man whom he found that his natural man detested. He recalled Mary's words as they walked up the hill Saturday evening, and her quiet acceptance of Jesus Christ as her own Saviour. His heart cried out that Mary Arden was in a different realm now from this man. She belonged in the heavenly realm, and surely that could not be true of this man. He found to his horror that he did not want that to be true of this man. He found himself wishing there was nothing at all in common between Mary Arden and Brooke Haven. Almost a groan escaped him right there before them all. The torture of his own desire and of the realization of his sin in not even caring for this man's soul was horrible to him.

"Oh, my God!" he cried out silently. "I need Thee now! Cleanse me afresh. Let me forget everything now except Thy Son. I'm just handing over to Thee all of this that seems like tragedy to me. Make me a clean empty channel for Thy word and let it work in hearts according to Thy will."

After the service that evening the people did not chatter as usual. They went home awed and silent. Their hearts had been deeply searched in that quiet hour, and it seemed as if each wanted to get to a place tonight where he could be alone before God. Even in Orrin's car which Mary had insisted on using tonight there was very little conversation. Mary had almost forgotten the presence of Brooke Haven in the little chapel, or even of Laurie Judson, while she listened, for she was conscious only of that Presence that had been growing more and more real in these last few days.

And Brooke Haven was silent most of the way home because he was turning over in his mind the best sentence he could devise that would cast dishonor upon the preacher. He found it difficult to frame his thoughts. He had heard very little of what the man said because he was taken up with hating him. Only a few scattered words reached beneath the surface of his thoughts, and these he found so disturbing that he tossed them out of his mind instantly.

Finally, he turned to Mary in the darkness, across Randa whom she had placed determinedly between them on the back seat, and said in a condescending tone:

"When a man dares to get up and preach to other people like he does, he'd have to be awfully good, wouldn't he! A bit of a sis."

"He is good!" flared up Randa hotly. "And he's not a

sis." And then she clapped her hand over her mouth and looked toward Miss Mary imploringly in the dark, to forgive her impudence to her guest.

"So?" responded Brooke amusedly. "I wonder."

But Mary simply leaned forward and spoke to Orrin in her usual sweet voice:

"Don't turn up our drive, Orrin, since Mr. Haven will be wanting to get his train, I suppose."

"No, I drove," answered Brooke quickly. "Just let me out here. My car's parked nearby." He chose to disregard Mary's absence of any invitation to come up to the house. He climbed out of Orrin's old flivver and pausing only to say to Mary, "It's been a pleasure to be with you again," he lifted his hat to her, ignoring the rest, and stalked away to his car.

With relief Mary watched him a moment and then let him slip out of her thoughts, preferring instead to dwell on the things she had learned that evening from Laurie's sermon.

She had had some idea of introducing Brooke to Laurie with the intention of letting Laurie try to "help" him, but when she started down the main aisle toward the door where Laurie stood shaking hands with his congregation, surprisingly enough it was Orrin who had pulled at her arm and almost shoved her out the side door, muttering something about it being "hot in here, let's get out quick! Can't get my breath!" And the rest followed, of course. Strange for old Orrin to feel the heat like that, or make anything at all of his own feelings. But Mary soon forgot all about it.

She did not, however, soon forget that parting slur of Brooke's. It had made her very angry. The more she thought of it the more she found she resented it. It rankled for several days. She thought she would like to get those two men together and show Brooke Haven in some way just what a manly man Laurie Judson was.

Fortunately she did not dream of the way in which her wish would come true.

IT was several days before Mary saw either Laurie or Brooke Haven again.

She spent the time happily, feeling more and more a sweet sense of security and friendliness in this pleasant little town. She hunted up some of her father's old friends, of whom she had often heard him speak. She spent an evening in the home of Mr. Winters, the president of the Arden National Bank. She enjoyed the time immensely, especially as Mr. Winters embarked at once upon the subject of the neighbors who used to live on the farm next to the Ardens.

"Jeremiah Judson was the finest man I ever knew," he said, then added with a warm smile "—until his son Laurie grew up. He's just like him."

Mary tried to keep her rosy color from giving away her delight at his remark. She smiled demurely and agreed that Laurie seemed a splendid young man. But she found she could only say it to her toes. She dared not raise her eyes to be searched by these pleasant friends. What on earth was the matter with her? She had never been used to having moments of embarrassment such as she had had lately.

Mr. Winters seemed eager to pursue his topic.

"Yes," he went on, "I always did like Laurie when he was a boy. Never anything underhanded or mean about him. I don't mean he didn't get into mischief sometimes, but not the kind some boys do. He was never malicious or destructive. And if he did happen to break a window or so playing ball, he always went right to the owner and apologized and offered to pay for it. He always insisted on paying, too, even though the people sometimes told him to forget. Just like Jerry in that. In fact," he hesitated, looked over at his wife, glanced back at Mary who was listening with a glow of interest, and then decided to take the risk and say what he had started.

"I've never told this to a soul," he said, "except my wife here, and didn't intend to until it's all over, anyway, for I know Laurie doesn't like his affairs talked about any more than his dad ever did. But you seem like family folks, being neighbors and knowing the Judsons so well for so many years. I think I can trust you to keep mum." He bestowed an admiringly confident look again on Mary, which she acknowledged with another pleased smile. Then he proceeded to tell of the transaction between Laurie and himself after Mr. Judson's death.

Mary felt her heart nearly burst with pride in that wonderful boy, a man now, taking more than an ordinary man's responsibilities, and taking them quietly, without a whine or a trumpet to let everyone know what he was doing. How fine he was. He was her childhood ideal of him come true. Misty tears came to her eyes as Mr. Winters told of some of the hardships he knew Laurie had deliberately faced in order to make good his father's debt.

"He has a splendid job at the radar plant," he explained, "and will no doubt be in charge of it himself before many years are past if he keeps on. If he were not making such a good salary so that he can, in a sense, afford to do this, I would not have heard to it."

Mary felt that some of the pieces of the picture puzzle that was Laurie Judson's life were slipping into their places. It gave her a keen sense of relief, besides the increased admiration she now had for him. For, if he was as smart and industrious as she had supposed, it had been a mystery to her why he could coop his mother up in that tiny little cottage that must be most uncomfortable especially in the hot weather. It seemed to her that a thoughtful son would surely have provided something better for his mother if it were possible. The answer was completely satisfying to her. Especially as Mr. Winters said that the time of payments was almost at an end. Then that would free Laurie to do many things, perhaps, that he had not been able to do because of his attempt to stretch his earning power as far as possible. Perhaps she would see more of him. Then she chided herself for the selfish thought and determined to be just glad for Laurie.

She was in a happy mood when she returned home that evening. And even the next morning. Nannie heard the lilt in her voice as she went about singing, and Nannie was pleased. But she wondered about it.

"Can't be from havin' that city fella here visitin' Sunday," she mused aloud to Randa as they picked over raspberries for preserving. "Although she mighta been pleased that he went to church with her. Yet she didn't seem happy when he was here." She shook her old head wisely. "An' if a fella makes a girl get glum then he ain't the one for her to marry, that's sure. I only hope she finds it out in time." Then she sighed heavily and Randa's expression grew more fierce and her hands flew faster and faster over the raspberries as if she were trying to catch up with young Master Cupid and tell him that he was doing the wrong thing this time.

Mary took one afternoon to visit here and there around the little town and renew girlhood acquaintances.

Several girls she had known were still living in Arden; a few were married, and most of these had little children toddling about. Mary loved playing with them and a little wistful feeling came over her as she watched these girls who were so happy in their new homes. She wondered if happiness like that would ever come to her. Their lives seemed so smooth, so untrammeled with other people's whims and wishes. Oh, of course there were probably times when their husbands were hard to please, or the babies were sick and cross, but they had a reason for living, and their way ahead seemed so ordered and sure.

She reached home that day with a pleasant feeling of having made a tiny niche for herself in the life of the town. She had promised to take one young mother to the doctor for the babies' check up since the mother had no car, and the way was hot and long. Another friend was coming up to have lunch with her the next day. Oh, she would soon establish herself here as a regular resident and wouldn't it be nice!

As she walked back to the house from the garage and glanced toward the pretty little summerhouse, it suddenly occurred to her that she had not thought once today of Brooke Haven. Good! He must have taken himself home after that church service and would not bother her again. One dose of churchgoing was probably enough to finish him completely. She sincerely hoped that if he were to be helped to better things someone other than herself might be the one to help him. Perhaps Laurie. If he came around again she would certainly arrange to introduce them.

Mary had not the slightest idea of what a miserable Sunday night she had given her friend Laurie Judson. Laurie had lain awake for three hours struggling with himself, trying to put out of his mind the thoughts of depression and jealousy that crowded him. It was long after midnight when he came to himself and was ashamed.

"Oh my gracious Lord," he cried out silently in his heart, "forgive! Give me *Thy* love for both of these people, not mine. Mine is selfish. Do as Thou wilt with us all, *at any cost.*" And then he turned over and went to sleep.

The next morning after breakfast Mary started upstairs to hunt out a bit of sewing that she thought would be nice to work on while her friend and she chatted after lunch. Then she heard Nannie's voice calling.

"Miss Mary, if you want them biscuits for lunch, I guess I'll have to have more flour. Randa's busy with her cleanin' an' I wonder if you could run downtown and get it for me?"

Mary agreed, pleased to be of use. She was beginning to feel quite at home in the clean airy grocery store where they usually traded.

As she pushed her cart along, contentedly looking about at the attractive tables of fresh fruit and vegetables, to see if there were any that she thought Nannie would approve of her buying, she heard a soft voice behind her call her name.

"Mary! Mary Arden!—isn't it?"

It was Laurie's mother. Mary ran joyfully over to her and threw her arms about her in a loving hug just as she used to do when she was a girl. Those same true, sweet eyes smiled up at her, so like Laurie's.

"My dear!" murmured Mrs. Judson lovingly. "Laurie told me you were back in town. Why haven't you been to see me? I have hoped you would come."

Mary flushed and drooped her long lashes, hesitating, conscious that she had been past the house twice, wanting to go in, yet shy of doing so because she had found she was not a little girl any longer, and Laurie no longer seemed much older than she. But she couldn't say all that to Laurie's mother! She did not know that Laurie's mother was reading it in her sweet confusion, and respecting her for it.

"I have wanted to come," Mary managed at last, raising her eyes honestly to Mrs. Judson's. "I wasn't sure you would want me—remember me, I mean," she finished in embarrassment. She was annoyed with herself that she should be so at a loss for explanation. She had been so carefully trained, and was always so well poised, never creating awkward situations. What ailed her?

But Mrs. Judson patted her arm understandingly.

"How could we forget you, child? It was always a joy to have you visit in the old days. Come soon, won't you? Why not have a bit of lunch with me tomorrow?"

Mary's face bloomed with pleasure.

"I'd just love to," she said. And suddenly the day was brighter, and life seemed full of delightful happenings.

Mary was more than usually gay during her friend's visit and all the rest of the day even after her friend had gone. She never realized that a large part of her happiness was bubbling up from the knowledge that she was to go to the Judsons' on the morrow. The thought nestled contentedly in her heart, giving just a flutter of excitement now and then.

This time Nannie found out the source of Mary's brightness that very evening, for Mary could not keep it to herself.

"Don't plan for lunch for me tomorrow, Nannie," she chirped as she stuck her head in the kitchen door before supper. She had tucked a rose in her dark curls and Nannie almost purred thinking how pretty she looked.

"I'm going out," Mary explained, then added as if it were too good to keep, "over to Mrs. Judson's."

After she was upstairs out of hearing Nannie cast a wise smile at Randa.

"Did you catch what she said? Ain't nothin' in a visit with a woman that much older'n her to make her sing her words like that! She's dead in love with Mrs. Judson's boy an' don't know it!" They chuckled together.

But Mary blissfully went on her happy way, pausing not to dissect this pleasant feeling of anticipation.

The next morning Mary had an appointment at the hairdresser's. She would not have made it if she had known ahead of time that she was to go to Mrs. Judson's for lunch, for she would have liked to have the morning free to savor, as it were, the coming pleasure, and her hair would have done well enough as it was! But she disliked breaking appointments, so she went. She was just going out the door to drive downtown when a telegram arrived.

She signed for it and kept on her way out to the garage, tearing it open as she went. Her heart sank for she had a feeling it would be from her mother. She had heard not one word from her since the day of the wedding. She did not know what her mother had done about that announcement in the papers, or whether she had done anything. It would be like mother to smooth everything over without any public gossip if possible. There was no telling what story her mother had concocted that would be near enough to the truth to pass, yet would not exactly deny the announcement. She sighed, wishing she could just throw away this message, and never have to meet the situation it might bring. But of course it must be faced. This time, however, she intended to remain firm and not be coerced into returning to the city, or Castanza, or wherever her mother was by now. It seemed hard-hearted but she felt that she must have a few weeks by herself to get her balance more securely, before she went back to try to straighten out all the knots in her life which her friends and her mother were bent on tying.

So she climbed into her friendly little coupe and opened the yellow page. It was from her mother:

Wire from your father says he is delayed another month in China. I am not able to be alone at Castanza. What are you going to do?

A weight seemed to descend on Mary again as she read the words and she let her head sink down on the wheel for a moment with a discouraged groan. She had counted so much on her father's companionship and help. Must she give up her coveted summer at Arden and go back to that frivolous life at Castanza that seemed so empty to her, especially now, after she had tasted a vital, more worthwhile existence?

She sighed again and glanced at her watch. Time for her appointment now. Well, nothing need be decided immediately. She would have the next hour or so to think it over. So she drove swiftly downtown and parked her car outside the natty little real estate office that she had seen when she first came back to Arden, the second story of which bore the name Sylva Grannis, Beauty Parlor.

Mary had chosen Sylva's shop simply because it was the only one she knew of in the town. There were probably several others, some she might later prefer to this one. But it would be rather fun to see what Sylva looked like by now, and see whether she remembered her or not.

So she climbed the short flight and mustered a smile as she entered the dingy suite of rooms, or rather stalls, that comprised the beauty shop.

14

MARY was not pleasantly impressed by her first glance
around the shop. The *décor* was gaudy—Sylva always had
been a bit loud in her tastes—and there were many
scraps of shorn hair lying about, stuck to the floor by
soapsuds, as if they had been there for quite a while. But
perhaps the girl was overworked and understaffed and
could not keep up the spic-and-span look that a good
beauty shop required. Thus Mary reasoned, trying to
control her prejudice.

A girl in a soiled uniform was lolling behind an untidy
desk reading yesterday's comic strips. She finished her strip
and laughed coarsely before she looked up and stared at
Mary Arden. She took in Mary's simple little morning
dress, its Paris lines and its fine quality, her white summer
sandals that looked as if they had been born on her slender
feet, her quietly expensive linen handbag, and then her
lovely soft hair and perfect complexion.

At last she said: "'V you nappointment?"

"Yes," answered Mary trying to retain her normal
smile, "at ten o'clock. With Miss Grannis. Arden is my
name."

"Oh." That was all. And the girl slouched in her huaraches into one of the red-curtained booths.

Mary could hear a low whispered conversation. It was several moments before the girl reappeared. "You can siddown. She'll be ready soon." Then she returned to her comics, now and then stealing another look at that outfit of Mary's.

It was at least ten minutes before Sylva Grannis released another customer, whose coiffure Mary shuddered at. Sylva slowly turned her eyes under their plucked brows in Mary's direction. At first her lids narrowed ever so slightly, then:

"Oh, it's really you, is it?" she greeted Mary. "I wondered, when the call came in. I did hear you were back here visiting. A boy friend told me." She laughed mirthlessly. "How dah ya like it back in the little old home town?" She spoke as if she too were accustomed now to greater things.

"I love it!" responded Mary. "I always did, you know. But you did remember me! I wasn't sure you would. I was here so rarely, of course." She was trying to make this meeting be what she considered the normal meeting of two old teen-age acquaintances would be, but somehow it wouldn't take the shape of what she had expected. She could not restrain another shudder at the greasy look of the comb Sylva was using on her hair, and the general slovenliness of the whole shop in spite of its glaring chromium fittings and black-and-red trimmings. The very air was stuffy, too, this hot day. There wasn't the clean sweet smell of fresh lotions and spic-and-span utensils to which Mary was accustomed. Well, this was one place her mother would have pointed to and said, "I told you so. Small-town stuff."

Then Mary remembered that telegram that was stowed away in her bag and her heart sank lower. Oh, how many, many disturbing things there were to face and go through with.

As their somewhat desultory conversation dragged on and Mary forced herself to submit to Sylva's ministrations, her mind was also working on the problem that lay in her handbag.

Then she became aware that Sylva was talking about "little old Arden" again.

"We do have some good towns around here, though," rattled on the older girl. "Take Weston, there's a coupla good night clubs there. I was at the Golden Orange Saturday night with a fella and we had a swell time. He really shot the works. Talk about dough! Maybe he didn't have a roll of it. And I didn't go easy on him, either! I really had me a time! An' was he a good-looker? Oh, baby!" Mary did not know that Sylva was exercising great self-control in not letting Mary know that the good-looker with the bank roll was also an acquaintance of Mary's. It was a great temptation to tell her. But Sylva had been sworn to secrecy on that point and she was going to enjoy this whole scheme too much on her own account, to risk spoiling it now by letting the cat out of the bag. But surely, just telling about a man with looks and money was not squealing. Plenty of men had those. Mary would never guess who her friend was.

So she chattered on, meanwhile letting a stream of soapy water run down into Mary's eye. Altogether, Mary decided, this was one shop she did not care to patronize again, one old-time acquaintance whom she would just as soon not see again. Yet there came back to her just then something she had heard last night about how children of God should let Him possess their hearts, so utterly that He can love others through them. Could she ever learn to love this sort of girl? Could she ever bring herself to speak to her of Jesus Christ? That was something to ask Laurie about sometime. The thought of Laurie was always delightful to her and she unconsciously fell to thinking of how splendid he had looked last night as he stood talking in his informal way, so utterly forgetful of himself.

But as if Sylva had read her thoughts she too began to speak of Laurie.

"Have ya seen that handsome Laurie Judson since ya been back? My! what a good-looker *he* turned out ta be. An' who'd ever have thought of him turnin' preacher? He never seemed like that when he was a boy. But he's no stuffed shirt, even now. He can really show ya a good time! You used to go with him, too, didn't ya?"

Mary's face flushed hotly. She was glad that her front hair hung down a little and hid her just then. She resented this girl's even mentioning the name of Laurie Judson. And she was furious at the suggestion that Laurie had been going with Sylva. Laurie never had, not in the old days, and surely not now.

Not for anything would Mary let this girl see that she cared in any special way for Laurie. As calmly as she could she said: "Oh, I used to know him a little. He lived next door, you know."

She was puzzled that Sylva should give such a sneering laugh then. She had not remembered Sylva as being so vulgar. She used to run after the boys and was counted rather silly, but her conversation now verged on the very common.

At last Sylva finished setting her hair and Mary was free from her for a little while as she sat under the dryer. Its whirring motor drowned the giggling chatter of Sylva and her assistant, except when Mary shifted in her seat and caught a word or two of it. Both girls were still on the subject of the boys they had been out with and they were comparing detailed notes of their recent "dates." Their intimate vulgarity sickened Mary. She was glad to draw back under the refuge of the big noisy hood so that she need not listen.

But then her other problem faced her once more. If her father were here, what would he think she ought to do? Go back and submit to being dressed up like a doll and paraded from one party to another, without any higher aim in life than to glean more flattering compliments than someone else did? Did her duty to her mother demand that? She had a feeling that her mother was not grieving for her, personally; it was just that she craved the pleasure of showing off her daughter. Yet Mary's newly awakened conscience made her wonder if she were misjudging her mother, and again she felt the weight of this problem and sighed heavily.

She wondered what Laurie would say. Would he think it right for her to stay and enjoy her own house in her own way when her mother had put it up to her in the way she had in that telegram? As if she had a responsibility to try to fill her father's place? How could she do that? It was not that her mother was really lonely, or that she could be a real companion to her mother, for Mary recognized all too well that they had very little in common.

When Sylva finally came to her and led her back to have her hair combed out, she was no nearer a solution than before.

She was extremely glad when she was pronounced finished and she could pay what she owed and take her leave. She managed a friendly smile of sorts and a good by to Sylva but she was too honest to pretend that she liked her or wanted her to come to see her.

Mary did not like the tight hard way Sylva had fixed her hair. She could scarcely wait until she was in her car and out of sight of the shop before she stopped by the roadside and combed it out into its usual soft waves. But still it didn't feel like her own hair. She made a wry face. "I'd like to go right home and wash it over myself," she said indignantly. "It doesn't feel clean! Ugh!"

The day that she had thought was going to be so pleasant was all upset. Everything seemed to have gone wrong. Then all of a sudden she laughed. "To think I'm such a little ninny that I'm upset over my hair! How silly! I came to Arden, and this is part of it. I'll take it and like it. Laurie Judson said last night that God was glad to have us take even the smallest troubles to him. I wonder if He could take away this disturbed feeling that keeps annoying me. Maybe He could help me solve that telegram problem too."

For the first time in her life Mary Arden lifted her distressed heart in a feeble little trusting cry to her Heavenly Father. It was wordless, as the cry of a babe is wordless. It would not have passed as a prayer in any formal gathering of petitioners, but a loving father understands the meaning of infant wails. Mary Arden was not aware of being answered at the time, but long afterward when she looked back the bewildering way she had come she realized that even before she called, God had prepared an answer.

The thought came to her that there was no need to rush back to Castanza immediately, for her father had not been expected for at least another week anyway. Perhaps something would turn up to show her the right way for her to go by that time. Meanwhile her mother was as well off as she had been for the past several weeks since her father left.

So she drove on to Mrs. Judson's.

And though the morning had turned out so unpleasantly, she was not disappointed in her visit here. As soon as she stepped into the tiny house she felt at ease. Mrs. Judson soon took her out into the little spic-and-span kitchen with her, to help with the last preparations for lunch.

"Just as if I knew how to do things," thought Mary happily. "Well, I certainly want to learn!" She set her pretty lips in determination.

As they sat down to the cosy little table that looked so tempting with its cool salad and iced drinks, Mrs. Judson bowed her head and spoke in quiet tones to the Lord who seemed to be seated there with them as a beloved honored guest, or rather host; for this gentle lady, as she thanked Him for the food and the sweet fellowship together, made Mary feel that it was in truth the Lord who had planned this little party and brought them together. It was a new thrill to her.

And as they grew closer in renewing their old friendship Mary found herself telling this other woman of her problem that seemed so hard to solve, especially since that telegram came.

"It's not that I don't love my mother," she tried to explain with a worried pucker in her sweet brows, "but she and I like such different things. I really don't care for that life at Castanza. It's just one useless party after another, with some of the people drinking too much and getting silly. I like people, and like to be with people, but those people never talk about anything sensible or interesting. I never feel after one of those parties that I'm glad I went. I like to think after I've been somewhere that I have something I didn't have before, or that I've given somebody else something to think about. Perhaps I'm too serious. They tell me I am. But I do like fun, too. Real fun. Getting half drunk isn't fun to me."

She dried another plate carefully and then turned her troubled face to Mrs. Judson's. This woman was so easy to talk to. She was not laughing or scornful. She smiled understandingly.

"I don't think you are too serious, Mary," she said. "Unless it's being too serious to want real gold instead of tinsel, or to enjoy real food instead of sawdust. What does your father think of your being here?"

"I didn't actually plan to come until after he had left on this trip to China. He went the day after I graduated, so I had no chance really to talk it over. But I mentioned it once some time ago and he was pleased. Then I wired him and he sent word I might come. I know he likes it here."

"Did he say anything in this telegram about your going back to be with your mother until he gets home?"

"Mother didn't say. She just sent a wire asking what I was going to do about her, alone up there." Mary spoke in a discouraged tone, like a little child.

"If I were you I'd write an air-mail letter, or cable your father direct and ask him what he wants you to do. Wouldn't that settle your mind? Then if he thinks your mother should not be alone, go back and give her the best time you can. Don't you think that is what the Lord would want you to do? Ask Him to direct your father in what to tell you."

"Oh!" breathed Mary wonderingly. "Could I? Would He? Just a little thing like that? I know Laurie said we could take anything to Him. But—I don't know how to pray. You see, I'm just—beginning, sort of!"

Mrs. Judson set up the last dishes on their shelf, then put her arm about Mary and drew her to the davenport in the living room.

"I'm glad you are 'beginning,' dear, and I know you will never be sorry. It's not an easy way to go, but it's a joyous way!"

"Yes," beamed Mary, "I'm beginning to find that out

already. But I know so little. I do want to learn more. When I listen to Laurie on Sundays it's wonderful but it makes me realize how very much there is to learn. I scarcely know how to read the Bible yet."

"Yes, that's a marvelous thing, that we never get to the end of all of God's wonders. They are always fresh and new. Would you like to learn some more of them right now? Shall we get the Bible and study a little?"

"Oh, I would love to," cried the girl.

And so for an hour they sat with their heads together as Mrs. Judson opened up some of the treasures of the Book to the child who had had so little training in spiritual things, and so much in the things of the world.

At last Mary gave a deep sigh of satisfaction.

"These are things I've always wondered about," she said. "Why didn't they tell us things like this in college? It seems to me that all they did was to make fun of the Book then."

"Yet God knew you were hungry for His truth, and it was He who sent you back to Arden, I'm sure," said Mrs. Judson. "He always satisfies a hungry heart. He's like that!"

She smiled and again Mary had the feeling that God was right there, a beloved one to whom Mrs. Judson had introduced her, and who had joined in their talk. She felt rested and utterly at peace.

Just as she was going out the door Mrs. Judson put her hand gently on the girl's arm.

"There is one thing you will need to know, dear," she said warningly. "Your way ahead now will be challenged at every step by the Enemy of God's children. Don't forget that Satan is still very active in spite of what your college professor said. And his chief activity is against believers. Some great trial may come into your life soon. I don't say that it will, but that is often the way it happens. You may be tempted to think that you were foolish to believe God, that all this is nonsense. Just remember that God allows such tests by Satan to strengthen your faith. If you stand firm you will find your faith is much stronger afterwards, when God has brought you out again into a bright place—for He *always* does! Now come again soon, dear, and call me any time I can help. Good by."

Mrs. Judson drew the sweet young face down to hers and kissed her tenderly. Mary gave her another girlish hug and went down the path. The tears came to her eyes as she waved good by from her car. How like a real mother this woman was. Why weren't all mothers like that? Was it because this woman knew the Lord so well that she was so lovely?

Those last words of Mrs. Judson's came back to her once on the way home, but the way seemed bright now to Mary and she scarcely gave them a thought at the time. Mrs. Judson had suggested some simple work she could do, helping with the children in the little chapel Sunday School, and tomorrow she was to take her friend with the two babies to the doctor. Oh, life looked very pleasant in this little town. She loved to think she could be useful here. That other problem, too, seemed not so troublesome now. She planned what she would say to her father in a cablegram. He would help her. And she had asked God to show her the right way, too. Yes, it would soon come out right.

15

AT supper that night as Laurie and his mother sat in the same cosy little dining nook where Mary and she had had lunch, Mrs. Judson made a suggestion.

"I believe Mary Arden is truly interested in spiritual things, Laurie. I think it would be wise if you would go up there rather often and help her with her questions. She is very intelligent."

Mrs. Judson knew her son well. She could tell that he was taking a firm grip on himself before he was able to say casually,

"I *don't* think it would be wise, mother."

Ah! Then she had been right. This girl was at the bottom of the mysterious sadness that seemed to cloak Laurie in spite of his brave attempt to keep up a cheerful front. But what could the trouble be? Laurie's immediate and decided disagreement was so unusual as to be like an explosion there in the room. Mrs. Judson was silent for some minutes, till the reverberation of it died away.

She hesitated a long moment even then before asking: "Why not?"

Laurie had always been straightforward. He disliked

beating around the bush. He did not always tell all he knew, but when he was faced with a direct question he would either answer it truthfully or refuse to answer it at all.

"Because she's engaged to another man, mother." He said it fiercely.

Laurie rarely spoke in that tone of voice and Mrs. Judson realized how intense had been his struggle. Her heart went out to him. But she did not commiserate. After another quiet minute she asked:

"Are you sure?"

"Yes, I'm sure. As sure as anyone can be."

"You mean she told you?"

"No, but I can't go around asking a thing like that right out of the blue, can I? Look at this."

He took from his pocket the clipping he had found in the newspaper: It was worn and limp now.

Mrs. Judson read the notice, looked at Mary's lovely face with its sweet true eyes, and was puzzled. There had been that in Mary's voice that afternoon when she had spoken of Laurie that had told Laurie's mother more than Mary intended to tell. Still, the girl had not voluntarily called to see her, and had seemed embarrassed when she mentioned her coming. Perhaps—? Yet Mary had always been straightforward, too. Why would she not tell her friends here if it was public news? There was something not just as it should be.

Mrs. Judson sat a long time, reading that notice over and thinking, while Laurie went on with his studying, or pretended to.

Finally she said, "I'd ask her, son, if I were you."

Laurie looked up astonished, but his mother said no more. She rarely disagreed with him and rarely gave advice.

Now that the subject had been brought out into the open Laurie wanted to talk.

"Of course I know she never was a girl I could have—could have hoped to—to go with," he finished lamely. He could not bring himself to say the word marry. It seemed too absurd now in the light of that clipping in the big city's society column that he, a poor boy who was nothing at all, should ever have aspired to such a thought as marriage with Mary Arden.

"Do you really think I should go and ask her?" Laurie asked after another long pause.

"'Could be,'" quoted Mrs. Judson with her lips pursed up and a twinkle in her eye. But more than that she would not say.

Friday was the day he chose to go. He had spent all the intervening days arguing with himself. Trying to decide whether it really was best to go or not. He ate his supper hurriedly, answering his mother's various queries in a preoccupied manner, suddenly bursting into brightness at odd moments. His mother wondered, but when he started off up the hill toward the Arden house, whistling, she smiled and nodded to herself contentedly.

It happened that Sylva Grannis had had a late appointment that Friday and was just closing her shop when Laurie Judson strode by, walking as if he had a pleasant purpose in view. Her eyes in their thick mascara setting narrowed and then widened as she twisted her red lips in a contemptuous smirk. She took her time locking the door to let Laurie get a little start and then she quickly slid into her little shabby coupe and started the motor. She seemed to have things still to do to her face and she let the engine idle several minutes, all the time keeping a keen weather eye on that tall straight figure striding along up the hill. She knew that in her car she could catch him easily, but she did not want to let him make a turn without her knowing it. Above all she did not want to be seen following him. It was important that she discover exactly where he was going.

When Laurie reached the end of the long street that stretched lazily along the slope of one of the low hills surrounding Arden, Sylva let her clutch in and chugged after him. She saw him leave the asphalt street and continue on up the dusty road. Quite plainly she could see him turn in the grassy back lane that led to the south pasture of the Arden house. A grim look of triumph came over Sylva's face. Yet she must be sure. She followed on up the dusty road and drove past the lane. She caught a glimpse far up the hill of Laurie standing in the back yard of Mary Arden's house, talking to Orrin who was just coming from the barn.

Sylva drove on a little farther and turned into the driveway of a neighboring farm, backed out the other way into the road again and drove past the lane once more. This time she was rewarded by seeing Laurie follow Orrin in through the back door. She drew her coupe into a wide spot in the road under an overhanging branch where she commanded a view of both front and back Arden doors. There she waited. She had had no supper yet but she was prepared to wait an hour or two if need be, to make sure of her prey. She had chewing gum, and she had cigarettes. If anyone came by she would tell them that something was wrong with her car and she had sent for the garage man. That would obviate the possibility of some kind, misguided, friendly farmer stopping to help her. She had no desire for company. She would prefer not to be seen, not here, at any rate.

But she had not long to wait. In the late summer sunset light she could see two figures emerge from the front door and wander toward the summerhouse. One was Mary Arden and the other was certainly Laurie Judson.

Only another few moments she waited there, to make sure that the summerhouse was going to claim them for a time, and to go over her plans carefully again. She had hoped for some chance just like this but had scarcely expected it so soon. She had kept a keen watch every night on Laurie Judson's house, and every night except one he had been in evidence there, mowing the lawn, weeding the little vegetable patch, or mending a screen door. That one night had been Wednesday and she knew very well that he was at the prayer meeting service in the little chapel on South Mountain hillside. She had driven past and seen him, and then waited what seemed an interminable time till the long prayers and hymns were over, to see whether he would escort Mary Arden home, or visit her house after the meeting was over. But he had walked home with old Mrs. Wescott who lived near the chapel and helped her up her steps. She was lame with her arthritis. And then he had gone straight home. What a dull life he lived, she thought. He was good looking, oh very! But not for Sylva. Too good! She shook her ringleted head! She must seek more lively escorts.

Swiftly she drove the half mile to her own home. It was a cheerless little house near the end of Main Street. It was between two larger houses, and had there been a bit of comfort in its aspect it would have been said to be tucked in; but so close it was, and so bare, that it gave the effect of having been rammed in in a last-minute effort to make the most of the space between the two larger buildings.

It was not Sylva's house, but it might well have been, to all intents and purposes. For it had been left to her old aunt who was now resident there, and with whom Sylva was supposed to be boarding. But the poor old soul was deaf and so nearly blind that she did not know the half of what went on there. Sylva bought the food for them both and let the old lady think that she was being generous in so doing, and therefore had the right to do about as she pleased in the house. Sylva had the future in mind, and reasoned that the house would descend to her in due time. Sylva had already taken possession of the two rooms upstairs for her "apahtment," philanthropically arguing that poor old Aunt Carrie ought not to climb the stairs, with her rheumatism and all, though Aunt Carrie as yet had not felt a touch of it. Still, she was likely to fall, as her eyesight was so bad, and so Sylva had ensconced her in a tiny cupboard of a room downstairs off the living room. Aunt Carrie sweetly let "Sylvie" take care of her and made no remonstrance. So Sylva had her own living room upstairs and received most of her own callers up there. Aunt Carrie being so deaf was not disturbed, or Sylva always said she wasn't, by their loud carryings-on over her head or their late departure down the bare creaking stairs.

This evening Sylva rushed in and waving Aunt Carrie aside went to the telephone.

"Arden 1714." she told the operator peremptorily.

Aunt Carrie saw her say a few words into the instrument and then wait, speak again and then with a satisfied sly grimace, hang up the phone. But she could not hear a word she said.

Sylva then put her hand to her head and coming close to Aunt Carrie shouted, "I have a terrible headache, Aunt Carrie. I think I'll go up and lie down. Please don't disturb me this evening. I'm going to be sick. No, don't worry about me, I've sent for the doctor. When he comes, just send him up, but nobody else, understand? No, I'm too sick to eat. Well—I'll just take a cup of coffee and a sandwich upstairs in case I feel like eating later." She went into the dining room and hastily put some food on a tray, standing between it and Aunt Carrie so that she would not see the large helping of pickles that might appear too much for a sick person with no appetite, though she felt reasonably sure that Aunt Carrie would not be able to tell without looking closely whether they were pickles or grapes. Neither could Aunt Carrie discern the healthy look of her, nor her strong voice. That was well.

So Sylva took her way up to her own abode and poor Aunt Carrie was left to worry about her and wonder who would help them if "Sylvie took real sick." She kept going to the door to be sure she would not miss the doctor when he came, for she might not hear the doorbell from the kitchen. There was no use, she well knew, in going up to try to do anything for Sylva, for Sylva was independent and did not care to be fussed over; she had often told her so.

It was about twenty minutes of nine when the doorbell rang.

Earlier that same evening Mary Arden had been in her room writing letters when she heard the sound of voices under her window. Someone was talking to Orrin. She caught the tone of a voice she knew, and her heart began a flutter of eagerness. It was Laurie. At last. It seemed so long since he had been up to see her. But probably he was busy and very tired these hot nights when he came home from his work.

She was ashamed of herself for allowing that little glad flutter. She was just like any silly young girl, getting foolish thoughts about a man older than herself! She was of age now, and, in a sense, on her own and she must not allow any nonsense to upset the balance she was trying to attain in her life. Laurie was just a good friend who used to be nice to her, and she liked him. Oh, she liked him, of course. Why not? He was a splendid young man, handsome, clean-cut, brave— she had been hearing in the town some of his exploits during the war when he was out in the Pacific. He seemed an ideal young man, but he had no particular interest in her, of course. He just thought of her as a little girl he used to know. He came here to see the others, Orrin and Nannie, in whom he felt a kindly interest since they had always been so friendly to him when he was a boy next door. Yes, it must be that he came to see them primarily, because he did not come any oftener now that she was here, as far as she could judge from what they all said; less often, in fact. Well, she must just go on in a friendly way and keep her head, not let herself even think in any special way about him. She had no desire to put herself in the position of caring for a man who was not especially interested in her. Of all situations she dreaded that.

So she walked downstairs very demurely, intending to be quite the dignified young mistress of the house. Yet somehow when Laurie came in and looked into her eyes in that glad adoring way, all her resolves and even the reasons she had made up for them vanished away. She found her heart ringing and she smiled up at him with pleasure as they met in the bright wide hallway. The sweet color came flooding up in her face as she realized that her hand was in his in joyous greeting and that he seemed glad to keep it there.

He did not hold it longer than was due a warm handclasp. Yet she did not soon lose the comforting feeling of his hand about hers. She found herself snuggling that hand in her other one to try to preserve the sense of having his upon it. It seemed a precious thing because he had touched it.

"I'm glad to see you," she said. A simple greeting, yet there was a lilt in the words that made his own heart stir with hope.

"Don't you think you have been rather neglectful of this needy parishioner?" she teased.

For answer he only gave her another of those smiles that seemed to envelop her in their warmth.

Suddenly conscious of each other's presence and nearness they became wordless as they sauntered into the living room. Searching desperately for something commonplace to say, Mary suggested,

"Let's go out in the summerhouse. I am so pleased with my new chairs out there." Then "What a silly thing to say," she thought. "So trite. Banal! Ugh! He will think I'm a featherheaded fool. I guess I am. What ails me that I can't even think normally when this man is with me?" She took a deep breath and tried to get hold of her thoughts with a firm determined mind. She had no idea that he himself was struggling to find words for what he wanted to ask.

Yet how ridiculous! The words were there. Few enough, to be sure. Just "Are you really engaged to be married?" Yet he could not find voice to sound them. She would think him a complete fool to come out with such a question right out of the blue that way. He had come here for the express purpose of setting his mind at rest about the question, though he feared there would be little rest when he had his answer. For how would she allow a notice like that in a newspaper if it were not so? And there was certainly no chance that a girl like Mary Arden would have an announcement made publicly without knowing her own mind; there surely could not have been a quarrel since that day the notice was printed.

No, it was all useless, futile, to wonder and wish. He had better put the whole thing out of his mind at once and consider this part of his life over with. Hopes gone, dreams a mirage. Well, if that was in God's plan for him, "even so, Thy will be done," he breathed in his tortured soul.

Mary did not notice the cloud of sadness that came again over his nice, lean tanned face. She had been trying to think of a start for conversation that would not sound inane. She grasped at a sentence she remembered of his sermon on Sunday and began to question him further about it.

Laurie came to with a start and remembered that his mother had said Mary was in need of teaching. Here was a legitimate reason for his presence here. Better let that other question go. So he took out the little worn red leather Testament he usually had with him in his pocket and turned to a chapter that would explain the answer to Mary's question.

But they had no sooner settled down together on the new chaise longue so that Mary might look over his shoulder at the fine print than Randa came hastening out the flagstone walk.

"Telephone for you, Miss Mary," she announced, rather regretfully.

She pretended not to have noticed their heads together over the Book, but when she returned to the kitchen there was not a detail which was not related to Nannie with relish.

"I'll go in with you," said Laurie. "I can't stay long tonight anyway."

They hurried up the path.

Laurie stood just inside the kitchen door saying a word to Nannie while Mary answered her call.

She was not thinking particularly about who might be

calling. She had her mind on what Laurie had just been telling her. Then a rather illiterate voice came over the wire demanding,

"What have you done with my boy friend tonight, Mary Arden?" and ending with a vulgar giggle.

"What—what did you say?" gasped Mary unable to believe that the call was not a wrong number. Yet the girl had spoken her name.

"Oh, *you know!*" came the coarse voice again insinuatingly. "I want my date! How did you manage to take him away from me?"

"I don't know what you mean!" responded Mary icily. "Who is this?"

"Don't you know me, dearie? This is Sylva. I had a date with Laurie tonight and you took him away. I don't stand that sort of thing, girlie. We were set for a high time tonight. I want him back. Let me talk to him!"

Unable to make any response, Mary laid down the telephone and turned with an awful sinking of heart to Laurie who was just coming through the kitchen door into the hallway.

Her face was ghastly pale, but the light was dim now in the hall and Laurie did not notice.

"The call turns out to be for you," she said in a flat toneless voice.

Laurie took the instrument, with a little frown of annoyance at being disturbed there, wondering if perhaps something was wrong with his mother.

"Yes?" he said, "Judson speaking."

A voice he did not know answered. It was a voice in distress. People in his little congregation often called him when they were in trouble. But he could not think who this might be.

"Oh, Mr. Judson!" the voice was weak now, as if the person at the other end was hardly able to speak. "I'm in terrible trouble! I wonder—if you—could come and—help me. I don't know but I'm—going to—to—*die!*" The word came out in a moan. "I am afraid to die, Mr. Judson. Oh, won't you come? I'm Sylva Grannis—you probably remember who I am. I live in the little house next to Simpson's on Main Street. Oh, would you? Thank you so much—" another sob. "Just ring and come right upstairs, please. My aunt is deaf and may not hear you. Oh, do hurry!"

Mary Arden was too well bred to listen to another person's telephone conversation. She had retired a discreet few steps into the living room. All she heard was Laurie's low "Yes, I'll be right over." Her heart stood still. Was Laurie actually going to leave her for that hussy? Could it be possible that he was attracted by her? Had he been going with her, then, all these nights when he had said he was so busy? But she would not for anything let him see that she was hurt. She must not show her feelings to him. It was going to be hard not to retreat into an icy reserve but not for anything would she put herself into contest with that girl.

Mary had not seen the disappointed puzzled frown on Laurie's face as he listened to Sylva's lament. He hung up the phone and came into the living room wearing a troubled look.

"I'm afraid I'll have to leave earlier than I thought tonight. I've just had a call from someone in trouble—a girl I used to know a little. She seems to think she is going to die or something and wants me right away. I guess it's a call I'll have to answer, though I'm no end disappointed. I had hoped to have a good talk with you." He looked down at Mary but her eyes drooped now and did not meet his.

Mary had difficulty in keeping out of her tone the sudden anger and contempt that flared up in her. It was one thing if Laurie Judson wanted to go with a girl like that. It was nothing to her. But to *lie* about it was something else. And she had thought him such a fine straightforward Christian gentleman. So this was what his Christianity amounted to!

"Certainly go, if your *duty* lies in that direction. Good night." She turned to go up the stairs almost before he had started out the hall toward the kitchen.

He wondered at her brusqueness. It was not like Mary to be discourteous. She might at least have walked to the door with him, or stayed until he was gone. Perhaps she was hurt, jealous at the thought of another girl—and his heart tried to give a painful twitch of hope. No, that was not like Mary either, to show jealousy. It must be that *she* thought *him* discourteous for interrupting his visit with her so suddenly. She was such a young Christian, so new to the ways of the life of faith that she would not have realized that a call for help was to a Christian like a summons from God. He had to answer. There was no choice. If this girl was really dying it might mean eternal life to her. He sighed as he hurried down the slope after a hasty explanation and good by to Nannie who was finishing up the last chores in the kitchen. Laurie's heart was heavy for he had not yet had what he considered a good opportunity to find out what he wanted to know. Oh, how lovely Mary had looked as she came down the stairs tonight and greeted him. That sweet glad light in her eyes seemed to say that she thought a great deal of him. But no, that was not possible. She had given her word to marry that other man and Mary was not two-faced. She simply did not realize how charming she was when she smiled that way. She would never play around with one man while she was engaged to another. And he should have known better than to go there tonight. It had just opened the wound again to watch her there in the twilight, and sit beside her. Hereafter he must keep strictly away from her.

And so he hastened his steps toward the house of Miss Sylva Grannis.

MARY Arden struggled up the stairs on feet that felt as if they weighed tons. Somehow she reached the refuge of her own room. She thought she never wanted to see Laurie Judson again. Yet in spite of herself she went straight over to the back window where she could watch him hurrying down the lane. Such a fine stalwart young man he looked! Was it possible that he had let himself be ensnared by a girl like Sylva Grannis? Not one word or trait of his nature had ever betrayed the fact that he had low tastes like that. And to lie about his going! To hide behind his ministry of helping others! What a farce. Did it mean that all Christians were false? Her heart protested. If that were the case all her newly found peace and joy were gone. No, Nannie was not like that, nor Orrin. And they looked up to Laurie as if he were God's very messenger. She had thought of him so herself. Oh, this thing had not happened! Could not happen! There *must* be some mistake.

Mary felt as if her heart had been struck a heavy blow. She had just been gradually getting her balance and learning to live happily again since that awful night of

Brooke Haven's deception. And now this! This was worse. The other had been only shame and public embarrassment, and anger at one whom she already despised. This thing was like a poisoned arrow aimed at her heart. It destroyed the very reality of the man she had almost worshipped. She had considered him far above other men, too fine and strong to stoop to deceit to cover his own weakness.

How different everything seemed from just one short hour ago. How happy she had been to hear Laurie's voice and feel the touch of his hand. To stroll with him about the yard, to sit with him and learn more of heavenly things. Oh! She gave a groan. Was the Bible false, too? Was there nothing on which she could rely? Nothing at all in this world of selfishness and sin and deceit? Was there nobody to whom she could turn for help? Nannie couldn't help. She would undoubtedly stand up for Laurie, make some excuse. What excuse could there be? Mary could not trust that childlike faith in him. Orrin had a lot of common sense, but she shrank from bringing this problem before his ironical judgment. She found it was too close to her heart to speak of to most people. She certainly could not have gone to her mother with it even if she had been at home. Mother would be the first one to condemn a poor boy. She would *expect* him to be disreputable. She would say triumphantly, "Didn't I tell you so, daughter?" Father might be able to help, but father was away. And she had had no answer yet to her cablegram. Anyway, father would probably bid her laugh at herself. But this was a trouble beyond such meagre remedy. She knew that if she tried that now and only that, she would soon grow hard and bitter.

She had asked God to show her the way the other day, but God seemed to be even farther away than China.

Of course there was Laurie's mother, but she couldn't go to her about Laurie!

Suddenly Mary flung herself down on the bed and sobbed into her pillow. Great shaking, heart-broken sobs that made no sound because they were too deep. It seemed that she was utterly alone. There was no one to go to. This dark place she had come to in her life was full of terrors and uncertainties and she must tread it alone. Would she ever get through it?

A long time she lay, letting her grief have its way. Her thoughts were in a riot of confusion. She kept hearing Sylva's coarse sneering voice demanding her "boy friend." Laurie Judson and Brooke Haven seemed to be one in her mind because of their deceit. She pictured Laurie at a night club or roadhouse dancing close to Sylva, and she felt like screaming. She was whirled ruthlessly round and round in a torrent of bewilderment. She did not hear when Orrin closed and locked the front door for the night. She wandered for hours in the maze of her own wonderings and reasonings.

At last in her despair and utter helplessness, feeling the need of someone outside of herself to rescue her from the frightening torrent of her distress, she cried out in her heart, "Oh, God, if You really are my Father now, if all this that I have learned is true, help me now!"

Then from somewhere in the depths of her memory came sounding words that she had heard, words from the Bible, spoken in Laurie's little chapel last Sunday evening by an old man with weatherbeaten face, but a look of peace shining from him, as he prayed in response to Laurie's request. His voice had been so confident in its quiet praise that Mary had raised her head a mite and glanced out of the corner of her eye to see who this was that knew God so well and had such cause for praise. His white hair was thin, his collar was frayed but clean and stiff with starch, his hands were worn with work, but his heart was glad. She seemed to see him now as the words he had spoken came back to her:

"And we praise Thee, Lord, for the way our Saviour measured all the deep waters in our path and brought us through. We know He always will! He'll never leave us to drown in them!"

Ah! That must be wonderful assurance, to know that as the old man knew it. And where else had she heard something like that? The words seemed familiar. "He'll always bring you through." Of course! Those were dear Mrs. Judson's last words to her the other day as she left the house. And she had given her some other advice, too, a warning.

Mary forgot to sob out her sorrow while she tried to recall what Mrs. Judson had said. It was something to the effect that the devil was going to put trouble in her path, and that God might actually allow it in order to test her faith. Strange, that trouble should come so soon. It was almost uncanny, after Mrs. Judson's warning. Could this thing that had happened to her possibly have anything to do with the step of faith she had taken last week? Most of the people she knew would mock the idea. But it was reasonable to suppose, if *any* of the Bible was true, and if she really was allied with God now in a new way, that whatever enemy of God there might be would try to hinder her progress.

"He will try to make you think that all this is not true," Laurie's mother had said.

In a sort of fright Mary sat up on her bed. That was just exactly what she had been tempted to do this last hour, to throw aside all that Laurie had taught her and Laurie's mother had taught her, and all she had read in the Bible, because she had found a weakness in one of her teachers. Laurie himself had said that nobody, not *anybody* was just right.

Then came the same disturbing little thought to Mary: "Perhaps he was trying to excuse his own sins in that way."

But she had read enough in the Book for herself now to know that "All have sinned" was God's word, not simply Laurie's.

At last she got up and went to her bathroom and washed and dried her eyes. Then she took the little red Testament from her pocket that she had slipped there when Randa came to call her to the phone, although it gave her a new pang to remember that it was Laurie's and its place was always in his vest pocket nestled close to his heart. She shook her head trying to throw off such thoughts.

"I will read and read, and read," she said to herself, "till I come to *something* that I can understand and be guided by."

The soft little book opened easily, yieldingly to her hand. She leafed over the pages, reading a verse here, a verse there, most of them those that Laurie had marked with a red pencil.

"Oh, God, show me! Give me some word from You. I'm so alone!"

Then she turned again and this time several pages slid by and she saw a long verse marked heavily in red.

"Beloved," she caught her breath. It was as if Laurie had sent that message to her—oh no, how foolish and confused she was—it was God's word, not Laurie's. She read the word again and dwelt on it, it was so comforting. "Beloved, think it not strange concerning the fiery trial which is to try you as though some strange thing happened unto you." Mary's eyes opened wide and she sat amazed scarcely ready to go on farther; the verse spoke her own situation so plainly. "Think it not strange"—she had been thinking it so very strange that all this should come to her! "Fiery trial." Oh, how fiery no one but God could know. To have her almost lifelong ideal smashed in an instant as hers had been and to be left alone to face the scorching fact! Oh, this Book knew about things like that!

Then she read on, breathlessly, eagerly, half thinking to find her own name and Laurie's there, and all the details of her life!

"But rejoice—" Rejoice! How on earth could she *rejoice* in what gave such frightful pain?

"Rejoice inasmuch as ye are partakers of Christ's sufferings—" Partakers. She was not alone in this, then. Some One had been through suffering like this before. She knew enough to realize that not a soul that ever lived had gone through such suffering as the Son of God went through. Then in some way she was being permitted by this thing to share in the mystery of what He went through. He had known what it was to suffer alone. He had promised never to leave His own alone. In a vague way Mary could see that as she stood with Jesus Christ in this trial, trusting Him in spite of everything, she was being given the honor of sharing what He went through. Oh, she could not have stated as a theological doctrine the reason for the suffering of God's children, but it thrilled her to think that she might have some part with Him by standing true to Him in this trial.

She looked down at the Book again. "—that, when His glory is revealed ye may be glad also with exceeding joy."

Mary could not understand much of that last part. The glory seemed a long way off to her. But she did realize that God had joy and brightness and glory waiting somewhere at the end of all this.

There was a recent date written in Laurie's hand on the margin of the verse. Had Laurie, too, been subjected to a fiery trial lately? A testing? And would God bring him through? Perhaps that was the reason for the sadness she had noticed on his usually merry face. She had not the slightest suspicion that Laurie's trial might have anything to do with her.

After that when the thought of Sylva came again she put it away from her. Let God work that out for Laurie and bring him through!

"And He has promised to *bring me through!*" she said aloud, wonderingly. She took a deep breath and laid the little book down reverently. "I guess that ought to be enough to rest on."

It was long past midnight but for the first time she realized that she was very tired. She undressed swiftly and crept into bed with more peace in her heart than she had had all the evening.

But she was wakened early in the morning by another telegram. This time it was not from her mother.

17

AS Laurie walked swiftly the long half mile to Sylva Grannis' house he tried to forget for the time being the girl he had left. He was still puzzled over her summary flight up the stairs before he had scarcely started away. Even though she might have been hurt at his leaving her she would not normally have left him as she did. But he had an errand to do now and he must be prepared. So he tried to fix his mind on some Bible verses that would make simple and plain the way of salvation for a dying soul. But nothing seemed to come to his mind but the scornful hurt look in Mary Arden's beautiful eyes.

At last he asked his Heavenly Father for help in this coming situation, whatever it might turn out to be, and mounted the three steep little steps up to the house. He could see a dim light upstairs. That must be where the sick girl was. He wondered what had taken her so quickly. He knew Sylva Grannis, that is, he had seen her about town ever since he was a boy. He had never liked her. Yet here she was calling on him as a messenger of God to point the way to Him. The old thrill came over Laurie as he realized the warmth that could come into his heart toward a seeking soul, even though he did not like her personally. What a miracle that he found himself willing and glad to give up his coveted time with Mary Arden in order to help this poor lost one across the border. How marvelous that God had chosen him to do it!

Such were Laurie's exalted thoughts as he rang the bell and pushed open the door.

There was Aunt Carrie popping up right at the entrance.

"Miss Grannis sent for me." He motioned upstairs. Aunt Carrie nodded to him to go right up. With serious mien he mounted the stairway.

He thought he heard a rustling sound and hurrying tiptoed steps as he neared the door where a dim crack of light showed. Perhaps Sylva was sick enough to have a nurse. But when he tapped and went in there was no one in the room except Sylva, and she was lying quite still in her bed, as if she were too weak to turn at his coming.

She was clad in a most revealing black lace nightgown. Her shoulders and arms were much too plump and fleshy for a sick or dying person, but of course a heart attack might have seized her suddenly. Laurie could not help noticing how coarse her skin was and how fat and pudgy her arms. But he discarded the passing thought as unworthy of his errand.

For several seconds Sylva lay without opening her eyes, to let her visitor take in the full effect of what she considered her appeal.

Laurie was beginning to wonder whether he should waken her, or whether he had better step out and come some other time. She did not look so very near to death, he thought. But the light was dim and he was not skilled enough in such cases to be sure.

Just at the psychological moment Sylva slowly opened her eyes.

"You've—come—at—last!" she breathed faintly.

"Yes," answered Laurie gently. "I've come. Is there some special question you want to ask me?"

Again the lids were closed for a long moment. They still did not open, only fluttered weakly as the girl barely moved her head sideways as if to say no.

Laurie was somewhat at a loss how to proceed. But as she had asked him here in desperation apparently, and said she was not ready to die, he began to repeat some verses in a low clear voice.

"'All have sinned and come short of the glory of God,'" he began. "And 'The wages of sin is death but the gift of God is eternal life through Jesus Christ our Lord.' That means that if you trust in Jesus Christ as your Saviour," he explained, "believing that He took the punishment for your sin when He died on the cross, that even though this body dies, you will never be judged for your sins and you will live forever with Him." He said the words slowly and plainly, as if he were talking to a little child. As there was no response he asked, "Do you understand that?"

A slow sad shaking of the head was all that gave any sign that she had heard.

So Laurie began with other verses, showing the plan of salvation from several different angles. Because she would not or could not speak or ask any questions it was hard to know just what point was not plain to her. He could not tell where to begin. He felt as if he were feeling an uncertain way in the dark. What word of scripture might possibly awaken this poor soul to see the light? It was the strangest situation Laurie had ever been in. Many seeking persons he had helped to see the truth, some on the battlefield and some at home, and he had joyously introduced them to his Lord. But this was a difficult case indeed. After some time of quoting verses and explaining them as plainly as he could he paused.

"Is that clear now," he asked again softly, for she was so quiet he had a feeling she must have gone to sleep. "Would you like me to stop now? Perhaps I'm tiring you."

Again that weak little shake of the head, but more decided this time.

At a loss, Laurie knelt down beside the bed and prayed. A harder heart than Sylva's there could not have been, for scarce a soul could have listened to such a petition as Laurie offered without at least a softening or a tear of gratitude.

Laurie finished his prayer and hesitated. He felt he was not getting anywhere. He disliked staying so long. Yet he dared not go if this girl was still in the dark, and might actually die soon. He would never forgive himself.

"You are tired now, aren't you?" he asked again. "You want me to go."

This time Sylva opened her eyes and looked at him pleadingly.

"No," she whispered. "Go on!"

Mystified, Laurie went on to give more and more scripture. There were whole chapters he knew from memory. But he could not yet discern any response in her, nor any indication of what he should say next.

He became aware of Aunt Carrie's worried footsteps downstairs coming to the foot of the stairs, then uncertainly going away again.

There was one angle he had not used to approach her. Perhaps that would be enough to arouse her. So he ventured:

"Sylva Grannis," he spoke her full name, more loudly than he had been speaking, as if to call her from the distance she seemed to be from him, "Sylva Grannis, I have given you faithfully the word of God. You have made no response, although you have asked for it. I can only hope that you have heard with your heart and accepted the Lord Jesus Christ as your Saviour. If you have not, and will not, I have only one more word to say to you: 'If our gospel be hid it is hid to them that are *lost!*' May God help you!"

Just then the town clock struck half-past ten. It had been only nine o'clock when he arrived.

Suddenly Sylva sat up in bed. In a loud tone, perfectly plain to be heard by the dwellers in the houses on either side or by late passers-by on the street—though of course not by Aunt Carrie—she said:

"Laurie Judson, you get out of my bedroom! If you don't I shall scream for help."

He stood up, utterly stunned.

"Get out!" yelled Sylva. "Go on back to your precious Mary Arden—if she wants you after this!"

In furious comprehension that he had been completely taken in, Laurie realized that he must somehow acquire witnesses of this evening's performance, or quite possibly his name and his job and his ministry at the little chapel were all gone. He thought fast. There were no witnesses, for Aunt Carrie was too deaf and blind to be considered. Then he would have to make some. He would take this girl by force down to the police station and make her tell the chief what she had done, and why. He was too distraught himself and realized too keenly the need for immediate action to try to reason out why on earth she had done this thing. But if he took the bull by the horns and made the thing public of his own accord perhaps he could forestall any scandal.

In a firm tone he commanded: "Sylva Grannis, you lied to get me here for some unknown reason. Now you put on some clothes and come with me to the police station. You are going to tell McNary exactly what you have done. You will be very sorry if I have to use force, but I will. Now hurry. I'll wait in the hall."

Laurie was not at all sure that Sylva would obey him. In fact he was nearly sure that she would not.

He intended to wait about ten seconds and if he heard no sound of her getting ready to go he would make another move.

It was quiet at first, then she laughed, a loud sneering laugh.

"Very well," he called, "then I shall call McNary here."

He started downstairs to the phone. But just then the doorbell rang.

He reached the foot of the stairs just as the door opened and in walked Orrin.

Aunt Carrie bustled up turning on lights, trying to see who the caller was.

"It's jes' me, Carrie," yelled Orrin into her ear. "I come by to see if this gentleman is about ready to go home now."

She nodded and smiled. "Is my niece better, doctor?" She whined in the loud voice of the deaf, peering at Laurie to try to make out which doctor he was.

Orrin glanced at Laurie who took his cue in an instant.

"I think she will be *much* better now," he shouted back. "She'll probably be able to get up tomorrow."

"Too bad she went out of her head so, weren't it?" sympathized Orrin in a voice he hoped neighbors might hear also.

But Aunt Carrie said, "Yes, she had a bad headache."

"Doctor had to give her a shot to quiet her, didn't ye, doc?" Orrin yelled again.

"Well, yes, she had *several* shots!" answered Laurie,

with a wry grimace. But Aunt Carrie did not understand.

She saw them out the door and then locked it carefully. She tiptoed to the foot of the stairs and cocked her head as if she could hear whether the patient needed her, then still tiptoeing softly she went to her own room and proceeded to get ready for bed. It had been a long anxious evening.

Laurie and Orrin made haste to the old racketey car and chugged off.

"Well, friend, you sure were God's angel of deliverance tonight!" exclaimed Laurie fervently. "How you ever happened to be there in the nick of time I can't tell! Did you hear what that girl said?"

Orrin chuckled.

"I heard a mite," he admitted, "though I don't gen'ally go in fer eavesdroppin'. Can't ya jes' leave how I got there with the Lord and take it fer granted He worked it?"

"I suppose I can," agreed Laurie humbly, "but it is tremendously interesting sometimes to have a glimpse behind the scenes and learn just how the Lord works. Isn't it?"

Orrin grinned again in the darkness as his old car lumbered on toward Laurie's home.

"Wall, I dunno as I can rightly explain it," admitted Orrin. "I guess I jes' happened to be comin' out tonight on an errand, and I heard your name as I was passin', so I thought mebbe I could give you a lift home. I kinda sized things up when I heered what she said an' what you told her, so I cum in to hurry things up."

Orrin made no attempt to synchronize the order of events as he portrayed them. How he could have heard Laurie's name over the roar of his ancient engine he did not say. And not for worlds would he have let Laurie know that he had followed from a distance that evening, wondering what errand could have taken the young man so swiftly from his beloved and left such a despairing look on her face as Orrin had caught on Mary's. He gave no sign that his amazement had surpassed any bounds when he had discovered the house where Laurie had gone to visit. He would have been willing to admit to Laurie, had that young man pursued the questioning further, that he had heard some of the low voiced scripture he had quoted, and that prayer, or at least a word of it now and then. Though how he could have heard that when he had been supposed to have stopped his car at the sound of Laurie's name shouted by Sylva, he did not stop to figure out. But Laurie did not ask further. He knew old Orrin well, and he smiled to himself in pleased confidence in Orrin's loyalty.

"Do you suppose there will be a grand scandal about town over this?" wondered Laurie. "Such things do happen, you know."

"I don't reckon so." Orrin closed his tight lips with determination. Whether he intended to start a counter plot Laurie did not know, but he trusted his friend's judgment, and more especially his Lord's overruling, and he let it go at that. Good old Orrin.

Then his mind went back to Mary. He was woefully troubled at having left her the way he did. He tried to voice some of his worry over it to Orrin, but found it meant too much to him. He dared not trust himself to talk about Mary yet to anyone. And besides, if he made anything of it, it would look as if he cared too much. Better try to explain to Mary himself the next time he saw her. But what could he explain? It did not sound plausible.

"Can you imagine why in blazes that crazy girl pulled

a trick like that?" he asked Orrin after a thoughtful pause.

Orrin put on his wise look, though it could not be seen.

"Young man," he replied, "you will have to learn that the ways of women are strange. They do things that have no rhyme ner reason. But ef anyone was to ask me I'd say—" he paused oratorically to let the terrible force of his next word be appreciated— *"jealous!"*

"Oh, for the love of Mike!" exclaimed Laurie in horrified astonishment. "That must be why she mentioned Mary Arden." Then Laurie, realizing that he had said more than he needed to say, added "Er—I mean, how on earth did she know I was up here at Ardens' and why would she care? You don't think she's—she's—" again he could not bring himself to say what was in his mind, that the girl was in love with him—"I mean, she's never seemed to—to—pay attention to me. And goodness knows I never looked twice at her. Oh, what an unholy mess!" Laurie was dumbfounded.

"Might as well forget it all," advised Orrin. "Like as not you'll never hear any more of it. Anyway, didn't you tell us on Sunday as how God promised that no tongue that shall rise against thee shall get away with it?" He did not state that by the time he and Nannie finished telling their version of it to certain acquaintances in the town, that the town would have very little use for Sylva Grannis. He did add, however, "Might be a good thing if that beauty parlor of hers found a better location in another town." But neither did he say what part he might have in urging Sylva to such a step.

He let Laurie out at his own home which seemed to be standing there in the quiet summer night waiting anxiously for its master.

But Orrin drove a long roundabout way home because he had a great deal to think out. First he had to decide just what to tell Nannie. Probably the whole truth would be best. Little as he pretended to value women's judgment he had generally found that it was wisest not to keep things from Nannie. Nannie was different anyway. She had a great deal of common sense. Her judgment nearly always coincided with his.

It might be that Nannie could help him with his next problem, namely, to crystallize the details of the story that must be circulated before that hussy got her own tale around. Also to decide what part if any he would need to take in evacuating Sylva Grannis and her beauty parlor.

But his hardest problem was going to be to explain matters to Mary Arden, and that right quickly, in order to remove from her beloved face that hurt look of utter despair. Could he tell her the whole story? It all sounded so outlandish he wondered if she would believe it.

Randa was asleep when he reached home, and Mary Arden's light was out so he assumed that she also had retired. But Nannie was waiting for him. He had known she would be. She had on her long sleeved tatted nightgown, and her gray hair was up in its usual leather curlers, but she was watching out the window in the dark room, and listening for the unmistakable sound of Orrin's car.

She was greatly relieved when she heard it. Orrin very rarely stayed out like this. She did not know what to make of it. He had told her nothing of his purpose when he left. For Orrin had thought there might be nothing to the excursion, and then he would return, to make some casual routine explanation of his hasty departure.

But Nannie must hear this.

As he told her every detail that his sharp ears had been

able to glean from their station beneath Sylva's window, Nannie's wrinkled old face blazed with indignation.

"The hussy!" she hissed. "To think of her doin' a trick like that to a minister!"

"Laurie's not a minister," corrected Orrin so worried that he stooped to picking at trifles.

"Well, he's just the same as," maintained Nannie. "It must be she has a crush on him and is jealous of his comin' to see our Miss Mary."

"Yes, I did think some o' that angle. But if she has why would she want to ruin his good name?"

"Oh, you never can tell what girls will do," asserted Nannie. "Besides, she's the kind of girl who wouldn't care if her man's name was ruined so long as she got him. There are such, you know." Nannie instructed her husband as if he were a callow young man not yet familiar with the evil ways of the world.

Orrin sniffed.

"She don't belong in our town," he said. "Town'd be better off without so many o' them fool shops anyways. Say! Didn't Miss Mary go down to that shop last week herself?"

"Why yes, I believe she did." Nannie took down one of her curlers that felt too tight and rolled it up again as she tried to puzzle out the tangle. "But you can't think our Miss Mary would have said anything that would get Laurie into trouble, do you? I don't believe she would ever let on how much he comes here. It isn't like her. What could her visit there have to do with this?"

"Dunno." Orrin was beyond his depth when it came to what might go on in those mysterious stalls at the beauty shops.

So they discussed the problem, far into the night, and slept late next morning. And that was how it came about that Mary Arden was gone before either of them awoke, and Orrin had no chance to explain what had happened the night before, even if he could have thought of a way to do it.

MARY was beginning to be tired of telegrams. This one, she thought, would be sure to be another insistent one from her mother, and she would simply have to make a decision one way or another about going to Castanza. She had still heard nothing from her father. No doubt he had moved on again and her cablegram had not reached him as soon as she had calculated that it would.

She tore open the envelope and then hesitated. How was she to know what to do? Must she go back there to Castanza and throw away all the rest of this beautiful summer? Suddenly she jumped out of bed and knelt down, the telegram still in its envelope.

"Oh my dear new Father, please show me so that I will *know* just what to do. I think I'm willing to do as You want me to. But I'm very slow at learning what You want. Thank You. Amen."

Then with a feeling of wonder upon her that she had thus dared to bring her pitiful little request before such a one as God, she took out the telegram and read:

Your mother hurt in auto accident. Come at once. Have cabled your father. Hetty.

Wide-eyed with distress Mary stared for a moment at the words, hardly comprehending that her prayer had thus accurately been answered. There was no question now as to what she should do.

With fingers that trembled in their haste she grasped her bedside telephone and called the airport.

"Yes, we have," the man cheerily answered her request for a reservation. "Just one seat. Plane leaves in twenty-five minutes."

Could she possibly do it?

She threw on her pretty little dark blue travelling dress, with the crisp white collar and cuffs that Nannie always kept spotless for her, gave a brush to her curls, and ran down to Randa in the kitchen.

"Make me a sandwich, please, Randa, and cool me a cup of coffee for now before I go. I have to make the plane in a few minutes. Mother has been badly hurt. No, don't disturb your mother if she's not down—explain to her why I had to go."

Then she rushed up the stairs and packed a bag, putting in several useless things in her excitement, and leaving out some that she later needed. But she was not worrying about equipment just now. The main thing was to get home. The telegram was from the city. Mother was not at Castanza then. But Mary had no time to wonder why.

"Randa," gasped Mary, as she took a hot swallow of coffee, "will you call Alvin Burgett at the garage as soon as you think it's open and ask him to get my car from the airport and store it until I get back. Or I may even send for it. Tell him I'll leave the keys at the airport office in his name and mine."

"Yes, Miss Mary, but shouldn't I waken dad and let him take you out? He'll be that upset. I don't know why they're not about yet. It's after seven and I never knew them to sleep so late."

"No, Randa. Let him sleep. They've both had a lot more work to do since I came," she gave a sad little laugh, "and I guess they need the rest. Give them both my love. I'll let you know how things go. Good by!" and she was off, racing down the driveway in her little coupe.

That early plane made good time back to the big city, but it seemed a long age to Mary.

Her first thought was one of shame to think that she had been so hardhearted as not to respond to her mother's plea and come to Castanza to be with her. Perhaps this thing would not have happened had she been there. She judged herself harshly.

But then she began to realize how marvelously God had answered her when she asked for guidance. Why would God answer her like that if she was so bad? Then she remembered what Laurie had said once: "God accepts us on the merits of His Son, not on our own."

Then the thought of Laurie sent a surge of pain through her. She had been awakened so quickly to this other disaster that the grief of last night had not yet marched into her thoughts until now. Oh, to think that just now when she needed Laurie most, he was suddenly farther away than he had ever been before! It seemed to Mary as if she were in a fiery furnace of troubles. Could it be that there was "the form of one like the Son of God" with her? It was a thrilling thought. The more because she had begun to experience in some small degree what it meant to walk with God.

She looked out the window and up at the limitless space. She had used to think God was far out there beyond all those fluffy white clouds. In fact she recalled with some discomfiture a fancy that had followed her childish mind for years when she was a little girl. Her mother had bought her a dream of a blue-and-white dressing table, all beruffled with white organdy in billows, over a blue background. It had been the little girl's ideal of beauty and she had subconsciously connected it with heaven, picturing the Almighty as seated upon a throne which closely resembled her dressing table, a throne all decorated with gold like her gold set that lay on her table, and angels flitting here and there in lovely groups like her organdy ruffles. She smiled amusedly. What a funny picture-God she had tried to worship, something like the paper pictures people pasted on their doors in China, perhaps, only prettier. There was no image that came to her mind as she thought of the One who now walked with her. There was just that sense of His nearness, His love. Was that what the Bible meant by walking by faith? Not being able to see or visualize anything, just knowing? She must ask Laurie sometime. Then again the pain came. Would she ever feel like asking Laurie anything again?

Then she wondered for the fiftieth time how badly hurt her mother was, and whether she was going to die. Mary had never had to meet death in her family before. That girl who had died at college was the first one to go in her circle of friends and she had not been especially intimate with her. She wondered how she could ever go through it, if father did not get home. How would she know how to plan? There would have to be a service, and decisions of all kinds to make. She sighed again, with the weight of this new dread. She had not yet faced the thought of the desolation her mother's going might bring. So far this was just another trouble. If only she could feel free to call upon Laurie as she would have done up until last night.

The roar of the plane's engine soaring on and on seemed like the inevitable march of disasters that were endlessly appearing in her life now. There was only one bright hope. That was that she could continue to count on the Presence that had begun to be real to her. He had answered her prayer this morning. In a startling way, to be sure, but the answer had come. She would go on in this strange uncharted way, and see if He would bring her through. At last the gentle wavering of the great ship told her that they were losing altitude. Soon the land rose into view and the gliding monster came to a standstill.

Mary hurried to the waiting taxis and gave her home address. She must speak to Hetty and find out where her mother was, and just how badly she was hurt.

It seemed another endless trip but at last Mary was back at her house, paying the taxi man with fingers that were nervous from anxiety.

Hetty came to the front hall immediately. Her face was a picture of woe, but then Hetty was so easily upset and she always made mountains of everything.

Without a greeting Mary asked, "Tell me *all* of it, Hetty. I want to know how bad it is."

Hetty twisted her stubby hard fingers as she talked.

"It's pretty bad, Miss Mary," she said in a voice that hesitated and trembled. "Your mother was on her way home from Castanza to attend a funeral here the next day, when it happened. It was a truck that got 'em, a big beer truck, that came across the highway from a side street and smashed right inta them. Henry's that upset, too. He says he wishes it coulda been him that was so bad. He has a broken arm and some bruises."

"But—mother? How badly—is she hurt?" quavered Mary.

"Well, I couldn't rightly say." Reluctantly the conscientious Hetty tried to escape telling the whole truth. "But the doctor says she may get better!" she triumphantly suggested.

Mary went over to Hetty and took her by the shoulders firmly.

"Hetty, tell me now! Right away. What is it?"

Hetty's honest eyes drooped, looked here and looked there, and finally at Mary's insistence, they looked straight up and she said,

"It's her head, Miss Mary! Concussion, they called it. They don't know yet if it's broken or not. Oh, I didn't want to have to tell you!" She put up her immaculate starched white apron and wept restrained sobs.

"Thank you, Hetty," said Mary quietly. "Now tell me where she is."

"At Temple Hospital, Miss Mary."

"Is Henry there, too?"

"No, Henry is out and about, though he can't drive a car."

"Where are the keys to mother's car?"

Hetty hastened to get them, and Mary followed, without waiting to go upstairs and freshen up.

Her mind dazed and whirling, Mary drove to the hospital, trying to go slowly, conscious that she was not up to driving, yet wanting to go at top speed for fear even now she might be too late.

She parked her car at a parking lot and found that her hands were icy cold as she handed the keys to the attendant.

She hastened into the elevator. Oh, how many many trips and vehicles there were to take! How interminable each ride seemed.

Then she stood in the white hospital room. The doctor was there, but he waited a moment while she went softly over to her mother and looked at that still face all swathed in bandages. The tears came to her eyes, tears of regret, perhaps, more than of sorrow. Mary had always felt it keenly that her mother and she seemed so far apart in thoughts and ways. Just to think that she had not responded to her mother's last request! Perhaps she never would have a chance to ask forgiveness.

The doctor motioned her to come out into the hall.

She looked up at him with wide sorrowful eyes and waited for his verdict. She knew this man. He had been the family doctor for years. She could trust him.

"You mother is hurt badly, Mary," he explained gently, "but we cannot tell yet just how badly. She may recover completely, or she may remain like this, unconscious for a long time, days or even weeks. There *may* be a brain injury, but we think not. We are going to take more pictures this afternoon."

That was all. There was nothing more to be learned. She would just have to settle down to waiting. Waiting and watching for some sign of returning consciousness.

Slowly, with reluctant step, like one taking up a very heavy load to carry for a long, long time, Mary went back into the bare white hospital room and seated herself in the big arm chair where she could look at her mother's face.

All the waves of trouble seemed to sweep over and engulf her as she thought over the last few weeks.

"Oh, God, where are You now? Do you know about all this? Do You care?" And as if in answer there came back to her Mrs. Judson's last words to her. How marvelous that she had been warned. What if she had not? Surely she could not have stood against this rushing tide of woes.

All the afternoon she sat there. The nurses came and went and did the few things there were to do for the sick woman. They wheeled Mrs. Arden out for X-rays, kept her an interminable time, and brought her back, still with no further word for Mary.

For a girl whose whole life had been filled with action and color, the waiting seemed the hardest trial of all. Would this go on just the same way for days, for weeks, perhaps? When, oh when, would father come? There had been no word from him yet.

The cable had been sent immediately after the report on the accident, which had occurred just before midnight. There should be some answer tonight or at the latest tomorrow.

Wearily Mary took her lonely way home that evening and tried to eat the nice supper the cook had prepared. But nothing tasted right and she found she did not care whether she ate or not.

The next day was much like the first one—just waiting. Toward evening a message finally came from her father, which heartened her a little.

Will be home as soon as I can get there. Much delay in getting reservations. Please send daily reports care of International Airlines.

Then followed several days, all alike. Mary began to feel as if she were in a sort of vacuum, where time did not pass.

At last one evening, feeling desperately lonely, she called up her house at Arden. It was good just to hear Nannie's voice. She could hardly speak to her for the glad tears that choked her. She had written her just a brief note that first night to let her know what had happened. Now she could give very little more news.

But Nannie could sense how hard the long testing was for her dear girl. And the next day she made Orrin drive her across town to Mrs. Judson's, ostensibly to take her some of her strawberry preserves, and to make a call. But Nannie had no intention of leaving the place without painting a thorough, sympathetic portrait of Mary sitting day after day beside her mother's bed, alone, waiting.

As a result, Mary received a loving note soon after that from Mrs. Judson. It was full of motherly sympathy and also a word or two of encouragement to "stand fast" through this new trial.

Mary searched the lines rapidly for some mention of Laurie or some word from him. There was nothing until the very end and then it simply said, quite conventionally, "Laurie and I shall be thinking of you and holding you up in prayer, my dear."

That was nice, and was probably meant to be comforting—yes, it *was* comforting, in a way. But Mary's lonely heart longed for the friendship she had learned to lean upon. Of course, if Laurie really cared anything about that other girl—it still seemed incredible!—then of course he would not be wasting his thoughts on her particular trouble.

But Mary was learning more and more about prayer herself these long days when she was set aside from all other activities. She spent many hours poring over Laurie's precious little red Testament. She was beginning to experience the faithfulness of her new Lord, and to exult in that, in spite of the uncertainty of earthly friendships.

Then one night about a week after she had left Arden, she reached home exhausted and discouraged, and as she walked in the front door she noticed a light in the living room. She stepped to the entrance and there was Brooke Haven.

He rose and came to meet her, holding out both arms

sympathetically. Mary had been so lonely she was almost glad to see even Brooke. For most of her friends were away, of course, at the mountains, or the shore, or on long summer cruises. Brooke would gladly have received her into those open arms, but she still drew back, putting out her hand instead.

"I'm just back from California, Mary," he said, "and I heard of your trouble. I had to come right over to you. How is your mother?" He really sounded as if he cared. At least he was someone to talk to, a live person out of the dream that was her past life.

"Thank you, Brooke," she responded with sincerity in her tone, which sign of capitulation Brooke did not fail to catch. "Mother is just about the same, I'm afraid. Sometimes she stirs and we think she is going to recognize us, but then she sinks back to unconsciousness again. The doctor says tomorrow will be a crucial day."

"Oh!" soothed Brooke with just the right amount of pity. "That is hard for you, isn't it!"

"Well, yes," she smiled deprecatingly, "but of course it's a lot harder for mother."

"But you look so tired. I'm sure you haven't done a thing since it happened but sit and watch her, have you? Now admit it. I thought so," as she sadly nodded. "Now you are to come right out with me and take a little ride, and we'll talk about something else than sickness. You will ruin your lovely looks if you don't have some recreation."

"Oh!" cried Mary. "As if that mattered! Don't you realize that my mother is facing death at any moment? And—" Mary hesitated, wondering whether to say this to Brooke or not, then spoke in a slow solemn way, "I don't think my mother is ready to go, Brooke!"

A sneer curled his handsome lip. "What nonsense, Mary. I thought you knew better than to go in for such hooey. What has your mother ever done that's so terrible? You talk that way and you'll have people thinking there's some scandal connected with her name."

"No, Brooke, you don't understand." Having gone this far, she felt as if she must explain. "God demands perfection, of course! Otherwise what would a heaven be for? And none of us have that. We only receive it as a gift, by accepting Jesus Christ as our Saviour."

Black fury raged behind Brooke's eyes and he allowed himself to rant more than he had intended ever to do. He had before made up his mind that anger and mockery would not win with Mary. Diplomacy was more powerful. But he could not control his disgust for a moment.

"Mary Arden! It's beneath you to give a thought to such cheap palaver. What kind of God do you want to worship? One who would decline to admit a person as good as your mother into His inner sanctum? How absurd! Come now, and ride with me, and we'll get all such forlorn thoughts out of your brain. We'll plan some fun for when this hard time is over. Come, my beautiful lady."

But Mary shook her head.

"No, thank you, Brooke. Not tonight. I'm too tired." She saw that there was no use trying to explain further to one who did not care to understand. "If you will excuse me, I must go straight to bed now. I want to get over to the hospital early tomorrow since the doctor thinks mother may rally. Good night, and thank you for taking the trouble to come."

Coolly thus she dismissed him, and he realized that his wisest plan would be not to push her farther just now.

And the next morning Mrs. Arden opened her eyes.

She saw Mary first, and returning consciousness showed in her bewilderment at first. She looked about the hospital room. Then she feebly put up a weak hand and felt of her bandages. But her mind was clear.

"Am—I—badly—hurt?" she demanded rather than asked of Mary.

"You were, mother," said Mary gently, leaning tenderly over the bed. "It was an accident. A truck hit the car. Do you remember?"

Her mother shook her head almost imperceptibly.

"Henry?" she muttered.

"He is bruised, but all right," assured Mary.

"Do you feel a little better now, mother?" questioned Mary anxiously. But her mother made no response to that and Mary saw she had fallen asleep again.

For two days more she was like that, waking for longer and longer periods. Then the third day her eyes opened wide again, and in a clearer tone, as if she were well able once more to take command of all situations, she asked:

"Where is Brooke? I want him here. You stay till he comes."

19

WHEN Brooke arrived Mrs. Arden opened her eyes again after having been apparently asleep for some hours.

Mary had called the nurse, and the house doctor had come in also. He announced that the patient seemed slightly better, but that any upset still might cause her to slip away suddenly at any moment.

After that report Mary sat with every nerve strained, praying, wondering, watching. The doctor had said that Mrs. Arden must be humored in every possible way, or he would not be responsible for the outcome. So Brooke had been sent for.

Mrs. Arden seemed to be aware of him as soon as he entered the room. Mary wondered afterward whether perhaps she had not been awake a long time. Mary did not understand her mother. She did not seem particularly glad to see Mary, only to have her wishes carried out.

Brooke came in looking pale, for he had always said he hated hospitals, that he was so sensitive to other people's suffering he could not bear to see it. His eyes avoided the sick woman as much as possible. His eyes

---

227

looked haunted. They fluttered from Mary to the nurse, then out the window, then back to Mary.

But when Mrs. Arden spoke, he had to look at her.

"Brooke?" she called. "I'm glad you've come." Her voice seemed stronger now. "I suppose this crazy thing had to happen to me to bring Mary to her senses. Now I want you to take her and marry her, today. I may not last much longer, and that is my last wish."

Mary's face turned ghastly white. With one trembling hand she grasped the cold iron of the hospital bed table behind her. Her knees shook so that she was afraid she would fall.

A gleam came into Brooke's black eyes, and he willingly walked across to Mary and put his arm about her.

"I'll be glad to do just that, Mrs. Arden," he said with a delighted little laugh. "Would you like me to get the minister here now?"

"Oh, *no!*" gasped Mary. She felt as if she were going to faint.

The nurse looked in a puzzled way at her, but decided that this was too intimate a problem for her to interfere with. She stepped out and called the house doctor back, for he had gone to the next room to see another patient.

In a word she told him what she had heard.

"I don't think the girl wants it. She's going to balk," whispered the nurse.

"She'll have to pretend she's going to, or something," replied the doctor, in what he tried to hope was a whisper; but Mary could hear his growl plainly from where she stood just inside the door, "unless she wants to kill her mother. If she just agrees to it maybe that will satisfy the old lady. Of course I can't order her to do it," he shrugged.

But Mrs. Arden was saying, clearly,

"Yes, Brooke, bring Dr. White here. Now. I don't want to have any slips in this thing again."

Mary's head swam. "Oh, God! You *must* help me now!"

Just then another man walked into the room. Mary threw a desperate glance toward him. Any interruption now would be welcome. Then all at once with a smothered glad cry she flung herself into his arms and clung to him. "Daddy, oh, Daddy!" she sobbed in relief.

He held her close and kissed her.

Then he stepped over to the bed and stooped to kiss his wife.

The doctor looked startled, and grabbed for his patient's pulse. But he was relieved to find it perfectly steady.

Without emotion Mrs. Arden said, "Well, John, I'm glad you've got back at last."

Mary's heart echoed her words in vast relief. Now surely father would find some way out of this.

"I've just advised these two to go ahead with their marriage plans, John, they've had to wait so long. I don't want them to think they must wait because I'm laid up." She spoke with determination and her husband looked up at Mary in mild surprise. He saw her desperation and glanced at Brooke, who smiled back a triumphant smile.

But he answered his wife soothingly. "We'll get them fixed up soon, Alice. I'll see to all that. Now let's get it quiet in here and you and I will have a nice talk after a while."

So the nurse, with a sympathetic glance at Mary, took the opportunity to show them all out except Mr. Arden and he settled down beside his wife's bed, motioning Mary to go and rest. "I'll be home for lunch," he whispered to her. "Wait there till I come."

With rejoicing in her tired heart Mary started home. But she could not escape the escort of Brooke Haven.

"I'll have you home in a jiffy," he said patting her as he almost shoved her into his car which he had parked illegally outside the front door at the curb.

"You must have a good rest now that your father is home," he said in what he meant to be a comforting voice, though he could not keep the elation out of its tone. "You don't want to be tired out for your wedding trip, you know," he added gleefully.

Mary kept her face stonily ahead. "I don't intend to take any wedding trip any time soon," she said scornfully.

"No? Well, it can wait, I suppose, till you are sure your mother is really better. But the doctor seems to think she is, and now that your father is here to take over the burden of all this you ought to think of yourself a little. After all, you have your own life to live. And you can see that your mother feels so too. She is anxious that you should not tie yourself down because she had been hurt a little."

"Hurt a *little!*" Mary blazed contemptuously. "How *can* you speak so when you know mother almost *died?* And she may yet!"

"Oh, I didn't mean to be unsympathetic," he quickly reassured her. "I'm only trying to show you that *you* don't need to carry all this burden now. It's wonderful of you, of course, Mary, and I always knew you were a wonderful girl. Most girls couldn't be bothered. It's just like you to spend yourself the way you have, and not give a thought to your own comfort or wishes."

Brooke tried to pile compliment on compliment to make up for his break in the role he had attempted, of being all tenderness and righteous sympathy. But Mary made no further answer. She simply stared straight ahead of her, too utterly scornful of him to answer him back.

At the house he started to follow her in but she waved him away.

"Not now, please. I shall have to rest if I can. Thank you for driving me. Good by."

There was only contempt and disgust for Brooke Haven in her thoughts as she opened the front door. All the terror of that moment just before her father walked into the hospital room seemed to rush back upon her as she stepped into the silent house. She shut the door and locked it, for fear Brooke even yet might return and force his way in, in spite of her dismissal. The dread of being married to him against her will seemed waiting there in the hallway to crush her.

Then she glanced on the hall table where Hetty always put the mail and there was a letter for her. In Laurie's handwriting!

As if she had a priceless treasure she caught it up to her and ran upstairs to her room, suddenly light-footed and eager.

It was not a thick letter, just one page, and it was only a conventional note telling of his sympathy and prayers for her, and hoping that her mother was improving, but it was signed "As ever your friend, Laurie."

"As ever"! Oh, could it be? Was he really just as he ever had been? How could she doubt it? Surely there was some strange answer to the peculiar happening that night when he had left her so suddenly. How could it be that he would have *lied?* Laurie Judson had never been known to lie in his life. Was not that what Mr. Winters had said? And Nannie too, when she and Mary had first talked about him? A man didn't change just overnight, not a grown man like Laurie. Yet, there came the old doubt: when there was a girl involved might not a man do any strange thing to protect his name?

Yet Laurie never was one to protect himself. He always would admit his own wrongdoing, even as a boy. Could it be, oh *could* it be that it was the girl who lied? Not Laurie? Mary had never even considered such a possibility before. It had never occurred to her. But how simple. It was not hard to imagine Sylva lying. For what reason Mary could not possibly conceive, but an answer might evolve, sometime. Till then, better trust God to work it out. Had He not saved her already, more than once?

With thankfulness, and a heart lighter than it had been for many days, Mary knelt down beside her bed and tried to think of some adequate way of expressing her gratitude to God for what she considered at least a reprieve from marriage with Brooke Haven.

She knew that people used various quotations from Psalms, or some such beautiful language when they addressed God, but she was not familiar with those. Finally she just folded her hands and with tears in her voice said aloud, "Thank you, Lord!" then bowed her head quietly a second and rose up again, feeling that she could take up her way again with cheer and confidence.

Mary tucked her precious letter inside her blouse where she could be constantly reminded that Laurie Judson was thinking of her and praying for her, and then she went downstairs to tell Hetty and the cook to prepare a nice lunch for her father.

Mary stayed in town another week, and her mother continued to improve. What it was her father had said or done that closed at least for the time being the subject of Brooke Haven and marriage Mary never did discover. When she asked her father he simply smiled and said, "Never mind, honey. That will work out all right. I know your mother pretty well, and I learned a long time ago how to handle her. Just leave it to me, and don't worry about it any more. If you don't want to marry that young fellow you don't have to. I'm not particularly in favor of him myself. In fact, I'd rather keep you to ourselves for a little while longer!" He smiled and drew her to him.

"Oh, daddy, I'm *so* glad you have come home!" cried Mary as she snuggled against him.

"Well, I'm glad, too. I thought for a while there that I never would make it. I was pretty desperate. But honey, you look tired. Your mother is so much better now, I think you ought to get away and rest a bit. Stay for a week or two anyway until your mother comes home from the hospital. She will want you then. Where would you like to go? To Castanza? She tells me there is a room already reserved there for you."

"Oh, no, daddy, please not to Castanza. Couldn't I go back to Arden?" begged Mary. "I love it so there."

"Why, yes, of course, if that is where you want to go. I think that's a splendid idea. I only wish I could go with you myself for a visit. But perhaps that will come later. Yes, go, child, and get some color into your cheeks."

So Mary said good by to her mother that night and left on the train very early the next morning. Strangely enough, her mother seemed fairly satisfied to have her go. Mary wondered about it. She never knew about the telegram to Brooke Haven that Mrs. Arden dictated to the night nurse that evening after her family had gone home. Its message was cleverly worded, implying that her daughter being free for a time might, with sufficient coaxing from the right person, be persuaded to spend some time at Castanza.

It so happened that when the telegram was delivered Brooke was in the company of several young people who were not Mary's choice of friends. They were quite devoted to Brooke, however, and perhaps more so to Brooke's bank account.

So when he announced that he was driving to Arden, starting immediately, they all clamored to go along. They asked no questions about how far Arden was, nor when they would return. It was a lark, and they were itching for a lark. Brooke was rather aghast at first, and produced various reasons why it would not be best for them to go, but they laughed him off, and finally he decided that possibly a gay throng might do more to induce Mary to come with them than if he were alone. So off they started.

Mary, when she reached Arden, went over to the garage and picked up her car. Then, just to revel again in the dear hominess of her beloved little town, or perhaps to catch a glimpse of a tall familiar figure, she took the long way home, and finally wound around until she reached the lane leading to her own south pasture. And that is why she failed to see the three cars parked at the front of her house.

20

NANNIE met Mary at the kitchen door. Her face was very red. Her mouth was set in severe lines. She was trembling so with indignation as she spoke that her glasses slipped down from their customary place on her front hair, and slid with a bump onto her nose.

"You've comp'ny, Miss Mary!" She said it tersely, as if to imply that it was Miss Mary's responsibility and of course if this was the type of company she desired it was up to her, but that Nannie would not approve nor have any part of it.

"Company? That's nice—or" she hesitated, puzzled by the normally hospitable Nannie's forbidding frown. "Who is it, Nannie?"

"I'm sure I don't know them, Miss Mary," she replied coldly. There was always much to be inferred from what Nannie did *not* say. This time Mary deduced that Nannie had no desire to know them, either.

"One of 'em is the young man who was here to supper that Sunday but the rest I never saw before." Then she snorted. Her cargo of indignation had been loaded for some time and its ship had strained at anchor long enough. She launched forth: "They come in here as if they owned the place an' demanded 'drinks.' I give 'em ice water an' they just laughed at me. At least I saw two of 'em snicker in back of their hands. 'No,' they wanted 'something stronger,' they said. So I told 'em I could make some pineapple or grape punch and this time those same two giggled right out loud. I never was so insulted in this house in my life." Her eyes blazed and the perspiration beading her hot brow began to run down as if it had remained in suspension longer than could be endured.

"Then they went into the living room," she went on, "an' I could hear them lookin' over everything in there. An' once they laughed! Miss Mary, they *made fun* of some of yer grandmother's things. I think they laughed at me. I can stand that, but they were makin' fun o' you, too, Miss Mary, for goin' to church. At least they said you were 'hipped' on religion!"

Then did the torrent that had been held back for a good part of the afternoon break forth and the unwonted tears streamed down Nannie's face mingling with the sweat and she put up her apron and sobbed heartbrokenly, but in a smothered, whispered way, as indeed she had related the calamity all along.

Comprehension had dawned on Mary as soon as Nannie spoke of Brooke. He had probably brought his own choice of friends to call. Perhaps to try to take her back to Castanza with them. No doubt Nannie's pride had taken quick offense at the first glance at these ultra-modern young people and she had thereupon highly exaggerated their rudeness without knowing that she did so. Her quick mind tried to plan what on earth she could do to entertain these wild young acquaintances of hers until she could think of a courteous way to send them back where they came from.

But when she saw Nannie's tears, a thing she had never seen before in her life, she just gathered the poor old woman into her loving arms and soothed her.

"Never you mind, Nannie, I don't care either, if they make fun of me. Nobody can hurt us just doing that! I can guess who they are and they don't have much sense, I'll admit. I suppose I'll have to feed them tonight and maybe even let the girls sleep here for it's a long drive back, you know, but I'll think of a way to get them out of here tomorrow. Now, don't you worry. You go ahead and plan for me the nicest supper you can think of so I can boast about you! And I'll try to calm them down."

So Nannie, comforted by the thought that Miss Mary did not seem to consider them welcome bosom friends, set about planning and giving orders to Randa with the greatest efficiency, to prepare a buffet supper for twelve that would equal or surpass anything these crazy youngsters had ever had in any of their fine city restaurants. But all the time she worked she kept that grim expression and muttered now and then to herself or to Randa. Meantime Mary greeted her visitors and then herded them out to the lawn and set them to playing badminton and tennis, while the others sat around talking and watching the games.

Floss Fairlee was not with them for she had gone with her bridegroom to Texas for two months. Another cousin of Brooke's was there whom Mary had met only once or twice. She was homelier than Floss and much more scatterbrained. She and her boy friend, a pale youth named Everett something, had come in the roadster with Brooke, and they had agreed to drive Brooke's car back and let Brooke drive Mary's car, if Mary could be persuaded to come back to Castanza with them.

The other nine of the party included Bill and Betty

Downs, one of the couples who had announced their engagement that horrible night of the rehearsal, and who had since decided not to wait any longer for their married life to begin. The rest were Brooke's intimates rather than Mary's. They belonged in the crowd at the Castanza Country Club, and Mary knew them all, but not intimately. She had seen them many times at the club, had played golf with them, and had been on swimming parties with them, but was not particularly friendly with any of the group. Floss, and two or three who were in another crowd entirely had been her especial friends at Castanza, but Floss only because she was the kind that was hard to shake off.

But it was not in Mary to be rude, and she graciously made them feel welcome, even though there was not any pleasure to herself in having them there.

She good-naturedly took their teasing about her "dry" household, stood up stoutly for Nannie and the others who served her and then cleverly diverted their minds by means of games and a funny story or two, until she had them actually enjoying themselves in what they had termed "this dump."

Mary was quite used to the loud rude ways of many of her contemporaries. She did not like those ways. She tolerated them in her friends and had learned to take for granted a certain amount of their free and easy violence, but her early training had given her a much higher standard of conduct.

She fully expected that some of her grandmother's furniture might be damaged, or her rugs stained, before she could manage to get the foolish pack back to their own den.

But Mary did not yet realize the change that had come over even her own high standards since she had been at Arden. Accustomed now to hearing gentle talk, clean and wholesome, it grated on her painfully to hear the loud, coarse, often profane chunks of speech with which these young people pelted each other. She wondered what she ought to do when they used the name of God in that empty senseless way. It had never struck her as so terrible before. But now she felt that she knew God in a way she never had before, and it seemed disloyal to let them speak so of Him. Once she objected to an unusually vulgar blasphemy, and when she did the whole crowd hooted with laughter and took up her quiet remark in a singsong ribaldry, merrily prodding her with it until she saw there was no use trying to make these hoodlums see what they were doing. Not by objecting to it, at least. For the first time in her life she realized that as a child of God she now lived in a different realm from these others, and that it was a physical and spiritual impossibility for them to see as she saw.

So for the rest of the afternoon she remained quiet, stealing away to the refuge of the house as often as she decently could, on the pretext of "seeing to something," though she well knew that Nannie needed no guidance in this situation.

Dinner was an uproarious affair. Mary had it served out on the flagstone terrace, hoping to safeguard some of her grandmother's precious relics. But the crowd swarmed all over the place in spite of her. Still, after the meal was over she stole into the living room and glancing around saw that there was no damage, at least so far, that a good scrub and furniture polish could not remove. She was very choice of her grandmother's antiques.

They idled around the yard, playing a little more, or walking off in pairs down to the creek. Some went canoeing, taking the paddles they hunted up in the hall closet without asking so much as by your leave, while Mary was outdoors.

But at last when all of them by common consent gathered again on the terrace they complained of terrible thirst.

Mary instantly said she would have Randa bring some of Nannie's raspberry vinegar—it was the best in the county—and slipped back to the kitchen to give the order.

Raspberry vinegar! Shades of all our archaic Victorians!" they snickered almost before she was out of the room. "That is one for the book! Ha!" And they all immediately instituted a series of noises that are for some reason connected with raspberries.

When that merriment had somewhat subsided, before Mary returned, a girl named Rosalie, a tall pale blonde who wore drippy chiffon and inch long fingernails, whined:

"Brooke, you've been in this burg before, isn't there any place within reasonable distance where you can get us something to drink? I'm positively going screwy if I don't have something soon. You brought us here and it's up to you to see that we aren't stranded in this desert. Hurry up, for heaven's sake!"

Brooke sat still, hesitating.

"Mary may not like it," he objected, for he had been taking great pains during this visit to be as courteous to Mary as possible. He intended to keep up the role he had begun last week. It did not occur to him, of course, that Mary detested the actions of the whole crowd, for he was so used to them that he did not realize that anything was amiss.

But they all snatched his objection from him with a hiss and a hoot.

"When did you begin caring so much about that, Brooke Haven?" teased Betty Downs. "After what you pulled that night we all announced our engagements—

whatever *did* happen then, goodness knows!—I wouldn't think you gave a rap about whether she liked it or not."

Brooke had the grace to be somewhat embarrassed. They all kept at him.

"Tell us where the taproom is, if any!" They urged.

At last he slowly rose, saying grudgingly,

"Well, I'll take you down if somebody else will buy the stuff. I don't want Mary in my hair. I wash my hands of it."

"Okay, okay, okay," they yelled, "Let's go."

It was decided that Bill and Betty should go and Bill would transact the deal. So they started off before Mary came back from the kitchen.

Mary was gone some minutes to get the iced drinks, offering Nannie loving apologies for making her any more work after the prodigious task she and Orrin and Randa had already accomplished. While she was gone one of the party, perhaps fearing an instant's empty interlude, had the bright idea of going into the house to dance.

They poured through the French doors and now the pale youth named Everett came to life. He had draped himself here and there over the most comfortable chairs all afternoon and complained of everything. Now he sat down at Mary's beautiful grand piano and, still without much apparent motion, ripped into a rhumba. His lanky body still drooped but a slight sinuous motion could be observed through his length from time to time in rhythm with the music.

Mary heard the sounds from the kitchen and her heart sank. She had hoped that she could ward off any more noise and confusion, or at least keep it out of her beloved house. It seemed a sacrilege. She sighed a long weary sigh. Nannie heard her and came over to be the comforter this time.

She patted Mary on her shoulder, after wiping the hot dishwater from her hands onto her apron.

"Don't you mind, dearie," she soothed. "They'll get tired sometime an' then it'll all be over. Sometime we'll laugh about it, I s'pose. You know, I was just thinkin' how the Lord Jesus Himself must've hated a lot that went on at that there weddin' in Cana. But He took it, an' somep'n good came out of it. Now maybe He's allowed this mess here so that somep'n good can come outa it. Cheer up, child!"

"Oh, you dear Nannie! That's wonderful of you to think of it in that way. After all the work it's made you, too. I'm more sorry than I can tell you. You know I never would have invited them!"

"Sure not, dearie. An' don't you mind the work. It's good for me. I didn't have enough of it all the time there was nobody here. It keeps me young!" She laughed brightly, mopping her hot face again with her apron. But Randa kept her grim expression as she dried and stacked the piles and piles of dishes. Randa had not yet learned the high ways of the Lord as had her mother.

But when finally Brooke arrived with the drinks—Mary had not even noticed his absence—she was aghast. Well she knew how wild this crowd could become when they had enough liquor in them.

She went forward to him quickly.

"No, Brooke, I do not care to have drinking in my house. I am sorry but you will have to keep it outside."

"Yes, we're sorry too," mimicked one of the girls in a stage whisper which Mary pretended she did not hear.

But one of the boys agreed cheerily: "We'll take it out on the terrace if you want. Sure! Come on, boys and girls!"

With rollicking hilarity they trooped out. But Mary stood with flashing eyes facing Brooke.

"I don't like this, Brooke! You will have to stop it. After all it is my house, and you brought these people here."

Brooke put on a pained sympathetic expression.

"I don't like it either, Mary," he agreed sadly. "I'll surely do what I can. They don't realize that you and I feel any different from the way we used to." His expression was pious in the extreme.

Mary looked keenly at him, astonished. She could not believe that there was any real change in Brooke Haven.

"Why did you bring them here, Brooke?" she asked.

"Oh, they found out I was coming and insisted that they would all come along and persuade you that we really miss and want you at Castanza. I didn't want them, but you know this gang. What could I do?" He put a large amount of wistfulness into his voice.

Mary did not pursue the question of how he found out so quickly that she was to be at Arden. She simply answered coolly:

"When I decide to leave here it will be because my mother needs me. I have no intention of going to Castanza at any time."

"Not if I promise to be good and do just as you say?" Brooke bent his shiny black eyes upon her in the ingratiating way he had long ago learned went well with women.

"That has nothing whatever to do with my decision," Mary answered coldly. "Now what are you going to do about this crowd?"

"What do you want me to do?" he asked meekly.

Mary tried to think. More than anything she wished he would take them away, immediately, never to return. But it was not in her to be actually rude enough to send her guests away, summarily, uninvited though they were. After all, she had occasionally played with them and laughed with them and even drunk a sip now and then with them at Castanza, not longer ago than last summer.

"I want you to see that they are reasonably quiet," she said, "while they stay, and then leave at a decent hour. The drinking is to *stay outside* if it must be at all, and I shall have to put it up to you to control them."

With the utmost sincerity gleaming from his eyes Brooke promised that he would.

But, as Mary had feared that it would, the party grew in hilarity.

She stayed away from them as much as possible. They did not seem to notice or care. They went on with their dancing and their outdoor tête-à-têtes and their drinking and wild singing until Mary wrung her hands in shame. To think that her grandmother's house should be degraded thus. To think that the dear people of this town, whom she was just beginning to know so well and love so much, who were beginning to count her as one of them, should witness such an orgy. What if Laurie or Mrs. Judson should stop by? Her face grew flaming hot with the shame and indignation of it all. Perhaps they would all try to stay all night! Nannie and Orrin could not exactly be considered official chaperones. What could she do? Would she have to call the police?

A light was still on in the kitchen. Had some of the guests left it, going out for ice cubes, perhaps?

No, there was Orrin. Blessed Orrin!

She went swiftly over to him, with difficulty restraining the sobs that wanted to come into her voice.

"Orrin, we'll have to do something! I can't have this

any longer. I asked Brooke Haven to keep it under control but I can't even find him now. What *can* we do?"

Thus appealed to, Orrin arose to his full height which was considerable when he really straightened up.

"You want me to stop it, Miss Mary? I 'lowed you would, 'fore long. That's why I set up. Don't you worry!"

Orrin strode into the living room.

Mary noticed then that he was dressed in his Sunday best.

In a voice that boomed over the tumult he shouted:

"This place closes at midnight! All out now! Miss Arden will show the—er—ladies to their rooms. Reservations have been made at the Arden Inn for the men." Then he turned out the lights.

A gasp of astonishment startled the hubbub into silence for a long moment. The piano stopped its rhythmic thumping. The dancers became rigid with surprise and almost fear. The weird sound of Orrin's deep voice combined with the darkness gave them an eerie feeling that it was a supernatural voice they heard.

Then out of the silent gloom came suddenly a high-pitched silly giggle, and Barbie's childish squeal:

"Curfew, eh? That's right in character, boys and girls. Okay with me, I'm tired!"

"Oh, sho itsh home shweet home, ish it? Where do we go from here?" mumbled a boy whose rumpled tie hung over his shoulder. He was clinging wildly to the girl he had been dancing with.

"The *front* door's this way," thundered Orrin with great dignity. He put just a slight emphasis on the word front, as if there were other ways of exit he could offer if anyone showed reluctance to use the usual one.

Then Orrin turned on the dimmest kind of light in the front hall near the door.

Meanwhile Brooke Haven had been sitting with Rosalie on the big willow couch under the front window in the sunroom. Brooke had spied a door to the outside near them, so when they wanted more to drink he would slip out and get it without having to be observed. They were having quite a cosy time. In his hazy state Brooke decided that Rosalie was a delightful companion, and she in turn was taking full advantage of her opportunity of having the prize man all to herself. By a well-aimed bit of wit she succeeded in putting Mary Arden in an extremely ludicrous light to Brooke, and they both joked about it.

But when the lights suddenly blinked out they were confounded. They heard Orrin's voice roaring orders, and Brooke said, thickly, "Well, come on. We might as well go. That tyrant in there will only rout us out if we don't."

But Rosalie was angry. She thought she had just got Brooke where she wanted him and in a few minutes more he might possibly capitulate to her charms so far as to kiss her and forget Mary Arden. Then, if only Mary herself would walk in, wouldn't there be the sweet dickens of a mess? And Rosalie would love it. Mary would have nothing more to do with Brooke, of course, Mary being the particular prude that she was, and Brooke would be left to Rosalie. There was absolutely no choice between Everett and the wealthy handsome Brooke Haven! So it was with great reluctance that she arose and tried to follow him.

"Give us a light, Brooke, for sweet Pete's sake!" she cried as she stumbled over a chair.

Brooke fumbled for his cigarette lighter, remembered he had loaned it a while ago to another boy, and reached for a match. It was a little paper folder of matches that he produced. He tried to light one but it flicked out of his unsteady hand as he scratched it. He swore and took another. His hand was shaky and he had difficulty because Rosalie was clinging to him all this time, giving foolish drunken cries. The second match burned his fingers and he swore again and dropped it.

"Now where the devil did that match go?" he muttered, feeling around the floor in the dark. "Maybe it dropped in the pillows."

"Oh, come on!" Rosalie pulled at him impatiently. "I don't like this darkness. It's gruesome."

"But that match was still lit!" Brooke explained.

Rosalie gave him another impatient pull. "Oh, it's probably out by now. Wouldn't be a bad idea to burn up this crazy dump anyway. Then Mary would have to come back with you." Then she laughed again in a silly falsetto.

Brooke was just enough out of his normal senses to consider that a good joke, and they tittered foolishly together as they made their uncertain way to the front hall.

Orrin was very much in evidence there. He glared at Brooke Haven when he came out of the dark sunroom escorting the tall blonde. But Brooke returned him an unctuously cordial good night, then asked if he could help to close the house, for all the world as if he were the most privileged guest there, as indeed he thought he was. But Orrin gruffly refused his help, and at last the good nights were over and two cars full of boys went roaring down the driveway. The third car belonged to Betty and she had already gone upstairs after agreeing to meet the boys downtown at the inn in the morning. So at last the Arden household quieted down and Mary, faint with relief, thanked Orrin and went to bed herself, still indignant, but weary enough to sleep heavily.

It was a little after one o'clock that Laurie Judson, on

his way home from a meeting in a rather distant town, stepped down from the bus on Main Street and started to walk the several blocks to his home.

There was one place where he could see through the trees the south wing of the Arden house, and without knowing that he had formed the habit of doing so, he glanced up that way.

Abruptly he stopped and looked again.

There was no question about it, that *was* a thin licking flame, and smoke, rising from the end windows of the sunroom. Mary's room was just above it!

21

LAURIE well knew that Mary had been expected back that day. Nannie and Orrin had taken care of that. They had hoped he would come to his senses and be there to welcome her. They could not understand why this romance in which they were so interested should not develop as they felt it should.

But Laurie had not come to greet her. The servants felt it was as well he did not, too, after all the goings on! Nannie wondered with growing horror whether Laurie had indeed been there unbeknownst and gone away again when he saw what was taking place. Oh, to think that he should find Miss Mary with such a crowd and such carryings on! What a pass things had come to in the Arden house! What would Grandmother Arden have thought!

Laurie had gone out of town to the meeting not of necessity but because he did not wish to stay in Arden and try to keep out of Mary's way. He did plan, of course, to come and call after a reasonable time. But it would not be the thing for him to rush up there as soon as she arrived, if she belonged to another man. So, hearing that a speaker whom he would enjoy was to be in Middleboro, he phoned his mother that he would not be home for supper and went.

But he heard very little of what the speaker said. He was thinking about Mary. Wondering whether she was home yet. Wondering if her mother was better. Wondering if that fellow Haven would be bringing her. If *he* were in Haven's shoes, that is what he would have done, and not let her out of his sight. More than likely they were having supper quietly together right this minute, he thought moodily as his bus jogged on toward Middleboro. Then he discovered that that was the real reason why he had wanted to get out of town, because he thought that Brooke Haven would be bringing Mary down. And he was still more thoroughly disgusted with himself than he had ever been before. It was not that he was afraid of the man. He could gladly have gone to battle with him with one hand tied. But it was the fierce pain of seeing them together that he found he wanted to run away from. So he sighed through the meeting and sighed himself home again on the bus.

It was not until he saw that stealthy flame that he sprang into life. He fairly flew up the hill to the house. The smell of smoke grew stronger as he went. Strange that Orrin had not been awakened by it! But the servants slept in the other wing.

As Laurie drew near the house a wicked knife of flame burst out of another window, directly below where Mary slept. It must be spreading quickly, he thought wildly. "Oh God! Let me get to her in time. Take care of her!"

The thought that he might even now be too late froze his heart. It seemed to him as if his flying feet were really only creeping, in slow motion. He did not take time to wonder at the strange car in the driveway which he had to dodge as he came up to it in the dark.

At last he reached a low front window. He shot his big fist through the screen, tore the wire and flung himself into the room. Choking and almost blinded he grabbed the rug from the floor and threw it over the couch where the worst of the fire seemed to be.

Just as he took the stairs, four or five at a bound, he heard sirens in the distance. Thank God! Someone had sent in an alarm. Perhaps Orrin was on the job.

Then he heard a terrific pounding of running feet and Orrin's voice roared: "Fire! Wake up, Miss Mary!"

Laurie reached her room first. It was full of smoke. He could not tell whether the fire itself had reached here yet.

The din of the sirens and the yelling had just wakened Mary. She was sitting up in bed, coughing and wondering what awful nightmare she had. She tried to scream but the smoke choked her. Then all at once strong arms were about her, lifting her gently, carrying her out of her own door down the hall to the servants' quarters. Did she dream it or had she heard a low thankful murmur in her ear: "My darling!" as those wonderful strong arms held her close? But when she was put down and she turned to thank her rescuer he was gone. Gone back that choking fiery way to get others. For Orrin had shouted to him that there were girls in both the guest rooms.

Most of the guests had been aroused by now. The fright had sobered them and they ran screaming out of their rooms, rushing this way and that. Rosalie was about to take off through her window when Orrin arrived and seized her struggling form. Then giving her a good shake he almost shoved her out to the back stairway.

Laurie was just returning from a tour of the other

rooms when he came upon Mary, and a tall blonde girl scantily dressed, who was crying in a high silly voice, "Oh, Mary! Isn't this perfectly *terr*-ible? And I know how it started. It was Brooke Haven did it. Oh-h-h! We might all have been burned alive!" She gave a horrible shriek and landed with both arms around the neck of the tall handsome stranger. In disgust Laurie pried her hands loose, propelled her into Nannie's room and banged the door shut. Then he gave a snort of scorn and turned around.

Mary still stood there, looking unbelievably lovely in a voluminous flannel wrapper of Nannie's. There was nobody else in the hall just then. The firemen downstairs could be heard shouting to those in Mary's room: "Okay now. Just about licked."

Mary looked up at Laurie with all her heart in her eyes. All that she had wondered and suffered and trusted for in the past weeks seemed to be calling to him.

Almost without his permission his own eyes answered her look.

She put out her hands. "Laurie! Dear!" She said.

And then he took her in his arms and folded her close. What blessed peace! What shelter! What a precious refuge after all the storms. No need for questions to be asked and answered, yet.

Their lips met, sealing the trust that each felt in the other. Somehow Laurie knew that Mary would never have yielded her lips to his if she loved another man. Somehow there must be an answer to the riddle. And for the moment Mary forgot that Laurie might ever have cared for another girl.

And so they rested, holding each other close, all the fire and the flood of troubles forgotten. For long minutes they stood, soul telling soul all that each had suffered and longed for.

Then all of a sudden there sounded a loud "Har-rumph!" down the stairway. They had not heard Orrin come up the stairs, stop in delighted amazement and retreat, waiting as long as he dared to give his message.

Laurie and Mary suddenly broke out into a laugh. Dear old Orrin! He had tried not to interrupt.

"The fire chief wants you should come down right away," called Orrin in a loud voice as if he were at a great distance.

Mary and Laurie looked at each other and laughed again with happy understanding. But Laurie did not let go of Mary's hand.

"Yes?" he called back. "Okay. Tell him I'll be down. I'm busy for a minute."

Mary giggled. "You must go—dear!" she said joyously.

At that he gave her a look that turned her heart upside-down.

Mary followed him downstairs.

"Hey, Jud!" called the chief. "How about you staying awhile here to make sure everything is out for sure? My wife's sick and I gotta get back as soon as I can. An' Jeff here is due on the early shift in a coupla hours now. He oughta get some sleep. Could you do it?"

"I'd be glad to, chief," agreed Laurie heartily. "Delighted, in fact," he whispered to Mary who stood behind him in the hall.

"That's swell. I know I can always count on you. Call me if you need to, but I think we're safe in leaving now."

"Oh, yes, go ahead, get back to your wife, Pete," Laurie shouted back through the window. "The sooner the better," he said mischievously again under his breath to Mary.

They watched the men climb into the trucks and roar

down the drive. They turned to each other once more but just then the excited girls made their appearance again, wrapped in various impromptu negligees which Nannie had produced. Mary had not stopped to wonder before how Nannie had managed to keep those unwanted girls out of the way all that time, but she knew that Nannie's wiles and devices were many, and thanked her in her heart.

The girls buzzed and chattered and laughed, now that the danger was over, for all the world as if the fire had been one more entertainment act in the party. They had been gaily drinking of the strong coffee that Nannie had made for the firemen, who had declined with thanks and said they didn't have time for it. The girls had delightedly devoured the crackers and cookies which Nannie had produced, and now they had come in search of more excitement. Rosalie had been telling them of the handsome stranger!

It was some time before Mary was able to herd them off to bed again. But at last she and Laurie were alone once more, or thought they were. Just as Laurie drew her to him an ostentatious cough sounded at the far end of the hall. Exasperated, Laurie threw a funny little grin at Mary and then called aloud,

"Orrin, are you there? How about helping me look around here a bit? We ought to see how badly damaged things are. I called to the men to take it easy with the property. But sometimes they get rough, you know, and break glass and douse on water when there's really no need."

The three went thoroughly over the damage.

"The sunroom's the worst," said Mary ruefully. "Mine is mostly smoke. A little paint and fresh paper will fix that up. It needed redecorating anyway. But I can't understand how the fire started. As far as I know there was nobody in the sunroom."

Orrin spoke up grimly.

"There *was* somebody in the sunroom, Miss Mary. When I turned out the lights they come stumblin' out. It was a tall gal an' that Mr. Haven. I heard 'em say somethin' about a match, too, but I was that riled up I didn't listen hard enough then. I should've looked around careful after they were in bed. I guess this fire was my fault. If I hadn't turned out them lights it might not uv happened." He sounded so contrite that Mary hastened to reassure him.

"Oh, no! Orrin, how could it possibly be your fault? You didn't know there was anything to check on. And if you hadn't turned out those lights that awful party would have been going on yet. It was the only thing that quieted them. Oh, I'll be so *glad* when they are gone. The girls said they were leaving early in the morning, and I hope they *never* come back, any of them!" Then she clapped her hand over her mouth and glanced at Laurie to see what he thought of her saying such a dreadful thing about her guests.

But he saw her chagrin and only laughed.

"You don't hope it a bit more than I do, young lady, if this is what they are going to do to you. At least, unless they all have a change of heart before next time."

Mary made a little indignant grimace.

"Brooke Haven—" she spat out the name—"pretended to have a change of heart, that time he came here and went to church but I never did think it was real."

Orrin barely repressed a delighted chuckle. And there was a strange sound like a whispered "Praise be!" from the kitchen door where Nannie and Randa had been cleaning up.

But Laurie looked startled and suddenly turned to

Mary, taking her arm and leading her toward the living room.

"That reminds me," he said seriously, "I have something to ask you." Then turning back toward Orrin he called, "You had better get some sleep, friend. I'll call you if I need you."

But the discreet and canny Orrin was already out of sight.

Laurie drew Mary to the big couch in the living room, where only a dim light was burning in a corner.

He seated her gently and then stood before her.

"Mary Arden," he said solemnly, looking deep into her eyes, "are you or are you not engaged to Brooke Haven?"

Mary gasped with amazement then burst into a peal of happy laughter.

"I most certainly am *not!*" she assured him.

Relieved, but determined to settle the whole question, Laurie took a worn scrap of newspaper from his inner pocket.

"Then what does this mean?" he asked in bewilderment.

Mary glanced at it. She had never read the column herself. She had seen it that first morning when Hetty had brought it but she had tossed it aside with horror, and never wanted to see it again.

She glanced it through and this time she did not laugh.

"Sit down beside me, *dear,*" she said gently. "I wanted to tell you long ago but I was ashamed to, it seemed so horrible."

With her hands held warmly in Laurie's strong gentle ones she told him the whole story, including the kisses she had carelessly received in the beginning of her acquaintance with Brooke, and most certainly not forgetting the photograph of Laurie that seemed to have brought her to her senses.

Laurie's grip on her hands tightened as she told of the night of the wedding rehearsal and a righteous anger blazed in his beautiful brown eyes. Mary thrilled to see it. He *did* care, then. He had all along.

Then she remembered.

"But Laurie," she said in a low voice, "there is something I want to ask you, too." She hesitated a moment and drew her hands from his as if to free him to answer as he would. "Do you—have you—" it was hard to say, but all must be clear between them. "Do you care in any special way for Sylva Grannis?"

In utter horror Laurie looked at Mary appalled. Then, grasping what she must mean, he in turn burst into uproarious laughter. It lasted only an instant, for seeing the hurt look on her dear face, he stopped and took her tenderly in his arms.

"My darling, my darling! Did you really think I could ever even want to look at that girl twice? Didn't I tell you that she called me to come when she was very sick, near to death, as she thought, though she seemed very much alive before I was done with her."

"Yes, you said so, Laurie," murmured Mary from her refuge in his coat collar, "but she told me on the phone that you had a date with her, that you were her boy friend. I never knew you to lie, but I just didn't know *what* to think. Oh *Laurie,* I loved you so!" Mary sobbed. The agony that had been pent up in Mary's wounded heart for the past weeks found outlet at last and Laurie held her close and comforted her, letting her cry it out, realizing the relief it gave her.

When she became quiet and he had kissed away all the tears he returned to the subject of Sylva.

"I can't think what would make that girl pull a trick like that. Did she ever dislike you particularly?"

"Not that I know of," Mary said piteously.

Then Laurie told her the whole story of that evening and they had a good laugh over it, and agreed that there was nobody in the world quite like dear old Orrin.

"We must tell them about us the first thing," said Laurie.

"About us?" questioned Mary wickedly, twinkling her blue eyes at him.

"Oh! Why—you will marry me, won't you, Mary?"

But for answer she drew his head down again and laid her lips on his.

"Oh, Laurie, I never knew there could be such joy on earth! I listened to the promises those two made each other at that wedding and wondered how people *could* take such vows. But it's all so simple when you love!"

"Isn't it!" he agreed. "And beloved, do you know where such love comes from?" He asked tenderly.

"Why, from—God, I suppose you mean?" she said with awe and wonder in her voice.

"Yes, dear. He says love like ours is meant to be a picture of the love between Christ and His real church—believers, you know. Those who really get to know Him love him so much that what they do or don't do comes from love for Him, not because they are bound by vows."

"Oh," breathed Mary. "Isn't that *wonderful*. I never heard it put like that before. Most people think so lightly of marriage as if it were sort of indecent."

"Yes," he said sadly. "I know. But it's not. It's the most sacred, holy relationship that could be. You see, we as His own, belong to Him, body, soul and spirit, and He first gave Himself to us in that way. Just as you and I shall belong to each other, each living for the other."

"Oh Laurie," cried Mary softly, "life is really just beginning, isn't it?"

"Yes, for us, my darling." He took her in his arms once more and they let the wonder of their new love roll over them in glad waves.

"But if I am to be allowed to care for you the rest of your life, darling, I must begin now. You have had a hard night of it and you must get some sleep."

Mary laughed brightly.

"And how about you, you dear big toughie, do you often rescue damsels from fires, and then go all night without sleep yourself?"

So at last he promised to go and they agreed that he would stop on his way home from the office the next evening and together they would tell the dear servants of their new joy.

"Then you are to come to supper at my house, and we'll tell mother," he planned.

"Lovely!" exclaimed Mary. "I do love your mother, Laurie. She is sweet." Then she added sadly, "I am afraid you can never love my mother that way. She is—different, you know. But you will love dad. I know you will. Why, you know him already, don't you? I had forgotten."

"Yes, I have always admired your father, dear, and perhaps when your mother learns to know the Lord we will understand each other better."

"Oh, do you think she would ever listen far enough for that?" said Mary wistfully.

"We shall be praying together for that, darling," he answered gently.

"Oh, Laurie it's going to be so wonderful with *you!*" cried Mary again. "You *are* wonderful, you know."

"No, I'm not at all, dear. I'm just a very plain fellow as you will soon see. But we do have a wonderful Lord, don't we?"

"We do," she sighed happily.

At last they parted, but neither slept for a long time for joy.

22

THE GUESTS having left, all the next day Nannie went beaming about her work, albeit wiping a furtive happy tear away now and then. Mary said nothing about Laurie but she was singing all day long. Even Randa managed to hum a bit of a tune as she scrubbed white paint and tried to erase the marks of the disaster as far as possible.

Mary spent quite a long time in the sunroom, looking and measuring. Finally she called up a plumber and had him come up. They conversed at length, and when Laurie arrived that evening, after their joyous greeting, she pulled him after her excitedly.

"Come and see what we are going to do, beloved!" she cried. "See this little alcove? Do you think your mother would be happy in a kitchen that size? Just for when she *wants* to be alone, you know. And over here the plumber says there is room for a little bathroom. That still leaves plenty of room for a dinette and living room combined. Then we are going to enclose the little porch out at the back here and it will make a beautiful bedroom for her. Oh, do you think she will come? Will she like it?"

"I know she will, darling," said Laurie putting his arm about Mary and turning her sweet eager face up to his. "But are you quite sure that is what you want to do?"

"I am quite sure—that is, if *you* would like it. I thought it would be so like old times to have you and your mother too up here on the hill where we all used to be. But—do you like this old house? Would you care to live here? And would it be convenient to your work? Because," she smiled adoringly up at him, "you know I would follow you to the ends of the earth if that were where you wanted to go, beloved!"

"Oh, my dearest dear!" he said again, drawing her close again. "I can't believe you really love me! I'm sure I don't see why you should."

"Oh, don't you? Well, just leave that part to me, sir," Mary laughed.

"Now, Laurie, there is one more thing we must plan to do. Then we can go ahead. That is to break this to my mother and father."

So down they sat on the remains of the burnt willow couch and schemed how they would go to the city that Saturday. Laurie could take the overnight express back and be home again in time for his service Sunday morning.

Before they left for the Judson house they stopped in the kitchen, hand in hand. Orrin was just coming in from the pasture.

The smile on their faces was so obvious that before they could say a word Nannie had thrown up her floury hands and cried "Praise be!" while Randa primly waited with a smile from one side of her square face to the other, for them to make their announcement.

"Would you all mind very much if this house should be taken over by a Mr. and Mrs. Laurie Judson?" asked

Mary with a twinkle. "Would you be willing to go on working for them instead of Miss Arden?"

Nannie could wait no longer, but flung her arms about her Mary lamb, flour and all, and held her tight while the happy tears flowed down her face.

"Oh, my lamb!" cried Nannie laughing and crying together. "And I was so afraid it was going to be that other—that river man!"

"River man!" exclaimed Mary bewildered.

"She means Mr. Brooke," explained Randa apologetically.

Then they all had to have a laugh again.

"Well," chuckled Orrin, "I thought 'twas about time you both came to your senses. How 'bout supper, Randa?"

"We're going up to mother's," said Laurie gaily. "We'll be seein' you again. Good by."

They went out to the garage and Mary said, "You drive, Laurie. This will be your car too, you know."

"Thank you very much, my lady, but I've just ordered a new one myself, if you please, and that will be yours, too, if you like it. I'll not be quite so strapped for money from now on, and I can do a few things that I've wanted to do all along."

Mrs. Judson met them with open arms. She did not need to be told the news, although they delighted to tell it again.

"Oh, to think that I have a dear daughter at last! I've always wanted one, and I can't imagine one I would love more than you."

They had a beautiful time there and then they had to bring Mrs. Judson back to the house on the hill to ask her approval for the plans of the little apartment.

"I'm really glad about the fire," Mary decided as she looked around the place happily. "I might never have had the courage to touch the dear old place, and now it's going to be so much nicer than ever before! Is that the way the Lord has to work with us?" asked Mary in sweet humility. "We don't have sense enough to know what we want sometimes, do we? So He has to let our old things be spoiled before we are willing to take His better ones!"

Laurie smiled understandingly at his mother and then took his beloved in his arms again.

"Mary has learned in a few days, mother, what it took you years to teach me. I must be a dumb thump!"

Mary put a soft hand over his mouth.

"Don't you dare to talk that way about the man I am going to marry!" she scolded prettily.

And Mrs. Judson was quite satisfied with the adoring look the lovely girl turned upon her son.

Then, on Saturday, they went to the city.

They took a taxi first to the Ardens' house. Mary had wired her father that she would be there, with a guest.

He was waiting in the library for them, pretending to himself that he was reading the evening paper, but in reality he was puzzling over the strange ways of his daughter, wondering why she would bring a guest just now. Her mother was home from the hospital but she was by no means ready for company.

At first he did not recognize the tall handsome young man with the beautiful glad brown eyes and the smile that seemed to light up the room.

Then as Laurie came forward and shook his hand he exclaimed:

"Laurie Judson. Man, I didn't know you! It's good to see you, sir."

He drew him into the room cordially and seated him and began to ask about his mother and the other friends at Arden before Laurie or Mary could tell their news.

But soon Mary broke into the conversation with, "Dad, I'd like to interrupt this, if you don't mind. Laurie hasn't long to stay and he has a favor to ask you."

She smiled demurely trying to hide the mischievous twinkle that would come into her eyes.

She could almost feel her father's imperceptible stiffening as he thought subconsciously, "Son of impecunious old farmer friend wants favor from wealthy magnate. We'll see."

But she gazed with pride at Laurie in his beautiful new brown tweed suit, impeccable in his grooming as ever Brooke Haven had been, and far, far more good-looking, she thought.

Laurie smiled that glad smile again. "Not the ingratiating smile of a job seeker," Mary exulted. "It's a glorious, triumphant smile of joy!"

"Mr. Arden," Laurie began without hesitation, but with humility in his voice, "I'm here to ask the greatest favor you could grant. May I marry your daughter?"

Then he smiled over at Mary, a smile ablaze with his great love.

The astonished Mr. Arden had no words for the instant. Then he stood up and came over to Laurie, taking his hand warmly.

"I can think of no man I would rather give her to, son," he said and the tone of his voice rang true.

Mary gave a little skipping run over to her father and kissed him and then went into Laurie's ready arms.

"Oh, daddy," she breathed, "I'm so happy! But do you suppose mother will—be pleased?"

Mr. Arden looked serious.

"Your mother is still very weak, of course, Mary. I'm not sure we should tell her yet. Let's have dinner and talk it over. Then perhaps I might go up and pave the way.

I haven't told her just when you would arrive, so we'll just wait a little, shall we?"

So they had a happy time together while Hetty served in wonder and stole many an admiring glance at the handsome young man who seemed to have dropped down out of the sky and who gazed so worshipfully at Miss Mary.

The cook and even Henry had to stand at the swinging door as Hetty passed through in order that they might take a peek at him.

"Every bit as good lookin' as that Haven fellow," adjudged cook in a loud whisper to Henry. "I never did think much o' him."

And all during the dinner, after the two young people had first poured forth the details about the fire, Mr. Arden was cleverly, diplomatically gleaning facts about Laurie's work, Laurie's experience, and Laurie's financial standing and possible future. Laurie fully realized what was going on and freely dispensed all the information he could, aware that this man was only protecting his daughter.

Then Mr. Arden betook himself up to the sickroom, armed with such facts as he felt would be advantageous to the cause of Laurie and Mary.

"Is Mary here yet?" called Mrs. Arden in tired impatience as he approached.

"Yes, Alice. She came in just a little while ago. She will be right up. But she has a little surprise for you. I wanted to tell you first a bit about it—"

"No," broke in Mrs. Arden imperiously, "I want her here, now!"

"But—" insisted her husband.

"No, John. Call her now!"

So he gave a little shrug and called her.

Mrs. Arden was weak, but not too weak to have keen

hearing. She noticed the two pairs of footsteps, one heavier than Mary's.

She glanced sharply at her husband. But he was looking blandly toward the stairway. She could not tell what he was thinking. Were those Brooke's footsteps?

Then Mary came in and gently leaned over to kiss her.

"Mother," she said, "I've brought someone I'd like you to know, for I've promised to marry him. And oh, mother, I'm so happy! Laurie, come where mother can see you. Mother, this is Lawrence Judson." Mary beamed at him proudly.

Startled, Mrs. Arden stared up at the handsome young giant as he courteously bent over her bed, taking her thin frail fingers gently in his.

"I shall try to take the best of care of your daughter, Mrs. Arden. She is the most precious thing on earth to me," he said solemnly.

"Stand off, young man, and let me look at you."

Laurie stood up to his full height and let Mrs. Arden stare him through and through. It was an ordeal. She missed nothing. Suddenly his glorious smile blazed out at her, with its twinkle of fun at the humor of his situation.

Mary was holding her breath. What would her mother do? She could make things pretty uncomfortable when she was crossed.

But when Laurie smiled Mrs. Arden relaxed her gaze.

"I guess you'll do," she said reluctantly, "if her father agrees and he evidently has. But don't fool yourself, young man. You have a very headstrong girl to manage."

Mary laughed with relief.

"I'll try to be good," she said meekly as she looked up at her bridegroom.

Laurie held her close, as he said diplomatically, "I shall try to do as well as you have done, Mrs. Arden."

Grimly the woman nodded and motioned to them to go.

Her husband stayed but she waved him away, too.

"Go on, John. I'll hear the rest later. I know when I'm beaten." And she closed her lips and turned her head to the wall.

MRS. Arden managed to be up and about in time to make plans for the wedding. She had looked forward to this event for twenty-one years and she had no intention of being cheated out of her rights in its minutest detail.

First of all, she insisted that the wedding should be in the city.

"You are going to iive at Arden as long as you like," she argued with pursed disapproving lips, drawing in her breath as if it was only by the greatest self-control that she spoke no more of her mind than that, "and I intend to have you here until that time!"

Mary looked hopelessly at Laurie, who was in town for the day. For she had confided to him how greatly she would like to be married at Arden, the old family homestead. Laurie smiled gently, sympathetically and shook his head, as much to say, "We'll be there in time, beloved, let your mother have what she wants now. Remember I'm taking you away from her for good, and it isn't easy for her!" All this Mary read in his loving glance, and then afterward wondered how she could know all his thoughts, when she had really been with him such a comparatively short time.

She looked over at her father. He was sitting in his big easy chair reading the newspaper as if he hadn't heard. But by the very way he held the paper Mary knew that he was hoping she would give in to her mother in this thing, since her mother had given in on the one thing that really mattered, their marriage.

And then, with just a little inward, hidden sob, seeing the pretty plan she had cherished about to be snatched away from her, Mary followed a habit that was becoming a fixed one with her; she cried swiftly in her heart, "Lord, show me what You want!" And suddenly all the pieces of her puzzle took their right places, the big things seemed important, and the little things shrank, and then Mary smiled. Looking joyously toward her dear bridegroom, knowing he would be glad, she said,

"Why, of course, mother, we'll have the wedding here."

And then began the weeks of shopping. It seemed endless to Mary as she followed her mother's directions in where she was to go, and what she was to look at, and which she was to have sent up for inspection. For Mrs. Arden was not yet able to do as much personal shopping as she would have liked.

But when the things Mary sent home turned out to be almost all sport clothes, or dainty cottons, with now and then a well tailored suit or two, Mrs. Arden saw that she would have to go herself if she was to be pleased.

"You have nothing here but the plainest things, Mary. This is not a trousseau! Only one evening gown and that is entirely too simple for most occasions."

"But, mother, you know, I'm to live in a small town, where the life is very simple, and I don't want to be

dressed up more than other people. You have always
taught me that it was not good taste to be overdressed."

"That may be, my dear, but I hope you will condescend to visit your parents *some* of the time, and I do not
intend to have you look like a country cousin, even if
you insist on trying to be one!" Her mother's words
ended with an ill-disguised sniff that brought back some
of the tired ache in Mary's feet. She had spent a long day
in the stores and had thought she had done well in her
selections.

She sighed. "I really liked these, mother."

"Oh, keep them, if you do. But I shall see that you
get others, even if you never wear them. You can hang
them in the closets here, if you don't care to take them
along with you. Perhaps that would be just as well."

"Well, I think it would," Mary responded brightly. So
her mother went along the next time.

Oh, it was not that Mary did not enjoy pretty things
as much as any girl. She had loved to pick out that little
pink flowered morning dress, for instance, with its airy
dainty ruffled collar and think that when she would wear
it she would be "Mrs. Judson," and "Mr. Judson" would
be sitting opposite at their cosy breakfast table. The
thought made her heart leap and her cheeks grew pink
until the salesgirl looked at her sweet face wonderingly.

But Mary had no desire to shine at showy parties and
dances now. Her whole interest was absorbed elsewhere
and the shining of her eyes drew all glances toward her.

Mary did not know that under cover of all the plans
and details and directions her poor mother noticed every
smile of delight and every delicate curve of beauty in her
precious daughter and reveled in it, trying to still the
ache of her heart as she realized that all that loveliness
would soon belong to another person.

Neither did she know that her mother had begun to

notice the new sweetness in her daughter's willingness to give up her own way. She no longer submitted in the old fretful, discouraged, beaten way, but as if pleasing her mother were a joy. Mrs. Arden had listened to Mary one evening as she told her father of her new trust in the Lord, and although Mrs. Arden said no word, she began to watch. Mary had not found the words to speak to her mother yet about the new life she was living, but she felt certain that her father was deeply interested.

And so the days went on, each bringing to completion some cherished long-planned dream of Mrs. Arden's.

There were six bridesmaids, their dresses shading from a luscious peach color, through tones of apricot, to a deep russet, for the wedding was in October. The flowers had to be chosen almost bloom by bloom, to carry out the careful shading of the garments. Rich heavy-headed dahlias they were, set off by delicate tracery of dark greens. And each girl wore above her brow a band of satin flowers cunningly fashioned like the flowers that she carried.

As they came down the aisle of the stately old church the evening of the wedding they seemed like a garden come alive.

But when Mary Arden, on her father's arm walked down to meet her bridegroom, it seemed to the admiring throng of their friends that the sun must have burst out at evening, for the light in both their faces was beautiful to see.

Floss Fairlee was back from her trip to be there, and all the others of the old crowd, some of whom were bridesmaids and some were ushers, as Mrs. Arden insisted on having some of the men in Mary's group as well as some of Laurie's friends. And of course Laurie courteously agreed.

But Brooke Haven was not there. He had already

started on a trip around the world. His name was not even mentioned except by a few whisperers at the wedding reception, and even the most scandal-loving among them had to admit that Mary's new bridegroom was equally as desirable as Brooke had been, in looks at least.

The morning of the wedding Mary received a card in the mail which had been forwarded to her from the Arden address. It was announcing a new beauty parlor to be opened in a town twenty miles away from Arden, and its manager was one Sylva Grannis. Mary read it and smiled a little twisted smile, and then put the card away to show to Laurie sometime. But it was months before she remembered it.

Of course Mrs. Judson was at the wedding, looking sweetly patrician in a lovely beige dress that Laurie had insisted on taking her to New York to buy. Mrs. Arden looked her over with obvious anxiety and then received her with as obvious relaxation. All of which Mrs. Judson observed and smiled at, all the while rejoicing that her dear new daughter had been so marvelously preserved all her life from all that was superficial.

Mr. Arden received his daughter's new mother-in-law warmly and graciously just as Mary had known that he would.

Nannie and Orrin and Randa were invited to the wedding, at Mary's insistence, but they had decided to wait at home and prepare for the couple's return.

For Laurie and Mary had planned that after a short trip together they would go straight home to Arden and have open house, greeting all their friends there.

So it was that at last they drove into Arden and up the winding drive.

The house had had its redecorating all finished including Mrs. Judson's cosy apartment, and it seemed to be watching expectantly along with the three loving hearts—four, now—who were waiting eagerly for the return of the new master and mistress.

Laurie and Mary, their hands closely clasped as Laurie turned the last curve, saw the bright lights and glimpsed the dear faces at the windows.

"Oh, Laurie," cried the lovely bride, "it's like getting to Heaven, isn't it? With all of real life ahead of us!"

Laurie drew the car to a stop at the door and bent over and kissed her.

About the Author

Grace Livingston Hill is well known as one of the most prolific writers of romantic fiction. Her personal life was fraught with joys and sorrows not unlike those experienced by many of her fictional heroines.

Born in Wellsville, New York, Grace nearly died during the first hours of life. But her loving parents and friends turned to God in prayer. She survived miraculously; thus her thankful father named her Grace.

Grace was always close to her father, a Presbyterian minister, and her mother, a published writer. It was from them that she learned the art of storytelling. When Grace was twelve, a close aunt surprised her with a hardbound, illustrated copy of one of Grace's stories. This was the beginning of Grace's journey into being a published author.

In 1892 Grace married Fred Hill, a young minister, and they soon had two lovely young daughters. Then came 1901, a difficult year for Grace—the year when, within months of each other, both her father and her husband died. Suddenly Grace had to find a new place to live (her home was owned by the church where her husband had been pastor). It was a struggle for Grace to raise her young daughters alone, but through everything she kept writing. In 1902 she produced *The Angel of His Presence, The Story of a Whim,* and *An Unwilling Guest.* In 1903 her two books *According to the Pattern* and *Because of Stephen* were published.

It wasn't long before Grace was a well-known author, but she wanted to go beyond just entertaining her readers. She soon included the message of God's salvation through Jesus Christ in each of her books. For Grace, the most important thing she did was not write books but share the message of salvation, a message she felt God wanted her to share through the abilities he had given her.

In all, Grace Livingston Hill wrote more than one hundred books, all of which have sold thousands of copies and have touched the lives of readers around the world with their message of "enduring love" and the true way to lasting happiness: a relationship with God through his Son, Jesus Christ.

In an interview shortly before her death, Grace's devotion to her Lord still shone clear. She commented that whatever she had accomplished had been God's doing. She was only his servant, one who had tried to follow his teaching in all her thoughts and writing.